—Praise for *Viscera*—

"It takes a brave and immensely talented writer to concoct a dystopian fantasy of earthquakes, killing fields, drug addiction, and routine eviscerations that is also profoundly humane and laugh-out-loud funny. It sounds impossible, I know, but Gabriel Squailia has done it. *Viscera* is ultimately a story of self discovery, of being who you know yourself to be down deep in your gut even when the world wants to tell you otherwise. There is extreme ignorance and savagery in *Viscera*'s fictional universe, but there is kindness and healing too—just like the world we know."

—Camille DeAngelis, author of *Bones & All*

"*Viscera* is a work of gleeful weirdness, set in a world that calls to mind China Miéville's Bas-Lag novels, and full of characters fighting to reshape themselves and their destinies, in search of deep and resonant truth."

—Kat Howard, author of *Roses and Rot*

"Exquisitely imagined, deeply insightful yet scathingly witty, *Viscera* barrels along at a scorching pace after vividly realized characters whose separate quests—for identity, for revenge, for release—find themselves on a collision course in a world that's simultaneously both grimdark and surreal. Lusciously weird and utterly unique."

—Nicole Kornher-Stace, author of *Archivist Wasp*

"In Squailia's world, trees can act as a living internet, the calcified organs of dead gods lie under a city and respond to spilled blood with earthquakes, and having your major organs removed is not necessarily fatal. Identity shifts and slides as characters attempt to shape themselves and are shaped by their swiftly changing circumstances. To what extent, *Viscera* asks, does who we are lie in our bodies, and to what extent does it lie in our actions?"

—John Langan, author of *The Fisherman*

"The most delicious kind of nightmare, *Viscera* is gorgeous, theatrical, and weird as hell. Squailia's voice, the world they weave with it, and the eminently human characters they build will linger long after reading."

—Phoebe North, author of *Starglass*

Also by Gabriel Squailia

Dead Boys

VISCERA

GABRIEL SQUAILIA

TALOS PRESS
NEW YORK

Talos Press books may be purchased in bulk at special discounts for sales promotion, corporate gifts, fund-raising, or educational purposes. Special editions can also be created to specifications. For details, contact the Special Sales Department, Talos Press, 307 West 36th Street, 11th Floor, New York, NY 10018 or info@skyhorsepublishing.com.

Talos Press® is a registered trademark of Skyhorse Publishing, Inc.®, a Delaware corporation.

Visit our website at www.talospress.com.

10 9 8 7 6 5 4 3 2 1

Library of Congress Cataloging-in-Publication Data

Names: Squailia, Gabriel, author.
Title: Viscera / Gabriel Squailia.
Description: New York : Talos Press, [2016]
Identifiers: LCCN 2016017985| ISBN 9781940456683 (softcover : acid-free paper) | ISBN 9781940456713 (ebook)
Subjects: LCSH: Imaginary wars and battles--Fiction. | Imaginary places--Fiction. | BISAC: FICTION / Fantasy / Epic. | FICTION / Fantasy / General. | GSAFD: Black humor (Literature) | Fantasy fiction.
Classification: LCC PS3619.Q35 V57 2016 | DDC 813/.6--dc23
LC record available at https://lccn.loc.gov/2016017985

Cover illustration by Gabriel Shaffer
Cover design by Claudia Noble

Printed in the United States of America

for Autumn,
for Ryan,
for me

BOOK ONE

—The Drash's Kiss—

R aindrops slapped the cowl of Rafe's cloak as he followed Jassa through the trees. She darted with ease between trunks and branches, clucking with irritation each time he was snagged by prickers or mired in the mud. Rafe was suffering from constant sniffles and a rising, bone-deep hunger, but Jassa's spirits had been high since they left the city. She told stories as they went, some of which he'd heard three times since leaving Eth. This one, however, a meandering travelogue about how much better life had been before Rafe had been able to enjoy it, was new to him.

"But all of it was richer back then," she called, as if from across a crowded room, "from the sauce in the dishes to the lottery payouts. You're too young to have visited the court of Malachi the Emperazor, I suppose. Ridiculous title he gave himself, but no one could load on the excess like old Mal!"

"Passed me in the street one time," Rafe said. He hadn't actually been too young to visit the court, but too poor. "He was riding in one of those—"

"Stop your mumbling! Can't hear a thing you say."

"Sorry. What I said was—"

"You'd have been in swaddling-clothes during his Festival of Sevens," she went on, loosing a sodden evergreen branch, which slapped him in the face. "Shame, too! He had a fetish for the number seven, and it was our shared obsession with numerology that got the Assemblage invited. Kindred spirits, he thought us, though he insisted there was no such thing as luck. Imagine! A madman, he really was, but so wealthy that no one gave a shit. Anyhow, there were to be forty-nine courses that night—seven mated with seven, you see; remind me to work on your arithmetic—and I was determined to taste them all, even if it made my belly burst. A few courses deep and I couldn't tell one dish from the next, my fingers were *that* coated in gravy, so I turned to the child who'd been kneeling next to my chair all the while and said, 'Where's my napkin, whelp?' And what do you suppose she says to me?"

"I don't know!" cried Rafe. "What did she—"

"'That's what *I'm* for,' she says, and flips her hair right over her face! Now, sure enough, I look around, and all the cronies of the Emperazor's court are wiping their fingers in the silken tresses of their own human handkerchiefs. I even saw one blowing his nose! There were dozens of these children, and all of them matched. They were the royal offspring of some Northern clan, won for the city in the Battle of— well, some big to-do, at any rate."

Rafe pushed the laughter out of his chest at what he hoped was the appropriate moment. "I wish I could have been there!" he hollered, hoping he was loud enough.

Jassa turned, scowling. "Boy, we're *hunting*," she hissed, water dripping from her nose. "Hush yourself, or we'll never catch our quarry."

Rafe bowed his head, trudging on behind her. He'd been incapable of saying the right thing since they'd left the city of Eth, a course he desperately wanted to reverse. Jassa had been so kind to him before he'd joined the Assemblage, buying him sweets, complimenting his looks, and introducing him to the basic principles of Fortune-hunting. She seemed to be around his mother's age—a road-weathered forty-something—and he'd found in her a patience his own mother had never possessed.

Since he'd become her Deuce, though, he'd tumbled into a world of codes and rituals he barely understood, and everything he did felt wrong. For a time, he'd thought her affections would return on their own, but by now he understood that until he learned how to give her what she wanted, he'd earn nothing but her scorn—and the odd kiss from the drash, just enough to keep him well.

The night they'd met, she'd promised him all he could handle. "You'll never go wanting again," she'd said.

The fault was his own. She must have meant that he'd have it all once he'd *earned* it.

He'd simply have to do better. Once they caught their quarry, she'd see.

"And that liquor," she called, every bit as loudly as before. "That brilliant, steaming, bubbling liquor! Mal's enchanters had rigged a way to distill hooch in the bladder of a living human, you see, so to get yourself drunk, you'd approach some squirming servant who'd been holding it for *days*, and hold your mug right under the poor thing's pizzle."

"Ha ha!" It was not a party Rafe would have cared to attend. "Whatever happened to that Emperor, anyway?"

"You mean the Emper*a*zor," she said. "The Emperor came four rulers before."

He blinked. "What's the difference?"

"Difference? *Difference*?" She hooted with laughter. "No parties during the Emperor's time, for one! Listen, this isn't complicated. Jaegen the Emperor, Preen the Laminator, Malachi the Emperazor, Kruks Thagvallion, then the Caninists."

"I don't know how you keep them straight."

"It isn't that complicated," she snapped, "if you've two hemispheres of a brain to rub together!—No, wait. Mal, then the Caninists, then Preen, *then* Kruks. So, right, the Emperazor was deposed by the Caninists, that's what happened to him. A few short weeks after that party, he was strung up by his own entrails in the Crunkshank Gallery. Last I checked, his corpse was still dangling there—and the guts still held, after all those years. Bless his wallet, Old Mal always did have a strong stomach!"

"The Caninists," said Rafe, struggling to show off a bit of history. "Weren't those the ones that put a dog on a throne?"

"Well, it wasn't a fucking cat, now, was i—*wait*." Jassa dropped to her knees, examining a rumpled stretch of mud and moss. "*Hush*, you hear me?" Lank hair slid out from behind one ear, dangling into the muck. "*Quiet*."

Out came her notebook, covered in the hide of some improperly-cured beast, its pages rumpled by dozens of stains. Pulling out a stubby pencil, she added to her collection of manic scribbles, muttering over the footprints in wet earth.

Rafe stared down, a familiar pain stabbing his lungs as his gut filled with a tidal fear. Ever since he'd joined the Assemblage, it had been rising and falling, highest in the morning and the still of the night, when Jassa snored beside him, more peaceful without the drash than he'd ever be.

Unless he found that peace once he proved himself. If these were the tracks of the stranger they'd been following, he'd have his chance soon enough.

Nothing terrified him more. Was it natural, he wondered, to fear the very thing he wanted?

Maybe it was better if it wasn't. As Jassa had whispered at the party where they'd met, *If Fortune loved what was natural, the birds would sleep in nests of gold.*

She raised a pale hand and bent two fingers. Squelching as softly as he could, Rafe lowered his ear to her lips.

"A woman, barefoot. Snared a rabbit here, less than an hour ago." She pointed vaguely to the markings in the mud. "Now tell me, Deuce: is she traveling alone?"

Rafe stared, watching his reflection wobble in a puddle. "I, uh. Does it—is it supposed to say in the mud?"

Jassa squinted at him, leathery skin scrunching around beady eyes. "How in hell would the mud say *that*? These are the tracks of a single woman, clearly. I mean wherever she's camped, boy. Are there more, or is she traveling alone?"

Rafe's mouth was dry. The hunger in him spiked, everywhere but his belly. "Am I—supposed to guess, Jass?"

Her hand came near his face, and he flinched, but she didn't clap him, just rested her cold palm on his neck. She tugged him close enough that he could smell her breath, like goat's milk. "What are you?" she said.

Various parts of him felt warm in complicated ways.

"I'm—I'm Rafe? Rafe Davin."

Her lip curled. "*What*, not who."

He'd already put a hand on his chest before he recognized what answer she wanted. "I am a member of the Assemblage," he whispered.

"What else?"

He paused. "I am your Deuce."

She stowed her notebook in the bag beneath her cape, about ready to throw him a beating. Where was the look she'd given him at his initiation, that pride so bright he felt like melting?

"I am Fortune's plaything."

She kept on staring. He almost blurted it out—but no, it was always about Fortune with her, and there was always something more he was meant to remember. Lists of leaders, lists of avatars, lists of rules for inviting luck, lists of things that might chase luck away—with no reference materials, and no time to study any of it, at least not when his head was clear.

Her fingers dug into the base of his skull. "What," she whispered, "is a Deuce to his Ace?"

Rafe's throat clicked.

"The *vel*—" she murmured, as if he were a child. "The *veeellll*—"

"Oh! 'The velvet beneath the rolling of your dice,'" he recited.

Of course: this had been part of his initiation ceremony, with a dozen other flowery phrases he'd instantly forgotten.

"That's right," said Jassa. "The velvet beneath the rolling of my dice, guiding me in a billion invisible ways. I am here to *take* the chance, you are here to *guide* it. And because Fortune loves beginners, the less you know, the better."

Rafe nodded with more passion than he felt. He knew nothing but the words in her lists, devoid of context, and beginner's luck was the only reason she'd offer for keeping him in the dark. But Rafe didn't feel lucky.

"So," said Jassa. "When I ask you a question as my Deuce, boy, what are you to do?"

It felt safer to guess than to stammer. "Let Fortune answer with my tongue."

Jassa clapped him on the cheek and took her head away from his.

She was smiling. He exhaled, slowly.

"Now show me," she said.

Rafe closed his eyes.

"All right. Well."

No visions lay in that darkness. No divine voice whispered the truth.

To hell with it. Guessing would have to do.

"No," he said. "The barefoot woman *doesn't* have company. Besides the rabbit, and he's dead."

Jassa laughed through her nose, tugging out her notebook, where she recorded this prediction in some cramped, illegible corner. "Then it's time you made your Goddess proud, boy. Do you have something to say to Her?"

He nodded, feeling the weird little twist of his coming sacrilege. The things they wanted him to say made him feel ashamed and giggly all at once. Every other church he'd been to wanted worship from its worshipers, but not the Assemblage—they wanted him to say the most awful things he could think of.

He wondered how long it would be before he got used to it.

He knew that Jassa loved it when he blushed.

"Fuck you in the ass, Mother," he whispered.

"Louder."

"*Fuck Fortune right in the ass!*"

"Good," she said, chuckling softly, brushing his cheek with her hand, feeling its heat. "You look like a little bruised plum, you know that?"

His face burned hotter.

Jassa reached behind her cape. "Now. Who holds the reins of rule, boy?" He stared as she pulled out a dagger in a leather sheath. "Who is it that hoards all the wealth in the world?"

His hands began to tremble. She tossed the dagger from hand to hand, waiting.

This part he knew. "The worst among us."

"The very worst," she said, laying the dagger in his palms. It was heavier than he'd expected, and he longed to give it back and to wield it, all at once. "Every time the guard changes, we hit a new low. More rottenness, more avarice, more slaughter, fewer parties. And these despots swimming in on their waves of filthy lucre, Fortune loves them, does She not?"

"At first."

"Only as they ascend," said Jassa, pacing. "And then, as fast as She can, She forsakes them—and why?"

Rafe drew breath to answer, but Jassa barreled on, digging in her pockets. "Because they bend their fucking knees for Her, that's why! Because no sooner have they taken the city than their bowels fill with cold water, and every last one of them begs."

She took out a tiny brass wheel, Fortune's holiest symbol, and dropped it into the mud between her feet. "And this is our secret, boy," she said, dropping her breeches and squatting. Rafe looked away from the source of the steam. "We know what makes our Goddess respond. As Gast the Foundation taught us, ere she died: *to catch Fortune's eye, you must spit directly into it.* Look at me, damn you!"

Rafe obeyed, heart pounding. Jassa stood, hiking up her breeches, and stomped into the puddle, burying the wheel in piss and mud.

"We will take the city of Eth," she said, eyes shining, "and we'll keep it. Through deviousness. Through perversion. Through *desecration*."

"'The more evil a man does,'" Rafe recited, unsheathing the blade, "'the more of the world he owns.'"

Jassa laced up. "Are you ready to become Her avatar, boy? Are you ready to own the world entire?"

He touched the tip of the dagger to his thumb, marveling at its edge. A little more pressure and his flesh would part like wet crepe. "I'm ready," he said.

For once, it was true. He might not believe in Fortune, but he believed in this.

When it was done, he'd feel the kiss of the drash.

Jassa smiled, showing all seven of her teeth.

"Let us pray," she said.

They found their quarry in a half-burnt farmhouse in the midst of a tiny clearing. With one wall missing and the others lined in charcoal-black, the building reminded Rafe of an outdoor stage. Crouching at the edge of the wood beside Jassa, he fought a paranoid suspicion that the dark-skinned woman they'd tracked here was playing a part to lure them closer. In any case, his guess had been right: she was traveling alone.

The woman salvaged a cleaver from the wreckage of the kitchen, then squatted before a chopping board that had once been a plank in the pantry wall. The rabbit hung nearby, already skinned. Rafe stared at her tall, taut frame in its mud-brown tunic, noting the economy of her movements. Her hair, bursting loose from braids that had needed attention months ago, was as gray as a storm cloud on a sunny day.

Why couldn't she have been young?

"I don't know about this," he whispered, the steady hiss of the rain covering his words. "Who gets that old without an army to protect them? Might be she's a mercenary, or worse."

"Keep your bladder buttoned," said Jassa, glaring. "Look at her *face*, boy. Smooth as a nugget of amber!" She pulled her pack around under her cape. "Someone's put a scare into her, that's all. Shocked her hair white."

Rafe squinted at the woman's broad-cheeked face, which didn't look old, he supposed, but nor did it look like the face of an easy target. "I just don't know."

"So you said. But Fortune does. And so do I." Jassa pulled something heavy and red out of the pack and into her palm. "You'll feel Her eyes swing down on you soon enough. Her gaze will grant you faith." She reached for his chin with her empty hand. "And when it comes, boy?"

Her finger was as cold as an icicle.

"Do not squirm from it. Do you hear me?"

Rafe nodded, pushing against his fear. If only he could have the drash *before* the deed. But he knew better than to ask. He squeezed the dagger's hilt, feeling dizzy.

"Remember that what we do is not for you," Jassa whispered. "It is for *us*. It will steer our fate. We will take the city, for Lady Eff, for Fickle Faena, for Left-Handed Luce, whose dart never goes astray. And it all starts with your blade."

Rafe was breathing hard, grimacing at the pain in his lungs as he watched the wiry woman. She lifted the rabbit by its back legs. She pulled its muscled stomach open and scooped its guts into a wooden bowl, then laid its body down on the plank of wood. She hefted the cleaver and swung it down time and again, dividing the body into gleaming sections of muscle and bone.

Thunk. Thunk.

THUNK.

"That cleaver, though," he whispered. "This dagger's sharp, but I'm not a killer, Jass. I mean, I've never even been in a—"

Rearing back, Jassa punched him in the ear, hard enough to bring tears to his eyes. He fell back into the mud, glancing up frantically at the farmhouse.

The wiry woman hadn't seen.

"Everyone's a killer, boy," Jassa hissed. "Some just haven't had the opportunity to prove it. And *this* should make your job less terrifying." She gave him a good look at the object in her hand, a bulbous red bottle encircled in a shining belt of wirework runes. "Fortune will provide. Do you hear?"

Rafe blinked, reaching out a hand. "Is that—an *enchantment*? Is it *real*?"

"Course it's real," she said, stowing it before he could touch it. "They're nearly as expensive to fake as to make."

"But that's—" His throat tightened with anger. They'd been scrounging pennies for weeks, barely able to afford a meal. "How did you pay for it?"

"With the help of these ten tiny soldiers," she said, wiggling her fingers. "The keeper of the inn at Idlet had an extensive cabinet of curios, and he was a sloppy drunk. Now steady your hand, boy, and show Fortune your steel."

An enchantment. They had an enchantment.

Rafe pulled himself up. His hands were steady.

Whoever the woman in the farmhouse might be, she was no enchanter, or she wouldn't be cooking her own meals in the cold. He no longer doubted that they'd bring her down. He simply wanted to see what would come out of that bottle.

The fire in the farmhouse's shattered hearth began to smoke and sputter, and the wiry woman rose to tend it. Once it was stoked, she slid an iron pot beneath the rope of rain pouring from a hole in the roof. The pot's black belly sang out into the trees.

"That racket is all the cover we'll need," whispered Jassa, pointing. "Position yourself on that end of the farmhouse and give me a count of one hundred before you distract her."

"What should I do?"

"Use your *brains*, boy. Make a birdcall! Toss a rock into the trees! But wait until the bottle breaks to make your move."

Rafe drew the blade.

Jassa closed her hand on his arm. "We'll move quickly, after. While Fortune's gaze is on you. First the harvest, then we play."

Rafe was off, sneaking through the trees. His body was buzzing, kiss or no.

This was what it felt like to put a thumb on the scales.

At the back of the farmhouse a half-burnt wall kept him out of sight. Leaning in, he caught a glimpse of his quarry dumping meat into the stewpot. Panting, pulling a fist-sized stone from the muck, he wound back his arm.

The stone cracked against the limb of a hollow tree.

The woman grunted. Hold steady! he thought, and then he heard the bottle bursting. He leapt around the wall and onto the farmhouse floor, blade at the ready.

Red glass had shattered between the woman's heels. The bottle's wirework frame skittered between her feet, landing between them. She looked down at it, then up at him, mouth agape.

For an instant, the liquid was acting as liquid should, dripping down from her bare calves.

Then the wirework flashed.

Words rang out from the runes, an echo of the enchant-er's voice, stretched to the point of incomprehensibility by time and power. Rafe reared back as the air between himself and the woman filled with the stink of burnt herbs and sew-age. The liquid surged, taking on volume as it rose, thick-ening into a dark wave of sinew that slithered up to enfold both of her legs.

She thrashed against its tendrils, twisting her body until she was nearly free. Rafe stepped back, spotting the cleaver a few feet away.

Then the sinew drew her deep, slurping her up from ankle to hip. Gripping her tight, it heaved her into the air, then slammed her on her back.

Her skull struck the floorboards. Rafe dashed around, kicking the cleaver into the clearing, crouching down over her body. She lay still, the tendrils binding her so tightly to the floorboards that wood splintered.

The dagger felt alive in his hands.

"For Fortune."

He swept the blade through her belly.

Her tunic yawned open, dark around the edges like a great, wet mouth.

Rafe goggled as if he was a witness to this scene, not its author. Jassa was there already, kneeling beside him, lay-ing out a leather belt stuffed with tools. She tossed him a satchel. He held it open as she began to harvest, dropping the woman's organs, one by one, through the dark ring of fabric between his hands.

"Hold Her," whispered Jassa. "Hold Her steady, now!"

He nearly set down the satchel to comply, but the wiry woman's body was already still. It was Fortune Jassa meant. Hold *Her* steady—hold Her gaze.

Was She watching him now? Was that why he felt such excitement?

He ought to feel sick, or guilty. That's what a normal person would feel. But no—he felt elated.

Like a good boy.

Jassa dropped the woman's heart into the sack. She was almost done, already. He hummed to himself, shuddering happily.

Was it really the gaze of a goddess that made him feel this way? Or was it just the promise of the drash's kiss?

Either way, Rafe had killed a woman, unless the sinews had killed her first. Her body was almost empty, and when it was they'd take her insides back to Eth, where the Assemblage would deliver them to the Puppeteer. Rafe and Jassa would be heroes, at least for a night. Maybe Jassa was right, and this would be the beginning of their lucky streak.

Things were changing. He could feel it.

"Is it time?" he said, his anxious excitation making his voice squeak.

"Yes, boy. You've earned your reward."

Rafe tied off the satchel, panting. Jassa cleaned her fingers on the edge of the mud-brown tunic, then pulled two metal boxes out of her own knapsack, along with her ever-present notebook. Rafe crouched next to her, and for once she didn't begrudge his closeness.

One box was the size of her hand, the other as large as a prayer book. Both were scratched and dented from frequent use. She fiddled with the latches on the smaller box, and Rafe inhaled deeply, his mouth flooding with spit.

The box reeked of molasses and musk. A single lump of tlak, sticky and brown, was all that remained inside.

He frowned. Had they burned through so much since they'd left Eth? They must've done most of it yesterday, he supposed, though he remembered getting up from that session with the hunger still lapping at his bones.

Rafe nearly bit his tongue, but hunger overwhelmed caution. "Why the hell didn't we bring *more*?" he grumbled. "That's barely enough for a session. What happens on the way home?"

"One kill," said Jassa, grinning, "and the puppy thinks himself a wolf." The glint in her eye suggested that he was lucky her hands were busy. "We buy from the Puppeteer," she said with exaggerated patience, searching the pockets of her bag. "He controls who gets tlak. Perched over the sacred catacombs of Eth, from whence Fortune's sweetness comes." Finding a pair of tweezers, she began to wipe them with her filthy shirt.

All of this he knew. "Right, and he's not taking coin any more, just guts. But—"

"But murder might cause quakes in the city," she said, like she was helping him complete a thought he was too dim to finish alone. "So we're out here, in the leftmost ventricle of no place at all, where the deed won't cause any aftershocks. Providing for the family. Hunting and gathering, just like a number of other Aces and Deuces. But we won't," she murmured, lifting the tlak and warming it with her breath, "be among them for long. You'll soon have all you can handle!"

He frowned. "But for safety's sake, shouldn't we—"

"Fix before we start sweating? Yes, boy, we damn well should!" She glared at him. "Well? Ready the board!"

He was already too hard-up to argue. From the bottom of the box he took up a stub of chalk, four leaden bumpers, and a set of dice. He scrawled out the diagram, set the bumpers at its sides, and laid out the dice, two for Jassa, two for himself.

He heard a scrabble.

He held his breath.

Jassa had opened the larger box. A mesh screen covered its wide floor. Through it, dim storm-light struck the dull, umber chitin of a palm-sized insect with long, jointed legs and an overabundance of mandibles. Annoyed at the intrusion, the drash struck twice at the mesh, then retreated with a wary clatter.

"Everyone's hungry, little love," Jassa cooed. She lowered the tweezers toward a tiny hole in the screen, dropping the tlak inside. Skittering over, the drash plucked up the grain, coating it in moistness as it worked it into its craw.

"Good girl," muttered Rafe, bouncing on the balls of his feet. "Make it sweet for us, now."

"For *Fortune*."

The drash stared up at them with gray, gelatinous eyes that flooded with blackness as the drug hit its system. The grain had already dissolved, and the sac beneath its carapace would be full of liquefied tlak in a matter of moments, along with enough poison to kill a cow.

Strip away all the ceremony, and it was plain enough why members of the Assemblage traveled in pairs: no one could withstand two stings in a row, but wasting one was unthinkable.

Jassa tipped the box to one side. The drash slid across its metal floor, its black eyes staring mindlessly up at the roof.

"Deuces first," she said.

Rafe had already tugged his collar open. She peeled back the mesh. The creature barely twitched as she plucked it up and set it down on the left side of his neck, its mandibles tickling his earlobe.

"Hello, lovely," he murmured.

The drash's long middle legs gripped veins and tendons.

Jassa stroked the long, stiff hairs atop its carapace with a grubby forefinger. With maddening languor, the drash unfurled a stinger three times the length of its body, then plunged it deep in the meat of Rafe's throat.

The liquid was as cool as the drash's body, but it felt like it was boiling as it hit his blood. Rafe clenched his teeth and rocked, waiting for the pain to subside. The first kiss held more poison, or so he'd been told; as Jassa's Deuce, he'd never had the opportunity to taste the second, which the aficionados of the Assemblage held to be perfectly decanted. Grinding his teeth, he waited for the agony to recede.

Before the Assemblage, Rafe had eaten his tlak, and there had been no pain.

But nor had there been pleasure like the wave that overcame him now, crashing on his tongue and then his body. As the poison burned his muscles, the tlak itself bubbled through his salivary glands, thick as caramel and twice as sweet. As he chewed it, satisfying his stomach's hunger as surely as that in his bones, a second rush came, flushing his bits, candying his nerves. All his aches were washed away, except for the stabbing pain in his lungs, which felt less like an ailment now than a private joke. Losing his balance, he held out his arm for Jassa, but fell too far, forcing her to steady him. Whispering unpleasantries, she tugged the stinger out of his throat, lying down on her side as she set the drash down on her neck. Woozy though he was, he tended to his duties; as Jassa closed her eyes, he coaxed the second kiss into her, waiting for the last of the tlak to settle out before he lifted the creature and locked it back in its box.

Giving Jassa time to savor the rush, he turned his attention toward the board he'd sketched on the floor, struggling to remember what he'd been taught. He'd only been given a fraction of the rules to begin with, but Jassa insisted this was immaterial. A Deuce, she'd said, should know how to sketch a serviceable board—which was intricate enough that he'd bungled it the first few times, done no favors by the tingling of his brain—but no more, for as long as possible. His job was to roll, not to question, and if he pressed her as to why, she'd only say that Fortune loved a beginner.

Not that She loved him well enough to let him win. He'd lost by a wide margin each time.

Yet what did it matter? What were they playing for, anyway, but the affections of an abstract concept, a goddess who didn't exist?

Rafe knew better. The Gone-Away gods were real, once. But even they were long dead, buried in the catacombs under

Eth. That didn't stop everyone around him from worshiping shadows and figments, pouring their money into fantasy.

He lapsed into a coughing fit, then realized he was doing it to keep Jassa from hearing his thoughts—which got him giggling.

Jassa opened her eyes, snorting as she leapt toward the board. "Hurry!" she cried, though she took the time to pick up her notebook and resume her scribbling.

"I've *been* ready," he said, wiping his eyes.

"Shut your orifice. I *saw* something."

He'd asked her once what she kept in those pages, but all she'd say was, *I'm studying to improve my chances, as should you.*

At last she gasped and dropped the book on the floor. He scooped up his dice. She scooped up her own. Both their faces were gleaming in sweat.

"For the luck you give us," Jassa said, holding her rattling dice in cupped palms above her forehead, "for the peaks and the valleys, for your patience and wrath, for the stonily twisting prayers of your catacombs under Eth, for the sweet troves of treasure they contain, for the moody thunder of their quakes, for the inscrutable path we travel toward owning them at last—"

She went on like this for a while. As he shook the dice over his brow, Rafe glanced over at the dead woman's body, its lower half still encased in naked muscle, its upper half a peaceful cave of rib and gore.

I made that, he thought.

"—for all these things we see, and all those we cannot, we say unto you: *fuck you, Fortune.*"

Rafe giggled. "Fuck your rotting body straight through the sewers on a boat made of cocks and shite."

Jassa looked impressed. "Ha!" she cried, still shaking her dice overhead. "And have you chosen an aspect, as I taught you?"

"Of course." He hadn't, and he struggled now to remember one she'd like, mentally pawing through yet another list—this time of Fortune's avatars. "I'll be, uh—I'm Left-Handed Luce."

She barked with condescending laughter. "Then why are your dice in your *right hand*, boy? Luce *has* no north paw—even a simpleton knows that!"

"Sorry," he said, too amused to be aggrieved. Shifting the dice, he shook them harder, delighting in the sound.

"Now roll," Jassa whispered, "while Fortune still smiles on the blood you've shed."

The dice clattered down so rapidly that it didn't matter whose hands were whose, not to Rafe. To Jassa, everything mattered: she kept score on the wooden floor, scrawling out her inscrutable calculations in tiny labyrinths of chalk, consulting her notebook with frequent murmurs and exclamations. Leaving her to it, he zeroed in on the parts of the game he could sense, like the way the dice jumped as they struck the pits and knots in the wooden floor, or the sound of them rebuffed by the bumpers that kept them from tumbling into the grass.

He must've got lost in staring at the clearing—all those blades pelted by the rain, all trembling at once!—because Jassa was shouting, and was red enough that she must've been at it for a while. "—out of the groove entirely, you baby-faced buffoon," she cried. "You're losing Her!"

Flecks of spittle darkened her chalky calculations. He tore his gaze away from that, too. "What do you want me to do?"

"Keep Her fucking eyes on you," she snarled. "I swear, idiocy like yours is perilously close to lucklessness." She reared back from him, as if he might be contagious. "Are you *sure* you haven't any unquiet dead following you about? At times you seem almost—blighted."

"No such thing as unquiet dead," he muttered. "When you're gone, you're gone, is all."

But the question brought Gingerbeard's face to his mind.

"You're about to learn whether that's true," shouted Jassa, "if you don't get back on Fortune's good side—and fast! Her *eyes*, boy!"

He bit his lip, seeking the clarity of pain. The weight of all this ridiculous ceremony was crushing him.

But Jassa would strike him soon, and it went worse when she was high.

Keep Fortune's eyes on you—what did it even mean? He sighed, then coughed. What did Jassa say about Fortune's fickle favors?

That She loved a beginner, and that She loved blasphemy.

Thus, in order to play along, all Rafe had to do was combine the two in some novel way.

Like telling the truth.

"I don't believe in any of this," he said, then flung the dice.

Jassa stared at the board, her pale face gone white. She scribbled on the floor, then in her notebook. Cursing, she rolled quickly. "I don't know what you're doing, boy, but you'd better do it again."

He picked up the dice again, smiling. He'd finally found something he was good at. "I don't even believe that Fortune is real. I never did. You promised me drugs, so I joined. But you don't give me near enough, not to fake all this forever. So fuck it, Jass. I'm done pretending."

Rattle, tink.

Jassa gasped, then sent her own dice tumbling in response. She wrote some more, then gasped some more. "Again. Roll again!"

Rafe closed his fist. "Why should I?"

She recoiled. "Wh—*why*? Because She's here, She's with us, She's in us—She *is* the *rolling* of our *dice*! Now bring us home, boy, bring us to glory, before She turns Her hateful head!"

Rafe slid the dice over into his right hand, rubbing them against each other between his fingers and palm until they squeaked.

Jassa's hands were shaking.

He let them shake a while.

"I heard them call you the Widow of Lank Street," he said. "They say you chew through Deuces quicker than a locust chews grain. For a minute or two you were kind to me, so I didn't want to believe, but I believe, now. You're gaming me, and I hope She does exist, you know it, Jass?" He ran his tongue over his teeth. "So I can watch Her game *you*."

Jassa's face went red. "*Roll.*"

He shrugged and let the dice slide off a limp palm.

The chalk snapped in Jassa's fingers.

"Oh, you bastard," she whispered. "Oh, you son of a tit-less sow!"

Rafe squinted at her scrawls on the floor. He was on the verge of comprehension when she stood and kicked at the board. The chalk spun over his head, the bumpers skittered into the mud, and one die struck his knee, rebounded, and landed an inch from the dead woman's face.

"What happened?" he said.

The sound of his voice surprised him.

It wasn't a question—it was a demand.

"You've no idea."

Her voice was cracked and thin. Was Jassa crying?

"How could you? Beginner's luck, they call it, but that's not what it is." She crushed her eyes against the heels of her palms. "It's Fortune's revenge! I had you on the edge. I *had* you! She was moving the world for me, She *was*, I was on the verge of ascension, and then—"

"Wait."

Rafe saw, or thought he did. He pointed at his score, then at hers, the skin on his neck prickling in wonder.

"Jass. Did I just—"

"I am the velvet beneath the rolling of your dice," she croaked. "You ragged little *cunt!*"

"My *Deuce?*" Rafe couldn't hold back his laughter, or the swift thought behind it—*Fortune will provide.* "But that means—"

"—that I'm yours to command." Jassa lowered her head. "May the Goddess help us all."

—A Thousand Little Men—

"**S**tew's ready," said the boy, poking a wooden spoon into the pot, but neither of them ate so much as a bite. He sent the woman to pick through the mud instead, where she searched for the pieces she'd kicked from their game. The storm had passed by the time she packed them up, and the two of them walked into the clearing, the boy leading with bleary pride, the woman trudging after with the satchel hanging over her shoulder, slapping against the backs of her thighs.

He stopped at the edge of the wood, squinting up at the rafters of the farmhouse. She muttered a question, and he shook his head, then led her into the trees.

Rain plipped from the leaves. The frogs spoke up in chorus.

A burning log slumped, embers tinkling from its middle.

Something scratched among the rafters.

There came the rasp of fabric on wood.

A tiny figure emerged, a man-shaped burlap doll who shimmied down a beam, steadying his boots on the hobnails that some long-dead homemaker had strung with dried flowers and herbs. As he landed on the countertop with a *tip-tap*, his breath rattled with satisfaction.

The mannikin stood no taller than an infant, despite his platform shoes. Dusting off his three-piece suit, he surveyed the room, his button eyes shining in a face stitched from thick, burgundy cloth. Hefting the slotted spoon the boy had tossed onto the counter, he crept to the edge with an eager, flat-toothed grin, peering down at the drawers below.

He pried them open with the spoon's handle, each drawer wider than the one above it, until they resembled a miniature flight of stairs. Testing his weight with every step, the mannikin descended to the floor, then crept across it, tapping each floorboard in turn with the rounded end of his makeshift cane.

He stopped when he reached the wiry woman's body, scrunching his burlap brow to squint at the sinews cocooning her legs. Inching forward, he reached out with the spoon, probing the mass of muscle—leaping back when it shuddered in response, like the haunch of some sleeping beast irritated by a fly. Keeping his distance, he pressed on, tip-tapping, into the shadows.

At last he reached a plank that gave a hollow knock when he rapped it. Tossing the spoon aside, he pulled up the board, muttering, "I *knew* those addle-pated dullards had left money on the table!" Flexing his glove-like fingers, he reached into the recess and gripped a strap of the woman's bag. After a prolonged struggle, he cursed, then dropped down into the floor, where the sounds of buckles opening were audible, just before a gasp of appreciation. "Trinkets!" he squealed, tossing a bag of glass vials to land with a clink near the woman's outstretched hand.

She snatched it up immediately.

"All right, Tiny, that'll do."

The mannikin's head popped up above the floor-boards in surprise, searching the room for the source of the voice.

Ashlan propped herself up on her elbows, and his puppet's mouth went wide with astonishment. "You heard me," she grunted, sliding the bag of bottles back along the floor, where it bumped against his chest and landed at his feet. The sinews cinched tight around her in protest at her sudden movement. "Get your mittens off my gear, and we still might leave here on good terms."

"Dear lord, girl," he said with a laugh, "are you actually *alive*?"

"More alive than you, kid," she said. "Your burlap's about to bust." The pain in her legs was incredible, but at this point in the day it was nothing but a drop in a very large bucket. "How long since you were animated, anyway? Fifty years? Sixty? I never heard of a mannikin so recent."

"I am ninety-nine years of age," he said, crawling out of the floor. "But I've still a few surprises left before I unravel."

"Damn." If the little man wasn't lying, it was remarkable, maybe even unprecedented. Something niggled at her mind as she shooed a fly out of her belly. "Seems like a hell of a feat for someone so fragile."

"Well, what can I say?" Planting one hand on his hip, shoving the other into the pocket of his worsted waistcoat, he thrust his little chin into the air. "I'm tenacious."

"Good on you. Around here, you're either a survivor or a maggot farm." She searched the floor for the band that had fallen from the red bottle. There it was—a few feet from her head. "Now. Are you going to give me a hand, or do I have to do this the hard way?"

The mannikin paused, cocking his head and examining her more deeply. "You're—a fascinating specimen, I admit," he said, folding his arms. "But seeing as you've caught me with a hand in your personal cookie jar, I'm unable to imagine a scenario in which helping you escape your predicament would do me a lick of good."

Ashlan exhaled irritably, laying flat on her back. "No trust in your fellow freaks, that's what your problem is."

"It's hardly at the top of the list."

Slowly, methodically, Ashlan began to relax her muscles, from the top of her scalp on down. She could feel the pain more acutely this way, but then pain was so familiar a companion that she was able, as usual, to embrace it. By the time she got down to her toes, the enchantment had eased its grip, ever so slightly, in response to the lack of resistance. Then, with a motion so slow and fluid it was barely perceptible, she moved her right arm overhead, reaching for the wirework band whose runes held the enchantment's trigger. But it was no use trying to trick the sinews; the band still lay an inch or two out of reach, and as soon as she exerted herself, the muscles squeezed all sensation from her legs, tugging her a precious inch farther from her goal.

She slapped her palms on the floor, annoyed. "Last chance to be a helper, little fella."

"I'll pass." The mannikin scooped up his spoon, twirling it as he circled her. "You know, most people I've encountered on this long, strange trip have been a bit more surprised to meet a puppet moving on his own. Yet you seem to know *just* what you're dealing with." Stopping beside her, at a safe distance from both her arms and the sinews, he leaned on the end of the spoon. "Which leaves me at a disadvantage, doesn't it? I've never seen a human survive half the damage you've taken, and I've seen my fair share of damaged humans. And, dear me, would you look at *that*!" Laughing, he pointed into her yawning stomach. "Your organs are regrowing, all clustered in your belly like an bunch of peeled grapes! What *are* you, exactly?"

"Hard to kill." She took a deep breath, then wrenched her body, tugging her hips as hard as she could against her constricting restraints. "The rest," she grunted, "is up for debate."

There was a resounding *crack* as Ashlan's femur snapped in two. She couldn't help but shout at a pain so deep and brilliant, but in the space of a single breath, she wrestled the outcry down to a whispery hiss.

She looked down at herself, not without satisfaction. With her body twisted unnaturally around the shattered pivot of her hip, she'd bought herself a good bit of reach.

Lunging for the wirework band, she caught it with a fingernail. Dragging it down, lifting it between her fists, she yanked as hard as she could, reducing dozens of carefully-wrought runes into a mangled silver line.

Just as she'd thought, the enchanter had cut some corners. You couldn't expect perfection these days.

Cut loose from their binding, the sinews thrashed wildly, gripping floorboards at random. Some tendrils snaked out toward the edge of the farmhouse floor, while others slapped against the kitchen cabinets, where Ashlan was amused to see the mannikin leaping back with a squeal of dismay, striking the back of his head on the wood with a dull thump.

Before he'd been caught, the mass of muscle gave out a piteous squelch, then burst in a wave of foul-smelling liquid. Crinkling her nose, she watched the potion slosh beneath her twisted legs, dripping down into the cracks between the floorboards. "Yeesh."

The mannikin giggled nervously, rubbing the back of his wooly head as he edged away. "I suppose I could have tossed it to you, after all."

"Would've been nice. Not that I expected it." Ashlan tried moving her leg, but stopped when the room went dark. Her hip was broken, and even masochists had their limits.

Then a breeze wafted the smell of the stew in her direction, and Ashlan let out a trembling moan. Though she still had only the barest vestige of a stomach, her body flooded with hunger.

Enough to make her hands shake.

Enough to make her mouth water.

Enough to make her think of how much closer the mannikin was than the stewpot.

Shaking off the thought, breathing as deeply as her fledgling lungs would allow, she flung herself onto her open belly, grunting as she landed.

"I *would've* helped, honestly," the mannikin was saying as he eyed the edge of the farmhouse floor. "But I got too curious, damn me! Wondering how you might escape, and precisely how much—well!—how much *pain* you might take to accomplish such a goal."

"How much you got?" she whispered. Hand over hand, she dragged herself toward the stewpot, trying to keep herself from looking directly at him.

Taking her desperation for a lack of murderous intent, the mannikin seemed to come to a decision. "A bite to eat, is that what you're after? Allow me," he said, tossing his spoon aside and stepping quickly toward the hearth. "My experiment was a little childish, I'll admit. Allow me to make amends. Perhaps it's time I—what was it?—put some trust in my fellow freaks! A friend in need, isn't that what the oldsters say?"

She stopped, squeezing her eyes shut. "You want to be—friends."

"Associates, at the very least!"

Wrestling with a welter of feelings she didn't care to acknowledge, much less name, she peeked as he hefted up the bowl of rabbit guts and dumped it on the coals. The smoky stink was fantastic, but the mannikin didn't recoil. They had no olfactory sense, she remembered. Taste and smell were finicky enchantments, and there was limited room for rune-work on the insides of their little hides.

Dragging a chair to the hearth, he maneuvered his way to the lip of the pot and labored to scoop out a bowl of stew twice as heavy as his body. Somehow, he got it to the floor without spilling a drop, then slid it between her hands with the proud air of a circus tamer bringing a lion to heel.

"Cheers." Ashlan lifted the bowl to her lips and gulped half of it down at once, disregarding her burning tongue. "So how long you been following those junkies?"

His head snapped up, a tuft of black cotton bobbing atop it. "Beg pardon?"

"C'mon." Ashlan swallowed another chunk of rabbit and pointed into the wood. "*They* are harvesting human innards. *You* are a talking sack stuffed with enchanted human innards. And we're in the middle of actual nowhere, so. Not much of a stretch."

"Hmph." He tucked an errant thread into his waistcoat, whose buttons, she noticed, were made of solid gold, with little dancing men on their faces. "You are awfully knowledgeable about my kind for a creature of your apparent age! I was under the impression that not many of us had been seen in quite a few generations, and given the lofty assignments given to the last of us left living, a woman roaming the countryside alone would seem ill-positioned to learn the secrets of our design. Not that I'm averse to an exchange of information, mind you! But perhaps you'd lead things off by enlightening me—just how old *are* you?"

"Stopped counting a while back. Got to be close to two hundred." She hadn't quite finished the bowl, but her rudimentary stomach was almost bursting. Mewling, she wrangled herself into a seated position, lifting her injured leg and forcing it out in front of her. "And yeah, I've met a few mannikins. Used to date a girl who did the stitching on the—" She wiped sweat from her eyes onto the back of one gore-spattered sleeve. "The puppets. That's what you look like, without the stuffing in. No offense."

"None taken. That's what we *are*, after all, however long the strings—puppets stuffed with walking, talking guts. What a world! So you're more than two centuries years old, are you? All that time to wander and scheme, well-nigh invincible. And yet your belongings amount to a small sack of ornamental gemstones, a handful of empty glass vials, and a few dog-eared books banned in most human societies."

"What else does a girl need?" An itchy wave of pain coursed through her gut as her body heat spiked.

Her stomach had burned through all that food in an instant.

"Hit me again." Tossing back the last few mouthfuls of stew, she held out the bowl, glancing at him despite herself, then staring sullenly out at the wood.

Damn if he didn't look just like an upright game hen.

Bowing without a trace of mockery, the mannikin trotted the bowl back to the hearth. "But you must've kept busy with *something*, all this while," he said as he scooped. "What is your profession, if you don't mind me prying?"

"You've *been* prying," she muttered. "What's a little more?"

He brought back the bowl of stew, and she all but snatched it from his hands. Another wave of prickly heat struck her as she gorged, this one bathing her hip. Even for her, this hunger was intense, and she wondered what had come over her.

"I don't work often," she said, thumping on her chest as she waited for her esophagus to catch up to her mouth. "Keep to myself, mostly. Easier for everyone that way. But when I'm really hurting for coin, I have a—a healer routine.

I show up at a village market, borrow someone's knife, and do myself some damage. Cut off a finger, or what have you. And then, when I've got a good-sized crowd watching, I drink a vial of berry juice, and—"

Closing her eyes, she braced herself against the floor and channeled her body's surging heat. Her broken femur went furnace-hot, then *popped*, loud enough to make the mannikin jump.

Groaning with relief, she lifted her leg into the air, wiggling its toes.

He put a hand on his chest. "Dear girl, did you just—"

"All better."

Dripping with sweat, she pointed at her midriff. Her ribs, visible only moments ago, were covered over by sheaths of muscle grasping to close the gap.

"I show them a little of this, and next thing you know, they're throwing money at me."

The mannikin whistled in appreciation. "With proof like that, what *wouldn't* they pay?"

"And there's a little song and dance to go with it. 'Heals everything from gout to gonorrhea. Even raises your fresher dead folk, if you're lucky.'" Ashlan had to put her hands behind her back to keep them off her belly—the itching was that intense. "'Unfortunately, I sold out of stock in the *last* town I was in, and the ingredients are rare.' That kind of thing." Feeling a shift inside as her organs began to blossom, Ashlan slurped down the broth at the bottom of the bowl.

She was still hungry, she realized.

What had come over her? She was used to a raging appetite when she got this banged up, but it wasn't usually so pronounced that she'd start looking for nourishment in anything that came to hand.

On the other hand, it had been quite a few years since she'd been disemboweled.

"An admirable confidence game," said the mannikin, still trying to feel her out. "And yet, as we've noted, you're a pauper."

"Well, I never claimed to have any damn sense. In business or otherwise. And when bodily harm isn't a thing, you tend to get a little lax where security is concerned." Sated for now, she stood and tossed the bowl onto the counter. "And I don't know if you've heard, but there's a war on. For the past century or three." Still jelly-legged, she staggered over to her belongings, digging through the pile until she found another tunic, identical to the one the boy had ruined.

"A war that profits many," mused the mannikin, "although, with few exceptions, they started rich." Ashlan caught him staring at her body, without prurience, as she pulled off her clothing. "In any case, despite your best efforts, you own nothing but a sagging bag of trinkets and your remarkable talents, which require naught but sustenance to activate. Have I got that right?"

"Sort of."

He was about to follow up with another question, but the sight of her stomach distracted him.

She let him look.

Smooth, dark skin was closing over the cavity like cloth tugged together by an invisible zipper—though it took all her will not to scratch at the seam her nerves insisted was separating the old flesh from the new.

"If I eat before I heal, it's easier all around. Saves me a monster of a headache. Stops me from slowing down."

Keeps me from doing anything I might actually regret, she thought as she pulled the tunic over her head. For good measure, she grabbed the bowl and scooped out the stewpot, which was empty now but for a pool of broth.

"With talents like yours," said the mannikin, "I'm amazed you haven't found work at the court of a king."

"What," she mumbled, her mouth full, "you mean as entertainment?"

"As a bodyguard!" He slashed his spoon like a tiny sword. "Invulnerable, and willing to work for nothing more than the odd pot of stew? I can't imagine that no one, in the past two hundred years, has proposed this to you."

"I tend to keep all this to myself." Slurping, she sat down on the edge of the farmhouse floor. "But you caught me at a—vulnerable moment."

"Well, and I'm no threat to you," he said, strolling out beside her. "You could rend my seams asunder with minimal effort."

"Anyway," she said, shuddering at the thought, "I'm not really bodyguard material. Never been in a fight, even."

"I can see why, if you're willing to take abuse like *those* two dished out."

She shrugged off his scrutiny.

This creature had a knack for bringing up things she didn't want to talk about, and she began to wonder what she was still doing here.

"So you're not a warrior," he said. "But could you be convinced to *preserve* life? Not a great deal of it—just mine," he said, sitting down beside her. "And only for a short while. Work for me, and you'd never again need to sneak away from a village market in the dead of night. My name is Hollis Runt."

He thrust a burlap hand at her. It was filthy, soaked with a century of god-knows-what.

She took it gently in her own. "Ashlan Ley. And I appreciate the offer, little man. But I travel alone."

"With holes in your tunics," he said with a merry laugh, "and empty vials as your only treasure! At least allow me to finish my pitch before you refuse."

She nodded, dimly understanding that she was already considering it.

Her behavior was unaccountable. She'd just spent more time talking to Hollis Runt than she had to anyone in decades.

She owed him nothing. She didn't even know him.

Had she ever told anyone but a relative this much of the truth about herself?

He dug into his waistcoat pocket, waggling his head. "You were correct, of course: I *have* been following those junkies, ever since they staggered across my path, some miles outside of Eth. I'd heard a rumor, you see, in my travels among the undersides of certain tavern tabletops—that *someone* in that fabled city was hunting for human organs. And when these two stumbling simpletons advertised to the entire wood that they were after *you*, and working for *him*, well, I simply made a point to reach you before they did. Not hard, considering their pace! I knew what they'd take from you, and it's true that I let them—without compunction. It's a marvel that you're alive, but I'll admit that I wouldn't have stopped to mourn you if you'd died like a sensible person."

"Gee, thanks."

From his pocket he pulled a silken pouch the size and color of a wild strawberry. "Innocents will die regardless of my actions, Ashlan Ley. I don't know if you've heard," he said with a gleam in his buttons, "but there's a *war* on. And those junkies, nincompoops though they may be? They're agents of a powerful cult of lunatics who do their harvesting for a man known only by a fanciful sobriquet."

Ashlan didn't like the sound of this. "Haven't heard of him. But I've been out of the loop a while."

"Word is this fellow haunts the catacombs under the streets of Eth, manufacturing drugs from the gland of some Gone-Away god. And yet, rich as this master criminal is, he's recently risked the attention of the Ethian guards to branch out into this rather unsavory collecting. They call him the Puppeteer—and since you're so sharp, I'd wager it won't take you long to guess what he's building with all those guts, eh?"

Ashlan's mouth went dry. "Either the world's biggest sausage," she muttered, "or more like you."

Hollis snorted, teasing open the little pouch's drawstring. "More that *look* like me, perhaps." Digging into the silk, he pinched something between his thumb and forefinger that looked like a red seed. "But *I* was made to assist and to entertain. I was sold as a jester, used as a nanny, and given access to far too many state secrets. After a while, they just forgot I was there."

"Where was this?"

"The Court of Cru, may it rest in peace."

Cru. Ashlan's skin rippled with gooseflesh.

No wonder this worn-out mannikin was making her feel so strange—Hollis Runt was the prototype.

She'd made him, a hundred years ago, with her own hands.

Sewn those button eyes into place. Painted the runes on his hide-lined insides.

Stitched up the burlap around a warm bundle of her own innards.

Damn it, how could she be hungry *again*? Carrying the bowl back to the pot, she scooped out the last bit of broth, disgusted with herself. "What happened to them?" she murmured between slurps. "The Court of Cru?"

"The Queen forced me to raise three broods of her children," he said. Ashlan vaguely recalled one of Her Majesty's trips to Eth, made in her ninth month, to take advantage of the city's enchantments, which multiplied any single birth into a brood of seven. "All twenty-one of those fist-faced hellions at once! And it was a special sort of hell they created for me. Torturing me for sport, over all those years, growing ever taller, ever crueler, their lives prolonged by enchantment. I was their toy, to be sure— and yet I had unlimited access to their minds, and not a one of them had the imagination to judge my character. Given the task of educating them, I taught them all the most violent secrets of statecraft, dwelling in particular on the blood-soaked histories of their ancestors. I paid lavish attention to any tales of fratricide—and told each of the demons that these special stories were for *his* ears alone. Ah, it took decades to turn them against one another, but

I did enjoy my work. It was the performance of a life-time—or twenty-one!

"And then, when the Queen had the good sense to die at last, stretched beyond any semblance of humanity by her philters and incantations, I set my full-grown monsters against one other, then did away with the few that still lurched through those cold, marble halls. You might be surprised how much damage one can do with a potion of a paralysis and a simple household sewing needle," he said, clambering down into the grass. "And I took it as the highest compliment of my career that each dying Cruvian, with his last gargling breath, proclaimed himself the one true King."

"That can't be," she blurted. "Your enchantment won't allow you to harm a living human, much less your pact-holder."

"Correct, once more," he said, giggling as he carried his seed to a patch of mud. "At least in theory! And yet, as Granther said in his *Incantarium:*

> *The stubbornest enchantment ever laid*
> *In gold or parchment, stone or breath or mud,*
> *Is but a debt the gods demand be paid*
> *In salty waterfalls of mortal blood.*

"There are numerous ways to change the terms of a pact, Ashlan Ley, though none that allow one's hands to stay clean." He peered at her, and she tried to bury her dismay. "Does it unnerve you?" he said, pushing his red seed into a patch of mud with a burlap thumb. "So be it! I saw no other way to break my pact with the Court, and I could hardly live out my lifespan peacefully once I'd heard rumors about the Puppeteer. I've met but a few other mannikins, and I could tolerate none of them—twisted little imps to a man, their faces like mockeries of mine, but devoid of my strength, my code, my character. Now I'm asked to abide an *army* of these little impostors, carving up the world in my image? When I, Hollis Runt, was robbed of my legacy to waste my life in a cesspool like Cru?"

He wasn't even looking at her any more, just gibbering down at his seed.

Ashlan couldn't deny how awful this army of puppets sounded. The project at Uni had been snatched out of her hands before Hollis had even awakened. They'd sent him to Cru against her will, with a wave of others cast in burlap and leather, then used the proceeds to weaponize the design. When she'd protested, they'd tried to sell her a story about prevention and precaution. They'd keep *more* people from dying with these hideous, armor-plated murder dolls.

At some point they'd fallen out of fashion, and Eth had moved to the next enchantment. But now it seemed like the Uni's redesign had been dredged up again. It wasn't her fault, of course—not hers alone. She'd never wanted this.

But she'd designed him, she'd filled him with herself, and every other mannikin had followed after.

And what did it mean that Hollis had turned out to be a murderer himself?

Queasy, she realized she'd been waiting for something like this to happen for years. She'd always known it would, and carried that knowledge close to her chest, pretending it wasn't there.

Ashlan had been born wrong, and no amount of avoidance could fix that.

Do no harm, she'd promised herself, and look where that had led.

"Well!" he cried, cackling at the mud. "I can't stand the thought of more like me. And nor should you, Ashlan Ley! Imagine: a thousand little men wielding a thousand poisoned blades, all their devious minds bent on slaughter. If the Puppeteer isn't stopped, and quickly, there'll be nothing left of Eth—and then they'll sweep like wildfire through the rest of the kingdoms!"

He turned his head from the mud to grin up at her.

"Unless, of course, you'll join me."

He was ninety-nine, he'd said. And his enchantment had been keyed to end after a century.

She'd meant it as a sort of inside joke. With constructs, you had to specify *something*. But no one had expected any of them to last this long.

He'd fall apart soon enough. Maybe before he put himself in harm's way.

But maybe not. If he was bound for Eth, there were a thousand ways he could get himself killed before he even waddled through the gates.

None of that explained why she cared. She'd never gone looking for him, after all. And it had been decades since she'd given the mannikin project so much as a passing thought.

Seeing him made it different, somehow. She stepped down into the clearing, annoyed at herself.

Hollis lowered his face to the mound of earth and began to whisper something rhythmic and unintelligible—then leapt back as his incantation started writhing through the air, brushing against her skin with a moist, eldritch heat.

He stopped beside her shin as the mud before them began to roll and buckle, as if a mound of snakes were buried just beneath the surface.

"What *is* this?" she murmured. The grass below their feet began to rumple. Runes resolved themselves in the mud, rising in a spiral around the planted seed.

"Your inheritance," he purred, "if you accept my offer."

Standing on tip-toe, he reached up and grasped her hand.

She took it, squeezed it, and hated herself for the gesture.

"Help me trail the junkies," he murmured, "deliver me safely to the Puppeteer, and all of this will be yours when I'm gone."

He gave her hand a squeeze back, bruising her knuckles.

She'd forgotten how *strong* they were.

"You've been around a while. But with a war chest like mine, Ashlan Ley, you'll really be able to *live*."

Four little hills rose around the seed, each one splitting open in a jet of steam. Cracks appeared in the mud between them, each one impossibly straight, forming a rectangle that began at once to shudder. Ashlan cowered as the muddy platform rocketed up, shooting clear above her head, clods of earth tumbling from the sides of a gigantic ebony cabinet whose doors swung open with a moan.

She peered up—and gaped.

Its deep, gleaming shelves were stuffed with ingots of solid gold.

Hollis dropped her hand, strode to a cabinet, yanked open a drawer, and plucked out a fist-sized nugget from a hoarder's trove of odds and ends. Whistling, he tossed it into her hands. "Just a taste, for now!" he called, then slammed shut the doors with a burst of whispered syllables. The cabinet sunk out of sight with a flatulent sigh, and the swarm of runes collapsed into a muddy depression and a roiling cloud of steam.

Ashlan felt the weight of the soft metal in her palms, still warm, either from the summoning or its place of origin.

She'd never been good with coin. She'd just lose it in some scheme, or give it all away once she got drunk, the way she always did.

But pretending she wanted it beat trying to explain whatever was driving her to stick by his side.

"Deal," she said, closing her fist. "I'll bring you to the Puppeteer. But I'm not your mercenary."

"A shame, too," said Hollis, clicking his heels. "I suspect you'd already be rich if you were! But don't think twice—I'm more than happy to put a knife in my accursed creator all by my lonesome."

She almost dropped the lump of gold.

He thought the Puppeteer had made him.

It'll be fine, she thought. He won't ask, and you won't tell him. If a creature as manically single-minded as Hollis found out his *real* creator was a few feet away, there would be trouble. More likely than not, he'd attack her.

She'd probably have to put him down, and she just couldn't bear it.

"Look, you want to stop the Puppeteer from making any more mannikins, I'll—I'll get you there in one piece," she said. "We'll track the junkies, and follow them to him. But no killing sprees. Agreed? He's—one murder is more than enough. Eth is too—volatile."

"Very well." He pursed his burlap lips. "Although I must confess that when you started moving around, all ripped to ribbons, I was hoping you'd be more—fun."

Ashlan shoved her things into her bag. "Let's go while we've still got some day."

"Oh, we're in no rush! We'll have no trouble finding *them*, not with your long legs beneath us," he said, trotting up to her. "Those two travel about as subtly as a herd of elephants."

Hollis held his arms up over his head, waiting expectantly.

Ashlan stared down, puzzled. Then she recognized the gesture.

Unsettled, she lifted him up like a toddler, shivering at his cool weight on her hip. "Let's hope they're still stoned enough to be taking their time."

"Undoubtedly. Besides, the ferret-faced woman made that urchin boy her leader at the end of their game. He's a babe in the literal woods, so I'm more concerned about finding them *too* quickly than not at all. Let's do our best to stay off their heels until they're in Eth, eh? It's better if they don't know we're after them until the very end."

"And then?"

He laid his head against her chest, giggling.

A spray of raindrops struck her face as they passed beneath a springing branch and into the wood.

—Thorns—

Rafe was running through the trees, crashing through the underbrush, sending deer and rabbits bounding, loosing startled birds with his footfalls. Prickers raked his skin, but he was high enough to laugh at the scratches. Now it was Jassa who kept falling behind, yelping out, "Have you gone mad, boy? You're lost—utterly lost!"

"Am I?" he cried, leaping up onto the trunk of a downed tree, its roots coated with clumps of dark earth. "Am I, Deuce? Or are *you* the one who's lost her way?"

Jassa stomped into view, wiping her nose with poorly-concealed fury. "Just about," she muttered. "But if we double back now, I can still get us back on the path."

"Fortune's found us a *new* path," he said, raising his left hand over his forehead and giving it a shake. "Isn't this what you wanted, Jass? Her eyes are on me, just like you asked!

Damn the Lady." He squatted down, licking his lips. "Damn Her eyes!"

Maybe it was just the tlak, but Rafe was beginning to wonder if there might not be something to all this. The game had done him a good turn at long odds, that was sure. Another stroke of luck or two, and he'd be willing to call this a lucky streak—and it was only a few short steps from there to full-blown faith.

Better to be an Ace who believes than a doubting Deuce, he thought, waving his hand in and out of a shaft of sunshine with pure, childlike glee.

Suddenly he stopped, looking down at Jassa.

"What are you doing?"

"Checking something," she mumbled.

He could *see* what she was doing plain enough.

She'd sat right down on a rock and pulled out that notebook of hers—and was flipping through pages and scribbling notations, as if her time was her own.

Jassa had ridden him like a fairground pony since the moment he'd become her Deuce, and now that the shoe was on the other foot, she'd given herself an unscheduled break.

Balling his fists, Rafe leapt down from the tree trunk. "This belongs to the Goddess now," he sang, swiping the book from her paws.

Jassa hopped up, ready to strike.

But Rafe whipped his dagger from its scabbard. "Easy there, Deuce—let's not forget who Fortune's chosen!"

The blood drained from her face. "Yes, my—my Ace," she whispered, like the phrase caused her pain.

"Don't start weeping, now," he cooed, tapping her chin with the flat of the blade. "These are the rules you taught me, Jass! Surely they're good enough for you, too?"

She nodded miserably, seeming to deflate. He caught a glance at the open pages of the book in his hand.

Gibberish. It was all illegible.

How long had he been following an imbecile—and *why*?

"Please, my Ace," she whined, "let's find the path."

"Oh, we've found it." Sweeping his cape aside, sheathing his dagger, he shoved her notebook into his bag, noting her distress with a rush of satisfaction. "Follow me, Deuce—I know the way!"

Off he ran, seeing bursts of color in the trees that probably weren't there, whooping as the branches swished around him. This wildness had been tamped down by Jassa's control for so long that Rafe had lost track of what he really was— even under the influence, he'd forgotten what it felt like to soar this high.

"But Fortune didn't forget!"

He tripped on a root, but landed on his feet. Another stroke of luck.

They were everywhere, now that he knew how to look.

He really was Fortune's favorite, wasn't he?

How had he ever let Jassa push him down so far?

Because he was used to following, in a way.

He'd been cared for, before all this.

Gingerbeard had been a kind of—

No use dwelling on it.

"It's a new day!" he barked, starting off again.

"But what will happen, my Ace," shouted Jassa, still lagging behind, "when night falls, and we're still in the wood? We won't make it far without the kiss!"

The thought almost stopped him. She was right—withdrawal would close around them in a day or two. If they didn't fix, they might well die out here.

But this was no way for an Ace to think. "Fortune told me to roll the dice," he shouted back, "and I'm rolling!"

Despite himself, Rafe was panting now, his breath short, a familiar stabbing in his chest reminding him that he'd taken things too far already. He'd have to use his newfound status to get some time alone tonight, and give his lungs a break.

Not for too long at a stretch, they'd told him, *and never when you sleep.*

He could feel his pace slowing, his faith draining—and then he saw the tree.

"Fortune will provide," he whispered, tingling all over.

"What's this?" panted Jassa, coming to his side and bending over with her palms on her knees. "A tree struck by lightning, is it?"

"No," he murmured, stepping closer to its dark trunk. "But the ignorant often make that mistake. This is a gazing-tree, Deuce—the biggest I've ever seen."

It towered over the wood like a grand, shining shadow. Every inch of the thing was blackened, from its twisting roots to its abundant foliage—but no fire had touched it. Its leaves hadn't burnt, just gone as dark and glossy as obsidian, from stem to blade. Nor were they moving, though a breeze rustled the branches of every other tree in the copse.

"So you're just going to *gaze* at it, then? How's that meant to help?"

"Hold your tongue, or I'll hold it for you."

Rafe reached out and grabbed at a low-hanging branch. Both the leaf and the twig that it clung to came off in his hand. He opened his fist, examining the dense, dark, pollen-like stuff that remained.

After a moment, the motes began to drift back to the branch, clinging to the stub they'd come from.

"That's—enchantment," whispered Jassa, agog.

"You're thinking too small." The powdered bits of stem and leaf were already fitting back into their former shape. "You could claw down this whole tree and scatter its bits to the edges of this wood, and it'd still come back to itself in a matter of hours. That's no enchantment, Deuce—it's the will of a god."

She shook her head, wide-eyed. "Never heard of Fortune doing anything of the like."

"Nothing to do with Her. The gazing-trees belong to Gone-Away Nex."

Through the haze of his high, a memory bobbed up.

Rafe was packing his bag, back at the boarding house.

He'd wrapped something old in a pair of moth-eaten socks, and stuffed it to the bottom.

"The Gone-Away," said Jassa carefully, "are buried under the *city*, my Ace. And we are miles from there, remember?"

"But all these lands were Theirs, once." He swung his bag onto the ground and opened its flap. "And Nex was the Goddess of Connection. She had a vested interest in keeping tabs on everything at once." Working his arm down through layers of clothing, each grittier than the last, he heard the drash skittering in its box. "The gazing-trees were Her eyes and ears. No matter how far She traveled, She could always watch these woods."

"And how do *you* know all this?"

He felt the forked handle and closed his fist. "Because my family used to be Her attendants. Generations ago, we kept Her temples, and were rewarded for it. Even after the Gone-Away died, traces of Them remained. Like Nex's gazing-trees. And *these*." He tugged the tool out, feeling its weight in his hands. "Every Davin has one."

"A pair of sacred socks." Jassa sighed. "My Ace, I beg of you, let us—"

"Shut your fucking mouth, Deuce."

He pulled the tool from the fabric, tugging open the ties on its leather case and sliding it free.

The blade was yellowed bone, worn and chipped. A scapula, or so he'd been told—the shoulder of some long-dead ancestor. He hadn't thought of it before, but given its size, it must have been a child's.

"Is that—a knife?"

"A spade," he said. "Not for digging, though. It's for this."

He turned to the tree, thinking of his Gran, all those years ago.

A Davin cares for the dead, preserving their connection to the living, as Nex willed it. A Davin quiets them for Her, easing them on their way from this world. And in return, a Davin can always find what's lost.

Struggling to remember what she'd told him, Rafe knelt by the gnarled root.

He was too stoned to recall the ceremony, but it probably didn't matter. His family loved pomp more than they'd ever loved each other.

"We're lost," he said, remembering his mother using her own spade in these very woods. "Bring us to Eth."

Then he sunk the blade into the shining flesh of the gazing-tree. The soft substance gave, slumping around the yellowed bone, a puff of black powder surrounding its forked handle.

Hearing a rustle from beneath, he yanked the spade out, laughing. "You see, Deuce?"

"I don't see a thing, boy," she said—then gave a gasp as the first green tip emerged, corkscrewing up out of the root.

Five more tendrils followed after, and Rafe stepped back, remembering how quickly this would go.

"Get back."

The site of his puncture was boiling with runners. Touching down on solid earth, they spun themselves into a thick, twining vine that sprouted waxy leaves. It was almost beautiful—and then it burst, dripping with a thick, dark fluid as thorns the length of his fingers split its sides.

Anchoring itself in the dirt, the vine shot off into the wood, growing faster than they could hope to run.

"Fortune's favorite, indeed," she breathed. "My Ace, do you know how much we could *sell* that thing for?"

"Not a lead slug, I'm afraid." Rafe snapped the spade's sheath onto his belt, opposite his dagger. "It only works for Davins—bloodline magic, they call it. But it'll carry us to the mountain of tlak we'll earn with that satchel!"

Jassa hefted up the bag of guts, giving a thin-lipped smile. "Now that's a prayer I can understand."

He couldn't tell if her crisis had abated, or if she was simply playing along. It occurred to him, though, that the role of an Ace was to have enough faith for the both of them.

Sliding on his pack, Rafe followed the flowing vines, savoring the tlak in his veins like never before.

You've earned this, he thought. It's high time things went your way.

Ignoring his warnings, Jassa cleaved too close to the vines and stepped on a thorn as long as her thumb. Despite her complaints, though, and the blood that squelched in her boot, they reached the edge of the wood in a little over an hour, then stood on the brink of a sudden expanse of untrammeled light.

The low sun gushed over a glistening hill, past the crest of which lay nothing but sky.

"There's a killing field, down below." The stench was powerful, and made Rafe oddly nostalgic.

Jassa squinted at him, then swallowed her objection. "What I wouldn't give for a map and a schedule," she muttered.

He shook his head. "If there was a battle on, we'd hear it. There's little danger of running into any soldiers-for-the-day, it's just—"

But what was it?

He traced the dark line of vines over the hill. Not far from the tree line, the path of thorns had swerved straight for this clearing.

He'd expected to see Eth in the distance, that was all. But this must have been the straightest route. Or perhaps the vines were keeping them safe, steering clear of some unseen danger.

Nothing was wrong. His high was simply fading.

"Fortune will provide," he whispered. Feeling dizzy, he struck out into the light, keeping his distance from the thorny runners.

The pain felt like an invisible knife stabbing him in the lungs time and again on his way uphill. He was panting by the time he peered over the crest.

He knew this place. It was the suburban battlefield known as the Thirteenth Designation.

A carpet of corpses stretched from the foot of the hill to the far edge of the wood, half a mile or more. Light and shade played among the fallen bodies as a series of clouds passed over the sun. The soldiers were sprawled just where they'd died, still clutching their weaponry, which was too cheap to loot—mostly sticks with bent nails driven through the ends, no swords. Their uniforms were so shoddy that the colors had dyed their skin in the rain, all green and purple like a garden of bruises. It was late in the day of their death, and they were beginning to burst. He couldn't see the maggots, but he could feel them thriving.

Gorging on discontent, his Gran would have said, as if worms fed on emotion, not flesh. *Every corpse is angry, at the start.*

A Davin soothes them until they have nothing left to say. Until their bones are cleansed of complaint.

A Davin who doesn't is just taking up space.

Something wasn't right. He could smell it.

One hand drifted to his dagger, the other to his spade.

"Oh, lovely," snarled Jassa, stuffing plugs of cloth up her nostrils. "Hundreds of the unquiet dead to offend—and each one ready to rip our luck to shreds!"

A murder of crows took wing, startled by the sound of her voice.

"*Quiet*, Deuce," he snarled, spotting the tents thrown up past the bodies, near the far edge of the wood.

But it was too late. A black-cloaked sentry had already emerged.

The sentry's hand dropped to his side—and pulled out a yellowed spade of his own.

"Oh, *fuck* me," whispered Rafe, raising a hand.

The spade had found what he'd lost, all right.

"What's happening?" whispered Jassa.

Rafe gave the signal. "Clan Davin," he said, his throat thick with misery. "The vines brought us to my family."

Rafe's uncle, down below, gave the all-clear, shaking his head.

They must've known Rafe was coming when they saw the vines. No one else had ever left the clan.

"Thought you were bringing us to the city, boy." There was acid in Jassa's voice.

"I—I tried." But instead of thinking of Eth while he'd stabbed the root, Rafe had been remembering his mother, working the magic herself. He'd *asked* for Eth, but the tlak had jumbled his thoughts.

"Fortune's favorite, eh?" muttered Jassa.

He couldn't argue. If Fortune *did* exist, she'd used all this to show him how little she thought of him.

The rest of his black-cloaked, olive-skinned clan came trudging out of hiding, pushing wheelbarrows, carrying picks and shovels, scowling up at the top of the hill. Half their number set to work on a pile of fresh corpses, lining them up neatly, stripping them down for their baths, setting out their ceremonial robes. The other half got back to scrubbing a row of skeletons exhumed from a pit at the far side of the field, where they'd been buried on the Davins' last journey through these lands.

"These are *yours?*" whispered Jassa. "You're a—a *gravedigger?*"

"Was." He'd forgotten people called them that. What a tiny part of it all the digging was.

He should tell her. Tell her now, while he still could.

Or he could run. They might catch him, or they might just let him go.

But for all he knew, the path of vines had already withered away behind them, and they'd never find that gazing-tree again. If he fought this, they might well end up dead in the wood.

"They'll throw us a feed," he said, "and help us find our way."

At a cost, he knew. But he couldn't think of anything else to do, and by now his uncle was halfway to them.

Gritting his teeth, Rafe started downhill. A breeze carried bleach and spices, vinegar and sweat, sweet curd and rotting flesh: the smells of home. "Come on, Deuce. You've nothing to fear from the Davins."

They stared as he came, and he supposed they had to. When he'd left, he'd barely begun to match outside to in. They'd known about the fights, but they'd never seen where they led. Whatever the changes, though, there was no mistaking Rafe, not with the resemblance so striking.

"Five long years since we've seen you," called his uncle, keeping his distance, "and *this* is how you return?"

Rafe said nothing. He saw shards of his reflection all around. His cheeks stood high in his third-aunt's face. His unbrushable hair rose like a nimbus from his cousin's scalp. His lower lip hung pendulous beneath his uncle's nose. The only thing that set Rafe apart was that the others wore their oily, black cloaks, and on every dark breast the symbol of Clan Davin had been embroidered—a white-bladed spade sprouting thorns from its forked handle.

Irritable, they all kept their distance, and he imagined for a blissful moment that he might pass through them without speaking, that he'd find a well-marked road to Eth on the other side of the killing field, that he could treat this moment like an unpleasant dream he'd wake from as soon as the drash crawled onto his neck.

Then he saw his own eyes staring back at him, as if from a mirror.

"Rafia," she said.

The syllables were flat. The name hit hard. Rafe stopped walking and faced her.

His lesser relatives stopped working, watching Lura Davin for their cues.

Jassa bumped up behind him, her satchel swinging. "Boy, is that—"

"The thorns said you were coming," she said. "I found it hard to believe them." Lura strode through the corpses, her callused feet landing neatly in the spaces between their elbows and their ribs, their necks and their gaping chins. How old she looked, though her eyes were as sharp as ever. They never left his face. "It's been far too long. But I'm relieved that you finally found your way home." She stopped in the midst of the field, folding her arms beneath her bosom. She was cataloguing Rafe's outfit with her eyes, peering at his tight bush of hair. He could feel her holding back a critique. "The spade helped you find your way, then. The old ways show us new ways, isn't that what Gran used to say?"

Rafe heaved a shallow sigh.

There were so many things he could have said just then.

All he could manage was, "Mother."

"Well. You look like you've been on the road a while. We'll eat." She couldn't help but glance at his hands. "Do take a moment and wash up, girl."

Rafe's face was burning. Jassa goggled at him.

"*Rafia?*" she said.

There it was.

Her startled laughter.

The first of many reasons he'd kept this from her.

Rafe clamped his hand on her arm. With the other on the hilt of his dagger, he twisted it behind her back and pressed his mouth to her ear. "Never call me that again," he spat, loud enough for the rest to hear. "Or *girl*, or *she*, or *her*."

Then he shoved her down, sprawling among the bodies. Rafe stomped through them, weathering the horrified stares of his relatives, wondering what might have happened if he'd explained himself to Jassa from the start.

She'd probably have sold him out to the Assemblage, or said the wrong thing in the wrong bar and gotten him killed. Deep down, he'd never really trusted her. So he'd said nothing, just labored to keep his body hidden, earning himself this stabbing pain in his lungs.

Not for too long at a stretch, and never when you sleep. That's what Gingerbeard had said, giving Rafe a binder bought dear at Mr. Rue's. But Rafe had sold it, after, and taken to using bandages, which was idiocy to begin with—and then Jassa had led him to the wood, and he'd spent every moment under her babbling scrutiny.

Now he'd earned his pain, and an itch that felt downright fungal besides.

"Keep up, then, Deuce," he yelled over his shoulder, reaching as deep as he could into the tight, filthy fabric and letting his fingernails fly.

They ate flatbreads, sour cheese, spiced meat, and pickled vegetables, all loaded onto waxy leaves. The Davins ate, anyhow; Jassa was too upset by the putrescent corpses sprawled mere steps from the cook tent to make so much as an attempt at a bite. She pushed at the plugs in her nose instead, making her look like a mannerless child.

For Rafe, it was disturbingly comforting to taste his family's food again, a feeling cut short the instant his mother wiped her mouth on her wrist.

"So," she said. "Whatever passed between us, I think we can all agree that five years is too long."

Rafe remembered the day she'd stopped speaking to him.

He'd stayed far too long, after. But if he admitted that now, they'd both start yelling, and he was tired already.

"It's a long time, all right." He couldn't very well admit that he'd come here by accident. But he needed directions. "We're hoping to get back to Eth by nightfall."

"Oh? So soon? I thought you'd stay the night, at least. The Davins can offer safety," she said, appealing to Jassa, "and there's always more than enough food to go around. Expecting ten, cook for thirty—that's the Davin way." She smiled, setting her own leaf aside. "I'm Lura," she said, smiling. "Rafia seems a bit too—" She glanced at the welts on their necks, holding her expression steady. "—too tongue-tied to introduce her—friend?"

Jassa worked her lips without a sound, choosing her words carefully. "I'm Jassa Lowroller. I'm, ah—that, is Rafe is—we're associates."

"Haiji, some wine?"

Rafe's cousin leapt up and fetched a wineskin for Lura, looking faintly terrified. Rafe himself waved it away, to Jassa's great disappointment.

"Jassa," he said, "is my *Deuce*. My subordinate."

"A business arrangement, then?" Lura drank deeply. "And what is your enterprise?"

"Harvesters," said Jassa.

"Trappers," said Rafe.

They glared at each other.

"We procure rare game, for wealthy clients," said Rafe.

The Davins looked at Jassa's sodden bag. "I see," said Lura, still smiling. "I thought the rich rather enjoyed hunting, no?

In any case, I'm sure it's—very lucrative. But I would like to point out to the both of you that there is plenty of work to go around here. We have the Thirteenth Designation, as you can see, and three other killing fields to care for, besides. Jassa, has she told you at all about what we Davins do?"

Jassa let out another laugh, this one more considered.

It would be better to go, with or without a plan. He was just about to stand up when Jassa found her tongue.

"I was told something about how you belong to the dead gods under Eth," she said. "But tell me, Lura—which loop of intestine do you lot call home? Is it Gone-Away Frig, or Gone-Away Frag?"

Lura's smile froze, and for a moment Rafe thought the act was over.

Then she drank. "I guess that's how it must seem, eh? A jumble of ancient guts, forgotten under the streets. Everyone disagreeing about which one belongs to which deity, and all the translations seem to argue with themselves. An endless fight, and all that power goes to the wayside." She was staring at Rafe now. "But the Davins are above all that. We belong to Nex, the Place Between. Her brain lies below the Uni, and Her gazing-trees surround the city. We know just who we are, Jassa—the Goddess' guardians, the keepers of Her temple, now as ever. We are they who quiet the dead according to Her wishes—and make a good living at it, too, I would add."

Rafe could see where this was going. "Look." He leaned forward, pointing. "See that pile, Deuce? All those bodies, heaped together?" Jassa followed his finger and nodded, disconcerted. "When the Davins are done washing those strangers' stinking feet, they'll dump them all in a mass grave, singing them lullabies. And then," he said, getting louder as he pointed at a row of skeletons, "they'll come back months from now, dig them up, and scrape all the rot from their bones. That's what *quieting* means—nothing more. A little song, a little dance, two burials, a heap of silver, and then rubes like you believe they're safe from the grasping fingers of Grandpa's ghost."

His face was red, and so was Lura's. She gripped the wineskin as if it might fly away. "Tell me something, daughter. Why is it that you believe in all the other wonders of this world, but the teachings of your own people are beyond the pale? Is this *really* about the unquiet dead—or have you something else to say?"

"I can keep it to this subject well enough," said Rafe, crossing his legs. "It's easy enough to see that the Gone-Away lived—we can tour their rocky guts. And there's no arguing with enchantments—they can squeeze us to fucking death. For any of your other wonders, there's actual *evidence*, but where are your unquiet dead? Jassa insists that they're chewing on her good luck! Uncle Grimple claims they've robbed him of an erection! We never see them, we just *blame* them—but the dead themselves? They're intangible. Invisible. Imaginary."

Lura must have put away a full bottle by now. "So you don't believe in what you can't see, is that what you're saying?"

Rafe could feel Jassa staring at him—thinking of Fortune, no doubt.

"You know I don't."

"Then how," said Lura, flashing her stained teeth, "do you explain your so-called manhood?"

Rafe shoved his chair away, heart pounding. "Deuce," he shouted, standing up. "We'll be on our way."

"Rafia, wait."

His mother lurched up, but Jassa hadn't moved.

"That was rude of me," said Lura. "What I meant to say—however poorly—is that there's a place for you here."

"Not as myself," Rafe said, quietly. "There never has been."

"For *you*, girl." She stumbled at him, slurring. "For my first-born daughter. Dress how you like. *Act* how you like. No more silent treatment, love. Just recognize—that we are *suffering* without you. With you and your father and your Gran gone, Rafia, we have too few hands to do the work. The other clans are at our heels, threatening to take our contracts out from under us. The Devourers, those filthy corpse-eaters, have all but convinced the Guvnor that we're useless. Help us, love. Please."

"I can't."

He wanted to say more. He wished he could destroy her with his words. Instead, he waved a hand at Jassa.

She smiled at him, as if all this were a grand entertainment.

"Up, Deuce!" he shouted.

"As you say, milady," Jassa said, under her breath.

Rafe cracked her so hard across the mouth that blood sprayed onto his uncle's lunch.

"Hell," said Lura, as if nothing at all had happened, "we'll even make room for your paramour. There's room for you both—and pay."

Jassa stood, wiping blood from her chin. "*Me?*" she cried. "His—her *paramour*? You must be off your nut, woman—I had no idea she was even *bent!*"

"Enough!" shouted Rafe.

The entire clan swiveled their heads.

Rafe's hand itched for the dagger.

He ought to do it here, in front of all of them. *The Widow of Lank Street*, they called her. She'd kill him, sooner or later.

And what would the Davins do? Call the guards on him, miles from Eth?

They'd bury her, that's what.

He saw then, quite clearly, that he couldn't do it.

Whatever he'd done in the farmhouse, whatever he'd felt, it was gone now.

"This—this was a mistake," he stammered, and started to leave the tent.

"Leave now, and you're leaving forever," said Lura.

"That's the idea."

"The *spade*," she shouted.

She wrapped a hand around the handle of her own, and every Davin in the tent followed suit. Even Haiji, who looked like she was about to weep.

Rafe stopped, and Jassa stumbled into him.

A dozen Davins drew. Bone gleamed in the sunlight.

They were bluffing. They had to be.

A rustling of tendrils shifted the field of corpses from beneath.

"Rafe. *Boy*!" whispered Jassa. "Let it drop."

Rafe tugged the tool from his belt and tossed it into the field. His cousin sucked air between her teeth.

"I don't need it, now," he said.

"It would seem you never did," Lura said. Scooping it up, she weaved close enough that Rafe could smell the wine on her breath, the oil in her hair. "Rafia?"

Rafe looked up.

"You will never be quiet, girl. Even if you plague me in death as you did in life, your soul will never leave these lands."

Rafe didn't look away, at least. But a muscle in his foot began to twitch, causing his whole body to shake.

"Is this what you wanted, when you left?" she said, pointing at the puncture-wounds on his neck, twisting her lips. "*Boy?*"

Rafe spit on the ground.

"Close enough."

He left the tent, stalking through the bodies, and Jassa followed, slowing their pace to a crawl as she hopped and staggered. Rafe kept his burning face tilted to the ground until they were clear of his relatives.

"Where are we going, boy?" Jassa hissed.

"I don't know, Jass."

That's when he saw them.

Hairless, pallid, and stripped to the waist, they were looking down at the corpses—and whispering.

"*Devourers!*" Rafe screamed, scrabbling at his belt.

On his left side, where his spade no longer hung.

He groped for the dagger.

They raised their hands, and the field erupted.

A geyser of black flame tossed Rafe through the air, sucking the heat from his skin. Jassa flounced up beside him, surrounded by red droplets. For an instant he thought her satchel had burst, that they'd lost their cargo, that the tlak they might have earned was lost.

But no—she'd been ruptured by a fist of fire.

Blood sprayed through the gaps in her teeth.

They were dead, he supposed.

Ah, well.

I t was night when he woke, and the moon was full and high. Rafe lay bleeding, surrounded by the bodies of his kin, some living, most dead. A ring of black flames burned in a wide circle around them, penning them in.

He couldn't see Jassa.

He could see his mother, though.

She was missing her head.

His cousin Haiji still lived. She was the only one who sat upright, listening to the flames hiss.

"Haiji," he croaked. "Haij."

She turned, a little. It took some time for her to decide to crawl to him.

"Don't make noise," she whispered. "They killed Draymun for crying. They don't need us alive."

"Is it the contracts?" he whispered back. He tried to sit up and regretted the motion.

Haiji shrugged. "I think. Maybe the Guvnor gave them our lands. Because their methods are faster than ours. Else they're just taking them." She wiped her eyes angrily.

"Gran used to tell me about them."

"Same. 'You don't mind me, child, the bald-heads will chew your bones.'" She looked with suspicion at the ring of flames. "They're not quieting anyone's souls. They're not letting them pass on into peace. They're *burning* them, Rafe."

Rafe didn't care what they did to him now—dead was dead. But he was glad that Haiji had called him by his right name, at least.

He'd landed between two soldiers, his head pillowed by their ribs. Inspecting them, he found Jassa, still breathing a bit, though so much of her body was glistening that it stung his eyes to look.

No wonder he'd thought the satchel had split. She was halfway disemboweled.

Somehow he laughed.

"So they'll eat us up, then?"

"Only a little," came a sonorous voice from the edge of the ring, where the flames were parting like a velvet curtain around a woman in a purple cloak.

Her head gleamed, hairless, browless, coated in grease. She didn't even have eyelashes, Rafe noticed as Haiji scurried away.

He noticed, too, that an infant slumbered on her chest, tied there with a purple sling.

A tiny greased baby. And why not? They were a clan, after all. They lived and died like any other.

"A dollop of bone marrow, that's all we actually swallow," she purred as she sat beside him, folding her legs atop a corpse's back. "One from each shank."

She touched Rafe's leg.

Not like Jassa would have touched him. Like a lover.

Her hands were very warm. Her baby was burbling.

"Some say we eat the whole corpse. But how many of us would there need to be, to chow on a field this size? We'd have to outnumber the armies we serve, and at that point we might as well *fight* them, and eat whatever we caught. No, just a taste of each—a dollop!—mixed together in a savory paste." She touched her throat as if it were a piece of expensive machinery. "I take it down slowly, enjoying the flavor. Anticipating the digestion that will bind the dead to this world. It is not a taking, but a joining. There is beauty, on both sides. But you'll see for yourself. For a moment."

Each time Rafe blinked, it took longer to open his eyes. He saw figures dancing in the darkness, where there were none. He couldn't be far from the end. He wondered if he'd been punctured, where his side ached. Maybe his bandages were the only thing holding him in.

"You're amusing yourself," he murmured, though he felt no anger. "That's why we're alive, isn't it? An audience."

"I *am* amused!" said the Devourer, brightly. The baby began to squirm, rooting for her breast, and she obliged, pulling out a breast and helping until the little mouth latched. The child gulped greedily. "I've waited for this a while. Your scrappy little clan has held these fields for an awfully long time. Everything else comes and goes, doesn't it? The rulers, the guilds, the babies, the soldiers, the enchantments. All turning over and over, making such fantastic mulch. Everything except the Davins, and a few other favorites of those tenured madmen at the University. Finally, it's our turn."

She touched Rafe's face slowly, very slowly, outlining his nose, his cheeks, his lips, with such hot consideration that he gave himself over to her touch.

At least someone would see him as he died, he thought.

He was surprised to learn that it mattered.

"But I *like* what you are, little Davin. Not like the others, are you? Something new, right at the end of the line. A *delicacy*. I'll eat you on your own. I'll make sure that *your* dollop isn't mixed with the rest."

"Thank you."

His eyes slid shut, then open again. It felt like his last blink.

"Oh! But I should be thanking *you*. I thought we'd have to fight the matriarch, and I wasn't entirely sure which way it would go. I've heard stories about her thorns. As big as trees, they say! But then you came along. Such a timely distraction."

Either the flames were parting a second time, or Rafe's brain had begun to drown.

The Devourer looked up, light playing on her gleaming face, and on the hairless skull of her child.

"Hate to interrupt," came a voice from the edge, "but we found this lurking in the wood."

Rafe must have been hallucinating again.

It was the dead woman from the farmhouse.

He didn't believe in ghosts.

She didn't seem to care.

"Always room for another at *our* table," the Devourer said, stepping across the corpses like stones in a pool.

The ghost looked at her—then glanced down at the baby on her chest and recoiled.

It was odd, wasn't it? That a ghost should be afraid of a child.

But she cringed, and started spitting.

The Devourer paid her no mind.

She was too busy staring at Haiji.

The girl's back was silently heaving.

"No crying," said the Devourer, and ruptured her body with a sudden burst of flame. Then she left him, and the ring of black fire closed behind her.

Rafe ought to feel something, he supposed, but there was no room.

The dead woman's ghost sat beside him, cradling a handbag in her lap, spitting occasionally. Everything went silent, except for Haiji's body sizzling and the whispers of the flames.

"Come for vengeance?" he whispered, his eyes crossing. "You'd better hurry."

The ghost didn't speak, but her handbag did.

"These dimwits will bleed out before the hour has rung," it rasped in a voice like two flat pebbles rubbed together. "And then we'll be sunk! Can't you *do* something?"

"I'd really rather not," said the ghost, sounding bored.

"Don't make me beg, Ashlan Ley. I'm worse at begging than at reaching high shelves."

The ghost sighed, leaned in, and pulled the dagger from Rafe's belt.

The one he'd used to kill her.

He deserved this. He wondered if she knew it was a mercy.

But she didn't stab him after all. As calmly as he might cut an apple, she slashed herself twice, once on the pad of each thumb. She stuck the blade in the dirt and shoved a bleeding digit in his mouth. The other was for Jassa.

Rafe squirmed from the taste of salt and copper.

The ghost pushed her thumb deeper.

"Suck," she said. "If you want to live the night."

Like a baby himself, he obliged.

—Nerves—

"**I**t's safe," said Ashlan, patting the side of her bag. "Relatively."

Hollis pushed the flap open and peered out, his burlap brow nearly folded over. "What *is* all that?" he rasped, pointing at the black flames.

"They call it hellfire. Burns cold."

"The name seems a trifle dramatic."

"Bloodline nomenclature usually is. Not a lot of outside opinions involved. And it's got nothing to do with hell, or fire—it's the decomposing effluvia of the gods. These jokers can control it—*some* shady deal must've gone down, centuries ago—but they can't get too far from Eth, or it dries right up. Why they're eating people, I have no idea. That is entirely unrelated."

He dropped down on the carpet of corpses. "Once again, Ashlan Ley, you prove remarkably well-informed for a small-time con artist."

"I'm a lot of things."

The ring had a circumference of fifteen corpses, give or take a few limbs. Those at the edges were thoroughly crisped, but the rest seemed unharmed by their proximity.

"Is there any way we can take it with us?" Hollis asked. "Just enough to cold-roast an eyeball or two, or maybe a gonad. I certainly wouldn't want to be as quick dispatching the Puppeteer as that hairless procreator was with this lot. Swallowing one of his favorite bits with cold fire, though—well, it appeals to my aesthetic sense."

The Puppeteer again. Every few minutes, Hollis looped back to the subject of his "creator," concocting ever more elaborate fantasies about his death.

Luckily, he hadn't noticed how uneasy this made her—he was too fixated on bloody vengeance for that—but Ashlan was increasingly eager to get all this over with.

Maybe he'd unravel along the way and save her some trouble.

That thought unnerved her, too.

"I mean, you could always ask the Devourers," she muttered. "The last one seemed chatty enough."

He turned on a platform heel, suddenly petulant. "Yes, and *about* them, Ashlan Ley. You ought to've slaughtered those depilated creeps—wrung their greasy heads right off their necks! There'd be two fewer captors to escape right about now."

"When we got here," she said, as patiently as she could manage, "you were telling me to pull the heads off the black-cloaks. Imagine where that would have landed us, Runt—once the Devourers showed up, we'd have been caught between the two clans. 'Kill it if it moves' isn't going to get us to Eth."

"It'll get us there faster than allowing ourselves to be imprisoned by every pack of half-wits patrolling the wood!" He climbed onto a dead soldier's back and gave it a petulant stomp. "I simply can't understand why you *allow* all this. For my sake, I'm glad that you didn't dispatch those junkies—but why did you allow them to ransack your chest cavity, when knocking off the two of them would've cost you nothing?"

"It's just—easier. Laying low. Keeping the spotlight off me—and what I can do. People take what they want, and they go away."

"That's a flimsy argument," Hollis muttered. "Pain seems hardly to bother you at all, and from what I can tell, there's not a weapon in the kingdom that can waylay you for long, if you set your mind to it."

She decided to let him believe that as long as he could.

"All of which makes your—your *pacifism* completely incomprehensible," he went on. "Such strength you have, such resiliency, and such size! Why *not* cut down everything in your path? Why *not* let the world know what you can do? What good can you do for me—for yourself? for anyone?—if we're bound by a cage of uncanny fire? And what difference could the destruction of your body possibly matter when you're an hour away from wholeness, regardless of how much damage you take?"

"It ought to matter to you, if you're hiding in my handbag."

But she knew the answer well enough. The thought had haunted her since childhood.

What if she started killing, and couldn't stop?

"I don't know, Runt." Ashlan stood, wincing. Her feet were all pins and needles. "I guess I might still be standing after I took on two dozen men. I've never tried it." She hobbled to the edge of the ring, peering down at the gruesome litter of the battle. "But I do know this: the second the Devourers lit me up, you'd be a lump of fucking coal."

She found what she was looking for: a severed arm, hacked off at the elbow. She chucked it into the wall of flame, where it crackled and shook, then rebounded.

Hollis stepped away from the cold, smoking twist of bone and gristle, his upper lip curling. "Well. Perhaps necromancers are a special case. But should we encounter a militia, for example, or an irregular group of bandits—"

"How many hits do you think I can take before you get skewered?" She found another severed limb and hefted it. "What if I drop you, and you get stepped on? Really, Runt, all it's going to take is one good whack, and your century's over. Plus, we've got these two to keep alive," she said, waving the leg at the woman and the boy, "or we lose our shot at the Puppeteer. Right?"

She could see him marshaling an argument.

It died on his lips as she rammed the leg into the wall.

The limb leapt into the air the moment it touched hellfire. Grappling it, bracing with all her might, she rammed it through the squealing resistance until it finally popped through the other side. She yanked her hands back before they touched the flame, feeling grimly satisfied.

"Ashlan, what are you *doing?*"

"Experimenting. We've got to figure a way out of here that doesn't fry the three of you."

"How is *that* meant to help?"

"I'll keep you posted." She wiped her hands on her tunic. "I was kind of hoping some space would open up around it. But at least we know it's not a wall. There's a lot of push-back, but I could get myself through if I really had to."

She pictured herself charred, still lurching on. Or falling down and being left alone a while.

It would be better to avoid it entirely. Hellfire didn't seem like it offered the kind of pain she cared to deal with.

To her surprise, Hollis was seething. "So you're openly planning on leaving me to die here," he said, flexing his little fists. "After all I've offered you."

"Easy, Runt." She came to his side, kneeling until she was as close to his level as she could get. "No one's ditching you. Worst case, I just—bury you, burn myself alive, and dig you up again when the Devourers are gone."

He looked aghast for a moment, then guffawed. "God's rot, woman, what a plan! But I can't very well cry claustro-phobia after asking you to dive unarmed into a small army of mages. Let's hope it doesn't come to that, eh?" Climbing over the corpses, he inspected the sleeping bodies. "As you noted, the real challenge will be keeping the junkies alive. They know where the Puppeteer is, and we don't—so we can't just let them burn, delightful as that might be. But are you sure they're even stable?"

Ashlan wasn't sure of anything, not in here. "I mean, I've used blood to keep someone alive in a pinch before. But they've always had medical attention after, from people with more field experience than me. I don't know how far it goes on its own." She lifted up the woman's cloak and winced. "This one isn't looking good. There are some things on the outside that ought to be in, if we're going to start tossing her around. I got some of my blood down her throat, but she really does need—packing."

"I'm really more of an *un*packer," he said, smiling. "Surely you can manage it?"

Ashlan looked down at her hands. "I'm not exactly hygienic. And I don't have the tools."

"Can't you just—" He gestured vaguely. "I don't know, *bleed* on her?"

"You want me to, what, cut off a hand and hose her down?"

He paused, considering. "Would that work?"

Ashlan sighed. "I would much rather not find out."

The two of them were sleeping soundly, at least— Ashlan's blood had a peculiarly soporific effect. And they looked almost childlike in repose.

The boy was olive-skinned, his nose aquiline, hair more curly than kinky. The woman was pale and road-worn, the sort of customer Ashlan could imagine reminiscing about some bygone crown her ancestors had never actually worn.

These were the people who'd scrapped her body to get themselves high. She'd expected to feel hatred, or at least some defensive twinge, but there was nothing. She'd have been more upset if they'd stolen her bag.

"I think the boy might be all right," she said. "Do we really need both of them?"

"Hmm. What with all the Ace-ing and Deuce-ing, I think it'd be safer—if only to avoid suspicion down the line." Hollis tapped his lips with a frayed forefinger. "Patch her up, and be quick about it. Meantime, I'll try and find us a way out of this infernal cage."

"Great." She watched him toddle over to the edge of the hellfire, thinking idly of tossing him over and seeing if he survived the fall. Instead, she pulled Rafe's dagger out of the dirt, wiped it passably clean, and held it to her wrist, frowning down at the woman's face.

"I can't *believe* I'm doing this for you," she whispered.

The cut was deep and confident, the blood intoxicatingly dark.

Ashlan appreciated how steady her arm remained. She felt her breath changing as her body flooded with panic, then nausea, then warmth. She noted that hideous certainty that always arrived when she began to take herself apart.

There is no end to this, it said.

The pain itself was like an old friend walking through the front door, telling the same jokes that made her laugh every time.

Then, hot on its heels, the hunger.

Again, she felt a curious pang—which warranted no reflection, because she was already wrapping it up, clenching her teeth and clamping her fingers around her forearm. It seemed like the woman had already absorbed enough of Ashlan's blood—she was breathing more steadily, her innards retracting, her black puncture blanching.

It would have to do. There was nothing clean to bandage her with, so if she fell apart when they moved her, so be it. They had no plan that could possibly get her out of this ring, anyway, and it could only be a matter of time before the Devourers returned.

Ashlan felt that boiling well of heat that always lay just below the surface of her skin. Over the years, she'd built a kind of wall to keep it from lashing out and healing every scrape she suffered. People reacted poorly, she'd learned as a child, when confronted with a regenerating girl.

And there were times when she just wanted to hurt awhile.

Now, with a long exhalation, she let the wall down.

Her arm began at once to prickle with emerging sweat. Her flesh seared, her mind went blank, and within moments she had a knitting wound and a splitting headache.

"Ashlan," Hollis rasped.

"Give me a minute," she muttered, pressing her temples.

What she wouldn't give for a rack of lamb right now.

"*Ashlan!*"

She whipped her head around, furious, famished, thinking how nice it would be to *bite* him until he shut his tiny mouth.

But Hollis was staggering backwards, tripping over corpses, scrambling up and doing it again.

He couldn't tear his eyes from the wall of flame.

It was moving toward the middle—quickly enough to gnaw through two or three lengthwise corpses every minute.

Ashlan stood, whispering a curse. The hellfire sizzled through the bodies at the edge, one cold, implacable inch at a time. She lifted Hollis, who squawked in indignation as she retreated to the center of the circle, watching it cinch toward them.

Down, she thought. That's all she could think, as if a magnet was pulling her from below. She had to get him *down*.

"Guess it's feeding time," she said, setting him down near the boy's feet. "We've got a few minutes, if we're lucky." Grunting, she heaved a corpse off of the matted grass. "Forget these two. We'll find another way. Let's get you in the ground. We need to start digging."

"With *what*?" cried Hollis.

"I don't know," she shouted back. "Look around!"

Hollis ducked as a hideous screeching erupted at the edge of the ring. The hellfire had caught a dying black-cloak where he lay. From the feet up, his flesh was turning to char, but the man was too weak to pull himself away.

Ashlan picked up the dagger and started hacking at the ground, though she didn't manage much besides loosening the grass. The earth was hard and rocky, and scraping it with the blade didn't gain her enough ground.

"Nothing but sharpened sticks," Hollis called from the edge, "and a satchel of your guts."

"Grab a stick," said Ashlan, dropping the blade. "Maybe I can get some leverage, break things up a bit."

Hollis hefted a makeshift spear, balancing like a tiny acrobat as he made his way across the corpses.

"Damn it, Runt, you're slow." Ashlan lunged toward him, swiping the stick from his hands. "I can't dig and keep track of you at the same time."

She snatched up the satchel of guts, too, and tossed them toward the center. She didn't feel like listening to them sizzle—not before the rest of her did.

Ashlan sank the stick into the unforgiving earth.

She pushed, and it snapped in half.

The black-cloak wasn't screeching any more. The hellfire had swallowed his skull.

"Stay close," she shouted, kneeling and clawing at the rocky dirt with her hands, earning nothing but dry, stingy palmfuls at first. She kept on, though, clenching her jaw so hard that her neck spasmed.

Before she'd cleared an inch, her fingers were bleeding. The earth was so studded with stones that she'd torn off several fingernails by the time she had anything she could call a hole. Pouring with sweat, she held back the full rush of heat and dug deeper, not even pausing to glance at the tightening hellfire. She dug until her fingers were pulped, then kept digging, flinging dirt beside her, hoping it was landing in something like a pile. She'd have to pack it over Hollis' body again, and it would need to be deep enough to protect him from the flames that would soon be closing over his head.

How deep could the hellfire *reach*? The further she went, the more futile all this felt.

She felt a harsh vibration running through her arms as her naked finger-bones scraped the surface of a stone even wider than the hole she'd dug.

"Hurry," pleaded Hollis.

"Toss me the dagger, Runt."

Gripping its hilt with fingers like gory talons, she fought through the pain, gouging desperately at the edges of the stone. "Even if this works," shouted Ashlan, "we're going to need to find another way to Eth. I might just be able to get you under, but these two—"

"Just *dig!*" yelled Hollis, hunched beside her.

Grunting, she pried up the edge of the stone. It loosened a good bit of earth as she wrenched it free.

She hauled it up, and her heart sank. Even if Hollis curled up like a fetus, the pit was still too shallow.

"There won't be time to bury an acorn," he moaned.

The wall of hellfire was ten feet away, starting on one of the pale woman's outstretched hands. She wasn't awake, but she was shrieking.

And the boy was next.

"We're *fucked*," Ashlan said. Out of sheer frustration, she hurled the stone back into the pit, where it thudded—and then kept falling.

She and Hollis turned to stare at the sudden hole in the ground.

"What enchantment is *this?*" he cried.

"I don't know." She seized him by the front of his waistcoat. "But it beats waiting around."

She dropped him, squealing, into the black.

"Hopefully."

She dragged the woman from the flames and wedged her, feet-first, into the pit. Clods of earth broke off all around her, and she tumbled out of sight. She shoved the boy in after, watching him slide into darkness.

For a moment Ashlan stood at the edge, watching the oncoming flames gleam in the grimy tendons of her hands.

The hellfire was close enough to make her shiver.

Her nascent fingernails itched as they emerged. New skin was sliding up around the muscle like sausage casing. She shouldered her bag, flinching from the sizzling and popping of her guts going up.

For a wild moment she thought of staying.

But Hollis was bellowing her name from below.

It probably wouldn't have killed her.

Ashlan stepped into the darkness.

She'd just pulled the woman and the boy clear of the long, diagonal shaft that led to the bottom, dragging them by their collars toward the sound of the manni-kin's voice, when the hellfire sent a wave of earth and flesh cascading behind her. She couldn't see a thing, but she could feel rocks and dirt striking her back. Bent double to keep from bashing her head on the tunnel's low roof, she dragged them farther on.

"Did the junkies live?" Hollis rasped.

"Give me a minute." Pulling them closer to him, she knelt beside one of them, groping for a pulse. "This one's all right. Breath's pretty shallow, though. And the other one's still hanging on, too."

"You sound disappointed."

"Well, are *you* going to carry them?"

"Hmph." She heard him pressing on, dragging his hand against the wall. "Even if I *could* help, how do we know it would do us any good? This might well be a dead end, where I'll languish until you dig your way out. Which would probably be the end of me, at the rate *you* dig."

Suffocation wouldn't slow her down forever, but running out of air would be markedly unpleasant. "Unless it's the burrow of some giant rodent. A blind mole as big as an elephant."

She heard his echoing gasp from down the hall. "Or a worm! Some massive, toothy lamprey of the earth."

He was trotting back already. "Probably looking for voles to eat," she said. "You're about the right size."

Hollis smacked into her leg and clung there. "Do you really think we ought to stay where we are?"

She rolled her eyes, invisibly. "Runt, if we're figuring the odds between a tunnel collapse and a giant worm attack, I'm going to say we should keep going. You can work on your bestiary of imaginary dirt creatures on the way."

He shoved away, huffing. "I'm sorry, does the invulnerable woman have something clever to say about cowardice? One day I'll learn what frightens *you*, and lower you into a pit of it."

"You just described every day of the past two hundred years," she muttered. "Really, Runt, you'd better hope that this tunnel lets out in a village. These two need help, fast. I don't think my blood's going to do much more on its own."

"Do you mean to say that dropping them from a great height didn't improve their condition? My, you *are* an expert, aren't you? Come along, then, before both of them die on us."

She swallowed her retort, focusing on how she was going to handle them. "Okay. What's your plan?"

"Pardon?"

He was powering on like this was going to be easy. "For *moving* them. What am I doing, dragging them on the ground? Carrying one toward you, then coming back for the other?" Either way, just thinking about it made her sweat. The air was close down here, and damp.

"My plan is for you to work it out for yourself," he called. "Come, now! If you don't dilly-dally, and nothing ferocious devours us, we'll be aboveground in no time."

But by the time they saw the light, her mind was as pulped as her hands had been. She'd expended so much heat healing the pain in her back and the gashes on her knuckles that her head was pounding. The tunnel never seemed to stop curving, and more than once she convinced herself that she'd lost an addict down some unseen fork. Her clothes were soaked, and there wasn't a drop of spit left in her mouth. By now, all she could think of was food and drink, to the exclusion of everything else—she couldn't even be sure that the addicts were alive, as it had been hours since she'd remembered to check their vital signs.

She couldn't see Hollis, though, and he drifted far ahead.

More than once, she wondered if that had saved him.

It wasn't sunshine that greeted them at the end of their path. The light was greenish-gray, and buckets of rain were pouring down the wide ramp that led to the open air.

"Ach." Hollis frowned as he stepped into a puddle at the foot of the ramp, his burlap skin caked with dirt. "We lost the whole night down here."

"Maybe our friends have horses," whispered Ashlan, dragging the woman up beside the boy.

"What friends?"

She pointed. "Whoever dug *that*."

The ramp was surrounded by a great, loose wall of displaced earth—except for a tidy path cut directly through its center. A shovel still jutted from the pile beside it.

"No horses," came a curiously lilting, reedy voice over the rush of the rain. "A bear, though." There was a thoughtful cough. "I am not the bear. And the bear is not alive."

Hollis stepped back, his button eyes wide. "We can't just walk up there," he whispered. "That could be anyone!"

"What's our option?" said Ashlan. "The tunnel is blocked, and I'm not leaving these two to die. Not after all this."

"Could you hurry up?" said the voice. "You took longer than we thought. The food is cold. So are my toes."

"I'm going." Ashlan lifted the woman's limp body for what she hoped was the last time.

"You can't be serious," hissed Hollis. "That's a lunatic, with untold powers!"

"A lunatic," said Ashlan, "with *lunch*. Do what you want." She carried the body to the top of the ramp, then stopped abruptly.

Somehow she hadn't been prepared for the actual bear. Standing upright, it was startling enough, little more than a piebald hide sagging over yellowing bones. Then it *moved*, lurching toward the shovel whose handle stood diagonally in her path, yanking it free with a surprisingly fluid motion. Its black lips flapped raggedly around its fangs, giving it an air of menace that its dull eyes belied. The fur of its chest swung, too, hanging open around some bright object that was splayed between its ribs with twine—a small, painted canvas, she saw, as it planted the shovel and came to a stop.

She peered at the painting, where robin's egg blue and a rich, yolky yellow swirled around a curious illustration.

Curious, because it wasn't a rune that seemed to animate the bear, but the likeness of a distant, ethereal face.

The face of the tall, paper-white woman with ink-stained fingers who stood beside it.

In her way, she was no less startling than the bear. Though her bare feet were muddy, she was quite dry, protected as she was by a vast, floating blanket of darkness. Some weightless substance of pure, shining black hung over her head, anticipating every diagonal drop of rain, writhing out to protect her from wetness.

As this otherworldly umbrella roiled, blotting out half the sky, the woman gave another pensive cough. "She's almost dead, you know." She stretched a stained finger toward the addict's limp body, not looking at either of them. "You'll want to put her in the sledge, with the other survivors." Something seemed to occur to her, and she peered into the space over Ashlan's shoulder. "Unless you wanted them to go—home?"

She stood a full foot taller than Ashlan, broad but slender. Her long hair was clean and combed, but full of burrs. She was dressed in hand-stitched furs and hides, festooned in feathers and animal bones, with the curled foot of a blackbird hanging from a length of twine around her throat.

"Home?" said Ashlan.

"Oh." The woman smiled, her eyes seeming to focus five feet past the back of Ashlan's head. "Not *your* home, of course. I meant death. You don't want them to go to death."

"No," said Ashlan softly, wondering if Hollis might be right. It didn't matter: the safest course was to humor her until they knew what she was after. "No, I don't."

"Then we'll heal them, you and I."

"You, uh—you sure you *can?*"

This was an absurd question to ask of anyone controlling a dead bear and a cloud of living night, and Ashlan regretted it immediately.

The woman looked irritated, then stroked a feather hanging from her hair, which seemed to calm her. "I am sure. I rarely heal—humans, other than myself. Never, really. But on the behalf of so esteemed a visitor, I'd be happy to. How many others have you brought?"

She'd heard them talking already, so there was no point in trying to hide Hollis. "Two. One other wounded, uh, human."

The woman arched an eyebrow, glancing down the ramp. "Rest assured. Between what I know and what you *are*, they will be well in no time."

"What I *am?*" Ashlan's heart thudded. "I don't know what you mean."

"Yes. You do." She looked disgusted, and rubbed at the feather again, more rapidly this time. "What need has an immortal to pretend? What company have you been *keeping*, Lady?"

"Look, you seem a little confused. I'm not—"

The darkness leaked out above Ashlan's head, an angry, shining mantle that looked ready to swallow her whole.

Untold powers.

Regardless of the chances it stood of doing her any per-manent damage, playing coy suddenly felt like a terrible idea.

"Okay," said Ashlan, shifting the limp weight in her arms. "So I'm—different. From most people."

The woman barked mirthlessly. "You are not some—car-nival act," she said, as if it was painful to explain this aloud. "A *contortionist* is 'different from most people.' You are not a *person* at all, Lady."

"Look." Ashlan nearly lost her grip on the body in her arms. "You obviously don't know me."

"No. But the gazing-tree does," said the woman, looking up into the cloud.

Something about the phrase niggled at Ashlan's memory.

Of course. The weird, burnt-looking oak beside the path of thorny vines. Hollis had leaned against it, and it had slumped away from his hand.

It's a gazing-tree, he'd said, wiping his hand furiously on the earth. *You've never heard of them? Something to do with the Gone-Away, or so they used to say at the Court of Cru. Their wood was lousy with them.*

And the clump of tree he'd displaced had drifted off—into a cloud of soft, black spores.

This woman's umbrella was made of them, Ashlan real-ized, peering up. At its edges, she could see the spores reach-ing out—and being rebuffed, by some unseen force, into a shape they were constantly resisting.

"That's a *tree?*"

"Not currently," said the woman. "But that's what peo-ple call them, isn't it? At one time, they were the sensory apparatus of Gone-Away Nex. Well, some say they belonged to Gone-Away *Nunce*, but that's absurd—He barely had a brain, let alone one that spanned five kingdoms. But such are the problems of a modern translator of ancient Ethian." She smiled to herself. "There was a time when each of the Gone-Away had their representatives in this world. Some, like the gazing-trees, yet remain, but they are—adrift, you might say, now that their gods are dead. This one," she said, making it whirl with a gesture, "has decided it is mine, and I asked it, long ago, to keep watch for someone like you. You must have passed by another one yesterday, and the ward went off. I was napping, and it came streaming inside to tickle me awake."

Ashlan struggled to keep her face blank. "Someone— like me."

"Yes. You could not all be *gone*, of course—where would you go?—but I thought perhaps you were gone from here. I longed to meet you, but I couldn't blame you for leaving. This wood was once so much more than a drainage ditch for the wars of Eth." She flicked her wrist, exasperated again. "Oh, put her down before you exhaust yourself."

Ashlan struggled to push all this from her mind. There was no reason to believe a thing this madwoman said. She wanted something from Ashlan, that much was clear—and Ashlan would need to negotiate with her, quickly.

"Where did you want me to put her?"

"Behind Umber," said the woman, crouching down to peer at an earthworm that writhed in the muck at her feet.

"Behind—"

"The bear." She pointed at a cape of serrated leaves woven into a long train that was tied to the bear's shoulders with red and green ropes. So much was happening out here that Ashlan hadn't even noticed. "I call him Umber. I call myself Tanka. Tanka Equinox."

"Tanka." Ashlan laid the body down behind the bear, grimacing as she looked at the blackened wreck of the woman's right arm.

The hellfire had taken her hand, and half her forearm. Charred bone extended inches beyond anything that could still be called flesh. If Tanka could heal this, she was a miracle worker.

"I'm Ashlan Ley," she said, turning away. "Or did you already know that?"

"Of course I didn't," she murmured to the earthworm, as if only it could understand Ashlan's profound silliness. "The gazing-tree told me you were *near*, Lady Ley. It did not peruse the contents of your mind, or eavesdrop on your conversations. It simply sent a branch to tell me you had come. And so I asked it to dig toward you. Being what you are, I assumed you could easily feel its presence, and use your considerable powers to follow its path." Her face fell. "I can see now that this was—overly optimistic." She stood, and sniffed. "And now our tea is cold."

"Right. I'll, uh, I'll get the others moving, then. Be right back."

Ashlan trudged through the mud and into the tunnel, shaking her head.

Being what she was?

She *had* felt something, though.

A tug from below the earth.

She put it out of mind. Forgetting things might well be the only area of expertise she had any faith in.

"Why are you being so *polite* to her?" whispered Hollis, hidden in the darkness.

Ashlan turned on him. "What did you *want* me to do, Runt? Kick her in the shins and find out how strong her bear is?" Sighing, she peered back at the ramp, hoping the rain was loud enough to cover their bickering. "She's crazy, yeah, but she's calm. Let's just keep her that way. She wants to have a tea party, so let's play along. Unless you'd rather stay here, and have me send your regrets?"

"No." He fiddled with the golden buttons on his waistcoat. "This is *my* expedition." He brushed himself off, aggressively. "Is she—frightening to behold?"

Ashlan lifted the boy, grunting. "Compared to what, exactly?"

Hollis stood by the ramp. "Follow my lead, and do try not to muck this up."

He waddled up confidently enough, then flinched as a sheet of rain struck his face. "Greetings!" he called when he'd recovered himself, giving a courtly bow. "My name is Hollis Runt, and I am the leader of this motley crew. My thanks for your unexpected and timely aid!"

"Lady Ley?" shouted Tanka as the cloud above her expanded to twice its size. "Why is that—*thing* talking?"

Hollis recoiled. "I beg your pardon!"

"He's a mannikin," said Ashlan, standing very still, hoping Hollis had the wit to do the same. "Like—like your bear. Animated by enchantment."

"Like my—no." Tanka frowned. "No, no, no. Umber is pleasing to the eye. And does not talk. *This* is a mobile excrescence in the shape of a doll."

"Come now!" cried Hollis, pointing a finger up toward her. "You may be powerful beyond reckoning, and bully for you—but there is no excuse for such rudeness, madam!"

Ashlan was surprised to find her ire rising. "Hey, Tanka, could you, uh—go easy on him?"

"You would like me to treat it like a *person*?" Tanka cocked her head. "But it is a construct. A childish forgery of the city. A cage built of meat and words. And its rune-work is weak."

"My *rune-work* has held for a full century!" Hollis shrieked.

"I don't know about *weak*," Ashlan muttered, feeling too defensive to control herself.

"Yes," said Tanka, glaring. "Weak." The black cloud had begun to descend, forming a bulwark behind Tanka that took Ashlan off guard. Even Hollis seemed cowed enough to shut his mouth.

Tanka seemed satisfied with their continued silence. "You should have a servant that better suits you, Lady Ley. I will happily paint you a helpmeet, when our work is finished."

"Servant?" said Hollis quietly, balling his fists. "'*Servant*,' did you say? Why, I'm afraid you misunderstand, Tanka Equinox."

"Easy, Runt," said Ashlan, "let's not—"

"I am no one's servant," snapped Hollis, "and I have taken too much abuse in my day to pretend otherwise. Your 'Lady Ley' is *my* employee, and this," he said, gesturing broadly, "is my enterprise. I will be happy to treat with you, and I am by no means ungrateful for whatever help you might give, but I demand that you give me the respect I am damn well due."

"Umber!" shouted Tanka, waving a hand. "Take the boy."

Dropping its shovel, the bear lurched toward Ashlan, scooping the body from her arms with shocking swiftness. Its paws were surprisingly agile as they laid him down on its leafy sledge. Turning away, it lumbered toward a grand, hollow tree in the distance, around which a wooden ramp spiraled. Its bark was swallowed in new growth, and near its elephantine boughs, Ashlan spied carven windows alive with flickering lights.

"Tell the doll I meant it no offense," said Tanka. She curled her fingers, and a long, black wisp emerged from the cloud, hissing down into the earth beside them, freezing both of them where they stood. "But it distresses me to think of *you* serving anyone. Much less—well. You belong to this wood, Lady Ley, as surely as it belongs to you."

"I don't know who you think I am," Ashlan murmured.

That was all she could manage to say. She and Hollis had turned to gape as the wisp became a stream. As it flowed, it settled rapidly into the outline of a gazing-tree twice the size of the one they'd seen along the way. The spores were gushing in, root-first, filling its shell with an inky solidity as they shoved piled earth out of their way.

"It is clear," said Tanka, "that you don't. And that is no impediment, Lady Ley. You must walk whatever path you have found under your feet. It is not mine to question, nor to divert. But it does seem to be leading to my door, wouldn't you say?"

Ashlan turned from the shining leaves. Tanka seemed to be waiting for her approval. Somehow this was more unnerving than any show of force.

"I mean." She glanced down at Hollis. "That all right with you, boss?"

"Hm!" The word seemed to help him find his tongue. "So long as whatever business you have with Ashlan Ley can be conducted while you tend to the junkies," he said, waving helplessly at the treehouse where they'd already disappeared, "I have no objection. As I said, I'm not ungrateful in the slightest for any aid you might give us! Or *have* given. I—I believe this little fracas was largely due to the long and frustrating night we spent underground. May we put it behind us?"

Tanka gave no sign that she'd heard him. She was still staring at Ashlan, waiting.

"Um." Ashlan struggled not to stare back. "How about that tea?"

"It is cold," said Tanka, striding suddenly into the rain, leaving the cloud of spores to finish unraveling.

Ashlan and Hollis stood for a long moment, watching her go.

"Runt, I think you're going to have to play the silent partner a while," whispered Ashlan, stepping slowly away from the looming shape of the gazing-tree. "This is—I don't know what this is. But it could probably kill you faster than I could react." Across the lawn, Tanka began to climb the spiraling ramp. "You good with that?"

"Yes. So long as we are clear," he whispered back, "that your new friend has eaten too many mushrooms without a guidebook."

"Agreed. So let's just find out what she wants and get out of here."

Hollis nodded, staring balefully at the gazing-tree. "As soon as possible."

Tanka waved from a platform at the top of the tree-house, then stepped through a broad doorway curtained with hanging white moss, which swung behind her as she disappeared within.

"For your sake," said Hollis, striking out, "let's hope that bear can cook."

I t wasn't moss.

Whatever white substance dangled from the doorway, sliding cold and rubbery across the nape of Ashlan's neck as she followed Hollis inside, it wasn't moss. Her whole body shuddered as she struggled through thick strands of the stuff. Once through, she twisted her arm behind her back in a futile attempt to brush the clinging sensation from her skin.

"Whatever is wrong with you?" said Hollis, squinting up at her.

"Sorry," she said, struggling to steady the pounding of her heart as her eyes adjusted to the candlelight. There was no sign of Tanka, or the bear. "Look." Kneeling, she turned her back to him, still pawing at the nape of her neck. "Is there something on me?"

"The rain has washed away the filth of the tunnel," he murmured. "Unless you mean that cobwebby stuff in the door?"

"Yeah." She rubbed her neck, peering up at the walls, spying dozens of tiny, unsteady lights among the riot of jumbled objects. That the whole place hadn't gone up in flames was a wonder, unless enchantment kept it from burning down. "I guess it's nothing."

"Not that I can see. Though there's certainly no dearth of—whatever it is."

Indeed, strands of whiteness hung from every carven ledge. As a breeze blew through the glassless windows, sheaves of it waved from hooks driven into the high, domed ceiling. Tiny brown birds swooped and dove around its irregular, hanging shapes. Ashlan even spied it tangled in the layered paint of a grand, red mural splattered on a wall on the far side of the room.

"*Nerves.*"

Tanka's voice rang through the grand chamber, but Ashlan couldn't find her, by sound or by sight. There was too much to see in all these dimly-lit nooks: bones and baubles, books and brushes, branches and antlers, chalky diagrams and animal skulls. Alcoves and sconces were hidden everywhere, with just enough candlelight to make out the riot of paint that covered every wooden surface, repeating, again and again, their creator's visage—though Tanka's face never seemed the same twice. Here, she was slender as a skeleton; there, round-cheeked and -bellied; and in a knotted carving almost completely covered by candle wax, she was muscled and square-jawed.

"I'm sorry," called Ashlan, pawing at her neck again, still feeling an echo of that rubbery wriggling on her skin. "Did you say—"

"Nerves."

The ruptured bear lurched out of a dark corner, bearing a tray laden with wooden bowls and clay mugs, depositing it smoothly on a low, wooden table.

"Drink," rang Tanka's voice. "Eat."

Ashlan mumbled an absent-minded thanks, then took a cup.

"*Ashlan*," whispered Hollis.

"Silent partner," she said, just before she guzzled.

The tea was cold, as Tanka had promised her, but it tasted pleasantly of honey and flowers where Ashlan had expected bitter roots and herbs. Chasing it with a berry cake that sent crumbs spilling over her tunic, she stared back at the over-lapping networks of pale fibers that hung over the door.

"Nerves, huh?"

Hollis sidled up against her. "*Ashlan*." He was peering around, slapping the back of her calf. "Where are they?" he whispered. "The junkies, can you see them?"

Ashlan, her headache abating, couldn't think of any reason to be so suspicious. Everything seemed fine here. If Tanka wanted any of them harmed, they'd be harmed, that was all—what good would worrying do?

"I don't understand," she called out, looking around. "You mean—nerves from *bodies*?"

"Of course," came Tanka's voice. "Where else would one find them? These—belonged to Umber, once."

Ashlan heard a chirping, and looked up.

"Here I am, Lady Ley."

She could see Tanka now, as if she'd allowed herself to be seen. She was perched on a high ledge framed in grassy nests, her fingers entangled in an extraordinarily large skein of white stuff secured to the ceiling above. Now that Ashlan gave it some consideration, it didn't resemble moss so much as an unearthed system of roots, organized around a long, central stem. That must be Umber's spine, she thought, and the four fluttering branches were his arms and legs, and all those tiny rootlets had once been spread through his heavy, breathing flesh.

She wondered how Tanka had managed to extract them.

It no longer felt awful.

It seemed wondrous, now.

And perfectly natural that the cold scrap of white that had landed on the nape of her neck had made its wriggling way down her spine. Warmed by the heat of her skin, it tickled, not at all unpleasantly, as it began to stretch itself around her ribs.

Smiling privately, she took a bowl of soup and drank. It was a delicious melange of broth and root vegetables, so hearty that she didn't mind its coldness, nor that Hollis was making such a racket as Umber carried him, by the ankles, down a shadowy hall.

"Are you curious about them?" said Tanka. "The nerves, I mean."

"You gathered all these," Ashlan said, sitting on the floor beside the table and cracking a boiled egg, "for your—collection?"

"For my research," said Tanka. She hopped nimbly from her ledge, down a series of wide platforms and onto the floor, where she pulled a massive basket from an alcove, almost too broad for her arms to bear.

It was full of writhing, furry creatures. The largest one, Ashlan saw as she peeled the shell, was the carcass of a mountain lion, with a little painting like Umber's in its own ripped chest. Tenderly, it was nuzzling the living kittens that were curled up beside it—and inside, since one was at play in its ribs.

"I had an ailment, once," said Tanka, feeding the kittens, one at a time, from a leather skin. "It dwelt in my nerves for most of my life. I'm younger than you are, do you know it?"

"Most people are." Ashlan, having devoured the egg, decided she was full. She sat back, cradling the teacup in her hands. The wriggling seemed intent on covering her entire body, as if she were being fitted with a very cozy suit—of warm rubber, perhaps, or supple skin.

"This ailment disturbed me deeply," said Tanka, batting the mountain lion's muzzle away from the milk. "It would often make me tremble. Sometimes it would make me shake. It distracted me from my work, and from the company of my friends. So I collected all of these, from people and other animals, to help me fix it. And fix it I did. I am pleased to say that I healed what the doctors of Eth said could not be healed, and that I have been healthy for many years."

Ashlan had to set down her cup.

She was afraid she'd spill the tea.

Tanka looked up in surprise. "Does my story please *you*, Lady Ley?"

Ashlan realized she'd been laughing, hard enough that tears were spilling down her face. "Yes, it does."

"Will you tell me why?"

"Because you can change living bodies," she said. Her amusement was gone. Only the warmth of her suit remained. "And I—I want mine changed."

She always had, she realized. Or at least for as long as she could remember.

Tanka turned her face away, smiling. "Then you have come to the right place."

Ashlan arched her back and let out a great yawn.

"Lie down, if you're sleepy."

She did, right on the floor, and closed her eyes.

"But don't go to sleep," said Tanka. "Not just yet. I must be—honest with you. It is important to me that we are honest with each other. You are an esteemed guest, Lady Ley, as is the stag when he carries his heavy antlers onto my lawn, bearing news from home. For this *is* your wood, however you have learned to think of yourself in your long, unpleasant travels. Are you still with me?"

"Yes." Ashlan could feel the suit closing around her fingers and toes, even the tip of her nose. She relaxed herself completely, surprised at how deep her breath could run, how slow.

"I have become a part of this wood, too, but for me it took effort, education. By now, I am more a part of it than of mankind. I have not spoken in words for many years—not since I dug the ailment out of my flesh, and replaced my faulty nerves with those of my friends and adversaries. No human has seen me in almost a decade, unless they were about to go home—or demanded to be sent there. Instead, I have given my life to my friends, and to my creation. I love both more than any troth could express, and I do not regret the time I have spent here. But what my friends tell me when they visit, more insistently each day—friends like Umber, when he was alive, and Lady Greatcat here, and all the unnamed others who still have breath in their lungs—is that I am missed, back home. Do you know what I mean by that?"

"Death," said Ashlan, the word as heavy on her tongue as gold in her palm. "You mean death."

"Yes," said Tanka, settling down beside her. A bird seemed to have settled down, too, chirping as it pecked at the food on the tray. "Although that name is unpleasant to me. It conjures an end, where I know there is a *land*. My homeland. Most names *are* unpleasant, though, or at least ill-fitting. Even the one I've given myself. It seems—an approximation. For something better painted, or sung."

Umber was dragging something heavy in. It had been some time since Hollis had made any noise, wherever he was.

"But I do not return home, not yet, for a single reason. Do you know what it is?"

Ashlan couldn't imagine one. She wasn't sure she'd ever been able to.

"No."

"What keeps me here is my desire to *create*." Another bird flapped down, and another. "I am a woman, both like and unlike yourself. But however far I have traveled, whatever I have woven with nerves and with flesh, whatever I might carve, or paint, or tell in song, the ultimate act of creation remains beyond me. And so I stand alone, unable to love, unable to give as I would—until I gain my final boon from this world. Tell me, Lady Ley, do you know what *that* is?"

Umber, by now, had dragged the heavy thing up to Ashlan's side and trudged off.

Tanka's riddle wasn't hard to answer. It just felt nosy to do so, with or without an invitation. But between her height and the peculiar timbre of her voice, which belonged to no category but its own, Ashlan could guess.

She was reminded of a woman who'd been her lover long ago—of Tay, who'd proudly called herself crosswise, and broken the will, if not the nose, of anyone who'd shamed her for it.

Until the Liniment Boys slit her throat—for confusing them, as they'd put it.

Crosswise. Ashlan couldn't imagine Tanka calling herself any such thing.

All the same, she'd asked her for an answer, and Ashlan had to give it.

"You don't—have a womb," she said.

Tanka gave a short, bitter laugh. "I do," she lilted, "it simply hasn't arrived yet. But I didn't mean the crucible, Lady Ley. I meant its proof. A child."

For a while they listened to the birds cracking seeds in a bowl.

"And this is where you will help me become myself—as Umber once did, with his nerves. I did not take his life, as I hope you have guessed. He died on his own, after we had been friends for a good while. It was painful to wait, but wait I did, and would have waited longer, for the sake of our friendship. But I have no such luxury now. My time is short, and you, Lady Ley, have no such—restrictions."

Ashlan thought of how freely she'd given her guts to the addicts, and wondered how she could possibly object.

Something about that thought troubled her.

She realized, foggily, that she *couldn't* object.

Nor could she say anything at all.

Because Tanka hadn't asked her a question. Everything else Ashlan had said, for quite some time, had been at Tanka's express invitation.

Umber was dragging a second heavy thing into the room. Ashlan struggled to open her eyes, and found that impossible, too.

"You may look."

The woman and the boy were laying in low cradles on either side of her, still fully clothed, but blanketed in deep piles of orange fronds. They seemed to be breathing easier, though the boy was wheezing.

Tanka was squatting near Ashlan's feet. "I care little for the lives of humans, as you may have gathered. But you, Lady Ley, are no human."

Ashlan wanted to object.

This was what Tanka had been getting at all along.

But Ashlan had a mother, once, and siblings. They just hadn't been—like her.

Cursed.

"It *must* have occurred to you." Tanka smiled, and the wrinkles around her eyes reminded Ashlan that she was vulnerable, despite her power, and aging, even now. "However you might have pushed the question out of your mind. You are more powerful than I, Lady Ley. More powerful than most anyone alive. But you do not know yourself—that much was clear from the moment I met you. I think you must be a foundling. And so I have bound you, rather rudely, because I have waited so long for your arrival that I cannot wait for your understanding. Still, I will not take what

I need without offering you an exchange. I might earn your exasperation, but I would not earn your enmity. And this is why it made me so glad to hear that you, too, are in need of change! That means that you can *see* me, doesn't it?"

"Yes."

That was the worst part.

Ashlan understand her perfectly.

She thought, without knowing why, that this must be the true reason she was keeping Hollis close.

Because she needed him as Tanka needed her.

Tanka reached toward Ashlan's face.

"May I touch you?"

"Yes."

The hand was warm and dry.

"Tell me."

Ashlan's breath thickened.

"Tell me what you are, that you would yet become."

She tried not to speak.

"You have been seeking some goal. That much is clear just from looking at you. You've folded yourself around it, until you can barely breathe."

The suit tightened around her skin until it felt like her eyes would burst.

"What have you been seeking, Lady Ley?"

Ashlan did not want to speak this truth.

She didn't even want to *know* it.

But it was slipping out on its own.

"What I want," Ashlan whispered, "is to die."

Tanka did not take her hand away.

She watched Ashlan breathe for a long while.

"You are aware, aren't you?" she said with a wistful smile. "That this is a far greater distance to travel, for one such as yourself, than for me to become a mother."

"Yeah." Ashlan looked at the ceiling, feeling her heart seize. "Is it impossible?"

"No." Tanka stroked Ashlan's cheek with her thumb. "I don't believe so, Lady Ley. Not impossible. Just very, *very* difficult. And requiring components that are, quite frankly, beyond my means to purchase. They'd cost a king's ransom. Now, you might find them and steal them, mind you, or kill their owners. But by then you might be asking these things of my child, and not of me—for by the time you'd won that war, I'd have gone home before you, whether I wished it or no."

Ashlan was laughing again.

This time Tanka did pull her hand away. "Have I—upset you?"

"No. No, it's fine. Just don't—don't hurt the doll. He has gold. A queen's ransom. Enough to buy whatever you need."

"Ah. Now I see why you tolerate him!" She laughed herself, a bright, musical sound. "But come, we have no need to delay what we've both waited for—not a moment more." Standing, she peered down at the cradles. "Which of these two would you rather be?"

The smile slid from Ashlan's face.

Something sought to buoy her mood, just as the suit held her body in place.

"Neither."

"You must pick one, Lady Ley." Tanka knelt next to the boy. "This one has fluid in his lungs. He hasn't breathed properly for some time. I'm not sure why, but perhaps his body will tell us the tale. Umber, the shears?" The bear withdrew to an alcove, digging through a pile of clanking tools. "But it is a minor pain, as such things go. The woman's arm is ruined, as you know. We can do nothing there, not without far more effort than she warrants. The pain will be excruciating, and constant. I'd go with the boy, if it were up to me. But you know them better." She folded her arms beneath her breasts. "Choose."

It hurt not to.

But it was only pain.

Now that she'd noticed Tanka's spell at work in her mind, she could struggle against it. Not enough to move of her own volition, but enough to disobey.

"Don't take me out of myself," she gasped.

Tanka frowned. "Hush," she said, flicking a finger at Ashlan's mouth.

Ashlan felt the wriggling, supple substance of Tanka's spell drawing itself over her lips, sealing them shut with comfort and warmth.

"This will not be quick, Lady Ley. This is untested magic. I have long theorized. I have imagined the forms extensively. I have filled sketchbooks with plans. But still, there will be—guesswork. It will take many drafts before I get it right. And while they are tested, I will not listen to a friend of this wood as she suffers interminably." She laid a hand on the boy's cradle. "To these two, I owe no such loyalty. So you and the boy will trade places, for a time."

The bear lumbered back with a pair of shears, their blades as long as Tanka's forearms. Kneeling, she laid one under his shirt, one over, and cut him out of it.

"Hm."

Ashlan wrested her head up, though it felt like it would split her skull. She saw another layer of fabric under the boy's shirt, startlingly filthy, wound tightly around his chest. The skin around it was angry, with open sores where the friction had been greatest.

No wonder there was fluid in his lungs.

"What—*is* this?" Tanka murmured. "What's he done to himself?"

The answer was plain enough, at least to a former student of the Uni: the boy was as bent as a thrown-away nail, and he'd been binding his breasts for so long that he'd given himself pleurisy. He must have been wearing the makeshift binder in his sleep, probably to keep his partner in crime from learning the truth—as a matter of survival, if modern-day Eth was anything like its forebear.

What's he done to himself? Tanka had never encountered a binder before, it seemed. So she'd asked a question, and Ashlan, focusing on her unspoken explanation, wedged her desire to answer against Tanka's order to keep quiet—with enough force to part her lips at one corner.

It was barely enough to pull air through. She'd been foolish enough to hope that the spell would break if she managed it, that she'd be able to grab those shears and get free. Instead, the warm weight of the suit pressed down harder, sealing her mouth shut again—and closing her nostrils, to boot.

Tanka lifted the shears again, her white brow furrowed as she slid a blade beneath the bandages, directly under his arm, where she began, with obvious impatience, to cut him loose.

"I'll get you settled in him quickly," she was muttering, "and we'll care for your new lungs before too much time has passed."

Ashlan couldn't draw breath. She could only watch as Tanka sliced the stiff fabric open, then began to tug it roughly from his skin.

Then she saw him, and her body froze.

She was staring at his breasts, marked deeply by the tight-wound fabric.

The shears clattered to her side.

Her face, so impassive all this while that each expression had come as a minor revelation, was roiling with complicated reactions that seemed to chase each other away, then recur. Several times she seemed about to speak, but nothing came.

Stars appeared in Ashlan's eyes as she began to suffocate.

She watched as a bird landed on Tanka's hunched back.

Tanka didn't budge.

At last, even Umber seemed to tire of her silence, picking up the shears and shuffling off. This seemed to stir Tanka from her reverie. Hearing Ashlan's body shaking behind her, she covered the boy's chest with the orange fronds, either with tenderness or a depth of sorrow that amounted, however briefly, to the same. Looking drained, she leaned over Ashlan's body and plucked at the back of her neck.

The warmth retracted from Ashlan's body, all at once, as she gulped down breath. "*Fuck,*" she shouted. Every muscle in her frame was convulsing from the sudden cold.

Tanka didn't look at her. She stared at the walls instead, settling at last on the grand, red mural. "Do you know," she said, "it is possible that I have been away from humans too long?"

Ashlan struggled up, rubbing her arms, looking for something heavy to swing.

"I—I noticed nothing," Tanka said.

Ashlan stopped herself. Don't attack, she thought. Don't run. Don't even move. Not without a plan.

In the meantime, if Tanka was feeling talkative, let her talk.

"Don't beat yourself up about it," she muttered. "The kid's doing a pretty solid job of passing."

Tanka glared at the wall. "I don't mean his—his *body*. That's none of my concern, or yours. Don't mistake me, Lady Ley; that the boy and I are not like you does not mean that we are like each other."

"Okay." Ashlan was peering at the shadowy folds in the walls, each one covered in a curtain of nerves, trying to determine where Umber had taken the mannikin. "So why'd you stop?"

She'd found the hall, she thought, but she still wasn't moving.

It could only be because Tanka had said she could help her die.

Ashlan realized that she believed her.

There might be other enchanters, of course, who could do the job.

But Ashlan was wondering how any of them would know what she was, when she herself never had.

Tanka claimed to. And Ashlan believed that, too.

"I hate the city," Tanka said softly. "I hate its denizens, in general. In groups, everything they do repulses me. The things that they build. The things that they believe. The men they choose to worship. But its people, alone—I know them not at all. Least of all the youth. And though I would prefer to forget it, I am one of them. I was born in Eth, under the bridge at Tunica Media." She folded her arms. "This boy is awful, I have no doubt. He has done awful things, at any rate. And yet—he's done none of them to me. And if I've proven anything in my short life, it is that I cannot see the future."

"Me either." Ashlan gave up.

For better or worse, she needed Tanka.

Let her call it home, if she liked. But Ashlan prayed that death *would* be an ending.

"Umber?" Tanka called. "Free the talking doll. I've gone about this all wrong."

While the bear shuffled down the hall, Tanka crossed to an alcove, finding a dusty bag of grass-colored velvet. Turning to Ashlan with a thin smile, she pulled out a slender bottle and held it out.

"Is that—"

"Greenfellow's Reserve," she murmured.

"Single malt."

Ashan was salivating. That distillery had burned down twenty years ago.

Since then, she hadn't tasted anything but moonshine.

"I've forgotten most of the manners I knew," said Tanka. "But I seem to remember liquor being essential to making amends."

Much as she hated to, Ashlan turned away. "I don't know. Let's see what the boss has to say."

Tanka's face fell. She tucked the bottle under one arm. "Very well."

Umber carried a large pillowcase out of the hall and dumped it, without ceremony, in the middle of the floor. Out of the mass of wadded cotton wriggled Hollis, who leapt away from the bear and ran, sputtering, to Ashlan's side. "There's *more*? I thought I'd be ground up by now, and sealed in this witch's next pie. But what has this despot of droppings and acorns *done* to you, Ashlan Ley?" He pressed against her leg.

The fabric of his body was still damp from the rain. She tried to shrug him off, to no avail. "I mean. Not much, in the end. She choked before she got to the good part."

"But she was *about* to do nefarious things. You can see it in her beady little eyes!"

Tanka snorted. "Am I to be tried in the Court of Almost, then? And who will be my judge?"

"At the very least, you altered the mind and body of my lieutenant," he huffed. "Why did you stop?"

"I've decided to let you live, Mister Runt. Explanations are not owed to you."

"Well," said Hollis, sticking out his chin, "what matters is that we're free to go. Unless you only brought me out to scramble *my* brains, as well?"

"Not unless you have the ability to imbibe." Stiffly, she held out the bottle. "I admit that I headed down a—an unstable pathway. But I hope that we might still—benefit one another."

Tanka treated herself to a generous slug of Greenfellow's, then passed it to Ashlan.

Ashlan gulped, her eyes watering, her mouth full of peat. "What's the move, boss?"

He squinted. "I don't see why we ought to treat with her at all," he murmured. "The junkies look stable enough to me."

"That all depends on what you want them to *do*," said Tanka. "Walking, for instance, is quite beyond them now. But it needn't be."

He looked to Ashlan. "You don't really *trust* her, do you?"

She didn't.

But she needed her.

"Yeah, I think she's on the level," Ashlan muttered. "Coming at it a little crooked, maybe." She swigged again. "If it makes you feel any better, she already knows all my dirt. Might as well tell her what she needs to know."

She'd take it anyway, if she wanted it, thought Ashlan, passing the bottle back.

Hollis scowled, and trotted away from her. "That doesn't make me feel better at all, Ashlan Ley. What it *does* is make me wonder whether you're still dazed from whatever whammy she laid on you while I was indisposed. No, I think I'd rather that Tanka Equinox set me at ease. Tell me—after all this skullduggery, why should I believe that you want to help us?"

Tanka had raised the bottle to her lips. She let it fall. "I've come to understand that Lady Ley and I share a certain—"

"I told her you want to kill your creator," blurted Ashlan, glaring over his head at Tanka, who snapped her mouth shut. "That he's building a, uh—a factory for murder dolls, and the addicts are going to lead us there."

He whirled on one platform heel. "That was not yours to *tell!*"

"I know," she said, dropping to a crouch. "I'm sorry, Runt. I was under the influence. Not whiskey, I mean. She—she put a whammy on me!"

His little shoulders were heaving. "You are both lucky that I have so little time left."

Tanka strode to Hollis' other side, arching an eyebrow. "But it is fortuitous, is it not?"

He gave a sour laugh. "How's that? Because you can stuff *more* of me in pillowcases now?"

She nodded. "Just so. It may not be pleasant to work with one who loathes all that you are, Mister Runt. But I would gladly join you, for a time, if it means working to eradicate such shoddy rune-craft."

"This shit again," Ashlan muttered, reaching for the bottle.

Tanka looked startled at her thirst, but gave it up readily enough.

"You take me for a rube," he said softly. "As if anyone with such powers would leave her stronghold just for the satisfaction of killing puppets."

"Ah, you mistake me," said Tanka. "Helping *you* helps Lady Ley. And helping Lady Ley helps me help myself."

He looked at Ashlan, shocked. "Do you mean to tell me, Ashlan Ley, that you've promised this witch a slice of your inheritance?"

Ashlan, who'd been wondering how all of this could possibly come to a conclusion, nodded quickly. "Yes," she said, wondering where she'd put the cork, then deciding that it didn't matter. "That is what I did."

She'd promised her *all* of it, she realized—whatever it took to get her spellwork up and running, at which point Ashlan would have no use for gold, because she'd be dead.

Hollis' enchanted cabinet had seemed like a convenient excuse to keep him close, but it was lucky there was a hefty payoff at the end of all this, after all.

"Well." Hollis scowled, but opened his palms. "I suppose it's yours to divvy up as you see fit, should all this come to a pleasant conclusion—by which I mean the Puppeteer drowning in a pool of his own fluids. Very well, Tanka Equinox! Let us find the man responsible for making more of me, and force him to put down his needle for good. Perhaps you could help me immobilize him with your nerve blankets, so that I might carve at my leisure? I have a particular pattern I'd like to try, a sort of fleshy gammon-board that I *think* he'd survive for an hour or two at the very—"

"Hey, time for a cheers! Cheers, everybody."

Ashlan drank enough to cover both of them and the bear, then sat heavily on the floor.

Tanka sized her up, judging her useless. "Tell me, Mister Runt, what you had in mind. The *larger* pattern, I mean."

"Very well." Hollis was stalking around the cradles, frowning prodigiously. "When I met your Lady Ley, these two ruffians were harvesting her organs on behalf of this vile Puppeteer, tearing the fruit from her basket while she played possum."

Tanka looked aghast. "You allowed *them* to remove your insides?"

"Easier than fighting," Ashlan murmured into the neck of the bottle. "Don't judge me."

"Our plan, at first, was to follow them to their lair in Eth, then gain entry with some degree of stealth," said Hollis, poking at the woman's charred wristbone. "But all that's gone to pot. The best we can hope for, by now, is that you might be able to meddle with their minds, so that they wake feeling friendly. That should be a doddle for you, I'd guess." He gestured at the ceiling. "Just slap a few of your dangling ganglia on their heads, and we're off!"

Tanka pursed her lips. "No."

"Damn you, Tanka Equinox!" He stamped his foot. "Have we forged an alliance, or no?"

She took a deep breath, then peered down at him. "Why would you want them to feel friendly toward you?"

Hollis looked blankly at Ashlan. "I thought *you* were the one who was drinking."

"I think he's trying to say that we need to know they'll cooperate," said Ashlan.

"No," said Tanka again, stepping toward the cradles. "You need to know that they'll *obey*. It is far easier to compel submission than friendship. Umber, my chalk."

Hollis brightened. "Are you going to put little paintings in their chests?"

"One would think their fellow humans might notice," murmured Tanka. Umber brought her a stick of chalk and a large shard of slate, and she sat between the sleeping bodies. "No, it would be best if we alter something simple. Like their relationship to what they love most."

Ashlan shooed an errant kitten, which padded off to Hollis' side, sniffing at him with interest. "Which is—?"

"Tlak," said Hollis, waving the cat away. "Stay sober enough to keep up, Ashlan, this concerns you, too! But it is tlak," he said to Tanka, "that is the very problem with any plan involving their obeisance. Should we try to bribe them, they'll buy an ample supply and nod off before they're useful. Threaten them, and they'll be that much more likely to sell us out. To say nothing of their bizarre religion, which seems to inform their every decision, and in consistently unexpected ways. So unless you're sitting on a veritable mountain of drugs, Tanka Equinox, with a direct pipeline to the whims of Fortuna, I fail to see how you intend to motivate them *without* mind control."

"Not a mountain of drugs," Tanka murmured, scribbling feverishly. "A valley."

"Are you—" Hollis tilted his head. "Are you being *purposely* obtuse?"

"It is possible."

Ashlan leaned over and peered at the slate. "Is that person—vivisected?"

"Opened," said Tanka, pointing. "I'll draw doors on their backs that will swing wide. All their soft parts will emerge, while your essence, Lady Ley, keeps them alive."

She sighed. "You're talking about my blood, aren't you?"

"Your blood," said Tanka, "and other vital magics."

"You'd better have some more of those berry cakes," said Ashlan, leaning back on her elbows. "At least a dozen. Maybe thirteen."

"All fine," said Hollis, "so long as your kittens don't get peckish. But toward what end? What *valley* are you speaking of?"

"A good spell requires symmetry. They took Lady Ley's insides," said Tanka, sliding her slate before him. "So we shall rebuild theirs. When we are through, their metabolisms will be altered, such that they'll get no pleasure from their addictions. They'll still *need* the tlak," she said, pointing to a labyrinthine squiggle in the midst of her diagram, "to fend off withdrawal. But they won't *feel* anything, ever again. Unless, of course, they do just as we say."

Hollis paused, dumbstruck.

"Oh!" he cried, giggling uncontrollably. "I suppose this witch of yours has her good points, after all."

Ashlan polished off the bottle of Greenfellow's as she stared at the sleeping bodies in the cradles, thinking of the hell they'd wake to. "You're cold, T."

Tanka smiled, rubbing the throat of the smallest kitten. "So they tell me."

—Pathways—

Rafe was leading the new girl down Carotid Alley, holding her hand like they'd been friends for years. "You'll want to step over those purple things," he told her, pointing down at the paper cylinders scattered on the broken stones. "Bangums, we call them, and you never know when they might have some bang left. Sometimes they'll just startle you, but Sixty-Leven blew off a pinky toe last night—and kept right on dancing, the fool! He was high as a knob on a flagpole, but so was everyone else. You really did show up at just the wrong moment," he said, smiling back at her.

It was the night after the Second Masque, and Rafe could still feel the party in his flesh—a constellation of aches and pains, some sharp, some dull, that aroused sweet memories with every cringe. He was glad when the girl smiled back, though it seemed to take too long for her to hear him, like she had to wait for what he'd said to be translated by some invisible imp flying near her ear. "There'll be plenty more parties, of course, and I doubt you'll have to pay for a thing—for a while, anyway. They'll get used to you around the boarding house eventually, so milk it while you can."

She was smiling now, all shy and golden, with jet-black hair cut at a steep angle that framed her jaw just so. It was a pity that she kept rubbing at her skin with her fingers— her chin, her upper lip, her forearms, anywhere she'd shaved, he guessed. She was probably worried that her stubble was coming in, but her fingers were so dirty—almost black at the tips.

Then again, Rafe had no room to judge anyone's bodily anxiety, not when he couldn't walk down the hall to the bath without being wrapped up tighter than one of Little Gem's unsmokable spliffs.

"Up ahead is Mr. Rue's. See, with the golden button on the sign, and the tiny dancing man on the button? Rue's is where you can get fitted for dresses that actually suit your frame. That's if you ever have any extra coin, mind, because he marks up the mods for our kind. He's bent himself, but he taxes *us* for being crosswise! It's like that, even here—though Gingerbeard's always telling me it's better than it's been for a generation."

It looked like the new girl was about to speak, but she just shrugged, almost compulsively, like something was itching under her shirt.

"Now, speaking of coin, don't bother trying to borrow at the boarding house. Everyone's always skint, except for Mrs. Dallow, and she'd rather set you afire than spot you a five.

Not that she's unkind, as landladies go—and she's one of the only owners in Eth who'll rent to the bent, as Gingerbeard puts it. But safety's harder to come by than coin—that's a Gingerbeard phrase, too. I'm full of those," he said, glancing back to see if his giddiness was getting on her nerves.

Then he stopped, fighting the feeling that they'd gone in a circle.

Hadn't they just left Carotid? Where was the turn?

With all he'd taken last night, it wouldn't be surprising if he was still high enough to get turned around. It wasn't like the two of them to go so far—Gingerbeard preferred a controlled buzz, and kept Rafe steady even when he wanted to get blitzed—but it *had* been a Masque, and those only came along so often.

Here was the turn, up ahead. Rafe had been on track after all.

"And if you *do* have any extra coin, be shy about it until it's spent. It's not that there's thieving, much—but if you're anything like me, you'll help your friends until you've nothing left to eat with. Where did you say you were from, again?"

The new girl, whose name he kept forgetting, opened her mouth to speak—then shut it, ducking into the doorway of Mr. Rue's.

Rafe was about to scold her when he saw what she'd seen and backed in beside her, just in time.

Six men with scab-brown helmets were hauling a bent boy down the street. His mouth was bloody, his eyes purple and swollen, his breasts yanked out of his top.

Rafe's stomach churned. He pressed into the shadows, trembling.

When the guards were gone, the new girl clasped him to her chest, her heart thumping in his ear. "It's all right," Rafe told her, squeezing her hard before he let her go, as much to comfort himself as her. "It happens, even here. If they come for you, just run, and if they catch you I'm sorry," he said, but then he stopped talking, because she hadn't taken her hands away.

She was rubbing his back, her long arms reaching down over his shoulders. There was a strange intensity to the action. It didn't seem sexual, but nor did she seem to be afraid any longer.

Maybe it was a custom where she was from, some way of showing thanks. Not wishing to be rude, he reached up behind and touched her the same way—then froze when he felt the nubs on her shoulder-blades.

Stubs, really.

He could feel the jagged edges where whatever had stuck out had been cut off.

Or ripped.

She opened her mouth, moving her throat like she was trying to coax her voice along. It never came, but he heard her all the same, in a faraway sing-song.

Those were my wings.

"Oh," he said, grinning as he backed away. "Well, there's all kinds at Mrs. Dallow's! I'm sure no one will look at them funny, if you decide to show your body. And I—I don't do that, myself. Folk will give you space in the bath, if you ask for it."

What a long night this had become. He just wanted to put his face in Gingerbeard's hair and breathe a while.

"Let's go, yeah? We'll be safe inside."

Rafe felt better as soon as the boarding house was in sight. The front door was crooked, its stone doorstep so old that it sagged almost to the street in the middle. There were chipped flower boxes in the windows above, all overflowing with butts and bottles. Someone inside was singing an aria—beautifully, but at a volume so high that it must have annoyed anyone in the rooms adjacent.

"Here we are, then: Mrs. Dallow's Cut-Rate Boarding House! The finest sanctuary for bent folk in all of Eth, or at least the finest that orphans like us can afford. All right, I'll tell you the bad news first: it's noisy, and someone's always bringing in lice. But it's warm, always, because it's built right on a stone-vent from the catacombs. Keeps your toes from getting cold at night, but you *will* get sticky as summer candy—another of Gingerbeard's phrases. Sorry, I'm smitten, I guess you can tell! You'll meet them presently." Rafe remembered when the pronoun had seemed strange to him, and looked back to see if she was confused. "You met any twains yet? No? Gingerbeard is crosswise, like us, but—different. Different from me, anyhow. They're neither man nor woman, unless it's a night when they're both, and those are my favorite kind. We call Gingerbeard 'they,' anyway, and some from abroad aren't used it, and think we're speaking of multiple people. But here, let's go in and find them."

But the new girl wouldn't go. She just stood on the corner, staring at the building like it might hurt her to enter.

"Come on! It's safe inside, and warm."

She shook her head, and pursed her red lips tight.

"You have to," he said. "It's not *safe* here."

Maybe he was still high. The word seemed to have lost its meaning.

Safe. Safe. Safe. Safe.

She was moving her throat again.

I'm not like you.

"Of course you are! A girl to my boy, naturally, but I see you. 'Like knows like, love.' That's another—" He stopped, stepping across the alley, squinting at her face, which seemed to be changing, though he couldn't say how.

"Was I wrong? Are you not—bent? Like me? Crosswise?"

That word has no place here.

A thought struck him as he noticed how smooth she'd become. No shadow of stubble darkened her lip now. Maybe she'd been taking her Esther, which meant she *did* have coin. And the poverty put distance between them, because if anyone had ever been dying to take his Tester, it was Rafe.

Esther and Tester, that's what Gingerbeard called them. *One makes you softer and one makes you rougher, and neither can we afford, my love.*

However spoiled she might be, though, he couldn't just *leave* her here. Not with those helmeted monsters roaming.

Rafe had a wicked idea.

"Look," he shouted, pointing behind her, "the guards are coming back!"

It was cruel, but effective. She scurried in, and he followed.

She was staring up at the walls in the lobby, and he remembered doing the same, once. Everyone who landed at Mrs. Dallow's was asked to tell about themselves on a big piece of paper, and the joke was that no one ever told the truth—so there were pictures, stories, and made-up songs about all sorts of faraway lands and lost titles. Some had even made certificates of origin. The entry room was plastered with papers, each one stuck up haphazardly with paste, and Rafe was just about to explain the custom to the new girl when he saw.

She was rubbing her back against the wall, like her stumps were itching, and all the papers were coming down.

It was raining castles and princes in gowns.

He stepped toward her.

"Are you all right?"

I need help.

"How can I help?"

Ask Little Gem.

Rafe felt sick to his stomach. He couldn't remember telling her about Little Gem.

He must have forgotten. It must have been the drugs. He must have been getting confused, because they were upstairs already, outside of the bathroom, and he couldn't remember climbing those creaky steps.

Don't worry.

"Right."

So they went into the bathroom.

Little Gem was there, in the tub, naked.

"We shouldn't be here," he said.

It was even harder for Little Gem to have her clothes off in front of people than it was for Rafe.

Ask her.

The new girl put her hands on his shoulder-blades and gave him a push.

Rafe didn't want to be rude to either of them.

Ask her how to help me.

His skin felt tight. It felt like he'd forgotten how to say no.

"Gemmie?"

All he could see was her brown back bent over in that deep, deep tub.

Something had been drawn on her skin.

A door.

"Gemmie, love, I need to help—what was your name again?"

"Let her touch your back," said Little Gem, her voice oddly raspy, like she'd been screaming all night.

It bothered him that he hadn't seen Little Gem's face. She was curled around something, or someone.

"Let her touch your bare back," said Little Gem.

This Rafe truly didn't want to do.

But he pulled his clothes off, feeling the pit of his stomach burning.

"All right," he told the new girl, "you go ahead."

Then he must have gotten confused again, because he was up high, his arms tied to the ceiling. He looked down at his body, feeling that awful rush that always came when he could see his breasts, rising into panic now because there were *people* around.

"This isn't right," he said, hating his high, plaintive whine as it echoed through the room.

"It's what she needs," rasped Little Gem, her voice echoing up from all the way down on the floor.

Rafe could see into the tub from where he hung. It was deep, very deep, and it seemed like it was getting wider. There was room for both of them in there, Little Gem and the wiry woman she was cradling in her arms.

She was broad-cheeked, dark-skinned, with a gray mess of hair that was months overdue for a braiding.

His flesh prickled as he realized that he knew her.

He'd killed her.

In the farmhouse.

She was his, he saw. His very own unquiet dead. She'd be with him always, following him from place to place.

That bothered him. Not that she was haunting him— that part he deserved.

It bothered him because that killing had happened in a world apart from this one, a colder, wetter place, full of trees.

Which meant that none of this was real.

The boarding house. Little Gem. Mrs. Dallow. All of it had gone away from him, and he couldn't remember why.

The new girl, very tall, her limbs and neck spindly and strange, touched his back. Her hand was wet.

She was washing him, with soap. He didn't like it, but he couldn't stop it.

He looked down at the floor. The tub was gone, and the ghost from the farmhouse was sitting on a stool. Little Gem sat behind her, both hands on her back, staring up at Rafe.

"She's better at it than me," said Little Gem.

She had gold buttons for eyes.

Tiny men were dancing on their faces.

"Better at what?" he called down.

"Lookit."

Little Gem was pointing.

Rafe looked.

The woman from the farmhouse was pulling paper streamers out of her arm, red and rustling, leftovers from the Second Masque. They were tumbling into a bucket on the floor.

There were so many, and the new girl was kissing his back. It didn't feel right. Nothing did.

"Gemmie?"

Something had begun to worry him.

"Gemmie, where's Gingerbeard?"

She gave a rattling sigh, and climbed out of the tub.

"Everywhere," she said.

There was something wrong with Little Gem's arms.

"Where's Gingerbeard?" Rafe said again.

"All around," said Little Gem, gesturing. Her arms were slashed open from elbow to wrist.

He was starting to remember.

It made him angry. He'd intended not to dwell on such things.

Behind him, the new girl made a sound like *ughhhhh*. She'd stepped in something, and she took her hands off his back to scrape it off her shoe.

"Stop fucking around, Gemmie," he shouted.

"Lookit."

Little Gem pointed down.

Rafe saw what the new girl had stepped in.

It was Gingerbeard.

There were pieces of them everywhere.

The pieces formed a trail, and the trail led out of the room.

Rafe struggled against his ropes. He had to get down and collect them, or he'd never be able to put Gingerbeard back together.

But Rafe couldn't get free. The new girl had opened her mouth wide and started licking his back, far down on the left side. Her tongue was cool and moved slowly, deliberately, up toward his neck.

The ghost sighed. She'd filled one bucket, then called for another.

But Rafe was looking past her, into the room he shared with Gingerbeard, number 17, where the lights were off.

It wasn't empty.

"*There* you are," he whispered, relieved.

Gingerbeard would get him down from here.

"Hello, lovely," Rafe called.

Gingerbeard, silhouetted by the light outside, turned their head.

They'd been looking down at the street, and now they were looking up at Rafe.

Their hair was up, all bushy and curly.

It would smell sweet and musky at once, like curried honey, and he couldn't wait to put his face in it and breathe.

Although they stood in darkness, Rafe could tell from the cut of their dress what they were wearing. It was the one with the purple flowers, the one Mr. Rue made. The two of them had nicked the fabric from the curtains of a house that burned down on Lank Street half a year ago.

My smoky lilac, Rafe had called them the first night they wore it.

But the dress was sagging tonight. Gingerbeard had a substantial body, and it was Rafe's greatest joy to wrestle it around. Now, though, they barely filled out the purple fabric, because of how much the—

"*Fuck*," whispered Rafe.

—because of how much the guards had left on the ground when they executed them on the corner.

They'd never come to bed last night.

Gingerbeard was walking toward the light.

Could hardly even tell who it was.

Worth risking quakes, to those pig-fuckers.

To make an example.

Of all of us.

Rafe closed his eyes, fixing his mind on the ghost from the farmhouse. If *she* was here, then none of this was happening.

Which meant that Gingerbeard wasn't here.

Rafe would not see them.

Rafe would not remember this.

It worked, somehow. When Rafe opened his eyes, room 17 was gone.

Not the new girl, though. She was still behind him, and her tongue had traced an archway up from his left side to a point between his shoulder blades, then down again, all the way down on the right.

A door, like Little Gem's.

It didn't tickle any more. It stung.

Then it *tugged*, like the new girl was sliding her hands into his flesh and pulling the door open.

"She'll climb inside," rasped Little Gem. "She'll be safe there, snuggled up in your chest. That's how you can help her. She'll sleep in you, and her wings will grow."

"Stop," he said, or tried to say, and something about the sound of his own voice made him frightened.

It wasn't like the other noises in the dream. This one was real.

He tried it again. "Stop."

It came out like a wheeze from behind him. It had nothing to do with his mouth or throat.

He struggled to open his eyes.

Light came through, a little.

It was enough to motivate him.

He pushed his tongue between his teeth and bit, hard.

The pain helped. His eyelids wavered up, offering him a blurry slice of the world past his dream.

This wasn't the boarding house. It was some wide, flickering chamber, full of animals and bric-a-brac.

Little Gem was gone, and the new girl, and Gingerbeard, for which he was grateful. But the ghost of the woman he'd killed in the farmhouse was here, sitting on a stool, bleeding into a bucket.

Her arm was open, not the sort of slice you made to keep your desire to die at bay, but the kind you made when you had finally decided to embrace it—a long, confident cut between the tendons.

The kind that had carried Little Gem away in the boarding house bathtub.

The ghost looked bored. Her blood had slowed to a trickle, which seemed to irk her. "Some more here, Umber."

A deflated brown bear came shuffling to her side, bringing a tray of tea and cakes. She nodded her thanks, shoving one cake after another into her mouth, swallowing them quickly, not stopping to chew. The sustenance seemed to replenish her arteries, though not her energy. Her blood came gushing back as she kept on chewing, looking like *she* might take a nap now.

But she was startled by another voice.

It was Jassa's.

Suddenly Rafe remembered more than he cared to.

"Ah!" Jassa cried, helplessly, like a dog chasing a rabbit in a dream.

With great effort, Rafe shoved his pupils to the corners of his eyes.

Jassa was hanging from the ceiling, too, her bare ass to him. A tall woman stood behind her, painting on her back with a brush.

He could tell the woman was crosswise, just barely—*like knows like*. She was beautiful, in presentation still more than in form, and he found himself aching at the sight of her.

Not because he wanted her. Because it had been so very long since he'd been among his people.

Yet something gave him pause about associating her with Little Gem, Gingerbeard, and the rest. Maybe it was the clear understanding he suddenly had that she would have had nothing to do with any of them at the boarding house, since they were the grubbiest possible sort of bent orphans and she was some sort of forest queen.

But then, maybe the distance he felt had nothing to do with being bent at all. Maybe it was because of what she was—*doing*.

She dipped her paintbrush in ink that seemed somehow too black, and started to paint a door on Jassa's back. It was a trapdoor, and she sang to it, a pretty melody in some dusty-sounding language he'd never heard before. The ink began to hiss, and the door swung slowly down and open, showing him the white tips of Jassa's severed ribs peeking out amidst her muscle.

The ink that lined the doorway flashed, though it was a flash that took light *out* of the room, not in. Rafe was blinded, for a moment, by that too-black darkness, and from the ghost's muttering it sounded like the others were, too.

When Rafe found he could see again, Jassa's back was cut neatly open, lying flat like one of those beds that swung down from the wall in Mrs. Dallow's tiniest rooms—*pansypantries*, she'd called them. That's where Rafe had hidden himself away after Gingerbeard's murder, at least until the tlak had run out, but he'd found a sort of claustrophobic comfort there that was entirely lacking in the swung-down trapdoor of Jassa's back.

It was a plank of raw meat, and her organs were lying atop it in a tidy little bundle.

Steam was rising off them.

Like a red loaf of bread.

Rafe couldn't stop staring.

Because whatever had been done to her had been done to him, too. He could feel it, the weight of his openness pressing down behind him, the lack of breath and pulse in the cavity of his chest, the dizzy wrongness that somehow hadn't killed him. Wherever his mind might have gone, whenever he might have escaped to, all this was really *happening*, and the carnage at the boarding house had passed. That one had led to the other was undeniable, but he struggled to keep himself here, in the present—and to survive.

He tried to anchor his thoughts with the details. Wondering why he and Jassa weren't bleeding out, he saw the ink shimmering around the edges of the doorway cut into her back, a shimmer that coated her workings, too.

They weren't dying because the tall woman didn't want them to die, at least not straightaway. It bothered him that he couldn't imagine her purpose in all of this—it was like no enchantment he'd heard of.

Witchery, that's what it was.

"Go ahead," the bent witch said. "Bring it here."

A tiny man with a face like a dried apple carried over a bucket full of blood, then poured it carefully into Jassa's innards.

Her guts bubbled happily, like an animal given a treat, and Rafe started laughing, though it wasn't funny, exactly. It was more like he'd filled to overflowing with all that he'd crammed inside over the past few months, from Gingerbeard's slaughter to the catastrophe of this moment, and now it all had to come out however it could. But the trouble with laughing, in the state he was in, was that his mouth was trying to make the noises that were actually coming from behind him, his lungs jerking on the trapdoor bed that the bent witch had swung out of his back.

"What *is* that awful noise?" rasped the tiny man, and then he looked up at Rafe. "Ach—the crosser's awake!"

"That word has no place here," the bent witch murmured.

Rafe stopped laughing.

"But calling *me* a—what was it?—a 'mobile excrescence' is fair game?" muttered the tiny man. "I see how it is."

The bleeding ghost sipped her tea. "Thought you said these two would be unconscious the whole time."

"I *did*," said the witch. "He should be."

She strolled around to look at Rafe's eyes, holding an ink-smeared wooden palette, its edges wrapped in tiny, curling vines. "Unless—hm." Setting it down, she consulted some arcane diagram. "It could be his withdrawal," she murmured. "Soaking up the effects of Lady Ley's blood."

"Hit him again," said the ghost, and Rafe, fearful that the bear would swing a balled paw down into his guts, began to twist around, trying to get his wrists loose from the rope.

The tiny man trotted over with the bucket and poured more blood into Rafe's organs.

Rafe calmed, immediately.

How warm it was inside.

Now he was sleepy, and glad for it. He felt like he might wake anywhere, at any time, even back at Mrs. Dallow's, before the Second Masque, with Gingerbeard's big, sweet-smelling arms wrapped around him.

He'd tell them to stay in that night, and all would be right.

But he couldn't allow himself to forget any of this.

What the woman from the farmhouse was doing to him went beyond vengeance. It would have to be answered, even if her gang of freaks killed him.

Maybe he'd come back to haunt her, if a ghost could haunt a ghost.

And the tall one, in the furs?" said Hollis, his voice like a nail file on a salt lick. "The human, I mean, not the bear. Tell me her name again, first and last. I'm not trying to be hard on you two, I just need to make sure you've been paying attention!"

"Tanka," gasped Rafe. "Tanka Equi—*fuck*!"

He was doubled over in pain again. Jassa wasn't even attempting to make words of her moans. Both of them had been writhing on the floor for hours, neither knowing nor caring where this small, dark chamber was, or why these freaks wanted them to know their names.

It meant something that they did, though.

It meant Rafe and Jassa wouldn't be allowed to die any time soon.

"I guess that's as close as they're going to get," muttered Hollis from atop the bear's shoulders.

Umber the bear, thought Rafe, because even their dead pets had names to memorize.

Hollis had climbed atop the awful thing after Jassa's fumbling attempt to crush his head in her hands. Rafe wished she'd managed it, if only to stop that excruciating voice, though it probably would've extended their misery once the others found out.

"I know! We'll put our heads together and come up with a mnemonic device. Something that rhymes; that's what seemed to help the kiddies at Cru, when all else failed.

Which it did, as a rule. Let's see: Hollis Runt, rhymes with flawless—"

"Equinox," sputtered Rafe. "Tanka Equinox. Please, just stop talking.—*Fuck!*"

The cramps about blinded him this time. His body was slick with sweat, all his muscles were spasming at once, and he could feel every red-hot bone in his body. Worst of all, he was *famished*, and had no hope of keeping down so much as a sip of water until all this had run its course.

It would take several days, if they were lucky. This was tlak withdrawal, and Rafe couldn't believe how deep they'd gone into it, or how quickly.

But then, he couldn't say how much time had passed between the killing fields and here. They'd woken on this floor, surrounded by these flickering mountains of bric-a-brac, wearing ill-fitting clothes of soft leather, already tlak-sick.

"I'm trying to keep you focused," said Hollis in that hideous voice of his, every syllable ripping through Rafe's head, "and distracted! I'd read you a storybook, if Tanka would lend me one. But we might as well accomplish something while we're at it. We have work to do as soon as you're well! You can even help me carve him, if you're so inclined—though more precision will be required than your last job."

"Let us be," said Rafe, as Hollis swam in and out of focus. "Please."

"They never will," said Jassa, clutching the blackened remnant of her forearm to her chest. "Can't you see? They want us—*broken.*"

"You got to broken all by yourselves," said Ashlan from the doorway. "You have any idea what shape you were in when we found you?"

Rafe shoved himself away from her.

She wasn't a ghost, as he'd believed when he'd seen her in the ring of fire. But he still couldn't reconcile her presence here with her death in the farmhouse.

His body was wracked with chills, only partly because of the sickness.

I killed you, he thought. Why didn't you die?

"Anyway," said Ashlan, looking up at Hollis. "It's time."

"Ah, lovely! The show begins. Hoist us up again, would you, Umber?"

The bear restored him to his perch as Tanka entered the dim, empty chamber, climbing atop a tall stool and folding her arms over her legs.

Rafe writhed onto his belly, panting. She was staring at him, but her face was impossible to read. He found no hatred in her eyes, but he still hadn't heard her speak.

Hollis patted the bear's ragged muzzle. It opened its jaw, and he pulled a pair of metal boxes from between its teeth.

Rafe's metal boxes.

"Give it," shouted Jassa, dragging herself toward Umber's feet as well as her muscles would allow. "You give it here!"

"Nothing *in* there, Jass," said Rafe. Nothing but game pieces, and a drash as hungry as they were.

But she kept on crawling, as if she'd gone over the edge.

Maybe she had. On top of everything else, her hand was gone, and half her forearm with it.

Hollis passed the larger box down to Ashlan, who set it on the floor and slid it toward Rafe with her foot.

"You still haven't worked it out, Rafe Davin?" said Hollis, flipping open the lid of the smaller box and plucking out a die. "Your companion here was holding out on you. She had a stash of her own all this while. Show him, Ashlan Ley."

She crouched beside him. "This was in her shoe."

In her hand was a blood-soaked scrap of cloth. Ashlan peeled it open, and a chunk of tlak tumbled out.

He should have stabbed her when he had the chance.

Jassa was coming, writhing along the floor like a snake.

She looked like she might try to gobble it off the floor if she could get there in time.

"That was *ours*," Rafe shouted, slapping a palm onto the crumb, rolling over to shield it with his back. "Open the latch," he said to Ashlan. He didn't have the coordination to pinch his fingers, but the tlak had stuck to his sweaty skin. "Please."

She frowned, considering.

His body shook harder. "I can't do it myself. Open the latch!"

"All right. But you're feeding that fucking thing yourself."

The drash let out a frantic clattering as she flipped open the lid, and Ashlan backed away.

The poor beast was starving. Rafe put his hand to the hole in the mesh, and it snatched at the crumb with its mandibles, taking a chunk of his palm along with it.

He was bleeding, but it didn't matter. He could hear it masticating. Everything was going to be all right.

Jassa had almost shimmied over to him. "My sins have saved us!" she babbled. *"Fortune favors the worst.* You see that, don't you? How even now She smiles upon us? My Ace?"

Rafe closed his arms around the blur of the drash beneath its mesh.

Its body was slowing. Its poison was growing sweet. It would be ready soon.

With shaking fingers, he pried up the screen.

Jassa's heel snapped his jaw shut. A second kick rolled him off the box. By the time he righted himself, she'd already scooped up the drash and pressed it to her neck. As it clamped down, she stroked its carapace with the back of her trembling hand—and bellowed.

There was no pleasure in the sound.

"Jass?" he called. "What's happening? *Jass?"*

She sat up, face white, raising her fingers to her neck, where the drash still clung.

It was over too soon.

The freaks were all talking at once, but Rafe wasn't listening. All he could see was Jassa, her hands steady now, tugging out the drash while its stinger retracted, still dribbling.

She hadn't even finished the kiss.

"It's all wrong," she was whispering. "Is it *this?"* She pointed at Rafe with her missing hand. "The dark flame? Is it in my body, still? Devouring the sweetness?" She held the drash out to him. "Take it, boy," she pleaded, sounding dazed, but not drugged. "Show me. Is it me, or is it *us?"*

It didn't matter what had passed between them, not now. Rafe, barely breathing, turned his head. As Jassa set the drash on his neck, he looked up at Tanka Equinox, still sitting on her stool, hands in front of her knees.

Her fingers were lacing and unlacing, again and again.

Their tips were stained with black ink.

He shivered, remembering something.

Too black.

It hadn't been a dream.

She'd opened him up.

She'd *remade* him.

He clenched his teeth as the stinger plunged, but no rush came. His tongue probed the edges of his teeth, but there was nothing to chew. Just boiling poison in the muscle of his neck, and the deep, sick-making pain of the stinger near his spine.

The nausea, the fever, all the signs of withdrawal were gone—but there was no sweetness, no pleasure, no high.

"It's us," he murmured. He clawed the drash from his skin, shuddering.

Its legs waved in ecstasy. At least *it* could still enjoy itself.

He dropped it in its box and closed the lid.

He and Jassa sat in numb silence as the freaks congratulated themselves.

The sickness was gone, but that only made it worse. It meant there was no *end* to this. They'd need to shoot again, within a day or two, and for nothing. And then again, and again, with no joy and no release.

He stared up at the freaks. They'd written the rules of this game.

It was time to find out how it worked.

Before he'd thought better of it, Rafe stood. The bear took a step toward him, holding out a paw.

Rafe wiped the sweat from his face, but didn't back down. They hadn't gone to all this trouble just to kill him now.

He pointed at Tanka. "You did this. You took us apart and you put us back together wrong."

"Not wrong. Different." She slid to her feet, looming over him.

How he wished he was taller.

"All of us, Mister Davin, are made of pathways," she said. "Some carry us to pleasure, others to pain. I changed a few of yours, as I've changed so many of my own."

"Fuck your pathways. You hacked us open," said Rafe, "and you played in our fucking guts."

"Hah!" cried Hollis, clapping his hands. "And are you playing the pot today, Rafe Davin, or the kettle?"

Rafe looked at Ashlan, his face burning.

She stared back at him, rubbing her belly slowly.

Jassa hadn't moved since he'd taken his kiss. If he'd ever needed one of her craven excuses, it was now—and she wouldn't so much as look up.

"Speechless, are you?" said Hollis, climbing down the front of the bear, using its ribs like a ladder. "And what could you say, really? Other than, 'Thank you, Sir Runt, for saving our highly devalued *lives*.' If you hadn't been necessary to us, you'd be halfway to some Devourer's colon by now. Or had you forgotten all that?"

He had. He'd forgotten most everything, and longed to forget more. "So we owe you," he said. "Is that it? You've experimented on us, and we should be *thankful* for it?"

"That depends." Tanka stepped forward, holding out her hands like a pair of scales. "Before we found you, did you want to live? Or die? If you wanted to die, then no, you should not be thankful. We brought you back, and to a version of your life that may well be worse than it was before. But if you wanted to live, Mister Davin, then things are more complicated. You were dying, and we stopped it from happening." She smiled, and Rafe stared, having no idea what lay behind it. Was she toying with him? "We gave you life, and then we changed your design, which is a kind of taking. So as it stands, we are even—a generous assessment, considering your prior involvement with Lady Ley—and for that, yes, you might well be thankful. It means you are free to go."

"Hold on a minute," said Hollis from the floor.

"No." She held up a finger, and the tiny man shut his mouth. "They are free to go, and live as they are. They may break their addiction, or embrace it as it stands."

Rafe kept expecting Jassa to interject.

But she wasn't even listening. She was cradling her blackened arm to her chest, rocking it like a colicky infant.

"If, however, you decide to help us," said Tanka, "I will restore you. When the job is done, you will be as you were, Mister Davin. Free to indulge, and enjoy your indulgence, without further interference."

"Those are just words," said Rafe.

She bowed her head. "As all promises are."

Rafe stewed a moment, trying to pretend, even to himself, even for a moment, that he might walk away.

Ashlan scratched her chin. "We're going to eat soon, right?"

Hollis threw his hands up. "Do you ever think of anything but your stomach, Ashlan Ley?"

Rafe remembered the tea and cakes. More than anything, he was hungry. Tlak's sweetness staved off hunger, for a day at a time—but when it went, it left the body ravaged.

He couldn't imagine himself hunting in the wood, especially with sickness looming.

He'd never get a mile from here, knowing that Tanka might give him the sweetness back.

And she knew it.

"So this is the game?" said Rafe. "Pretending I have any choice in all this gets you off. You're gods, is that it?"

That got a reaction from Jassa, though whether it was a laugh or a sob, Rafe couldn't say.

"I," said Tanka, "am no such thing."

"Nor I, sadly," said Hollis, "but I'll play the part if you insist on prostrating yourself."

"Look, this is business," said Ashlan. "And considering how we met, it seemed like it might be more effective than asking nicely."

"Then I hope you have a solid supply of tlak," said Rafe, hating how petulant he sounded, "or we'll only get sick again."

"Isn't that how the Assemblage pays you?" said Hollis.

Rafe looked down at him, startled. How much did they *know*? "Pays us?"

"For the harvest you collected. For Ashlan's guts."

"You kept the satchel?" It could hardly be fresh, but it would be better than returning empty-handed.

"Well, no." Hollis patted Ashlan on the leg. "But she'll make all you need."

She glared. "*Runt.*"

"Oh, come, don't get shy about it *now*. She's invulnerable. A regeneratrix! But it makes her very cranky."

Rafe's mind was reeling. "And what's your plan, exactly? You want—to take down the Assemblage?"

He looked back, worried, but Jassa still had no reaction. The Widow of Lank Street was gone.

He was shocked at the change, but only for a moment.

Rafe himself felt like seven kinds of hell, but he was standing. Advocating for the both of them. Fighting for their restoration, with whatever he had left.

Because, for all her bluster, she didn't have half his strength.

What we suffer takes half of what we are, Gingerbeard once said, *but it makes us twice as strong in exchange.*

"No, we have no beef with your cult," said Hollis. "It's simple, really. You want to get high, and we want the Puppeteer. Have you ever asked yourself what he *does* with the organs he collects?"

"I thought—" Rafe looked uncertainly at Jassa. "I thought for some reason he was making us better tlak." But it sounded like a lie, something she might have told him to keep him from poking into deeper truths.

"Ha! Sweeter candy from the store, is that it? No, Rafe Davin, the Puppeteer wants to send a million of *me* out into the world, to fill up all its dark closets with leaping, rasping puppets of death. Imagine the courts overrun with mannikins—the streets awash with the slushy runoff of our mayhem! Imagine every city in the world dancing at the end of his strings. Or—or you can help me imagine a better future.

One in which he's tied down and dissected before his nefarious plan begins. One in which he's rebuilt in ways that will make *your* change seem like a kiss from an angel."

"If you want him," said Rafe, "then he's yours."

The Puppeteer was a criminal Eth's guards couldn't find, much less prosecute.

Rafe didn't know him by name or by face, and he'd never expected to.

But he'd have promised them anything at all.

D awn was deafening, both the birdsong and the light itself. The very air he breathed felt thin, intoxicatingly so, and sobriety only fed the feeling. It was as if he'd woken in the mountains, or like a quake had subtly tilted the ground below and no one else had noticed. His muscles were tight, his heart hammered, and yet something thicker and richer than blood seemed to flow through his veins. He could feel everything—every nerve, every twitch, every thought—and the glory was excruciating.

The freaks had given him his own chamber, with windows carved into the wooden walls and more hand-carved furniture than the space warranted. The bear had brought him a tray of food, though there was no meat, and he'd eaten, with a gratitude that ashamed him, before lying down on the bed.

What he'd done there couldn't be called sleeping. It was more like a ceaseless line of thought that dipped a little from time to time, any rest it might contain constantly threatened by the sheer drop of panic.

The sources were many. He counted them on his fingers. Withdrawal, the loss of sweetness, the memories his dream had stirred. Jassa's betrayal, the sight of his clan, the slaughter of his clan. Ashlan Ley, Hollis Runt, Tanka Equinox.

And then, older and more insistent than the rest, there was his unbound body.

The slightest change in his physical position could tip his heart over the edge. Another wave hit whenever motion caused his breasts to shift. Looking down at their curves, even clothed and buried under sheets, was intolerable. He wished the freaks hadn't taken his bandages, filthy though they'd been. He thought of ripping up the witch's sheets and winding them around his chest, tying them tight enough to break his ribs if he sat down too quickly—just like the first time he'd bound himself, hiding in his uncle's empty tent.

Cringing, he reached beneath the soft leather shirt he'd woken in and felt his skin. There was no sign of the doorway on his back, nor the sores and scabs the bandages had left. They'd healed him—at least they'd call it that, though it felt to Rafe like another violation.

Fighting against the tightness of his muscles, he drew in a great breath and pushed it out.

Not a twinge of pain remained in his lungs.

He pressed a hand against his chest, feeling the gallop of his heart. The only thing that kept him from seeking out death as quickly as he could was the promise Tanka had made.

If he helped her, there would be sweetness.

The thought plunged him into desperate excitement. How malleable he felt, how raw. The last time he'd felt this way, watching the blue light stream through the windows for minutes that felt like hours, knowing that nothing would ever be the same, it had been the morning after the Second Masque. Someone had come before sunrise to tell him they'd found Gingerbeard. Rafe, high and numb, had nodded as if it was expected news, then lain back down and tried to sleep, as if that might let him forget. But sleep never came, and by noon his shock had hardened into sweaty decision: he would lock himself up in one of Mrs. Dallow's windowless pansy-pantries until the fist-sized brick of tlak was gone.

They hadn't even bought the stuff. They'd tried it only once before. It had been a party favor, given to Gingerbeard when they won some ludicrous game of chance at a party on Lank Street. Already drunk, the two of them had taken too much, then lost hold of each other in the crowd.

Lying on that tiny, plank-like bed, he bit into it.

The darkness filled with its slight, nutty sweetness, and everything became irrelevant.

He needed nothing, neither food nor light. He drank nothing, and scurried to the bathroom only twice, when everything was quiet. He ignored every knock, every voice at the door. He'd paid through the end of the week, though he had nothing left over—Gingerbeard had kept their collective wealth in a leather purse strapped to one thigh, since Rafe was always losing things. And the job Mrs. Dallow had found him, working as a courier to the maintenance crews in the upper levels of the catacombs, would be long gone by now.

He heard a great commotion once, when they found Little Gem's body in the bathtub—shaken loose, Rafe imagined, by the sudden loss of Gingerbeard, her closest confidante. Rafe heard the sounds of grief, and understood that they pertained to someone else he should have mourned, but he still had enough of the brick left to make that irrelevant, too.

It wasn't quite forgetting, but he felt sure it would lead there, in time.

But the tlak ran out before he could manage it. He stayed in the dark long after it was gone, centering on the sickness, feeling it grow until it pushed him out the door, so late at night that no good-byes were necessary.

He hurried back to the bar on Lank Street, where they needed no Masque to continue the party. Sliding through the crowded room, he found them in the corner, the ones who'd given Gingerbeard the brick, still throwing dice as if the fate of the world depended on it. Their teeth were ruined and their necks were marked, and the one they called Jassa Lowroller, that night's champion, took stock of Rafe and saw nothing but need.

Like knows like.

Going with her hadn't felt like a decision, and neither did what followed.

Neither did *this*—this sudden arrangement with the bent witch, to assassinate the city's sole supplier of tlak. From what Rafe knew, the man was hidden deep in the catacombs, and was connected enough to avoid the guards, or wealthy enough to own them.

Now that his body had recovered, Rafe wondered what he'd been thinking. When he'd left the Assemblage, he'd been an initiate, as ignorant about the structure of his church as the rules of the games they played. It wasn't as if he could stroll back into their next gathering and be welcomed as a leader without explanation—it would require a careful, informed performance, one he felt ill-equipped to script, and wasn't sure he could pull off. So far, the freaks had been content with his vague assurances, but sooner or later they'd want a plan.

Jassa knew enough to get them in, he was sure of it. But her mind was gone.

With or without her help, it would fall to him to concoct a plan and smuggle them in.

He heard footsteps coming down the hall. Rafe struggled up, his panic doubling, his arms squeezed tight around his chest.

It was Tanka, wearing a leather skirt and corset, with tall boots. Without a word, she shoved a bundle at him.

He forced himself to take it. "What's this?"

"Equipment," she said, turning her back. "Put it on."

He opened his mouth, then closed it, his hands shaking.

He'd expect this callousness from the rest of them, but not from her. She ought to know what it *meant* to be naked in front of a stranger.

He'd had enough trouble taking his clothes of in front of—

Enough. Tanka wasn't offering him a choice, and he wouldn't show weakness by begging.

He stood, feeling light-headed, and gripped the bottom of his shirt.

Tanka strode out into the hall, slamming the door behind her.

Alone, confused, Rafe unfolded the bundle.

It was a sturdy, sleeveless garment of black leather. The front was flat and stiff, the inside lined with soft cotton. At the back, two slim runners of hard, black wood fit together with a sturdy series of hooks and eyes, to be cinched tighter by the laces that zig-zagged up the sides.

A binder.

Rafe stared at it for a long time, then pulled off his shirt and slipped into it. It took work to snap the back together alone, and more to cinch the sides tight enough, but he was far too stubborn to ask for assistance. He worked it out eventually, though he'd broken a sweat. There was a glass in the corner, and with the binder on—fitting snugly, pressing hard, but a damn sight more comfortable than the bandages he'd been a fool to wear so long—he stared at himself a long while, then slipped the shirt on over it.

Flat-chested, he looked like himself again. His heartbeat gradually steadied.

It was better-built than any he'd seen. This pressure was different than what he'd grown accustomed to—a comforting tightness, so evenly distributed that he knew there would be no chafing, no cutting into his flesh.

He pulled the door open. Tanka stood in the hall, arms crossed, back turned.

"Why did you do this?" he said.

She pushed past him, shutting the door behind her, and stood for a long while, composing herself before she glanced at him.

"That'll do."

"Why," he said slowly, "did you *do* this? It's not like you just had this lying around."

She did a funny thing with her lips, as if it cost her great effort to speak to him. "We need you to be as—inconspicuous as you were."

"*Inconspicuous?*" A bitter laugh came unbidden from his throat. "Is that what you call it? The rest of us call it *passing*, you see, and it's a matter of life and death—for us, at least, who have to scrabble just to survive. That's what most of us are doing, you know? Stuck in Eth, with no way to escape the trap we're in. While you're safe out here, aren't you? With your dead pets and your buried stashes of coin. And now you've outed me to a bunch of strangers, and you'll march me right back into the city with nothing but a scrap of leather to protect me. And why not? This is what *you* need. For me to put my faith in people who know nothing of our ways, and hope that they don't let the wrong word slip and get me hacked open on the street. Let me get on with your errands, then, so you can get back to finding yourself—while they're killing the rest of us just for walking free."

When the words had stopped, he turned and started making the bed, just to give his hands something to do.

No response came. He wondered what he'd expected. Some chip in her mask, he supposed. Some sign that she felt as awful as he did.

Instead she drew breath, and sighed.

"When I—stepped out, in public, for the first time, as I am—"

You're *bent*, he wanted to scream as he tugged the blankets into place, you're *crosswise*, just call it what it is!

"—I lived in Tunica with my family, all sixteen of them."

Tunica Media. That was Northmost Eth. Not the best neighborhood, but far from the worst.

"Back then," she said, "a woman called Jaena was in power. Jaena the Joiner, they called her. She hailed from the High Andrils, where every child, when they come of age, is asked if they are a boy or a girl. For a brief time, it was— fashionable to do the same in Eth."

Rafe stopped fussing with the sheets.

No wonder she didn't call herself bent, or crosswise, or anything at all. According to Gingerbeard, these words had been slurs in the old days.

Poisoned blades, before we hammered them into armor.

"Have you heard of Jaena?" she said.

"Yes."

"And what came after?"

Rafe nodded, feeling sick.

His grasp on Ethian history was shaky, but everyone at Mrs. Dallow's knew of Jaena the Joiner. Gingerbeard had spoken of her reign as a golden age. She'd chosen a cabinet of advisors and functionaries who were native-born, and a crosswise woman had served on her High Council.

We breathed easy, then. For a few years, anyhow.

Then Radmun came, with his army of addicts—paid in lassia, to ensure their loyalty.

And Radmun had slaughtered so many citizens on his way in that the catacombs boiled over. The calcified organs of the Gone-Away gods, dormant for decades, were awakened by blood, reordering the streets in a seizure of dark enchantment.

After, Radmun had ruled in peace—or so he'd called it. He'd punished urban murderers with enchantments considerably worse than death.

But there had been a notable exception. He blamed the catastrophe on Jaena's excess—on the sins of the bent. It became legal to remove them, and their kin, from the streets of Eth.

Tanka's family, Rafe guessed, had been cleansed.

How she'd escaped was a question he had no intention of asking.

They stewed in silence for a long while.

He sat heavily on the bed, sliding a finger into his collar now and then to touch the top of the binder, just to make sure it was still there. Tanka stared through the slatted window, her face blank for a very long while.

Finally, he tried to guess how much his binder would have cost at Mr. Rue's. "You made this in one night?" he said, a hand on his chest.

"Umber did," she said, looking down at him. "It's still not meant to be worn while sleeping."

"I know that," he said. "I *know* what's right. Not that I do it, much." His face was burning. "But you—*you* ought to know better than to let others know what I *am*."

She jerked her head. "I will not justify my decision, Mister Davin. But nor am I ignorant of its impact. We must be as safe as we can, both of us. As safe as anything can be, there."

"*You'll* be safe enough. Unless your powers only work in the wood."

"No, I'll be just as strong in Eth. Lady Ley and her doll, as you know, have business with the Puppeteer. I'll do what I can to aid them, but I'd make a poor spy—and I have matters of my own to attend to. So I will promise to aid you, if things go poorly. Up until you've settled into your plan, at least. But keeping your secret safe from the Assemblage, as you've done well enough so far, will be up to you. Construct your plan carefully, Mister Davin, and everyone will profit."

Rafe bit his lip. The careful construction of plans was a talent that had so far eluded him.

He'd better pick it up quickly.

"I have faith in you—or, rather, in the depth of your desire." She walked to the door, and Rafe stood, wondering if he ought to follow.

"But understand this, Mister Davin." She stopped, one hand on the doorway. "If, whether by accident or by design, you render it impossible for Lady Ley to achieve her goal, there will be no restoration of your altered pathways. I will keep you alive if I can, but unless the doll has its satisfaction from the Puppeteer, you will live, and die, as you are."

"Understood," he muttered.

"You'll find your things in the common room," said Tanka, taking her leave. "Meet me down below."

He did as she said, though he was uneasy in the hollowed-out body of the treehouse. Even in daylight, it was hard to say what was shadow and what was a doorway, and that bear of hers might be lurking anywhere. Rafe packed his things, as anxious about the fact that someone had tossed them all over the floor as any of the rest of it.

The sound of the drash scuttling in its box hardly soothed him. "But there's sweetness at the end of this road," he whispered to himself, though it was only true if he could manage to get them all to the end of this winding, uncertain path.

Sliding on his pack, then wrapping his filthy old cloak around his shoulders, he saw the blur of a body pacing on the porch, through a doorway with white curtains tied off to the sides. It was Jassa, he realized as she returned to lean over the railing. The sight of her was startling, not least because she'd pinned one overlong sleeve over the ruin of her right arm.

Until this moment, it hadn't occurred to him that it was the *right* hand she'd lost. No wonder she was so out of sorts, he thought, walking slowly toward her. After a lifetime of rolling dice and stabbing folks in the back with it, she was bound to miss it more than she would've the left.

Then, too, she looked strangely pious, staring silently into the sunshine like some leather-clad nun. Leaning on the porch's railing—built, like the rest of it, out of living wood the witch must have coaxed into shape—Jassa was scribbling in her notebook, even more furiously, even less legibly than usual.

She'd rifled through his pack to get it. He suppressed the urge to shove her over.

Instead he joined her at the railing. He'd expected her to look haggard, but she looked a good deal more rested than he did, and as calm as he was nervous.

You're the Ace here, he thought.

"Deuce."

"My Ace," she cooed, without looking up from her sprawl of incomprehensible symbols.

"What nonsense are you scribbling now?"

"Plans." She bobbed her head, finishing a long line and tucking the pencil between the pages. "Oh, *new* plans, my Ace. Full of Fortune's blessings! Things are looking up—sky-high!"

He stared at her.

She was waving her book above her head.

Overjoyed.

"Focus, Jassa. *Jassa*. Look at me."

She seemed to notice him for the first time. "My Ace!"

"That's right." Bend her to your will, he thought, or it's over before it begins. Use her faith. "Your Ace. And I'm telling you—*Fortune* is telling you, through me—"

"*You're* Fortune's favorite," she said, beaming.

"Of course I am," he said. "And Fortune says only one plan matters, Deuce."

"To win all the games," she said, suddenly serious, turning to open her book again.

He slapped it from her hand, gripping her by the shoulders. "*No*."

Her face went white. "No? No! No, my Ace."

"All that matters," he hissed, "is that we get the sweetness back. Do you understand me?"

"Yes," she breathed, eyes wide. "Yes, my Ace."

He let her go before he lost control.

He wanted so badly to push her over that he could almost feel the thud.

It took him a moment to master his breath.

"You need it," she said, bathed by understanding. "You *need* the sweetness, don't you?"

He sighed, grateful that she'd gotten that much. "Yes, Deuce. We both do."

"Because—they're gone. All of them."

He turned, frowning. "Because who are—"

"Your family," she said sadly. "Gobbled right up. Yum!"

He was on her in a moment.

The air whooshed out of her as she struck the floor of the porch. She held her arms before her face, and he grasped them, one in each hand, wrestling them away so he could beat her face into pulp—with his forehead, if he had to.

But he'd no sooner gripped the folded leather of her right sleeve than she gave a gulping scream, her eyes swimming in and out of consciousness.

The flesh of her truncated forearm crackled beneath his fingers.

It was still cold. He could feel the jutting bone.

"Hurts, does it?"

He stood up, still holding her right arm.

"Yes," she moaned.

"Then hold your fucking tongue," he snarled, shoving her away.

He stood at the railing, struggling to collect himself, feeling sick to his stomach.

It didn't matter that he hated this, hated *himself*. All of it was temporary. "We'll get the sweetness back," he said again. "We'll bring them to the Puppeteer. We'll win *this* game. But speak out of turn, Deuce, and you'll feel that pain again in an instant."

She staggered up, stowing her notebook in her bag, then lifting a dark blue sack from the floor and slinging it over her left shoulder.

He'd been so distracted by her demeanor that he hadn't even noticed it. It swung slightly, though she stood quite still.

"What is that?"

"It's *her*."

Rafe remembered what Hollis had said about Ashlan.

"You mean—"

Regeneratrix, he'd called her.

"Fresh-baked numbles!" cried a voice from behind him.

Rafe spun on a heel. Hollis was tucked away in Ashlan's handbag, jabbing a cloth finger at her stomach. "That's right, Rafe Davin, your supply's replenished. Piping hot guts, and enough of them to buy you a hearty helping of your favorite street drug, I have no doubt."

Ashlan was cramming a loaf of bread into her mouth, swatting Hollis' hand away from her belly. "You enjoyed that too much."

"What, splitting you open? I've been patiently waiting my turn ever since the man-boy showed me the way."

Rafe looked down at the lawn, his face burning. He didn't care for the way Hollis had spoken, or his horrid little leer, but he knew that the doll would never own up to it. And a drop of his rage would kill the thing in an instant.

At least he knew who to be wary of.

Down below, Tanka was striding across the grass. "Shall we, then?" she called.

As Ashlan started down the spiraling ramp, Hollis poked his head out of her bag. "Saddle up, boys and girls, and you'll be back in the comfortable arms of a debilitating addiction in no time!"

"Knock it off, Runt, or someone's going to toss you in a river along the way."

Rafe walked down before Jassa, who seemed perfectly placid again. She even smiled at him as he passed, showing no sign that she remembered what he'd done to her moments ago. He wondered if she'd ever be what she was. Maybe his own sanity was just a veneer of shock that would crumble, in its own way, before long.

So long as Tanka put him back together first, he couldn't see that it mattered. It had been a long time coming—if he could even call himself sane, as he was.

They made their way around the tree's enormous trunk, until Ashlan stopped abruptly ten feet from the ground. "You've got to be kidding me," she said.

Rafe, stopping himself before he stumbled into her, followed her gaze. Lumbering up behind Tanka was Umber the bear, dressed in a greatcoat, dragging a massive, silver-buckled, two-wheeled trunk with one paw.

Hollis pulled himself halfway out of the handbag. "Surely you don't mean to bring him with us to *Eth*?" He craned his neck up at Ashlan. "Surely she doesn't?"

"Umber will be just fine," Tanka sang. "And I don't go anywhere without him. Unless one of you wants to carry my trunk in his place?"

"Inconspicuous," muttered Rafe.

Maybe sobriety wouldn't be such a problem.

Not if they all died before they passed through the shining wall of Eth.

BOOK TWO

—Homecoming—

Ashlan was hanging back, scratching some more at the angry rash that had covered her legs, when the rest of them broke through the tree line. She could tell from the noises they were making that the city was in sight.

Tanka began singing to the wood, one last time before they left its safety, seeking its goodwill in her endeavor. Rafe sighed so hard it sounded like he was deflating. Even Jassa, who'd been quiet all these miles but for some brief consultations with Rafe and the occasional burst of babbling while she wrote in her book, let out a gasp and a fevered prayer.

Hollis peered up from Ashlan's bag, whispering, "Are there strangers about? I'd love to get my first glimpse of Eth."

"Knock yourself out," Ashlan muttered. She'd had her fill of the place a century ago.

She seemed to remember swearing an oath that she'd never return.

One more to break before the end.

Itchy and ill-tempered, she made her way forward and joined the rest of them in the brush at the top of the hill. Down in the valley, open fields were divided by the packed dirt of Southway—a long, winding road whose trickle of travelers swelled into a dense crowd toward the end.

There, in the distance, stood Eth, its high, serrated wall gleaming like mother-of-pearl in the pink light of the sunset. The story went that its bricks were carved from the scales of some sea-beast slain by the heroes of old, back when the bodies of the Gone-Away gods were still warm underground, and the ocean was a damn sight nearer. Above the wall rose the city's fabled architecture: the Nail of Naywen, Clumthrullion's Keep, and that triple-cluster of crystalline towers known only as Shiny Clump.

The city was a showboat, to be sure, but none of its wonders had the power to stir Ashlan's heart. She'd seen it all too many times, from too many angles, seeking too many things that never came to be.

That's what she told herself, at least. Then she caught the barest glimpse of a low, silvered dome, and it felt like her pulse had caught on a pricker bush.

The University at Eth.

How happy her mother had been to see Ashlan, firstborn in her brood, accepted. Then Elil Ley had been killed, along with half the population of Eth, including the vast majority of Ashlan's classmates—all trotted out into the fields and executed, a hundred at a time.

That was the first time Ashlan had been slaughtered in public, and she'd later slipped off the back of the burial cart and into the wood, waiting for years until the Professoriate had forgotten her face.

There was a second chance, and third, and a fourth. Again and again, she'd emerge from the wood and put herself through the same entrance exam, always under a different name, all the while noting the subtle ways that Eth was changing around her. The Professoriate, after all, was influencing the magics of war, learning to shape the Uni into a powerful body whose knowledge would outlast even the shrewdest, most devious leaders of Eth.

But Ashlan was learning, too, albeit through sheer repetition. By the end, she whipped through the entrance exam so quickly that she was taken for some kind of prodigy. Through it all, she'd always half-expected one of the professors to recognize her eventually, but there were so many students, so many of them identical brood-mates, that the moment never came.

No one was there to watch when she finally graduated. But Ashlan was proud—not *of* herself, but *for* herself, in her mother's stead. She'd still had hope, then, and it was the memory of that emotion that shocked her now.

How alien it seemed. She'd *believed* in this place. She'd loved its streets, even its people.

That was a hundred years in the past now, though, and in all that time, the one thing she'd never allowed herself to do was come back.

Seeing the shine of that faraway dome, she knew why.

It felt like she'd turned to coal inside, gray, cool, and cracked—and now the sight of the Uni had her splitting open, surging with a long-buried brightness.

She wondered how something so old could burn so hot.

"Come on, then," called Rafe. "That's a long line ahead of us, and we can't afford to lose any more time." Without a glance at the rest of them, he started down the hill. Jassa followed close behind, holding her ruined right arm overhead and singing.

"If anyone needs me, I'll be in my office," rasped Hollis, tucking himself back into Ashlan's bag.

"I don't know if I'm ready to follow that kid's orders," said Ashlan, watching Rafe zig-zag downhill.

"I'm afraid you'll have to be, Lady Ley," said Tanka, starting off after him. "While you're dispatching the Puppeteer, I'll be—" She glanced at Ashlan's handbag. "Otherwise occupied."

Figuring out how to kill *me*, thought Ashlan, then rewiring the addicts, then using my regenerating body to get yourself a womb.

Only then—after everyone else had gotten theirs, and with Hollis' magical bank in pocket—would Ashlan be allowed to end this journey.

She stopped to scratch her feet again, staring daggers at the Uni.

She'd been waiting for death since she left the place. She could wait a little longer.

Rafe looked up from the bottom of the hill, irritated. "Can't you heal that up," he called, "instead of slowing the rest of us down?"

"Looks contagious," said Jassa, pursing her lips.

Ashlan shook her head, cursing under her breath as she worked her nails over the mottled skin of her ankles. For all these miles, Rafe had been dragging his feet, complaining about the worsening symptoms of withdrawal—but from the moment Ashlan stumbled through a scratch-patch and got her bare feet covered in this maddening rash, their lateness was *her* fault.

"I'm not hacking off my feet just to get rid of a rash, Rafe." She wished Hollis hadn't been so forthright about her powers. "It'll pass."

Unless she sloughed off the skin first, she thought, forcing herself to give it up. Sick of his nagging, she picked up her pace, overtaking him quickly—then forcing him to jog, panting, in order to keep up.

Now, from the front of the group, she noticed how deep the crowd was, and how tightly they'd packed the Southway. There were hundreds of them, mostly mercenaries, coming back from a day's work in the killing fields. Most were in rough shape—sliced up, held together by bandages and tourniquets ripped from their own uniforms, slumped in the dirt or carried on their fellow soldiers' backs. Ashlan was startled to notice there were no medics or supplies out here, yet for all the suffering, there was no sense of urgency either—the portcullis was closed, and folk were playing cards in the dirt while their brood-mates slid helplessly closer to death beside them.

It was hard to watch. But taking care of this endless war's wounded wasn't her job anymore. Hadn't been for a century.

"The hell's the holdup?" she said.

"The Guvnor locks the gates," said Jassa, digging out her notebook and tucking it in her right armpit, "whenever there's too much blood!"

"A real splatter-fest this week, too," said a woman leaning on a pike near the side of the road. Her eyes kept drifting to the bear, though she looked too exhausted to make much of a fuss. "And his guards just finished knocking hell out of a protest over in Greater Splanchnic. Pushed the murder line right up into the red. Ground got a little wobbly yesterday."

Ashlan blinked at her. Eth could only take so much killing before the catacombs came to a boil. Too many violent deaths, and the guts of the Gone-Away started to shift under the streets, shivering the city with quakes and rogue enchantments.

But armed conflict took place outside the wall.

At least, it was supposed to.

"He's—killing citizens? Inside?"

"By the scores. Plus, the city medics got a raise recently. So they'll wait for the worst of the wounded to die out here before they let the rest of us in. Just in case." The pikewoman hawked and spat, philosophically. "You'll probably want a guide. For a few coins an hour, I could—"

"*She's* new," said Rafe, glaring as he waved them on toward the line. "The rest of us aren't."

"Right," muttered Ashlan, too distracted to argue, "that's my problem."

She was trying to imagine how many deaths it must have taken to push things this far. The shining wall kept a number of useful enchantments from spilling out over the countryside, where they'd lose their power—but at the cost of this constant instability. A ban on urban violence was the most expedient solution, but it was notoriously difficult to enforce—and people were murdered all the time, mostly by guards.

Half the times Ashlan had been cut down in her student days had been within the walls, and still the city stood. It must've taken a massacre to get this close to the edge.

"Better play it safe, Runt," she whispered as they neared the throng. "Just the big guy. No minions. A bloodbath could bring the whole city down."

Umber was drawing a great deal of attention as they came to the back of the line, but Tanka was supremely non-chalant. Ashlan looked closely at the crowd gathered around him. It wasn't just the walking wounded who were shielding their faces from the glare of the low sun on the wall, as she'd originally thought. There were merchants' carts, too, surrounded by armed escorts, and itinerant families with dusty faces, and a fair number of extremely pregnant women hoping to make it inside before they popped. The most famous of Eth's enchantments was brood-birth—mothers never had single children here, but identical batches of seven, which made it far more likely that one would live until adulthood.

Ahead of them in line was a woman who hadn't been able to keep herself from birthing. She clutched the lone baby to her breast, weeping as she insisted that it would be all right.

Ashlan glimpsed wet, matted hair and tiny, purple fingers—and all but broke into a run, spitting copiously, hands on her stomach.

"The hell are you *going*?" shouted Rafe.

"Change of plans," called Ashlan.

"What are you up to, Ashlan Ley?" hissed Hollis from her bag.

She couldn't wait to get him out of there—his weight against her body was more maddening with every step she took. Carrying him around for so long, so close to her body, she'd even caught herself thinking of him as her *son*. They did have a great deal in common, biologically, but the thought still felt too bizarre to entertain. "Trust me," she whispered back, though it occurred to her that Rafe might not follow.

Luckily, Tanka was right behind her, Umber pulling the squeaking wheels of the silver-buckled trunk at their heels. "Is something wrong?"

Ashlan glanced back. Rafe's face was red as the setting sun, but he'd taken off after them with Jassa following in his footsteps, moronically serene.

"We don't have an extra day to wait for that gate to go up," Ashlan barked, pressing on into the fields around the wall, where the pong of sewage wafted toward them. "By tomorrow night, these two will be sweating hard enough to forget their names. We've got to find another way in."

"There *is* no other way in!" shouted Rafe, struggling to keep up. "They've locked the place down, except for Pharynx Gate—and every other chink in the wall, however tiny, is crawling with guards."

"The sun will set in a matter of moments," said Tanka, "and we'll be blanketed by night. As for the guards, they're nothing but armored flesh. They won't slow *us* down any longer than we allow them to, will they, Umber?"

The bear, which had done nothing but shuffle along all this while, let out a rumbling gargle—not a roar, exactly, but a long, deep vibration that seemed to come from its bones. As Ashlan and the others startled, it opened its ragged mouth, shaking its head in a clear sign of assent.

"I—I don't know, Tanka," said Ashlan as Hollis wriggled against her hip. She was worried, now, about what she might have started. "We can't just cut our way through the armed forces of Eth. Spill that much blood, we could bury a whole neighborhood."

"Perhaps." Tanka waved a hand across the field, where the nacreous wall was steadily darkening. "If we slay them within city limits, we risk awakening the remains of the Gone-Away. But draw them *outside* of Eth's walls, and we suffer no such quandary."

"A murder out of Eth is no murder at all," offered Jassa, patting her blue sack of guts with affection.

Rafe had folded his arms tightly around his chest, tapping his sternum with two fingers. "How do you intend to draw them out, exactly?"

"There are tunnels used to dispose of the bodies of those they murder inside the city," said Tanka. "There's one not half a mile from here—I know it well."

"What are you going to lure them out with, though?" Ashlan said, peering down the length of the wall.

Tanka smiled. "With *you*, Lady Ley."

Rafe looked like he'd just gotten a bit of good news. "It could work."

It was a sign she'd been spending too much time with these people that Ashlan could be comforted by Jassa's assurances, if only for a moment. She kept tossing her dice on the pitted stone that rose from the reeking muck near the tunnel, muttering as she scribbled down the results. "Another kiss! Another kiss from Fortune's lips."

"Stop saying 'kiss,'" pleaded Rafe, hunched beside her. Both of them were sniffling, their faces sheeted with sweat, but only he seemed shaken.

Ashlan stood before the moonlit mouth of the tunnel, knee-deep in bilge. She could feel the slippery bones in this slurry, and was glad for the cover of darkness.

Under the wall it was black as pitch. To one side of the round entrance stood the bear beside its wheeled trunk, Ashlan's bag slung over its massive shoulder—she'd been relieved to get Hollis away from her for a while—while Tanka stood on the other, idly flexing her fingers.

From the far-off line before the gate, Ashlan heard the death of another mercenary, marked by a distant burst of ritual wailing as the brood marked its loss.

It was a fitting accompaniment to this idiotic mission, but there was no one to blame for this mess but herself. So, setting her jaw, she bent down and plunged inside.

The faint glow of moonlight left her. Unseen bodies bumped her shins—whole or in pieces, she'd never know—and she sloshed on ahead, stumbling suddenly over the rising floor.

At least she wasn't wading through filth any more. She picked herself up, waving a hand overhead. The tunnel widened, and as she climbed through the darkness she stood straighter, seeing a glow far ahead.

She opened her mouth.

A match flared in a recess beside her.

She whirled around in surprise.

"Oi there!" came a voice. "Who's that, now?"

The tunnel behind her brightened, a blue glow that seemed to burst from everywhere at once.

Voices rose in excitement, at least four of them, deep and as similar as echoes.

Ashlan tore down the incline—and tripped over a loose stone.

She sprawled twenty feet away from the muck. "I'm down!" she shouted, hearing the guards at her back, cursing herself. The plan had been to lure them out, not give herself up.

"Damn right you are," came a voice from behind her. Something swung down and smashed her in the ribs.

She groaned. They'd broken a few, and kept on swinging.

"There's more outside," called another. "She's called 'em. Rucks, get the bottle, bruh—we'll take 'em out where they stand."

She looked up, drawing breath.

The guards all had the same face—bald heads, bulbous noses, thick necks.

One swung a boot into her stomach before she could get a word of warning out.

Winded, she twisted her head around. The one called Rucks was dashing, whooping in excitement, toward whatever nasty surprise they had in store.

What a treat this must be. It wasn't often they got to uncork an enchantment.

If he gets to that bottle, she thought as the truncheon swung down at her face—

Then stopped.

The guard above her was hanging in the air.

His three brothers looked up, gaping, then joined him.

Rucks called out, caught by the ankle himself.

Then all five of them whipped past her, helmets banging against the walls and floor, hollering as they were dragged, splashing, through the slurry.

They weren't screaming long. As Ashlan pulled herself up, wondering at the silence, she heard a deep, gurgling rumble, followed by a raspy giggling.

She staggered out through the mire, holding her side as she ducked into the moonlight.

It shone on the glossy, black bark of the gazing-tree that had burst from the open lid of the silver-buckled trunk. Its spores must have been roiling in there for all these miles, held at bay by the force of Tanka's will. Now each guard was caught by one of its branches, which were wound, tight as snakes, around their bodies, filling their open mouths with smooth darkness.

Umber the bear, letting out a bone-deep rumbling, grasped tight to one of the guards with its claws. Pawing his belly open, it dipped its wide, wet jaws inside—where it gave a bubbling roar, shaking its hoary head.

"Long after the ability to take sustenance departs," said Tanka softly, "the hunger still remains."

Ashlan sighed, her ribs aching. Tanka's arms were extended, her fingers twisted, her hands sweeping through the air—and the tree responded, keeping every terrified wriggle of the guards under wraps.

"He is, after all, a predator," she breathed. "We mustn't begrudge him his nature."

Umber had moved on, its empty ribs gleaming and red. At a safe distance, Jassa gave trembling praise, while Rafe breathed between his knees, overcome. The bear took another guard, gnashing through his abdomen, as Hollis danced in the slimy carnage beneath—pretending, no doubt, that these were the workings of his own creator.

"The bear's nature, or yours?" muttered Ashlan.

Tanka seemed not to have heard her. When the last guard fell still, she worked her fingers as if she were massaging lather into wet hair. The gazing-tree strode out onto solid ground, its roots writhing along the surface like tentacles.

Rafe stumbled back, staring with a peculiar intensity at the carcasses of the guards as they dropped to the earth like half-eaten fruit.

"Gather their helmets," said Tanka, "and anything else that might identify them. We'll pack their things in the trunk, where the spores will keep them hid. The bodies we'll sink in the muck, where they'll soon be indistinguishable from the rest."

"You're taking trophies," said Ashlan.

Tanka turned, furrowing her brow. "Lady Ley, are you displeased?"

Ashlan couldn't stop staring at the faces of the men they'd killed.

Five of them, all the same. The other two in their brood were probably gone already. These ones would have joined them before long, anyway, during one overthrow or another. It was rare for a city guard to see thirty.

But they'd died tonight instead.

This is what you've done, she thought. This is what you *are*.

"Guess I can't help but think of my own brothers."

Tanka hummed. "They were city guards?"

"Wanted to be. They died in the killing fields before they had the chance."

"*My* brothers died here," Tanka murmured, "along with the rest of my relatives, all at the hands of men like these, who dragged them through this very hole."

Ashlan decided to leave it alone. "How long do you think we have before anyone notices they're missing?"

"Until the next change of guard, probably at dawn. We can press on at our leisure."

Jassa was looting the corpses, singing as she worked. Hollis had put an oversized helmet on his head and was drumming gleefully along, his palms slapping something he'd retrieved from the muck, where Umber's jaws had tossed it.

"See, this right here," Ashlan muttered, turning, "is why I keep to myself."

A shlan shoveled spiced lamb and rice into her mouth, swallowed, and repeated, taking no time to savor the taste.

The girl carving meat for the next dish looked up, eyes wide.

"Lady, you have to *breathe*."

"Piece of advice, kid." Ashlan wiped her mouth on the back of her hand. "As long as I survive the meal, eating like a pig just makes me a better customer." She dumped the rest of the meal down her throat and tossed the bowl onto the counter. "See? Quickest turnover you'll have all night."

As Ashlan rose, letting the heat in her bones surge out into her chest, the girl's father upbraided her.

"Poppa, she didn't even chew!"

Two broken ribs popped back into place, and Ashlan sighed with relief, scratching her stomach as she walked on.

Hollis, hidden in the handbag she held close to her stomach, wriggled in dismay. "This," he whispered, "has been one of the most disgusting experiences of my life, and I changed diapers for three broods at once."

Ashlan let out a belch that turned heads all the way back at the cook stall. "Three broods, all in diapers? Sounds like they had a terrible nanny."

"Feh. They resisted the chamber pot just to *spite* me."

"Can't imagine why," Ashlan said, scanning the crowd. Closing time had come and gone, and the place was thronged with raucous drunkards. Among this company, they were filthy enough to blend right in, and a blood-streaked bear was just another story. Unfortunately, it was now so busy that she had no idea where the others had gotten to.

"Ooh, honey cakes," she murmured, stopping before a stall full of baked goods. "Let me get two of those? Better make it three."

"How can you still be *hungry*?" Hollis whispered as she handed over the rest of her coin.

"I don't know," she mumbled, pushing the third cake into her mouth and swallowing. She wished he wouldn't keep talking to her about food. "It's comforting, maybe. The food's the only thing in this town that hasn't changed."

She wasn't sure why she'd expected anything to be where she'd left it. Banks, bookstores, even entire *streets* had shifted. She'd stepped into the Lidless Market—which used to be between Nuchal and Coracoid, and had since taken over half of Iliac Square—and started haggling over a handmade gammon board, just to make sure she still had what it took. Only after the vendor had tossed her out of his shop had she bothered listening to Rafe. According to him, Lady Such-and-Such of the Vermilion Rutabagas had long ago decreed that selling wares for anything but the advertised price was an abomination in the eyes of the Goddess of Fictitious Deities, so now there was no more haggling. Or something along those lines.

Ashlan couldn't keep up, and she'd stopped trying. She didn't stand a chance of tearing this city down, or getting anywhere near the Uni, even if she'd set her mind on it. That was just the old her flaring up, always trying to change things. This trip wasn't about her, she had to remind herself, and never had been.

They'd made it inside the city walls, and if the kid wanted to lead, she'd let him lead.

She spotted him at a bend in the sprawling, canvas-ceilinged market. Ashlan ducked around produce stands and carts full of clothing. She'd almost trampled a display of clockwork toys on a blanket when Hollis jabbed her in the gut, hard.

"Easy, killer."

"Stop," he growled, not even bothering to whisper.

The woman on the blanket looked up, her brow furrowed.

"Sorry," Ashlan said in her gruffest voice, "not you." She turned her back. "Okay, I stopped."

"I'll have that, Ashlan Ley."

She glanced back. "The clapping monkey or the waltzing babies?"

"Across the way. The *knife*."

Ashlan sidled up to a wide island of conjoined stalls, one of which overflowed with kitchenwares. Nodding through the vendor's speech, she followed Hollis' abdominal prods until she found what he wanted—a thin-bladed boning knife with a curved wooden handle.

"This? Comes with a nice leather case." The vendor slid it into the world's smallest scabbard, snapping it shut and smiling. "Your husband likes your cooking?"

"You know. Always stuffing his face, that guy." She dug a hand into her bag, then remembered that she'd spent the last of her coin. All she had left was the chunk of gold Hollis had given her at the farmhouse, and she couldn't wave that around here.

"We have spices aplenty, here at our sister shop. What's his favorite dish?"

"Uh." Hollis pushed a coin into her palm, and she passed it to the vendor. "Chitterlings."

The man stopped his pitch, staring at what he'd been handed. "I'll make change!"

Ashlan sucked her teeth. She'd just given him a solid-gold button from Hollis' waistcoat, emblazoned with a dancing mannikin.

"Subtle," she murmured.

"I'll *have* that *knife*."

"I got it, Runt."

She let out a long, purse-lipped breath as the vendor returned. He gave her a brown paper package, but no change.

"These others, madam," he said with a backward gesture, "at our other sister shop, they say they are with you. Is that correct? Will you settle up all at once?"

Jassa and Rafe stood on the other side of the island, Tanka and Umber lurking behind them.

Rafe was staring at her, his head cocked, daring her to object.

"I don't think my husband would like me spending all his—uff."

Hollis had thumped her again from inside the bag.

"Never mind. What he doesn't know, right?"

"Have a look, though," whispered Hollis.

"Right. I'll just, ah, have a look at what they're getting first."

Ashlan came around to the other side of the island, passing Tanka, who seemed more interested in the crowds pouring out of the public houses than anything Rafe and Jassa were doing. She looked tired, thought Ashlan—less *full* somehow, as if the city was slowly sapping her.

The two of them had made a small pile of equipment on a clear stretch of counter. "What's all this?" said Ashlan.

"Things we'll need," said Rafe.

He'd picked out an awl, a thick needle, and a spool of sturdy thread. Jassa had cupped her hands around a set of elaborate ivory dice and a devotional carving that stood nearly a foot tall.

"We're sewing our way in?"

Rafe sucked his teeth. "The plan involves mending."

"It's fine," whispered Hollis.

Ashlan nodded to the vendor, who started wrapping things up. "I think it's time you explained what we're doing."

"I will," he said, looking pointedly away. "When we get where we're going." The vendor handed him a packet, giving Ashlan what little was left of the change, and Rafe was off without another word.

Inside Eth, it was Rafe's show—that was the deal. She'd meant to follow him without question, as even Tanka was doing. Only he and Jassa had any idea what they were getting into, and Jassa only barely.

Why, then, was Ashlan thinking of absconding with Hollis and ditching the rest of them in the crowd?

"Trust in him," Jassa murmured, right in Ashlan's ear. "The boy is *favored*!"

Ashlan shuddered. She hadn't even known Jassa was behind her. "I hope to hell you're right."

Jassa knelt, setting her sack on the ground as she tore open the brown paper packet with her teeth. "Your feet," she grunted, tugging her devotional statue free. "Are they feeling better?"

"Uh. Yeah, I guess. They don't itch any more."

"Good. Good! All is as it should be, in Her eyes." Jassa hefted the statue with her left hand.

The carven woman had one arm, too. She wore a beggar's robes and looked vaguely maniacal.

"Left-Handed Luce," purred Jassa. "An aspect of Fortune. See? She's smiling!"

"She's a statue," muttered Ashlan. "That's all she *can* do."

But Jassa had run off, purring to her inanimate friend about their tremendous luck.

At least one of them was feeling optimistic.

Dwarfed by the tall, clustered buildings outlined in moonlight, Ashlan wondered if Eth had always been this grimy. It had seemed so imposing to her once, so full of power and possibility. Now all she noticed were the gouges of artless graffiti and the reek of inadequate sewage.

Years ago, this city had been her home. She'd shared meals and stories with the students who'd lived around her, in these very buildings. Back then, it felt like they had a common past, or enough of one to fake it, and that they'd share a future, too.

But none of the others had lived to see twenty-five.

Ashlan was exhausted. She couldn't remember the last time she'd slept. Neighborhoods melted by as they walked, each one clotted with memories she'd prefer to avoid, mostly succeeding. Once, though, Rafe spotted a group of guards, their backs turned, their prey cornered. Swiftly, noiselessly, he turned down an alley, leading them all into a neighborhood known as the Lower 'Ninges.

Ashlan stumbled. Above her stood the unchanged façade of a flat she'd rented downtown, on her second attempt at her degree, once she'd confirmed that she was the last living Ley. She took up a fake name and played the role of a student she'd known before, a funny girl who was drunk all the time.

Now she stood staring through the open archway on the second floor at the same old staircase where she'd taken a spill one night, breaking a tooth in her fall. The story spread of how she'd spit out blood and enamel and stood up cackling, laughing too hard and for too long, like the pain itself was funny to her. For months after, she had to hold back the heat in her bones, keeping it from rushing toward the ache. She'd always had insomnia, but that's when she nearly stopped sleeping altogether, for fear she'd wake up and the tooth would be healed—and she'd have to break it again, by hand, before anyone noticed.

Later, when a coup wiped out her Reparative Anatomy class, she'd been relieved to withdraw to the forest—because of the tooth, but also because exhaustion had caused her to test dead last.

The memory receded as they turned again.

"Just around this corner," called Rafe, slipping out of sight with Jassa in tow.

Ashlan hadn't noticed them getting so far ahead. Even the bear seemed to be dragging his paws. The only sounds on that dark street were their footfalls and the insistent squeak of the silver-buckled trunk.

"We'll leave you here," said Tanka softly, "Umber and I. Now that we know where to meet you."

Ashlan stared at her. "You're—leaving?"

Tanka frowned. "You sound so sad, Lady Ley. But there are other preparations we must make while here in Eth." She seemed uncomfortable discussing it on the street, and Ashlan was too tired to press her. "And there is no room for me in Mister Davin's plan."

"She has a point," said Hollis from below, startling Ashlan. "The time for grand gestures has ended. We must be *precise*."

She'd drifted so far out that she'd forgotten he was even in the bag.

It was good that she'd been reduced to an accessory in all of this. She was coming unraveled—or maybe that had happened long ago, and only her solitude had kept it hidden from sight. How else could she have grown so different from the girl who once lived here?

"When the job is done," said Tanka, stepping into the shadows as they rounded the corner, "I'll meet you near here. A fragment of the tree will keep watch for your return, and I'll be along soon after. Best of luck, Lady Ley."

"Right. You too."

Ashlan found Rafe standing stock-still in the middle of the street, Jassa slouching behind. Before him was a crooked green door atop a wide stone step so worn that it looked like it had melted. Face covered in a sheen of sweat, Rafe was staring up at a fresh-painted sign that read THE KING GUV.

"Something wrong?" said Ashlan, approaching.

"No," said Rafe.

"What's happening?" whispered Hollis.

"Everything's fine," said Rafe, sniffling. "Other than withdrawal." He flung open the door, and Jassa followed him in.

"I don't know, Runt," she whispered into her bag. "I'm having second thoughts about following this kid around. He's looking even shiftier than usual, and that's saying something. You don't think he'd sell us out the first chance he got?"

"Oh, pull yourself together," Hollis hissed. "Shifty, indeed! What he *looks* like, Ashlan Ley, is a junkie on the verge of total breakdown, which is precisely what we want. The harder those two sweat, the more useful they are. Now hustle on in, and let's find out what manner of plan they've concocted."

The lobby was cramped, its walls speckled with yellowed dots of paste. The scraps of torn paper that clung to them looked like tiny, irregular flags, their shadows waving in the dim candlelight. Behind the counter, a sallow man with wild, silver hair sighed up and slapped a key on the wood. "Just the one night? Or what's left of it?"

"Two," said Rafe, staring down at the key. "But we— we'll need a different room."

Ashlan frowned. What was he playing at?

"Don't like this one, huh." The inn-keep pulled his lips back from his teeth. "Not this room." He swiped up the key, peering at the number 17 as if he might find a flaw in its design. Then he shook his head like he had water in one ear, peering closely at Rafe. "What's wrong with *this* room?" said the inn-keep. "Perfectly good. Warm and all. Nice view."

They all stood perfectly still, like idiots.

"Does this boy speak for all of you? How *old* is he? Does he speak for *you*?"

He was looking at Ashlan.

She felt Hollis wriggling in her bag, and heard the pop of the button on his new knife's leather case.

"Easy," she whispered.

Not that she had the vaguest idea what else to do.

"My Ace speaks for all of us," said Jassa. "And more. For *Her*." She hoisted up her statue, giving the inn-keep an earnest smile that looked just as crazed as the carving.

He turned back to Rafe. "Ace, huh. You stayed here before, I gather? Because, you know, the old lady, the fruit-bat, Mrs. D, she had a—particular sort of clientele."

Ashlan wondered what the hell was going on.

Rafe had said this was a place he knew, but he'd clearly never met this inn-keep.

But the inn-keep knew of *him*, or his people—which wasn't working to their advantage.

Maybe he had a stash in one of the rooms he was now hoping to recover. If not, why would he risk all this attention?

"That what this is?" said the inn-keep, getting up, getting loud. "Because I've had enough of you people coming back to the roost, making sad eyes under your false lashes. Hasn't been an oasis for the bent in this city for some time! Party's over, you understand? I burnt whatever knick-knacks were left behind, just like the guards rounded up the last of your friends and burnt all of *them*—and that's sad, yeah, but that sort of trouble is the *last* thing I need. So shuffle off, all of you," he said, staring at Ashlan and Jassa, trying to decide if they fit the bill, "before I stop being neighborly and call the guards on *you*."

Jassa was the only one of them who had an idea, it seemed.

Ashlan decided to run with it.

"Hey, you got us all wrong," she said, smiling as she stepped up to the counter, her arms in the air. "I don't know who you pegged us for, but this is all about *luck*." She swiped up the key, rattling it in his face. "You know about luck, don't you? The *kid* sure does. Seventeen's his unlucky number. We're gamblers, get it? Fortune's playthings. Sure, he's little, and he's kind of spoiled—but we let the kid call the shots, because he always wins! And when *he* wins, *we* win. He's like our, what do you call it, our insurance policy. Our lucky charm, or whatever." She reached out and tousled his hair, and Rafe wrested his head away, his cheeks flushed.

"Lucky?" said the inn-keep, rubbing his nose.

"Oh!" cried Jassa, taking up Ashlan's cue. "Very!" Stumbling over to the inn-keep, she dropped down to her knees by the edge of the counter, setting her statue on the floor and following it with a rattling fistful of dice. "See? Can't argue with those. Lucky! That's my Ace's luck. Ha! That would have been four times the prize, had we bet at the table. Look there. And there!"

Hollis jabbed Ashlan in the gut again.

Reaching into the bag, she sighed, flipping another golden button onto the counter.

Was he *naked* in there?

The inn-keep was nodding now. "All right," he said, grinning. "All right. So you had a good night, and he's riding high. Just a boy. He's just a boy! I didn't mean to be rude, you know, it's just that you don't *look* like you have coin. Let's get you another room, then. Nothing but the best for the golden child!" He flipped a key to Rafe, who caught it as it fell. "Anything you need, you just let me know. Full service for you lot, all right?"

But Rafe was already on the stairs, jumping them seemingly at random.

"You *still* don't think this is shifty?" she whispered, climbing up behind him.

"No shiftier than the rest of you," said Hollis.

Ashlan ducked down a hall, finding the keychain swinging from the lock. Pulling it free, she stepped inside a large, dusty room, where Rafe was shrugging out of his cloak, setting things on a crooked table.

"What was all that *about*, Rafe?"

"Does it matter? We're alive."

"Not for lack of trying."

As Jassa closed the door, Hollis rolled from the handbag and hopped right up, showing no sign of cramp or fatigue, though he'd been curled up in there for hours on end. He was nothing if not well-built, she thought as he pulled his little knife from its case. It looked like a rapier in his hand, an impression that only strengthened as he began to lunge and parry.

Ashlan sat back on one of the beds, her feet on the floor. "You cut me, Runt, and I'll boot you right in the face."

"Hah!" He swiped at a corner of the blanket beside her, loosing a burst of feathers. "I'll lop off your toes for trying, giantess."

Jassa dropped her blue sack and began to set up her things in the corner, speaking to her dice as she arranged them in front of Left-Handed Luce.

Ashlan cracked her knuckles. "All right, you've pushed this string long enough, Ace. Let's hear this plan of yours."

Rafe stared down through the window at the street, looking sweaty and haunted.

There was no stash in here after all, Ashlan thought, watching him. He was just in a state. He'd seen how much his neighborhood had changed and gotten spooked, just like her.

Then he'd panicked, and brought them all through the lion's jaws.

He'd better have something sensible to say for himself now.

"They sent us out to find organs, right. Human organs, to trade the Puppeteer for tlak. The fresher they are, the more we get paid. So, Ashlan, you're going to be our mark."

Of course she was. Whatever the plan, she was always the mark.

"We met you while we were harvesting. Far from Eth, the last surviving member of your clan, wandering the wood, looking for help. Now you've seen the light, and you want to join the Assemblage. Because you've seen what I can do."

Hollis held his blade up to the light. "And what is that, exactly?"

"He plucks the strings of Fortune's harp," purred Jassa from the corner, "and makes them *sing*."

"Aha," said Hollis. "And when was this, exactly? I must have missed it."

"Look," said Rafe, turning, "it doesn't matter what you two think of me. She's my Deuce now, and I'm barely an initiate. That'll be remarkable enough to them. And Jassa will bolster her claim with tales of my extraordinary luck, which she'll send ahead in a letter. Sounds like that inn-keep will help us send it—there are couriers running before dawn in this neighborhood."

"A letter?" said Ashlan, feeling uneasy. Jassa had pulled out her notebook, and was using Rafe's new knife to cut out the pages she'd been writing.

"The Assemblage moves its base of operations every fortnight. There's always someone at the pub on Lank Street, but it would be dangerous to trot you in unannounced. You might end up disappearing in a way that doesn't serve the plan, is what I mean. And besides, I'd rather—" He set his jaw. "They think I'm a child. Just like that man downstairs does. That's—the only way I've ever been able to pass. So I'm not walking in there without a solid introduction from my Deuce, saying how things have changed. Without it, none of this works."

Jassa gave him a fawning look, and Ashlan resolved to read the letter closely. But this seemed to be more about Rafe's ego than anything else, so she let it slide.

"Most important, though, is that I'll have plenty of proof—a harvest of human organs in the sack, and another set, even fresher, inside *you*. That's what you'll look like to them, going in—a full purse for the Assemblage, and a body with no ties to the city for the Puppeteer, still steaming. And that's what they'll care about. How much tlak we're about to bring them."

"Okay," said Ashlan. "So you, what, knock me out?"

Rafe shrugged. "Bash your skull in, probably. More convincing if they see your brains."

How nonchalant he was. He was expecting her to protest, and he was expecting Hollis to side with him.

"Fine," she said, refusing to give him the satisfaction. "But what about Hollis?"

"They'll check your bag." Rafe sat down on the bed beside her, his lips curling up at the edges. "So we need a way to get Hollis in, and to get you both to the Puppeteer."

Hollis looked, for all the world, like a child eager to hear the end of a bedtime story.

"Okay," said Ashlan. "So—"

"So that's where *this* comes in," said Rafe, holding up his oversized needle.

"Congratu*la*tions!" sang Jassa, giggling.

"I'm—missing something," said Hollis, frowning.

Ashlan wasn't.

"They want to gut me again," she said, closing her eyes, "and sew you up inside."

Hollis stepped back. "That's—a bit much. Isn't it? That is, a handbag is one thing, but—to be entirely surrounded by—by—"

"Unless you have a better idea," said Rafe, "this is the plan. They've told us, time and again, that the Puppeteer wants fresh harvests, and untraceable ones. They don't give a damn about quakes—it's the trail leading back to the murder they want to avoid. So you'll play the perfect mark, Ashlan, and after you fall, we'll run your body right over to the Puppeteer. And when he goes to collect his prize, Hollis strikes."

"With my knife at the ready," he whispered, stroking the flat of his blade. "All sewed up inside, ready to meet the warm jelly of his eyes! Yes. And we'll have a code word, Ashlan Ley, so I know when to slash my way out. How about—*Father*."

"You've warmed right up to this idea, haven't you," she muttered, taking a deep breath and pushing it out slowly.

Carrying Hollis might be the nastiest thing she'd ever done to her body, and she'd done a lot.

I am a vessel, she thought, nothing more. I will carry them all, and then Tanka will allow me to sink.

Just a little longer.

Just a little more of Rafe's bullshit.

That didn't mean she had to go out of her way to make it pleasant for him, though.

She thought back to the farmhouse, when he'd cut her open. She remembered how shaken Rafe had been.

He'd barely been able to watch Jassa scoop her clean.

"All right then," she said, clapping her hands. "If that's the plan, that's the plan. Runt, give me your knife."

Rafe, sitting beside her, moved back.

She held out the blade. "Get the sack ready," she said to Hollis, then pressed the hilt into Rafe's palm.

He looked at her, startled. "What?"

"Sun's almost up," she said, standing squarely in front of him, pinning his knees between her legs, tugging her shirt off. "You're the big man around here, right, Ace?"

She saw the tremor in his hand.

"So carve the fucking roast."

Grasping him by the elbow, she yanked it in, hard.

There was a pop as the blade punctured her belly, then a hiss as she dragged his fist across.

The pain was brilliant. It was hers.

She could hear Jassa's dice rattling in the corner.

Ashlan leaned close to his ear.

"Attaboy," she whispered.

—Lady of Perpetual Revolution—

Rafe was pacing, sweating, sniffling, his boots off so he didn't flinch from the sound of his own footfalls. Withdrawal had its claws in him, but he was stuck in this room, unable to do a thing to help himself—other than wait.

Jassa had somehow fallen asleep in the corner, curled like a dog around her hideous statuette, somehow able to sleep, though her tlak-sickness had to be as bad as his own. Ashlan, meanwhile, was sitting on the bed, hunched over her stomach. Every time he passed, she glared, and she cringed whenever Hollis moved inside her.

It was worse for Rafe, though, than for both of them combined—because for some reason he'd gone and brought them here, to this horrible, haunted imitation of Mrs. Dallow's Cut-Rate Boarding House.

What had he been *thinking*? What had he hoped would happen when he'd led them up this street, when the fire that licked his bones was just beginning to smolder?

It had barely been sensible at the time. But he'd wanted to be safe.

The city felt like a gauntlet he was running. He was hiding everything at once, so much that there was no room to think. Back at Tanka's treehouse, it had seemed like Jassa and the freaks would be the source of all his danger, but now he could see what a threat he posed to himself—compromised by withdrawal, he was terrified to speak, to act. He felt constantly on the verge of slipping out of character, revealing some facet of himself that had to stay concealed.

In his panic, he'd headed straight for the familiar. *I know a place*, he'd told them, and walked toward Mrs. Dallow's, driven, perhaps, by some half-formed hope to show off to the boarders that people were following his orders now, or to prove to Jassa and the freaks that there were people out there who knew and respected him.

It was only when he saw the street that the obvious struck him.

Everyone at Mrs. Dallow's knew him as crosswise, making this a decidedly curious place to prepare himself for passing as an uncrossed boy-child.

Yet it made a certain sense. No one knew more about battling through the outside world in the armor of make-believe than a bunch of bent orphans.

All of whom, as it turned out, had lost the battle—chased away at best, killed at worst. This place wasn't Mrs. Dallow's any more.

But Rafe, too crazed to change his course, had plunged inside regardless, and now here they were, two rooms down from 17, a hallway removed from the pansy-pantry where he'd gotten himself hooked.

The memory of that first high seized him now, and his hands started shaking, moving him one step closer to total uselessness. He had until nightfall, he guessed, as did Jassa, who was flinching and murmuring in her sleep—like a dog, he thought again, like a barely-conscious animal.

A terrible thought struck him. Was she too unsteady to pull this off?

He paced back to the far wall, leaning his palms against it, panting.

Now he was simply ricocheting from one fear to the next. He had to steady himself. He tried to breathe.

But Ashlan's breathing was louder—as she shifted her weight, cursing at her belly.

She'd need to hold it together, too, and she hadn't stopped complaining, either in word or in deed, since he'd finally managed to sew her up. Everything hinged on her performance, and Rafe had no evidence that she had the skills to pull off a con of this magnitude.

His whole plan felt riddled with fractures.

He stared at the wall, shutting them all out of his mind.

And ricocheted again, from the sight of the peeling wallpaper.

He and Gingerbeard were fighting. Screaming, red-faced. Little Gem was pounding on the wall, shouting back at them for quiet.

But they couldn't stop. As if possessed, they ran through their invisible tally-sheets of wrongs done, promises forgotten, crimes of negligence, acts of love spurned or ignored.

Then they fell, after hours of this, into bed, without touching.

Where they stared at the walls. The peeling, dingy, once-purple floral paint of the wallpaper, coming down in brown-glued sheets.

Our house will be fancier than this, though.

This was how the game began.

Our house will have a dumbwaiter in every room.

Hot and cold running rosewater.

They'd describe it, in detail, for hours, hauling themselves out of the nightmare of their conflict and back into this recurring dream. Their House for Wayward Bent Folk, where the two of them would take better care of their crosswise orphans than Mrs. Dallow ever had.

Rafe wouldn't have to be a courier any more, pretending he was a child. Gingerbeard wouldn't have to dress like a man and tend bar.

The kids will call you Mister Davin.

Will you be Missus Beard, then?

Naturally, love.

As if that word were the triggering rune that ended their enchantment, Gingerbeard would lay a large hand on Rafe's back, and the two of them would be safe again.

Rafe shoved the memory away, staggering back from the wall.

It didn't matter, he realized as a wave of nausea assailed him, that he couldn't get high. He'd settle in a heartbeat for the tlak to simply take away this sickness, this infirmity, this constant swooping of his mind. It would leave him exhausted, miserable, and miles from where he wanted to be, but he wouldn't be like this—so vulnerable he felt *flayed*.

He flexed his hands, turning to Ashlan. "We have to get *out* of here," he said, with enough force that Jassa roused, red-faced, from the floor.

"Where," said Ashlan under her breath, kneading her stomach with both hands, "do you suggest we *go*?"

Rafe stared at her, momentarily unable to put her question in context. Too much was happening—too much in his mind, still more in his body.

The letter. They were waiting on the response to Jassa's letter.

He and Ashlan had read it over, separately, before dawn. In an awkward, left-handed scrawl that was mercifully comprehensible, the missive was stuffed with knotty, worshipful language that told the Assemblage to expect a wealthy mark at that day's Meeting for Worship. It hinted of a Gift that would sweeten their relationship with the Man Who Held the Strings. Then it went on, and on, speaking of Rafe's ascension and many other subjects, rambling as her mind must have been for the past few days.

The inn-keep had sent it to the grubby pub on Lank Street, and they began waiting for word of where that day's gathering would take place.

There came a pounding at the door.

Rafe jumped, shivering, as if his feverish thoughts had invoked it.

Jassa dashed over, pulling the door open before his para-noia peaked. A boy stood on the other side, his hair combed, his eyes dull, the torn page of a broadsheet in his hand.

A courier. Rafe's old job, when Rafe had been pretend-ing to be a child himself.

He snatched the broadsheet from Jassa, glaring until she shrank back.

"The inn-keep will pay you," he said, searching the page for a message.

The boy was as irritated by the snubbed gratuity as Rafe would have been, but Rafe shut the door all the same, find-ing the letters between the lines—hidden without cunning. He wondered why they'd even bothered writing in code.

"Sulcus Station," he said. "We're heading to the aban-doned entry to the catacombs."

Jassa let forth a stream of blearily worshipful language regarding the infinite wisdom of Mother Luck, but Rafe wasn't listening. He was hurriedly packing up, sniffling and snorting, feeling the sweat trickle down inside his binder.

He laid his hands on the dented metal of the drash's box.

The scrabbling soothed him, for a moment.

Then his blood answered, scrabbling at his veins.

He lurched to his feet. "Deuce," he barked. He wanted the thing away from him, until the time came.

"My Ace," said Jassa, dropping her own belongings to scurry to his side.

"Take this," he said, passing her the box, "and keep it safe until we're flush. We'll take the kiss when we're paid, to stave off sickness. And then, after the witch restores us, we'll hole up for a while." He'd need her, for a while at least, if only to get himself high. He'd have to figure out the rest of his plan from there. "But there's no need for anyone in the Assemblage to know what's been done to us."

"A wise plan," cooed Jassa, holding the box to her breast, "as befits Fortune's favorite."

"Hope you're up to this, *Ace*." Ashlan lurched up, making a groaning, flinching production out of her discomfort.

At least there was no bulge, he noted as she walked past. He was surprised that Hollis fit without protruding, however he'd contorted himself—but then, a mannikin was nothing more than a bundle of processed human guts, give or take a bit of cloth and a pair of tiny shoes.

Rafe turned to lock the door, and stopped, head pounding.

They'd told Tanka they'd meet her here tonight, when the job was done. But the room was empty.

They hadn't left a single thing behind. When it came down to it, not a one of them had any faith that they'd be back.

The last time Rafe had been anywhere near the Sulcus Catacombs Entry Station, he'd been a courier himself, ferrying messages, meals, and small servings of drugs to the workers in the catacombs below. It was a child's job, and he wasn't a child. But the work was steady, and showing any sign of wit earned him enough in tips to make it worth the drudgery. *You're gonna be all right, kid*, the supervisor at the Station used to say. *Once you're grown, you've always got a place down here.* Rafe often thought that he'd rather be murdered than go to work in the innards under this neighborhood—not that it would be an issue, since with his frame, they'd never accept him as a man.

Then the station had closed, after all the workers Rafe used to pester for cigarette money were crushed mid-shift during a dig into the calcified liver of some forgotten deity. The organ of the Gone-Away had shifted enough to tilt the whole of Sulcus, sending shockwaves through Eth early one morning. Now there was no official entry into the catacombs here, and the enchanters who'd ordered the dig—nowhere near the site at the time—blamed their loss on shoddy work practices, moving the operation elsewhere and leaving the building ripe for squatters.

"*That's* where the Assemblage is?" muttered Ashlan.

He looked up as Jassa made a beeline for the crumbling mass of the entry station, riven almost in two by the quake. Ever since, the back half of the building had stood four feet higher than the front. The street itself was empty—except for the pair of Deuces guarding the front door, giving Jassa a hero's welcome.

"We're on," said Rafe, grinning through his queasy terror as he threw an arm around Ashlan's waist.

She stiffened as the Deuces looked up, and for a moment Rafe felt trapped in a nightmare.

This was Ashlan's entrance, but she wasn't speaking. She didn't move.

Sweat gushed from his every pore, hot and cold at once. He thought he might scream, or run.

Then she laughed—a wild, throaty sound, full of life— and reached down to tousle his hair. Slumping against him, walking like she was half-drunk, she looked up at the Deuces and shouted, "This kid's a *nut!*"

Rafe, too surprised to speak, tried to laugh along, but he was blushing so hard he feared he'd already spoiled the effect.

"Would you look at Lickle Dee," cried the Deuce known as Stankjar. "Would you just look at him! Our boy's become a *man* out there in them woods! Who's the bird, Lick?"

"Wedding bells, huh," said Yabli beside him, her fingers roving the panoply of sores on her neck. "Congrats seven times. The other six are implied. I'm not saying them."

Ashlan shrieked right in Rafe's ear. "Oh, he's not my *boyfriend*! You guys are kidding, right? They're too much!"

"Guess we would be too much," said Stankjar with a leer, "if you're used to Lickle Dee's lickle dee, there."

"What's that mean?" said Ashlan, looking blearily from Jassa to Rafe. "Why do they keep calling you Lickadee?"

"Little Dee," said Yabli. "Stank talks funny. It's a nickname. Short for Little Diaper."

Rafe's face felt frozen in an empty-eyed grin.

"Because, you see," crowed Stankjar, his eyes already wet with tears of laughter, "because on his first night with all of us, he got so stoned that he—that he—"

"He crapped his pants," said Yabli.

He had no defense for this—for feeling so small, so young, so full of shame.

At least, he thought miserably, he'd managed to get into character.

"He's no child now."

Jassa spoke softly, but her solemnity quieted the others. Her eyes were shining, too, but with worship.

He shivered with relief. She wasn't too far gone to play her part, probably because she really believed it. He'd never been so grateful for her faith.

"This boy is the chosen of Fortune," she said.

The Deuces were rolling their eyes from Jassa to Rafe and back again, waiting for the joke.

"Didn't you get the letter?" Rafe said, confused for a moment.

"We—delivered it," said Stankjar. "Wasn't for our eyes, was it, though?"

Of course—it wouldn't have been shared with anyone so low on the ladder. All this was news to the Deuces.

"Well!" Jassa smiled beatifically. "Now you know. Rafe Davin is my Ace."

"Guess you really are a man now," said Yabli, rubbing the side of her chin against her shoulder.

"Won't call you that again," murmured Stankjar. "Sorry, Ace."

"*Sooo*," said Ashlan, wriggling into the awkward silence, "my name's Reena, Reena Greeshom, and if today's enough fun you might be calling *me* Little Diaper next!"

They all laughed at this, except for Rafe, who was beginning to wonder if stony silence and the occasional glare might be enough to carry him through the day. Things seemed stable enough now, but he still had a horror of speaking. It was lucky they'd been in the wood so long—his obvious withdrawal gave him a good excuse for all this sweating and flinching, which might well have happened either way.

"Probably just piss though," Ashlan was saying, "cause we've been on the road so long I haven't *eaten* enough to crap. You guys got anything to eat?"

"Snake eyes, Jassa, but what happened to your *hand?*" said Stankjar, kneeling down.

"I noticed," said Yabli. "But I didn't say anything."

"It's from when we met Reena," said Rafe quickly, before Jassa or Ashlan could butt in. This much he'd rehearsed, if only in his mind, and he wanted to be sure the details were set out right from the beginning. "Reena and I had gone off into the woods to pray. Her first time, with a drash at least." The others looked suitably impressed—both that he'd taken the blasphemous step of hooking a stranger, he imagined, and that he'd brought Jassa so far to heel that she, of all people, would forego her kiss. "When we came back, her home was going up in black flame. Whole family died. Jassa barely escaped alive."

"Nice one!" called Stankjar, clapping Jassa on the back. Yabli, too, made sure to touch her, as she'd have laid hands on anyone who'd had a close call. *Luck is contagious*—that was one of the Seventeen Tenets written by Gast the Foundation in the Ecstasy of her First High, and very possibly the least nonsensical of the bunch.

"It was *bad*," drawled Ashlan, her eyes half-lidded. "Everybody burnt. Everybody I ever knew. But you know what I saw, up in the smoke? The Lady Fortune was holding up Mister Rafe, like a baby. And Mister Rafe was rolling a pair of golden dice, and the dice said—" She closed her eyes, wrinkling her brow. "Seven—nine—two—four—aaaand three."

Stankjar began mouthing those numbers to himself, striving wildly to memorize them. Yabli, meanwhile, reached deep under her collar to scratch. Noting her discolored skin, Rafe wondered if she'd let drashes prowl her entire body by now. She was known as the Public Deuce—hiring herself out to take the poison-heavy first kiss for tlak tourists all over Eth—and Rafe was amazed she was still alive. For most of the faithful, two kisses in an hour were enough to risk death, but Yabli's tolerance seemed bottomless.

"That's tough," she said. "Your lucky hand, wasn't it?"

"It's even luckier now," said Jassa, raising her right arm with a bright smile. "The Lady cares more for *change* than for *charms*."

"Ha!" cried Stankjar. "I can see now why the Lady saw fit to give Rafey the Ace-hood, if that's your line of thinking these days." Stankjar had pulled out his namesake, rattling the dice at its filthy bottom. "Ask anyone. I'm far luckier using the same charm every time—that of nature's lubrication." He spit forcefully into the jar, then shook it and rolled.

Yabli looked down at the gleaming dice. "Not that time."

"But on average, though."

"Actually," said Jassa, pulling out her notebook and flipping through its lead-darkened pages. "I kept *extensive* notes during our time in the wood, and what I've found—praise Fortune!—amounts to a new truth, revealed through the doings of my Ace." She gazed at him with such peace that he wondered if her own shivering and sweating even bothered her. "Charms are useful, yes. Blasphemy is useful, too. But these are but tools in the kit. The kit itself—that is, what Fortune *really* favors—is change itself. Perpetual revolution."

She lowered her eyes. "It's been the start of a new chapter for my Lady and I. Now I begin again, at the bottom."

Rafe frowned, wondering why she was going on so damn long. "In any case," he said, stepping toward the door, "I'm sure that, ah—that Reena is ready to meet the others. She's been hearing about this Meeting for Worship, and she's eager. Aren't you, love?"

"I sure could go for a kiss, I'll tell you that for free."

Yabli turned to the heavy doors and tugged them open, one after the other. "Right, right. Yeah, you all are the last ones. Head on in."

Shivering with relief, to say nothing of his anticipation, Rafe led the way into the dim-lit warehouse. The place was echoing with voices—somewhere under this ruptured ceiling, the rest of the Assemblage was preparing their daily Meeting for Worship—but the entry itself was choked with rows of dusty crates rising all the way to the ceiling. Behind these boxes, the wide floor and its collapsed tunnel were hidden from view.

The noise only increased as the doors shut behind him.

Someone threw the bolt. "What's your sermon going to be, Lickle—I mean, Mister Rafe, sir?"

Rafe froze, staring at the leavings of the Sulcus Catacombs operation. "My—sermon?"

"Sure," said Yabli. "You're today's incentivizer."

"Newest Ace and all."

"He's a wonderful speaker," purred Jassa.

Rafe's mind was racing.

He'd have to *speak*, to demonstrate his faith and authority, or they'd know this had all been a ruse.

"I was—thinking of—"

He was thinking of nothing.

He was thinking of shitting himself on stage.

He had no faith. How could he have hoped to fake this?

"—of blasphemous steadfastness in times of adversity."

He didn't even know what the words meant, but he was already racing to work out his opening remarks.

The sound of Ashlan grunting, then sighing, stopped him.

Skin crawling, he turned.

The Deuces were standing over Ashlan's limp body, grinning at him.

Her neck was obscured by the backs of three sleepy drashes.

This wasn't the plan. Rafe was meant to drop her later, thumping her in the head with the collection plate in front of them all.

It was *his* moment. Why had Jassa taken it?

"Now, Deuce."

She was walking toward him, head held high.

"It's time we completed your education."

Eyes wide, he turned to run.

Right into the swinging truncheon of the Ace behind him.

There was blood in his eyes, blurring his vision. He was barely tied up—loose ropes, desultory knots—but the pain made any hope of escape laughable.

It hadn't come from being beaten, but from his blooming withdrawal. The sun was low, a dim, red light trickling through the door from the open windows of the warehouse. Hours must have passed while Rafe had been unconscious. His limbs responded to his urgings, vaguely, but even if he'd managed to stand, he couldn't have hoped to outrun Hollis, much less his captors.

He dragged his head up. Ashlan lay beside him, belly-up on a plank of wood, her face swollen from an overdose of drash poison. Someone had folded her hands neatly on her stomach.

He could hear voices in the warehouse beyond, rising in a roar that threatened to split his skull, then plunging into moaning and grunting. Rafe laid his head down, his mouth uncontrollably flooding with spittle as he pictured the Meeting for Worship.

They were getting high without him, he thought in panting desperation.

He was still wrestling with his ropes, thinking without much conviction about dragging himself hand over hand and begging for a crumb of tlak, when two figures stumbled in.

"Lickle Dee's up and sloppy," said Stankjar, his eyes glazed. "Living up to your name again, are you?"

"Eh," said Yabli, a fresh welt on her spotted neck, "happens to the best of us. I mean. If there *was* a best of us."

She stood over Rafe, and he braced for the blow—only to find her yanking the ropes from his ankles and wrists.

He looked up, blearily.

"Don't get excited," she said. "You're gonna die. I'm just not carrying you there."

"Still confused, eh, Licks?" Stankjar leaned against the doorway, inspecting his cuticles. "I say we deserve an award

for advanced thespianism. Shoo-ins for Ace-ing, after wink-
ing his hood like that! You never suspected we was in cahoots
with your Jassa, didja?"

"Course he didn't," said Yabli. "When you're that green,
you think everyone is."

"But *we* been at this for years." Stankjar squatted, leer-
ing in Rafe's face. "I joined up myself when she was just
a baby Widow. Barely older than you, we was. And even
then, Jass was thinking ahead, talking about pushing over
the doddering leadership of the Assemblage, and that. Why
should we forever slob the knob of the Puppeteer when we
could be running them catacombs ourselves, and et cetera.
Always planning, in that grotty little notebook, isn't that
right, Yabs?"

Yabli, who'd nodded off halfway through, snapped to
attention. "Always," she said, once Stankjar had repeated the
question, "always planning. That's our Luce."

"Luce?" Rafe whispered. His face rumpled in confusion,
and the very expression seemed to burn his sodden skin.

"Why, sure, Left-Handed Luce," said Stankjar, wiping a
thread of drool from Yabli's chin. "That's the Widow's name
now, fuck Fortune in the good ear. Goddess in the flesh, you
know? She's ascended, so She has!"

Rafe stared.

Jassa's arm. The carving.

Her madness had been an act. And he'd clapped right
along.

"You don't believe that," he grunted. "Even you can't be
that stupid."

Yabli laid a hand on his face and let it sit there, limp. It was worse than being hit.

"Just saw Her chomp on a ball of tlak the size of a grapefruit, hon. Your girl wasn't even buzzed."

"Turned to candy when it passed Her lips," breathed Stankjar. "That's avatar power, right there. And we took the leadership down for Her this morning. A proper coop, top to bottom. This dead one over here, this—what was her name, Stank?"

"Y'mean Aslan Loo?"

"Right," said Yabli, patting Rafe's sweaty cheek. "She's gonna earn us a *heap* of tlak tonight. The golden goose, with the endless guts. He'll pay out the nose."

"And then Aslan Loo's body will take out the Puppeteer, too, somehow or other. Wasn't clear on that. But it's a good trick, Luce says!"

"Then after the party, we'll rule the city," said Yabli, standing. "Whatever's left of it. Shame you won't be there to see it, Lickle Dee. Real shame. But you made your bed hard, boy!"

They hauled him up, their hands under his armpits.

"Ashlan," Rafe moaned.

But she didn't stir.

He hadn't really expected her to.

The Deuces laughed. "*She's* not gonna help you, kid," said Yabli.

"This is it for you, I'm afraid—that Ace business cost you dear. Luce says we're to gut you along with the rest—all the top brass of the Assemblage, all tied to posts just as neat as you please—and that wave of blood will carry us straight to the top!"

"Course, all that killing'll prolly crush the city, too," said Yabli. "But Eth had it coming."

"All a big laugh to Fortune, though, innit? She'll roll her dice on a carpet of bodies, and bless us all!"

They'd carried him out onto a jagged path. The collapsed tunnel stood beside them, its wide, shattered perimeter dotted with crates strung together with twine. On its other side milled the Assemblage, Jassa's shrill voice rising above them, promising them the moon in exchange for the blood they'd spill.

The crowd cheered and surged. "Shit," said Yabli, "they're about to gut the bosses without us! Haul ass, Stank."

The Deuces broke into a run, but between their intoxication and Rafe's withdrawal, he ended up stumbling, sprawled on the floor.

He started to crawl then, shuddering from the effort, with no idea where he was going.

He stopped when the floor began to crumble under his palms. Delirious, he'd dragged himself right up to the mouth of the tunnel. Moist heat hissed from the blackness below, jetting between the boulder-sized rocks that choked the fallen entry.

"Grab this little jerk, Stankjar. They're already carving, I don't want to—"

But the city rumbled, then shook, and there was a moment of stunned silence.

Across the warehouse, a lone woman found her voice.

"Fuck you, Mother Luck!" she shrieked, in ecstasy.

Then the ground heaved, like a sleeping giant shifting its weight.

Blocks of stone tumbled down the tunnel's throat as it opened wide. Darkness yawned, belching heat.

Then, before the Deuces could reach him, the floor tipped—and the catacombs swallowed Rafe whole.

—Kin—

When Ashlan's father left—not her brood-father, who'd died before she and her six brothers were born, but the man who'd taken his place—her mother took them out through the gates one night, wearing their bedclothes. When the guards asked where she was taking them, Elil Ley said, "The wood. To visit an old friend." She had changed lately, as she had before and would again, speaking more quickly, spending more money. She wouldn't tell the children who she was going to meet, as if she couldn't name the person, or wouldn't. Then she left them, far from any trail, promising she'd be back. They slept fitfully on the leaves, and Ashlan's brothers woke before dawn.

Ashlan didn't. She'd inadvertently made her bed over a snake hole, and the last thing she remembered was a flash of excruciating pain. *This isn't fair*, she thought.

What she meant, she'd reflect later, was that it wasn't fair that such pain even existed, that the human body was capable of producing such a thing.

At least it didn't last long. The snake that bit her was called a mudbrown, and its venom clotted her blood before she'd woken anyone. She died, as anyone would.

When her brothers found her, they took up wailing, having learned the way through the frequent deaths of their neighbors. It was a good thing, too, because the noise was the only thing that led their mother back to them. She'd gotten lost, she claimed, with the fiery intensity that afflicted her every so often, sometimes for months at a stretch.

She told them to hush, because their sister would be just fine. "You wouldn't be, if it were any of you, but she's different. In case you hadn't noticed."

This was both a family joke and a source of constant unease. Everyone who'd ever met them knew Ashlan was different. Broods were composed of *identical* children, and Ashlan, even if she'd been given the same haircut and dressed in the same clothes, was very much unlike the rest—darker, sharper, and taller, with different bits between her legs.

Her mother insisted that they were all born in the same brood. "They're your brothers, Ash, you're not adopted." But she never elaborated, saying only that it would get harder as they grew. "For now, the neighbors can pretend she's crosswise and I'm swimming with the current by putting her in dresses," she told them once. "But it won't hold for long. Your paths are going to split when you come of age, maybe even before. Nothing lasts forever. Even family shatters. I might do it, you might do it, we all might at the same time."

On this particular morning in the wood, her brothers couldn't tell whether they ought to believe their mother when she said Ashlan would be fine. She said so many strange things, and Ashlan's body was getting cold.

But then, as their mother instructed them in her rapid-fire way to build something out of branches and vines they could use to carry their sister home, it began.

Ashlan's body was spitting out the poison—and everything the poison had touched. Her coagulated blood, her stiffened veins, her actual heart itself were expelled, slipping out through sudden channels in her skin. The moment all of it was gone, she closed right up again, burning so hot that her brothers could feel the fever from a foot away. Then Ashlan started breathing, wearing her gore like a woven blanket.

They loved telling her, repeatedly and in great detail, how she'd split open and reformed, and she loved to hear it, at least before they came of age.

That morning they carried her blood-smeared body back with incredulous pride. Their sister was a magical creature, a secret they'd eagerly keep from the world, at their mother's urging—and *they* were the only ones who could tell her about herself.

When she finally woke, she was bathed and in bed. "I'm starving," she said, and they fed her all the porridge she could eat before presenting her with the discolored wonder of her own rejected heart, still attached to the fretwork of her circulatory system.

"No one can know, which is fine, because no one would believe you," her mother rattled from the kitchen. "But now you see why she can never go to war. She'd get cut, then she'd heal, and they'd know. And once the world knows, once the *city* knows, they'll take her. With coin or with force, doesn't matter. They'll change her. They'll have enchanters, and they'll sew her up, and she'll never be free, and she'll never be good. If they learn, your sister will turn into a monster. You might even have to fight her, all of you, and you wouldn't survive that. None of us will," she said, smiling incongruously, "after they turn her."

Ashlan learned to hide herself, for her brothers' sake, and they loved her enough to make up for it, for a while.

But when they came of age, her brothers would come to hate her, as the war took one after another from their brood. Partly because she couldn't die, but mostly, she suspected, because she was never there to wail.

She was too busy learning, about her body, about her limits. She experimented with rocks and knives, shattering her fingers, slicing her muscles, yanking fistfuls of flesh from her bone. She mastered many things, the heat included, but poisons always eluded her—the best she could do, if she'd eaten bad meat, was force her stomach out through her skin, and it seemed better to simply wait it out.

She visited home, sometimes, but her mother never told her why she was what she was, or what it was called. "Don't worry yourself, Ash. You've got enough on your plate, and honestly, you always will. Too much, maybe. So keep in mind what really matters. You're a healer—never lose sight of that.

It's in your blood, and I mean that exactly how it sounds. Never stop helping people. That's who you *are*—you're here to help. *Do no harm.* Don't let them take that away. They'll do it if they can. Make you a killer. A monster."

Ashlan's mother wasn't well, but Ashlan heeded her all the same—maybe more than she would've if Elil Ley had been stable, whatever that word meant—for a solid century, at least. And along the way, she managed to avoid any doses of poison as conclusive as that mudbrown's bite.

Until the drashes struck her neck, two at once.

They were drugged. For a split second, as her mouth overflowed with dark, nutty sweetness, Ashlan could understand the rush these cultists were chasing.

Then the screaming pain of the poison overwhelmed all her other senses, and she was plummeting, her vision going dark even as another stinger slid in—a third, for good measure.

There was no telling how long she was out.

Beat out her brains, and she'd still be conscious, somehow. But poison took her down, past sleep.

She called it death, because she didn't know what else to call it.

But unlike death, it ended, and she woke with her mouth tasting like burnt caramel. She wondered when the plan had changed, and why. Maybe it had been one last nasty gift from Rafe. She hoped he was proud of himself, then.

Ashlan still wasn't breathing, and her eyes refused to open. Worse, she could feel her veins sliding in bundles through the cool flesh of her body—cold, heavy, and rubbery, like one of Tanka's nerve trees was being born through her skin. The sensation was so disgusting that she had to work to keep still, but she did it, because she could hear that she wasn't alone.

A man was here, and he sounded delighted to be witnessing it.

"Well, that's just fascinating, isn't it? Look at her face! Look at that *eyelid*! It's like a lattice—like a pretty little doily all soaked in beet juice. Why, her whole head is hooded in veins." That explained the darkness, she supposed—her body itself was blinding her. "What a wonder she is. I mean, with one of her and a well-stocked cabinet, what couldn't you teach? Ha! That's a thought, eh? A school of our own, when all this is done. She might even help! You know, I bet she will, once she sees the students' enthusiasm. Who *isn't* curious about anatomy?"

He was talking to himself, she realized in time, his voice robust, musical.

Was this the Puppeteer?

She couldn't give the go-ahead until she'd identified him first. Hollis had to be hearing this as well, however muffled it was in there—and he'd probably heard a lot more while she was out.

Father. That was the magic word—once she'd made their target, once she'd lured the man close enough to her loaded stomach, she'd say "Father," clearly enough for Hollis to hear. And then it'd all be over.

He'd have his bloody fun, and she'd be free.

She could feel the tensed weight of the mannikin tucked into the hollow skin of her belly. She'd healed it carefully, pushing out Rafe's clumsy stitches, back at the boarding house. She hadn't grown her organs back—with a dose this big, poison kept her from healing anything else until she'd worked it out. Hollis shifted inside her, just a tiny bit, but enough that she could feel the point of his knife pressing up against her ribs.

Heat rolled through her flesh as the last of her veins slipped through the soles of her feet. She focused as intently as she could on leaving her organs in their fledgling state—so Hollis would have more room to maneuver.

The man gasped as her skin sealed up. "How *toasty* this girl gets. You could fry an egg right on her belly! Pity we don't have any eggs. But no, that wouldn't do—she might wake up while I was using her for a skillet. Plus, the omelet would be all bloody! Who'd want that? Not me."

He paused. "I mean."

At the sound of his voice, she felt Hollis bump against her ribcage, with a fist or a boot.

He was eager to know who it was.

It was time to help him find out. Holding back a wave of heat, Ashlan sat up.

Or tried to. She clanked and fell back, instead, restrained by her wrists and ankles.

The man made a noise like he'd just seen a pony do a backflip.

He actually clapped his hands, *pat-pat-pat*.

Then, humming excitedly, he peeled back her caul of veins.

She almost blurted out *Father* right then.

But they'd only get one shot at this. She had to be sure. Forcing her blood-gummed eyelids open, she kept blinking until her vision cleared.

The man was handsome, tan, and tall, with features so sculpted that she thought of a statue with the hair painted black. He'd seen a barber recently—the lines of his beard were ornate and precisely defined. Either he was a dandy or he was trying to impress her, or both.

"Well, hello, there! You're up and about! I wasn't sure what to expect, after all you've been through. A minute or a week, I don't know all that much about how this works—not the particulars, I mean. But I just couldn't bring myself to get things going until we'd been introduced. Ach! Listen to me, I'm so excited I've forgotten my manners. You *lead* with the introduction, *then* you gush."

He held out a manicured hand, close enough to her shackles that she could have clasped it, had she wanted to.

"What is this?" she croaked. How could he think she'd be friendly, given the circumstances?

"Right," he said, laughing at himself, moving his hand away with an apologetic wave. "We're not on equal footing. Not yet. I'm getting ahead of myself! I do that sometimes. Just tell me when, I'll back right off. My name's Ram Annathanker the Ninth. Yes, like the warlord. And yes, we're related, but no, I don't want to follow in his footsteps."

The words were practiced, timed, down to the chuckle.

"And I know *your* name, of course. Not 'of course'—why would you assume that? Sorry, it's just that I'm *such* a fan,

Miss Ley. Miss Ley? That feels a bit formal. Ashlan? Too familiar? Oh, what works for you?"

A fan.

The Puppeteer—if that's who Ram Annathanker was, and she hadn't lost the thread completely—was a fan of her regenerating body.

Rafe, the little idiot, must have told him what she could do, angling for a larger payment, no doubt.

And he'd given her name up, too. Not Reena Greeshom, but Ashlan Ley.

"Ram." She yanked her wrists against their restraints. "You've got me strapped to a—to an operating table, is that what this is? I could give a fuck what you call me. All I want to know is what I'm doing here."

"Oh, dear!" he said, swooping backward.

His voice soared, like he was telling a joke.

He was performing dismay.

"I've gone and crossed you already. That took even less time than I'd feared!"

Ashlan looked more closely at the room as he drifted over to a metal table by the wall. They were in a long passage that bent at both ends. It had no corners, just rounded edges, and the ceilings, walls, and floor were covered in deep furrows. The chair beside her was crooked, and all the tables had wooden blocks under their legs to keep them even on the bumps.

"Maybe, if I may, if it's not too presumptuous, I could ask if you're angry because you're—hungry? At least in part. I mean, all this—situating you've done, it takes it out of you, right? What was the phrase—ah! *Nothing stimulates appetite like forcible regeneration.*"

Ashlan's skin was covered in gooseflesh.

Ram lifted a little silver bell from a tabletop and rang it.

Nothing stimulates appetite—

She couldn't place those words. But it sounded like he expected them to impress her.

"Look, maybe you've got a point," she said. "I could eat, I guess." She'd get him closer with a plate of food, then find a way to confirm his identity when he was in range. "I—I *do* get irrational sometimes. I'm just feeling a little confused. Disoriented, you know? One minute I was up above, and now—where are we, exactly?"

"Right! It's unexpected all around! We never imagined having *you* here. This was not a meeting I ever thought would happen! But I knew as soon as the Assemblage described you what was going on. And how could I pass up this chance? It's like, I don't know, raising Granther from the dead to give a lecture on rune-work."

She felt dizzy.

What had Rafe *told* him?

He couldn't have put together that Ashlan was Hollis' creator.

Could he?

"*That's* what you want from me?" she said, confused. "My—expertise? Because, you know, Ram, given the way the Assemblage was talking, I was starting to get the impression that you were about to scoop my insides out, then get me to heal so you could do it again."

"Oh!" Ram laughed, his shoulders bouncing. "You are a pip!"

"Hey, let's be honest, I've been through worse," she said, rolling her eyes. "And in worse company. But—listen, could you tell me what you need them for? Just so we're on the same page. Call me crazy, but I like to keep track of where my parts have gone. And, hey, I sure could use that food."

Hollis tensed, rumpling the skin of her stomach.

"You want me—to explain how it works?" he said, beaming. "To *you*?"

"Knock my socks off." She wiggled her bare toes.

Anything to keep him off the subject of her *expertise*.

"Sure, sure! I mean, I'd be happy to give you an update," he said. "Honored, really! This is the house you built, Ashlan—we're just adding a new wing."

Dread overcame her as two young women entered the room, brood-mates. Clean, wearing medical smocks, smiling brightly at Ashlan. "I'm glad you're up!" said one, her cheek adorned with a tattooed numeral III. "How are you feeling?"

These were students.

He'd been talking about schools, lectures.

The house she built.

He knew about the prototype. But *how*? The Uni had scrubbed her name from the mannikin project, and her confiscated notebooks had never been logged. Before she left, she'd called in every favor she was owed to try and find them. She'd had plenty of friends who worked in the stacks—and they turned up nothing, suggesting that the books must have been lost in a quake.

She kept a smile plastered on her face. It wasn't worth panicking over. She just had another ball to keep in the air, because if Hollis found out, all of this was for nothing.

"Something we can do, Ram?" asked IV.

"Oh, yes! Some breakfast, I think. Just for Ashlan—I ate already."

Ashlan looked at the walls again as Ram and the students talked over the menu. This was no manmade tunnel. Everything was covered in protruding, finger-shaped bumps.

Villi, for the absorption of nutrients.

She was looking at the lining of a calcified intestine.

That's where they were—up the asshole of Eth.

In the catacombs, near the God-Gland, where they were mining their tlak, then selling it off to build their army.

A thousand little men.

This *had* to be the Puppeteer. It wasn't as good as an admission, but she could probably convince Hollis that she had enough evidence.

Now she just needed him alone—and close enough for Hollis to strike.

III and IV were mouthing pleasantries, taking their leave. "Nice to meet you, too," Ashlan said.

Forget the food—she had to get Hollis in gear while they were making her meal, then knock them out in the kitchen.

"So," she said, propping herself up on her elbows, "you were about to tell me what I'm here for. Right?"

"Right! Sorry for the delay. Let's set you at ease, shall we?" Ram sat, all the way over by the wall. "I just want to start by saying—I mean, you called yourself our 'prisoner,' but that doesn't feel accurate, considering."

"I don't get your meaning."

He cocked his head. "Considering—*you*, Ashlan."

She stopped smiling. "I'm—a very private person, Ram. But what I really want to know is who *you* are."

"Okay." He smiled, clearly making a concession. "Let's put a pin in that conversation, then. We'll talk about me! You have every right to ask. *I* am a student of history. Not a student at the Uni, though my parents would have loved that, may they rest in peace. They were both tenured professors, and they had very—*specific* ideas about what I should be. A ruler, for one. But can you imagine me on the throne? Just like Ram III, because *that* went so well! Anyway, I ended up—going another way." He folded his hands. "I always had the feeling that this, *all* of this, had to change. Eth, for starters. This carnival of slaughter, you know? We're better than this!"

This was better than talking about her, she supposed. But he was still too far away.

Maybe if she could get him talking about her insides. He seemed—enticed by her, somehow.

Like he was really looking forward to watching her regrow.

"You know, I guess what I'm really wondering is what you want with my—"

He held up a finger.

Damn it, he was midway through a rant.

"Ambition, that's the problem! That, I came to believe, is the drive that's hurting us. But is it learned—from our parents? Or is it innate—in our bodies? Well, it was while I was really digging into that question that I learned about *you*, Ashlan. I found you down here," he said, waving at the walls, "buried in the catacombs, in a pile of junk under the stacks at the Uni, when I was barely more than a kid. Not you yourself, of course! I found your notebooks. Your *designs*."

Fuck.

She lost control of the heat.

The tiny cluster of her organs surged, swelled.

Hollis was crammed down, toward her pelvis, the point of his knife shoved up against the inside of her navel.

Nothing builds appetite like forcible regeneration.

She had written those words, a century ago.

She had to distract *both* of them, fast. She could cover this with Hollis later—but how?

She'd come up with something. She had to.

"Ram," she shouted, grinning. "For fuck's sake, buddy, level with me. You're the Puppeteer, right? Isn't that what they call you?"

She felt Hollis' entire body tense.

The point of the knife was rising, coming through the skin, a tiny bump under her leather shirt.

Ram sat back, taking a deep breath, rolling his tongue against his lips as he slowly crossed his legs.

"The Puppeteer?"

He stood.

Started pacing.

Come on, she thought. A little closer.

"That name, that concept—I mean, we have to give them something, right? The Assemblage. The Uni. The people of

Eth. They expect certain things. A man—well, usually a man, almost always a man—grasping for control, power, coin. They're not ready to see that paradigm change quite yet. They will be, that's what all this is about! But for now, what we do is, we always send the same fellow to meet them. I don't mean to be *cruel*, but he has, let's say, a very distinctive face! And then we let them think what they think. So, am *I* the Puppeteer? Is *he*?"

He was five feet away. Looking right at her, smiling.

Then he turned, pacing the other way.

"There are twenty-four of us, mostly students or graduates of the Uni. We have all sorts of enterprises—the sale of enchantments, the refinement of tlak from a spot around the corner we call the God-Gland. The whole kit and caboodle is known, informally at least, as the Puppeteer Initiative. So, if you want to be reductive, you could say I'm one-twenty-fourth of the Puppeteer. I don't know, does that answer your question?"

"Sort of." She tilted her head. "I mean, are you the one who's going to pull out my insides?"

His cheeks got ruddier.

He must've been thinking about this for years.

He was walking over.

"Over and over again?" she said softly. "I mean, you'll make all the little men you can dream of. Right?"

Here he came.

"And they'll take over everything. A thousand little men. All full of me."

"Ashlan."

A few feet more.

"I am *so glad*—"

Another step.

"—that you invented those mannikins."

"*Father*," she barked.

There was an awkward silence.

Hollis didn't move.

Ram looked confused. "Your—father? Inspired the design?"

She closed her eyes.

Everything was over.

Except that it never would be, now.

"Well. They inspired *me*, anyway. But you only got the chance to make one, isn't that right?"

"Let's not dwell on the past."

"*A prototype, just to test the waters. Rune-work bound in leather and cloth.* But the Uni sold it off, before you'd even given it life, to some backwater kingdom miles and miles from here. The Kingdom of—what was it?" He snapped his fingers. "Oh, right! The Kingdom of Cru."

The knife inside her dropped.

She could feel its point, stuck near the base of her spine.

She laid her head back on the table.

"But Ashlan, we've taken it so much further, now. After a few trial runs, with the little guys! They're tough to control, though, at that size, and with that much zeal—a few ran amok, I'm afraid to say. That's not to pooh-pooh your design. It's still an absolute *marvel*, I want you to know." He leaned over the table, his eyes twinkling. "You made the mannikin. And now, together, we'll make the Kin of Man. I am—*so* eager for you to meet him. A little later! After a bottle of wine, maybe? Maybe—" He lit up. "I know! I'll bring your notebook, the one where you first sketched the design. That'd be a kick, right? And I think it would help you to get reacquainted with the Ashlan *I* know." He walked away, smiling. "This must seem unfair. You're here against your will, I get it. It's just that I—I don't think *she* would be. The old Ashlan, I mean. Deep down, who you *really* are—well, gosh, I just can't believe you wouldn't want to make the world better!

"So we'll start here. With the gentlest possible rough stuff. We'll take your guts, yes. But I have every faith, Ashlan, that you'll *want* to give them before long. You and me, we'll end up as friends."

Pleased with himself, as he always seemed to be, he winked.

"Stranger things, right?"

Ram left her.

Ashlan lay in silence for a long while.

So did Hollis.

She came close to speaking, a number of times.

Twice, she felt Hollis take up the knife.

But neither of them did a damn thing.

After a long while, the students brought in her food—a ptarmigan, stuffed with bread and mushrooms, which they set on a crooked tray. They let out her restraints enough that she could reach it. But they didn't speak to her, and she didn't move, even after they'd left.

She just stared, her mouth watering. There was no fork, no knife. Did they expect her to gnaw the meat off? Her hands were still covered in her own blood, the cuffs of her shirt dangling with veins.

But none of that would have stopped her, normally—her head was splitting, her stomach groaning—and that was what pushed her over the edge.

She owed Hollis an explanation, and forcing him to listen to the symphony of her digestion seemed one cruelty too many.

When the bird had stopped steaming, she sighed.

"I was working for the Uni," she said. "Just graduated. I was in Reparative Anatomy. Regenerative techniques for a proposed unit of battlefield medics. Truth is, I was never really that good at school. I'd just been in it so long, I learned to fake it.

"I was going for tenure, anyway. I had plans. Wanted to make a better Eth, from the inside out. You'd be amazed how naïve I was, even with my hundredth birthday around the corner. Or maybe you wouldn't.

"I'd just gotten my first big grant. I was celebrating with my research team when some faction or another set off a building-sized enchantment in the middle of the Market. They could never figure how many it killed. Hundreds, maybe thousands. There was a quake, a sizable one. The pub we were in was right at the edge of the destruction. We walked out to see dust in the sun. A whole neighborhood went under. People buried in the rubble, everywhere.

"So we went to work.

"I could see pretty quickly that my blood was more useful than I was. I had a good cover in my research—I'd been running tests on myself for so long that everyone thought I was inventing the stuff. They thought I was a genius, I guess. But it wasn't my work, just—what I am.

"I went off to get my supplies. So I said.

"What I really did was requisition all the bottles I could find in the Lidless Market, then cut myself open. Emptied my heart three or four times before I was done.

"We put it to good use. By the time the guards arrived, there was nothing left to do. Nothing but kill the looters—and those were mostly merchants, taking supplies out of their own shops. Good old Eth.

"Anyway, there was one guy I met, an out-of-work actor. Fillibrand Drinkwater, he called himself. The whole time, he kept everyone laughing. I started writing down the things he said, all this archaic language he used. We all started writing things down, in my notebook.

"It was a joke, at first. Someone saw my notes about battlefield medics. So they drew all these tiny Fillibrands, running around and fixing people up, feeding people vials of my blood while they talked this endless stream of fancy-sounding bullshit.

"By sunup a group of us, Uni folk and civilians both, were planning out how we'd build these replicas. Give them strength, intellect, medical knowledge. Ram thinks it's my design, but there were a dozen hands in there, at least.

"So I took it back to the lab. Soon enough, the city changed hands again. Things got—tense. But I kept working on the mannikin project."

She picked at the bird, chewing. She couldn't help herself.

"I built you, Hollis," she said. "I sewed you by hand.

"They gave me organs, and I never asked who they were from. I went down to the lab late at night and replaced them with my own. I—wanted you to last.

"Then you were gone. They took you, and made a bunch more. The first wave, the cloth generation, they were all sold off to the wealthy. Toys for kings and rich toddlers. Jesters and nannies. Not a one of them made it onto the battlefield. But they raised funds for the next wave—and those ones did.

"The Uni confiscated everything, and I thought it was lost forever, until now.

"I turned one hundred. Things started to—get to me. I didn't have interest in much. Except drinking.

"I don't know what happened. It felt like it was the project slipping out of my hands. But maybe that was just an excuse. Maybe I just got tired.

"My work slipped. They busted me down to professor's assistant, learning students' names just in time to hear that they'd died.

"And I started hearing stories, toward the end. Little men with poisoned blades, dropping out of trees. Sturdier than you. Armored. Running around the killing fields, slitting the throats of the wounded.

"The next build. Same as you, they'd found a way to break the one thing I really *did* write into the rune work: *Do no harm.*

"Whatever you learn about saving a life can be used just as easily to destroy it. But nobody knows that better than you, right, kid?"

He'd been still so long she wondered if he'd come unraveled midway through.

She couldn't bear the thought.

"Hollis," she whispered.

She rested a hand on her belly.

"I'm sorry."

She saw the flash before she felt the pain.

The thin tip of his boning knife was jutting through the back of her hand.

She yanked it away, less angry than startled. He'd stabbed up through her navel, and now he worked the blade down, sawing through her skin.

There was no sense in fighting. Reaching to the edge of her restraints, she tugged her shirt up.

Hollis crawled into the light, his burlap skin wet and dark. He dropped to the floor, his shoulders bowed, the knife in his hand. "I knew something was wrong. The way these people were talking about you when we arrived—"

"Hollis."

"What was I *thinking*?" He shook his head violently. "That anyone who could bring a puppet to life must be able to make himself live a long while, I suppose. A century— what trouble could it be to survive a century, for someone who could create life out of whole cloth? And I was right, wasn't I? My mistake was assuming that the Puppeteer and my creator were one and the same."

"Look, I should have told you. I just—"

He turned, his button eyes shining with her blood. "You'd only have broken me sooner. What I dreamed was that I'd find him—and for some reason he was always a man, in my mind—in the same workshop where he made me. A workshop! All of this came straight from a fairytale, and I never questioned it. An actual puppet-maker—can you imagine? I thought I'd catch him in the act of sewing up one of my brothers. 'I'm home,' I would call—and then the two of us, my brother and I, would hack him into pieces small enough that we could tie them all to strings.

"And then, Ashlan Ley? We'd make those pieces *dance*, just as he made *me* dance, all these years."

"It shouldn't have been this way," she said. "You were—misused."

"*Me*? Misused?" Laughing, he shoved the chair over to the side of the table and climbed atop it, waving the knife in her face. "Whatever your intentions, I am precisely what you made—a sad little echo of yourself!"

She kept her hands down.

Let him do what he liked.

She wouldn't risk hurting him to save herself a little pain.

"Look at you," he snarled, waving his blade. "Immortal! Invulnerable! And what are you, Ashlan Ley, but a great puppet? What do we do, either of us, but make the same mistakes, time and time again, as we lurch toward some grim and unattainable fantasy? Look!"

He held up his arms, doing a grotesque little jig on the seat of the chair.

"I'm dancing for you even now! Helpless to do anything else. All I ever wanted was to murder my creator," he said, thumping his chest, "for telling a joke this bad. But I can't even do that, can I? Here we are! Here's my knife! I could carve you to gleaming ribbons, right now—but you'd only laugh at me, like you laughed at Rafe Davin.

"You're sick enough that I'd get my vengeance—and you'd *enjoy* it. How's that for a punchline?"

Turning, he dropped from the chair.

She felt a manic urge to rip herself from her restraints— to chase him, to catch him, to pull him close—

Then Hollis stopped, standing in shadow.

"There's only one sort of vengeance I can take, I suppose," he said softly, "and that's the truth. That you could've *fixed* this mess you've created, years and years ago—that you could've told me the truth, and fought *beside* me—that you could've built yourself a life worth living, had you not been so damned busy. Even now, you're too busy, aren't you? Too busy to pick yourself up and stop the madman strolling down the hall. Too busy—on your endless quest to nowhere."

"What is it you think I could *do*, Hollis?" The words sounded hollow even as she said them. "Kill him? Kill them all? Bury the whole city, just to—"

"Oh! Oh, yes." He sounded happy, suddenly. "There's one more thing I'd have you know. That this," he said, pausing to let her hear a tiny *pop*, "is the only thing of value I have left."

He rolled it across the bumpy floor. She caught a glimpse before it fell through the cracks.

It was the last gold button on his vest.

The red pouch came sailing after, its seeds spilling everywhere, bouncing down.

"The enchanters at Cru called this trick the Shining Future. They were full of cons, those fellows! The Court itself was bereft, by the time my babies were grown. Twenty acts of fratricide—all over an empty treasury. That nugget of gold I gave you was all that remained, and you couldn't even hold onto that, could you?"

"You little prick," she said. "You had me feeling bad for a second there."

The room went silent. For a moment she thought he'd gone.

Then, from around the bend, she heard his faint, rasping voice.

"May you live forever, Ashlan Ley."

When the students returned, they asked if the silk purse belonged to her.

"I don't need it," Ashlan said. She healed her stomach before they noticed the gash.

They looked annoyed when they saw how much was left on her plate, so she put away the bird while they watched. That seemed to please them. They took off her wrist cuffs, student III holding a vial in her hand—a threat—while student IV bathed her.

She hadn't decided whether she should try to escape. Not now, while IV scrubbed the grime from her back, hard enough that her body jerked, but in general. She had nowhere to go. And ripping herself free would mean fighting them, and what if she couldn't stop? What if she got a taste of blood and slaughtered them all, and the city came crashing down?

You could always just endure it, she thought. Like you do everything else. Sooner or later, it'll just end, and then the next thing will begin.

Again, and again, just like this, forever.

Hollis' words were still ringing in her ears, and she let them ring—until they sounded like every other meaningless thought competing for space in her head.

The students rubbed her down with oil, then dressed her. One kept watch while the other braided her hair, far too loosely, as if she was afraid of hurting her. They showed her a mirror, after they'd wiped down the table and locked her wrists up again.

This was for him, she understood. For Ram.

He confirmed it when he returned, complimenting her lavishly. She looked like a meal, he said—no, like a feast. A sumptuous feast.

She stared at him, not sure whether to encourage him or shut him down.

He didn't seem to mind her glazed expression. He went to great lengths to explain their anesthetic techniques. It was important to him to know that she wouldn't suffer.

She thanked him, and smiled weakly, as if she'd been overcome by shock, and might come back to herself soon.

They put her under, and when she woke, she'd already healed.

She let herself bob along like this for a day or two. They took five loads of innards from her—contributions, they called them—and fed her constantly. The students were good cooks.

Ram visited her often. She didn't say much, but listened attentively to his long, self-congratulatory stories.

Sometimes she caught him staring at her belly.

She started to wonder what he was doing with all of her. The thought started to bother her. The discomfort reminded her of another time.

They'd just taken the nameless prototype from her lab.

She'd sat there all night, looking at her empty desk. A part of her was out in the world—and she had no way of knowing what it was doing.

This time she'd learn.

The next day, when he brought a meal to share with her, she apologized for shouting at him when she'd arrived. It made him glow, instantly. Encouraged, she gave him more.

The lies came easily. She knew what he wanted to hear. "I was hungry, you were right. But it was more than that, Ram. My—my *body* got the better of me. Sometimes I feel like I'm not in control. It's like my blood keeps flooding with substances that are working against me." She lowered her eyes. "Against you, too, I guess. But I—I do want to see a better Eth. A better world. I *do* want to help."

"Hey," Ram said, leaping up, too excited to finish his plate. "I promised you something, didn't I? And then we got caught up in building Kin One—we're going to have to name them, maybe you can start helping there—and I plumb forgot." He bounded to the curve in the passage. "I'll be right back. Don't go anywhere!"

She rattled her manacles.

He laughed.

Their little joke.

He brought her the last of her notebooks, convinced the students to leave her lanterns on that night, and left, promising that they'd have a drink together when she was done. "A toast to the Ashlan *I* know." She read through it, more irritated than inspired.

Then she got to the quake, and was surprised to find she remembered every word.

Except for the names. She must have passed the book around their camp in the rubble, and everyone who'd helped her design the mannikin had signed.

She was startled when she got to her own.

She'd been using a pseudonym, then, after one of her many resurrections, but she wrote *Ashlan Ley* that day.

When it was done—when she got to the point when the Uni had confiscated her books, that is—she closed the cover and lay back on the table.

Ashlan had spent the past hundred years in a fog. Her history was partly to blame, surely. But there had been a kernel of truth in what she'd told Ram. Her biology had conspired with the rest of it—the Uni's betrayal, her serial solitude, the violent deaths of more or less everyone she'd ever met—to make it all seem insurmountable.

Her body had made up her mind.

This made her angry, in a foggy way.

"My life has not been an utter waste," she said aloud, as if she was trying on the words.

They didn't fit.

It wasn't long before Ram brought the wine, a bottle in each hand. He was already drunk.

She threw her head back, thanking Fortune, and while it was theatrical, she meant it. The moment after he opened her manacles, she downed her first glass in one gulp.

"I can tell I'll have to work," he said, raising his eyebrows slowly, "to keep up with you."

"Maybe." She slid off the table, sitting on the bumpy floor and holding out her glass. "Probably. Tell me something?"

He sat beside her, pouring, then scooted closer. "Name it."

She gulped that glass down, too, running her tongue over her teeth. "What are they? Your Kin, I mean."

He set down his glass and hugged himself. "When I was young, Ashlan, I had this fantasy. Have I told you yet? No— that I was singly born."

"Huh."

"That surprises you?"

"It does." It did. He sounded Ethian.

"It wasn't—the usual way. I mean, I *was* born in Eth. But my parents, who loved to complicate everything, they got their own home-brewed enchantment approved. A sort of birthing circle, one use only, that would take all the best elements of my seven iterations—and fold the whole brood into one. The best possible offspring." He sipped his wine. "I am the basket where the chickens put all their eggs."

She snorted. "And they named you Ram Annathanker. Just to make sure you stayed humble."

"I *know*! I was grown, in a lab, to unite the kingdom. Rule for a lifetime, plus conquer the lands all around. It was a lot to live up to. So I didn't." He leaned back on one palm. "Anyway. This fantasy I had—I was a kid, mind you—was that I'd find a way to divide myself back into seven. And instead of ruling Eth, alone, the way my parents wanted it—I was supposed to reconcile the Uni and the throne, see—"

"No pressure." She filled her own glass this time.

"Exactly." He finished his and poured another. "So after I magically extracted all my brothers, we'd rule the whole world. One of us in each kingdom. I guess we would have annexed some, to even things out."

"Wouldn't that have led to brother fighting brother?" she said, squinting. "I mean, *you're* the student of history, but I have read a few books."

"Ah, but you see, we wouldn't really *be* brothers. We'd all be me! And I'm perfect, so." He made a face to show her that he was kidding. "But you're right. As I got older, I started doubting how harmonious I'd really be with myself. Power always seemed to go in the same direction. Toward its own destruction, not to mention the destruction of everything else. And right around then, I found your notebooks.

"You taught me what I could be. Through your words. Through your designs. But most of all, Ashlan—through your hope."

He closed his eyes. "*I will do no harm. I am here to help. And if I do not, I have become a monster.* When I read that, Ash, I have to tell you, it changed the course of my life."

Despite the rush of confused emotion, she kept her voice bright. "So the Kin, they're your—identical rulers?"

"Actually, no. They're—well." He drained his glass and set it on her table, standing, holding out his hand. "Why don't I show you?"

"I'd like that." She stood up, making a show of her unsteadiness.

He took her arm. "I developed something new, so far as I can tell." He led her around the first bend. She was unsurprised to see more of the same—room after room set up in the bends of the Gone-Away's intestine, lit by flickering lanterns. "It's a piece of rune-work that senses a certain constellation of psychological stances. What you might call—lust for power. It can sniff it out, even at a distance."

She made approving noises as they came around the corner, into a far larger chamber, crammed full of cabinets.

Seeing the great metal chamber at the far end of the room, she stopped.

It was fifteen feet high, built of solid steel.

"The Kin of Man is in—*there*?"

"The first of them, yeah. We're almost ready to start the second, thanks to you." He held up his hand, as if she might race toward the box and throw the door open. "Now, I know he can't do anything to you that's going to last." Ram smiled, picking up a lantern.

"But?"

"But this seems like a good time to ask you if you've ever thought of yourself as a leader. Wished it was maybe you who was holding the throne, bossing people around, smiting your enemies, that sort of thing."

She laughed, though her stomach was sinking. "Your mannikin can read minds?"

Ram's chest expanded. "More like—he can sense these cocktails of aggression, the residual physical effects of ambition, if you will—but yes, in effect, that's what he does. I call it the Alpha Scan. It's named after an outmoded theory, but—"

"But he tracks down people who want power, and then—"

"Then he changes the world."

With a bow, Ram pulled the bolt and tugged the door open.

Light licked the floor, where six helmets lay.

The seventh stood atop the shoulders of a ten-foot-tall man. Its fingers were made of stout blades, splayed apart, cruelly recurved. Every joint was a spiked bludgeon, every metal surface covered in acid-eaten runes.

But Ashlan was staring at its face.

It was a cast-iron sculpture of a bulging human heart, and though it had dull, immobile chambers instead of eyes, she could feel it regarding her.

Reading her.

For a moment, she was afraid of what it might find.

Then Ram walked up to it, striding through the empty helmets—each one representing another of the body's organs, from brain to liver, all intricately detailed—and placing his palm on its broad stomach.

The Kin of Man folded its blades away inside the empty chambers of its forearms and knelt, putting an arm around him.

"You're not afraid," she said softly, "that it might kill you?"

"Oh," he said, laughing. "That's what I *made* him for. My parents, they engineered me—to be a monster, in your for-mulation. Right? So it gives me a lot of comfort to know that if I ever were to do what would make them proud—well, he'd find me, and put a stop to that." He patted his creation and closed the door. "Six more to go! Then we'll set them to work. Our Kin will spread out all over the world, and keep the human race from getting the better of itself. This is the world you wanted, Ashlan—the end of the worst of man!"

"It's—incredible," she murmured.

But all she could think was what it was *made* of.

From boot to helm, that thing was packed full of her enchanted insides.

He put his arm around her as they walked back.

She saw something moving in the shadows, emerging from a dark furrow behind the chamber.

She looked away. Ram hadn't noticed.

It was Hollis, his face crumpled, his vest hanging open, staring not at Ashlan, but at the door.

It took all she had not to run to him.

But she had no idea what she planned to do.

They drank the other bottle then. Ram was talking about his plans. His schools, their curricula formed around the interests of the students. The way he'd redesign the city. "You've thought of everything," she said, and he almost purred.

Before he said good night, he put her manacles back on. "I don't think we'll need these for much longer," he whispered. "The others want to be sure, that's all. They haven't gotten to know you the way I have."

"I don't mind," she whispered back.

He smiled, weaving across the room.

She could feel his desire.

"Ask me," she said.

"Tomorrow. Do you—do you want to be awake? To be—with me?"

"For—the surgery?"

"Yeah. It might be educational," he blurted. "You might—you might learn something about yourself."

I'm learning something about *you*, she thought.

His face was red, and he was breathing quickly.

She understood. To him, this was an act of love.

He saw the two of them as parents, about to birth a new world.

"Sure," she said.

"I mean. Without the anesthetic, it's going to hurt."

"Pain doesn't bother me." The words came easily. She knew what he wanted to hear. "I just keep thinking about the Kin. How it's *me* in there. I'm ready to be more—involved."

"Yes. You will be, Ashlan," he whispered. "But—don't let the others catch on, okay? Just for today. I'll need to get them used to the idea. They're—" He glanced over his shoulder. "They're still not sure if you should be walking around."

"No problem." She winked, and went limp.

All night she struggled to decide.

Two hundred years, and she'd never taken a human life, while everyone around her seemed to be a murderer, or in training to become one.

Kill Ram, though, and all that was over.

So she'd never killed.

How much harm had she done regardless?

Leave him alive, and he'd make *seven* of them.

How much harm would the Kin do?

How many lives would they end?

She couldn't sort out the calculus. She still hadn't made up her mind by the time III and IV came in. They took their time, chatting with Ram, earning his laughter. Ashlan kept very still.

He placed his blade against her belly. She could feel his hand trembling.

"Everything all right?" said IV.

"Oh!" said Ram, chuckling. "Too much to drink last night. I must have the shakes."

He steadied himself, and had just swept his blade from one side of her belly to the other when the room went strange.

"Is it me, or—"

All of them stopped moving.

"That was something," said IV. "Wasn't it?"

They must have felt the same queer lurch that Ashlan had.

"No, look." Ram pointed at a bottle on a shelf. It was rattling, seemingly on its own.

"Damn it," said III, crouching down as the floor seemed to roll beneath them. "*Another* quake?"

"It's really going to hell up there," said IV.

Ram sighed as it settled down. "It's probably the fucking guards," he said, "going to town on the Assemblage. Or the other way around. Gosh, we really created a—"

This time the whole room shook. "My goodness—it's a big one!" called Ram, starting to look concerned.

Tables crashed. Instruments fell. The shaking grew so intense that chunks of calcified innards fell from the ceiling, then crashed onto the floor.

It calmed for a moment. Then the rolling began, then the shaking, again and again, sending hunks of stone to the floor, until IV was helping III up from the floor, her face bloody.

"It's not stopping," Ram shouted at last. "Get into the chamber with the Kin. It's the safest place. I'm right behind you."

They ran.

This might be the end of Eth, or the beginning of Ram's new world.

Either way, Ashlan had been shaken into a decision.

This wasn't calculus after all—it was arithmetic. Two monsters were better than seven.

Ram had staggered over. He reached for Ashlan's wrist— then stopped.

"Shit!" he said. "I was about to bring you along. But the others would be suspicious! I mean, we can just pull you out of the rubble later if it gets bad, right?"

He turned his back before she could answer.

Ashlan ripped her hands through the metal cuffs, shearing off her thumbs.

Ram heard the clank and paused, turning as another rumble began.

Leaping to the floor, feeling the slippery mass of her insides spilling out, she let the heat rush into her arms. Her thumbs sprouted back—the bones, at least.

Ram saw her just as she'd gathered a slippery loop in her hands.

A chunk of ceiling took him to his knees.

Ashlan did the rest, garroting him with her entrails.

He stabbed at her arms, however briefly, with his scalpel.

"You're adorable," she said.

—Rites—

Withdrawal was in full bloom.

A flower made out of lack.

A ball made out of tlak.

If all the tlak the Assemblage had taken was rolled into a ball, how big would it be?

Bigger than the fruit Jassa had bitten?

Littler than the wad Gingerbeard had won at the Masque?

Larger or smaller than Rafe's own beat-skipping heart?

"You didn't kill me," he said, or imagined saying, as if Jassa could hear him, as if dying in the catacombs instead counted as some sort of victory.

There was a score sheet that tallied all the times he'd taken the drash's kiss.

The only trophy he cared to win was Most Times High.

There was no getting around the fact that he was failing.

Unless he was winning, in reverse.

No one had gone this deep into tlak-sickness before.

Anyone else would have killed themselves to feel so much pain.

Especially if they knew, as he did, that it was permanent. That he could never awaken from this dream.

Life was full of possibility, but one thing was certain, and that was that Tanka would sooner kill him than bring back the sweetness now.

Jassa had taken that away from him.

She'd taken it away from *herself*, too, which almost seemed saintly.

He'd never again taste it flowing into his mouth, from a spigot under his tongue, that tide of sticky sugar sweeping all his memories out of reach, washing him from himself.

He'd never see his drash again, never calm it with the drug.

Never watch its eyes turn black or stroke its long-haired back.

He'd never feel its kiss sliding between the tendons of his neck.

Instead, he'd die like this—mourning the loss of a bug.

If Rafe was crying, it was less because this was happening than because it refused to end. It might have been going on for hours, though it felt more like days, but there was no light down here, and he could hear no sound that didn't come from the vents or his own body. The noise he made astonished him. He cried like a newborn calf, pathetic and unrestrained. Later he understood that the raw flesh of his bottom lip, which was split in a dozen places, was due to his facial contortions. He'd been ugly-crying, as Little Gem would say, so hard he'd cracked himself open. I have nothing to do with this sound, he told himself as his bare chest buckled and hitched. This is happening *to* me, not *in* me, because I do not cry. When was the last time I cried? It never happened, and it's not happening now. But someone was spending saltwater down here like they had a full tank. Someone was asking the walls why. Someone was listing all the people who'd gone away, calling their names like they might hear him and come back.

"Just come back."

H e could see death turning, drifting his way.

It wasn't a specter or a personification, no bugbear in a hooded cloak.

It was the total absence of Rafe Davin, and it was very close.

Seeing its face, every pitted feature the exact inverse of his own, did he welcome death, or wish it away?

An avatar of the Inbetween, he had perfected the art of doing both at once.

B roken and whole were no longer distinct.

A false binary, Gingerbeard would have said. Like wicked and good, or man and woman.

You were either one or the other. But Gingerbeard had lived between, and Rafe suspected that everything did.

Absolutes are the hallucinations of culture.

That was a Gingerbeard phrase. He was full of them.

Take his body. Perhaps it was broken, and perhaps it was whole, but he thought it was both at once.

If his stomach was ruptured, was it any less his stomach?

Was his stomach ruptured?

No. That had been back on the killing fields.

That had been Jassa's stomach. Hadn't it?

It hadn't been a dream, he was sure of that. It only felt like a dream because he'd been healed.

Wounds were the body's nightmares, diseases their fever dreams.

Dreaming and waking—another false binary. Rafe was doing both.

He focused on what he could verify. His nose was broken, crooked, plugged with blood. Look, he could hardly breathe.

Of course, that was partly because he'd been sleeping in his binder, down here in the dark.

Somehow he worked it off, loosening the ties and wrestling his way out. His sweat made that easier.

If it was sweat.

His stomach kept on heaving. The floor beneath him was slick, whether with sweat or less prosaic fluids. He didn't know, and didn't care to.

He pictured a wave of blood pouring down into the maw of the catacombs from the sacrifices of the Assemblage. He heard the hissing and gurgling, and the sound was enough to drive him mad.

Or maybe that was just the vents jetting warm, wet air from below.

Rafe was not, in fact, lying in bathwater. But tell that to his body. It believed he could swim out of himself. He wished it was right.

When the heat went away he was grateful, until the shivering began. But before that he'd been relieved to know he wouldn't be boiled alive.

Not from without. His bones, though, they were burning.

A skeleton built of embers was ready to slide out of his flesh, then slump, tinkling, into a mass of gray ash.

First the pain was excruciating. Then it went on for so long that it became excruciatingly boring.

"Is it worse to hurt or to get used to it?"

Speech struck his skull like a bell. Why he'd been talking, he didn't know. Who could say what he'd been saying?

Who could say whether he was living or dying?

Who could say which pain belonged to the fall and which to the tlak?

"Without tlak," he roared at the crowd, "there is no life. Yet I have no tlak, and still I live!"

They raised their dead fists, opened their dead mouths, and cheered. It sounded like the Masque at its peak, when no one could remember what their own faces looked like, and no one cared.

These were *his* dead, from his black-robed clan to the hundreds who stood behind them—thousands, even, and more, always more, because the dead who belonged to Clan Davin could not be counted. All the dead were Davin dead, which meant that all who'd ever lived had been neglected by

Rafe. *Until everyone is quiet, our people cannot leave this place*, his Gran used to say, and now he was the last of his line.

And there she was, his Gran, toward the back of the crowd. With her bony hands, she was shepherding this mass of corpses, urging them to stand toward the front, to hear his speech.

"I *will* keep on living," he cried, "and I *won't* get high again!"

The crowd lapped it up. What he said was conclusive and loud, and they were dead, after all—they'd cheer just about anything.

Except for the two in front. Rafe could feel their disappointment, see the tall one one sigh.

It was Gingerbeard, wearing their purple dress, standing with their arm around Little Gem, who looked like Rafe's speech might kill her all over again.

"Brave words, my love," called Gingerbeard, their voice ringing out through the chamber.

The dead stopped cheering and stared.

"Brave words," they went on, "but you don't *have* any tlak, and never will again. You're framing an inevitability as a choice. And what valor is there in failing to drown when you're strapped to a raft?"

Little Gem sighed, taking their hand and pulling them away.

"Wait," shouted Rafe, but Gingerbeard had already turned, showing Rafe the curls that spilled down their broad, shapely shoulders.

Their body was *whole*, he saw with a shock—set right by some unknowable force.

Gingerbeard had been quieted, and not by Rafe.

It should've been him who undressed them, who washed their broken body, who spoke to their life.

It had been his job to bring them peace—and where had he been instead?

He was crying again, the weakness spilling out of him like milk from a cracked pitcher.

The dead turned, frowning at the sound of his sorrow.

He was no leader. They carried him down from the platform.

Toward the back, they'd lifted someone else on their shoulders.

It was Lura Davin, holding her own head in her lap.

"No one left to quiet *you*, girl."

Rafe was aware that he had been passing in and out of consciousness, and that his consciousness had been compromised by withdrawal, and that his brief moments of lucidity were getting longer, and that his body was slowly cleansing itself of tlak, and that sooner or later he would be completely sober, and that he would die this way, of thirst.

Did he know how long it had been since he'd fallen down here, tumbling around corners in a long, snaking tunnel that led to this chamber?

He did not. He guessed: two days.

Could he guess how long it had been since Gingerbeard was hacked apart on the street outside his window while Rafe was too high to tell the difference between their screams and the twilit songs of drunken partygoers?

Three months. Four at the most.

Was he aware of how far he had fallen in such a short time?

He was.

If Gingerbeard knew, would they be so disgusted that they'd look at him with eyes gone cold with hate?

He wanted to say yes. In a sense, he *had* been saying yes, all this while.

Why couldn't he say yes?

Because Rafe had not been the first among their chosen family to lose himself this way. Because Gingerbeard had not hated the other addicts at the boarding house.

Had Rafe?

Neither of them had. They knew how easy it would be to join their number.

What had Gingerbeard said?

We all do strange things to keep ourselves from dying. And when it comes down to it, love, no one knows which of those things might lead us back to life.

S till alive, Rafe crept toward the edges of the chamber. He couldn't see the walls. He could feel them, though, irregular and rough. The space was larger than he'd thought. There were cracks in it, but no passages.

He laid down again. All he could feel was his papery mouth, his clicking throat. Even his bare breasts hardly bothered him, not next to his thirst.

He started to think about water the way he'd been thinking about tlak.

Wondering how much of it he'd sweated and pissed away. Gallons, it felt like.

How long before his organs rebelled, shutting down one by one?

He pictured the stone breaking open overhead, filling the chamber with cool, gushing liquid—which would drown him before he'd taken a gulp.

He almost laughed. But it felt like laughter might split his belly wide open.

The earth ruptured, again.

Rafe was tossed around, flying and thumping, pelted with rocks. His body was flung against the floor, against the walls, his eyebrow split. The pain brought him brief, airborne clarity.

This was no tremor. The city's streets were shaking like a dirty rug.

He could hear the clatter of buildings falling. He smashed onto the ground again, wheezing.

The earth undulated. He touched his own blood, amazed that his body still had wetness in it.

Eth was coming to an end.

He wondered who'd done the killing that started it. Maybe it was Jassa. A real goddess now, remaking the city in her own jagged image.

It was awful to admit, but it made him feel better to think that he wasn't dying alone.

He flew up again, feeling like he might never come down.

When he opened his eyes, there were people with him, reeking of sweat.

"Shitfire," shouted one, leaning down and shining a blue-white light on Rafe, "this girl's alive!"

Irritation roused him. Rafe opened his mouth to identify himself as crosswise, not caring if these strangers killed him or left him to die, needing more to be seen than to live.

Dazed, he stopped and squinted. The radiance was bound in a tiny bottle. The man holding it was grizzled and brown, with flyaway eyebrows.

His partner, a slight, dark woman in tailored clothes that were torn and dusty, squatted beside him. "So she is." She sat down by Rafe's side, her hands flying over his body, checking to see how bad things were. "Got off easy, at least where your bones are concerned. But you've been down here since the *first* quake, haven't you? Hold tight," she said, then turned, slipping down a passage the quake had ripped open in the side of the chamber.

The grizzled man pulled Rafe's binder from under some rubble and draped it over his chest. "You're in good company down here," he said, shining his light over the walls. "We might be trapped, Chuck, but we're trapped without guards. Safer that way."

Rafe moved his mouth again, but his voice was gone.

"Name's Graven Jacks," said the grizzled man. "Set your mind at ease—I've lived through forty years on the killing fields, and I'll be damned if I'm dying now, just because of some sneaky fucking temblors come up out of the blue!"

Rafe blinked. The man was shouting at the walls.

"Careful, Jacks," called the woman, returning to kneel by Rafe's side. "You'll tantrum your way into an avalanche. Here. I'm Loxia Lydus."

She put a canteen to Rafe's lips.

Rafe put his hands to his mouth.

The water was hot and tasted of leather, but it was life.

After a while, he lifted his head. "Help me with this," he croaked, patting the binder.

Loxia nodded, holding it up, peering with curiosity at the hooks and eyes on the back.

"Come on now, Chuck," Jacks shouted—he seemed always to be shouting. "She won't fit in that thing! She's confused, poor critter. It ain't even *hers*." He'd come close, his hands starting to tremble from heated worry.

"It's a binder," Rafe said.

They stared blankly.

"I'm a *man*," said Rafe, too irritated to dance around it any more. "Bent, you know? Crosswise. Open the back, cinch up the sides."

"My mistake," said Loxia softly. With a little more prodding, she figured out how to get it on him, then worked slowly at the laces. "The thing you have to understand about Jacks here," she murmured, "is that he gets very nervous when he's not doing anything. Like a very large, very old puppy. And I'm not entirely sure," she said pointedly, "that he knows what 'crosswise' means."

"Don't you fucking patronize me, Chuck!" There was no threat in Jacks' voice. It had gone so high with indignation that he was almost singing. "You have some sort of monopoly on the understanding of people? Is that what you think?

I know about people, you know," he growled, hopping up, beginning to pace. "People of—of all denominations!"

"All right, Jacks, all right, you're a man of the world. Now pull it together. We need to get this man topside."

"True enough," said Jacks, calming immediately as he put his broad, cracked hands under Rafe's arms.

"I can walk," moaned Rafe, and both of them laughed.

"Like a newborn colt, you can," said Jacks, hefting him up as Loxia took his knees. "But it's quite a ways up, and we'll only be walking halfway."

"Save your strength," said Loxia. "We'll need your help once we're up above. You're doing well, all things considered."

"What's up there?" Rafe said.

"You mean what's left?"

"We'll know when you do," said Jacks.

"There was damage enough after the first quake that we came down to hunt for supplies," said Loxia. "And then— well, this was unprecedented. Worse than Radmun's quake, from what I can tell. I'm glad we found so many of you alive, but I don't have high hopes for what's above."

They carried him through a jagged corridor, Jacks holding his bright bottle in his teeth. They emerged into an enormous cavern, some long-abandoned transport hub sprouting shattered tunnels in all directions. A massive pile of debris stood in the middle, mostly the remains of a stone stair whose last few steps still clung to the ceiling, plus a building or two that seemed to have smashed down from the surface.

There were a dozen other people here, half of them wounded. There were bodies, too, and pieces thereof. The healthiest among the survivors were rifling through the rubble, pulling out anything whole enough to be of use.

A dozen wounded lay around him, their eyelashes coated in dust. Some of their heads were bloodied, some of their limbs crushed.

He'd live through this, given nourishment. They couldn't say the same, not with any surety.

There was a clatter of debris sliding down the heap. Graven Jacks stood at its highest point, surrounded by a group of other scavengers pointing up at the hole in the cavern's roof.

Swiftly, and with a minimum of argument, the group worked out a way to build tools from the wreckage, then mark out the safest path to the top of the hill. The ideas that flowed between them were disseminated quickly enough that splints and stretchers were soon in play. Loxia Lydus pulled a red glass bottle from a crate and began to describe to the others how they'd use it.

Rafe shrank back. It was the very same sort of bottle that Jassa had used to bind Ashlan.

Loxia produced a short, curved blade from the box.

This had been a trap all along.

They meant to sacrifice him to save themselves.

In a panic, Rafe began to struggle against his bonds, attempting to free himself without making any noise. If only he could get away from them, he might lose himself in the tunnels, and—

And he could barely move.

The sky above cleared, sending a shaft of sunlight down into the cavern. He caught a glimpse of Loxia pouring her potion, suddenly illuminated, all over the bare, brawny arm of Graven Jacks, who laughed as the sinews swallowed him up to the armpit.

With the tip of her knife, Loxia drew them out, speaking to the writhing tendrils with the same sort of sunny, inane babble she might have used to encourage a dog to go for a walk. Seemingly entranced by the glint of the sun on her blade, the sinews took on the shape she desired—a long, powerful limb many times the length of Jacks' body.

Rafe watched as she repeated the process on Jacks' other arm. Then, grinning, he lifted his tentacular appendages above his head, gripping the broken stairs and soaring up with a hoarse but childlike whoop.

"I had no idea you could use those things that way," Rafe croaked as Loxia and another woman hefted up his stretcher.

"That's why I defected from the Uni," she said. "I have some experience with enchantments. And they were hoarding what we needed to keep this city alive, from looters who never came."

Before long, it was Rafe's turn to be hauled up by those sinewy limbs. He shut his eyes as the sky loomed closer, then felt a blast of cool air as Jacks set him down on the gritty street.

Rafe looked around, feeling faint, as the others were brought up behind him. Over the toes of his boots he could see how many buildings had been reduced to dust and brick, how many neighborhoods had sunk out of sight. Shiny Clump was jutting at a madcap angle some hundred feet lower than usual, and the silvered dome of the Uni was simply gone—swallowed whole by the catacombs. Eth was in ruins, and at its edges he could see its pearly wall in pieces, the sun shining on the open fields beyond.

I'll run, he thought. As soon as I can move.

The Assemblage will never find me, because I'll never come back.

Then Loxia touched down, a tentacle patting her on the head.

Seeing her shocked face in the sunlight, an unrecognizable mask of dust and blood that surely mirrored his own, made him feel safe for a moment. If Jassa was looking for him, she wouldn't be able to spot him until he bathed.

She seemed so far away. All of it did. This chaos had swallowed so much.

A curious gratitude overcame him. The city seemed too broken to hurt him, for now.

They gave him food, water, and enforced rest, but Rafe was too stubborn to stay down—within a day, he was blearily working, helping Graven Jacks organize the waves of survivors coming into an abandoned schoolhouse at the inner edge of the shattered wall. Though he and the others from underground had joined a far larger group of complete strangers, they labored without any noticeable hierarchy—people popped in and out of rooms, shedding and taking over responsibilities as their areas of expertise became needed elsewhere. Jacks himself, in addition to lending brute force where needed, seemed to act as the building's living reference library for such skills. He called everyone Chuck, even Loxia and Rafe, but he seemed always to know what each individual Chuck was best at.

"Ah, found some unspoilt meat, did you?" he roared as two boys carried in a side of beef peppered with rubble. "You'll want squinty Chuck, tall white fella with the broken spectacles, last seen on the third floor, I b'lieve. He was a chef, or at least a mess cook—can't recall, but at any rate he won't add a finger to the stew!"

Rafe himself had been carrying messages and fetching people for hours, ignoring his body's complaints as best he could, when Jacks waved him over. "Got a job for you, Chuck," he said, with no less volume than usual, though his grizzled visage was far more somber. "A woman was just brought in, over off the western hall. She's not going to make it. I need you to see her out, now."

"You want me to—"

"Sit with her while she shoves off, yeah."

"You really think that's the best use of our resources, Jacks?" Rafe was instantly red-faced. "It's not a favor she's likely to remember. And there's need all around."

Jacks rolled a massive shoulder. "Seems pressing enough to me. I don't believe anyone ought to go alone, especially strangers. Might be because I'm a bachelor, and it makes me feel like *I* might have a hand to hold."

"Maybe *you* ought to do it, then," Rafe snapped.

"Hm." Jacks scratched his stubble, looking at Rafe like a puppy nipping at him. "Suppose I misread you, Chuck. Looked like you've seen your share of endings. But if you're too squeamish, I'll find someone with a tougher lining."

"Squeamish, my ass."

Rafe stomped away.

And into the schoolhouse.

Was he that easy, that a tossed-off taunt could change his course? If so, he hadn't changed a whit.

I could leave, he thought, fuming. I could duck out the back and slip through the broken wall. No one would know until I was far, far away from here.

There was nothing to keep him. He didn't know these people. Whatever contract he'd held with the freaks was broken, and though he'd heard nothing of the Assemblage in the jumbled rumors about camp, a living Jassa would be a certain threat.

Rafe could run.

But where?

His eyes danced in the dust that swirled through the sunlight. He pictured himself in the wood again, without weapons or food, getting good and lost. Or trudging along some dusty road, hoping the next place was kinder to bent folk than Eth had been.

Then Loxia passed by, carrying a crate of supplies down the hall. "Five doors down on the left, Chuck." Everyone was saying it now—it was easier than learning so many names at once.

"Thank you," said Rafe, and then his feet were carrying him down the western hall.

The woman's brown skin was ashy, her hair a curly cloud. She was just about his age—he wondered why he'd thought she'd be older. Her amber eyes were very mobile, and seemed only intermittently to be able to focus on his face.

He could feel himself trying not to look down.

Don't be ridiculous, he told himself. You've seen this enough.

You've *done* this enough.

So much of her flesh was open to the air that he couldn't believe she was awake.

This was why people believed in ghosts. It felt as if she might reach out and take him with her.

But that was the opposite of what he'd been taught— when he'd sat beside his father, with Gran and Lura at his side.

His father's head had been carved open by some drunken soldier's blade. They'd showed Rafe his brain, telling him not to fear, that this is what they all were made of, and a Davin didn't flinch from the truth inside.

The soldier had seen their cloaks and mistaken them for an army. His father spoke words that had no business standing together.

Rafe hadn't run then.

Surely he hadn't grown *less* brave in twenty years.

We will carry you along with us, Gran had told his father at the end, *until you're strong enough to go.*

And Rafe had said it, too, and believed himself.

"Hello," said Rafe, his heart thudding as he approached the side of the dying woman's bed.

Thinking of Graven Jacks' words, he forced his hand out.

She clasped it. Her grip was both desperate and weak.

"You're not alone," he said, looking back at her eyes.

She looked dubious.

He couldn't manage all that talk about carrying her with him. They were strangers, and the words wouldn't come.

"Let me tell you a story," he said instead.

At this, her forehead smoothed.

Rafe had no idea what he'd say next. But the story he'd pasted up on the wall of Mrs. Dallow's Cut-Rate Boarding House came to mind, about his childhood adventures on a pirate ship.

Feeling absurd, he closed his eyes and let the words come. He didn't need many of them, in the end.

After sundown, Rafe was chewing slowly, staring into a shifting field of his own exhaustion, when Graven Jacks came back to the table, a bottle of whiskey in his paw. "Here," he shouted, "and no more apologies from you!"

The woman across the table was shaking so badly that Jacks had to pull out the cork for her. "But I *am* sorry," she grumbled after she'd gotten a few slugs down. "People dying all around, and these are my priorities." She noticed Rafe staring, and held out the bottle.

He considered it.

Finally he shook his head. "Too bitter for my taste."

"Cut yourself some fucking *slack*, Chuck," shouted Jacks, waving away the bottle from the woman. "You've a sickness, not some moral fucking failing! I mean, hell, I don't know you, maybe you've got both. But in a city like the one we've been living in, I've never seen the point in blame. Am I to be hung for murder, when I was paid to kill? You steadied your fucking hands, Chuck, now work your hardest, and have your little slap-fight with your personal demons when there's solid ground underfoot."

Rafe waited until Jacks' cloud of bluster had blown on. "Easy for him to say," he muttered.

"Sure is." She'd nestled the bottle between her feet and was staring at it guiltily.

"Rafe Davin."

"Rainer Mory." She didn't look up.

The urge to tell her more nearly drove him from his seat. But everyone here seemed to be confiding in a stranger. Rafe leaned forward on his elbows, shoving his bowl away.

"I was a junkie before this," he said, tapping his neck. "A tlak addict. Then I—I took a fall. Down below, I couldn't get any for a time, and—well, now I'm clean." He glanced around, unsure who it was he thought might be listening. He left the freaks out of it, just in case. "But it wasn't by choice. It's like I was—like I was enchanted. Like someone *took* it from me. It doesn't feel like anything I deserve."

"You know how lucky you are?"

Thirsty as she'd been, he'd expected Rainer to understand, not hand him platitudes. "Lucky," he muttered, "would have been if I'd *asked* for it." He started to go.

"No, no. I don't mean that." She drank, then corked the bottle, leaning forward herself. "You really haven't heard?"

"Heard—what?"

"About Left-Handed Luce."

Rafe gripped the edge of the table.

Loxia Lydus slid in next to them, setting down her bowl. "The name on everyone's lips," she said, raising her eyebrows.

"I haven't heard." Rafe was finding it hard to breathe. "What happened?"

Rainer shied away now that Loxia was here. "The word is," said Loxia, "all this mess was triggered by the Assemblage. The sweet-necks went on a killing spree." She broke her bread and dipped it into her bowl. "Their leader, some junkie who styled herself Left-Handed Luce, had promised them a lifetime supply of tlak if they slaughtered a bunch of elderly folk from a hospice."

"Elderly folk? Ha! I heard it was a sack of forty-nine babies, snatched from a nursery." Jacks tossed a loaf of fresh-baked bread onto the table and sat before a second bowl.

"Whoever it was," said Loxia, "it brought on the little quake. And the guards lost control after that, and clamped down hard enough to cause the big one."

"And the *big* quake," said Jacks with a grin, "collapsed the fucking God-Gland, didn't it?"

Rafe laughed out loud, too horrified not to. "You mean—"

"The only known source of tlak, in Eth or beyond," said Loxia, holding her hand out for the bottle of whiskey, "is now buried under a city's worth of rubble, thanks to Luce."

"See what I mean?" said Rainer Mory, smiling a little. "You got out at the right time."

"Loxia," said Rafe.

Amusement had blown right through him. He was shivering now.

"Hm?" She passed the bottle back to Rainer.

"Did you—happen to hear what became of her?"

"Luce?" She nodded. "Her gang took control of Crunkshank Gallery just before the big quake hit. They were set on taking a run at the Guvnor. Then her followers got the news about the God-Gland."

"Carved their leader up like a side of beef," said Jacks, waving a meaty spoonful of stew. "She's strung up there now, I hear."

The table moved on, and Loxia scooted closer. "Question for you."

"All right."

"Met a kid yesterday. Crosswise girl, younger than you, looking for razors and feeling pretty scared to be so—out in the open about it, all the sudden. All I told her was that I might know someone she could talk to, if she wanted. But I didn't say who, because I never asked how out in the open *you* want to be."

"As far as it gets."

His cheeks were hot. The words surprised him.

But Loxia just nodded. "I'll send her your way, then."

Rafe sat, skin buzzing, and watched a number of smaller decisions ripple out from that one.

He knew what he was about to do, but had to work through convincing himself regardless.

Then, when he couldn't ignore it any longer, he turned. "Jacks."

The big man looked irritable at being interrupted midway through a gory description, then saw Rafe's expression. "What's on your mind, Chuck?"

"I'll need your help." He gripped Jacks' shoulder, standing. "To bury our dead."

Jacks nodded. "Quite a few of 'em by now. Be good for morale, no question. I'll gather up some diggers."

"I'll handle the rites," said Rafe.

Rainer looked surprised.

"I don't look the part, I know. But I come from a— religious family, you could say." Rafe made a stack of bowls, and more started coming down the table at him.

He set a fistful of spoons in the top bowl on the stack and lifted the lot. "Jacks, in the morning, when the diggers are all organized, let's carry a stretcher over to Crunkshank Gallery."

"Chuck?" Jacks looked confused.

"Left-Handed Luce," said Rafe, "is one of mine."

Rainer went down to the creek once more while Jacks dug holes with the rest. Everyone was sweaty from hauling bodies and swinging shovels in the sun, but they left the pails of water alone, watching Rafe work with a wary admiration. What he was doing—undressing the dead, bathing their bodies, whispering to them about their lives, even when he didn't know them—must have looked, to them, like a sort of magic.

He could even see it in Jacks' eyes when the big man looked his way. For all the death in his life, he had no intimacy with it. For centuries, Ethians had relied on clans like the Davins to stand as their intermediaries, leaning on a ludicrous superstition about the malice of the unquiet dead.

The dead will eat your luck. The dead will give you gout. The dead will smother you in your sleep.

The dead, Rafe thought, dipping his hands in cold water, could care less about the living.

Even still, what he'd told his mother—that the Davins were preying on the superstitions of suckers—no longer felt quite right.

This business of quieting the dead wasn't an outright lie. It was a useful fiction.

He was quieting *someone* as he washed this stranger's feet.

It just wasn't the corpse.

It was Rafe himself.

And that, in turn, was calming all the people watching, who had, for reasons unimaginable outside of this catastrophe, put their trust in him.

He finished washing the body of this young man, and leaned in, his lips next to its ear.

"Sleep well, love."

It was a daft thing to whisper. But when he stood, he could feel that the attention around him had tightened, as it did every time he spoke to one of the dead.

Carrying the strange weight of their respect, he came to the end of this long line of bodies, now prepared for burial according to the methods he'd been taught by his mother and grandmother.

Only a single corpse remained.

He'd saved Jassa for last, hoping exhaustion might make it easier.

Rafe and Graven Jacks had met the keeper of the Gallery that morning, just past dawn, trekking through streets that the quake had rendered into peaks and valleys, some of them shifting at the merest footfall. The Gallery itself still stood near the back of an unshaken peninsula clinging to the northern wall, its high marble columns a testament to the city's one-time commitment to architectural stability. The keeper, a young woman with very long hair, had been relieved to hear what they'd come for. "These others are *kings*," she said, pointing at various blotches on the walls.

"I'd have had to throw her out on the street! By the rules, you know, not out of callousness."

Rafe and Jacks stood for a while, staring up at the shelves. They'd only have been allowed in Crunkshank Gallery on a Feast Day, otherwise, or as part of a heavily guarded train after a coronation. This was Rafe's first glimpse of the story of Eth, told in bodily leavings—the solemnity of its ancient crypts overwritten, in the past few centuries, by a proud display of butchery. A row of crowned heads, devoid of their bodies and rotting to dust, stood above a skeleton reordered so that its skull was lodged in its pelvis. Rafe spotted a tangle of dried intestines, which the keeper confirmed as belonging to Malachi the Emperazor, strung over a chandelier of mummified hands, each boasting at least one gaudy ring. "Your friend here's simply out of place," said the keeper, still sounding worried about it. "She *did* rule, on a technicality, for a moment or two—but there were none of the necessary rituals performed, just a riot of drugs and gambling before the second quake hit. And then, when her—*disciples* heard the news about their drug supply, they—well, I guess you can see well enough for yourself."

"Cut her down," said Rafe, and Jacks had complied.

Now she was lying in the open field, far from the broken wall of Eth, near to the edge of the wood, her body a pincushion for daggers. In place of her eyes stood a pair of dice that had rattled in her sockets as they'd carried her, blanketed and secured to a homespun stretcher, out to her resting place.

The digging was done. The others crowded as close as they dared. Rafe tugged out the blades, one by one, noting how the people around him flinched every time, showing her corpse a compassion he doubted they'd have felt if she was still alive.

It was almost time for the ceremony. He'd meant to invent a new one, but there was precious little left in his mind.

He'd use Clan Davin's framework, then. It was as good as any. Better than the Devourers saying grace, at any rate.

Rafe washed the daggers clean. The bucket's water gone red, he waved for Rainer to switch it out, and she did so with a woozy solemnity that seemed somehow appropriate. The blades themselves would be buried with Jassa's body—by the customs of his clan, whatever killed a person became part of their flesh. Then, when the corpses were dug up again, all this would be cast aside, and their bones scrubbed, before their second burial. Only then would they be proclaimed quiet.

On second thought, maybe he'd skip the second burial. He was the last living Davin, after all, and it wasn't as if any-one else would miss it.

Rainer brought a fresh pail. Rafe set his jaw, peeling off the leather clothes Jassa had been wearing since the tree-house, stuck to her body now.

He'd never seen her naked before. Jassa had hated to be touched, though she never seemed to mind doing the touching.

For the purposes of preparing his ceremony, he tried to stop thinking ill of her as he dipped his hands in fresh water and washed her feet.

Then he fished the dice from her sockets, and placed them in the pocket of her shirt, to be burnt. He rinsed her face, not that it did much good, then leaned close to her ear.

"Let's hope there are no Aces or Deuces where you're going," he whispered.

He stood, and the others looked at him with heavy expectancy. Graven Jacks was leaning on a shovel, standing before a voluminous grave, big enough to bury the entire row of bodies. Beside him was Layna, the crosswise girl Loxia had sent him, watching Rafe with a kind of hilarious awe, as if his proximity to these mangled corpses was both a brilliant joke and an act of heroism.

Rafe cleared his throat, feeling like a child playing a god in a Feast Day performance.

"I speak for Jassa Lowroller," he started, hating his high-pitched voice.

He wished he had Gingerbeard's comfort with language.

He might as well just borrow their phrasing. They'd hardly mind.

"You never know what's to come in another person's story, any more than you know the end of your own. Had she lived, Jassa might not have done any good, the way things were going. But she might have done—better than this."

He looked at the shattered body of Eth. With the wall down, stories were circulating of eggs with seven yolks, of trees in the wood turning wobbly and pink, like giant lungs. The catacombs had collapsed, and the streets were such a mess he couldn't imagine how they'd ever be set to rights. Making a home here was madness—but no one had seen a guard in days, and so here they stood, surer with every hour that all this mess was some kind of beginning.

"It might seem odd to bring her out here, among all of these people who died because of what she started. But my family believed that saying what you know of a person soothes them on their way out of this world. Quiets them down, so they won't disturb any of us. And that the dead folk around them will follow the quiet one.

"So we'll give it a try. What do I know of Jassa?"

What *did* he know?

That she shot her snot out of her nose like a rocket, even indoors?

That she'd steal the cake from your plate if you so much as turned your head?

"She had six sisters," he said, "and all of them served on the killing fields, and died there."

That played well enough. Graven Jacks grunted, thumping a fist on his chest, and a number of others followed suit.

"She loved to win, and would stop at nothing to do it."

More of them nodded.

"And she loved to tell stories. Repeatedly, and with an— with an ever-changing variety of details."

That was all he had, if he was keeping things neutral. He looked down at Jassa.

She was grinning up at him, her face a skinless mask of muscle and clotted blood.

Knowing the Assemblage, he doubted she'd been dead at the time.

"My family taught me, too, to begin every burial with these words, which my mother said were true of everyone who lives long enough to walk and talk—from the most honorable person lying here, down to the very worst."

He closed his eyes and touched his chest.

"'How they tried,'" said Rafe. "'How long, how hard they tried.'"

—Gone Away—

Turning from the open door, from the ringing sound of seven infants screaming, Ashlan ran from the city of her birth.

She ran with the century-old child pressed to her chest, her grip the only thing keeping his insides in, her blood on his burlap the only thing keeping him wheezing.

She ran from the chamber where she'd found him smashed on the floor, the seams of his belly burst by a fallen stone, his button eyes still staring up at the locked metal door that kept his giant brother in, just barely able to whisper, *I only wanted to see his face.*

She ran from the dark tunnels where she'd wandered without food or water, growing wilder as she rammed blindly against walls, fell cursing down pits. She ran as her body's fluids slowed and stopped, as she healed again and again, reviving her organs until she'd summoned a second skin of pain, a full-body migraine that made every step an agony.

She ran from her hunger, from the things that it wanted, which never left her, and never would.

Still she ran, from the overturned streets of Eth, which finally looked as it did in her dreams—hemorrhaged, tumbled, choked with the dead and the living.

Ashlan ran, and would keep on running.

From the people in their tents at the outskirts of town.

From the shining sun and the promises it would break at dusk.

From all that Eth had been and would be, into the wood, where her mother had gone before her.

Elil Ley, stripping leaves from green branches, talking for days without pause, crashing through the forest as she searched for someone who wasn't there.

Just as Ashlan had, every time her life outgrew its pot.

Slaughtered at the Uni? Come to the wood.

Lost another lover? Come to the wood.

Money all spent? Come to the wood.

To the wood, where she'd go wild like her mother, praying to her mother's nameless god. A god who was always just about to save her from her mess, her pain, her appetite.

"Always *about* to," she spat, for she'd been talking a while now, rapidly, heatedly, "but He never quite does it. Always on the edge, never over. Until the edge pulls away and it all starts up again."

Ashlan stopped, staring at a shaft of light that fell through the leaves, striking a heart-shaped rock riven by the roots of a lightning-struck tree.

"Been here before," she murmured. "Been *everywhere* before. That's the problem, isn't it? Always repeating. Never changing."

"But your blood," rasped Hollis, "might have changed any number of things."

Ashlan startled. The heat came roaring out of her bones, reviving her heart, which started up at double-time.

She'd forgotten he was even here, though his body was tucked under her tunic, pressed close to the bare skin of her breast.

"Those people," he said. "All the wounded of Eth. You could've healed them."

"You want me to go *back*?" She shook her head, incredulous. "What is this, a change of heart? You want to make things *better* before you go?" She looked back, noticing how deep they'd already come, how far away the city was.

He was right. She was a healer.

She knew it as surely as she knew that no force could make her return.

"No," said Hollis, chuckling weakly. "Not my style. I only mean that you're *not* repeating yourself, Ashlan Ley. In your tale of the last disaster, you fed the multitudes with your blood, like a noble fool. Yet here we are."

"Well, I'm done caring," she said.

But her body ached to let its blood, to pour it again over his torn skin, to give him just a little more life.

And why?

Because she *cared* for him?

Because he was, what, her *son*?

She let out an ugly, snorting laugh as she dashed around the shaft of sunlight, into the trees again.

"I mean, what's the point," she said, dodging branches, trying to avoid anything that looked like a path, because there might be other people out here, too, survivors trying to find their way to wherever else, and she wanted only to be alone. "So the Ethians heal up, build themselves something worth living in out of the rubble? Doesn't matter. Somebody's going to take it right out of their hands. Some new faction, some other kingdom. In a matter of days."

"Even with the guts of the Gone-Away buried?" Hollis said. "Isn't that what everyone's been fighting over all this while? The power beneath the streets?"

"You could crush it to dust and bury it under *three* cities. Somebody's going to find a way to boil it down and strain it out."

But that had nothing to do with her running. This wasn't about the heartbreak of her disillusionment. She'd been an idealist once, but that was long ago.

What lay behind that heavy metal door, though—that haunted her.

It had been shut and bolted. She'd checked it, and checked it again.

And still she couldn't scrub the thought from her mind— that the Kin of Man would get out, sooner or later, and come bursting through the streets, churning through any citizens whose hearts harbored secret ambitions.

He'd slaughter them for their thoughts.

And he was full of her. *Made* of her.

But this was a lie, too, she thought, filling with sourness as she'd filled with heat. It wasn't what she was running from.

It was just another mask laid on top of the truth.

Fuck, but she was hungry.

Ashlan ran faster, branches scoring her skin.

"So you're escaping the cruel and repetitive cycles of history," said Hollis, sounding dubious. "But where to, Ashlan Ley? Where are you taking me?"

"I don't know," she snapped, startling a deer up ahead, which bounded wisely away. "Would you rather die alone, Runt? In the dark, where I found you? I could always dig you another hole! I've got nothing but time."

His little body gripped her.

He was afraid, and she was afraid, too.

It didn't seem right, that he should be the one to die. All he wanted to do was live, and she'd have given anything to trade places with him.

The urge ripped through her again. Her headache made her want to scream. Soon she'd have to stop and set a trap, or else—

She was running.

Her mouth kept going, spittle flying.

She barely knew what she was saying. She hated herself for saying it.

Hollis had stopped interjecting. She gashed her palm on a sharp rock and bathed him with her blood, peeling him back from her skin to get at his insides. He roused, a little, but she could tell he was fading.

"Hang in there, Runt," she muttered. "Stay with me."

"Why," he whispered, "is that so important to you?"

"It's just—"

But she didn't know.

All this time, she'd been trying to keep him safe. Or else she'd been chasing his gold, a treasure that never existed. All in order to die, and she couldn't, now.

Was that all this return to the wood was? Some manic echo of her former quest?

Did she long to stop living so badly that she couldn't see the hope was gone? Or was she simply her mother's daughter, an echo of the madness of Elil Ley, looking for the cure to a sickness of the mind, an ailment that couldn't name itself?

Ashlan turned, ready to run again, at random, forever.

That's when she saw the hand.

It hung three feet above the earth, its skin black and shining, its wrist atop a band of spores that snaked across a carpet of fallen leaves. Its palm was flat, perpendicular to the earth.

Stop.

"Tanka."

Ashlan wasn't sure whether to be irritated or relieved.

But whatever she'd been running from, or running toward, she wasn't any more. She'd felt unseen before, except to Hollis, who was so close to death he barely counted as a witness. Now, shamed by this phantom sign of Tanka's watchfulness, Ashlan packed all her wildness, all her weakness, away—as she'd done dozens of times before, as she would again, and again, so long as the world went on around her. She sat down heavily, no longer talking, just feeling the pain of all that unfed healing in her body and rocking, ever so slightly, over the cool weight on her chest.

In time the bear came shuffling through the forest, a roast bird dangling from its claw. Ashlan snatched it with one bloody hand, ripping through its meat, spitting out the bones. Only after its flesh was gone did she notice the thing had been salted and spiced.

"Thanks," she murmured, belching.

Umber looked down with sunken, glassy eyes and beckoned her.

She followed after the loose swing of its fur, feeling guilty for feeling better.

There was no point in running now. If Tanka wanted her to dance, she'd dance, whether she resisted or not.

Squirrels and birds burst from the wood before the bear's lumbering step. It led her to a hill encircled with trees, its grassy face inscribed with a subtle pattern of shining black rings.

"Is it alive?" came a lilting voice from above. "The talking doll?"

Tanka lay on her side in the boughs of a sparse-limbed tree, her fingers playing cat's-cradle with a floating skein of blackness. The branches around her were laden with the substance of the gazing-tree in patterns no less complex than those on the ground, though whether all this was play or incantation Ashlan couldn't say.

Then again, she thought, glancing at the painting that hung from Umber's ribs as the bear dragged the silver-buckled chest onto the hilltop, that distinction might be meaningless where Tanka's magic was concerned.

"Yeah." Ashlan folded her arms around Hollis' body. "He's alive."

"Tanka Equinox, I didn't know you cared," he whispered, turning his head as far as he could.

"Things have changed," said Tanka softly, swinging a loop of spores around the branch and lowering herself slowly onto the earth. "For all of us, I suspect."

"Sure," said Ashlan. "Jassa sold us out, probably to get the Puppeteer out of her way. That part worked. But Rafe is probably dead. And Runt never had any gold to begin with. Oh, and I'm the one who made him."

"I realized this some time ago."

"Of course you did."

"'Weak rune-work.' Your irritation spoke volumes."

Ashlan sighed. "So how was your week?"

"Similarly tumultuous." Tanka gestured to Umber. Scrabbling at the sides of the silver-buckled trunk, it began to rummage inside. "I spent some time at the University, doing a bit of research. What I found was—unexpected."

"What does that mean, Tanka?"

"That we should not be too hard on your talking doll," said Tanka, smiling bitterly, "for we'd have been disappointed regardless of its pocketbook. Both of us, Lady Ley." She strode to the hilltop. "I'd only just gotten the bad news when the quakes began. I wasn't surprised when none of you materialized at the boarding house, given the rumors of Jassa's sudden rise. I spent days there all the same, witnessing both carnage and kindness. Yet however deeply I dabbled with human company, I still ended up withdrawing, without finding any true connection. I began to doubt—well, that

I might ever find a suitable father for my child. But perhaps my thinking in that direction was influenced by my research."

The bear lifted a rubbery curtain of nerves from a sack of black silk, holding it up for inspection. "Yes, Umber dear, that's perfect." With help, she draped the curtain over her shoulders and sat, cross-legged, at the center of the pattern of spores.

"What are we talking about, Tanka? What is all this?"

It looked like another trap. But Tanka seemed to be ensnaring *herself* in it this time.

"I was wrong again, Lady Ley," said Tanka, adjusting the white, rubbery shawl on her collarbone. "I believed that I understood what you are. But where I had envisioned you as one of many—an immortal child of an immortal, raised as a foundling by human parents—what I have learned is far stranger.

"There's only you, Lady Ley. And you cannot die, not if you had all the resources in the kingdom at your disposal. And I cannot give birth, at least not with *your* body as my guide—for you are as infertile as you are invulnerable. Yet you possess a curious flexibility on both counts, and so I propose that we join together all the same."

She smiled, though it was laced with melancholy. "Let us almost get what we want, you and I."

Ashlan's urge to run had returned, redoubled.

"I don't have a clue what you're talking about."

"Of course you do," Tanka said, rolling her head back. "You always have. But your obstinacy, Lady Ley, is the stuff of actual legend."

The pattern of shining black lines surged up from the earth, soaking her shawl of nerves until it was black as jet.

"What was your name when you were born?" Tanka said, shivering as she lowered her chin.

"Just—Ashlan Ley. My mother didn't believe in middle names. Enough trouble coming up with all seven, she said."

"Untrue. According to the Ethian rosters, the first-born of Elil Ley's only brood was named Hempstead."

"Imagine being saddled with *that*," whispered Hollis.

The fear was no less powerful for being utterly formless.

"Fuck this," Ashlan muttered, and started to run.

Only to find her ankles ensnared by loops of spore-stuff. She thudded to her knees.

"Hempstead Ley was born completely identical to his brothers," called Tanka, shuddering as the nerves tightened around her, beginning to pulse. Her skin was flushed, pink and shining. "But one week later, his name was changed to Ashlan—and he was no longer the same. He was *you*, Lady Ley. I propose the following theory."

What's out there? Ashlan had asked. *Why are you always out walking in the wood?*

I'm not well, Elil Ley said. *Anyone can see that. But there's someone you can meet, sometimes. Someone who can heal any wound, any disease, anything at all. And even when you can't see* them, *you can feel* them. *Like an echo, Ash. Like a ripple.*

"That Hempstead's mother was the last of a long line of temple-keepers.

"That she was—uniquely suited to hear the call of the Gone-Away goddess her family served.

"That she took her infant to a being deep in the wood.

"That this being," said Tanka, raising a trembling hand to pluck at the pulsing nerves, arranging them on her chest, "was the avatar of Gen the Reviver—come to the end of a long century of life, ready to die and be born again.

"Your mother heard the call.

"*Your* call."

Ashlan tried to move, to *crawl* into the wood if she had to, away from the rest of this.

The black spores tugged her back, their slender shapes strong as iron.

"Oh, settle down, Ashlan Ley," said Hollis, hanging under her like a sloth. "It's not as if she'll let you *go*.—I'm confused, Tanka Equinox. Aren't the Gone-Away *dead*?"

"They are, yes," said Tanka. "But living parts remain. Such as the gazing-trees," she said, gesturing all around them, "once the belongings of Gone-Away Nex, the Connector. Lady Ley, in any incarnation, is like a gazing-tree in human form. An avatar, if you will—a fragment of Gone-Away Gen."

"So Ashlan's mother," wheezed Hollis, "met this avatar, and her baby boy was—transformed?"

"Eaten," said Tanka.

Ashlan ripped at the black loops writhing around her wrists, hard enough to pull off her hands.

But they let her go.

Then seized her up again.

"The brood," Hollis gasped. "*That's* why you ran!"

They'd passed a house on the city's edge where a tall, gaunt man, mistaking Hollis for the world's ugliest child, had invited them to share his shelter. Tempted by the smell of food, Ashlan had glimpsed his wife sitting on a dusty blanket, surrounded by their seven newborn babies.

Their fingers and toes so tiny, so impossibly fragile.

She could almost feel them bursting between her teeth.

It was hunger that had sent her running, a bottomless void that she'd spent a century trying to forget.

Who needs seven? its voice always whispered. *Would life really be harder with six?*

No one could stop you if you tried.

"Okay," she said, laughing desperately, her mouth watering even now. "You got me. I'm a monster."

"You are a living fragment of divinity," said Tanka. "Monstrosity is a concept that simply doesn't apply."

Ashlan looked up as Tanka pulled the darkened veins from her skin. Shining with sweat, she rose, her breasts impossibly swollen.

She'd given herself milk.

"The temple-keepers once viewed it as a great honor to give their first-born to the Shard of Gen. The child did not die, after all—it joined with the avatar, and became her." She passed the blanching shawl back to Umber, who packed it carefully away. "According to the legends, each incarnation will live a hundred years, then reach the end of her natural span. By then, she desires nothing but to devour a human infant and be reborn."

Ashlan remembered it happening.

She'd gotten drunk the night before, and woken to hear a baby crying.

You've finally lost it, she'd thought. Not long after, she'd gone away.

"The child lives on, and so does Gen, each folded into one another—though the avatar remembers nothing of what she was.

"It was the temple's job to raise you, you see. But the temples fell, Lady Ley. And without the truth, you've—struggled."

"That's one way to put it," whispered Hollis.

Tanka climbed down the hill and stood before her. "You are no monster, Lady Ley. But you've been fighting your nature for a full century. So long as you keep fleeing, you'll never find rest. Aren't you *tired*?"

"You know I am." Ashlan gripped the black reins, testing their hold. Tanka flicked her wrist, and they slackened. "But I'm not doing it," Ashlan said, struggling to her feet. "I'm not stealing someone's baby."

Tanka laughed. "You don't have to! You devised your own solution, just before your will to live ran out. Out of instinct, I suppose." Tanka looked down at Hollis. "Though it seems you barely understood what you were doing at the time."

Hollis gave a grunt. "Surely you don't mean—"

Tanka pulled a torn sheet of parchment from a pocket, unfolding it. "The language is tricky, here, as it always is in Ancient Ethian. *Once a century, the Shard of Gen must devour an infant to live again.* Now, *infant* is one possible translation, but I would call it—oversimplified. The actual phrase is closer to *a child given life who has not yet grown.*"

"Oh, you *would*," muttered Hollis.

Umber was pulling something from the trunk.

A handmade quilt.

Ashlan pulled away.

And stepped backward, her legs freed.

Tanka had twisted her fingers, and the threads of the gazing-tree were now pouring into the silver-buckled trunk, and all around it.

Into the shape of a wheeled black cradle.

"I won't force you, Lady Ley," said Tanka. "But you have a chance to die and live at once. And I will raise the babe you become—as my own."

"But it'll all be the same," said Ashlan. "I won't know it, that's all. But even if I start again, it'll all be exactly the same."

"Oh, I doubt that," said Tanka, giving her a stern look. "Any child of mine would have better sense than *this*. At the very least, Lady Ley, you would grow up shaped by the knowledge of what you are—in place of this yoke of shame."

Something in Ashlan broke.

The heat came rushing out, healing the gash on her wrist, bringing her skin to the boil.

Beneath it, the hunger swelled.

She wanted devoutly to die. She'd been careening towards it for a hundred years, for any number of reasons. And this might not be death, exactly, but she wouldn't know any better.

It would be the end of *her*. And the only cost she could see was the brief knowledge that she'd be stuck with Hollis Runt forever.

Which, now that she thought of it, had been true all along.

He rolled his head up, his scuffed buttons regarding her with disgust. "Of all the reasons to create a life, Ashlan Ley, this is, by far, the worst."

"At least you'll get your wish," she muttered, peeling back her tunic.

"How's that?"

She pulled his body away from hers, and decided not to bother undressing him, for fear that he'd simply collapse.

"You wanted to destroy your creator, didn't you?"

"Bah." He pursed his lips. "A technicality, at best."

She shrugged. "Looks like we all have to compromise, Runt."

Umber had finished making the bed. Tanka cleared her throat, one hand at the front of her dress, where her milk had soaked through the fabric. There was sadness in her, and a touch of panic. "Have you two come to a decision, then?"

"I mean, fuck it." Ashlan sighed, with finality. "I can always eat."

Her jaw came unhinged, both sides at once, with a startling double-pop.

With the barest yelp of protest, the tiny, broken body of Hollis Runt slid down her distended craw, boots and all.

Then, bathed in a sweat whose beads boiled as they emerged, Ashlan's body shuddered. Her arms slowed as they fell, and through the lattice of her bloody fingers she saw the sudden swelling of her belly, watching as the skin blistered and peeled. Below, the flesh was gray and shifting, like muscular stone, or living ash.

Then her round, stony stomach burst in a wave of heat and brightness, just as Tanka approached.

There was sadness in her stride. What she'd sought, after all, was to be the *creator* of a new life, not its steward. But with every step, she seemed more possessed by a sudden, trembling certainty—and as she reached into the other-worldly forge of Ashlan's womb, she, too, was renewed.

As for Ashlan, she could see no more, because her eyes were sizzling into streams of liquid rock. But her hearing persisted a moment longer—and as it went, she could hear the cry of the child she'd become, righteous and aggrieved, with lungs strong enough to shiver every leaf in her mother's wood.

© Bill Wright

Gabriel Squailia is an author and professional DJ from Rochester, New York. An alum of the Friends World Program, they studied storytelling and literature in India, Europe, and the Middle East before settling in the Berkshires of western Massachusetts with their partner and daughter. Squailia's first novel, *Dead Boys*, was published by Talos Press in 2015.

D.J. MaCHALE

razOr
bill

An Imprint of Penguin Group (USA)

A division of Penguin Young Readers Group
Published by the Penguin Group
Penguin Group (USA) LLC
345 Hudson Street
New York, New York 10014

USA / Canada / UK / Ireland / Australia / New Zealand / India / South Africa / China
Penguin.com
A Penguin Random House Company

ISBN: 978-1-59514-666-3

Printed in the United States of America

9 10 8

*For all the wonderful teachers, administrators,
and staff at Grand View Elementary School
in Manhattan Beach, California.*

FOREWORD

I love to travel.

Doesn't everybody?

Besides getting a break from the regular old routine, traveling is like going to school. In a good way, I mean. In school you are constantly exposed to new information, shown different ways of thinking, and introduced to people and places that you wouldn't ordinarily come across. I would love to go back to school for a while. Seriously. As long I could skip the tests and sleep late. But since that isn't likely, I'll stick to traveling.

Like most writers I enjoy exploring unique places and talking with people who have lives that are totally different than mine. You never know what you might discover. I was once in Venice, Italy, where I met a guy who said, "If you come across small alleyways that look dark and forbidding . . . walk in. That's where you'll find the hidden treasures." I thought that was great advice. (At least in Venice. I'm not so sure it's wise to go down small, dark alleys just anywhere.) His point was that it's important to be open to new experiences and to always look beyond the superficial. That's where the adventure lies.

As a writer it's critical to explore those dark alleys, and the sunny streets, and everywhere else in between.

Young (and not so young) writers often ask me for writing advice. My number one suggestion for them is to write about things that they know. When you write about the people and places and emotions and conflicts you're familiar with, you will be writing with authority and readers will respond. The bottom line is that the more you know, the more you'll have at your disposal to write about. That's one of the reasons I love to travel. I am intrigued and inspired by the places I've been to. Inevitably, they end up playing a role in my books.

It was while sitting on a remote beach in Hawaii shooting my TV show *Flight 29 Down* that I came up with the idea for the tropical island of Ibara in *The Pilgrims of Rayne*. A trip to Rome sparked the idea that brought Marsh and Cooper to the Coliseum in the Morpheus Road trilogy. The climax of *The Black* took place in New York City's Grand Central Terminal . . . a place I have been through thousands of times. The abandoned subway station where Bobby Pendragon first entered the flume in *The Merchant of Death* was inspired by an empty subway station that I passed through on the train every day on my way to college classes. I can still remember straining to catch fleeting glimpses of the dark, forgotten platform and imagining what real-life stories might have unfolded there.

Images like those are constantly being gathered up and stored in the hard drive of my memory, waiting patiently for me to come calling in search of ideas.

Like *SYLO*.

When I was in college my friends and I would take road trips from our hometown in Connecticut to an island off the coast of Massachusetts called Martha's Vineyard. I'm sure many of you have been there. Those who haven't might know it because it was where the movie *Jaws* was filmed. "The Vineyard" (as they call it) is a timeless throwback to a simpler time. I hadn't been there since 1985 and it's not an exaggeration to say than when I visited last year I found that it hadn't changed a bit. I half expected to find the can of Coke I'd left on a fence near the beach in Menemsha twenty-five years earlier.

Okay, maybe that's a little bit of an exaggeration but there was something comforting about visiting a place that has held true to its time-honored traditions in spite of the chaotic changes that have swirled around it. It was like a secluded oasis, stuck in time.

It was perfect . . .

. . . and the perfect setting for a story about ordinary people fighting for their lives while friends are dropping dead all around them on an isolated island that is suddenly invaded by a mysterious, deadly force.

Hey, what did you expect? You didn't think I was going to write a story about some old farts rocking on a porch by the seashore sipping tea, did you? Give me a break.

A new adventure is about to begin and I'm thrilled that you'll be joining me. Before heading for the island, I'd like to acknowledge some of the people who have helped bring this book to you.

This is the first book I'm publishing with Razorbill, and I couldn't be happier about it. The team there has been wonderful from the get-go. Especially my editor, Laura Arnold. Laura embraced the *SYLO* story as if it were her own and has been its constant champion. She put an incredible effort into wringing the best out of every last word . . . and out of me. Her insight and talent show on every page AND . . . she did it all while pregnant, no less. Amazing. I've told her how much I appreciate her work a million times so this isn't news to her, but it's always nice for readers to know who deserves a boatload of credit. Thanks to her and to everyone at Razorbill.

Big thanks go to my personal team of Richard Curtis, Peter Nelson, and Mark Wetzstein. They have been with me through good times and not-so-good-times. I'm very fortunate to have those guys helping me steer the ship. Or the dingy. Or whatever it is we've got. Thanks.

My wife Eve and daughter Keaton are the best support group anyone could ask for. Eve is still my first and best critic, while Keaton is now weighing in with her own opinions about my stories. I'm not sure if that's good or bad, but it's inevitable . . . and I couldn't be prouder.

Of course a lion's share of thanks must go to you, oh holder-of-this-book. Whether you've been with me since Bobby Pendragon first jumped into the flume or the only reason you picked this up was because you wanted to know what the heck "SYLO" means, I am sincerely grateful that you will be reading my story. I hope you like it.

I've made countless friends because of my books. I love answering your letters and corresponding online. Whenever I receive a note that begins, "You must be sick of reading letters like this . . ." I want to shout out, "No! Keep 'em coming!" (Sometimes I do.) Trust me, it's a great feeling to know that somebody has enjoyed one of my stories. Thank you.

Okay, housekeeping done. Time to kick this off.

It's an exciting moment when you begin to read a new series. You haven't met any of the characters yet. You don't know what they look like or if you're going to like them or hate them or root for them or hope they die an excruciatingly painful death. Right now you have no idea what kind of challenges they're going to face. Who will rise to the occasion? Who will crash and burn? Who knows the truth? Who has secrets?

Who will survive?

It's the same deal when you start to write a story. In the beginning you have no idea of what's going to happen. You just have to hold on and learn as you go. It's kind of like taking a trip . . . and I love to travel.

I hope you do too because we're about to begin another wild ride.

Hobey ho.

D.J. MacHale

ONE

It was the perfect night for a football game.

And for death.

Not that the two have anything in common. When you hear the term "sudden death," you normally don't expect there to be an actual loss of life, sudden or otherwise, but there was nothing normal about that night.

It was the night it began. The night of the death.

The first death.

I was sitting on the end of the team bench, more interested in the cheerleaders than the game. To be honest, I didn't have much business being on the team. There weren't many freshmen on the Arbortown High varsity, but with a student population that barely squeaked past two hundred, if you had two legs and didn't mind being brutally punished by guys who were older, bigger, and faster than you, you were in. I'm not exactly sure why I accepted the role of living tackling dummy, but I liked football and figured that in a few years I'd be the one running over hapless freshmen. So I guess I was paying my dues.

My main duty during a game was to be the sprinter on the kick-off team. That meant I had to run directly for the guy who fielded the kick . . . which made me the first to get taken out by the wall of blockers who were intent on stopping that very thing. It was an ugly job but at least it meant I'd come out of a game with a little dirt on my uniform.

My other duty was to be the backup for our senior tailback, Marty Wiggins. That's why I spent most of my time on the bench watching the cheerleaders. Marty was a legend. He'd had big-time colleges sniffing around him since he was a sophomore. He was that good.

But on that night, he was just sick.

The stands were packed. For Arbortown High that meant maybe five hundred people. It wasn't exactly the Rose Bowl but you wouldn't know that from the excitement Marty was generating. The place went nuts every time he got his hands on the ball because he was running over guys and knocking them aside like bowling pins. When he was tackled, which wasn't often, it took three players to drag him down. It was like watching a pro beating up on Pop Warner boys. He was in for most every play of the game until, with only a few minutes left, he dropped down next to me on the bench to take a rare breather.

He sat there gulping air, staring back at the field.

I figured his night was over so I held up my fist for a knuckle-bump and said, "Dude. Awesome."

Marty looked at me . . . and I froze.

He had a fiery, wild look in his eyes that made me think for one terrifying moment that he was going to hit me. The guy was totally charged up with . . . what? Excitement? Anger? Insanity? He didn't bump knuckles. Just as well, he might have broken my hand. I sat there like a fool with my fist hovering, un-bumped. I didn't want to say anything else for fear he'd drive his helmet through my face. Instead, he grabbed my forearm in a grip that was so fierce I had black-and-blue marks the next day.

"What's happening?" he whispered through gasping breaths.

He said it with a disturbing mix of fear and confusion that made me believe he truly didn't understand what was going on around him. Or with him.

"Uh . . . what do you mean?" I asked tentatively.

"Wiggins!" barked Coach.

Marty jumped to his feet and sprinted back into the game as if he had been launched from a catapult.

I was left on the bench, not knowing what had just happened.

The play was called and the team went to the line. Marty was pitched the ball and he rumbled around left end for another fifteen yards. All was well. Marty was fine. I chalked up his odd behavior to adrenaline and the excitement of the game and went back to my all-important cheerleader review.

Arbortown is a pretty small place, so going to a high school football game was the best thing to do on Friday nights in the fall. Okay, the *only* thing to do. As I scanned the crowd, I saw many people I knew, including my mother and father. Dad gave me a big smile and a thumbs-up. Mom wasn't as enthusiastic. She hated that I played football. Her deep frown meant she was expecting me to get injured just by sitting on the bench.

I gave them a small wave, then looked away . . . to notice a

3

strange face in the crowd. It belonged to a man with longish blond hair wearing a hoodie. He looked like a surfer dude, complete with beard stubble and a single earring. He stood out amid the sea of fans because he was the only one not cheering. Instead, he wrote furiously in a small notebook. I figured he might have been a college scout. It would explain why Marty was playing like he was possessed. This could be a scholarship showcase for him.

"Button up!" Coach ordered as he strode past. "We're going to score again."

That meant all the wretched scrubs, like me, had to be ready for another kickoff. We were on the ten yard line and about to go in. There were only a few seconds left in the game and I was surprised that, seeing it was a blowout, Coach hadn't pulled Marty. Maybe he knew there was a scout in the crowd taking notes. Or maybe he didn't trust Marty's backup—me.

I stood up with the rest of the team and cheered for the offense. It felt cheesy to be screaming for another score since the game had been over since halftime, but what can you do? It's football.

The team came up to the line, the QB called signals, and the ball was snapped. Marty took the handoff—no big surprise—and blasted into the line off right tackle. The defense had had enough. They didn't want any part of him. There were a few halfhearted arm tackles that didn't even slow him down as he burst into the end zone.

Touchdown.

The crowd exploded once again, cheering ecstatically while the band kicked in with our fight song, "Jericho." The cheerleaders jumped around and hugged each other like we'd just won a championship when all we'd done was add pad to an already lopsided score.

Marty sprinted to the back of the end zone, turned to the stands, threw his arms up in triumph . . .

. . . and dropped dead.

Of course, I didn't know that at the time. All I saw was Marty fall over and land on his back. At first I thought it was some new kind of celebration dance, like spiking himself instead of the ball. Our players were jumping on each other, chest-bumping and high-fiving. When they finally got around to focusing on the guy who was the cause of the celebration, they pulled on his arms to help him up . . . but Marty didn't respond.

In seconds the emotion of the moment flipped from elation to concern.

"Hey!" our guys yelled while waving to the sideline for help. "He's hurt!"

The crowd noise died instantly. It was a rude jolt to experience the sudden and dramatic change from joyous cheers and music to absolute silence.

Coach sprinted onto the field, waving at the other players to back away. He was quickly joined by a paramedic. With the rest of our offense huddled nearby, watching expectantly, the paramedic knelt down to examine Marty.

There was no doubt in anyone's mind that something serious had happened to our superstar. As he lay still on the grass, two more paramedics ran onto the field with a fracture board.

I turned around to look at my parents. Dad's expression now matched Mom's. They knew something horrible had happened. Everyone knew. A few seconds later we heard the urgent scream of a far-off siren.

I didn't look back to the field right away because I was mesmerized by the communal look of anxiety and horror on the faces of each and every person in the stands. All eyes were on the end zone and the guy who lay on his back, not moving.

People cleared a path for Marty's dad, who pushed his way through to get to the field. The poor guy was about to find out that his son had just gone from playing the game of his life to taking the final breath of his life.

Every last person feared that they were witnessing something horrific. Something they would never forget. Nobody moved as they waited for the news they knew wouldn't be good.

Almost nobody, that is. As I stared at the stands, I noticed that one person had already left. He hadn't even stuck around long enough for the ambulance to arrive.

The surfer dude with the notebook was gone.

It was the night of the death.

The first death.

And it was only the beginning.

TWO

I needed a midnight ride.

Gotta get out.

I sent the text to my best friend, Quinn Carr. He would know what it meant. It was a custom that Quinn and I had started shortly after we first met in middle school. Whenever one of us couldn't sleep, we'd sneak out of our houses and meet up with our bikes near the town pier at the end of Main Street. From there we'd saddle up, turn on our headlights, and race each other along the frontage road that circled Pemberwick Island, our home. We usually went after midnight, which meant there was little or no traffic to deal with, especially since we always took a remote route that traveled along the beach and away from civilization. It was ten miles of frantic insanity since most of the time it was too dark to see beyond the throw of our headlights and neither of us would bow to safety and slow down. A major crash might change that thinking, but neither of us had ever been thrown. So far.

Quinn came up with the idea. He said the rides would release endorphins into our systems that would shoot electrical impulses to the brain that helped reduce stress and create a feeling of well-being. Quinn was always coming up with things like that. I think he spent too much time watching Discovery Channel and reading Wikipedia. All I knew was that the rides were a perfect outlet for blowing off steam and working out problems . . . and that night I was definitely having a problem.

I couldn't stop thinking about Marty. How could somebody that young and in such great shape just . . . die? I lay in bed, only hours after the game, trying to keep my mind from replaying his final moments over and over, but it was no use. Sleep would not come.

I threw on my sweats, grabbed my helmet, and left my bedroom the only way possible at that hour of the night—through my window. My parents wouldn't have been too happy if they knew I was flying around the island in the middle of the night, so I quietly made my way across the roof over the porch and shinnied down a column to the ground. I kept my bike in the garage (which was separate from our house) so there was little chance of my parents hearing. I'd done it enough times that I had it down to a quiet science. Less than five minutes after I had sent the text to Quinn I was in the saddle and pedaling toward town.

It was long past midnight and Arbortown had shut down for the night. The restaurants closed by ten and the shops long before that. It was a tourist beach town, not an after-hours hangout. I rode straight to the town pier, where the ferryboat that made the five-mile run between Pemberwick Island and Portland, Maine, was tied up. It was a huge old thing that carried not only people, but trucks and cars as well. During the busy summer months, it was incredible to see the number of people and vehicles that would flood off that vessel. It was like watching one of those circus clown cars. I have no idea how it could handle so much weight and not sink. I'm sure Quinn knew. He'd have read it on Wikipedia.

At that hour the ferry and the pier were quiet. The ferry boat wouldn't be fired up again until five in the morning, when it would start making round trips to the mainland. I coasted to a stop at the head of the pier and pulled out my phone to see if Quinn had texted back, when . . .

"What took you so long?" came a familiar voice.

I spun around to see Quinn lying on a bench.

"No way!" I exclaimed. "I only texted you like ten minutes ago."

Quinn sat up, stretched, and rubbed his face.

"I've been here since midnight," he replied with a yawn.

"But . . ." I thought a moment, then said, "You knew I'd want to ride."

"It's amazing how insightful I can be."

"Did you hear what happened?"

"Seriously?" Quinn exclaimed sarcastically. "We live on an island, Tucker. News like that travels at the speed of heat. Besides, I was there."

"At the game? You hate football."

"True, but I wasn't going to miss you playing in your first varsity game. Not that there was much *playing* involved. But you did have some all-pro bench-sitting action going on."

"Give me a break. Most of those guys are three years older than me."

Quinn laughed. "I know. I think it's cool that you're even on the team. Crazy, but cool."

Quinn and I couldn't have been more different from each other and maybe that was why we got along so well. He was tall and thin like a lanky scarecrow with a wild mop of curly blond hair that rarely saw a brush. He wore heavy-framed glasses that sat on his big nose, making him look like he was wearing one of those Halloween glasses-and-nose combos, but it worked for him. It didn't hurt that he was incredibly smart—and enjoyed the fact that he stood out in a crowd. I, on the other hand, was more of the "blending in" type. I stood a good head shorter than Quinn and kept my brown hair cut short. I wouldn't consider myself particularly brainy, though I weighed in with a solid B-minus average in school. Not bad, in my book. Unfortunately my parents had a different book. I was tired of hearing: "Tucker Pierce, you are not living up to your potential." How did they know what my potential was? How could anybody know? It was a constant argument that often led to a midnight ride.

Quinn jammed his helmet down over his bushy hair and pulled down goggles over his glasses. He looked like a dork and couldn't have cared less.

"What do you think happened to Marty?" I asked.

Quinn shrugged. "We'll know more tomorrow."

"Why's that?"

"My parents are doing the autopsy as we speak."

The quiet night suddenly got quieter. I'd forgotten that Quinn's mom and dad were doctors at Arbortown Medical.

"Oh, right," I said softly. "Thanks for that image."

"Hey, you asked. Let's ride."

I did my best to shake the gruesome reality as we mounted up, flicked on our headlights, and pedaled out of town. Quinn and I rarely spoke during these ten-mile rides because the whole point was to push ourselves physically and mentally. It took serious concentration to keep from hitting a pothole or a patch of sand that would lead to a painful case of road rash, especially at the speed we were going, at night, with only a small light focused on the pavement ahead. The winding road was full of dips and turns, which meant we had to stay focused or end up with broken bones.

The route took us along the perimeter of Pemberwick Island. We traveled counterclockwise, which meant the ocean was to our right. The four-lane road never got much closer than a hundred yards from the beach. At times there would be thick forest between us and the water; other times we'd pass sandy bluffs covered in sea grass that gave us a clear view of the water. We occasionally passed a darkened house, but most of the route was through undeveloped terrain that hadn't changed in, well, ever.

There was no moon out, which normally meant a dark trip, but it was one of those nights that was so incredibly clear you could see most every star in the sky. Downtown Portland was well over five miles away across the water so there were no lights to prevent the sky from lighting up with millions of tiny sparkles. It was so bright that I considered turning off my headlight but figured I still needed to see obstacles in the road so I directed the beam to hit just ahead of my front tire.

It didn't take long before I was breathing hard and sweating, which was exactly what I needed. I could feel the tension drift away. I don't know if it was about releasing endorphins or about forcing myself to focus on something as simple as working out, but the ride was doing the job. Quinn was a genius, not only because he knew this would help but because he knew that I needed it.

"What's that?" he called to me.

"What's what?"

"Listen."

All I could hear was the sound of our tires rolling over the blacktop and the turning of our chains.

"I don't hear anything," I replied.

"You don't hear that?" he asked. "It's like music."

I listened again . . . and heard it. It was a single, steady note that drifted on the breeze. It was faint, but definitely there. It didn't sound natural, like wind through the trees or a migrating whale. It was too precise for that. The note changed and hung there for a few seconds, then changed again. It wasn't a tune, but a series of notes held steady, as if being played by an unseen electric piano. It came and went, sometimes loud and clear, other times hardly audible.

"What is it?" I asked. "There aren't any houses around here."

We slowed and sat up on our seats.

"It wouldn't be from a house," Quinn said, using his analytical voice. "It's gotta be moving because we haven't passed it."

"Look!" I shouted, pointing out to sea.

Something was moving over the ocean. I saw it move beyond a dip in the bluffs. It was a shadow. A big one. We had gained elevation and were traveling along a section of bluffs that rose and fell. When the terrain dropped down, we could see an odd mass moving over the water. When the bluffs rose again, we'd lose sight of it.

"Speed up," Quinn commanded, and we both dug in to catch the strange shadow.

"Is it a whale?" I asked, breathless.

"It's not in the water, it's moving above it, like a boat."

"A boat with no running lights?"

It was pitch black and looked to be the size of a small airplane. The only reason I thought it could be anything other than an actual shadow was that it was giving off the musical sounds. Shadows didn't do that. When it cleared a bluff, we could hear it. When it was blocked by a dune, so was the music. It was treacherous trying to stay with it while keeping one eye on the shadow and another on the road ahead.

"Somebody's on the bluff," Quinn called.

Sure enough, with the stars providing light, I could see that somebody else was keeping pace with the shadow, too. It was a rider on horseback, charging across the dunes. It was impossible to see who it might be because they had to be a hundred yards away from us. Whoever it was had to be an experienced rider because they were galloping over some treacherous terrain.

I saw the shadow again as it appeared beyond a dip in the bluffs.

"It could be a low-flying plane," Quinn offered.

"Again, no running lights," I countered. "No engine sound either."

The guy on horseback passed a pickup truck that was parked on the bluff. Pickup trucks weren't unique on Pemberwick, except when they were sitting on top of a bluff in the middle of nowhere . . . in the middle of the night.

"It stopped," Quinn announced.

I looked ahead to a break in the dunes and didn't see the shadow.

The horseback rider realized the same thing, pulled up, and trotted back the other way. Quinn and I put on the brakes. Though we could no longer see the shadow, we could still hear it. The music was growing louder.

"This is freaking me out," I said. "Where did it go?"

Quinn didn't need to answer, for the shadow suddenly reappeared, this time rising straight up above the bluffs.

"That's no boat," Quinn said, dumbfounded.

The shadow lifted ever so slowly toward the sky as the notes began changing more frequently, as if the rising movement required more energy. I looked to the sky, hoping to see a source of light that could be creating a huge, moving shadow. There was nothing but stars, except for where the shadow was.

The entity seemed to be sucking up light, looking more like a dark gash in the sky than something with substance. It was oval-shaped, like a flying manta ray. There was no way to tell how big it was or how close it was to shore because there was nothing to give it perspective.

We stood there straddling our bikes, staring at the rising shape, dumbstruck.

Quinn put it best. "What . . . the . . . hell?"

A brilliant streak of light appeared so unexpectedly that there was no way to know what it was or where it had come from. It was blinding, especially since we had been straining so hard to see the shadow in the near dark. Quinn and I threw our arms up to shield our eyes, which was smart because the streaking flash was only a prelude.

Boom!

The shadow exploded like a massive Fourth of July skyrocket. Sparkling particles blew out from the center of the black hole, lighting up the horizon, momentarily turning night into day.

The horse on the bluff reared up in surprise, its silhouette burned into my eyes. I had no idea if the rider stayed in the saddle because a second later we were hit with a wave of heat and sound that knocked us off our feet. I fell back, getting my feet twisted in my bike and landing on my butt. Still, I kept my eyes open to see what was happening. If I had had a few seconds to think, I probably would have run for cover, but it all happened too fast to think.

Like an exploding firework, thousands of dazzling sparkler-like particles spread across the sky. They hovered for a moment then fell to the ocean. Seconds later the fiery storm hit the water, extinguishing each and every bit of light. The event lasted no more than fifteen seconds. Once again, it was dark. The shadow was gone. The music was gone. I couldn't even see if the horseback rider was still on the bluff. The only sign left of what we had witnessed was the ringing in my ears.

I turned to Quinn. He looked as stunned as I felt. He gave me a wide-eyed look through his glasses and goggles . . . and smiled.

"Well, there's that," he said with a shrug.

Under other circumstances I might have laughed.

"This has been the freakin' longest night of my life," I said with dismay.

"Yeah," he replied. "And it's not over yet."

THREE

It's amazing how much action you can generate by punching three simple digits into a cell phone: 9-1-1.

The quiet solitude of the desolate shoreline was once again disrupted by a blinding white light and a sound so loud that it rattled my teeth, only this time it was explainable.

A Coast Guard helicopter hovered low over the ocean with its searchlight sweeping the water, looking for . . . what? We didn't know. Charging in to join the search was a Coast Guard rescue craft out of Portland. I could see its lights from a few miles off as it sped our way. On land were two Jeeps from the sheriff's department with their blue hazard lights flashing. Rounding out the spectacle were two more cars, SUVs, that belonged to my parents and Quinn's.

Right after the explosion, Quinn and I debated what we should do. Calling in the authorities meant calling in our parents and a possible end to our midnight rides. As much as we didn't want to have to face their wrath, it didn't take long to make a decision. This was too huge to keep quiet.

Twenty minutes later the two Jeeps arrived with their sirens wailing and lights flashing. I was impressed, considering that the sheriff and his deputy must have been asleep when they got the calls. It's not like there's a whole lot of criminal activity on Pemberwick. Those guys mostly dealt with tourists who got dumb when they drank too much beer or kids who raced around the island in their parents' cars.

Shortly after the sheriff arrived, the Coast Guard chopper flew in, which meant the sheriff didn't want to handle this alone. Smart move. I'd met Sheriff Laska a few times and he seemed like an okay guy, though not exactly a highly trained crimestopper. He was overweight . . . okay, fat . . . which didn't matter much because it wasn't like he ever had to chase down fleeing perps. The most chasing he ever did was with a beer after a buttery lobster roll.

Deputy Donald wasn't any more impressive. He looked like he had graduated high school last week. He was a little guy who wore his sheriff uniform really tight, like some badass state trooper. Maybe he thought it made him look bigger. I think it just made him look like he was wearing a Halloween costume that didn't fit anymore. I wasn't even sure if Donald was his first name or his last. They were both good guys but not crack detectives. I was glad that they had called in the Coast Guard.

When Laska and Donald got there, they instantly separated Quinn and me. It didn't take Sherlock Holmes to realize they wanted us each to separately give our version of what had happened to see if the stories matched. Laska questioned me and Donald took Quinn. I told the sheriff everything with as much detail as I could remember. The only tricky question came when he asked me why we were riding our bikes out there in the middle of the night. But I had a good answer for that too: I couldn't sleep after what had happened to Marty so we took off on a ride to blow off steam. It helped that it was the truth. Besides, what had happened over the water was a lot more disturbing than finding out a couple of guys went out for a late-night bike ride.

After asking me the same questions about five times, Laska told me to wait in the back of his Jeep while he went to talk with Deputy Donald. Quinn was in the back of the other Jeep, out of earshot. I caught his eye and he gave me a big smile and a thumbs-up. Dork. He was actually enjoying himself.

Our parents drove up shortly after and were asked to stay by their cars. After they loaded up our bikes the four of them stood together, talking and looking—what? Nervous? Angry? Worried? Probably all of the above. They'd just gotten calls in the middle of the night to say their sons were witnesses to an inexplicable explosion on the other side of the island. That had to be a shocker. But were they anxious about the explosion? Or the fact that Quinn and I were on the other side of the island when we were supposed to be at home in bed? That was a toss-up.

I didn't think we'd catch any serious flak, though. Quinn and I were usually upright citizens. Okay, we were *always* upright citizens. Our parents shouldn't be too upset that we went out for a nighttime ride, they should be grateful that we were normally pretty boring.

Living on an island like Pemberwick makes it tough to find good friends. It's not like you have unlimited choices, and I was lucky to find a guy like Quinn. The island sits five miles off the Maine coast. The only way on or off is by boat or small plane. The entire island is about eighty-five square miles with a town on either side: Arbortown, where I live, is on the west coast facing the mainland and Memagog sits on the east coast facing open ocean. The rest of the island is grassland, farmland, or beach. To the north is a separate island called Chinicook, which you can only get to by a half-mile-long bridge. I think they used it as a submarine-spotting outpost during World War II, but nothing's out there now but scrub and seagulls. The south end of the island is made up of tall cliffs of red clay that loom over the sea. It's all very postcard picturesque, and that attracts two very different kinds of people: those who live here year-round and those who vacation during the summer. Quinn and I fall into the year-round category, though neither of us had been born on Pemberwick.

Quinn's family came from Philadelphia when his parents chose to trade the high-pressure life of working in a city hospital for a more laid-back island lifestyle.

My family's journey was more out of necessity. Dad was a civil engineer who worked for years in city planning in my home town of Greenwich, Connecticut. When the economy went sour, he got laid off and decided to move us to Pemberwick to try something new, which turned out to be starting his own gardening business. It wasn't the most glamorous job but there was definitely a need, seeing as so many rich people wanted their summer places to look brochure-worthy. So Dad went from planning the growth of a city to planning the growth of petunias.

Though he was raking in a lot more grass than money, Dad seemed to like living here. Mom did too. She was an accountant who did freelance work for many of the small businesses on the island.

She often talked about how much fun she was having meeting new people and helping them with their work. As far as I could tell, neither missed our former life—which was cool—but it didn't seem fair that somebody like my dad could work so hard to get through school and earn a big fat degree and slave for years to build a career only to be tossed on the trash heap because some budget needed to be balanced. That wasn't right. My parents always tell me to work hard in school because it'll lead to a good career and a good life. Well, my father did exactly that and got dumped like a dead battery. If it could happen to him, a guy who does nothing but the right thing, it could happen to anybody.

It makes me wonder what the point of it all is. Why work so hard to try to get ahead if the rug can be pulled out without warning? Or you drop dead during a football game? Maybe that's why I don't try all that hard in school. I figure that whatever comes my way I'll deal, but I won't bother sweating about it until then. That way I'll never have to feel as though I got burned.

Quinn doesn't agree with that. He's all about piling on the AP courses and building his resume to get into some great school and set himself up to do something important . . . whatever that might be. It's pretty much the only thing we don't agree on. But that's okay. Whatever happens, we'll always have each other's back.

As I sat in the cruiser watching the helicopter make passes over the ocean, another vehicle drove up. The headlights were right in my face so I couldn't tell exactly what it was, but it looked to be a pickup. It stopped about thirty yards away. The driver got out as Sheriff Laska came over to greet him. He was an older guy wearing a plaid shirt and jeans. Because he was backlit by his own headlights

I didn't recognize him, but he looked to be tall and solid—your basic islander. He spoke to Laska and they shook hands as Deputy Donald joined them. Laska introduced them and started back toward me. As he walked, he motioned for Quinn and our parents to join us. We all converged at his Jeep.

"Who was that?" I asked, pointing to the guy in the plaid shirt.

"Another witness," Laska replied. "Guess he was the fella you two saw riding his horse on the bluff. Deputy Donald's taking his statement now."

"So he's okay?" I asked. "We thought he got hurt by the explosion."

"Seems fine," Laska said. "And his story matches yours."

"Of course it does," Quinn exclaimed. "Why would we make this up?'

"Quinlan!" Quinn's mom scolded.

"Aw, c'mon," Quinn protested. "We've been getting grilled like we're trying to pull off some kind of prank. Is that what happens to people who do their civic duty?"

"Enough," Quinn's dad snapped.

"It's okay, Doctor Carr," Laska said. "We *have* been putting them through the ringer."

"See?" Quinn exclaimed. "Whose side are you on, Dad?"

Doctor Carr rolled his eyes. He was used to Quinn being argumentative.

Quinn gave me a quick wink. I knew what he was doing. He was putting everybody else on the defensive so we didn't have to be. There was no way we were going to get in trouble for lying about being in bed and riding our bikes out there.

"Look," Laska said with patience. "You have to admit it's a wild story. You can't expect us to buy it just like that. We have to do our job."

"I understand," Quinn said. "Continue."

I had to keep from smiling. Laska may have been the law but Quinn was calling the shots.

"The Coast Guard's leading the inquiry," Laska said. "It's their jurisdiction. So far they haven't had any reports of a boat or a plane missing."

"I don't think it was either," Quinn said.

"And what exactly do you think it was?" Doctor Carr asked.

"A UFO," Quinn stated bluntly.

That got nothing but surprised gasps from our parents, and from me. Quinn hadn't mentioned that before.

"What?" Quinn said defensively. "I'm not saying it was from Mars. But it was flying, and we couldn't tell what it was. It didn't look like any kind of plane I'd ever seen. Isn't that pretty much the definition of a UFO?"

It was hard to argue with his logic.

"Whatever it was," Laska said, "we believe you saw something. So does the Coast Guard and they're going to figure out exactly what it was. So why don't you all go on home and we'll let you know if anything turns up."

"What about the truck?" I asked.

"What truck?" Laska replied.

"The pickup I told you about that was parked out on the bluff a little way back."

"Yeah," Quinn said. "I told Donny all about it."

"Deputy Donald," the sheriff corrected.

"Whatever."

"There's no truck back there," Laska said. "We checked that out first thing."

Quinn and I exchanged looks. Of all the things we had witnessed, the lone pickup truck was probably the least strange—until now. Had something happened to it when the shadow exploded? Or had there been yet another witness on the bluffs who drove off after the fireworks?

"We'll check it out," Laska added. "Now head on home and let us do our job."

Quinn's mom put her arm around Quinn's shoulder. She looked tired. So did her husband. I'd almost forgotten that they had been working late that night. I wondered if they had gotten the call from Quinn when they were in the middle of Marty's autopsy. I did my best to shake that image.

"We still working tomorrow?" Quinn asked me.

I looked to my dad, who said, "That's up to you guys."

Quinn and I worked for Dad on Saturdays, helping out with his gardening business.

I shrugged. "Better than sitting around."

After a few quick goodbyes, we got in our respective family SUVs and headed back toward town. I sat in back, fully awake, wondering if I could calm down enough to sleep. Ever.

"Are you okay, Tucker?" Mom asked.

I shrugged.

"Hell of a night," Dad said.

"Understatement," I replied.

"So you snuck out of the house to go riding in the middle of the night?" Mom asked.

There it was.

"I couldn't sleep," I said.

There was a long silence. There were two directions this questioning could take. I didn't particularly want to follow either of them.

Dad said, "So it was a moving shadow? Then a flash of light and it exploded? Are you sure it was an explosion?"

The new direction was set.

"I don't know," I admitted. "It's not like I've seen a whole lot of explosions outside of the movies. It was a big flash of light and a huge boom and we were knocked to the ground. To me that says explosion."

Mom and Dad exchanged worried looks.

"Could be a naval exercise," Dad said. "They do all sorts of things without making an announcement."

"Maybe it's some new secret weapon," I offered. "Like a drone."

"Could be," Dad said thoughtfully. "If that's the case, you can bet we won't be reading about it in the paper. Five cents says we'll never know."

Mom wasn't going to let it go as easily. Not the shadow-explosion, though; the after-hours tour.

"You shouldn't be going out like that so late at night," she said. "What if you got hurt?"

"I'm not a kid, Mom," I argued.

"I don't care how old you are, Tucker Pierce," she shot back. "Traipsing around in the dark is dangerous."

"I hear you. I'm not an idiot. I just wish you'd worry about something else besides me getting hurt all the time."

She threw me a stern look over her shoulder and said, "Sorry. It's my job."

"And might I add that you're very good at it," I said.

That made Mom smile. Dad too.

It was indeed her job. After all I'd seen that night, I wanted to embrace that fact. I wanted my parents to take care of all the bad stuff and make it go away. I didn't want to have to deal with unexplainable phenomena and police interrogations and mysterious witnesses, and most of all I did not want to have to deal with death. All I wanted was to hang out on my island home, play a little football, and help my father dig gardens.

Pemberwick was an incredible place to live . . . the kind of place that people chose to visit when they could go anywhere else. They came to my island to enjoy the warm days and mellow atmosphere and swim in the ocean and eat lobster and watch the sea grass sway while the sun sets over the rolling surf. For most people it's an escape from reality. For me it's home. I didn't want to deal with disturbing events that made it seem like something other than paradise.

Was that too much to ask?

FOUR

"**N**ots?"

"Not *nots*," said Quinn impatiently. "Knots. With a *k*, like they put on the front of *knife* for some reason I never understood. You can tell a lot about people by the way they tie knots."

"You are so odd."

Quinn and I were taking a lunch break from work. It was Saturday morning, the day after the game. Saturday was the day that football players rested up and healed. Most of them, anyway. I'd only been in the game for a total of five plays and didn't need a whole lot of recovery. Any soreness I felt wasn't from football. It hurts to get thrown off your bike by a mysterious exploding shadow.

Working for my dad meant grunt work. We raked leaves and mowed grass and pulled weeds and did any number of other brainless tasks that weren't exactly fun, but Dad paid us pretty well and it was work he didn't have to do himself, so everybody won.

"It's true, Tuck," Quinn continued. "Observe."

We were sitting on a bench in the town square drinking canned iced teas, trying to stay cool in the shade. It was early September and hotter than it had been all summer. Across the street was a vintage Ford pickup making a delivery of live lobsters to Lesser's Fish Market.

"How do you come up with these bizarre theories?" I asked. "Was it on one of those cable shows you watch at two in the morning?"

"No. I'm just a brilliant student of human nature," he replied quickly. "Watch and tell me I'm wrong."

A girl carrying a Styrofoam cooler strode out of the store, headed for the pickup. It was Tori Sleeper, a girl from our class. *Her* Saturday job was to help her father with his lobster business. Tori was cute, but odd. She had long dark brown wavy hair that she kept tied back in a practical ponytail. She usually wore equally practical jeans and T-shirts, along with a faded University of Southern Maine baseball cap. I never saw her hanging out with anybody our age, which was strange considering how small our school was. The few times I tried talking to her she answered in monosyllables. I couldn't tell if she was brilliant, aloof, or brain-dead. I guess you'd call her an enigma.

I kind of liked that.

"And we begin," Quinn announced.

Tori tossed the cooler into the back of the pickup next to a bunch of others and grabbed the edge of a bright blue tarp. She deftly yanked the tarp over the coolers, then grabbed a rope that dangled from a grommet and in one quick move threaded it through a tie-down hook. She snapped the line tight and expertly tied a . . . whatever knot to secure the whole rig. The procedure took less than five seconds.

"Impressive," I said.

"I'm telling you, Tuck," Quinn said. "That shows confidence, intelligence, and creativity."

"Or it just shows that she can tie a knot."

Quinn shook his head in disappointment. "Look beyond the superficial, my narrow-minded friend. There's so much to be learned from the minutia of human behavior. Now, go talk to her."

"What? Why?"

"You've been wanting to ask her out for months. But you haven't. Why? Because she's intimidating and you think you've got nothing interesting to talk about. But that's not the case anymore, is it? Now you can tell her all about unexplained celestial phenomena."

I felt panic rising. "No! I mean, who said I wanted to ask her out?"

"Be serious," he said impatiently. "Whenever she's around, you get all quiet and start this hypnotic staring thing. It's kind of creepy, to be honest."

"Maybe I think she's a freak."

"And maybe you've got to start taking some risks. Nothing ventured, and all that."

"I don't want to ask her out."

"You don't want to get shot down. There's a difference."

He killed his iced tea, tossed the can to me, and stood up.

"Where are you going?" I asked.

"To prove my theory," he said and headed for the truck.

I couldn't be sure what theory he was talking about, he spewed so many, but before I could stop him, Quinn marched right up to Tori and started talking fast. I couldn't hear what he was saying but he kept waving his arms for emphasis while she occasionally glanced across the street—at me.

Uh-oh. I sat up straight, suddenly self-conscious. But Tori didn't seem particularly amused or even interested. To be honest, I did think she was—what's the word?—different. But in a good way. I didn't go for the giggly girls who always seemed to be hatching plots against one another. Tori couldn't be bothered with that kind of drama. Question was, what sort of drama *did* interest her? I kind of wanted to know, but Quinn was right. She intimidated me.

Thankfully, a guy who I figured was Tori's father came out of Lesser's and that broke her away from Quinn. The two got into their truck and drove off, leaving a cloud of exhaust.

Quinn watched them for a second, then strode back toward me wearing a smug smile.

"See?" he announced with pride. "I was one hundred percent correct."

"About what?"

"She's not only astute but incredibly intelligent."

"How did you get that? She didn't say a word."

"She didn't have to. Her look said it all."

"What look?"

"The look she gave me when I told her you think she's hot. She wants nothing to do with you, by the way."

"What!" I shouted, horrified.

"No, this is good. Most girls would have giggled and blushed but she didn't even blink. That shows self-confidence. I'm telling you, son, it's all in the knots."

I threw his crumpled can at him, bouncing it off his chest.

"I'll put a knot in your head!" I shouted.

Quinn laughed and backed off. "I was just proving a point! Now you don't have to suffer the rejection of getting shot down. You owe me."

He turned to run and I was right after him, more embarrassed than angry. I never knew what Quinn would do next, though that's one of the reasons I liked him. He pushed people's buttons just to see their reaction. I was used to it, even when it was at my expense, which was often. It's what made Quinn Quinn.

We went back to work at the Blackbird Inn. It was a huge old Victorian mansion that had once belonged to some sea captain but had long since been converted into a hotel for people who liked to pretend they were vacationing in another era. It was one of Dad's biggest accounts because of its huge lawn and dozens of flower beds. Our job that day was to mow the expansive lawn. It was grueling work but I always took pride in how good it all looked when we were done—which would have been a lot sooner if the two of us hadn't been moving like zombies. It's tough doing manual labor on two hours of sleep.

"I can't believe you haven't asked me yet," Quinn said as he dumped a tarp full of grass clippings into a wheelbarrow.

"Asked you what?"

"About Marty. Don't you want to know why he died? The autopsy, remember?"

"I was trying to forget. What happened?"

"I can't tell you."

I whacked him on the back of the head with the handle of my rake.

"You're such an a-hole," I said.

"I'm not! It's unethical to discuss medical cases."

"Then why did you bring it up?"

"Because I can't tell you what happened." He lowered his voice and added conspiratorially, "But it isn't unethical to tell you what *didn't* happen."

I stared at him for a long moment, then whacked him on the back of the head again. "Cut the riddles," I commanded.

Quinn looked around to see if anybody was listening, then continued softly. "The autopsy turned up zip."

"Define *zip*," I demanded. "There had to be something. I mean, the guy died."

"There wasn't. He didn't have any heart problems; there was nothing wrong with his brain; there weren't any drugs in his system or disease or abnormality of any kind. The guy just stopped living."

That was disturbing news. I had hoped to hear that Marty had a previously undetected heart condition or rare genetic defect or anything else that would explain why the most athletic guy in school had suddenly become the most dead guy in school. A rare medical condition would have meant his problem was a tragic but understandable fluke. Having no explanation meant the same thing could happen to anybody.

"Tucker!" called a sweet voice.

Olivia Kinsey was waving to us from the porch of the hotel. On a table next to her was a pitcher of lemonade and some glasses. On her body was a tiny red bikini.

"That looks great," Quinn said longingly. "The lemonade looks pretty good too."

We dragged our sorry selves over as she poured some icy-cold drinks.

"You guys look like you could use a break," she said sweetly. "It is so hot."

"Really," Quinn agreed while giving me a sideways look. "Really, *really* hot." He wasn't talking about the weather.

Olivia was from New York City and had been spending the summer on Pemberwick with her mother. It was her first time on the island. All season I volunteered to work at the Blackbird because, well, Olivia was there. That's how we met. I was weeding the garden one day and—bang. She appeared like somebody out of a magazine ad for ridiculous hotness. Dad figured out my motives pretty quick and warned me about getting involved with an off-islander who I might never see again. We were actually having that conversation one day when Olivia returned from the beach in the aforementioned bikini. Dad took one look at her and said, "Uh . . . never mind."

Dad was cool.

Olivia was really out of her big-city element on Pemberwick, so I volunteered to show her around the island. Come to think of it, she came right out and asked me. I wasn't about to refuse. We went to a lot of movies. She loved movies. Didn't matter what it was. I also introduced her to most of the people who ran the shops in Arbortown. For somebody who came from the city, she seemed overly interested in how our simple island worked, which was cool, I guess. She had blonde hair that was cut short like a guy's, but there was nothing else remotely guy-like about her. I never put a move on her, either. Not that I didn't think about it, but she was way out of my league. She was older than me by a couple of years and went to some uppity prep school in New York and hung out with future captains of industry. I went to a public school on a remote island and hung out with future captains of lobster boats. There wasn't a whole lot of future for that kind of relationship but it was fun to dream.

Quinn liked to dream too. His mouth hung open as he stared at her unashamedly. I gave him a small shove to bring him back to reality before the line of drool hit his shoes.

"Thanks, Olivia, this is great," I said as I took the cold glass that was already wet with condensation.

"I'm sorry to hear about the guy from your team," she said. "What happened?"

"Funny you should ask," Quinn said as he stepped forward to begin a lecture on the subject.

"Nobody knows yet," I said quickly, cutting him off. "It's not good to start rumors."

Quinn backed off.

Olivia frowned. "So sad. He was having such an amazing game."

"You were there?" I asked with surprise.

Olivia gave me a coy smile. "I wanted to see you play."

I wasn't sure if I should be flattered or embarrassed.

"Oops," Quinn said and pretended to be focused on his lemonade.

"Oh. Well, sorry," I said. "I didn't play much."

"I didn't see you play at all," she said bluntly.

There was no pretense with Olivia—and no filter. She wasn't malicious; she just said what was on her mind.

"Tucker's on the kickoff team," Quinn said, jumping in to save my dignity. "The most dangerous part of the game because they give up their bodies with no concern for their own well-being. They call them Kamikazes."

"No, they don't," I said, scoffing. Then quickly added for Olivia's benefit, "But it is pretty dangerous."

Olivia gave a pouty frown. "I don't know much about football. I just wanted to see you play."

"I'm afraid you'll get that chance," came a voice from inside.

The screen door opened and Kent Berringer stepped out. Kent was the starting middle linebacker on our team. A junior. He was a tall guy with blond hair that was always perfectly messed up and a tan that lasted through the winter. His family was old-school Pemberwick. They'd lived there for centuries and acted as though they owned the place . . . because in some ways they actually did. His family owned the Blackbird Inn, meaning Quinn and I had been mowing the grass for Kent. Indirectly.

He stood next to Olivia, looking down on Quinn and me from the porch like he was the lord of the mansion . . . which I guess he was.

"How do you figure that?" I asked. "Freshmen don't play much."

"Unless a starting senior drops dead," Kent said with an incredible lack of tact.

It hadn't hit me until that moment. I was Marty's backup.

"That's right!" Quinn exclaimed. "That makes you the starting tailback."

"You up for that, Rook?" Kent asked, as if he didn't think I was even close to being up for it.

My head was spinning. "I . . . I guess."

"You better be," he added.

It came across like a threat. There's a fine line between arrogance and confidence, and Kent came down firmly on the arrogant side. The Blackbird was the nicest hotel on Pemberwick Island, which meant that Kent's family was rich and Kent was set for life. He knew it, too. He treated most everyone like he was their boss. Of course, in my case he actually *was* my boss.

"I saw you play, Kent," Olivia said, suddenly all coy and flirty. "You were so . . . violent."

She emphasized the word "violent" as if it made her all tingly just to think about it.

Kent shrugged with fake modesty.

Quinn rolled his eyes.

I had no right to be jealous, but I was.

"So does this mean you'll come watch me play again next week?" I asked, trying to reclaim the conversation.

Olivia frowned. "I'm not sure. School starts soon, so I don't know how much longer we'll be staying."

"Your school starts late," Quinn pointed out.

Olivia shrugged. "What can I say? Private school. They make up their own rules."

"But you're not leaving today," Kent said. "Let's catch a movie."

Jealousy growing.

Olivia brightened. "Kent Berringer! Why did you wait until the end of the summer to ask me out?"

I knew why. She'd been hanging out with me. But now that I had been revealed to be the bench-jockey scrub and Kent the violent star, the dynamic had changed.

"I wanted to," Kent explained with a shrug. "From the minute I met you, but hotel policy says we can't socialize with guests."

"Too bad," I said, not meaning it.

Kent added, "But seeing as you won't be a guest much longer, I think it'll be okay."

Quinn kept looking back and forth between me and them, hoping I would say something to stop the Kent-train from gathering speed.

"Why don't we all go!" he declared with a touch of desperation. "You know, a group thing like you see on TV."

"That sounds like fun," Olivia said with genuine enthusiasm.

Quinn beamed. He had successfully derailed the express.

"Sorry, Rook," Kent said. "Your father agreed to finish the lawn today and you're not even halfway done." He lifted up the lemonade pitcher and added, "Too many breaks, I guess."

And the train was back on the tracks.

"Rook?" Quinn asked with mock confusion. "What's with the chess reference, Kent? You strike me as more of a checkers guy."

Kent glared at him. Quinn knew full well that "Rook" was short for "rookie" and that Kent didn't know a pawn from a bishop, but as I said, Quinn liked to push buttons.

Kent ignored him and faced Olivia. "You should get dressed. As much as I'd like to hang out with you like that, you might get cold in the movie theater."

Olivia giggled and backed toward the front door. "You are so bad! Back in a jiff!"

She spun away and skipped inside.

"Jiff?" Quinn repeated with confusion.

Kent gave me a triumphant smile and said, "Finish the job, go home, and rest up for Monday."

He left us standing there holding our lemonade glasses.

"What's Monday?" Quinn asked.

"Practice. I'm the starting tailback now, remember?"

"And you just lost the hottest girl on the island," Quinn added. "You're oh-for-two today, my friend. Let's hope you do better on Monday."

As it turned out I didn't have to worry about practice the following Monday. It was canceled out of respect for Marty. There was no practice for the rest of the week and Friday's game was postponed. I'd never had to deal with the finality of death. All four of my grandparents had died before I was old enough to understand how it all worked. It was a strange feeling to know that I was the last person Marty had ever spoken to. The memory of his final few moments haunted me. What had been wrong with him? Did he know he was about to die or was it just the excitement of the game talking? I wondered if I should tell somebody about it, like his parents, but decided it would only make them feel worse if they knew Marty's state of mind at the end had been so—so what? Troubled? Confused? Frightened?

The funeral was held on Tuesday afternoon at the big white Congregational church near the town square. The whole football team was there. Coach asked us to wear our game jerseys, which I thought was a bad idea. Marty had died during the game. His parents didn't need to be reminded. But I was part of the team so I went along.

The church was packed. Looking around I saw many of the same faces I had seen watching with worry from the bleachers as Marty lay still in the end zone. I had never been to a funeral before so I didn't know what to expect. I imagined everyone would be all weepy but it wasn't like that at all. I think everyone was in shock. Especially Marty's family. He had two younger sisters who sat with their parents, stone-faced, in the front row next to the coffin. I couldn't imagine a sight more tragic than that.

The service lasted a long time, with many people getting up to talk about what a great guy Marty was. I hadn't known him that well because I was three years younger, but hearing the speeches made me truly sad that such a good guy had died . . . and that his last few moments had been so troubled.

Looking around, I scanned the faces of the people who had come to say goodbye. It was a gut-wrenching scene. Quinn sat next to me and his parents next to him. He hadn't known Marty very well either, but in a small town, you showed up. My eyes wandered over the crowd to see the gaunt looks on so many familiar faces—

And one unfamiliar face. It was the surfer dude from the game. He stood in the back of the church, still wearing his hoodie and sunglasses.

I turned to Quinn and whispered, "Who is that guy standing in the back?"

Quinn twisted around to look and said, "What guy?"

"The guy with the—"

I turned to point him out, but the man was already gone.

FIVE

"What more proof do you need that football is too dangerous?" Mom asked as we walked along Main Street toward home after the funeral service. "Young boys aren't built to take that kind of punishment."

Mom didn't want me on the football team in the first place but had been outvoted two to one at the beginning of training camp. I had to hope that the situation hadn't changed enough for her to convince Dad to rethink his vote . . . especially not since I had become the starting tailback with the chance to impress a girl in a tiny red bikini.

Dad said, "You're overreacting, Stacy. I played organized ball for six years and lived to tell the tale."

"And you've got an arthritic knee to show for it."

"That's not from football," Dad countered.

"No? It sure didn't come from jazz band."

That was a good one but I didn't laugh. I was on Dad's side.

"Look," Dad said. "Marty died and that's horrible but it doesn't mean we should keep Tucker from playing. Things happen. Heck, he could get hit by a bus tomorrow."

"I hate that saying," Mom groused.

"But it's true," Dad pressed. "People have to live their lives and do the things that make them happy. We've got to remember that."

That seemed like an overly philosophical argument for such a simple issue but Dad was on a roll so I didn't point it out.

"We moved here to make a better life," Mom argued. "A safer life. You know that as well as I do."

"I do," Dad said. "But we still have to be who we are. If we can't do that, then why are we here?"

The argument had gone from philosophical straight into weird.

"What was so unsafe about our lives before?" I asked. "I thought you just got fired and wanted a change."

Mom and Dad exchanged looks and fell silent. It was like they had said too much and regretted it.

"Am I missing something?" I added.

"No," Mom said, now calm. "I'm just . . . worried."

"Jeez, Mom, it's just football. It's not like I'm going to war."

That ended the argument. They both backed off without reaching a decision, which meant I was still cleared to play. But I was left with an uneasy feeling that had nothing to do with football. The idea that we had come to Pemberwick Island to get away from a life that was somehow unsafe was something I'd never imagined. It had an ominous ring, but I didn't press the issue. I thought it best to leave well enough alone. I was still on the team and for that I was grateful. . . .

Until the following Monday when practice began again.

Putting it simply, I got my brains beaten in.

"Pierce!" Coach screamed. "Don't save it for the prom!"

Coach was full of colorful sayings that made little sense but got the point across. Up until then I had been flying under the radar as a glorified tackling dummy. Now I was the starting tailback trying to fill the shoes of an all-star. I felt like a little kid playing with the big boys—because that's exactly what I was. And the big boys wanted to hurt me.

"Rip, knock-six on two," our QB called in the huddle.

It was an off-tackle handoff to me. The same play that Marty ran for a touchdown. His last. We came up to the line, got set, the quarterback barked, "Go!" and I launched forward. It was a perfect handoff, right into my gut. I wrapped my arms around the ball, kept my head up, and charged ahead. Running through the hole, I planted and cut for the sidelines. I was ready to turn on the afterburners when I got hit so hard I saw colors. The next thing I knew I was on the ground with Kent Berringer looking down at me through his face mask.

"Olivia's here to watch you get your ass kicked," he said with a smile.

I hated hearing that, which was probably why he told me. I staggered to my feet and trotted back to the huddle. A quick glance to the sideline showed Olivia standing there wearing white short-shorts and a blue halter top. She gave me a wave and a sympathetic smile. Swell. I had an audience for my undoing.

"Quit fiddle-farting around, Pierce!" Coach shouted. "Stick your shoulders in there and keep your legs pumping."

Shoulders . . . pumping . . . farting. Got it.

It was a trial by fire and I was getting burned. Kent had the defense all riled up and raring to get out their frustrations—on me. I didn't get any sympathy from the offense, either. They had lost their captain and all they had to replace him was an inexperienced freshman. I wanted to believe they were making an effort to block for me, but it sure seemed as though I was taking an above-average pounding.

Mercifully, practice came to an end before I was knocked unconscious. Coach gathered us together to congratulate us on a good workout and to let us know we'd be playing the rest of the season in honor of Marty. That brought on a big cheer.

"We were dealt a bad hand," he said. "But we'll do the best we can with it."

I wasn't sure if the bad hand was because Marty had died or because they were stuck with a pathetic running back to replace him. Probably both.

As we left the field, none of the players acknowledged the fact that I had so valiantly withstood a brutal pounding. I shouldn't have been surprised. Rooks didn't get respect, no matter what the circumstances.

Olivia was already gone. Just as well. Neither of us would have known what to say.

When I got home I was exhausted, and sore, and embarrassed, and I had homework, and, and, and—the whole situation had me ready to explode. So after dinner I got out of the house and went for a walk to clear my head. I didn't want to go anywhere near downtown for fear I'd run into some football fan who would remind me of how inadequate I was. Instead I headed for the beach. One of the great things about living on an island is that you're never far from the water.

The sun cast a warm red glow on the ocean and lit up a ribbon of thin clouds that stretched across the horizon for as far as I could see. I had gone there to clear my head, but looking out over the ocean reminded me of the exploding shadow. By now over a week had gone by and no information had come out about what it was. There was a short article in the local paper that talked about "two local boys" who witnessed the strange event, but that was it. All week the paper had been filled with articles about Marty. Nobody cared about what Quinn and I had seen.

We had both gotten phone calls from the Coast Guard and were asked to repeat the story, but they didn't have any more information to offer back. It was the same as Sheriff Laska had said on the night of the explosion: No boats or planes were reported missing. It was beginning to look as though Dad was right. The military might have been performing some secret tests.

Either that, or Quinn and I had been hallucinating.

I sat down in the cool sand to stare out at the ocean . . . and the mainland far in the distance. It seemed so far away, as if it were another world. In many ways, it was.

In spite of the recent disturbing events, I liked living on Pemberwick. The islanders who lived here year-round were pretty cool. I guess you'd call it a neighborly place where everybody knew most everybody else. Most of the men worked on fishing or lobster boats. That's what Pemberwick was all about. That and tourism. The summer crowds brought in the big bucks, which supported the people who owned the inns or worked the ferries or clerked in the shops or did any one of the other thousand jobs that kept the island humming with summer fun. Quinn and I had even pulled traps on a lobster boat that past summer. It was tough work, but we learned a lot about boats and the sea. It was a pretty simple life—and there wasn't much chance of getting cast aside like they did to my dad back in Greenwich when some corporation needed to cut expenses to increase profits. That world scared me. Pemberwick, on the other hand, made sense. It was safe. I could see myself living here for a good long time. Who needed the real world?

Those few short minutes on the beach had me totally relaxed and feeling good for the first time in over a week. It was a welcome vacation that I wish could have lasted a lot longer than it did.

"Hey! Tucker Pierce?"

A man's voice was calling to me from the road. I was afraid it might be an armchair quarterback from town who wanted to tell me how I'd never fill Marty's shoes. I debated sprinting down the beach to escape, but after the practice I'd been through, my legs felt like lead.

"Is that you?" the guy asked.

He was coming closer. No way I could duck this.

"Nope," I called over my shoulder. "Don't know anybody by that name."

The guy laughed and walked up behind me.

"I don't blame you, man. You've had a hell of a day."

Finally! Somebody who understood what I was going through. I turned to see who this sympathetic stranger could be—and came face to face with the surfer dude from the game. And the funeral. He was trudging through the sand wearing sunglasses and a big friendly smile.

"Who are you?" I asked.

He held out his hand to shake. "Ken Feit," he said with author-ity. "Good to meet you, Tucker."

I tentatively shook his hand. His grip was strong and confident.

"I've seen you around," I said. "What's your deal?"

Feit laughed. "No deal. I'm on vacation. Been kicking around for a couple of weeks. The surf's been outstanding along the East Coast so I've been working my way north from South Carolina, chasing waves."

It sounded like the kind of life I wanted to lead.

Feit added, "It's been great but I've got to get back to reality soon."

"What's with the note-taking?" I asked.

Feit pulled his small journal from the front pocket of his hoodie.

"This?" He shrugged and said, "I guess you'd call this a work-ing vacation. I heard about Marty Wiggins and wanted to see him play. So tragic."

"Are you a college scout?"

"Nah. I work for a company that makes nutritional supple-ments. You know, ergogenic aids."

"No, I don't know."

Feit laughed again. He laughed easily.

"It's not as complicated as it sounds. We manufacture nutri-tional substances to help athletes improve their performance."

"You mean like steroids?"

"No! It's all natural. We've got a new product that I've been testing and I thought of giving a sample to Marty but, well, I never got the chance."

"That's why you were at the game?"

"Yeah. Whenever I come across a serious athlete, I offer them a sample. It's the best PR possible because the results are incredible."

"What does it do?" I asked.

"Walk with me and I'll tell you."

The guy seemed harmless so I figured it couldn't hurt to take a walk. I took a step and stumbled a bit.

"Whoa, you sore?" he asked.

"I had a bad practice."

"Dude, that wasn't bad. It was brutal."

"You were there?"

Feit shrugged. "I told you, I'm always looking for serious athletes."

"Then you shouldn't have been watching me."

"C'mon," he said with a charming smile. "Let's walk."

I had to work to keep up. His idea of walking and mine were two different things. His was closer to a jog than a stroll. He looked to be in his thirties and in decent shape. I was half his age and in football shape, but my legs were still heavy from practice. At least that's what I told myself. I didn't want to admit that an old guy had more stamina than me.

"Check this out," he said, reaching into the front pocket of his hoodie.

He pulled out a clear plastic medicine bottle that was filled with brilliant red crystals.

"This is what my company makes. We call it the Ruby, for obvious reasons."

I took the bottle and held it up to the dying light to get a closer look.

"Looks like chunks of quartz," I observed.

"It's mostly sea salts. We've been experimenting with the stuff for years and I think we've finally hit the right formula. It's all about helping an athlete's metabolism function more efficiently, which dramatically improves performance."

"How?" I asked.

Feit laughed. Again. I wasn't sure if he found everything funny or if it was a put-on to make him seem like a friendly guy.

"You'd have to ask our research team about that. I just promote the stuff. But I guarantee you, once this hits the market, it's going to revolutionize sports and athletic training."

He took the bottle back and twisted off the cap. "Here," he said. "Give it a try."

"Whoa, no. I don't think so."

"It's totally safe, Tucker," he assured me. "It's basically salt. Some sugars too."

"And it's not illegal?"

"How can it be illegal? Nobody even knows it exists."

"I don't know . . ."

"I saw you play today, if that's what you call it. Do you want to repeat that performance again tomorrow? Or in a game?"

I didn't have to answer that.

"Here," he said, grabbing my hand.

He tapped a few tiny crystals into my open palm.

"That's, like . . . nothing," he said. "Let it dissolve in your mouth."

I stared at the red crystals. They were almost pretty.

"I don't even like taking aspirin," I said.

Feit laughed.

47

"Why is that funny?" I asked.

"Look, it's an absolutely harmless natural salt. I'll prove it to you."

He tapped a much larger portion into his hand, screwed the cap back on the bottle, and jammed it into his pocket.

"If it was dangerous, would I do this?" he said and licked the crystals from the palm of his hand. He then licked his lips, and smiled. "Tasty too."

I watched the cocky guy closely, not sure of what to expect.

"Yeah, so?" I said.

"Race you to the lifeguard tower," he said with a smile.

"No way. I'm too sore."

"Or maybe you're afraid to get beat by an old man."

He took off his sunglasses and gave me a wink and a smile. He then took off running faster than I thought was humanly possible. He blasted along the shore, digging through the soft sand like he was on turf.

I stood there staring, stunned. The lifeguard tower was at least a hundred yards away and he was there within seconds. How could that be? Was he really that fast? Or was it the Ruby?

I examined the crystals in my hand. It was salt. From the sea. What harm could it do? I was torn between fear and curiosity. I raised my hand and took a closer look, as if I could possibly unlock the secret of the stuff by staring at it.

I may have been looking at the crystals, but what I was seeing was Kent Berringer's smug smile as he stared down at me through his face mask after nearly knocking me cold. I didn't ever want to see that again.

I licked the rough crystals off my palm.

They were sweet in more ways than one. An instant wave of warm energy flowed through my body. Through my veins. My legs no longer felt heavy. Miraculously, impossibly, the soreness was gone. Everything snapped into focus as my senses perked up. The sunset seemed redder, the surf sounds louder, and the smell of the ocean more distinct. I didn't question what was happening. It felt right and I knew there was only one thing I could do.

Run.

I took off sprinting along the shore. The pain from the punishing practice was a dim memory. I felt the suddenly powerful muscles in my legs flex quickly, driving me forward, pushing me faster than seemed possible. Within seconds I was standing next to Feit at the lifeguard tower. I wasn't even out of breath.

"And that's the Ruby," he declared with a proud smile as he stood leaning against the tower with his arms folded.

I stood there, flexing the muscles in my arms, making a fist, experiencing my newfound strength. It was exciting . . . and frightening.

"This is . . . this is wrong," I said.

"Wrong?" Feit said with a scoff. "What could be wrong about unlocking your full potential? Now you can show the team what you've really got . . . and Olivia too."

I snapped a look at him. How did he know about Olivia? My blood was racing and I didn't think it was only because of the Ruby. It was like the salts had increased my brain power as well as my physical ability . . . which was probably why a thought came to me.

A horrible thought.

"Did Marty take this stuff?" I asked, though I feared the answer.

"No," Feit said quickly. "I told you, I didn't get the chance to give it to him. Who knows? Maybe if he had used the Ruby he'd still be alive."

Nothing felt right. I didn't like what was happening to my body and I didn't want to be hanging with this stranger who had seduced me into taking a substance I knew nothing about.

"I . . . I don't want it," I said, backing away.

"Really?" he asked. "You don't want to be a star?"

"I . . . I don't know what I want, but I don't want to feel like this."

"That's your choice," he said with a shrug. He wasn't laughing anymore. "If you change your mind, I'll be around."

I turned and ran up the beach, headed for town, sprinting impossibly fast. I tried to slow myself down but my body had the throttle, not my mind. I made it off the sand and kept going until I reached the small park at the end of Main Street. Thankfully nobody was around. I lay down on the grass and stretched out, willing myself to relax. I don't know how long I lay there. Five minutes? Twenty? Eventually I felt the effects of the Ruby leaving my body. The first sign was that the soreness in my legs returned. I never thought I would be relieved to feel pain. A weariness then washed over me as if the effort I had been putting out had sucked every last drop of gas from my tank. I sat up and rubbed my face. What had happened? Whatever the Ruby had done, it was wrong and I knew that I would never use it again . . . no matter how great a player it could turn me into.

I got up and jogged home at a normal pace and went straight to my room. I didn't want to talk with my parents because I didn't know what I would tell them. I don't claim to know how the human body does what it does, but I didn't believe for a second that what those crystals did was natural or legal, no matter what Feit said. I laid down on my bed in the dark, flexing the muscles of my legs and my arms, trying to sense any lingering effects.

After convincing myself that I would live, I went to my computer and feverishly Googled any key words that might lead me to answers: ruby, Feit, fight, "fite," sea salts, steroids, even ergogenic aids. The last search gave me some information about increasing athletic performance but I couldn't find anything about a red sea salt that could instantly transform someone into Superman, let alone a company that manufactured the stuff.

I decided to keep my adventure on the beach to myself. I didn't want anybody to know I had been stupid enough to take a strange substance from a complete stranger. Still, I couldn't stop thinking about what those red crystals had done for me. For those few moments when I was under their spell, I was invulnerable.

I wanted to know more about it . . . for all sorts of reasons.

SIX

"What's wrong?" Quinn asked.

"Why? What do you mean? There's nothing wrong."

I answered too quickly, which was a sure tip-off that something was, in fact, wrong. My adventure with the Ruby had been the night before and I could hardly think about anything else.

"Whoa, easy," he said defensively. "I was just wondering why you were letting Kent move in on Olivia without a fight."

"Olivia?" I asked, momentarily baffled. "Oh. That. Sorry."

"What did you think I meant?" he asked with confusion.

"Not that. I mean, not that there's anything else wrong but, I mean, there's nothing wrong. Why do you ask?"

Quinn stared at me suspiciously as we walked along Main Street toward school. He knew something was up and it bugged him that he couldn't put his finger on it. I had to get him thinking in the wrong direction, which wasn't easy to do.

"There's nothing between me and Olivia to fight over," I added quickly.

"There could have been," he said sternly. "But you blew it."

I shrugged. "Kent's an all-star."

"And rich," Quinn added. "Don't forget rich."

"Jeez, are you trying to make me feel bad?"

"Yes!" he shouted. "You can't let that guy intimidate you just because he's smart and good looking and athletic and—"

"Rich. Don't forget rich."

"Doesn't matter!" Quinn snapped. "The only real difference between him and you is that he gets what he wants because he believes he can."

"And he can brutally dominate me on the football field."

"You're making me nuts, Tuck. Where's your head? Good stuff doesn't just happen. You have to fight for it. But you don't. You don't even have the guts to talk to Tori Sleeper."

"Forget Tori! Who says I want to go out with her anyway? That's just you pretending to know everything about everything."

"But I do."

"No, you don't. Why are you so obsessed with me getting a girl anyway? Worry about yourself."

"I've got a girlfriend."

"Who?"

"Neema Pike."

I laughed. "Really? Just because she friended you on Facebook doesn't make you a couple."

"Whatever. This isn't about me. We're talking about you and Olivia."

"There's nothing to talk about. She's leaving the island soon anyway."

"Irrelevant, but go on."

I took a breath to calm down, then said, "I like Olivia. I liked hanging out with her this summer. But if she only likes guys who have a boatload of money and can wreak havoc on a football field, I'm not interested."

Quinn shook his head with disappointment. "Typical. Whenever you think something's out of reach, you back off and say you didn't want it anyway. What are you afraid of? Losing? Looking bad? That hasn't stopped you from playing football."

"Yeah, well, I'm quitting the team," I said softly.

"What!" Quinn shouted. He hadn't expected that. I thought his head was going to explode. "You're giving up on that too?"

"What's the point? I'm getting killed out there. I'm telling the coach today that I'm done."

"This is so typical. You were fine when nobody expected you to be any good but now that you've got to step up you just . . . give up."

"I'm being a realist."

"Realist?" Quinn spat as if the word left a bad taste in his mouth. "What does that mean?"

"It means I pick my battles."

"It means you're afraid of failing," he said with disdain.

"What makes you such an expert on football anyway?" I asked. I was losing patience with Quinn's accusations. "And girls?"

"This isn't about football or girls. It's about vision. You gotta have a vision."

I laughed. "Really? What's *your* big vision?"

Quinn went uncharacteristically silent. That threw me. I was expecting another quick, cutting comeback.

"I don't know yet," he said with total sincerity. "I'm being honest. I don't know. But I'll tell you something I absolutely believe: One day I'm going to leave this island and do something that people will remember me for. Something important. Bet on it, and don't laugh. I see you starting to laugh."

"I'm not laughing," I said, suppressing a laugh.

"My parents want me to go into medicine but I'm thinking politics. I'm smart. I could run things as good as the next guy. Or maybe research. There's a lot of undiscovered stuff out there waiting for somebody like me to uncover. Big stuff. But whatever happens, the one thing I will *not* do is stay here and grow old on this chunk of sand."

I wasn't sure how to react to that. So many thoughts flew through my head, not the least of which was the odd reality that Quinn had given me a straight, heartfelt answer for a change. The other was that I was somehow a loser for being happy on this "chunk of sand."

"Then go for it," I said. "I'm sure whatever you do, you'll be brilliant. But just because you feel that way doesn't mean I have to. There are lots of important things you can do. They don't all have to be written about in history books. It's just as important to take care of the little things."

Quinn let that roll around in his head for a while, then nodded thoughtfully and said, "Okay. I buy that. So do me a favor."

"What?"

"Start taking care of the little things."

Arguing with Quinn made my head hurt. He had turned a simple debate about whether or not I should compete for Olivia into a philosophical speech about our futures. He was thinking years ahead while all I wanted was to get through the day.

I didn't quit the team, and not because Quinn had shamed me out of it. The idea of facing the coach to tell him I was quitting was actually more daunting than getting pounded in practice. Maybe Quinn was right. I was even afraid of failing . . . at failing.

Practice was marginally better because I knew what to expect. I felt as though I was finally earning some respect from the other guys if only because I didn't whine about getting hammered on every play. By Wednesday we stopped hitting and concentrated more on timing and getting me to execute the plays without thinking. By Thursday I was actually starting to have some fun. We wore our game uniforms and basically ran through plays at half speed. There was a moment where I stood back, took a breath, and thought about how cool it was that I was going to play a major role in the spectacle that was Friday night football.

Then a harsh reality hit: I was going to play a major role in the spectacle that was Friday night football. Meaning, we had a game. If my own team wanted to take me apart, I couldn't imagine what would happen playing against guys who actually had a reason to want to destroy me.

We were playing Greely High in Cumberland on the mainland. Living on an island made it a challenge to travel to away games. As soon as school got out, we boarded a bus and the bus boarded the ferry. I'd made the crossing a hundred times and never felt so seasick. It probably had more to do with nerves than ocean swells but either way, I felt like ass. The bus ride to Cumberland took another half hour.

The best thing about that night was being introduced before the game with the starting offense.

"At tailback . . . number fifteen . . . Tucker Pierce," came the announcement and I ran through the gauntlet of cheerleaders and onto the field. Only a handful of fans from Arbortown had made the trip but it didn't matter. To me it was as good as running onto the field at Gillette Stadium.

There was a moment of silence for Marty, after which a couple of guys came up to me, pounded my shoulder pads, and said things like, "We're with you, Rook" and "Let's get 'em." I was over the moon. These were my teammates. We were in this together.

Kent grabbed my face mask, pulled it close to his, and hissed, "Don't screw up."

Not exactly a "win this one for the Gipper" speech but I didn't let it get to me. This was football and it was game time. The ref blew his whistle, the ball was kicked to us, and we returned it to the twenty-five. The impossible then became reality as I trotted out onto the field and into my first official huddle.

And that was pretty much where the fun ended.

The game was brutal. The Greely guys were like hungry sharks and I was bloody meat. It was much faster than in practice and I was one step too slow—not good for a guy who was carrying the ball. Fortunately we had a solid defense, so the game wasn't a blowout, but I was fairly useless. When all was said and done my stats showed fifteen yards gained on twelve carries with one fumble lost and two dropped passes. We lost by ten points. Brutal.

When the game ended, I jogged off the field trying not to look as beaten as I felt. I glanced into the stands to see my parents cheering gamely. I didn't know if I should be grateful for the support, or embarrassed that they were there.

Behind them was another fan who stood out from the crowd because he wasn't cheering. Mr. Feit had come to the game. Seeing him made me stop short. He gave me a sympathetic smile and a shrug as if to say, "Hey, don't blame me."

I briefly imagined how differently the game might have gone if I had taken him up on his offer to use the crystals he called the Ruby, but there was no way I could use that stuff again.

Could I?

The next day I was so sore I could barely move. Luckily it was the weekend of the annual Lobster Pot Festival and Dad had given me the day off. I took advantage and slept until noon.

"You gonna sleep all day?" Dad asked, poking his head into my room.

"No," I said, groggy. "All weekend. Set the alarm for Monday, would you?"

He laughed and sat at my desk, which meant he wanted to talk . . . which also meant I had no hope of getting back to sleep.

"What?" I asked suspiciously.

"Nothing," he said with a laugh. "I just wanted to tell you how proud we are of the way you're handling things."

"I'm getting my ass kicked."

"True, but you're hanging in there and that's what we're proud of. At least *I* am. Your mother would just as soon you pack it in."

I sat up, trying not to wince in pain . . . and happy that I hadn't quit the team. Hearing that Dad was proud of me was worth it, at least at that moment. Next week would be another deal.

"Maybe she's right," I said. "I don't know what I'm trying to prove or who I'm trying to prove it to."

"You don't have to prove anything to anybody, except yourself."

"That's pretty much what Quinn said."

"He's a smart guy," Dad said. "Annoying, but smart."

Dad had that serious "father-son important talk" face on. I wasn't in the mood but I was too sore to run away.

"I'm feeling a lecture coming on," I said.

Dad chuckled again. "No lecture. I want *you* to talk."

"About what?" I was getting nervous that he might know something I didn't want him to know . . . like about our midnight rides or my adventure with the Ruby.

"Do you like living on Pemberwick?"

"Yeah. You know that."

"I do. I just wondered if you missed Connecticut."

"A little, I guess. But we've been here for five years. This is home now."

Dad nodded but he looked troubled. I thought back to the strange conversation he and Mom had about moving to Pemberwick because it was a safe place.

"What's going on, Dad?" I asked. "Is there something you're not telling me?"

He sat up straight, as if surprised by a question he wasn't prepared for.

"No," he said, too quickly. "I just wanted to make sure you didn't have a problem with being here."

"I don't have any problems," I said sincerely. "Quinn's another story. He can't wait to get out so he can do something historic, but I'm in no rush to go anywhere. What's wrong with working in gardens? Though I was thinking we should make it sound more important and call it landscaping."

I smiled, thinking he'd laugh at the comment, but he actually looked sad.

"Did I say something wrong?" I asked.

"Nah," Dad replied. "Just know that you don't necessarily have to travel to do something important."

"That's what I told Quinn."

Dad shook off his dark mood, smiled, and stood up. "Well, you're a smart guy too. You take after your dad. Now get up and go into town and have some fun."

He left me alone with an uneasy feeling. My parents and I always got along great, which was a good thing considering I was an only child. (A term I hate, by the way. It sounds so forlorn or something.) We talked about everything. Even uncomfortable things like hygiene and sex. When Dad lost his job, I think it brought us even closer. It was like us against the world. We had to stick together and we did it by moving on and making a whole new life on Pemberwick. It sounds clichéd, but we were a team.

So it was strange to think that they might be keeping something from me. I suppose I shouldn't judge. We all have secrets. But if they asked, I would tell them about the midnight rides. And the Ruby. I had to trust that they would do the same for me and let me know if anything was seriously wrong.

Of course they would. Why would I think otherwise?

I was tired of stressing. It was the day of the Lobster Pot Festival and I was ready to kick back, eat some bad food, listen to corny music, and basically spend the day having the kind of fun that a lazy weekend on Pemberwick Island was all about. More than anything else, it was a day to try to forget all of the lousy things that had happened over the last few weeks and just enjoy the moment.

The moment.

I think back on it. A lot. It's like revisiting a favorite place. A place you wish you could go to again. But I can't because that place doesn't exist anymore, except in my memory.

SEVEN

The Lobster Pot Festival was the annual blowout that marked the end of summer. Three blocks of Main Street in Arbortown were closed off to traffic, making the whole downtown feel like one big party. Restaurants set up carts loaded with hot dogs, sodas, and lobster rolls. There was a band on every other corner playing rock oldies. Red, white, and blue banners hung everywhere. It was bigger than the Fourth of July.

This was my fourth Lobster Pot Festival and the most crowded by far. Oddly, there were a lot of faces I didn't recognize. Since the festival fell so late in the season, it was geared mostly to locals, but there were plenty of non-locals there to enjoy the day. I figured it must have been because the warm weather had stuck around longer than usual, so many tourists did, too. That was okay. I liked the energy. Kids ran everywhere. People wandered around in their khaki pants, Izod shirts, and Topsiders while downing loads of ice cream and cotton candy. Arcade booths were busy with guys trying to impress girls with their ability to knock over bottles with a baseball or hit free throws. Old folks danced in front of the bands, not caring what anybody thought of them. There was a sailboat race in the harbor and fireworks at the end of the day to cap it all off. It was always a great event . . . the last blast of summer.

I wandered through the crowd, looking for Quinn. Instead, I found Olivia. She was off by herself in a small alleyway, pacing and talking on her cell phone. As I walked closer, I could see that she was deep into a conversation. I didn't want to interrupt, so I stood on the sidewalk, waiting for her to finish . . . and heard what she had to say.

"No!" she cried. "No, this isn't what I agreed to. I've already been here too long."

She was pissed off.

"I want off, now. Right now," she demanded. "Before it's too—"

She kept trying to get a word in, but whoever she was talking to wouldn't let her. I felt bad eavesdropping and started to move away when she spotted me. Her eyes widened as if she had been caught doing something wrong. I froze, not sure what to do. She looked me square in the eye and I saw that she was not only upset, she was crying.

"Stop," she said into the phone, suddenly cold. "I get it. Goodbye."

She punched the phone off.

"I'm sorry," I said nervously. "I didn't mean to—"

"It's okay," she said, wiping her eyes. "That was my mother. I'm so embarrassed."

"Don't be. Is she coming to the festival?"

"No," Olivia said curtly. "She went to the mainland to do some shopping . . . while I'm here." She said this with a shrug and a big fake smile as if this were the last place she wanted to be.

"Are, uh, are you all right?" I asked.

She sniffed and nodded. "Yeah. Just homesick. I didn't think we'd be staying here for so long. But hey, things change."

I wanted to put my arm around her and tell her it was okay and I'd make sure she had a good time at the festival, but I didn't get the chance.

"Homesick?" Kent exclaimed as he walked up with a swagger. "That's not allowed on such an awesome day."

Olivia smiled bravely. "It's okay. I'm okay."

Kent stared me down and said, "I'm surprised you can walk, Rook." He looked to Olivia and added, "It was an ugly night for our boy."

I wanted to argue and defend myself, but he was right.

"Sorry, Tucker," Olivia said with sympathy. "Maybe football isn't your sport."

I opened my mouth to argue with her, too, but stopped. She was probably right too.

Kent put his arm around her waist and said, "C'mon, let's have some fun."

Olivia giggled coyly and nodded. "Yes. Let's."

She seemed to have shaken her dark mood, though I couldn't help but think it was an act, because she reached out and touched my face and in that brief moment I saw the sadness return to her eyes.

"You are such a good guy, Tucker. I'm sorry."

"For what?" I asked, genuinely confused.

"Take care of yourself," she said as Kent led her off.

It was a weird thing for her to say. "Take care of yourself"? It sounded so final, like we'd never see each other again. Who knew? Maybe we wouldn't. Her mother might give in and take her away from Pemberwick at any time. Her school had to be starting soon. All the more reason for me not to care that she had picked Kent over me.

I decided not to give it another thought. The day was about having some festival fun. I bought a hot dog and a soda from a cart, downed both, and was about to go for seconds when I caught sight of Tori Sleeper. She stood by herself in front of Molly's Candy Store, leaning on a parking meter and sipping a Moxie. A band was playing an '80s song (badly) and she was bopping her head to the beat. Her hair was down and loose for a change and she didn't have on her baseball cap. I almost didn't recognize her.

I wanted to walk right up and ask her if she was having a good time. I wanted to tell her about what Quinn and I had seen on our midnight ride. I wanted to ask her why she always looked so sad. I wanted to . . . but I couldn't. Quinn had said she wasn't interested and that was good enough for me. So I put my head down and walked past.

"Tucker!" she called out.

I stopped dead. Had I heard what I thought I'd heard? I turned around to see that Tori was looking right at me. I pointed to myself dumbly as if to ask, "Me?"

"Got a minute?" she asked.

I sure did. I put my hands in my pockets and walked back to her as casually as possible, which meant I had to force myself to keep from running.

"What's up?" I asked, trying to sound equally casual.

Tori didn't smile, but kept her eyes locked on mine. Quinn was right. The girl was confident. And intimidating. I couldn't tell if she wanted to be social or punch me in the face. The terrifying thought hit me that she was going to rip me a new one for telling Quinn I thought she was hot. Even though I hadn't. Even though I did.

"You guys were out on the bluffs last week," she said with no emotion.

I don't know what I expected her to say, but it wasn't that. I did my best not to register surprise.

"We were riding by," I said, trying not to reveal anything. "Why?"

"Quinn said you saw something."

"When did he tell you that?" I asked, giving up on being coy.

"Last Saturday. Outside of Lesser's Fish Market."

Right. The knots. He hadn't been embarrassing me in front of Tori after all, he was telling her about what we saw. It made me slightly less pissed at him.

"I don't know what it was. There was a big shadow floating over the water and it just . . . blew up."

Tori nodded thoughtfully. I could almost hear the wheels turning in her head. She dumped her empty soda bottle into a trash can and said, "What was it?"

"My dad thinks it was a military exercise. Quinn thinks it was a UFO."

"What do *you* think?" she asked, her eyes boring right into me. Challenging me. Why did this girl make me so nervous?

"I—I have no idea."

Tori thought about what I had said, then looked away from me and back to the crowd. It was like she was done with me and had retreated back into her own world. I stood there awkwardly, not sure of what to do or say next.

"You know this song?" I asked. "It's from an old movie. *Back to the Future*. My parents make me watch it once a year whether I want to or not."

Tori didn't react. She wasn't being obnoxious; it was more like her mind had traveled somewhere else. She stood there leaning on the parking meter with her arms crossed.

"Ever see it?" I asked.

"No."

"Oh," was all I could think of saying. I waited a few seconds then said, "Good movie."

It felt as though the temperature had suddenly dropped twenty degrees but there was no way I was going to skulk off like some loser.

"A lot more people here than last year," I said, lamely.

Tori didn't look at me when she said, "I hate this."

"What?" I asked. "The song? The band? The festival?"

"Yes."

Yikes.

"Tucker!" Quinn exclaimed as he jogged up, thank God. "I just parked the DeLorean, Future-Boy!"

Tori didn't react.

"You know, *Back to fhe Future*," Quinn said to her, hoping for a reaction.

"She's never seen it," I offered.

"Seriously?" Quinn asked, sounding shocked. "I've got the DVD. How 'bout if we all go over to my house tonight and watch it?"

Tori continued her non-reacting.

"I've got Junior Mints!" he added temptingly.

I had to laugh.

Quinn sniffed the air and said, "Hmm . . . who smells so lemony fresh?"

Tori finally showed life. Her back went stiff, she jammed her hands into her pockets, and she hurried off.

"See ya," she said and disappeared into the crowd.

Quinn and I watched for a second, then I punched him in the arm.

"Ow!" he wailed. "What was that for?"

"Idiot. We worked on a lobster boat all summer. What did they tell us to use to get rid of the fishy smell on our hands and clothes?"

Quinn thought for a second, then winced when the realization hit him.

"Lemon juice."

"Her dad is a lobsterman."

"Ooh. I guess that wasn't cool. But at least you finally talked to her."

"Probably for the last time, thanks to you."

"Sorry, man. I'll apologize."

He started to follow her but I grabbed his arm to stop him.

"Don't make it worse. Let's just go watch the end of the race."

As we made our way through the crowd, I thought about Tori's sudden, embarrassed reaction. After having worked on a lobster boat all summer, I understood that it was not a glamorous job. At the end of the day, you were tired and cold and yes, you smelled like fish. Quinn and I did it for extra summer cash. But Tori was a pro. That one brief moment had given me a little peek into her odd personality. She didn't seem like a happy person, especially with the comment about hating everything. She may have been confident, but she was also self-conscious. It made her seem less odd, and a bit more human.

"C'mon," Quinn called as we pushed through the crowd, headed for the town pier. "The boats are coming in."

The Lobster Pot Regatta was the centerpiece event of the festival. It's a sailboat race that's open to year-round residents only—no weekend sailors with more money than skill. The one-mile course looped around Arbortown harbor, beginning and ending in front of the town pier. The winner got bragging rights for the year and his or her name engraved on a battered old lobster pot. It's kind of like the Stanley Cup, but rather than drinking champagne out of it, the winners drank warm beer.

The race was singlehanded, which means only one racer per boat. There were all different classes and types of boats in contention but most were over thirty feet, which meant there weren't any amateurs. Still, it wasn't exactly an officially sanctioned event. I think most of the guys drank too much beforehand, but they're all expert sailors so there were never any problems, except for the occasional puking over the side. Those who hurl might have actually gotten style points, but I can't confirm that.

Quinn and I pushed our way through the crowd to get as close as we could to the seawall. The race was nearly done, so there were lots of people crowding in to see who would win. Or hurl. Or both. A huge orange float was moored about twenty yards offshore to mark the finish.

"Just in time," I declared.

Several boats had rounded the final buoy and were headed for home.

"Oh, man," Quinn said. "It's a close one."

There were three boats in contention, all with their mainsails up and their jibs full. That wasn't always the case. Usually one sailor took a huge lead, probably because he was the least drunk. But this year was going to be different and the crowd sensed it. This was a real race. Everyone started shouting, cheering, and blowing ear-splitting air horns.

"You know anybody racing?" I called to Quinn over the noise.

"Yeah," he yelled back. "The guy in second place in the Catalina. He's a friend of my dad's." He cupped his hands around his mouth and yelled, "C'mon Mr. Nelson!" as if Mr. Nelson could actually hear him.

The boat in the lead was a hundred yards from the finish, but Mr. Nelson was closing fast, which made the crowd scream even louder. I don't think anybody really cared who won, they just wanted to see an exciting finish and this had all the makings of one.

Mr. Nelson cut aggressively inside of the lead boat, looking like he was trying to steal the wind from the leader and then edge him out at the last possible moment.

"Nice," Quinn commented.

The crowd saw the maneuver and went wild. They sensed a last-second lead change and roared their approval.

Mr. Nelson's boat picked up speed. The sailor in front tightened his jib, trying to grab every last bit of energy from what little wind he had left, but he was going to lose.

"Any second now," Quinn said. "He's going to hang back until the leader loses all of his speed and then cut across his bow."

That's exactly what happened. The leader's boat lost its inertia and Nelson's boat surged forward. He cut the wheel hard and turned to slip in front of the leader.

"Yeah!" Quinn exclaimed, then suddenly froze. "Whoa. Too hard."

The crowd realized the same thing. As one, their cheers turned to shouts of warning.

"No! Cut back! Drop your sails!" Everyone was yelling advice that couldn't be heard.

"They're gonna hit!" I shouted.

A second later Nelson's boat collided with the bow of the leader's boat, knocking it toward shore.

The crowd groaned.

"Jeez, what's he doing?" Quinn said with a gasp.

I expected Nelson to come around and try to get back on course, but he kept turning. To get to the finish line, he had to travel parallel with the shore. He didn't. Nelson continued across the bow of the leader's boat and headed toward the line of floating docks that were strung out from the pier.

"He's out of control," Quinn yelled.

The crowd started shouting at him and waving him off, as if

that would do any good. Nelson's sails were full and he was headed directly for the first line of floats.

Someone blew an air horn as a warning, but the boat kept coming.

Several race officials were on the pier, waving frantically, trying to get Nelson to steer off. It was useless. If anything, the boat picked up speed.

"He's going to crash!" I exclaimed, stating what everybody already knew.

The race officials bailed, scrambling desperately to get off the float and out of harm's way. The last terrified official leaped from the float onto the pier moments before impact.

Nelson's boat hit the long float at full speed, its bow raising up like a breaching whale, revealing the underside of the hull. The two structures jackknifed, the bow rising into the air while pushing the float up onto its side. The boat would have kept coming up and over but the keel hit, stopping its forward momentum and twisting the doomed boat until the starboard side of the hull slammed into the float.

There was a horrific wrenching sound as the heavy boat unloaded on the semimovable float. The sails luffed, and finally the boat came to rest.

Nobody moved. Not the crowd on shore or the race officials down on the pier. I think everyone was in shock. That wouldn't last. Soon the officials would hurry out onto the dock to secure the boat. But that wouldn't happen for several more seconds.

The quiet pause wasn't due to the shock that came from witnessing such a horrific crash.

There was something much worse to be seen.

Anybody within viewing distance knew exactly why the boat had crashed. Mr. Nelson was clipped in using nylon lines, standard safety procedure when racing singlehanded. The line was taught, pulling against Nelson, who hung over the aft hatch, not moving.

"Oh man. Is he—?" Quinn said, barely above a whisper.

He was.

It was the day of the second death.

EiGHT

Race officials and paramedics sprinted to the damaged float to get to the foundering boat and Mr. Nelson. I had no doubt what they would find. As at Marty's last game, I focused on the crowd of faces who stared down at the scene in stunned silence. The band closest to the marina, unaware of what was happening, continued to play their version of the Ramones' "Blitzkrieg Bop," which added a surreal touch.

A woman cried out in anguish and pushed her way toward the float.

"Mrs. Nelson," Quinn announced in a soft voice.

I figured that.

I continued to scan the crowd, mesmerized, not only by the communal look of shock, but also because I expected to see Mr. Feit standing somewhere, taking notes in his journal.

"What's that sound?" Quinn asked.

I listened but heard nothing unusual, except for the lame band.

"I don't hear anything . . . wait." The sound cut through the band's three-chord symphony. It was a low bass sound that could have been far-off thunder.

"Is there a storm coming in?" I asked.

There wasn't a cloud in the sky, but the deep thumping sound grew louder and became so intense that it rumbled the pit of my stomach.

Quinn said, "It sounds like—"

His words were cut off by the thundering sound of six military helicopters that flew low over the town.

All eyes shot skyward.

"Marine choppers," Quinn pointed out. "Since when did the festival book fly-bys?"

The helicopters flew in tight formation out over the harbor then divided, three banking to the right and the rest turning left as they began to make wide circles back toward land.

"Look!" I exclaimed.

Two more aircraft flew by at a much higher altitude. These were military transport planes that were carrying . . .

"Skydivers!" Quinn shouted.

The rear cargo doors of both planes opened and a line of paratroopers spilled out. One after the other, seconds apart, their chutes opened and the divers drifted toward the island.

Poor Mr. Nelson was suddenly forgotten, even by the paramedics. Everyone stood still, staring up at what looked like hundreds of soldiers drifting down on top of us.

The band finally stopped playing as everyone at the festival, not just those by the shore, turned their attention to the sky.

A shrill horn sounded from out in the harbor. I looked out, and my knees nearly buckled.

"What the hell is that?" I gasped.

Far off shore, maybe a mile out, a huge naval vessel had appeared on the horizon. From this large ship came smaller boats that looked like amphibious troop-transport landing craft. They were in the water and churning toward shore. Toward us.

"Why do I feel like a German soldier who just woke up on D-Day?" Quinn said.

The crowd came to life, buzzing with wonder and pointing at the spectacle that was unfolding before us.

"This has got to be some kind of show," I said. "Right?"

"The ferry!" someone shouted.

All eyes went to the large transport ferry that was inbound full of cars and passengers lining the railing to gawk at the scene. It was a sight we had all witnessed thousands of times before, but this time it played out very differently. Two high-speed Navy gunships had taken up position on either side of its bow, changing its course and forcing it back out to sea.

"This is no show," Quinn exclaimed, stunned.

The troop transports were getting closer by the second. Soon they would reach the line of sailboats that were still on the race course. In the sky the paratroopers were seconds from landing. It looked as though most would touch down on the far side of town where there were vast stretches of open land covered with sea grass. The choppers had circled back and were hovering beyond the shops on both sides of Main Street. The doors slid open and zip lines were dropped down. Instantly, dozens of soldiers slid down the lines to land on the beach and the parking lots of Arbortown.

Whoever they were, they knew what they were doing.

The crowd noise grew, along with the tension. People had no idea what was happening or what to do. Most moved back from the shore in fear. Some grabbed their kids and ran off. Others pulled out their cell phones to call . . . who?

Quinn grabbed his.

"I'll call my parents," he said, breathless. "Maybe there's something online about this. Or on the news. Or something."

Quinn punched in his number, listened, and . . .

"It's not working."

"Is your battery dead?" I asked while pulling out my own cell.

"No. There's no signal."

I had the same problem, as did everybody else around us who was trying to use their phones.

I heard the high whine of a motor scooter engine and looked to see Tori Sleeper tearing out of town, headed for the coastal road. Tori lived a few miles outside of Arbortown. She was probably headed home.

The troop transports had reached the scattered racing boats. I was afraid they would run them down but instead they pulled up close to each boat, allowing soldiers to leap from their transport onto the decks.

With rifles.

"I think we're being invaded," Quinn said with a gasp.

"No!" I shouted without thinking. "Why? By who?"

The soldiers took command of the racing boats and they all quickly changed course, headed for the harbor.

"It's like they didn't want the racers to escape," Quinn declared.

"That's insane!" I countered.

The transport vessels pulled up, forming a line in front of the marina. A small, fast gunship tore into the harbor and pulled up about twenty yards from the pier.

"Attention!" came an amplified man's voice. The booming voice echoed through town as everyone fell silent. "Return to your homes. Immediately. I repeat. Return to your homes. Once the streets are cleared and secured, you will be given further instructions."

Nobody moved. It was like we had all reached a new level of shock. Nothing that was happening made sense.

"What's that?" Quinn asked, pointing skyward.

More parachutes had opened, but rather than soldiers dangling beneath the canopies, there was equipment. There were Jeeps and pallets loaded with boxes of . . . what? More weapons? Ammunition?

The booming voice continued, "Move off the streets in an orderly fashion and make your way to your homes or to the hotels where you are staying. The streets must be cleared immediately."

The shock had worn off and people started pushing back. You don't invade a town in New England where people have spent their entire lives without a fight. While those with small kids hurried off, most stayed and lined the seawall.

Quinn and I were right there with them.

There were angry shouts of "Who are you?" "Stay off our island!" "You aren't welcome here!"

Nobody had any idea who these invaders were, but we knew for sure that we didn't want any part of them, especially if they were giving orders. You don't tell a Mainer what to do in his hometown. It was a bold stand, but not exactly practical. There were maybe two hundred brave and belligerent locals who took a stand on the seawall against what looked to be a massive military invasion.

"We will be landing shortly," the voice continued. "Please clear the streets."

The reaction was a chorus of boos and shouts as the people literally tried to wave them off. Quinn and I got caught up and shouted along with them, waving our arms and screaming at the invaders to go away. What else could we do?

"This is not an act of aggression," the voice announced. "We need the streets to be cleared immediately to allow for our landing and everyone's safety."

"Let me through!" a guy shouted gruffly as he pushed his way forward through the crowd.

I turned to see Mr. Toll, a lobsterman who was older than dirt, making his way forward, clutching a shotgun.

"Uh-oh," I said. "Bad idea."

Mr. Toll was on a mission. He jumped up on the seawall and raised the shotgun.

"Whatever you got, we don't want any!" he shouted, and before anybody could stop him, he unloaded both barrels.

The ships were too far away for the shots to do any damage. All it did was escalate the situation from confusing to dangerous.

"They're firing back!" a lady yelled.

Sure enough, a soldier stood on the bow of the gunship and raised a large-bore rifle that looked a good deal more lethal than Mr. Toll's twelve-gauge. Before anyone could move, the soldier fired.

Several people screamed in terror but nobody was hit.

What the soldier fired was tear gas. The shell exploded not ten feet from Quinn and me and spewed a cloud of smoke that forced people to scatter. Another shot was fired and a second tear gas canister exploded further along the seawall.

The caustic smoke was already in my eyes, making them burn like I had been rubbing them with hot peppers.

"We gotta get outta here," I said to Quinn and grabbed his arm to pull him back from the water.

Most people had the same idea. No matter how badly they wanted to defend the town, they were no match for a well-armed military invasion. Kids everywhere were crying as people staggered away from the marina in fear and confusion. A handful of older guys stayed and continued to shout at the boats but it was a futile gesture.

Pemberwick Island was being invaded whether we liked it or not.

"Let's go to my house," I shouted to Quinn.

The two of us dodged through the crowd, which wasn't easy because everyone was moving in a different direction. It didn't help that festival booths lined the streets. It was bedlam that bordered on panic. People started getting nasty, shoving one another to get out of their way.

"Let's get off of Main Street," I said, and pulled Quinn toward a side street.

We didn't get far because the paratroopers had arrived. They stood at each intersection, blocking the way to keep the people all flowing in one direction out of the downtown area. It was the first good look I got at our invaders.

They were definitely military but with uniforms like I'd never seen before. They wore camouflage fatigues in various shades of deep red rather than the familiar greens or grays. They also had on dark red berets and black bulletproof vests. Most daunting of all was the fact that they carried wide-bore rifles, held across their chests at the ready. The weapons looked to be the kind that fired beanbags rather than bullets. Or more tear gas. These guys definitely meant business, but at least it didn't seem like they were ready to kill anybody. They each had a black baton hanging from their belts, along with handcuffs and a few other pouches that contained . . . I didn't know what. They seemed to me more like hardcore riot-control policemen than combat troops . . . not that that explained anything.

"SYLO," Quinn muttered.

"Huh?"

"The patch on their sleeves."

Each soldier had a colorful round patch on his left shoulder. The background was green, with a simple yellow design that could have represented a rising sun. Stitched in bold black letters beneath the sun was one word: SYLO. The same rising-sun design was on the front of their berets. On their right shoulders was another patch: an American flag. That at least answered one question. These guys were U.S. military.

They stood at the street intersections, funneling the people in one direction: out of town.

The roar of multiple engines filled Main Street. Quinn and I ducked into the doorway of a store and looked back to see a few stragglers still near the shore. The paratroopers moved them gently yet insistently away from the pier. We soon saw why. They were clearing the way for the landing craft. The amphibious vehicles had finally arrived and motored up to the town launch until their wheels hit land. The engines whined as they continued up the cement ramp and onto Main Street. I counted ten in all. They roared out of the water and lined up next to one another. On someone's signal the ramps dropped in front to reveal they were loaded with more SYLO soldiers, all armed with the same riot-control gear as the paratroopers. The soldiers jogged quickly and efficiently out of the landing craft and fanned out as if they had practiced this landing more than once.

"Keep moving, boys," a soldier called to us as he approached with his rifle still across his chest. "You need to head on home."

I didn't want to give him any reason to use the rifle, so I pulled Quinn out of the doorway and we started up the center of Main Street.

"Who are you?" Quinn called to the guy as we backed away. "What do you want?"

The soldier didn't answer.

We were the last people to leave Main Street. There was us and what looked to be about five hundred soldiers. We picked up the pace and started jogging toward my house. Overhead, more helicopters roared past, giving the impression that not only was the town secured and under control, but the sky over the island was too. We already knew that the invaders controlled the sea.

The reality of the situation was clear, but incredible: Pemberwick Island had been invaded by a mysterious branch of the United States military.

"This can't be happening," Quinn said, out of breath, as we jogged toward my house.

"Yeah, it can," I replied. "But what is 'it'?"

We didn't say another word until we got to my house. Mom and Dad were both there and nearly collapsed with relief when they saw us.

"Oh thank God," Mom cried.

She hugged me so hard I could barely breathe. I felt pretty sure that after all this she wouldn't stress over football anymore.

"I'll call Quinn's parents to tell them he's here and safe," Dad said.

He grabbed the phone, punched the speed dial, and waited.

"Doesn't work, does it?" I said. "Our cell phones don't work either."

"What about TV?" Quinn said.

I found the remote and hit the power button. The TV came on but there was only static.

Mom said, "We can't get online either."

"So what do we do?" I asked.

Dad was the most calm. Surprisingly so, considering that I doubt he'd ever experienced a military takeover before.

"What we *don't* do is panic," he warned. "There has to be a logical explanation."

The four of us stood there, staring at one another, unable to come up with one.

"Another guy died," I announced. "A guy in the regatta."

"Oh no," Mom said with a gasp.

"Nothing to do with the invasion?" Dad asked with concern.

"I don't think so. He died at the helm and crashed his boat," I said.

"That's when everything hit the fan," Quinn added.

The TV suddenly came to life. The annoying static ended and was replaced by a simple card that read: PLEASE STAND BY. The four of us ran to the screen and stared at the words. I willed the TV to show us a picture. I needed some proof that the rest of the world was still functioning normally. It could have been *Phineas and Ferb* for all I cared.

A full five minutes went by. I was about to give up when the screen flickered and a new image appeared. An impossible image, though the man on screen was about as familiar as could be. He stood behind a podium, prepared to address the world.

"Good afternoon," he said in grave, measured tones. "I'm here today to speak to all Americans, but in particular to the residents and visitors on Pemberwick Island, Maine."

Hearing him say those words was almost as shocking as having been through the invasion. It wasn't every day that you were spoken to directly by the president of the United States.

NINE

"Tell me this is a dream," Quinn mumbled.

President Richard E. Neff stood behind a podium that had the seal of the president of the United States displayed boldly in front.

Why do people always say a president's middle initial? It's not like you could mistake them for somebody else. Same thing with serial killers. Hopefully there's no correlation.

"Today at noon, a special task force attached to the United States Navy, known as SYLO, under my direction, landed troops on Pemberwick Island," the president announced gravely. "This is an unprecedented action but one that I approved for the following reason: The CDC in Atlanta—the Centers for Disease Control— requested the action following reports of several deaths on the island that by all accounts were natural but, as of this moment, unexplainable. The fear is that there is an unknown viral threat that has manifested itself on Pemberwick Island."

"Holy jeez," I said with a gasp. "Were there more deaths we didn't hear about?"

Neff was an older guy with short gray hair and piercing blue eyes. He always came across as easygoing, but at that moment he looked pretty intense. I guess that's what happens when you order an invasion of your own country. He spoke slowly and clearly, making sure that everyone understood exactly what was happening.

"This action is about creating a swift and airtight quarantine of the island so that the cause of these deaths can be identified and eradicated while preventing the possibility of the threat from spreading to the mainland."

"Yikes," Quinn said. "I guess the soldiers are the least of our problems."

Dad had his arm around Mom and hugged her close.

"Until the CDC can do their work and neutralize this potential threat," the president continued, "Pemberwick Island will be under strict quarantine. Ferry and air service has been suspended. No private boats will be allowed to leave or land, including commercial fishing boats. I understand that Pemberwick is a vacation destination and there are many visitors who are now stranded there. Of course this is an unfortunate and regrettable situation. To you folks, please know that you will be compensated and your living expenses will be taken care of for the duration of the time that you spend under quarantine."

I immediately thought of Olivia. If she was upset about being trapped here before, this was going to make her head explode. And what about her mother? Was she stuck on the mainland?

The president continued, softening his tone. "I want to stress that we don't believe there is an imminent danger to anyone on Pemberwick. No one in authority believes that this infectious agent is easily spread. Our actions are of an overly cautious nature. In spite of the dramatic nature of the SYLO presence, I urge everyone to remain calm."

"Ha," Quinn cackled. "Easy for *him* to say."

Neff continued, "Early investigation has shown that the cause of these deaths may have as much to do with genetics as with any infectious agent. In other words, the victims may have been genetically predisposed to be susceptible to what might possibly be a deadly agent. There is little chance that anyone else on Pemberwick is in danger. However, when considering the larger threat to the rest of the country, and the world, we have chosen the prudent path by initiating a total quarantine in order to stop the threat in its tracks."

I asked the screen, "So are we in trouble or not?"

The president didn't answer.

"No apology would be adequate to give to the people on Pemberwick for this sudden and, I'm sure, frightening invasion of their home," the president said. "I deeply regret having to make this decision, but I firmly believe that it is the correct one. The SYLO team will be setting up their operations in a central part of the island. The CDC will use this location as a base to conduct their research and bring an end to this problem as quickly and safely as possible. I will ask two things of the people on Pemberwick. First, as impossible as this sounds right now, please try to go about your life as normally as possible."

"Ha!" Quinn shouted.

"The SYLO team will do everything in their power to keep the intrusion as minimally invasive as possible. Second, please be patient and give your full cooperation to Captain Granger and his

SYLO team. They are there to help you. This swift action was taken without warning, I understand that. But it was the most prudent way to proceed in order to completely ensure that the quarantine would be effective and complete. Again, I apologize for creating such a disturbance to your lives and trust that you appreciate the importance of this action. I know there will be some confusion at first, but every effort will be made to keep you aware of changes as the situation develops. I thank you for your understanding, and your patience. God bless you, God bless Pemberwick Island, and God bless America."

The picture faded to black and was soon replaced by static.

The four of us stood staring at the TV. I couldn't even begin to process the information we had just been given, and I'd bet there were a whole lot of people staring at a whole lot of televisions feeling the exact same way.

"Well," Dad finally said with ironic cheer. "Other than that, how was the festival?"

Mom gave him a shove. "Not funny."

"This doesn't make sense," Quinn said. "How many people died? There was Marty, but Mr. Nelson just died a little while ago. The order to quarantine the island must have been given long before that."

"Maybe your parents know," I offered.

Quinn grabbed his cell phone and punched in a number. "Still no service," he announced. "Everybody must be doing the exact same thing and crashed the system."

I added, "And we're supposed to act all normal, as if nothing is going on?"

"That's what the president said," Mom offered weakly. "What else can we do?"

"I gotta find my parents," Quinn announced.

He strode toward the door but suddenly stopped before going outside. He stood staring at the door as if not sure he should go out.

It wasn't hard to guess why.

Quinn said, "You don't quarantine an entire island unless there's some threat of this thing spreading."

"Seriously," I agreed. "The rest of the world is protected, but what about us?"

"I don't think we have to worry," Dad said. "You heard what the president said. Very few people are genetically susceptible."

"So how do we know if we're genetically susceptible or not?" Quinn asked.

Dad gave Mom a dark look, took a deep breath, and said, "If we are, then it's probably too late already."

"Not comforting," Quinn said gravely.

"But it's a long shot, right?" I said hopefully. "I mean, odds are against us getting this thing."

"That's what it sounds like," Mom said.

Quinn shook his head. "It won't matter. People are going to panic. This doesn't add up. We've gotta—"

The TV flickered back to life. What appeared was an image of the front entrance to the Arbortown town hall. On the steps were two SYLO soldiers, standing at attention. In front of them, closer to the camera, was another soldier in fatigues who wasn't wearing a beret. He had steel-gray hair that was cut short, military style, and he stared right into the camera with such intensity that it was hard to look away. It was as if he was looking right at me. I wondered if everybody else thought the same thing.

"Good afternoon, Pemberwick Island," the man said with tight precision. "My name is Captain Benjamin Granger. I am the commanding officer of the SYLO division of the United States Navy. I trust that you have all seen President Neff's address, so you understand the circumstances that brought about this intrusion."

"Intrusion?" Quinn said. "That's a nice way of putting it."

"Yeah," I added. "A minimally invasive invasion."

"It is my mission," Granger continued, "to ensure the safety and well-being of each and every person on Pemberwick Island. I am also charged with securing the island so that during the quarantine period, no individual will leave and no individual will arrive. There will be no exceptions, other than my SYLO team and the scientists from the CDC who will soon arrive to begin the process of identifying and eradicating the threat."

Granger didn't waste words. He was a serious, no-nonsense soldier.

"As the president stated, we ask that you go about your business as usual. There should be little or no disruption to your lives."

"Who is he kidding?" I complained. "I'm feeling pretty disrupted right about now."

Granger continued, "I ask that you give your full cooperation to the team from the CDC, as well as to the men and women of SYLO who selflessly volunteered for this mission. They are here to help you."

"Help us what?" Quinn asked. "Not leave?"

"I cannot stress enough," Granger said, "that this quarantine is absolute. Do not attempt to leave the island. The SYLO team has been instructed to ensure that there is full compliance. That is our mission and we will not fail."

Quinn shot me a grave look and said, "Is it me, or was that a threat?"

"I will offer periodic updates on the state of the quarantine," Granger announced. "Our goal is to complete this mission as quickly and painlessly as possible. In large part, that will be up to you. Good luck. Granger out."

The screen went black and we were once again left staring at static.

"Wow," I said sarcastically. "What a warm guy."

"Seriously," Quinn added. "Why didn't he just say: 'Try to leave the island and I'll fire more tear gas up your—'"

"Quinlan!" Mom admonished.

"Sorry," Quinn mumbled.

"Look," Dad said. "We don't have a whole lot of choices here. Let's just keep our heads down and ride this out."

"But how are we supposed to be normal?" I asked. "There's a virus out there that's—"

"Potential virus," Dad corrected.

"Okay, there's a *potential* virus out there that's *potentially* killing people," I shot back. "Forget leaving the island. Nobody's going to leave their *house*."

"I'm not so sure about that," Quinn said.

"What do you mean?" I asked.

"The soldiers," he replied. "They're not wearing gas masks or hazmat suits. They knew what they were getting into and none of them took any precautions."

"There you go," Dad exclaimed. "That proves the threat is pretty slight. The best thing we can do is what the president said. Be patient and act normal."

"There's another thing," Quinn added.

"What's that?" Mom asked.

"I don't care what Neff said, there haven't been a whole lot of deaths. I would have known. Mom and Dad would have said something. Heck, we *all* would have known. You can't fart on Pemberwick without people knowing about it."

"So then what's the point of the quarantine?" I asked.

Quinn shrugged and said, "I don't know, but I'll bet you a nickel there's more to this story than we're being told."

We all shared looks, then Quinn took a quick breath and went for the door. This time he opened it. He leaned out and took a deep, exaggerated breath.

I couldn't help but wince, as if the action might increase his chances of dropping dead on the spot.

"I don't smell any killer virus," he announced. "Later!"

He bounded out of the door, jumped off the porch, and jogged off.

"What do you think, Tucker?" Mom asked cautiously, as if she were afraid of what my reaction might be.

"I don't know. I guess we just have to ride this out."

It seemed as though my answer allowed Mom to relax.

"It's the only thing we can do," Dad said, agreeing.

He sounded relieved. I wasn't sure why my reaction made them feel any better, but whatever.

Mom gave me a big hug. "We'll get through this," she said, though it sounded as though she was trying to convince herself.

"I'm going to lie down for a while," I said. "I'm still pretty sore from the game."

"Take a nap," Mom said. "We'll have an early dinner."

I nodded and went for the stairs. My legs suddenly felt heavy. I needed some downtime. I started climbing the stairs and glanced back at my parents.

They hadn't moved except that Dad was giving Mom a hug as if to reassure her that everything would be okay. I realized that they were putting up a good front so I wouldn't be scared, but they were plenty worried. I was about to continue on when I saw that Mom was crying. She was definitely a whole lot more upset than she was letting on. I started moving again, not wanting to intrude on the private moment. Their reactions made perfect sense, until I heard Mom softly say something that was intended for Dad's ears only.

"This is it," she said.

"Sure seems that way," Dad replied soberly.

I wanted to ask what he meant, but I had already heard more than I wanted to. Besides, they were my parents. They were always looking out for me. If there was something I should know, they would tell me.

So I kept my mouth shut and ran up the stairs.

TEN

Arbortown had become a ghost town.

At Dad's insistence, he and I went out the next morning to Schatz's Bakery to get bagels and try to pretend like all was normal, but one look at Main Street proved that it was anything but. The day before, the town had been packed with people enjoying the Lobster Pot Festival. Now, only a few brave souls hurried along the sidewalk while keeping close to the storefronts, as if they might offer some protection against . . . what? Some people even wore surgical masks. Abandoned festival booths lined the street. Paper napkins blew past overflowing garbage cans. The festive bunting and smiling-lobster banners swung lazily in the offshore breeze as cruel reminders of a happier time. Yesterday.

"Everybody must be hiding under their beds," I observed.

"That can't last," Dad said. "Life has to go on."

Every so often we'd see a pair of SYLO soldiers strolling together. They weren't walking with obvious purpose, but it definitely felt as if they were on some sort of patrol. Still, they each made a point of smiling and offering a friendly "Good morning."

"They aren't wearing any protection," Dad pointed out. "That's gotta mean we aren't in any real danger."

"Or maybe they've already been given some kind of vaccination," I offered.

That made Dad pause, but he shook it off. "No. If that were the case, why not just come out and give it to everybody? I'm thinking there's no real threat."

"Really?" I said skeptically. "That looks pretty threatening to me."

I pointed out to the water where a Navy warship stood guard over the harbor like a silent, shadowy specter—with big guns.

"Whatever's going on," Dad said, "I'm sure we'll be told everything real soon."

Something (besides everything) had been bugging me all night. I needed to talk about it with somebody. Dad was the logical choice.

"Do you think there's a connection?" I asked. "I mean between the quarantine and what Quinn and I saw the other night? You know, the explosion?"

Dad stopped walking, as if my words had struck a nerve. He gave me such a grave look that I expected him to blurt out, "You're right! I hadn't thought of that!"

He didn't.

"What makes you think that?" he asked cautiously.

"I don't know. You're the one who thought it might have been a military exercise. It seems like a pretty big coincidence that a dramatic military event happens right before we get dramatically invaded by the military."

"We weren't invaded," Dad corrected.

"Whatever."

Dad looked out to the water and the warship that was anchored at the mouth of the harbor.

"I don't know," he finally said. "I guess anything's possible. But like I said, I think we'll find out sooner rather than later."

I had to agree. There was no way an entire island of people could be cut off from the rest of the world and kept in the dark for very long.

We continued on to Schatz's Bakery only to discover it was closed. No big surprise. None of the other businesses on Main Street had opened either.

"It can't last," Dad said with conviction. "It's Sunday. By tomorrow things will start getting back to normal."

We spent the rest of the day at home. Cable was back. So was phone service. We stayed glued to the TV, watching for any news on the quarantine and talking to friends and family who lived on the mainland. The phone never stopped ringing. We had become national and probably international news. Friends from Connecticut called, wanting to know what was going on, but we didn't have any more information than they did. I kept expecting—or hoping—that President Neff would break into regularly scheduled programming to announce that all was clear. I wouldn't have minded if he did it during the Pats–Jets game since the Jets were kicking the Pats' butts up and down the field. But there was no such announcement.

In the afternoon Dad and I took another walk down to the harbor, where we found an entirely different scene from what was there in the morning. There was an amazing amount of activity going on. Transports were arriving and dumping off tons of equipment. As each ship emptied out, it would then shove off and quickly be replaced by another. More troops were arriving too. Helicopters flew overhead, dangling wooden pallets holding large, heavy crates. The president said that SYLO would be setting up somewhere on the island. I had to believe that these choppers were making round trips to deliver equipment to their temporary base, wherever that was.

In just a few short hours, Arbortown had gone from a ghost town to a hub of military activity. The SYLO soldiers controlled the streets (and the water and the air) while the islanders kept to the sidewalks, watching in stunned wonder as their quiet little island was overrun.

"That's a lot of gear," I said. "Looks like they're planning on staying a while."

Another troop transport arrived, but instead of soldiers, these boats carried a load of people in civilian clothes pulling rolling suitcases. It was a mix of men and women who could easily have been mistaken for tourists.

"CDC," Dad said. "The cavalry has arrived."

"They're not wearing protection either," I said.

"See?" Dad declared brightly. "If anybody should know if there's a danger, it's them."

Waiting for them was Captain Granger. The guy was tall and thin, towering over most of the other SYLO soldiers who were part of the reception committee. He definitely carried himself like a soldier, with straight posture that made it look as though he had a pole stuck up his back. Or somewhere else.

Granger didn't welcome the newcomers or shake hands or salute or anything. He just stood there, quietly observing. A few of the arriving scientists gave him a nod as they passed him but Granger didn't return the acknowledgement. He stood with his arms folded, staring at them with his steely eyes as if sizing them up.

A stream of black Humvees (when had they arrived on the island?) pulled up to the wharf. The scientists moved quickly up the ramp, handed their bags over to a few waiting SYLO soldiers, and jumped into the vehicles. The soldiers loaded the bags into the backs of the big cars and seconds later they roared off.

Granger never said a word. He stood observing the process until the last Humvee had driven off, after which a military Jeep screamed up to him. He got in the passenger seat, and the Jeep took off after the line of Humvees. The whole process took only a few minutes.

It was a disturbing scene. I'm not sure if that was because it had to happen at all, or because of the intensity of the moment. You could feel it in the body language of the arrivals, and definitely with Captain Granger.

In a word, it was tense.

"Those guys mean business," was my comment.

"Yeah, well, they didn't come for the chowder," Dad replied.

On the way home we walked past the Blackbird Inn. It was Dad's biggest client and he wanted to get a heads up on any work that needed to be done. We were about to turn off the street onto the pathway that led to the house, but I stopped him.

"What?" he asked.

I motioned toward the big house.

On the porch were Olivia and Kent. We couldn't hear what they were saying, but it was clear that Olivia was upset. I didn't need two guesses to figure out why. She'd wanted to leave Pemberwick even before the quarantine and now she was stuck here without her mom. Kent leaned against the porch railing, pretending to be interested in what she was saying. I knew he was faking because no sooner did Olivia turn her back to him than he glanced at his cell phone, probably to see if the Pats had come back against the Jets. He wanted to be anywhere else but there.

I wasn't sure if I was ticked off by the fact that Kent had the opportunity to get tight with her, or relieved that I didn't have to give her sympathy for being in the exact same mess that I was in.

"Got it," Dad said when he saw the tense scene. "It can wait."

We headed home in time to see another live message delivered on TV, again from Captain Granger. He sat at a desk, behind which was a big SYLO logo.

"What exactly is SYLO?" I asked Mom and Dad.

Both shrugged. They didn't know either.

I added, "I Googled it but didn't find anything to do with the military."

"Good afternoon," Granger began.

He tried to smile, but it looked painful. It was like somebody had told him he had to lighten up or he'd intimidate the natives, but it was so forced that it came out more as a sneer.

"As some of you may have observed, the team from the Centers for Disease Control has arrived. They are now hard at work and I assure you that they will do everything in their power to isolate and neutralize the alleged agent as quickly as possible. I urge you to cooperate with any request they may make so that they can do their work quickly and efficiently."

"I'll give him that," I said. "They definitely looked efficient."

Granger continued, "I observed today that most of you chose to stay in your homes. While that is certainly your choice, I urge you to carry on with your lives as normally as possible. There is no health risk in going about your daily activities. That is, of course, unless your daily activities include taking your boat for a sail." He smiled as if this was a clever joke but it came across more like an evil scientist who got his jollies by delivering veiled threats. I half expected him to let out a "Muhahahahaha!"

He quickly dropped the smile and lowered his voice an octave. "As we have made abundantly clear, until the quarantine is lifted, there will be no leaving the island. I trust that today's unfortunate incident was an aberration and will not be repeated. There will be no exceptions. As soon as there is more information to share, it will be. Good night."

The screen went black and a few seconds later it returned to the football game.

The three of us stared at the TV for a moment, letting Granger's words sink in.

"What incident?" I asked, the first to say what we were all thinking.

"I don't know," Dad answered.

"Whatever it was didn't sound good," Mom added.

We stared at the game, though the action meant nothing to me. It felt odd that the rest of the world could be turning normally when our boring little corner of the universe had been turned upside down.

✦ ✦ ✦

I didn't want to go to school the next day but couldn't come up with any good reason not to. Dad had left for work early and sitting home fretting with Mom wasn't appealing, so I sucked it up and headed out the door.

I had to walk past Main Street to get to the high school and saw that Dad was right. The town was slowly getting back to normal. The military presence was mostly gone. Whatever gear they needed had been delivered the day before. The festival booths were gone and the banners had been removed. I wondered if the people who had run the booths had decided to crawl out of their cocoons and pack up their stuff, or if it was the work of the SYLO soldiers. The scene wouldn't have seemed out of the ordinary at all, if it weren't for the occasional duo of soldiers walking by . . .

. . . and the warship sitting in the harbor.

The school was half empty, which meant there were a lot of people still hiding under their beds. But it also meant that at least half of the families had decided to do what we did, which was try to be normal.

"Did you hear?" Quinn asked as he jogged toward me on the way to our first class.

"I've been hearing a lot of things," I answered. "There's a long list of possibilities."

"I mean about the Catalina."

"What Catalina?"

"A thirty-five-footer that some guy from Cape Elizabeth sailed here over a week ago. He had it moored at Memagog and was staying at the Hob Knob Inn, but he didn't stay in his room Saturday night. Then yesterday morning the boat turned up on the rocks, nearly cut in half. Nobody's seen the guy since."

"Jeez," was all I could say.

"I'll bet that's what Granger was talking about on TV last night," he declared. "He said something about an unfortunate incident."

"So what are you thinking?" I asked. "That the United States Navy murdered a guy who was trying to escape from quarantine?"

"Well . . . yeah."

"Get outta here!" I said, scoffing.

I continued walking toward class and Quinn kept right up with me.

"I'm telling you, Tuck," he said, "this whole thing doesn't add up."

"So you're saying there's some kind of conspiracy going on, headed by the president of the United States, to harass the people on Pemberwick Island?"

"I don't know what I'm saying," Quinn shot back. "But I don't think we're hearing the whole story and that means that when we do, we're not going to like it."

"Or maybe it's exactly what they say and those scientists are going to figure out what caused those people to die and avert a huge catastrophe by saving Pemberwick and the rest of the world."

Quinn snickered. "Yeah, and then we'll wake up from that dream."

"That would be okay with me too," I said and headed for class.

The whole school was talking about the quarantine and SYLO and the people who died and the president and . . . and . . . and.

In some ways it was annoying to hear so much speculation, but I guess it helped to talk about it. At least none of us felt as if we were in it alone. Pemberwick Island was a tightly knit community, especially among the people who lived here year round. We took care of our own and that wasn't going to change because of a little old invasion.

After school I went to football practice but we didn't do much. Half of the guys weren't there and Coach wasn't even sure if there would be a game the following Friday. So we did a few drills and called it a day.

On the way home I took advantage of the extra hour with no practice and detoured into town. I grabbed a can of iced tea from Molly's and took it to a bench on the edge of the park on top of Main Street where I could get a good view of the entire downtown area. It all looked so normal, though I knew it wasn't.

Arbortown was still quieter than normal. There weren't even any cars moving on the streets. The only sign of life came from the fact that many of the shops were open, which meant business was being carried on, even if there were few customers. Since the quarantine had kept so many tourists on the island, I had to believe that they were all holed up in their hotels and inns with their bags packed, ready to blast out of Dodge. It seemed as though they'd be waiting for a while, based on all the equipment and personnel that SYLO had shipped in.

There were only three ways off the island. Most used was the ferryboat, but that service was shut down when SYLO landed. Another way off was by airplane, but I doubted anyone could even get close to the small planes at the airport with SYLO all over the place. The final way was by private boat, which brought up the mystery of the destroyed Catalina. I didn't even want to think about the possibility of that boat being attacked because the owner had tried to escape.

I did my best to convince myself that whatever the problem was, it would soon be solved, the missing sailor would turn up, and we could all get back to normal. I really wanted my life back.

The loud blare of a car horn tore me from my thoughts.

I turned quickly to see Tori Sleeper on her motor scooter, zipping quickly through an intersection. A light pickup truck was in the intersection, too, blaring its horn. I quickly realized what had happened: Tori must have sped through the intersection and cut the guy off—

And the guy didn't like it. He gunned the engine and the pickup jumped forward. With a squeal of tires, the guy made a U-turn and jammed on the gas. He was after Tori.

Tori rounded the far side of the park and glanced back to see the pickup charging toward her. I expected her to gun the engine but she did the exact opposite. She put on the brakes and hopped off, pulling her scooter up onto the sidewalk.

The pickup roared toward her. For a second I feared it was going to jump the curb and hit her, but it stayed on the road—and kept after her. I looked around quickly, hoping there was somebody around who could help, but there was no one in sight. Tori was on her own, unless I did something. I leaped over the back of the park bench and ran across the expanse of grass, headed her way, not sure what I was getting myself into.

The pickup screeched to a stop not five yards from Tori.

Tori didn't flinch. She stood next to her scooter with one hand on the seat and the other on her hip in defiance. The pickup had barely stopped moving when the driver jumped out.

I knew him. His name was Gary something-or-other. He was a carpenter who lived in Memagog. I'd guess he was about thirty and was known as a hot head. In that moment, he was living up to his reputation. He charged around the pickup, headed for Tori—with a baseball bat that he held up like a weapon.

Uh-oh.

"You messing with me?" Gary screamed.

Tori didn't answer. Or move.

I sprinted toward them with no idea of how I could stop a rampaging guy swinging a bat.

"Come on!" he screamed, his face red with anger. "You want to mess with me now?"

Gary wound up with the bat and took a swing that knocked a metal garbage can into next week. The garbage can flew five yards and the bat splintered, leaving Gary holding a sharp wooden spike that he waved at Tori as he moved closer.

Tori finally took a step back. She may have been cool but she wasn't *that* cool.

"Gary!" I shouted. "What are you doing?"

Gary shot me a look and I saw a fevered glare in his eyes that instantly brought back bad memories.

"She cut me off!" he screamed as if it were a heinous crime worthy of the death penalty.

"I didn't see you," Tori said softly but with certainty. "I'm sorry."

"Sorry!" Gary screamed. "You don't know what sorry is! But you will!"

He moved closer, ready to swing the sharp spike.

I don't know how I had the guts to do what I did, probably because it wasn't me who Gary was angry with, but I stepped in front of Tori.

"She didn't mean to cut you off," I said, trying to keep my voice calm. "She didn't see you."

Gary stopped moving. He seemed confused. He looked to the weapon in his hand as if he was seeing it for the first time.

"You're right," I said, even calmer. "She shouldn't have done it, but it was an accident."

"No, it wasn't," Tori said, but in a soft whisper that only I could hear. "I didn't cut him off."

Gary looked around as though not sure what to do.

"Maybe you should let it go, Gary," I said.

He let it go all right. He wound up and with a chilling scream threw the handle of the bat. The sharp splinter of wood flew further than I thought possible, sailed across the park, and embedded itself into the roof of the gazebo that sat in the center of the park.

That got Tori's attention.

"My God," she said under her breath, her cool finally cracking.

"Thanks, Gary," I said, trying to keep my voice calm. "Now it's over."

But it wasn't. Gary let out another scream and ran for his truck. He covered the twenty yards so quickly he seemed like a blur. He jumped behind the wheel, threw it into gear, and hit the accelerator. His tires squealed and smoked as he took off and flew down the road, taking a corner so fast it seemed as though the truck went up on two wheels. Seconds later he was gone. The only proof that the incident had happened was the lingering smell of burning rubber and the baseball bat lodged in the gazebo.

"What the hell?" Tori said, aghast.

She had no idea what had just happened.

I, on the other hand, had a pretty good idea. Gary losing it like that answered a question I hadn't even thought about asking until then.

Mr. Feit had been caught in the quarantine.

He was still on the island.

And he was still pushing the Ruby.

ELEVEN

"I didn't cut him off," Tori said softly, with a slight nervous quiver. "He just came up behind me and . . . flipped."

Before I could respond, the sound of screeching tires once again cut through the park. Tori and I both looked around quickly, expecting to see a crazed Gary behind the wheel of his pickup, headed our way.

Instead we saw a silver sedan speeding out of a side street and skidding onto the main road as it turned toward town. The driver gunned the engine and picked up speed, going way too fast for the quiet lane. Behind the car a black Humvee sped out of the same street, in pursuit.

"Now what?" was all I could say.

The silver sedan continued to accelerate, but didn't get far. An ambulance with a SYLO logo on each side turned onto the street in front of it and sped toward a head-on collision. The two vehicles had the sedan boxed into a three-way game of chicken.

Tori and I could only watch and brace ourselves for what was sure to be a horrific crash.

The driver of the sedan bailed. He turned hard, bounced over the curb and onto the grass of the park. The move may have prevented a head-on crash but he was moving too fast to make such a sharp turn. The car skidded sideways, digging up grass and spewing dirt, then slammed into a cement bench and came to a sudden stop. The impact spun its nose until it was facing back the way it had come, just as the pursuing Humvee arrived and skidded to a stop, blocking his way. A moment later the ambulance arrived, pinning the sedan in place.

The sedan's passenger door flew open and the driver scrambled out. It was a woman I didn't know or recognize. She wore a yellow sundress and sandals and looked like any one of a thousand moms you might see walking along Main Street in Arbortown with a toddler in tow, shopping for sunscreen. She leaped out of the car, landed on her knees, then quickly jumped to her feet and started to sprint to get away.

"There's nothing right about this," I mumbled.

An older mom-looking preppie lady fleeing from the police wasn't something you saw in Arbortown every day. Or any day. The Humvee doors flew open and several SYLO soldiers sprang out. One ran to the rear of his vehicle and went down on one knee to steady himself—as he took aim at the woman.

"He's going to shoot her!" I exclaimed.

Tori grabbed my arm out of surprise and fear. She had the strong grip of someone who had worked on boats all of her life. If I hadn't been so shocked at what we were seeing, it probably would have hurt.

The soldier fired, but what he had wasn't a gun. My guess: It was some kind of Taser because there was no *crack* sound that would normally accompany a gunshot. The only reason I knew he had fired was because the woman suddenly stiffened, stood straight, and fell to the grass. Hard. The SYLO soldiers were on her instantly, picking her up and dragging her back to the vehicles. The woman was limp, her sandaled feet trailing across the grass. They bundled her into the back of the ambulance and the other soldiers jumped inside. One ran back and got into the Humvee, another got behind the wheel of the silver sedan. Moments later, they all drove off the grass and disappeared down the side street.

The only sign that there had been an accident were the tire marks on the lawn.

"What the hell?" I said with a gasp.

Where I was stunned, Tori seemed totally freaked by the scene and sprinted for her scooter.

"Hey!" I shouted. "Where are you going?"

She jumped onto the scooter, fired the engine, and sped off without saying a word.

"You're welcome," I called after her.

She didn't hear. Or didn't care. In a few seconds she was gone and the park was quiet once again.

It took me a minute or so to get my head back together enough to remember how to move my feet. I went straight home, rolling over in my head the two different events I had just witnessed. As much as the attack on Tori was frightening, in some small way it made sense. I had no doubt that Gary had been introduced to the Ruby because of his over-the-top energy and the fact that he moved with inhuman speed. It was wrong, but explainable. What disturbed me more was seeing the SYLO soldiers chase down and Taser that mom-looking lady. Everything I had heard was that those soldiers were here to protect us. But from what? Ladies who rolled through stop signs? The fact that they zapped her and dragged her away in handcuffs like some escaped prisoner seemed pretty extreme. What could she possibly have done to deserve that?

The event was so disturbing that I couldn't bring myself to tell anybody about it. I had to hold on to the idea that SYLO was there to help us. I mean, President Neff told us so. What else could I believe? Before pointing fingers and making accusations, I wanted to know more about what was happening. But I had no idea how to do that.

The rest of the week passed without any more disturbing events, unless you count the fact that Pemberwick Island had become the butt of jokes for every comic on TV. "Looking for a hot vacation spot?" Jay Leno asked. "Try Pemberwick Island. You'll never vacation anywhere else . . . because they won't let you leave!" We even made David Letterman's Top Ten list of reasons to vacation on Pemberwick Island. "Number one: Free CAT scan with every cup of delicious, creamy chowder."

I might have thought the jokes were funny if I lived anywhere else. Letterman's line wasn't even that far from the truth. Every person on the island was required to go to the town hall and give a blood sample. When my family went, I recognized several of the CDC people who had gotten off the troop transport under Granger's cold glare. It felt a little creepy to have to give blood, mostly because we weren't given a choice. But if they were trying to isolate a potentially deadly virus and feared that some people were genetically predisposed to contracting it, then I guess it would be stupid not to get tested.

It was one test I desperately wanted to ace.

In spite of the CDC's bloodletting, Arbortown had started to feel close to normal. The tourists were poking out of their rooms and beginning to go back to the shops and restaurants. And why not? There was nothing else to do and the government was picking up the tab. I even saw people posing for pictures on the pier while pointing to the warship that sat ominously off shore. It was a surreal experience. A thin veil of normalcy had returned, though we all feared that just below the surface was a truth that we didn't necessarily want to learn.

On Wednesday the announcement was made that there would be a football game on Saturday morning. We were scheduled to play Memagog High, from the other side of the island, in November, but under the circumstances the date was moved up. Captain Granger made the announcement on TV, saying that it would be good for everyone to get out and enjoy a game; and since there were actually two teams on Pemberwick, we were nominated to be the day's entertainment. I guess that made sense. It wasn't like either team could travel off the island, so why not play each other? My only problem was that with nothing else happening on the island, the game was sure to be a sellout. That meant I'd have an even bigger crowd to witness my lame attempt to fill Marty's shoes.

I tried to talk to Tori a few times at school, but she avoided me and it was starting to tick me off. I had stood in front of a raging, armed maniac to protect her; the least she could do was acknowledge that I existed. I tried not to let it bug me and turned my focus to the challenge at hand . . . Memagog High.

Saturday came up fast. The game was on our home field because our stadium was twice as big as Memagog Field. It turned out to be a wise move. When we came out on the field for warmups, the stands were already packed. I'd never seen that before, even when there was a county championship on the line. It seemed as though everyone on Pemberwick had shown up because we were the only game in town. Literally.

As exciting as this was, there was an ominous touch. Armed SYLO soldiers casually circled the field. They walked in pairs, keeping an eye on the crowd. They seemed to want to keep a low profile, but it was hard to miss them. None went into the stands. They weren't there to watch the game . . . their eyes were on the people.

Kent was in his glory. During warmups, he ran around the sidelines, screaming things like: "This is our house! Nobody messes with our house!" It was all totally clichéd football psych stuff that was more for the crowd than for us.

When warmups finished, I jogged back to our locker room under the bleachers. Glancing up to the crowd, I saw Mom and Dad give me a thumbs-up. I also noticed that many people were wearing surgical masks, a grim reminder that we might all catch something deadly. I did a quick scan of the bleachers, looking for Mr. Feit. I didn't see him but that didn't mean he wasn't there. The crowd was too big for me to see everybody.

One person I didn't miss was Olivia because she was standing near the tunnel to the locker room. It was a warm morning and she looked incredibly cute in an Arbortown Wildcats T-shirt (that I'm sure Kent gave her) and mini jean shorts.

"Tucker!" she called, waving me over.

I took off my helmet and went to her.

"How're you doing?" I asked.

"As good as anybody, I guess," she said with a shrug. "It's weird being here without my mother. It's weird being here at all."

"I hear you," I said.

"I haven't seen you all week," she said.

It was my turn to shrug. "I've been keeping a low profile."

"I miss you."

She did? I couldn't think fast enough to say something clever in return.

"Do me a favor?" she asked.

"Sure."

She leaned forward and gave me a big kiss. Right on the lips. It wasn't one of those friendly pecks-from-your-aunt kisses either. This was like . . . a real kiss. It's not like I hadn't kissed a girl before. I had. Once or twice. Or once. But Olivia was a couple of years older than me and, well, she knew what she was doing. In that one brief instant, I forgot all about the game. And SYLO and the Ruby and the mysterious exploding shadow. What can I say?

After a few seconds, she pulled back and gave me a sweet smile that was even more electrifying than the kiss. I blinked, cleared my throat, and croaked, "Uh, and what exactly is the favor?"

She touched my cheek and said, "Make me proud."

I instantly went from the height of ecstasy to the depths of despair. Olivia had opened the door wide for me to impress her and maybe start a real relationship that held the promise of more kissing like that. But there was no way in hell that I could deliver on that favor. That door would slam shut two seconds after I was handed the ball for the first time.

"I'll see what I can do," I said with about as much casual cool as I could muster . . . which wasn't a whole lot.

She gave me a flirty wink. I headed into the locker room.

The game was a good one, a real back-and-forth battle that kept the fans cheering until the final gun. I think it probably helped everyone to forget the mess we were in, at least for a couple of hours. The best thing I can say about my own performance was that unlike the first game, I didn't embarrass myself. I guess that's saying something. On the other hand, I didn't make anybody proud, either. Coach tried working me into the offense early, but I couldn't do any better than stumble for a few measly yards per carry. I guess the worst came when I was thrown a quick outlet pass in the flat. Our quarterback really put some heat on the ball. I wasn't ready for it and the ball bounced off my hands— incomplete.

Normally during a game, you don't really hear the crowd. It's all just white noise and there's too much to worry about on the field to even think about it. But the moment that ball bounced away, I heard a collective sigh of disappointment that meant everyone was thinking the exact same thing: "Pierce sucks." It's a horrible sound, one that most people never have to hear. But I heard it and it stung.

I have to admit, in that brief instant I wondered what would have happened if I had taken a small sample of the Ruby before the game. Would I have made that catch? Would that massive groan of disappointment and disapproval been turned into ecstatic cheers and the approval of my teammates? And Olivia? I shook the thought quickly. As tempting as the idea was, it was wrong. No, worse, it was dangerous.

As the game went on, I handled the ball less and less, which was probably for the best. The undeniable truth was that I wasn't as fast or as strong as the other players. It wasn't for lack of trying. I just didn't have the physical ability.

Kent, on the other hand, played the game of his life. He kept up the steady cheerleading and pushed the defense to attack. I don't know how many solo tackles he made, mostly after blasting through a couple of blockers to get to the ball carrier. He had two interceptions, one that he returned for a touchdown, and he caused a fumble that he recovered himself. That play ultimately led to the winning score. I was genuinely impressed . . .

. . . until I went over to him on the bench to give him some encouragement. I banged his shoulder pads and said, "Unbelievable, man. Great game!"

Then I saw his eyes. They were wild . . . just like Marty's. Gary's too. In that brief moment I realized the truth. Feit had lied to me. Marty Wiggins had taken the Ruby before he died. I must have been in denial to believe that his incredible performance had been natural. There was no doubt in my mind that he had been under the influence of Feit's sea salts.

And now it was Kent's turn.

The rest of the game passed in a blur. I couldn't take my eyes off Kent, fearing that he might drop dead at any second. He played every play with the same speed and ferocity that he'd started the game with. The Ruby was indeed an amazing substance. When Kent fell on the fumble that gave us the ball for the last time, the crowd on our side went nuts.

I turned away and looked into the stands again because I knew he had to be there.

And he was. Feit was standing in the center of the bleachers, surrounded by a group of ecstatic fans who had no idea that Kent's life was in danger. He stood out because he was the only one who wasn't cheering.

He was looking straight at me. When we made eye contact, he pointed to Kent as if to say, "That could have been you."

My mind was spinning wildly. What was I going to do with this information? Feit was pushing a wonder drug that helped people perform at superhuman levels . . . and could be deadly. It made our victory feel hollow because Kent was definitely the MVP of the game. If he hadn't taken the stuff and played like a monster, we might not have won.

One other disturbing thought tickled the back of my brain: If Marty died after taking the Ruby, did this supposedly harmless ergo-whatever supplement have anything to do with the mysterious virus that SYLO was looking for? It wasn't all that crazy to think that somehow they might all be connected. I wasn't about to start running around telling people that the sky was falling though. I tried that once before and got nowhere. Nothing happened after we told the sheriff and the Coast Guard about the exploding shadow. Before pointing fingers I wanted to know more.

The game ended shortly after we scored the go-ahead touch-down. After the gun the crowd erupted with enthusiastic cheers for both teams in appreciation for the amazing game and the short vacation from the grim reality of the quarantine.

I showered quickly and was the first to blast out of the jubi-lant locker room. A crowd was waiting outside to congratulate the players on our first win, but nobody stopped me. I had been a non-factor in the game. I rounded the building to head for home and saw the one and only person who had stuck around to see me.

"Great game," Mr. Feit said.

I was so shocked that I stood there with my mouth open.

Feit added, "Then again, you didn't do much, but that was your choice."

"Kent took the Ruby, didn't he?" I said.

Feit's answer was to smile.

"And Marty did too," I added. "That's what killed him."

"Whoa," Feit said. "We don't know that. Did he take it? Yes. I told him to take only a few granules but he downed the whole vial. Hell, you can't swallow an entire bottle of aspirin without getting sick."

"You lied to me," I said flatly.

"I didn't want to scare you," he said.

"Scare me!" I shouted. "You're handing out drugs that are killing people and you're worried about scaring me? You're respon-sible for Marty's death! Did Mr. Nelson take it too? And that car-penter, Gary. He nearly killed a friend of mine!"

"Hang on," he cautioned. "Don't go throwing around accusa-tions. The Ruby is totally safe."

"Tell that to Marty's family," I sneered. "And the SYLO people. Is that why they're here? Is it the Ruby they're looking for?"

"I don't know what they're looking for," Feit said. "But it's not my sea salts."

"No? Is that a lie too?" I asked.

Feit walked slowly toward me. It took all of my willpower not to back off but I didn't want to give the guy an inch.

"Look," he said. "You saw what the Ruby can do. You felt it. Do you think Kent could have played like that without it? He took a small dose, the amount he was supposed to take, and what happened? You won your first game. He's a hero, and the hero always gets the girl. That's what it's really about, isn't it? That cutie with the jean shorts. Olivia, right? I'll bet she's outside that locker room right now waiting for Kent just so she can throw her arms around him and tell him how great he was. And you know what? That could have been you. I saw how she kissed you before the game. Don't expect a repeat performance."

He broke into a big smile and added, "Unless . . ."

Feit pulled a vial of the red crystals out of his pocket and held it up to me, shaking it temptingly.

"You can't be serious," I spat at him.

"It's totally safe if you take it properly. Marty didn't. But you're smarter than that. What do you say? Don't you want to be the one who gets the girl?"

I stood there, mesmerized, staring at the sparkling red substance. The dazzling glow that came from the crystals was almost . . . hypnotic. It was so tempting. Marty *had* overdosed; that much was obvious because Kent was fine. The Ruby could be used safely.

What harm would it do? Nobody would know. I could finally compete. I could make that catch. Without it, I didn't stand a chance. It would be so simple. Just a little bit and things would be so different.

I started to reach for the vial when . . .

"No!"

Somebody knocked the vial out of Feit's hand. I came to my senses to see that it was Tori. She stood with her legs apart and her fists clenched, facing off against Feit.

"Get out of here," she ordered Feit. "Take that crap with you."

Feit was momentarily thrown but recovered quickly and scooped up the vial. He backed off with a smile.

"Easy now," he said calmly. "No need to get all worked up."

"I'm going to the sheriff," Tori threatened.

Feit stopped walking and gave her a curious look, as if he didn't understand what she had said.

"The sheriff?" he said and laughed dismissively. "Let me know how that works out for you." He looked at me and added, "It's your call, Tucker. I'll be around."

Feit turned and strolled off, whistling as if we had just had a casual, friendly conversation.

My brain had locked. Too much had happened too quickly, not the least of which was the realization that I had actually considered taking the Ruby again.

"You're welcome," Tori said. "Now we're even."

"You know about it?" I asked, desperately trying to collect my thoughts.

Tori kicked at the ground, as if buying time to decide on how to answer.

"Would you have taken it?" she asked.

I had to think about that for a second.

"I don't know," was my honest answer. "I'm being publicly humiliated. Taking that stuff would be dangerous, and totally unethical, but man, it's so tempting."

Tori nodded as if to say she understood where I was coming from.

"But I think it killed Marty," I added. "And maybe Mr. Nelson. That makes Feit a killer. I think that guy with the baseball bat took it too, and he nearly brained you. You're right, we've got to tell the sheriff. This could be what SYLO is looking for."

"But we need more than theories," she said. "We need proof."

"Fresh out of that," I said.

Tori gave me a small smile. It was the first time I had ever seen her smile. I liked it.

"Come with me," she ordered and strode toward the parking lot.

"What? Why?"

"You need to see something," she said without breaking stride.

I followed obediently until we arrived at her motor scooter.

"You want me to get on that? With you?"

"Unless you want to run alongside," she said.

The seat was barely big enough for two, but there didn't seem to be much choice.

"What about helmets?" I asked.

"Do you have one?"

"No."

"Then I guess you don't wear one."

I slung my gym bag over my shoulder and sat on the back of the seat. Tori turned the key and the engine whined to life.

"Hang on," she said.

"To what?"

She hit the throttle and I barely had time to grab her around the waist. The bike wasn't big, but it was fast. At least it seemed pretty fast as we hurdled along with no protection.

"Where are we going?" I asked.

"I'm going to show you what a huge mistake I just kept you from making . . . and how we're going to get SYLO off this island."

TWELVE

I decided not to ask her any more questions until we had arrived at wherever she was taking us. The whine of the scooter was too loud and besides, I wanted her to focus on not wrapping us around a tree. Tori liked to go fast and take sharp corners. It felt just shy of reckless but I didn't want to sound like a weenie by complaining.

Our trip took us past the Oak Hills Country Club where we saw that it had been transformed into the SYLO base camp. Dad had a contract with Oak Hills, so I'd spent a lot of time there tending the clubhouse gardens and knew the layout pretty well. Flashing past, though, I barely recognized the place. There were dark green military-looking tents erected up and down the golf fairways. Some were small and looked to be where the soldiers slept while others were massive, circus-tent-sized structures. I also saw the tops of some wooden structures that were going up. That made me nervous. They may have been prefabricated quickie buildings but it gave the impression that they planned on being there for a while.

Humvees and Jeeps came and went. A helicopter swooped

overhead and skimmed the treetops before landing somewhere within. I caught a glimpse of a truck that had sprouted a dozen antennas, all pointed in different directions. The amount of equipment that had suddenly appeared on Pemberwick was incredible. The once-perfect golf course had a new personality. There had always been a tall ivy-covered wall surrounding the property but now with armed soldiers at every entrance, that wall had taken on a different, more ominous character. I saw the glint of silver razor wire peeking over the top as if another, more secure barricade had been erected within. This was now a secure military base. There would be no sneaking in to walk your dog or going for a run on the wide fairways as long as SYLO was there.

"I guess the members aren't going to be playing a whole lot of golf for a while," I said to Tori above the engine whine.

"So sad," she replied with total sarcasm. "What'll all those rich guys do with their time?"

"Seriously. I just hope my dad gets the contract to clean it up."

Tori had probably never set foot inside the country club, I realized, unless it was to deliver a load of lobsters. Being so close to her, I caught the unmistakable scent of lemons. I couldn't help but think that it was her way of masking who she really was. Was she ashamed? Or embarrassed? She said she hated Pemberwick, but was that because she hated being the daughter of a lobsterman? Or did she resent the "rich guys" who spent their days playing golf while her dad was out on the ocean pulling lobster traps? The more I learned about Tori Sleeper, the more I wanted to know.

We shot quickly out of town and sped along the winding Memagog Highway, which was a fancy name for the four-lane road that circled the entire island. It was the same road that Quinn and I used for our midnight rides. Every so often the road dipped closer to the shore, where glimpses of the ocean could be caught through the trees. A few times I thought I saw a military ship moving far offshore, but it was hard to get a good look through the dense foliage. It was a sobering thought. Did the Navy have the island surrounded?

We passed a farm where I spotted a familiar structure that I'd seen a thousand times before and never gave a second thought to . . . until then.

"Silo," I said aloud without thinking.

It was a tall red-and-white grain silo with a rounded dome that was used to store feed for a small herd of dairy cows. Was that what we were dealing with? Was SYLO doing the same with us? Storing us for some purpose other than what they would admit to? It was a silly thought that I shook off quickly. There was no sense in letting my mind spin to possibilities that didn't make sense.

After fifteen minutes of butt-numbing, teeth-rattling travel, Tori turned off the highway onto an unpaved road that led toward the shore. The sandy road was packed enough so that we didn't spin out, but I had to fight to keep my balance as we bounced over the washboard-like surface. Finally, we arrived at our destination: a house that sat on the edge of a quiet salt pond. The place was classic Pemberwick Island, with steel-gray shingles and a porch that wrapped around the three-story structure. There was a narrow yard in back covered with a checkerboard of grass and sand that definitely could have used my dad's expert touch. Beyond the yard was the water. A dock was built out from the shore that led to a long float where two lobster boats were tied up, bow to stern. It was a tidal pond, which meant the float would rise and fall with the tides.

A man was sitting on the float wearing a plaid shirt, jeans, and a worn Sox cap, working on a lobster trap. The place was classic Maine, like you'd see on a postcard.

Tori got off the scooter and strode toward the house.

"Wait here," she commanded. She climbed the porch and went right into the house.

I wasn't about to sit there like some barnacle, so I got off the scooter, dropped my gym bag, and followed. The place was old, but well taken care of. Across from the house was a gray barn that was nearly as big as the house and just as weathered. The expanse between buildings was nothing but hard-packed sand with sprouts of sea grass poking through everywhere. I walked onto the porch but rather than knock on the door, I rounded the house on the porch until I was on the pond side.

Tori had gone through the building and out the back door. She strode quickly across the yard, headed for the dock. It was low tide so the ramp at the end pitched down at a sharp angle. The pond must have been deep because even at low tide the lobster boats were floating. They looked to be twin thirty-five-foot Duffys. Or maybe Beals. Both had white hulls. One had a navy blue wheelhouse; the other was painted bright red. The red boat's name was painted on the bow in fancy, scrolling letters: *Tori Tickle*.

Cute.

The blue boat looked to be older. The paint on the white hull was yellowed with age. It was probably the backup vessel. Its name: *Patricia*.

The guy on the float must have been Tori's dad because she went right up to him and gave him a big hug. It was the same guy she'd been with when she made the lobster delivery to Lesser's Fish Market. It felt like a hundred years had gone by since then. I never met the guy but I must have seen him around because he looked familiar.

I had no idea where her mother might be.

Though Quinn and I had spent the summer working on a lobster boat, I didn't know much about the business end of lobstering. But I knew enough to understand that the only way a lobsterman makes money is by dropping traps and hauling up lobsters. The quarantine was keeping the lobster boats at their docks, which meant none of these guys could work. There was nothing good about this quarantine.

Tori said something to her dad and playfully pushed his cap down over his eyes. It was nice to see that she wasn't cold toward everybody. At least she liked her father. When she started back toward me, I quickly shot around the porch and went to the scooter. No sooner did I sit down than the front door of the house opened and Tori came out.

"This place is like . . . classic," I said. "Where's the closest house?"

"I told you to wait," Tori scolded.

Busted.

"I was just looking around," I replied. "Is that your dad?"

"Yeah."

"It's gotta be tough," I said. "Not being able to work his traps."

"You think?" she snapped angrily, as if I had insulted her.

"Whoa, easy. Just making conversation," I said defensively. "I work with my dad too."

"Let's go," she said and walked toward the barn.

"Go? We just got here."

She held up her hand to show me a key on a ring.

"We're not there yet," she explained.

Tori opened the barn door and I was hit with the distinct smell of horse.

"You can ride, right?" she asked.

The truth was I had been on horseback a couple of times but to say I could ride was a stretch.

"Sure," I said, and instantly regretted it.

"Don't sweat it," she assured me. "It's an easy ride, but we can't take the scooter."

Made sense, but it didn't make me any less nervous. If Tori rode horses the way she drove her scooter, I was in trouble.

Tori quickly and expertly saddled two beautiful, golden palominos. It made me think of Quinn's theory about people and knots. I wondered if the same applied to saddling horses because Tori definitely knew what she was doing.

She handed me the bridle of one, then led the other out of the barn.

"Does he have a name?" I called.

"It's a she," she replied.

Oh.

"Then what's *her* name?"

"I don't know."

Tori was starting to annoy me. I looked up into the big brown eyes of the horse that I was about to trust with my life. She looked harmless enough.

"Are we cool?" I asked her.

The horse blinked. I hoped that meant we were cool.

"I gotta call you something so how about . . . Lassie?"

The horse blinked again. I took that as a yes and led her out of the barn.

Tori was already mounted and waiting. With only a minor amount of awkward struggling, I managed to get my foot into the stirrup and hoist myself aboard.

"Hi-ho Silver," I said with a smile.

Tori didn't think that was funny and/or charming. She reined her horse around and started off. With a small kick, Lassie and I followed. Seconds later we were bouncing back along her driveway the way we had come. Lassie was a calm old girl, which was fine by me. Tori led us back toward the highway, but before we reached the main road, we turned onto another sandy road that I hadn't seen on the way in. This one was less used and the sand was soft, which was why the scooter wouldn't have worked. The road traveled roughly parallel to the highway while gradually moving closer to the shore.

I trotted up to Tori and we walked side by side.

"You going to tell me what this is all about?" I asked.

"You'll see when we get there. It isn't far."

We walked along in silence, which was making me crazy.

"You know, I've known you for four years and I don't—"

"Five," she corrected. "We've been in school together for five years."

Oh. That was interesting. I didn't even think I was on her radar.

"Okay, five years, and all I know about you is that you work with your father and don't talk much."

I wasn't sure if Tori was going to say anything and was about to give up trying to draw her out when she finally spoke.

"That's all there is to know," she said flatly. "That's the trouble with this island."

"What do you mean?" I asked.

"Don't you ever get tired of living on a rock?" she asked.

"You mean Pemberwick? Uh, no. I kind of like it here."

"Well, good for you."

"That means you don't?" I asked.

Tori gritted her teeth. She obviously wasn't used to talking about herself. Or about anything.

"My father works hard," she said. "He drops traps, pulls out spiders, drops more traps, and argues over prices. That's his life. He's a good guy. He deserves more than a bad back and a house that's falling down."

"Is that what *he* thinks?" I asked.

"No, but this is all he knows."

"What about your mom?"

Tori's expression turned dark.

"Sorry," I said. "Don't mean to be nosy."

"She left when I was three," Tori said, suddenly cold. Colder than before. "Never even said goodbye. I'm not sure if I should hate her for bailing on us, or envy her for escaping. I guess maybe I'm more like her than like my dad."

"That sucks. Where does she live now?"

"I have no idea," she said with no emotion, as if she couldn't have cared less. Or at least acting as though she didn't care.

I was beginning to get the picture of why Tori was so closed up . . . and hated Pemberwick.

"I wouldn't do what she did to my dad," she added. "So maybe I'm not exactly like her. But I wouldn't hate it if we moved somewhere else and started over."

"You sound like Quinn," I said. "He's ready to blast out of here the first chance he gets."

"And you're not?" Tori asked.

I shrugged. "I don't know. Maybe there's something wrong with me but I like it here. My parents chose to come here and Dad loves his garden—uh, landscaping business. I can see going into business with him someday."

"And spend your life spreading manure on other people's flowers?" Tori asked, as if I had said I wanted to be a professional assassin.

"Yeah," I answered sharply. "Sorry if that doesn't meet with your approval."

Tori opened her mouth to say something quickly, but then thought better of it and stopped. "Sorry," she said. "I didn't mean to insult you."

"Yeah, you did. Why don't you cut the mystery. I'm tired and I'm sore and I want to know why the hell you dragged me out here."

"We're here," she said.

We had arrived at a fence with a gate that was shut and padlocked. Tori dismounted and went to unlock it.

"The horses don't belong to us," she explained. "Some rich

guy pays us to board them so he's got some toys when he comes out on weekends. Nice, huh?"

"You really resent rich guys, don't you?" I said sarcastically.

She shot me a cutting look, swung the gate open, then climbed back on her horse and we walked through the gate.

"This whole area is fenced in. I think it may be the biggest parcel of undeveloped land left on Pemberwick. The guy said I should let the horses run free and get as much exercise as they wanted. Nice life."

"His or the horses?" I asked.

"Both. It's a great gig for me. I love the horses and ride whenever I want. It's like they're mine."

"But you didn't name them," I pointed out.

"Derby," she said. "Her name is Derby. This one is Racer."

I patted Derby on the neck. "Sorry, Lassie."

I thought I saw Tori smile, but it quickly vanished.

"There were two others," she said softly. "Remi and Nimbus."

"'Were'?"

She fell silent and gazed out over the ocean. Her head had gone to another place, just like when we were at the Lobster Pot Festival. I'm not sure what made me finally realize the truth. Maybe it was seeing her on that horse as if she were born to ride. Maybe it was being out there on the bluffs. Or maybe it was the way the tears were growing in her eyes. It was probably all of the above, because in that moment, I understood.

"It was you that night, wasn't it?" I asked. "You were the one riding on the bluffs when the shadow exploded."

Tori didn't answer right away, which was her answer. I looked around to realize we were very close to where we had chased the shadow down.

"It was your dad who spoke to Deputy Donald, right? I thought I recognized him."

Tori kept her eyes on the ocean and said, "He didn't want me to get involved. He's always protecting me. He told them he was the one who got thrown from the horse when the shadow exploded."

"Did you get hurt?" I asked.

"Just bruises," she replied, trying to control her emotions. "I know how to fall."

The image of the massive explosion that silhouetted the rearing horse and rider was one I thought I'd never forget. Now that I knew it was Tori, there was no chance I'd ever forget it.

"So then whose pickup truck was parked on the bluff that night?" I asked. "I thought it belonged to the guy who said he saw the whole thing, but if that was your father and he wasn't out here, whose truck was it?"

Tori shrugged. "I don't know. I wondered that myself. When I rode back to my house, it was gone."

"So maybe there was another witness," I said.

"Maybe," Tori agreed.

"You could have told me this sooner," I said. "I'm not a bad guy."

Tori finally looked at me with a pained expression that I truly didn't understand. She was hurting and it wasn't from being tossed off the horse.

"What did you bring me out here to see?" I asked gently.

Tori took a deep breath and said, "A few days after the explosion,

I rode Derby out here to round up the other three. Racer was waiting by the gate. The other two were . . . ”

Her throat convulsed as if she had trouble saying the words. “I saw them coming over that rise,” she said, pointing. “They were galloping. Fast. Like, impossibly fast. I thought it was an optical illusion but they flew by me like they were, well, flying. Saliva was spraying from their mouths and their eyes were wild. They pulled up just beyond that dune and started jumping. Up and down, like bucking broncos.”

She was fighting to keep her emotions in check.

“I didn’t dare get off Derby. I was afraid they’d trample me. So I cautiously walked her over, calling to them, trying to get them to focus on me and calm down. It didn’t work. They were out of control. Their whinnying was horrible, like they were excited and in agony at the same time. Then suddenly they took off together, charging back the way they came.”

I was afraid I knew where this story was going but didn’t interrupt. Tori had to tell it her way.

“I galloped after them but there was no way I could keep up. They were just so fast. Eventually they circled back toward here and—”

The words caught in her throat as tears starting streaming down her cheeks.

“When I got over that rise, I saw them. Both on the ground. Dead. Just like that.”

“Just like Marty,” I said.

“They actually looked like they were at peace. Nimbus had her head on Remi’s belly. Those two loved each other.”

Tori sniffed back tears, then nudged Racer to walk, headed for the shore. I followed on Derby, quietly. After about twenty yards, we came to what looked like a pile of rocks that had washed up from the sea. When we got closer, I saw it for what it really was . . . two large graves. We stood over them silently.

After a few moments, I couldn't take it anymore and said, "You think Feit gave them the Ruby?"

Tori's look turned hard. "Is that what he calls it?"

I nodded and said, "How did he give it to them?"

"He didn't."

Tori reined Racer and continued toward the shore. We approached a sandy bluff that led directly down to a small, rocky beach. It was a beautiful view, looking out over the ocean and a brilliant, cloudless sky.

"They found it themselves," she said and pointed down to the beach.

I wasn't sure what I was supposed to be seeing. It took a few seconds for my eyes to adjust and to register the horror that lay below. What at first looked like a beach covered with rocks, wasn't.

Instead of tide-washed stones, the beach was littered with chunks of red crystal. Most of them were baseball-sized, but some were as big as grapefruits. The larger chunks rested on a bed of smaller, shattered crystals. There had to be a ton of the stuff, just sitting there as if it had washed up like so much sea glass.

It was the Ruby.

"I saw Remi and Nimbus an hour before they died," she said. "They were down there, grazing. Whatever that wicked stuff is, it turned my horses into demons and then killed them. And now that Feit character is feeding it to people."

"I took some," I blurted out, without thinking.

Tori shot me a look of surprise and confusion.

"He said it would improve my performance," I added. "Serious understatement. I only took a few tiny crystals but the result was incredible. I felt like like . . . Superman."

"But you're okay now," Tori stated, confused.

"Because I hardly took any. Feit said Marty took too much, and obviously so did the horses. I guess your body can operate in overdrive for just so long before it crashes." I looked at Tori and said, "You're the only person I've told."

"What is the stuff?" she asked. "Why is Feit pushing it?"

I got off Derby and walked to the beach where the Ruby was spread out.

"I don't know," I answered. "Maybe it's an experiment gone wrong or some new toxic substance or something from Mars, for all I know. Whatever it is, it's—"

I didn't finish the sentence because I saw something else on the shore. Something out of the ordinary. Scattered throughout the field of red crystals were chunks of a black material that looked to be anything but natural. They were all sizes and shapes. Some as small as crackers, others the size of dinner plates. I picked one of the larger pieces up to see that it was like a piece of sheet metal, but much lighter, and paper thin. All the pieces were paper thin. It seemed to be made of some kind of plastic, which meant it was definitely man-made.

"I think that stuff washed up with the crystals," Tori said. "It might be pieces of a boat that was carrying the stuff. Looks like it broke up on the rocks."

"Smashed up is more like it," I said. "It was totally destroyed. I mean, there's nothing left but bits and pieces, like it was . . ." The words caught in my throat. I looked up to Tori and finished my thought. "Like it was blown up."

Tori's eyes went wide as the possibility hit her.

"Like maybe that shadow wasn't a shadow," she said, numb.

I quickly put one of the smaller pieces into my pocket, then knelt down, pulled my sleeve over my hand, and picked up a golf-ball-sized chunk of the red crystal. I didn't want to touch it with my bare skin in case the poison could somehow leach through my pores.

"We'll bring this stuff to the SYLO compound. This has got to be what they're looking for. Those CDC brains can analyze it and—"

The sound of a speedboat powering up cut me off. We both looked up to see a high-speed cigarette boat blasting away from the island, headed out to sea.

"Where did that come from?" I asked.

"There are private docks up and down the coast," Tori replied.

After watching the speeding boat for another few seconds, I said, "I think he's making a run for it."

The boat had huge twin outboard engines that churned up the water. Only one person was on board, standing at the wheel.

"What's that sound?" I asked.

Tori listened. "All I hear is the boat. What does it sound like? Wait—I hear it."

It sounded like the sharp, tearing sound of a jet engine. It quickly grew louder, which meant it was drawing nearer. Fast. Tori and I both looked back over the island and saw a slim, streaking shape flying high overhead. It had short stubby wings and a rounded nose.

The thing was moving so fast it was hard to focus on, and it was headed out to sea.

"Oh my God," I said with a gasp.

"What is it?" Tori screamed.

I didn't have to answer. A few short seconds later my fear came true. The streaking shape was a missile. It tore by overhead, zeroing in on its target.

"Is that—?"

The missile hit the cigarette boat and exploded into a ball of fire. It took a few seconds for the sound to reach us, but when it did, it was deafening. The horses panicked and reared back. It was all I could do to hang on to Derby. The impact point had to be half a mile out to sea, but I felt a wave of heat wash over us. That's how intense the explosion was as the boat's gas tanks ignited.

"Easy! Easy!" I commanded Derby.

We both got our horses under control and turned our attention back to the water. The only thing left of the cigarette boat and its skipper were a few pieces of smoking wreckage. I looked back to the sky, wondering where the missile might have come from, and saw the dark speck of a military helicopter flying back inland.

"This can't be happening," Tori said, her voice shaking.

"Attention!" came an amplified voice.

We looked up the coastline to see a military Jeep with a SYLO soldier standing in the passenger side, holding a megaphone.

"Do not move," he commanded. "Hold your position."

"No way," I said.

"What do you mean, no way?" Tori cried. "They're the good guys."

"Really? Well the good guys just blew somebody out of the water. I don't care why they're here. That's murder."

I climbed onto Derby's back and slapped the reins on her butt. The old horse still had life and charged forward. I had no idea if I could even stay on the back of a galloping horse, but at that moment I would rather have taken my chances with her than with an army of murderers, no matter whose side they said they were on.

THIRTEEN

I rode Derby back the way we had come, leading Tori up the rise that led back to the sandy road that snaked through the long stretch of sea grass.

"This is crazy," she called. "We can't outrun a Jeep."

I didn't care. They may have worn uniforms with official-looking arm patches and had the backing of the president of the United States but what we'd just seen was murder. If they could blow an innocent guy out of the water for trying to leave the island, they could just as easily do the same to a couple of kids who had witnessed it.

I crested the rise and was about to kick Derby into gear when I caught sight of two people sprinting across the open field. They were tourist types wearing khakis and sweatshirts.

"Hold up!" Tori commanded.

I looked back to see the Jeep speeding after them.

"They aren't after us," she declared.

I reined Derby to a stop as Tori joined me.

The Jeep bumped over the rough surface, closing on the two.

"Hold your position," came the command through the bull-horn. It wasn't directed at us but at the two running men.

The two guys didn't stop. They split up. A soldier jumped out of the Jeep and chased after one while the Jeep went for the other.

"I don't think they even know we're here," Tori said.

"Let's keep it that way, c'mon."

"No," Tori shot back. "I want to see."

The Jeep was gaining ground on the one guy. There were two soldiers on board. The driver and . . .

"Granger," I said. "The head SYLO guy."

The steel-haired soldier stood up in the Jeep as casually as if he were on solid ground—and lifted a rifle. He had done this before.

"No," Tori said with a gasp.

Granger raised the gun with the calm authority of someone who had done it before and took aim at the fleeing man.

The guy dodged and weaved, trying to make a difficult target.

Tori said, "He wouldn't—"

He would. Granger fired. There was a quick *crack*, and the man fell. Unlike with the woman who was run down and captured in the park, this weapon fired bullets. It was like seeing hunters chasing down and killing a fleeing animal, except that the animal was human.

The Jeep skidded to a stop right next to the fallen victim as the driver jumped out and went to the guy. Granger didn't move. He didn't even look down at the body. It was like he couldn't be bothered. That job was left to his subordinates. He rested the rifle casually on his shoulder while scanning the horizon, maybe looking for his next victim. The driver hoisted the body onto his shoulder and dumped it in the back of the Jeep like a sack of fertilizer. Or a dead deer. He then quickly got behind the wheel and took off the way they had come.

They soon caught up with the other soldier, who came trudging toward them with the other guy draped over his shoulder. He had bagged his own kill. He dumped the body in the back of the Jeep, on top of the guy's dead friend, hopped on, and the hunters charged off, headed for the road.

"Did that really just happen?" I said, stunned. "They could have captured those men easily. Same with the cigarette boat. They're the freakin' Navy. They could have caught that boat and arrested them but they killed them instead."

"What do we do?" Tori asked, sounding equally numb.

We had just witnessed a triple murder carried out by the U.S. Navy. What possible explanation could there be that would justify that?

"The sheriff," I said. "We'll get this piece of the Ruby to him and tell him what we saw. He can get it to the CDC people. Or the FBI."

"There's nothing right about any of this," Tori said, still stunned.

We trotted back toward the barn near Tori's house. The whole way I kept glancing over my shoulder for fear that Granger would come blasting out from the brush in the Jeep with his rifle up and ready. It was a nerve-wracking ride, but we made it back safely and started to pull the saddles off the tired horses.

"Maybe we should tell your father," I offered.

"No," she said instantly. "He's got enough to worry about, and . . ."

Her voice trailed off.

"And what?"

Tori struggled to find the right words, as if she was wrestling to understand her own feelings.

"I don't want him to be in danger too."

"You think we're in danger?" I asked.

Tori shrugged. "I think we saw something they didn't want us to see."

"Damn," I said. "Let's get this stuff to the sheriff."

We went right to Tori's scooter and she drove us back into town. Neither of us said anything on the way. I think I was in shock. In the last few weeks I had seen more people die than, well, than ever. As horrible as the deaths of Marty Wiggins and Mr. Nelson were, they were nothing compared to what we saw out on the bluffs by Tori's house. Those people didn't just die, they were killed. Shot. Hunted down. Was it murder? Could it be justified? I had trouble believing that our military had a policy of killing unarmed civilians, quarantine or no quarantine. There had to be another way to deal with people who were trying to leave the island. I wanted to talk to my parents about it, but Tori's words kept ringing in my ears. Maybe it was better if they didn't know. My hope was that we would drop the sample of the Ruby and the mysterious black material off with the sheriff, he'd get it to the proper authorities, they'd figure out that it was the cause of all of our problems, and then the SYLO soldiers would get the hell off Pemberwick.

Riding into Arbortown, I was struck by how normal the place looked. Boredom had replaced fear and people had returned to the streets. The only sign that things were different from any other typical September day were the soldiers that patrolled the streets . . . and the warships lying offshore.

Tori took us right to Sheriff Laska's office, which was a small one-story building on the opposite end of Main Street from the harbor. There was nothing official looking about the place. From the outside it could have been a candle shop or a bookstore. Tori and I stepped into the lobby area, where a receptionist sat behind a desk doing paperwork. Or a crossword puzzle, I couldn't tell.

"Is Sheriff Laska in?" I asked.

"Sure is," the lady replied brightly. She could have been some-body's gray-haired grandma. "Who should I say has come calling?"

I looked to Tori to see if she wanted to answer for herself, but she had gone back into silent mode.

"Tucker Pierce and Tori Sleeper," I answered. "We have some-thing important to show him."

"Well, then," the lady said, putting on an official tone that I didn't believe for a second. She had a hint of a condescending smile as if she thought we were two children who were there to report a cat stuck in a tree. "I'll get him right out here."

She stood and walked quickly down the hallway that led to offices in the back of the building.

"She thinks this is a joke," Tori said.

"That won't last," I replied.

Sheriff Laska came right out, rolling his ample gut into the room. His receptionist followed and sat at her desk.

"So," he declared. "Young Master Pierce and Lady Sleeper. What brings you here?"

I looked at Tori. Tori looked at the ground.

It was up to me.

Seeing this guy standing there in an official uniform suddenly made me tense up. This was no joke. We were about to throw down some serious accusations. I had to be careful. I decided to start with the Ruby and the black debris before jumping right in with the murder stuff.

"I . . . I think we found what SYLO is looking for," I declared.

The sheriff lifted a surprised eyebrow.

"That so? And what exactly might that be?"

I looked around and saw a box of tissues on the receptionist's desk. "Can I?" I asked the lady.

"Help yourself, sweetie," she said with a smile.

I grabbed a tissue and used it to pull the chunk of Ruby out of my pocket. Using the tissue as a protective pillow, I held it out to the sheriff.

"It's called the Ruby," I said. "A ton of it washed up on shore not far from Tori's house. There's a guy named Feit on the island who's been grinding it up and pushing it on people, trying to get them to take it. He's calling it a sports supplement. Marty Wiggins took some before he died. That's why he was playing like he did. I know some other players who took some, too, but not as much. They said it suddenly made them stronger and run faster."

I decided not to throw Kent under the bus for having taken the stuff. Or myself, for that matter.

"Then a couple of horses that Tori was taking care of got into the load on the beach. They ran around like super horses, then dropped dead. Just like Marty. For all we know that's what killed Mr. Nelson, too."

The sheriff wore a scowl that seemed to deepen with every word I said. He glanced toward Tori.

Tori offered a small shrug as if to confirm what I'd said was true.

"We think this is what's causing the deaths on Pemberwick. But the CDC people can tell for sure."

Sheriff Laska stared at the red crystal and reached out to take it, but then pulled his hand back quickly and rubbed his chin thoughtfully. He was afraid to touch it. That was good. It meant he was taking us seriously.

"There's more," I said and showed him the chunk of black plastic. "A bunch of this stuff washed up on shore in the same spot. We think it's wreckage from the boat or the airplane that was bringing this stuff to Pemberwick."

"Airplane?" Laska asked, raising his eyebrow.

"We found it all really close to where Quinn Carr and I saw that shadow explode a few weeks ago."

I intentionally didn't mention that Tori had seen the explosion too. As far as the sheriff knew, the only witnesses were her dad, me, and Quinn.

I added, "We still haven't heard any news about what that was. If you ask me, it's got something to do with SYLO. It's just too coincidental."

Laska took the piece of material and looked at it with a frown. He kept turning it over and over as if expecting to find an answer to the puzzle written on the back.

"That's some story," he finally said. "You say there's a bunch of that red stuff washed up on shore and some fella is going around giving it to people?"

"His name's Feit," I replied. "He's an off-islander. He tried to get me to take it, saying how great I'd play if I did."

Laska wheezed out a laugh. "Well, you couldn't play much worse, now could ya?"

I didn't appreciate the humor and stared at him blankly.

Laska stopped laughing.

"Sorry, that was a cheap shot," he said sheepishly.

"There's something else," Tori said.

This was it. We were about to drop the bomb on SYLO.

"And what's that?" Laska asked.

"Yes," came a voice from the corridor. "I'd like to hear more."

I froze. I recognized the voice from TV.

Laska stepped aside to reveal Captain Granger walking toward us from the sheriff's office. The guy was as calm and cool as if he had just been sipping a lemonade on the porch, not gunning down a fleeing man.

"These kids seem to think they've found our culprit," Laska said, pointing to the chunk of Ruby that I was still holding out.

Granger was more interested in the black plastic. He grabbed it out of Laska's hand, examined it, then tossed it dismissively on a desk. He then held out his hand to me as if demanding to see the Ruby.

I gingerly held out the chunk. Granger snatched it with his bare hand—too tough to worry about something as trivial as being contaminated by a substance that might kill him. He examined the rock with a cold, appraising eye.

Laska said, "They said that some fella named—"

"I heard," Granger said, cutting him off sharply.

147

It was obvious that Granger had no respect for the sheriff.

"Where can I find this fellow?" Granger asked.

"I . . . I have no idea," I replied. "He's not an islander. Said he was passing through but he keeps on popping up. He was at the football games. And Marty's funeral too."

Granger nodded thoughtfully.

"We'll find him," he said as though it was an absolute certainty. "It's a tall tale but we can't afford to discount anything. Thank you both for bringing this to my attention. I'll dispatch a team to clean up the beach immediately."

"What about that plastic?" I asked. "Do you know what that is?"

Granger gave me a smile that showed no warmth whatsoever. "My guess is that it's a piece of a boat's hull, but you would probably know better than me."

Tori said, "That was no boat."

Granger shot her a look. I was afraid that we had just put ourselves into his crosshairs.

"We'll collect everything and determine its origin," he said as if annoyed that he was being challenged.

"Great," I said quickly.

Granger strode past us, headed for the door. He was about to exit when he pulled up short and turned back.

"You said there was something else?" he asked.

This was it. I looked at Tori. Her eyes were on the floor again. I looked to the sheriff with his belly hanging over his belt. Compared to the steely Granger, he was a joke. Granger was a professional soldier who looked as though he would ruthlessly impose his will on friend or foe. And why not? He had the power of an armed, occupational force at his disposal. All Sheriff Laska had was Deputy Donald. I trusted Laska, but there was no way he could protect us from Granger once we accused him of murder.

"Yeah," I said before Tori could say another word. "I'm embarrassed to admit this but . . . I tried some of the Ruby. That's how I know what it does. I only took a little but it was enough to feel the effect. It's bad stuff."

Tori shot me a surprised look, but didn't say anything. She'd gotten the message.

Granger walked back to me, staring me down. His sharp gray eyes sent a chill up my spine. Did he know I wasn't telling the whole truth? Worse, did he know we had seen him gun down that man? It was all I could do to keep my knees from knocking together.

"That's it?" he asked, as if he knew there was a whole lot more.

"That's it," Tori said with conviction.

Granger shot her a look as if surprised she had dared to answer when he was addressing me.

"Yeah," I said. "That's it."

"All right, then," he said. "I'm sure the CDC people will want to talk with you."

"No problem," I replied. "I live over on—"

"I know where you live," Granger said.

That one statement chilled me more than anything else he'd said or done. It meant Granger knew a lot more about Pemberwick Island and the people who lived here than some military officer who just so happened to be assigned the oversight of a quarantine. It was a warning.

"I'd like to ask you all to keep the information about this

"Ruby" stone to yourselves and let the CDC do their investigation. It wouldn't serve anyone to start rumors."

"Makes sense," Laska said. "Right, kids?"

Neither of us replied.

Granger put on his red beret and said, "I'm sure I'll be seeing you again, Mr. Pierce. Miss Sleeper."

He turned and strode toward the door.

"Captain Granger?" Tori called out.

My stomach twisted. What was she doing? Granger stopped, did an about-face, and looked at Tori with impatience.

"How's it going?" she asked.

"Going?" he repeated, puzzled.

"With the quarantine. It can't be easy to keep people happy under the circumstances."

Granger gave her an ironic smile. "It's not my mission to keep people happy. I'm here to keep them safe."

"Right, by keeping them on the island. What would happen if somebody tried to leave? Or should I ask, has anybody tried to leave?"

Granger stared at her, evidently trying to read her. My knees went weak. Tori was not only good at knots, she was pretty good at playing with fire. It would have been interesting to watch, if I wasn't standing in the fire with her.

"No," Granger finally stated. "Everyone has been very cooperative. Nobody has tried to leave."

"But if they did, what would you do?" she asked. "I mean, what kind of force are you authorized to use?"

Granger gave a condescending smile that looked as painful as the time he tried to be charming on TV.

"That's a situation I don't anticipate having to deal with," he said, trying to hide his obvious arrogance. "We're all in this together, Miss Sleeper."

"Yes, we are," Tori said.

Granger gave her a nod and turned.

"Captain?" Tori called again.

I winced.

Granger stopped and looked back at her. Again.

Tori said, "How can you send a team to clean up the beach when you never asked us where it was?"

I wanted to scream at Tori for baiting the guy but couldn't in front of the sheriff and the receptionist.

The smile dropped from Granger's face. Tori had hit a nerve.

"You told the sheriff it was near your house," he said. "And I know where you live as well, Miss Sleeper."

With that he turned and left . . . and I started breathing again. Sort of.

Tori spun to the sheriff and said, "Who exactly is in charge here, sheriff?"

Laska sighed and shrugged. "Until this quarantine is lifted, it's Uncle Sam. I'm stuck here just like everybody else."

For a second I thought Tori might tell him about the shooting. I didn't want that to happen and if she started I would have cut her off again. I didn't want anyone to know what we knew, especially not somebody who was under Granger's thumb.

"Let's go," she snapped and went for the door.

I could finally relax. At least we were on the same wavelength again.

"I hope you're right," Laska said to me.

"About what?" I asked.

"That red stone. Who knows? Maybe you two will be the heroes that end this nightmare."

"Yeah, who knows?" I said and ran after Tori.

She hurried toward her scooter and I had to run to keep up.

"There's more going on with this quarantine than we're being told," she said angrily. "This has to be far worse than they're admitting or they wouldn't be killing people who try to escape."

"You keep saying escape, like we're in prison."

"It's starting to feel that way," Tori said with a slight quiver in her voice that told me she was as scared as she was angry.

"So what should we do?" I said. "We have to tell people what's really happening."

"Yeah, but not yet," Tori said quickly. "At least until they figure out if the Ruby is causing the Pemberwick virus. If it is, then this nightmare will be over. When SYLO leaves, we'll tell the authorities everything. We'll tell anybody who'll listen."

"And what if it isn't the Ruby?"

Tori frowned and looked at the ground.

"Then I don't know. If they're killing people to keep them from escaping, then whatever it is that's on this island has got to be a lot scarier than anything Granger can do to us."

We stood there for a long moment, not sure of what else to say. Tori and I had traveled in different orbits for years, but the events of the last few hours had thrown us together with a shared secret that meant we had no choice but to trust each other.

"Strange days," I said.

"Tell me about it."

"I'm not sure if I can keep this from my parents."

"I can't tell you what to do," she said. "But I'm not telling my dad. Not until I have a better idea of what this is all about. We're on Granger's radar now. I don't want my dad there too."

I nodded. "I hear you. Let's talk tomorrow."

Tori didn't respond to that. She turned, climbed on her scooter, and took off, leaving me alone on the far end of Main Street.

It was getting late in the day. I was exhausted. All I wanted to do was get home, grab something quick to eat, and go to bed. The less of my parents I saw in the process, the better. I didn't want to be tempted into spilling my guts.

The walk home brought me past the Blackbird Inn. It was a quiet evening, but it was suddenly broken by a harsh, wrenching sound that was coming from behind the property. I'd spent a lot of time on the grounds working for my dad and couldn't imagine what it could be. In spite of my being exhausted, curiosity won out and I went to investigate. I walked up the driveway of crushed seashells and around to the small parking lot out back.

The loud squeaking continued, followed by what sounded like something being thrown to the ground. Again and again. It was coming from beyond a row of tall hedges. The only thing back there was a dilapidated old tool shed that the Berringers wanted torn down, but Dad and I hadn't gotten around to it yet. I walked across the lot and along the path that led through the bushes and up to the old structure. When I stepped through, I saw something that was disturbingly wrong.

It was Kent. He was dismantling the shed. It was strange

enough to see him doing any kind of work because Kent never lifted a finger to do anything useful, but what went beyond strange and straight to unsettling was *how* he was doing it. Kent was tearing the place apart with his bare hands. The squeaking sound came from boards being ripped off the frame and tossed onto a pile as he worked at a fever pitch to dismantle the structure. He yanked on the boards, pulling out four nails at a time, as if the slats were made of Styrofoam. The guy was sweating and breathing hard, his total focus on the act of disassembling the shed.

Or destroying the shed.

He was still on the Ruby.

"Kent!" I called.

He shot me a surprised look. His eyes were wild, just like they were in the game.

"What are you doing?" I asked.

Kent dropped the board he had been holding and suddenly charged at me. I was so surprised that I didn't even think to move. He came at me like he did the running backs from Memagog . . . with mayhem on his mind.

"Whoa, dude," I said, taking a step back.

Kent picked me up by the front of my hoodie and threw me with such force that I must have traveled five feet in the air before my feet hit the ground. I stumbled back, trying to keep my balance, but the force was too much and I landed on my butt, hard. Kent was after me again, just like in practice, only now we didn't have pads on and Kent was Ruby-fueled. He leaped at me and put his knee on my chest.

"It's you she talks about," he said, breathing hard, spitting in my face. "I win the game and all she talks about is you. Maybe she won't like you so much if I mess up your face."

He reared back, ready to punch me.

My arms were pinned by his knees so I couldn't defend myself.

"Kent!" came the voice of my savior.

Kent froze and looked up to see Olivia standing at the opening in the hedge.

"What are you doing?" she screamed.

Kent was torn. He wanted to beat the crap out of me but not in front of Olivia. Still, he had to fight the urge to crush my face. With an anguished cry, he threw himself off me and knelt with his hands on the ground, breathing hard.

"Are you all right?" Olivia called to me, nearly in tears.

I was fine. The guy who was in real trouble was Kent.

"You took it again," I called to him. "Didn't you?"

Kent turned to look up at me. His eyes were still wild but the anger was gone. What I saw instead was confusion and fear . . . just like with Marty.

I added, "How much more did you take?"

"I didn't," he said, gasping for breath. "It never wore off. I have to keep moving . . . keep the blood pumping . . . work it off. I . . . I need to control it."

Olivia ran up to us and cried, "What is wrong with him? He's . . . he's acting crazy."

"I'll take you to a doctor," I said to Kent.

Kent jumped to his feet and backed away toward the half-demolished shed.

"No!" he screamed. "Nobody can know."

"Know what?" Olivia shouted.

I ignored her and focused on Kent. "You're in trouble, man. If you don't get it out of your system, you could die."

Kent went back to pulling boards out of the structure.

"I can work it out. Gotta keep the blood moving. Gotta keep breathing."

I took a chance, went up behind him, and put my hands on his shoulders. I felt incredible tension, as if every muscle in his body was flexed.

"That's the worst thing you can do," I said, trying to sound calm. "Keep this up and you'll flame out. Your body can't handle this. You have to relax."

He made a move to start pulling off more boards but I held him tight. He didn't fight me. I had gotten through to him. Whether or not he could control himself was something else altogether.

"Listen to him, Kent," Olivia pleaded, in tears. "Calm down."

Kent looked at her, and I actually saw his eyes soften. He really did care about Olivia. It wasn't me who got through to him, it was her. I felt the tension leave his shoulders. It was slight, but it happened.

"Okay," he said. "Let me sit down."

We both backed away from the shed until we hit a patch of grass. It took incredible self-control, but Kent sat down. I kept my hands on his shoulders in case he lost it again. Olivia joined us and held his hands.

"It's okay," she said to him soothingly. "Relax. Just breathe and relax."

Olivia starting humming a song, like a mother might hum to a baby who can't get to sleep. I didn't know what the song was, but it worked. I felt the tension leave Kent's body. Olivia was doing it.

She shot me a questioning look and asked, "Is it . . . the virus?"

"I don't know. It might be. But he can fight it. He just has to relax. If he can do that, he'll be okay. I think."

"People were taken out of the inn," Olivia said, her own panic rising. "These ambulances came up and the soldiers took them away. I think there are more people infected than they're telling us."

"I think so too," I said. "But they're going to figure it out soon."

"How do you know that?"

I didn't want to get into it with her. Granger was right about one thing: It wasn't good to start rumors. If Kent wanted to tell her about the Ruby, that was his choice. I wasn't going to rat him out.

I thought fast and said, "Because now they've got people who are still alive. That'll make figuring it out much easier."

I had no idea if that was true or not, but it sounded good. I was just happy that she didn't ask me what the Ruby was.

Olivia nodded. It sounded good to her too.

"You're such a good friend, Tucker," she said.

She leaned over Kent, and kissed me on the cheek.

I instantly felt Kent tense up.

"Whoa," I said to him. "Take it easy."

I shot Olivia an *Are you crazy? Why did you do that?* look.

She gave me a sly smile and an innocent shrug. Olivia was trouble. She cared about Kent, but I wasn't sure if she felt as strongly about him as he did about her. It was a potentially dangerous situation that I wanted no part of. I stood up and backed off before things escalated again.

"Talk to me, Kent," I said.

Kent was fighting the aggressive urges, but he was winning.

"I'm okay," he said with labored breaths. "Or I will be."

"Good. Then I'm gonna go."

"Pierce?" Kent called. "I don't know why I went after you like that."

"I know," I said. "You're not going to do anything else stupid, are you? Like before the next game?"

I was hoping he knew what I meant without having to spell it out in front of Olivia.

"No chance," he said.

I believed him.

"Good. Sit there and stay calm for a while."

"What is it?" he asked like a confused little boy. "How could it do this?"

"I don't know," I said. "But I think we'll find out soon."

I took off and ran the rest of the way home with my eyes on the ground. I didn't want to stumble across anything else that would add more drama to the already too-bizarre day. When I got to the house, I blasted in so quickly that I surprised Mom and Dad. Mom tried to hide it, but she had been crying.

So much for ducking more drama.

"What's going on?" I asked.

Dad started to answer fast, but held back. It was like he hadn't expected to have to explain anything just then and still needed time to figure out the proper response.

"Nothing," was his eventual answer.

"Nothing?" I repeated, incredulous. "Why are you crying, Mom?"

"I . . . I'm just worried. That's all."

"About what?" I asked. "Besides everything?"

Dad was reluctant to answer, but he knew he didn't have a choice.

"The TV works," he said.

I waited. He didn't continue.

"I'm not getting the tragedy in that," I said, confused.

I looked at the TV. On the screen was the nightly six o'clock CNN news. Dad watched it every day. He liked the news guy, Dave Storm, but mostly it was because every night at six sharp, they had *The Pemberwick Report.* It was a live segment that told the world about what was happening on our island. Or at least they told the world what the government had been telling CNN. Mom thought Dave Storm was cute. I thought his name was probably made up . . . like he thought he was going to be a weatherman and ended up reading the news.

Dad took a deep breath and said, "We're getting a TV signal. Radio too. We get news and shows and everything else."

"So then what's the problem?" I asked.

"What we're not getting is *out*."

"Out?"

"Phone service is gone," Mom said. "So is the Internet. We can't call, or text, or send e-mails."

"Nothing is coming in either," Dad added. "Nothing private, that is."

I said, "So, maybe it's just a power outage or something."

Both Mom and Dad gave me these looks as if I were the most naïve person who had ever walked the face of the earth.

I said, "So we can't talk to the rest of the world?"

"That's right," Dad said, "And that's why Mom is crying."

FOURTEEN

We spent the rest of the night watching TV, hoping for any news about why Pemberwick Island had had its communications cut off from the mainland, but there was nothing. The only update was that a few new cases of the virus in its early stages might have been identified and people had been brought to the hospital for observation and testing. The reporter said that the CDC was making steady progress and there was hope that they'd get to the bottom of the problem soon and blah, blah, blah.

There was nothing about the Ruby or the field of debris. There was no mention of the cigarette boat that was blown out of the water and the fact that two people were gunned down by SYLO killers, but I guess that was no surprise. It was torture not telling Mom and Dad about what I had seen but I followed Tori's instincts. The less they knew, the better. It would all come out eventually. Of that I was certain. Once Granger and his army were gone and I felt safe, I'd talk to anybody who would listen about what we'd seen. I wondered how I might get in touch with somebody at the *Boston Globe* or the *New York Times*.

It had been an incredibly long day. The morning's football game seemed like it had been played weeks before. My mind was racing in a million directions and if I hadn't been totally exhausted, I never would have been able to fall asleep. Thankfully I nodded off fast and didn't wake up until early the next morning.

When I got dressed and came out of my bedroom, Mom and Dad were already up and glued to the TV. I would have asked if they had been up all night but they were wearing different clothes.

Mom's eyes were puffy and red. She had been crying again.

"Anything new?" I asked, not really sure that I wanted an answer.

"No, but there's going to be an announcement soon," Dad said. "Grab some breakfast."

My heart started beating hard. Was this it? Did they figure out that the Ruby was to blame for the Pemberwick virus? Had somebody found the wreckage of the speedboat? I wasn't hungry but couldn't sit still so I grabbed some Cheerios and brought the bowl into the living room to join my parents. They were watching a Sunday morning news show that had nothing to do with Pemberwick Island. I watched the talking heads but didn't register a single word anybody was saying. I couldn't have cared less about what was happening with the rest of the world.

After about fifteen minutes, the screen went black. Seconds later, a SYLO logo appeared.

We all sat up straight. The logo stayed on the screen for a solid sixty seconds before it faded out and was replaced by the image of Captain Granger seated at a desk. The guy didn't look any more comfortable than the last time he had been on the air. Only this time,

I knew a little bit more about him and what he was capable of.

"Good morning," he began. "I'm sure many of you know that there has been a massive failure of the communications infrastructure here on Pemberwick Island. While we are still able to receive digital data, the use of telephones, both hardwired and cellular, has been sporadic."

"Sporadic?" Dad said, incredulous. "Try nonexistent."

"Also, we are not able to access the Internet," Granger continued. "Rest assured that the utility companies both here on Pemberwick Island and on the mainland are hard at work to identify the problem and restore service. Military communications have not been affected, so we are keeping tabs on the situation and will report the moment we have found a solution. We hope that we will all be back online and in touch shortly. Until then, we ask for your continued cooperation with the SYLO team during this time of inconvenience. Thank you."

The picture dissolved back into the SYLO logo and moments later the news program picked up, in progress.

"I guess that's it," Mom said. She seemed relieved, as if she had been expecting some bad news.

"He's full of it," I declared.

"Why do you say that?" Dad asked.

"If there's cable service, there's Internet. And people have satellite phones. Satellites didn't start falling out of the sky, did they?"

"Why do you think he'd lie?" Mom asked.

"I don't know. But I'll bet anything that Granger knows exactly why we've been cut off. Heck, he probably has something to do with it."

I jumped up and headed for the front door.

"Where are you going?" Dad asked.

"We can't use the phone but we can still talk," I said. "I want to see what other people think."

Dad ran ahead and cut me off.

"I think we should do what Granger suggested. We have to have patience."

"Seriously, Dad, do you trust that guy?"

He thought about the answer then said, "I have no reason to doubt him."

"Well, I do," I shot back. "And I want to know the truth."

I started back toward the door but Dad grabbed my arm and said, "We'll all get that soon enough."

He stared me straight in the eye as if he were trying to tell me something without actually saying it. I looked at Mom. Tears welled in her eyes again.

"What are you guys not telling me?" I asked with determination.

For a second I thought Dad was going to answer. Instead, he let go of my arm and backed off.

"Nothing," he said, sounding defeated. "I just don't want you getting in any trouble. Stay close to home, would you?"

"Where am I going to go?" I asked. "We're on an island, remember?"

Dad gave me a shrug and a nod. Mom got up and went into the kitchen.

"See you later," I said and headed out.

My parents were starting to piss me off. I didn't like how they were so willing to accept what was happening. These were good people who got shafted, had to pull up their roots in Connecticut and then move to another town to find a better life. That took guts. Why weren't they showing those same guts when their life here was being threatened?

I left the house, not sure of where I would go or what I was looking for. I wanted to be around people who were as upset as I was, and it didn't take long to find them. I went to Main Street and quickly discovered that my instincts were correct: People didn't accept Granger's explanation for why our phone and Internet had been cut off any more than I did. People I recognized from all over the island, and many more I didn't, were slowly gravitating toward town hall. It was the center of government for Arbortown and as good a place as any for people to vent about how they were being treated, even though it was Sunday and the offices were closed.

It started out as a few groups of people scattered here and there but the numbers soon swelled. They were all talking about the fact that we had been cut off, and nobody was happy about it. Everyone wanted to be heard, but nobody was doing much listening. I heard bits and pieces of angry outbursts coming from all around me.

"Who is he kidding?"

"It's not right!"

"I haven't pulled a single trap in weeks."

"My kids are in Boston. I have to talk to them."

"Without a phone, I'm out of business."

It went on and on.

"The natives grow restless," came Quinn's familiar voice. He walked up to me and said, "I was wondering how long it would take before people started getting antsy."

"I think SYLO cut us off," I said.

"Really?" he said with exaggerated surprise. "That makes you . . . and everybody else. The question is, why?"

I didn't tell Quinn about Granger for the same reason Tori and I hadn't told our parents.

"If they're not telling us the truth to keep us calm," Quinn said, "it's backfiring."

The crowd had grown and spilled into the street, choking off traffic into town. Car horns blared but it didn't help. It was gridlock.

"Not that I have any experience in these things," Quinn said. "But this has all the makings of an angry mob. Kind of exciting."

"Exciting?" I asked, incredulous.

"Yeah, in an anarchistic, overthrow-the-government kind of way. History is being made here and we're part of it."

I watched with apprehension as the small groups of angry islanders gradually drifted into one big group.

"I'd rather have things go back to normal," I said.

"Ah," Quinn scoffed. "Normal's overrated."

I gave him a sideways glance. "Do you mean that?"

"That depends," he replied.

"On what?"

"On whether or not we live to tell our kids about it all."

"Jeez, man, don't even joke about something like that."

"Who's joking? This is going to get hairy."

People started shouting to be heard. You could feel the energy growing, and it wasn't positive. I only hoped that nobody had decided to sample the Ruby. That would have been like lighting a fuse on dynamite. Slowly, the crowd pushed toward the steps of town hall, where people stopped talking to each other and started shouting their questions at the empty building.

"Why have we been cut off?"

"Tell us the truth!"

"Check this out," Quinn said. He cupped his hands around his mouth and started chanting: "Sy-lo, Sy-lo, Sy-lo . . ."

"Stop!" I commanded, pulling his hands away. "You don't want to mess with Granger."

"Yes, I do," he replied and continued his chant. "Sy-lo, Sy-lo, Sy-lo . . ."

The crowd actually picked up on it and soon the chant was booming across town with the combined voices of a thousand angry islanders.

I grabbed Quinn by the shoulders and got right in his face.

"Don't do this. It's not a game!" I shouted at him over the chanting crowd. "You're pushing the wrong buttons."

"Or helping to start a revolution," he said, then pulled away from me and continued to chant.

I didn't know what to do. Quinn was having the time of his life . . . and helping to whip the crowd into a frenzy. Finally, a woman's amplified voice came over a loudspeaker that was set up on top of town hall.

"Attention. Please clear the street to allow for the flow of traffic."

"No!" was the basic response as everyone shouted her down.

"Please disperse," the woman said calmly. "This assembly has become a public hazard."

Her voice only seemed to rile the people up even more. The

angry crowd had suddenly become an enraged mob. People I knew who were usually normal and friendly were showing their darker side. I saw my football coach and an art teacher. There were parents of my friends and even little kids. But the familiar faces were few and far between. Most of these people I had never seen in my life. No matter where they had come from, they were all getting swept up in the emotion.

A handful of guys broke from the crowd, charged up the stairs, and started banging on the doors. Everyone was yelling something different but the general sentiment was the same: They were tired of being held prisoners. Cutting off communications was the last straw.

"Come on!" Quinn said.

We pushed our way in the opposite direction and climbed up onto the second-floor balcony of a hardware store across from town hall. From there we had a perfect view of the action.

The street was jammed with people of all ages. Another chant began: "Sy-lo . . . Sy-lo . . . Sy-lo."

Quinn smiled with satisfaction.

The guys in front of the town hall continued to pound on the doors. It seemed like it was only a matter of time before they'd break a window and overrun the place. I doubted that Granger was inside, but that didn't matter. It was more about letting out frustration.

The announcements continued, "Please disperse immediately. This unlawful assembly has become a public hazard."

The crowd reacted instantly and angrily to that statement with a new chant, "Un-law-ful . . . un-law-ful . . ."

"Not as catchy as my chant," Quinn commented

"Where's this going?" I asked.

The answer came from the crowd itself.

"The ferry!" I heard someone yell.

The men who had been pounding on the town hall doors immediately moved as one toward the harbor while continuing to chant and scream in protest.

"Enough!"

"We're getting off!"

"They can't stop us!"

The crowd parted to let the men through and they picked up speed, headed for the harbor.

"Are they seriously going to try to take over the ferry?" I asked, stunned.

"This is awesome!" Quinn declared.

"Awesome? They could get killed!"

"Nah," Quinn scoffed. "Do you seriously think the United States Navy would hurt their own people?"

That was exactly what I thought.

The rest of the mob followed the guys, who began sprinting for the wharf.

"Let's go with 'em," Quinn said and made a move to climb down.

I grabbed his arm and pulled him back.

"Stop," I commanded. "You want to live to tell your kids about this?"

"Aww, you're no fun."

To Quinn this was all an exciting game.

I knew better.

Up until that moment the SYLO soldiers had not shown themselves. That was about to change. In the center of Main Street, at the top of the rise that led down to the wharf, a dozen soldiers ran into position, forming a wall to block off the street. Each had rifles slung over their shoulders. Real rifles. Not the kind with a wide barrel that fires beanbags.

"Ooh, not good," Quinn said, suddenly serious. "Maybe it is better we stay here."

The crowd of guys charging for the ferry started whooping a battle cry.

"Somebody's going to get hurt," I said soberly.

"Look," Quinn said, pointing to a rooftop across the street.

Captain Granger had arrived. He stood looking down on the action along with two SYLO subordinates. One of the soldiers had binoculars that he used to scan the crowd. Granger stood ramrod-straight with his hands clasped behind his back. If he was worried about the developments below, he didn't show it.

"That is one cold dude," Quinn commented.

He had no idea how true that statement was.

The angry sprinters were about twenty yards from clashing with the line of soldiers when the soldiers opened fire—with water. Fire hoses positioned on either side of the street spewed powerful blasts of water directly into the mob. Some people fought to keep going, but the force of the water was too strong. Many were knocked off their feet. Others were pushed back, only to hit the huge crowd that was following them. It was a madhouse. There were screams of anger and frustration floating everywhere. The people in the back didn't realize what was happening up front and kept surging forward which made it harder for anyone to retreat.

Granger remained as calm as if it was all a day at the beach. He motioned to one of his soldiers to come closer to him. Without taking his eyes off the action below, he said something to the soldier, who immediately got on a walkie-talkie to relay whatever Granger had said.

"He's running this show," I said.

The crowd kept surging forward. The waterworks might have worked if it were only the handful of guys who were running for the ferry, but there were so many people behind them that they were caught between SYLO and the surging mob that kept pushing them forward. It was looking as though this was going to lead to an even more violent clash when . . .

BOOM.

There was an ear-splitting eruption that came from the sea. It was so loud that it instantly quieted the crowd. All eyes looked out to the warship that was floating at the mouth of the harbor. A cloud of dark smoke drifted up from its deck.

"I think they just launched something," I said with dismay.

"I don't believe that," Quinn said, stunned.

A second later, he believed it. We all did.

A shrieking sound followed that meant something was headed toward us. Fast.

Pemberwick Island used two ferryboats. One had been turned back the day the island was invaded. The second sat empty and unused at the end of the pier. That ferry was an iconic image of Pemberwick Island that was duplicated on postcards and posters and photographed by every family that had ever experienced the idyllic pleasures of our island in the Atlantic.

But it would never carry another passenger, for a few seconds later it exploded. It was a solid hit. Flames spewed from the doomed craft as its fuel tanks erupted. I felt the heat from as far away as we were. It must have been searing hot down on the street.

The emotion of the crowd instantly turned from anger to panic. Dozens turned and fled. Women picked up small children to keep them from being trampled. People stumbled and fell, only to be stepped on by those desperate to get away from the wharf. Many of these people had been friends and neighbors for decades. None of that mattered when fear took over. Everyone wanted out and they didn't care who stood in their way.

The soldiers kept washing them with the fire hoses until the crowd had fled out of range. A few dazed men stumbled away, staring back in disbelief at the ferryboat that burned at the end of the wharf.

A number of soldiers turned the fire hoses from the crowd to the boat to extinguish the inferno. The water hit the fire to create billows of black smoke that floated up and formed a dark cloud over the small harbor, blocking out the light and warmth of the sun. Within minutes, Main Street was nearly deserted. All that was left of the riot was wet pavement and the burning hulk of the ferry.

I looked to see Granger's reaction to the mayhem—and gasped. He wasn't looking at the street. He was staring directly at me. I could feel his sharp glare boring into my head. Once again I had witnessed him committing a ruthless act. There was no doubt in my mind that he had called in that missile strike on the ferry.

"We're prisoners here," I said numbly.

Quinn nodded. "There's only one reason they'd do this. The

Pemberwick virus has got to be way more deadly than they're letting on. Why else would they go so far to keep us here?"

I started to climb down from the balcony.

"Where are we going?" Quinn asked as he followed.

"I want to see how Kent is."

"Berringer? What the hell for?"

When we hit the sidewalk, I looked up to see that Granger had stepped to the edge of the roof so he could still see me. What was he thinking? Was he worried that I might know too much?

As we hurried away from Main Street, headed for the Blackbird Inn, I confessed to Quinn. There was no way I could keep it to myself any longer. I told him the truth about the Ruby and about how I had taken it. I told him about Feit and about my fear that the Ruby had killed Marty. I also told him that I brought a sample to the sheriff to examine and how Granger was there and said he would bring it to the CDC scientists. But that's all that I said. I didn't want him to know *too* much and be on Granger's radar along with Tori and me.

At first he was pissed that I hadn't confided in him earlier, but the revelation of the possible cause of the Pemberwick virus topped his anger.

"So . . . what did the Ruby stuff do to you?" he asked with wide-eyed curiosity.

"I felt like I could do anything, and it wasn't just in my head. You saw the way Marty played. Kent was the same way. It gives you incredible strength and speed, but it's impossible to function at that level for any length of time. If you take too much, you flame out."

"So you think Kent is, like, dead?" Quinn asked.

"No, I think he beat it. But I want to know for sure."

"Jeez . . . ," Quinn said, stunned. It was the only time I had ever seen him at a loss for words.

"You were right from the get-go," I said. "There's more going on here than they've been telling us."

"More than they're telling *anybody*," Quinn added. "I think this is why communications have been cut off. They don't want the rest of the world to know what's going on either."

The realization hit me like a punch in the gut.

"Oh my God," I exclaimed. "Communications were cut right after I took the Ruby to the sheriff."

"You were getting too close," Quinn said.

The idea that Tori and I were the cause of the communication blackout was both stunning and frightening. If Granger was willing to execute people for trying to escape, what would he do to people who were in on his secrets? My only consolation was that I hadn't told my parents. They couldn't know until the rest of the world knew . . . which meant that somehow we had to tell the rest of the world.

We arrived at the Blackbird Inn to see an ambulance parked out front, along with two black Humvees.

"Uh-oh," said Quinn.

We ran up the driveway in time to see SYLO soldiers stepping out of the front door carrying a stretcher. On it was Mrs. Berringer. She was strapped down, but not to keep her from falling off—it was to keep her under control. She fought against her restraints, desperate to break loose.

"They're coming!" she shouted. "We have to protect our home! Let me go!"

Moments later, Mr. Berringer sprang from the front door and sprinted off the porch. He was an older guy. There was no way he could run like that. Not normally, anyway. Two SYLO soldiers sprang from behind a Humvee and tackled him. Mr. Berringer fought to get away, but the guys were too strong and quickly wrestled him toward the dark car.

"You can't do this," he railed. "We'll be overrun. They're coming!"

A second stretcher was carried out of the inn. This one held Kent.

I couldn't stand it anymore and ran for the house.

"Kent!" I called. "What happened?"

The paramedics put Kent's stretcher down and helped the others who were struggling to get Mr. Berringer into the Humvee. Kent had mostly come down from the effects of the Ruby, but when he saw me, his eyes flared. Not with power, but with anger.

"Why?" he snarled while straining against his restraints.

"Why what? Did your parents—?"

"The island's in chaos. They wanted to protect our property from the rioters. What else could they do? And you turned us in."

"What? No! I didn't tell anybody."

Olivia hurried out of the inn and stood close to me.

"This is horrible," she said with tears in her eyes. "They just started going . . . crazy!"

She held on to my arm like a frightened child, pressing her body close to mine. It only made Kent angrier. He struggled against the straps that held him onto the stretcher, but he wasn't going anywhere.

"You're dead, Pierce," he growled. "I swear I'll kill you."

The paramedics returned and one put a firm hand on his chest and said, "Easy. Calm down."

"Where are you taking them?" Quinn asked.

"The hospital," the paramedic answered. "Back away, please."

They lifted Kent up and quickly slid him into the ambulance.

"I'm coming for you, Pierce!" Kent screamed as they closed the doors on him.

Seconds later the Humvees took off, followed by the ambulance with lights flashing and sirens blaring.

Olivia buried her face in my chest and cried. "Why is this happening? What is wrong with them?"

I wasn't about to stand there and explain the Ruby to her.

"It's the Pemberwick virus," I said. "Hopefully they'll catch it in time."

Olivia looked at me and through sad, teary eyes said, "I'm never going to leave this island, am I?"

"Why don't you go to the hospital and try to calm Kent down," I said.

"No," she said, backing away as if I'd suggested she pay a visit to a leper colony. "I'm not going anywhere near that place."

She turned and ran into the house, slamming the door behind her.

"Well," Quinn said. "We've got all sorts of drama going on."

"The Berringers took the Ruby," I said. "It's spreading. Those CDC scientists can't ignore it anymore. They have to put out an announcement to keep people from using it."

"They won't," Quinn said. "Or they would have already."

"You think they're hiding the truth too?" I asked.

"I think the whole bunch of them know what's going on and they're doing everything they can to keep the truth from leaving this island."

"But there's no way they can keep it secret for long. I mean, people on the mainland are going to start asking questions."

"Maybe," Quinn said, sounding grim. "Or maybe this is bigger than we can imagine."

"What do you mean?"

"Let's go to my house," he said. "I want to show you something."

We left the inn and walked to Quinn's house without discussing it further. Arbortown was deserted. The stores were all closed. A riot will do that. People must have gone back to their houses to hole up out of fear for what SYLO might do to them if they poked their noses out. I wasn't worried about the soldiers so much. It was Granger who scared me. He was in charge. He knew it all. And I knew how ruthless he could be.

Worse, he knew I knew.

Quinn's parents weren't home. I figured they were doing extra duty at the hospital since so many cases of the Pemberwick virus were being brought in. We went right to Quinn's room, where he fired up his computer.

"Have you been watching TV?" he asked while the laptop booted up.

"Sure. What else is there to do?"

"Have you noticed that there isn't much news about Pemberwick anymore? When the invasion first happened, we were all over the place. I mean, Jimmy Kimmel did a whole sketch about being trapped in preppie prison where everybody was forced to wear bright pink and green and eat deviled eggs. But since those first few days, zip. We're already old news."

"What about CNN?" I asked.

"Ahh, *The Pemberwick Report*," Quinn said as he keyed in some words. "Every night intrepid reporter Dave Storm comes on at exactly six o'clock with a live, up-to-the-minute report on the latest news from our troubled little island. Check this out."

He brought up a media player and hit "play." The familiar image of the CNN anchor Dave Storm came up. He sat at a desk in front of a busy newsroom to deliver the evening report on Pemberwick. There was a logo and everything. *The Pemberwick Report*. Quinn let it play, but the sound was muted.

"This was the first report. The day after the invasion. I set the DVR to record them all. You know. It's history. I transferred it all to my laptop."

"What's your point?" I asked impatiently.

Quinn stopped the playback, hit a few more keys, and said, "I edited together a few seconds from every report. Check this out."

He hit "play" again, and the image of Storm came up from the next day's report. Everything was exactly the same except for his suit. It played silently for a few seconds and then cut to the next day's report. Again, it was the same thing, only with Dave Storm wearing yet another different suit.

Quinn said, "I've got seven reports here. All live. All recorded one day apart at six o'clock."

Two more clips went past.

"What am I watching?" I asked. "Is he saying something weird?"

"No," Quinn replied. "He's not saying much of anything. It's all about how SYLO is doing a fantastic job and everybody's fine. In the later reports he mentions the possibility of a few new cases of the virus, but that's it. There was definitely nothing about the Ruby."

"So then what am I looking at?"

Quinn scrolled back to the first report and let it play.

"Check out the digital clock deep inside the newsroom."

I looked over Storm's shoulder and saw a red digital clock that read 18:00. Six o'clock, using military time.

"Yeah—so?"

"Keep watching."

The next clip came up. The clock again read 18:00. The third clip was different. The clock read 2:04.

"Whoa, freeze it," I said.

Quinn hit "pause."

"I thought it was live at six o'clock?" I said.

"Yeah, me too. Watch."

Quinn hit "play." When the next clip came up the clock read 2:45. The clock in the following clip showed 4:06. The rest were different as well. The clock never read 18:00 again.

"So what does that mean?" I asked.

"It means the reports aren't broadcast live," Quinn replied. "They were shot at all different times of the day and then passed off as live."

"Is that normal?" I asked.

"Not for a live newscast," Quinn shot back.

"Maybe they pre-taped the reports," I said. "That's not a crime, is it?"

"No," Quinn said patiently. "But it's weird if they're calling it live, and so it got me thinking. I watch a lot of TV. I admit it. Don't judge me. After seeing that clock thing on CNN, I started paying closer attention to what was on in general, and you know what I realized?"

"That you have to stop watching so much TV?"

"Since the day SYLO invaded, there hasn't been a single new episode of anything. No reality shows. No prime-time shows. No daytime stuff. It's all reruns. Everything. Even the rest of the news. That's the weirdest thing. There are no big stories. None. It's like nothing newsworthy has happened for over a week. All they're showing is a bunch of fluff stuff like . . . like . . ."

"Like it was all recorded a long time ago," I said.

"Exactly. Nothing we're seeing is new."

My head started to spin.

"So that means—"

"It means we're not only cut off from talking to the outside," Quinn said. "It means the outside isn't getting through to us either. We're totally isolated."

FIFTEEN

"I've seen some stuff," I said tentatively.

"Who hasn't?" was Quinn's flip response.

"I mean, stuff I wish I hadn't."

"Again, who hasn't?"

"I saw Granger murder somebody, okay!"

For the second time that day, Quinn was speechless. He sat there staring at me with his mouth hanging open. I hadn't wanted to tell him about it. Not until we were all safe. But events were spiraling out of control. Safety seemed like a long way off. I wanted another ally.

"Details, please," was all Quinn finally managed to croak out.

I told him everything. About Tori telling off Feit and how she showed me the horses and the Ruby that washed up on the beach along with the debris from what could have been the exploded shadow. I told him about the cigarette boat that was blown out of the water and the two guys who were hunted down and killed by SYLO soldiers . . . and by Granger. I also admitted to him that Tori was with me when I turned the Ruby and the wreckage in to the sheriff—and Granger.

He took it all in without a word. His nimble brain was taking each bit of information and placing it into an equation that would hopefully bring us to an answer that made sense. When I had finally gotten it all off my chest, I waited for his response.

Quinn nodded slowly then announced, "I *knew* you liked Tori Sleeper."

"Seriously?" I shouted. "That's all you got from that?"

"I'm kidding," he said, then jumped to his feet and paced. He had gone from passive information gathering to full-on calculation mode.

"Okay, we know we're being lied to," he said, his words only a few steps ahead of his brain. "Or at least we're not getting the whole truth about this so-called Pemberwick virus."

"I think it's all about the Ruby," I declared.

"It can't be that simple," Quinn argued. "If that were true, all it would take is one announcement—'Don't eat the Ruby'—and poof, no more virus."

"So then what do you think the Ruby is?"

"No idea," Quinn said. "I'm more interested in SYLO. They're grabbing people off the street but we're only hearing about a few new cases of the virus. And now they're so desperate to control the quarantine that they're willing to kill people who try to escape."

"I think the guy in that cigarette boat was trying to escape," I said. "I don't know about those men Granger hunted down and shot on the bluffs."

"Whatever. It all comes back to the virus, and the reason SYLO is here," Quinn declared.

"It's gotta be about the Ruby," I offered.

"But that doesn't make sense," Quinn said with frustration. "If the Ruby was causing the virus, why would they keep it a secret?"

"I don't know! To keep us from panicking," I shot back. "Look at what happened downtown. Reasonable people turned into an angry mob when they suddenly couldn't log on to Facebook. Imagine what would happen if everyone found out that we were all . . ."

I couldn't finish the sentence.

"What?" Quinn asked. "Being poisoned?"

We let that hang there for a second.

"I don't buy it," Quinn said. "There's gotta be more to the virus than that."

"But if SYLO truly has no idea of what they're dealing with, why would all those soldiers volunteer to come here?"

"Who knows?" Quinn replied. "Maybe they were vaccinated. They might be here just to keep us calm until the end."

"Don't say that," I said, sober. "That's like . . . beyond horror."

"So what do *you* think is going on?" Quinn asked. "What exactly *is* the Ruby?"

"I don't know," I said quickly. "But you're right. It comes back to the virus. If we knew more about it, this would all make more sense."

Quinn gave me a sly smile. I knew that look. It meant he had thought of something that nobody else had . . . including me.

"What?" I asked.

"I know how we can find out more about the mysterious Pemberwick virus," he declared.

"How?"

"My parents. They're doctors at Arbortown Hospital. Dad's in the ER. They've got to know about every case of the virus that's been brought in."

"That's right!" I exclaimed. "What have they said about it?"

"Nothing. They never talk about patients. Confidentiality and all that."

"But this is a little extreme, don't you think?"

"I do, but they don't."

"So they're a dead end."

"No," Quinn said, once again offering the sly smile. "They might not tell me anything about their patients . . . but their computers will."

Minutes later we were on our way to Arbortown Medical. We grabbed bikes from Quinn's garage and pedaled our way to the far northern end of town along roads that we had all to ourselves. Nobody was out for a casual drive. They were too busy hiding.

I'd only been to the hospital once, when I fell off my bunk bed and broke my wrist. It was a painful memory. The process of resetting bones hasn't changed since medieval times. It was the longest four seconds of my life.

"Act casual and nobody will question us," Quinn instructed as we stepped into the lobby.

"I wish you hadn't said that," I complained. "How exactly do I act casual?"

"By not acting."

"You're killing me."

"Quinn Carr!" called the elderly woman who sat behind the

information desk at the dead center of the large lobby. "I haven't seen you around here in ages. You're growing up to be quite the handsome young man."

Under his breath Quinn said, "She says the exact same thing every time I see her."

"Hi, Mrs. Guimond," he said politely. Then in his most charming voice he added, "Are my parents around? I figure you're the one to ask since you pretty much run this place."

The sweet old woman chuckled and gave Quinn a coy smile. He knew the exact right thing to say to get people to do what he wanted. I was beginning to think he really was a brilliant student of human nature.

"Hang on a sec, sweetie," the woman said. "Let me see."

She checked her computer monitor, looking over her half eyeglasses.

Quinn leaned in to me and whispered, "She pretends to read the screen so people will think she knows how to use the computer."

"Nope," the woman announced. "They're not checked in. Come to think of it, I haven't seen them all day. Are you sure they're scheduled?"

Quinn frowned. "They said they were. You absolutely sure they didn't check in?"

"Sure as sugar," she said with a smile.

"Okay, maybe I'm wrong. No worries. I've got to get something from their office. Homework."

Before she could respond, Quinn grabbed my arm and hurried me past the desk.

"Wait, I'll write you a pass," Mrs. Guimond said.

"That's okay, we won't be long," Quinn said and kept us moving.

"Shouldn't we get a pass?" I asked him.

"Not if we don't want any record that we were here," Quinn said softly.

"What about your parents?" I asked. "I thought you said they were working today."

"That's what they told me," Quinn said. He sounded troubled.

"Maybe she made a mistake," I offered.

"Nah. Mrs. G may be a little dizzy, but she doesn't miss a trick. If she says they aren't here, they aren't. What I want to know is why they said they were coming to work and didn't."

I didn't want to speculate on the answer. There were too many bad scenarios.

Quinn led us quickly to a stairwell and down two flights to the ground floor and the emergency room, where his parents worked. A few people were being treated for what looked like scrapes and bruises. I wondered if they had gotten them on Main Street when the SYLO soldiers turned the hoses on the crowd. We didn't stop to ask and kept moving down a long corridor of offices until we reached the end, and the office that was shared by Dr. and Dr. Carr, Quinn's parents. Quinn gave a quick glance back toward the ER. There was nobody in sight so he opened the door and we slipped inside.

"Lock it," he said as he hurried to one of the desks and fired up the computer. "Let me know if anybody's coming."

I twisted the lock and positioned myself near the door where I could see the corridor through the window.

"Doesn't the computer have security?" I asked.

"Sure," Quinn said as he keyed in a code. "High security. The passcode is my birthday. Then they each have their own personal codes . . . their birthdays. My parents may be great doctors but they're clueless when it comes to computers. Got it!"

"Got what?"

"I'm on the secure hospital file server. I use the term *secure* with full sarcasm."

"What's there?" I asked while keeping an eye on the corridor.

"Everything. Schedules, budgets, equipment requests, even the cafeteria's recipes. You name it. If it has to do with this hospital, it's in here."

"And what exactly are you looking for?"

Quinn continued to click through screens while he talked.

"The charts on the patients with the Pemberwick virus," he replied.

"Aren't you breaking a few dozen laws by looking through people's personal medical history?"

"Absolutely. Ethical, moral, and criminal. But as far as anybody knows, my dad is the one who logged on and he's allowed."

A doctor hurried past the far end of the corridor and I ducked back so he wouldn't see me.

"Whatever you're doing, do it fast," I said.

"Here, I got it," Quinn declared. "Man, I am good."

I couldn't resist and hurried to the computer. Quinn was scrolling down a long list of file folders and came upon one that read PEMBERWICK VIRUS.

"That was easy," I said.

"I told you, security is not their strength."

Quinn dragged the folder onto the desktop and double-clicked it. The next level of files opened up, showing three different folders. They were marked DECEASED, ADMITTED, and UNDER OBSERVATION.

"Start with deceased," I said. "We already know about them."

Quinn clicked on the file and two more file folders appeared. One was marked MARTIN R. WIGGINS, the other PETER NELSON.

"That's them," I said. "Both dead."

"Yeah, let's see what the medical report said."

Quinn clicked on the Nelson folder. It opened to reveal . . . nothing.

"How can it be empty?" I asked.

Quinn quickly clicked on Marty's folder. It, too, was empty.

"Weird," Quinn declared. "This should have all of their information, from the doctor's evaluation to a death certificate and the autopsy report."

"Check out ADMITTED," I suggested. "The Berringers should be listed."

Quinn closed out one folder and double-clicked on the ADMITTED folder. A new window opened. Quinn and I stared at it, neither comprehending what we were seeing.

"I don't get it," he finally said.

"Where are the files?" I asked.

"There *are* no files," Quinn shot back. "According to this, not a single person with the Pemberwick virus has been admitted."

"But they were," I argued. "What about all those people that SYLO grabbed? And the Berringers?"

"I know," Quinn replied with frustration. "That's what I don't get. I'll check UNDER OBSERVATION."

He closed out the file and opened the final folder. The result was the same.

"How can that be?" I asked.

"I don't know," Quinn said, sounding shaken.

"Maybe there's some kind of medical setup at the SYLO camp," I offered.

"Then why did my parents tell me that all the suspected cases were being brought here? And those paramedics told us they were bringing the Berringers here."

We both stared at the blank screen, hoping that it would provide some other clue.

"There has to be a mistake," I said. "Are you sure this is the only record of patients for the hospital?"

"Yes!" Quinn shouted impatiently. "And it's not just for this hospital. This is the database for the entire island. Even if patients were taken to some other place, the information would be entered here."

I said, "Do you think that SYLO is hiding the information? Like a cover-up?"

"Maybe," Quinn said tentatively. "There's one other possibility."

"What's that?" I asked.

Quinn turned from the screen and looked at me. His face was gleaming with nervous sweat and his heavy glasses had slipped down to the end of his nose.

"Maybe there *is* no Pemberwick virus," he said softly.

"Dr. Carr?" came a voice from the corridor.

We both froze.

There was a knock on the door.

"Dr. Carr?" the man's voice called again.

This time he tried the doorknob. Quinn shot me a questioning glance. I nodded quickly—I had locked the door. Did the guy have a key? Four seconds went by. Four seconds that felt longer than when they had reset my broken wrist.

Finally, the guy gave up, and we heard footsteps walking away.

Without a word Quinn logged off the computer and shut it down. After a quick check to make sure nothing was out of place, we headed out. Neither of us spoke as we cautiously opened the door, checked that nobody was in the corridor, and hurried back through the ER.

"Quinn!" a man's voice called.

Quinn's back went straight as if he'd been hit with a cattle prod.

A guy dressed all in white and with a name tag on his shirt approached us. He looked like a staff guy, not a doctor.

"Hey, is your dad scheduled today?" he asked. "I've got some requisition forms for him to sign."

I willed Quinn to hold it together and think fast.

"You know," Quinn said, sounding way more casual than he deserved to, "I thought he was, but I can't find him. He must be around somewhere."

"No problem," the guy said. "I'll catch him tomorrow."

The guy hurried off and we could breathe again. The two of us did all we could to keep from running out of there. We hit the stairs, climbed back to the lobby, and hurried out the front door without stopping to say goodbye to Mrs. Guimond.

Once outside, we finally gave in and started running. We grabbed the bikes, blasted out of the parking lot, and didn't stop pedaling until we hit the war memorial on the edge of the village green.

There, we finally dumped the bikes and sat on the edge of the large cement sculpture that had the engraved names of all the war dead from Pemberwick. We were both breathing hard and trying to catch our breath when I looked up at the long list of names . . . and was hit with an odd thought: All those guys had died fighting for our country. I wondered what any of them would have done if they had been asked to be part of an outfit like SYLO.

"Why did my parents lie?" Quinn said, gulping for air. "What do they know?"

"Don't get all paranoid," I cautioned. "They're probably just as clueless as the rest of us."

"No," Quinn shot back. "My dad doesn't miss a thing. Neither does Mom. They're like . . . like surgeons. That's how precise they are. No wasted effort. No wasted words. They say what they mean with no room for wiggle. They said they were both going to work."

"So maybe something came up."

"Sure. Okay. Possible. But they've definitely been lying about the virus patients. Why would they do that unless . . ." His voice trailed off.

"Unless what?" I asked.

"Unless they're hiding something," Quinn declared. "Tuck, could they be involved with this somehow?"

"No," I answered quickly, then thought for a second. "I mean, that's crazy. Right?"

He didn't answer.

My mind raced ahead, trying to understand what it was we had uncovered, and what to do with the information. There was nobody to turn to. The sheriff was useless, we were cut off from the rest of the world, and the people who were supposedly protecting us were the ones keeping all the secrets.

"We gotta tell my parents," I finally declared. "I didn't want to before but this is getting out of control."

"What can they do?" Quinn asked, skeptically.

"I don't know!" I shouted. "But I don't want to deal with this alone anymore."

"Okay. Right. I'm with you."

We had gotten our wind back enough to get on the bikes and ride to my house. It felt good to focus on riding. It helped keep my thoughts from spinning out of control, kind of like our midnight rides. My entire focus was on getting home, dumping everything I knew on my parents, and getting some sage parental advice that would help us figure out the right thing to do. That's what parents did. It was their job. I was actually starting to feel a little bit better . . .

. . . until we turned the corner onto my street.

"Oh, crap," Quinn muttered.

Two black Humvees were parked in front of my house.

My stomach hit the sidewalk.

"They must be looking for you," Quinn said.

I didn't know if that was true or not but wanted to find out before they knew I was there. We walked behind my neighbor's house, past the hedge that bordered my backyard, and right to my back door. We dumped the bikes out of sight, then followed in reverse the route that I always took when sneaking out of my room at night for our midnight rides. I climbed onto the porch, shinnied up the column that held up the roof, and snuck across the shingled surface to my window. I was in my bedroom in under a minute.

Quinn followed seconds later. We quietly moved across my room to the door. Luckily it was open a crack. From there we could hear what was happening in the living room below.

My parents were there. I recognized their voices. But I also recognized another voice.

"It is absolutely imperative that we find them," the man said. "Both of them."

A chill rolled up my spine. It was Captain Granger. He was in my house. Talking to my parents.

Quinn saw the look on my face and turned pale. There was no way to know how many other SYLO soldiers were in the room, but there had to be at least one since there were two Humvees parked outside.

"I have no idea where he could be," Dad said.

"This is a critical moment," Granger added. "All signs indicate that the event is imminent. The arks have all been secured. If there's any trouble here on Pemberwick Island, then—"

"You don't have to remind us," Mom said. "We get it. All too well."

I shot Quinn a look. His eyes were already wide behind his thick glasses.

What event? What were they talking about? What were arks? More importantly, how would *my mother* know about any of it?

"There were no casualties during the rogue insurrection this afternoon," Granger said. "But I can't promise that being the case the next time, especially if your son starts riling folks up."

My knees went weak. My fears were correct. I was square in Granger's sights.

Mom said, "You could be mistaken."

"There was no mistake, Mrs. Pierce," Granger shot back curtly. "We have the satellite intel. It was your son and the Sleeper girl who witnessed our ambush of the rogues out near the Sleeper house. I only wish we had seen them at the time."

I had to hold my breath to keep from letting out a gasp. We were done. Granger knew we had seen him kill those men—and apparently so did my parents.

Granger continued, "This island is a powder keg and the fuse is burning quickly. If those two children start throwing accusations around, it will get very ugly very fast and it will be well within my mission to use whatever countermeasures are necessary to keep the peace."

Dad said, "When he gets home, you'll be the first to know."

I knew that tone. His teeth were clenched in anger as he fought to keep from boiling over.

"I can't wait for that," Granger declared. "We're going to find them." It sounded as though Granger had stood up and was headed for the door.

"You mean like you found that Feit person?" Dad called sarcastically.

My head started to spin. Dad knew about Feit too! He knew everything!

"We'll find him as well," Granger shot back. "This entire operation is about timing. I want to minimize casualties but if your son interferes—"

"He won't," Dad assured him.

"I need you to understand," Granger said sternly. "There is far too much at stake here to jeopardize our mission by protecting them."

"We understand," Dad shot back sharply. "We've all worked too hard and too long to let this get out of hand now. I can't speak for the Sleeper girl but you won't have to worry about Tucker."

"I'm going to make sure of that," Granger said. It sounded like a threat.

Someone's cell phone chirped. I didn't think for a second that phone service had been restored to everyone. It had to be one of the SYLO guys.

"Granger," said the captain, answering the phone.

There was silence for a few seconds as he listened to whomever was calling him.

"When?" Granger barked angrily, sounding even more annoyed than he had been a second before. He listened for a few more seconds, then added, "Understood."

He cut off the phone and announced, "Less than an hour ago, Dr. Francis Carr logged on to the Pemberwick Medical Database at the hospital and opened the files concerning the Pemberwick virus. However, Dr. Carr and his wife weren't at the hospital. They are assigned to the SYLO base. But their son was seen at the hospital, along with another young man."

"My God," Mom said. "Quinn."

Quinn let out a gasp that I feared was loud enough to be heard from downstairs.

"Quinn's a smart kid," Dad said. "If he smells a rat, he'll find it, and this bogus virus is a very big, smelly rat."

I had to keep from screaming. It was true. There was no Pemberwick virus—and my parents knew it all along.

"I want all three of those young people in custody," Granger said, the tension in his voice rising.

"I'm going with you," Dad declared. It sounded as though he was moving across the room.

"I'll wait here," Mom called. "And captain?"

"Yes?"

"Do not harm those children. Any of them."

I'd never heard my mom talk with such intensity. It wasn't a request; it was a threat.

Granger didn't respond to her. A second later I heard a door slam, and soon after that, one of the Humvees roared to life. Only one. Whoever was driving the other vehicle was still downstairs with my mother.

I was ready to puke. How was this possible? My own mother and father knew exactly what was happening on Pemberwick Island . . . and they were working with Granger to capture me.

I didn't know what to do, but Quinn and I couldn't stay there, not with a SYLO soldier downstairs waiting to grab us. I motioned to the window and Quinn nodded. We were on the same page.

It took every bit of willpower I had to climb out of my room—the room that always felt so safe but was now just a room in a house of people I wasn't sure I could trust. Quinn followed as I climbed out, and we made our way back to the ground. Without a word I sprinted to the far end of the property and dove through some tall hedges until we were out of sight and earshot of the house.

"What the hell?" Quinn exclaimed, with tears growing in his eyes. "What was that?"

"I . . . I don't know," I stammered. "They've been acting strange lately. Mom has been crying a lot and they've been talking about having moved to Pemberwick because it was 'safe.' What was so unsafe about Connecticut?"

"You didn't ask?"

"No! Jeez, they're my parents. They're supposed to be looking out for me, but—"

"They're looking out for you, all right," Quinn said, interrupting. "And when they find you they're going to turn you over to Granger. They're working with him, Tuck, and so are my parents. There is no Pemberwick virus. The quarantine is just a cover for— what? Genocide? Or some freak experiment? Are we all going to be fed this Ruby stuff?"

"I don't know," I said, numb. I felt like I was falling and that there would be no soft landing.

"What was that about an event?" Quinn asked, clicking back into analytical mode. "Granger said it was imminent. And your parents knew what he was talking about. It sounded like they've known for a while. You heard the threat. Granger would sooner kill us than risk us telling anybody about it."

We stood there, both trying to understand what it was we had heard. I didn't know what bothered me more: the fact that the people of Pemberwick had been fed a steady stream of bull since the moment SYLO invaded our home or that my parents had known about it from the start. No, worse—my parents were actually part of it. Quinn's parents too. They had lied to us. All that time my parents and I had spent wondering what was going on, it was all an act. The people I relied on the most, whom I loved, couldn't be trusted.

"What are we going to do, Tuck?" Quinn asked softly. "They're coming after us. We can't hide forever."

"I've got to talk to my parents," I said.

"What? No! They'll turn you in!"

"They're my parents, Quinn. I don't care what we've heard, there's got to be some reason behind this that makes sense. I don't believe for a second that they'd just turn on me like that. Your parents either. It just doesn't fly."

Quinn calmed down, which ended up being worse. In many ways anger and confusion were easier to understand and deal with than betrayal. He had to fight back tears.

"How could they lie to me like that?" he asked, as much to himself as to me. "Does that mean our whole lives have been based on lies?"

"I don't want to believe that," I replied. "I can't. It sounded bad, but they were still trying to protect us. You heard. I'm going to hold on to that and I think you should too."

Quinn nodded and wiped his eyes. "Well, we can't talk to any of them now because we're on the Pemberwick Most Wanted list and if we—"

"Oh no!" I shouted as a thought hit me like a bat to the head.

"What now?"

"Tori's on that list too."

I pulled out my cell phone and started dialing before realizing what a waste of time that was.

"Damn." I exclaimed, snapping the phone shut.

"Yeah, you're not on SYLO's calling plan," Quinn pointed out.

"C'mon," I said and took off for our garage.

"To where?" Quinn asked nervously.

"We've got to warn her," I shouted back.

"How?"

I didn't answer because I wasn't sure myself. It was like I was on autopilot. My legs were ahead of my brain as they carried me to our garage, where Dad's pickup was parked.

"We'll drive to her house," I announced, jumping behind the wheel.

"You can drive? When did you get your license?"

"Yes, and about two years from now."

Quinn crawled into the passenger side.

"Seriously? You're going to drive us out to the far end of the island and you don't have a license?"

I turned and looked Quinn square in the eye.

"Maybe you're right," I said sarcastically. "The island's about to explode, people are being abducted and murdered, we've got the United States Navy hunting us down, and our parents are helping them. Wouldn't want to add a driving violation to that."

Quinn gave me a weak smile. "Point taken," he said sheepishly. "Just keep us on the road."

I had driven with Dad many times on the more desolate roads of Pemberwick, so handling the truck wasn't the problem. Making it to Tori's house without getting caught was the real challenge. I turned the engine over, eased into gear, and slowly drove out of the garage. Our driveway ran right by our house, which meant the SYLO soldiers inside would definitely see us. I had to take an alternate route. Rather than head straight along the driveway, I made a U-turn around the garage, drove across the grass, and straight through to our neighbor's property. The folks behind us had a perfectly manicured lawn. Not anymore. It killed me to drive a truck over it and dig in deep tracks . . . but not really. There were way bigger things to worry about than lawn care.

"You realize this isn't a road, right?" Quinn cautioned nervously.

I ignored him and drove slowly, hoping it would draw less attention. Gratefully, our neighbors didn't come out screaming. I managed to get to the far end of their property and navigate across their bed of marigolds before hitting the gravel driveway. I made a mental note to replace their flowers as soon as I got the chance. The thought actually made me laugh. Why the hell was I worried about replacing flowers when we were fugitives?

"Now go!" Quinn yelled.

We hit the main road and I gunned it. Part of me wanted to jam the pedal to the floor and speed as quickly as possible out to Tori's, but that would have been inviting attention. Our only chance was to blend in and avoid any SYLO soldiers who had been alerted to look for us.

Tori's house was about ten miles out of town along the Memagog Highway. There was no alternate route. I gripped the wheel so tightly I was afraid it would snap, and I constantly glanced at the rearview mirror, expecting to see a black Humvee speed up from behind. My stomach was in a knot, waiting for the worst to happen at any second.

Quinn must have felt the same way because he didn't say a word. I think he was holding his breath.

We were about two-thirds of the way there and I started to think we might make it, when a black speck appeared in the road far ahead of us. A red flashing light shot from the grill. It was a Humvee.

"Damn," Quinn cursed.

I looked left and right, hoping for a side road, ready to roll the dice and turn off in the hopes that they hadn't seen us. There was nothing but an unbroken line of trees. It was the worst possible spot to cross paths with the enemy.

"Turn into the woods," Quinn cried.

"That's crazy. We wouldn't get twenty yards."

"But we can't just give up!"

I squeezed the wheel even tighter. The black speck with the flashing light grew larger as we sped closer.

"Maybe they don't know it's us," I offered.

"Yeah, right, and maybe Granger's really a good guy," Quinn said sarcastically.

The odds of either weren't good, but we had no choice. We had to keep going.

The Humvee loomed large. I took my foot off the gas in anticipation of the car skidding to a stop on our side of the road, cutting us off.

"Duck down," I ordered.

"Why?"

"They're looking for two guys. Maybe if they only see one they'll—"

Too late. The Humvee screamed by without stopping.

Quinn and I kept looking ahead, both afraid to turn to see brake lights, which would mean it was going to come after us. Seconds passed and I finally looked in the rearview mirror to see the Humvee disappearing toward town.

We both let out a relieved breath.

"So then, who are they after?" Quinn asked.

My mind raced ahead to our destination, making the answer obvious.

"Maybe they already found who they were after," I said and jammed the gas pedal to the floor.

The truck skidded on sand, the wheels bit, and we took off. My fear was that SYLO had already gotten to Tori and she was a prisoner in the Humvee. I didn't care about being inconspicuous anymore. I wanted to get to her house as fast as possible. It took only a few more tense minutes before I saw the turnoff to the Sleepers' lagoon-side house. I made the turn while barely slowing down and screamed up the sandy driveway. We bumped along until we hit the clearing that was their yard, where I slammed on the brakes, killed the engine, and ran toward the house.

"Tori!" I called.

I ran up onto the porch and right to the front door, where I hammered more than knocked.

"Are you in there?" I called.

My answer was a shotgun blast that blew out the window next to the door.

"Whoa!" Quinn screamed as we both hit the ground and covered up.

"The next one's aimed at you!" Tori yelled from inside.

"It's Tucker! And Quinn! Don't shoot!"

Neither of us dared to move. I didn't want to have to deal with Granger, but at that moment I was more worried about tangling with Tori. I dared to look up at the door and saw the curtain pull aside to reveal Tori inside, peering out.

A second later the door opened and Tori came out holding a shotgun to her shoulder, ready to fire again.

"You alone?" she demanded.

"Yes!" I shouted without getting up. "We came to warn you. Granger knows we saw him shoot those guys. He's coming after us."

Tori's eyes were wild. She scanned the yard as if looking for any hidden threats.

"They've already been here," she said, and I sensed the confusion in her voice. She was putting on a good show of strength, but she was upset.

"We saw a Humvee screaming the other way into town," Quinn said. "What happened?"

"They took my father," Tori replied. Her voice was shaking. Gone was the bold protector of their property.

Quinn and I stood up cautiously, neither convinced she wouldn't suddenly turn the gun on us again.

Quinn said, "And they left you here?"

"They couldn't find me," Tori replied. "There's a root cellar you can get to through the pantry. If you don't know it's there, you'd never see it. Dad made me hide down there just before they barged in and starting shoving him around. They wanted to know where I was. Dad reacted the only way he knows how, with his fists. He wasn't about to let some thugs take his little girl."

Tori lowered the gun and started to cry. Seeing that was almost as unsettling as her pointing the shotgun at me. The girl who rarely showed her emotions was finally breaking down.

"They dragged him out like . . . like some criminal," she said, her words clutching. "What the hell is going on?"

I didn't know where to begin to answer that question. The only thing I knew for certain was that the three of us were about as alone as could be. There was nowhere for us to go and nobody to turn to for help.

Quinn said, "Tuck's parents, and my parents . . . they're working with SYLO."

Tori stiffened with surprise.

"What? How is that possible?" she asked.

"We don't know," I said. "But we heard that something is about to happen. Something huge. They're afraid that if we tell people about what we know, there'll be a riot and the island will explode."

"What's going to happen?" Tori asked, sounding lost. "What could be so bad that they're willing to kill people to keep it quiet?"

My ear caught a faint sound that broke through the normal ocean and wind sounds of the remote property.

"Wait," I said, holding up my hand. "Listen."

We all stood still, straining to understand what the alien sound could be.

Tori heard it too. "What is that?"

The sound grew louder. It was a steady thumping noise that quickly grew louder.

"Helicopter," Quinn announced. "They're coming back."

SIXTEEN

"That root cellar!" Quinn declared, taking off on a dead run for the house. "We'll all hide down there."

Tori started right after him.

"No!" I shouted. "The truck!"

Dad's pickup was sitting right in front of the house, a dead giveaway that we were there. Seeing that, SYLO would tear the place apart looking for us. Tori put on the brakes and changed direction.

"The barn," she declared.

There was no need for her to explain. I sprinted back to the truck and jumped in the cab while Tori went for the barn and swung the doors open. The engine fired quickly, though I could still hear the sound of the rapidly approaching chopper over its rumble.

"Hurry, man," Quinn urged through the driver's window.

I hit the gas, spun the wheel, and drove straight for the barn. There was no way of knowing if they had already spotted the truck. All we could do was hope they couldn't see this far ahead. And pray. Tori had barely gotten the doors open when I tore through, careening toward the back wall. I jammed on the brakes, skidded across loose hay, and crashed into a stack of lobster traps that came crashing down onto the hood. Racer and Derby reared up and whinnied at the sudden intrusion. Tori went right to them and calmed them down.

We were in, but was it too late? I killed the engine and jumped out in time to see Quinn swinging the big barn doors closed.

"Did I leave tracks out there?" I asked, breathless.

"Too late to worry about that now," he replied.

Quinn and I leaned against the door, listening intently as the roar of the helicopter grew louder. Tori stayed with the horses, petting them and getting them to relax as best as she could. I couldn't say which was beating faster, the rotors or my heart. The ground trembled as the powerful chopper flew closer. I wanted to peek out of the window next to the door but was afraid I'd be seen, so all I did was close my eyes and wait. A shadow moved across the sky, blotting out the sun that streamed through the glass. The helicopter was hovering directly overhead. The sound was so deafening that Quinn put his hands over his ears. The shadow remained for a good thirty seconds. Did they spot the tire tracks? Had they seen us scramble to get inside? Were soldiers dropping down on zip lines?

The shadow finally moved off and the sound of the chopper lessened. I held my breath. They might be gone, or they might have been drifting further down the driveway to find a safe landing spot.

The sound grew fainter. They weren't landing. They were leaving.

I looked toward Quinn. His wide, frightened eyes asked the same question I had: Are they gone? It took several seconds for the sound of the helicopter to disappear altogether and that answered the question. They were gone. But had they left any soldiers behind? None of us moved for a solid five minutes. Once the ringing in my ears from the monstrous engine dissipated, I listened for any sounds of movement outside. There was nothing.

Tori was the first to move. She left the horses, grabbed a long, wood-handled boat hook, and tossed it to me. What was I going to do with that? Skewer a soldier? I wasn't about to do that . . . but I didn't give it up either. Tori raised her shotgun back to her shoulder and motioned for Quinn to open one of the barn doors.

He slowly eased the big door open, the squeaking of the hinges tearing through the silence. We all peeked out, fearing that we would be faced with a squad of armed soldiers.

The property was empty.

"Let's go to the house," Tori whispered. She still had the shotgun up and level to the ground.

The three of us moved quickly across the stretch of gravel between the barn and the house while constantly glancing around to see if any of the SYLO soldiers had been left behind. We made it inside and Tori quickly closed and bolted the door. It seemed silly to lock it, but if it made her feel better, I wasn't going to criticize. Once we were in and feeling relatively safe, we had to face the reality of the situation.

"What is this thing that's going to happen?" Tori asked. The wild look in her eyes was gone. She was back in control of herself.

"I don't know," I replied. "Granger called it an *event* . . . whatever that means. They don't want anybody on Pemberwick to know about it for fear there'll be a riot."

"They don't want anybody *anywhere* to know about it!" Quinn exclaimed. "Why else would they cut off communications with the mainland?"

"Is it about the virus?" Tori asked.

Quinn and I exchanged looks.

"There is no virus," I announced. "We hacked into the hospital database. There's no record of anybody having been treated for the Pemberwick virus."

Quinn added, "And we heard Granger admit it, so that pretty much is that."

"And that's why they're after us," I added. "They know we know the truth and don't want us to blow the lid off the deception."

"So then, what about the Ruby?" Tori asked. "And the people who died?"

"I don't know," I said, trying not to sound defeated. "I don't know how any of this fits together."

We let that frustrating thought hang in the air.

Tori broke the silence by asking, "Your parents are with them?"

I wasn't sure if she was talking to me or Quinn. Didn't matter. We both had the same answer.

"Yes," we answered simultaneously.

"How?" she asked. "Why? I mean, are they just going along with Granger or is it something more than that?"

"I don't know!" I yelled with frustration. "I'm suddenly questioning everything I ever knew. Why did we move here? Why this island? My parents talked about moving someplace safe but it sure didn't seem all that dangerous in Greenwich. Whatever the truth is, my parents haven't been honest with me for a long time."

Tori gave a questioning look to Quinn.

"Don't look at me," he responded with a shrug. "I don't get it either. But it makes me think that this started long before last week."

"What do you mean?" Tori asked.

"How could our parents suddenly be up to speed so fast? Whatever it is that's got this island in its grip, it stands to reason that they've known about it for a while. Before SYLO showed up. Before people started dying. Probably before either of us moved here. Heck, for all we know it may be *why* we moved here! I have no idea. The implications make my head hurt."

Quinn's logic was flawless, as usual. But if he was right, my parents had been keeping a huge secret from me for a very long time. A secret that changed our lives. I loved Pemberwick Island. Unlike most of my friends, I expected to live there the rest of my life. Now I had to accept the fact that I might not want to live here for another minute.

Tori walked over to a window that looked out onto the lagoon behind her house. It was getting late in the day. Shadows were growing long. Her father's two lobster boats bobbed gently against the dock. Under other circumstances I would have thought it was the perfect postcard image of Maine.

"We're prisoners on this island," she finally said. "All of us. What we don't know is why."

"The three of us are worse than prisoners," Quinn said. "We're fugitives."

Tori kept staring out at the lagoon but her mind was somewhere else.

"What will happen if they catch us?" she asked.

"Who knows?" I replied. "They don't want us telling anybody what we know, so I guess they'll lock us up until, well, until the event happens that they're talking about. That's the best we could expect."

"And the worst?" Tori asked.

I didn't have an answer for that.

"People have to know," she said flatly. "Not just here on Pemberwick. On the mainland. They have to know what's happening. The only way to stop it is to shine a light on it."

"We don't have a light that big," Quinn said. "Or a cell phone that works. There's no way."

"I'm not so sure about that," Tori said and pointed out of the window.

She was pointing at her father's lobster boats.

I didn't understand. Did her father have radios on board? That didn't seem to matter. If SYLO could disrupt cell service, they could definitely jam radio signals.

It was Quinn who put it together first. "Are you serious?" he asked, stunned.

"About what?" I asked, stupidly.

"This is a small island," she said. "We can't hide forever. God knows what they'll do once they get us. We've seen what Granger's capable of. If he's going to hunt us, I say we make it as tough for him as possible."

"And how do we do that?" I asked.

Tori looked me square in the eye and said, "We escape."

The idea was so far-fetched that I actually laughed.

"Why is that funny?" she asked, dead serious.

"It's not," I said. "It's just . . . it's just . . . dumb. How would we do that?"

"We'll take one of my father's boats. There's no moon tonight and the sea is calm. I'll bet we can slip past those warships without anybody even noticing."

I couldn't believe what she was suggesting. I looked to Quinn, who stood next to her, gazing out at the dock.

"Tell her," I ordered. "It's crazy."

"I don't know," he said thoughtfully. "Maybe crazy is a good thing. They'd never expect us to try something that was so totally nuts."

"What?" I screamed with surprise. "It's not nuts, it's suicide. You didn't see what happened to that cigarette boat. They blew it out of the water."

"That boat made a run in broad daylight," Tori said. "At full throttle. Those are some big ships out there. If we go quietly, they might not even notice us."

My mouth hung open in shock for several seconds before I declared, "You're both crazy."

Tori whipped away from the window and stalked toward me.

"So what do you want to do?" she said in a tone that was more accusing than questioning. "Sit around and wait until we get arrested and locked up? You can't even go home or your parents will turn you in."

"I . . . I still don't believe that," I said, though I wasn't so sure.

"She's right, Tuck," Quinn said. "There's nothing right about what's going on. Granger's a murderer and whatever the deal is with our parents, they're cooperating with him. We're alone here." He turned to Tori and added, "It's about five miles to the nearest landfall. We can ditch anywhere, then flag down a car and head for Portland."

Tori said, "We'll go to a local TV station. Or radio. I want to go on Big Hits Y100.9 and tell the world what's happening."

"Chris Mac!" Quinn declared. "I love that DJ. Can you imagine if we went on his show to blow the lid off this thing?"

"Stop!" I shouted. "You guys are talking like this is some big adventure. I know you both hate living here but you can't use what's happening with SYLO as an excuse to go looking for a little excitement."

"I think the excitement came looking for us," Tori said flatly.

"But this is serious," I argued. "People are dying and I don't want to be next."

"Neither do I," Tori said coldly. "That's exactly why we have to get out."

"No," I shot back. "My parents wouldn't let anything happen to us."

"Neither would mine," Quinn said. "But you heard Granger. Whatever's going on is serious enough that he's killing people to keep it quiet. You think our parents can stop that guy? Hell, he's part of the United States Navy. He's got the president on his side, which means he's got the whole freakin' government behind him. You think any amount of pleading by our parents would stop them from doing whatever they want to us?"

"There's only one thing that can stop them," Tori interjected. "They have to be exposed. This whole mess has to be exposed. We can do that."

I looked from one to the other. They totally believed in what they were saying.

"Exposed," I said. "What if that's the exact right word? What if we're mistaken? What if the virus is real? We could be carriers. If we left, we could spread it to the rest of the population."

"You're reaching, Tuck," Quinn said dismissively. "You don't believe the virus is real any more than I do. Not anymore. There's some other reason we're being held captive here. If you want your life back, the only way to do that is to let the rest of the world know too."

Quinn looked at Tori and added, "I'm with you. We're outta here."

"I don't think so," came a strange man's voice.

We all spun around to see a soldier standing in the doorway that led to the back porch. His right hand was at waist level, holding a pistol—aimed at us. He wore the dark red fatigues and red beret of SYLO.

The chopper had left someone behind after all.

The three of us stood frozen for what seemed like an eternity.

"We're leaving," Tori finally said. "You can't stop us."

The soldier flicked his gun to the right and calmly fired a shot that was as loud as it was shocking. The three of us flinched as an old vase on Tori's mantle exploded.

"My orders are to bring you in," he said coldly. "Ideally it would be alive, but that isn't a requirement."

He was an older guy with a cold look in his eye that made me believe he had seen more than his share of mayhem. Or caused it. I didn't see a drop of sympathy or concern for us. He had his mission and I didn't doubt that he would do anything necessary to carry it out.

It was over. They had us. To be honest, I felt a touch of relief. At least we wouldn't be making an insane escape attempt in an ancient boat, trying to sneak past the U.S. Navy.

"Let's all step outside," the guy said coolly as he reached for a small walkie-talkie that was clipped onto a web belt.

"No," Tori said.

Both Quinn and I shot her a surprised look. What was she doing? The soldier shifted slightly, aiming his pistol on her.

"Don't be stupid," was all I managed to say to her.

"Listen to your friend," the soldier said, smiling condescendingly.

Tori was wearing a navy blue peacoat. She put her hands into her coat pockets and took a step toward the soldier. I couldn't believe it. I wanted to reach out and grab her to keep her from taking another step, but with somebody pointing a gun on us, I didn't want to risk things getting out of control.

"You're not going to shoot," Tori said with confidence. "Unless you're a murderer."

The soldier raised the gun and with his eyes still locked on Tori's, he fired, blowing out a ceiling light. The explosion made Quinn and I jump again. The ringing in my ears was painful.

Tori didn't flinch.

"Stop!" Quinn shouted.

I wasn't sure who he was talking to.

Tori kept walking toward the soldier, who brought the gun back around to her.

"You are making a very big mistake," he said.

Was his voice cracking? Was Tori right? Was he going to be the first to blink? He didn't step back but he didn't seem as confident as he had a moment before.

Tori stepped right up until the muzzle of the gun was pressed against her chest.

"The only mistake here would be if you hurt any of us," she said, her cool unshaken. "Is that what you want? You want to be known as a kid killer? Your picture would be on the front page of every newspaper in the world."

The soldier laughed. He actually laughed. It wasn't maniacal or condescending. It seemed oddly . . . sad.

"Would it?" he said. "That would be good news."

Quinn shot me a curious look.

"That's good news?" he asked the soldier. "You want to be known as a kid killer?"

The soldier looked at him, then at me. His eyes focused like he was seeing us for the first time as something other than prey. He then spoke in a voice that was so soft I could barely hear him.

"It would mean people still cared."

As he looked me straight in the eyes, I saw a brief glimpse of a real person. A person with a family and history and friends. It didn't last long. His eyes quickly turned cold.

He looked back at Tori while reaching for his walkie-talkie. "Do us all a favor," he ordered. "Take a step back and—"

Tori thrust her right hand forward, the hand that was in her pocket, and hit the soldier square in the gut. It wasn't exactly a punch, but the guy reacted dramatically. His back went straight, he let out a pained gasp, and fell to his knees. Tori stepped out of the way and the guy fell flat on his face. She quickly kicked the pistol out of his hand.

Quinn and I didn't move. I can't speak for him, but I was in shock.

"There's line on the porch," Tori shouted at me. "Get it."

I didn't move. I couldn't even think.

"Go!" she demanded.

That kicked me into gear. I ran out to the back porch, found two hanks of heavy-duty line, and brought them back inside to find Tori kneeling on the soldier and twisting both of his arms behind his back. Quinn hadn't moved.

"Hurry!" she ordered. "He won't be down long."

I fumbled with the line, unfurling it as quickly as I could and feeding it to her as she expertly tied the stunned guy's wrists together.

"What the hell was that?" Quinn finally managed to say.

Tori reached into her pocket and pulled out a black device that she threw on the floor.

"Taser."

"Where did you get that?" I demanded to know.

"Dad gave it to me before I went into the root cellar."

She continued to truss the soldier.

"Why does he have a Taser?" Quinn asked.

"Same reason we have a shotgun. Those boats are his life. We protect them."

The soldier moaned. The electric shock had stunned him but he wasn't unconscious.

"Help me," she said. "We'll put him in the cellar."

I was operating in a daze. The three of us half-dragged, half-lifted the heavy man into the kitchen. Inside the pantry was a trap door in the floor that opened onto stairs that led down to a dark, damp chamber. We wrestled him down, feet first, until he hit the dirt floor.

"Lean him against the stairs," Tori commanded.

The guy was still too stunned to resist. We sat him up while Tori looped the line under his arms and around the frame of the stairs. Her last move was to lash his legs together so he couldn't kick. The entire operation had taken less than two minutes.

He was our prisoner.

"I told you," Quinn said to me.

"Told me what?"

"It's all about the knots."

The guy couldn't move. Tori had trussed him like a Thanksgiving turkey.

The soldier shook his head, trying to pull himself back to reality.

"That was incredible," I said.

Tori began to tremble. It was as if the reality of what she had done had finally gotten through to her.

"You okay?" I asked, rubbing her shoulders.

She nodded quickly. "Yeah, I just gotta breathe."

"We should gag him," Quinn offered.

Looking around, I saw a worn rag that was draped across a work bench. It was filthy. I didn't care. I grabbed it, rolled it up, stretched it across the soldier's mouth, and tied it behind his head.

"The walkie," Quinn said.

I snatched the walkie-talkie off his belt and jammed it into my back pocket.

"Can you hear me?" Quinn asked the soldier. "Do you under-stand?"

The guy focused on him. He was back with the living. He heard.

"We didn't hurt you," Quinn said. "Remember that."

The anger in the soldier's eyes told me that if he had the chance, he would not extend the same courtesy to us.

Tori leaned down and locked eyes with him. "And make sure somebody takes care of my horses. I'm holding you responsible."

I think the guy wanted to take her head off, but she had trussed him so well that all he could do was shake with rage.

"Let's get outta here," I said and led them up the stairs.

Once the others were up, I slammed the trap door shut and Tori clipped on a padlock.

"That won't keep him forever," Tori said, "but it buys us some time."

Quinn said, "Hopefully enough for us to get to the mainland."

"Whoa, stop," I said quickly. "You can't still be thinking of escaping."

Quinn looked me right in the eye and said, "Wake up, Tucker. They're coming after us. They sent that guy for Tori, and I have no doubt that he would have shot us if she hadn't saved our butts. There's another guy at your house right now and I'll bet you any-thing that somebody's at my house too." He reached down and picked up the soldier's pistol. "They're not going to stop until they get us, one way or another."

I looked at Tori. She still seemed shaken.

"There's no place to hide," she said in a small voice.

The two of them stared at me, waiting for a response.

"I'm not like you guys," I said. "We're talking about changing our lives forever. I like things the way they are."

"You mean the way they were," Tori said.

"Yeah, the way they were," I said wistfully. "I don't want to believe my parents are doing anything wrong."

"You think I do?" Quinn asked. "I'm their only kid. Same as you. You think I like knowing they're part of some villainous plot? I can't even begin to get my head around it. But people are dying, Tuck. That's real. We can't pretend like things are going to be okay."

"They took my dad," Tori said. "I'd do anything for him, but I can't go blasting into that SYLO compound with a shotgun looking for him. I want to find people who will. I'm going—with or without you guys."

Quinn looked me straight in the eye and said, "You promised me you were going to start taking care of the little things, remember? Well, sorry, we have to deal with a few big things first."

I truly didn't know what to do—other than to run home and demand that my parents tell me the truth. They had to have answers that would make sense and bring us back to normal. They were my *parents*. They watched out for me and complained when I wasn't trying hard enough in school. My mother didn't even want me to play football because it was too dangerous. How could they be part of a plot that could lead to my murder? I wanted answers and I wanted them to come from my mom and dad. That's what I wanted. More than anything.

"So where does that leave us?" Tori asked.

I took a deep breath and said, "It leaves us in the dark and I don't like being there. I want to know the truth . . . and I don't believe we're going to find it here."

"So?" Quinn asked.

"So let's get the hell off this island."

SEVENTEEN

The sun was setting, casting a warm orange glow over the calm ocean.

It was beautiful, but in this case beautiful was bad. As far as I was concerned, the sun couldn't drop fast enough. There was no telling how long it would take the SYLO soldier to free himself and let Granger know that the three of us were on the loose and on our way to the mainland. Our best hope of getting out of there undetected was under cover of night. If we left too soon we'd be spotted for sure. If we waited too long, somebody might come sniffing around, wondering why our pal in the basement hadn't checked in. It was going to be a race.

Tori reached up to the telephone that hung in her kitchen, pulled it off the wall, and yanked the jack off the end of the wire. At least when the soldier got free, he wouldn't be making any calls.

"Smart," Quinn said. "Any more phones?"

Tori shook her head. She grabbed two heavy coats that were hanging by the back door and threw them to us.

"It's gonna get cold," she said with cool efficiency.

They must have belonged to her father because they had the faint smell of the sea. Or maybe it was lobster. What they didn't smell like was lemons. That was Tori's deal. She picked up the shotgun and peered out of the window for the twentieth time, hoping, like us, that it had gotten significantly darker since she had looked twenty seconds before.

"Can you navigate?" I asked Tori. "I mean, I don't want to end up in Greenland."

She shot me a withering glare. It was all the answer I needed.

"I think we're making a mistake," Quinn said.

"Seriously?' I shouted. "Now you're having second thoughts?"

"No. I'm just saying we've got to do all we can to make sure we get there."

"It's not rocket science," Tori snapped. "We head due west and pray they don't see us."

"But we can increase the odds of getting there and getting the word out," he said.

"How?" I asked.

"By taking two boats," Quinn announced with conviction. "Tucker and I spent the whole summer pulling traps for the Willards. I can handle either of those boats. You and Tori take one, I'll take the other."

"You want to go alone?" I asked, incredulous.

"Not really, but with two boats there's a better chance of one getting through."

"That's a bad idea," I said dismissively. "We shouldn't risk both of the Sleepers' boats."

Tori laughed. "Are you serious? My father's been arrested, killers are hunting for the three of us, and you're worried about risking a couple of boats?"

"Well, when you put it that way . . ."

Tori flipped open a bench on the porch, pulled out two ICOM walkie-talkies, and tossed one to Quinn.

"They're charged and good for about twenty hours. Range is good. Maybe twenty nautical miles. Stay on channel twenty-one."

Quinn examined the device and powered it up. He didn't need any instructions.

"I don't like this," I said nervously. "We should stay together."

"No, he's right," Tori said sharply. "This is as much about getting the word out as about escaping. With two boats we've got double the chance."

"Then I'll take the solo boat," I said.

It was Quinn's turn to laugh. "No offense, Tuck, but with your navigation skills you'd be *lucky* to end up in Greenland." He looked at Tori and added, "The one time he took the helm of the Willards' boat, we ended up stuck on a sand bar for six hours waiting for high tide."

"Well, you're not exactly Magellan either," I snapped at Quinn. "We're talking about navigating five miles of ocean in the dark with the Navy hunting for us. Are you seriously up for that?"

Quinn chuckled nervously. "Jeez, don't sugarcoat it. Of course I'm not up for it, but what choice do we have? I can get there."

"Then I'll go with you," I said.

"No," Quinn snapped quickly. "Stay with Tori because, well, because—"

"Because I'm a girl," Tori said sarcastically. "It doesn't matter to me. Go with your friend."

I looked at the two of them, horrified that we had come to this point. I had to make a decision . . . go with Quinn or with Tori. I'm not sure why I made the choice I did because Tori had way more experience on the water than both of us put together. But it didn't seem right to let a girl go by herself, which meant she was absolutely correct about my thinking.

"I'll go with Tori," I said softly.

"Whatever," she said and strode off the porch. "I'm tired of waiting. Let's go."

She walked quickly across the scrubby grass that was her backyard, headed for the docks.

"Jeez, Quinn," I said. "Aren't you scared?"

"Terrified," he responded with a nervous chuckle. "But I'm more scared about what's happening right here. At least out there we've got a chance."

"Has it come to that? Do you really think Pemberwick is . . . what? Doomed?"

Quinn looked out at the lagoon and watched Tori step onto the dock and board the forward boat.

"Doomed? I don't know. But we're in serious trouble," he said with no trace of his usual sarcasm. "Whatever it is that's happening here, I think it's wrong that we haven't been told the truth. If it's as bad as we think it is, or even if it isn't, we have the right to know. Getting out of here and reaching people on the mainland will force the truth to come out."

"Yeah," I said soberly. "If we make it."

Quinn gave me a playful shove and said, "We'll make it. We'll have lobster rolls at Newick's and hold a press conference. I like the idea of being a hero."

I chuckled, but my heart wasn't in it.

"So you're going to get your wish," I said.

"What wish?"

"You're going to leave the island and do something people will remember you for. I never doubted you would. I just didn't think it would be so soon."

"What can I say? Destiny calls. I've already got the name picked out for the story I'm going to write about this adventure."

"Really? What is it?"

Quinn gave me a beaming smile and said, "The Pemberwick Run."

I had to smile too. "I like it."

"I'm telling you, we're going down in history, man. And it won't be the only time," Quinn said, with more than a touch of cockiness.

"I don't doubt that either," I said.

"Look, Tuck, I like it here too," he said, turning serious. "I might complain and say I want to kick the sand out of my shoes and live in the real world, but Pemberwick is my home. I like the place. I want it to be home again."

"Me too," I said.

"Then let's make it happen."

He reached down and picked up the soldier's pistol. It was an automatic, like a Walther or a Glock.

"You know how to use that?" I asked.

Quinn shrugged. "Let's hope I won't get the chance to find out."

We hurried down the porch steps and followed Tori's route to the dock.

The boat with the red wheelhouse, the *Tori Tickle*, was tied up in front of the older boat with the navy blue wheelhouse, the *Patricia*. Tori was on board the *Tori Tickle*, preparing to get under way.

"Help me with these," she commanded and started tossing over the lobster traps that were stacked to the stern. "We don't need them to be slowing us down."

Quinn and I caught the traps and stacked them on the dock. We had plenty of experience with lobster traps.

"Yeah," Quinn said, scoffing. "The extra weight might keep these fine vessels from outrunning one of the Navy's high-powered gunships."

I didn't laugh at the joke.

Neither did Tori. She stood with her hands on her hips, staring at Quinn.

"Sorry," he said. "Just trying to keep it light."

"Can you start those engines?" she asked.

"I think so," Quinn replied.

"Then do it."

Quinn gave me a quick look, rolled his eyes, and headed for the *Patricia* while I helped Tori offload the rest of the traps.

"I get *Tori Tickle*," I said. "Who's *Patricia*?"

Tori took a few seconds before she answered.

"My mother," she finally said with no emotion.

"Oh."

They say that it's bad luck to change the name of a boat, but I couldn't imagine keeping that particular name, bad luck or not. It would be a constant reminder of the person who had abandoned her family.

"It's because my father still loves her," Tori said. "In case you were wondering."

"How do *you* feel?" I asked.

"I don't," was her quick answer.

It was not a good subject to get into on the verge of making a suicidal escape, so I dropped it. When we finished unloading the traps, Tori stood up and scanned the lagoon. Dusk had settled in. The sun was finally giving up the day.

"We gotta get going," she said. "It should be dark enough by the time we clear the lagoon."

Quinn fired up the engines of the *Patricia* and they caught with a throaty roar. Each of the boats had powerful twin diesels. They were built to be working boats, not speed burners. In spite of Quinn's bad joke, we wouldn't be outrunning any other ships, Navy or otherwise.

Tori jumped out of the *Tori Tickle* and walked back to the *Patricia*.

Quinn was at the wheel, tuning the engines. I was impressed. He actually looked as though he knew what he was doing. I could have handled the boat on my own just fine, but Quinn was right: I would have handled us right into getting lost.

Tori waved for him to come over.

"Dad always keeps the tanks topped off," she said. "There's more than enough fuel to get us to the mainland."

"How should we do this?' Quinn asked.

"We'll go out first," Tori explained. "Give us a five-minute head start. When I get to the mouth of the lagoon, I'll head north for five minutes before turning west. You head south for a minute or two before making the turn."

"So we'll be what?" I asked. "About a mile apart?"

"More or less," Tori replied. "Definitely within walkie-talkie range."

Quinn said, "I don't think we should use them unless there's an emergency. They might be able to lock onto our band and track us."

I hadn't thought of that. Damn.

"Right," I said.

Tori said, "If we both head due west from that point, I'm guessing you'll hit land somewhere around the Portland Head Light. We'll be north of that. Beach the boat. Not that it really matters, but try to hit sand. Or find a dock. I'd like to think my dad will get these back in one piece someday."

"I'll do my best," Quinn assured her. "Then I'll call you on the walkie."

"What do we do from there?" I asked.

Quinn and Tori exchanged looks.

Tori said, "Let's worry about that when we get there."

Good point.

The three of us stood staring at one another. Up until that point, the idea that we were going to make our escape from the island was all theory. It had suddenly become a reality. We were about to try to sneak through a blockade enforced by the United

States Navy. The only others who had tried were blown out of the water.

"This suddenly doesn't seem like such a good idea," I said, my stomach twisting.

"But it's the only idea," Quinn assured me. "We'll make it. Keep your running lights off. Go slow and we'll be on land sucking down a Moxie before soldier boy even gets out of the root cellar."

I was glad that one of us was confident, even if it was for show.

"Good luck," Tori said to Quinn.

There was an awkward moment where they weren't sure if they should shake hands or hug. Tori finally took the lead and gave him a quick hug. Quinn actually looked over her shoulder and winked at me like I should be jealous. Dork.

"See you on shore," he said.

"I'll fire up the *Tickle*," she said and jogged for the forward boat.

Quinn and I were left alone with an uncomfortable silence.

"Hell of a thing," he finally said.

"Seriously," I replied. "I, uh, I think what you're doing is incredibly brave."

"Yes. Yes it is," he replied, matter-of-factly.

I had to chuckle.

"But you guys aren't far behind," he added.

"Maybe I should go with you," I offered.

"Nah. She's all tough talk, but she's still a girl."

"Yeah, a girl who took down a professional soldier. Jeez."

"Really," Quinn said, then added, "but you saw her afterward. She nearly lost it. I think she needs somebody steady to roll with."

"And you don't?"

"Nah," Quinn said, scoffing. "I've got ice water in my veins . . . which is a saying I never understood. How would that work exactly?"

"I don't know," I said, chuckling.

I really would have preferred to go with my friend. The two of us stood there awkwardly, neither wanting to leave.

"I don't know what to say, Quinn," I finally got out. "I mean, I always talk about how much I like Pemberwick and a huge part of that has to do with you."

"Okay, stop right there," he said quickly. "I hear you. I feel the same way, but I'm not about to stage some dramatic farewell scene like we're never going to see each other again. I'm serious. Even if we get caught, I don't see them blowing us out of the water. They'll board us, take over the boats, and bring us right back here, where we won't be any worse off than we are right now. So let's not get all weepy. We'll either see each other on the mainland or on the deck of the U.S.S. *Gotcherass*."

"Do you really believe that?" I asked.

Quinn stared at me for a good few seconds, then said, "Yeah. Of course I do."

"Yeah," I said. "I do too."

Neither of us were telling the truth.

"Excellent. Now don't go puttin' moves on Tori out there in the dark."

"I'll try to control myself."

We stood there for another long moment, putting off the inevitable.

"Let's go!" Tori called.

A second later she fired up the engines of the *Tori Tickle*. Both boats were alive and humming, ready to take us on the next leg of our adventure. Or our escape. Or whatever it was we were doing.

"I'll cast you off," I said to Quinn.

He hopped back on board and I ran to the stern, unlooped the line from around the cleat, and tossed it on board. I then ran to the bow and unlashed the front line. I walked that one back and handed it to Quinn.

"There you go," I said. "Good luck."

"The Pemberwick Run, baby," Quinn said.

I gave him a smile and watched him standing there for another full second. I don't know why but I felt as though I wanted to remember that moment. Quinn was doing an incredibly brave and selfless thing by going alone.

"C'mon!" Tori called impatiently over the rumble of the engines.

I unlashed the stern line of the *Tori Tickle,* tossed it on the deck, then ran forward and released the bow line. Both boats were now drifting free in the pond. I jumped on board and stood behind Tori, who manned the large, chrome wheel.

"Nice and easy," she said as she reached forward with both hands to grasp the dual engine throttles. She pushed both ahead gently and the engines rumbled louder.

We were under way.

I looked ahead through the Plexiglas windshield of the wheelhouse out to the horizon. It was still light but growing darker by the moment. That was good. By the time we maneuvered through the twists and turns of the lagoon to reach the ocean, it would be near dark. That's when the real fun would begin. For a moment I let myself believe that everything would be okay. We would get away from the island and make it to the mainland without a problem. I didn't want to think any further ahead than that. One step at a time. I settled in and took comfort in the familiar sounds of a rumbling engine and the far-off cry of seagulls.

My moment of optimism vanished when my eye caught something leaning against the console to Tori's right. It was the shotgun. I hoped to God that we wouldn't have to use it.

Tori stood straight at the wheel, her eyes focused on the course ahead. She had the brim of her USM cap pulled down low, though there was no sun to block anymore. It was probably out of habit. Or maybe that was just her style. Tori wasn't exactly an open book. But she was an experienced sailor. She guided the *Tori Tickle* with confidence through the labyrinth of waterways that twisted through the marsh grass toward the sea. The tide was high, so I didn't think there was much chance of grounding. At least we had that going for us. Still, she kept the small boat directly in the center of the narrow channel, just in case.

I caught the faint smell of lemons. It reminded me that, as confident as she was, part of her was self-conscious as well. It made me like her all the more, but at that moment I didn't need her to be self-conscious. I needed her to be steely eyed and focused.

I glanced back to see the *Patricia* slowly drifting away from the dock. Quinn wouldn't be following for another few minutes.

"I hope he knows the way out," I said.

"He can follow our wake," Tori said without breaking her focused gaze. "We hit this just right. There's just enough light for me to navigate out of here and by the time we hit open water it'll be dark."

"Yeah," I said. "We're as good as home free."

She gave me a quick, sharp glance. She didn't appreciate my sarcasm.

The boat was a thirty-five-foot workhorse that was used for one purpose: catching lobsters. Quinn and I knew the routine all too well. There were empty bins on the deck behind the wheelhouse that normally held bait or the day's catch. Bait would be put into a mesh bag and stuck in steel-cage traps. The traps would be lowered overboard and marked with a buoy. Every lobsterman had his own colors, so everyone knew whose was whose. After a few days, they'd travel back and haul them up with a winch to see how many dumb lobsters had wandered inside. They'd be measured to make sure they weren't undersized and the lucky runts would be tossed back overboard. The bigger boys would have their claws strapped with rubber bands so they wouldn't kill each other, and then they were all dumped into the deeper plastic bins that were filled with seawater to await the market and an eventual date with melted butter. The traps would be rebaited and dropped over to once again lie in wait. It was a Maine dance that had been going on forever. I couldn't help but wonder if the tradition would continue on Pemberwick when things got back to normal.

Actually, I couldn't help but wonder *if* things would get back to normal.

"You like lobstering?" I asked Tori, trying to make small talk that would take my mind off the steadily growing tension.

"If you had asked me that a couple of weeks ago, I would have told you how much I hated it."

"And now?"

She shrugged. "Right now I'd give anything to be out here with my dad, just hauling out spiders. Funny how perspective changes things."

"Yeah," I said. "Perspective. Don't it always seem to go that you don't know what you've got till it's gone?"

Tori gave me a surprised look as if she were seeing me for the first time.

"That's fairly profound," she said sincerely.

I thought about taking the compliment and shutting up, but that wasn't me. "It is," I said. "And whoever wrote the song I stole the lyric from really knows what they're talking about."

I gave her a winning smile. She rolled her eyes and looked back ahead. So much for impressing her with my poetic observations on life.

"Keep an eye out," she commanded.

As if on cue, I felt the boat rock as the V-shaped hull was buffeted by the surge of a wave. After chugging along for nearly ten minutes, we were one turn away from hitting the open ocean. I looked back to see the vague, gray shape of the *Patricia*'s wheelhouse making its way along the same route we had just taken. Quinn looked to be exactly five minutes behind us and finding his way without a problem. Ahead of us was the unknown. I ducked out of the wheelhouse and looked up to see stars appearing in the rapidly darkening sky. We had timed it perfectly. Tori wheeled us to starboard, skirted the last scrub-choked outcropping of sand, and gently pushed the throttles forward to help break us away from Pemberwick's grasp. We motored through a protected cove where the surf was minimal. Still, I felt the *Tori Tickle* rise and fall on a wave as if we were being lifted up and given a gentle nudge that would send us on our way.

"And here we go," I said without thinking.

We were officially in harm's way. I scanned the horizon, hoping not to see any patrolling Navy vessels. If there was a destroyer waiting outside the cove, our journey would have been a short one. But there were no ships to be seen. I looked back to Pemberwick, scanning for any sign of a missile-carrying helicopter. The sky was clear. We had already gotten further than the cigarette boat had.

"I'll get us out of the cove before heading north." She looked at me and added, "Don't want to run aground."

It was a dig over what I had done with the Willards' boat a few months before, but I didn't call her on it.

She kept the running lights off and the engine throttled down. I wanted to lean forward and jam both throttles to the max to pile on the speed and get away from there, but knew that could be a fatal mistake. The whole plan was to move as quietly as possible and slip under their radar—perhaps literally.

The cove was on the western shore of Pemberwick, the side that faced the mainland. That was huge. If we had had to circumvent the island, we would have certainly run into one of the Navy ships. As it was, we only had to travel a straight line. It was five miles from shore to shore.

Five really long miles.

Tori spun the chrome wheel, turning us to starboard and on to a northbound course that would run us parallel to shore. I would have preferred that we just kept going west, but the whole point was to put some distance between Quinn and us. We'd be headed west soon enough. At least that's what I kept telling myself.

The sea was calm, as predicted. At least seasickness wouldn't be an issue, unlike the last time I had been out on the ocean when we traveled by ferry to my ass-kicking at Greely High.

I looked west to see the hazy outline of the mainland. It seemed much closer than five miles but that's how it worked over the water. Distances always appeared smaller than they actually were. It was far enough away that I couldn't make out any lights. The area where we would land was fairly remote anyway. It wasn't like Portland was right there. Once we hit land, we'd have to find our way to the city. It was a problem I hoped we'd get the chance to face.

"Enough," Tori announced. "Let's get outta here."

She was as anxious as I was. We hadn't been traveling north for anywhere near five minutes but I didn't complain. The longer we stayed near Pemberwick, the better the chance of being spotted from shore. Tori spun the wheel and we turned again, back on our original heading, due west. The island was behind us, the mainland ahead. I wondered if I would be able to hold my breath for the entire five miles.

"You see anything?" Tori asked, as if I would have kept it to myself if I had.

"Nothing," I replied.

I kept moving my gaze from side to side, scanning up and down the coast for any signs of a Navy vessel. I didn't think they'd be hard to spot. They had no reason to be out there with their running lights off, like us. At one point I thought I saw a single light bobbing far north of us, but couldn't tell for sure if it was a ship, or a star reflecting in the water. I chose not to sound the alarm, not that we could have done anything about it, anyway.

"I don't see Quinn either," I said as I gazed south.

"Good," Tori replied. "That means nobody else can either."

We traveled in silence for several minutes. It was excruciating. I kept expecting to hear the shrill whine of a missile that was headed our way, or the bright floodlights from a Navy destroyer that had spotted us. Instead, there was nothing but the low, steady growl of the twin diesels and the lapping of the dark sea against our hull.

I stood right next to Tori and whispered, "Are we there yet?"

It was a joke. She didn't find it funny.

"We've gone about a mile," she whispered back.

We were both whispering for fear that the sound of our voices would carry over the water.

"A mile is good," I whispered. "Two miles would be better."

Pemberwick was shrinking behind us. I wondered how tight the naval blockade was. They had to be fairly close in order to spot any boats trying to leave. It wouldn't make sense for them to hang too far back. That would only increase the area they had to monitor. My spirits started to rise. Was it possible? Could we have done it?

I stared south, trying to spot Quinn, but there wasn't enough light. Again, that was good news. Visibility was low. By complete dumb luck we may have taken off on the perfect night. I fought the urge to grab the walkie-talkie and call him.

"What's that?" Tori asked, listening.

I didn't hear anything but the engines.

"Is something wrong?" I asked.

"Listen," she commanded.

I did—and immediately heard it. An alien sound cut through the rumbling of the diesels. It was a sound I'd heard before. It sent a chill up my spine.

Tori said, "It sounds like—"

"Music," I said, finishing her thought.

I instantly looked skyward.

"I've heard that before," she declared.

I held my hand up to quiet her. It was the same sound we had heard on the bluffs the night the shadow exploded. It was a single, sustained note that could have been coming from some celestial instrument.

Only this time I sensed a slight difference.

"There's more than one," I declared.

The single voice was joined by another. And another. It was like a heavenly orchestra, with each instrument playing different notes that slowly grew louder . . . as if they were coming closer.

"Kill the engine," I demanded.

Tori reacted quickly and shut down both engines. With nothing but the sounds of the open ocean to compete, the musical notes became more distinct. I scanned the sky but saw only stars.

"Is it the same thing?" Tori asked.

"Sure sounds like it."

Tori ran to the stern and gazed out over the water.

"I don't see anything at water level," she declared.

The notes grew louder. I couldn't tell how many were joining in. Five? Ten? A hundred? There was nothing threatening about them, except for the fact that they existed at all—and that they were growing closer.

"Maybe it's the SYLO navy," Tori offered.

"There they are!"

I exclaimed, pointing to the sky.

It was the same as before. A single shadow sailed high above, headed west. When it passed over us, the sustained note reached a peak and then dissipated as it moved west toward the mainland.

"So it wasn't a boat," Tori said, spellbound.

"And it's not alone," I added.

Another shadow sailed overhead, followed by another. The only time we could see them was when they blotted out the light from the stars as they crossed over us.

"Are they giant bats?" Tori asked.

"Giant musical exploding bats?" I replied skeptically. "That carry cargo?"

All of them were the same size and shape, like stingrays with no tails. They each traveled in a straight line with no obvious mechanical movement or engine sound to reveal how they were staying aloft. It was hard to tell how big they were because I couldn't judge their altitude. If they were close, then they weren't big at all. They could have been the size of dinner plates. But if they were far away and high in the sky, they were massive. I couldn't judge their thickness either. All we could see in the dark were two-dimensional black shapes—shapes that floated by while playing musical notes.

"Are we hearing their engines?" I asked. "Is that what's making the music?"

"I don't know, but there are hundreds of them," Tori said in awe.

A crackling voice came through the walkie-talkie. "Are you see-ing this?"

It was Quinn. I grabbed the device and squeezed the talk button.

"Yes. Just like the other night," I said.

"Maybe they're angels," Quinn responded.

I looked to Tori. She frowned.

"Be serious," I called back. "And keep the air clear. We don't want to be tracked."

"I guess it could be SYLO," Tori said. "Maybe they're some kind of reconnaissance drones."

"Then they're not looking for us," I announced. "Or they suck."

Tori said, "But if they're SYLO, it raises another scary possibility."

"What's that?"

"The explosion, the wreckage, and the Ruby. Does that mean SYLO was bringing the Ruby to Pemberwick Island?"

I snapped a quick look to her. "I don't want to even think of that possibility."

She shrugged. "Just sayin'. If they're military, then they might really be from SYLO. And if the thing that exploded was full of the Ruby . . ."

She let her voice trail off.

Quinn called, "That's the last of 'em."

The sky was clear again, with nothing but twinkling stars shin-ing down on us, unobstructed.

Quinn continued, "Let's keep on going and—whoa, look!"

Without seeing where he was looking, I had no idea what he was talking about.

Tori did. She pointed toward the mainland.

"There," she declared.

The sky over the mainland was lighting up, backlighting the contour of the horizon. It was a spectacular light show that stretched to either side but seemed concentrated over the area near Portland. There was no sound, only light. The colors were brilliant, as if a rainbow was erupting in the sky that was even more dramatic than the explosion we had seen weeks before. It looked like the aurora borealis had descended on the coast of Maine.

"Is there some holiday light show happening in Portland?" Quinn called over the walkie.

I keyed the talk switch but didn't say a word. I couldn't think of any.

The stunning lights silhouetted the swarm of black shadows that flew toward shore. There were too many to count. They flew together, as if—

"It's a formation," Tori said with a gasp. "They're coordinated. Are they creating those lights?"

I had no answer. We floated there, watching the light show for several minutes. Unlike my earlier sighting of the mysterious shadow, there were no flashes of light that came from the ocean. The impossible display had momentarily made us forget our own dire situation . . . until reality came flooding back.

"I got trouble," Quinn announced over the walkie.

"What?" I called.

"I killed the engines so I could hear the shadows and now I can't start 'em up again. I think maybe they're flooded."

I looked at Tori and said, "We gotta get out of here. If we're seeing this, so is the Navy, and they might come to investigate."

"Damn," Tori snarled and grabbed the walkie to talk to Quinn. "You may have a gas fume buildup. Put the throttles in neutral and run the electric bilge blower. It's the silver toggle to the right of the ignition. Do you see it?"

We waited. I couldn't take my eyes off the mainland and the spectacular light show.

"Quinn?" she called.

"I got it," he replied. "The blower's working. How long will this take?"

"I don't know. Maybe five minutes. Be patient. When you crank it, don't do it for any more than ten seconds or you'll flood it again."

"Understood," was Quinn's response. "What the hell is going on over there?"

The light show not only continued, it grew more dramatic, rising high into the sky and blotting out the stars above Portland.

"What about *us*?" I asked, nodding toward the throttles.

Tori cranked the ignition and the engine fired. The second started just as easily.

"Maybe we should go get Quinn," she said.

I kept staring at the mainland as if hypnotized by the display. I don't know how long we floated there. Minutes? Many minutes?

"Tucker? Are we going after Quinn?"

A shrieking sound tore through the sky. There was nothing musical about it. The sound was so painfully deafening that we had to cover our ears. We both fell to the deck and dared to look up to the sky to see . . .

"Fighters," I cried.

Four fighter planes, also silhouetted against the stars but much more recognizable as military aircraft, tore over us, headed in the same direction as the shadows. They traveled in formation for several more seconds, then broke apart. One went left, another right. The two in the middle stayed the course, headed straight for the shadows. We could see them easily because of the backdrop of flashing lights over the mainland.

"What the hell is going on?" was all I could say.

My answer came quickly. The fighter jets opened fire on the shadows.

"It's a dogfight!" Tori screamed.

The fighter jets started launching missiles that blasted from beneath their wings and tore into the formation of shadows. Several were hit and exploded in the air, erupting into spectacular fireballs similar to the one we had seen near Tori's house. Some splashed into the ocean; others crashed and erupted on land.

Another four fighter jets arrived and bore into the fight. They swooped in and out in an aerial ballet that would have been fascinating to watch if it had been some CGI movie.

When the fighter jets arrived, we got more of a perspective on the shadows. They weren't dinner-sized plates at all. They were nearly as large as the fighter planes—plenty big enough to be carrying a pilot or two. Or a load of the Ruby.

I grabbed the walkie and yelled to Quinn, "We gotta go. Crank the engine again."

We waited, glued to the aerial battle that was playing out over Portland, Maine.

"No good," Quinn called back. "It's starting to smoke and—no! I've got a fire!"

Tori grabbed the walkie and shouted, "There's an extinguisher aft of the wheelhouse."

I was torn between worrying about Quinn and the impossible air war. As we floated halfway between Pemberwick Island and the mainland, we had no idea who was attacking and who was defending or who was who, for that matter. The fighters were all about taking out the shadow craft, but there was no way to know *what* the strange shadows were or what they were doing. After what we'd seen from the military on Pemberwick, I wasn't so sure who were the good guys and who were the bad guys.

Up until that moment, the shadow craft were being shot out of the sky without putting up a fight.

That didn't last.

A laser-like white light streaked from three of the shadow craft at the exact same moment. All were focused on a fighter. The three lights hit the jet—and the plane vanished.

There was no explosion. No flash of light. No fire. No sound. The plane glowed for an instant and disappeared.

I fell to my knees on the deck, realizing that I had just once again witnessed death . . . along with a deadly technology unlike anything I had ever heard of.

"Did you see that?" Quinn screamed over the walkie.

I think I was in shock. I couldn't move, or think. I kept staring at the mainland and saw the same scene play over and over. Three shadow craft would target a fighter, hit it with multiple streaks of light, and the fighter would disappear. One by one the fighters were being picked off. They continued to do damage, splashing several of the shadow craft with their missiles, but it was clear that it would only be a matter of time before every last fighter was evaporated.

Tori's head was clearer than mine. She went for the boat's ship-to-shore radio—the same radio we didn't dare use in case we would give away our position. That fear had been replaced by a much greater one. She flipped on the power and the radio hummed to life.

"Who are you trying to call?" I asked.

"Nobody. Somebody might be on the air to say what's going on."

She spun through the frequencies, searching for a call. A voice. Anything. What we got back was a garble of static and confusion. Multiple voices seemed to be screaming over one another. It was such a mess that nothing understandable came through.

It was the same with every other frequency. All we could hear, loud and clear, was something horrifyingly unmistakable—the frantic sounds of panic.

Tori gave me a grave look. "Are we at war?" she asked.

"Who is 'we'? And who would we be at war with?"

"I can't find the extinguisher," Quinn yelled over the walkie. "The fire's spreading."

I forced myself to focus. "We gotta get him. Jeez, we've already waited too long."

"We're coming," Tori shouted at the walkie. "What's your position?"

"I don't know!" Quinn called back. "Somewhere south of you."

"There!" I yelled. I saw a faint flicker of light on the water that had to be the fire. "Let's go!"

Tori hit the throttles, the engines roared, and we were on our way.

All thoughts of stealth were gone. What we were witnessing over the mainland made the quarantine of Pemberwick Island seem trivial.

As we roared closer to the burning boat that held Quinn, I kept staring at the sky over the far shore. There were only two fighters left. Each launched missiles that took out a shadow craft, but there were too many of the mysterious planes. Unless the fighters flew off, they wouldn't be in the air much longer. They wouldn't be anywhere for much longer.

Tori screamed.

I spun to look ahead of us to see a massive black creature rising up out of the water between us and Quinn's boat. The light from the boat fire was soon blocked as the enormous black shape rose up like some monster from the deep—and kept coming.

"Turn!" I bellowed and grabbed the wheel.

Together we spun it hard and fishtailed into a turn to starboard without easing back on the throttles. I didn't know what it was in front of us. I didn't care. All I wanted to do was avoid hitting it.

"Guys! Get me outta here!" Quinn shouted over the walkie.

I heard the desperation in his voice, and it terrified me—even more so than the rising monster. Tori got her wits back and kept control of the boat. We spun clear of the leviathan until we could once again see Quinn's boat.

The wheelhouse was ablaze. Quinn stood on the stern, waving his arms.

That's when I heard the music return.

Tori and I looked up to see several of the flying black craft headed our way.

"We're coming!" I shouted into the walkie.

"I'm bailing out before this thing explodes," Quinn shouted back.

"Go," I yelled. "We'll pick you up and—"

Three white laser streaks flashed out of the sky. All were focused on the *Patricia*.

"Jump!" I screamed into the walkie. "Get off the boat!"

The last image I saw of Quinn Carr was him stepping up onto the deck rail to jump into the water . . . too late.

The beams hit the boat, there was a quick burst of light, and then it was gone. The fire. The boat. Quinn.

Tori pulled back on the throttles. There was no longer a need to hurry.

"My God," was all she managed to say.

We stood there watching the dark sea where the *Patricia* had once been. I kept expecting to see it reappear. Or to hear Quinn's voice over the walkie. Neither of those things happened.

"No," I said numbly. "No, no, no!"

I grabbed the walkie and screamed, "Quinn! Come in! Quinn!"

I was so out of my mind I don't think I was even pressing the talk button. It didn't matter anyway. We were close enough to the spot where the boat had been that Quinn would have heard my screams even without the walkie-talkie. I threw the walkie to the deck and leaned out over the rail.

"Quinn!" I cried. To nothing.

Tori came up behind me and held my arms.

"He can't hear you," she said, crying.

"Yes, he can," I shouted. "He could be in the water. He could be out there."

There was a rumbling, and then a sharp *whoosh* sound that came from our left. I barely had the will to look and see what it could be. I was aware of two eruptions coming from underwater, followed by a roar and the sight of two streaking cylinders. Missiles. They flashed into the sky toward the flying shadows that had targeted Quinn.

They found their mark. Two of the flying shadows exploded above us and crashed into the sea not fifty yards from where we were floating. The third escaped.

That solved the mystery of the rising leviathan. We were hit with a bright searchlight. I didn't even bother to raise my hand to shield my eyes.

"Attention," came an amplified voice. "Are you armed?"

Armed? We had just witnessed an aerial war using unheard-of weapons and this guy wanted to know if a couple of kids in a lobster boat were armed?

Tori was more together than I was. She grabbed the shotgun and threw it over the side.

"Prepare to be boarded," came the voice.

The dark, massive shape that had risen up before us loomed closer and I now saw it for what it was. It was a conning tower. The giant sea beast was a submarine. Painted boldly beneath the bridge was a logo.

SYLO.

My best friend was dead. His adventure was over.

But ours was only beginning.

EIGHTEEN

My head hurt.

That was the first conscious thought I'd had since staring up at the giant SYLO logo on the side of the submarine. After that, everything had gone black. What had happened? Had I been shot? Knocked out? Drugged? Or was I dead? Dead probably wasn't an option. Not that I had any experience with the afterlife, but I didn't think being dead involved having a pounding headache.

I opened my eyes, I think. It was hard to tell because it was dark. I was lying on a thin mattress that didn't do much to cushion the hard floor. A quick check of my body showed no injuries. The only thing that hurt was my head.

And my heart.

Quinn was dead. It was hard to imagine, let alone accept.

His last moments were the ones that kept playing in my head. It was like a horror movie on an endless loop. Three converging streaks of light hit the *Patricia* and . . . did what? Vaporized it along with my best friend? There was no sound. No explosion. No cry of surprise or agony. One second the boat was there, the next it wasn't. It simply disappeared—along with Quinn. I couldn't even kick my brain into searching for explanations. All I could do was dwell on the fact that Quinn was gone. He had made a selfless decision to fly solo. If he hadn't, all three of us might be dead. The attack could just as easily have been directed at the *Tori Tickle*.

Could I have saved him? What if I had gone with him instead of Tori? Could I have gotten the engine started and put the fire out? If I had been there, we might have been under way and out of there before the shadow planes arrived. But I wasn't there. I was on the other boat. The second Quinn put out the SOS about the fire, we should have gone for him. But we didn't. Tori asked me to. I remembered that. But I was too caught up with the light show over the mainland to worry about a little thing like my best friend needing me. What if I had been just a little more selfless? Would he still be around? I'd have to live with that guilt for the rest of my life.

Quinn had always talked about one day leaving the island to do something important, something that would be remembered. As far as I was concerned, he had done just that. He had saved our lives—and sacrificed his own to do it.

"Tori?" I called out.

All I got back was the sound of my own voice. It seemed as though I was in a small room on land. That much I figured because there was no rocking motion. I reached out and banged my knuckles into a wall. Fighting the kettledrum-like pounding between my ears, I managed to sit up and lean my back against the solid surface.

"Hey," I yelled. "I'm awake."

Soon after, a bright light flashed on, blinding me. Squinting against its glow, I looked to see the silhouette of someone standing ten feet away.

"How are you feeling?" the silhouette asked.

I was feeling horrible and hearing that voice made me feel even worse.

It was Granger.

"Where am I?"

"In the SYLO compound," was his simple answer.

"Why am I hurting?"

"You were tranquilized," he said matter-of-factly. "The discomfort will pass."

Discomfort? That was a nice way of describing a pain that felt like I was being thumped by a sledgehammer . . . not to mention the anguish over having lost my best friend.

"Where is Tori Sleeper?" I asked.

"In the same situation as you," was his reply.

"What situation is that?"

"That is what I would like to know," he said. "Why were you out on the water?"

"I want to talk to my parents."

"You will first answer my questions. Why were you out on the water?"

"To get away from here," I shouted angrily. "And from you. Why else?"

"To what purpose?" he asked, emotionless.

"Purpose?" I repeated, incredulous. "We're prisoners and you're the warden. I saw you hunt down and kill people. How many others did you take out? Why? To contain some mysterious virus that doesn't even exist? And you killed my best friend. The only thing he did wrong was look for the truth."

My tirade had no impact on Granger. He glanced down at a tablet computer he was holding and said, "You are familiar with Kent Berringer?"

"Why?"

"What is your relationship to him?"

"We're on the same football team. What's the big deal?"

Granger stepped forward into a light that allowed me to see his face. His cold eyes were locked on me. There was no humor or sympathy coming from this guy.

"How long have you known him?"

"I don't know. A while. My father works for his family. Why are you asking? Is he okay?"

Granger looked back down to his tablet.

"Tell me about the man known as Feit," he said coolly.

"No!" I shouted and struggled to get to my feet. "First you tell me what the hell is happening here. I just saw a war in the sky and whatever was flying around up there killed Quinn with a weapon like I never knew existed. Why don't you tell *me*. Who are you? What is SYLO? And what is really happening on Pemberwick?"

Granger stared at his tablet as if he hadn't heard a word I'd said.

"You sampled a substance you call the Ruby, is that correct?"

I started walking toward Granger.

"Do my parents work with you? Do they know what's going on here? Do Quinn's parents? Do they know that he's dead because of you? Who gets to tell them? I hope it's you."

I charged toward Granger. It was idiotic, but I was out of my mind. To me, he was responsible for the entire nightmare that had gripped my home and killed my friend. I wanted to hit him. Maybe wrap my hands around his throat and squeeze until he told me the truth. I wanted to see fear in his cold eyes. I suppose I should have realized how foolish a move that was, especially because he stayed focused on his tablet and didn't even brace to protect himself. When he didn't react, I had a fleeting thought that my move was a complete surprise and that I might actually have a chance against him.

The thought ended abruptly when I ran full speed into a hard, clear surface. I slammed my shoulder and was knocked backward. For my effort I was rewarded with a sore shoulder to go along with my aching head.

Granger was standing on the opposite side of protective glass. He looked down at me over his tablet with no sympathy.

"You will be moved to more comfortable quarters," he said, simply stating fact. "I trust that you will control your impulses or you will find yourself back in here. Alone."

"You killed him!" I shouted. I was trying to hold back tears but it was a losing battle. "He was a good guy. He got nothing but straight As in school. He read every book he could get his hands on and he liked every one of them. He was the smartest guy I know. He made me laugh. And now he's dead. Why? Why are people dying? What are you doing here?"

Granger stared at me with no emotion as I blathered on.

"We'll talk again when you are in control of yourself," he said. The light behind him went out and the room went black.

I slid down to the floor, crying and gasping for breath.

"Granger!" I screamed for no better reason than to let out my frustration.

I was back in the dark, in every way. I've heard about people "hitting bottom" and hoped I'd never have the experience. Lying there hurting, having lost my best friend and everything else to do with my life made me think the bottom was actually being hit because I couldn't imagine anything lower.

I sat there for a few minutes, crying. Why not? I didn't care who was watching or what they thought about me. I guess that's what happens on the bottom. Once I let my emotions take over, my sorrow and self-pity were slowly replaced by another more powerful emotion. Anger. These people had come to my island and taken over our lives. What did any of us do to deserve that? Nothing. We were victims. We all were. Yet Quinn was executed. Yeah, I'll use that word. Executed. We were in a war. We didn't ask for it, yet we were in the middle of it. But who were we fighting? SYLO? That was just the Navy. The military needs orders and a mission. Did that come from Granger? He was calling the shots but it was dumb to think that he was solely responsible for the nightmare. He was taking orders too. But from whom? He had the backing of the president of the United States. Richard E. Neff. Was he the villain here? That was too much to get my head around. I had to stay focused on what I knew, and what I knew was Granger. He may not have been acting alone but he was in charge. Granger was the enemy.

That was something I could understand.

As I sat on the floor in that dark room, lost in rage and confusion and sorrow, I made a decision. I couldn't just wish for the trouble to go away and for my life to return to normal. I couldn't hope that my parents would tell me the truth and it would all make sense and somehow go away. That wasn't going to happen . . . unless I made it happen. We were in a war. I had made a decision. I was going to fight. For me, for my old life, and for my best friend.

I promised myself that someday, somehow, Granger would pay for Quinn's death. I owed my friend that much.

I don't know how long I sat there in the dark. A couple of minutes? An hour? It was long enough to get back some control. I couldn't let my emotions rule my actions. I had to be as cold as Granger. Every move I made had to be calculated while taking one step at a time—and I knew what that first step had to be. . . .

I had to escape.

I had to make another Pemberwick Run.

A door opened, flooding the room with light. Standing there was a SYLO soldier with a pistol in a holster on his hip.

"Come with me," he commanded and stepped back outside.

I struggled to my feet, fighting the pain of my bruises and the residual effect of whatever it was that had knocked me out. I saw that the wall I had run into was a mirror. A two-way mirror. Was Granger still watching me? I didn't care. I staggered toward the door on stiff legs and stepped out into bright sunlight.

The dark room was actually a small stand-alone hut. It was one in a long line of similar prefab wooden huts with no windows that had been erected along the par-5 sixth fairway of the Oak Hills Golf Course. I wondered how many of the other huts were occupied by prisoners of SYLO . . . and if Tori might be one of them.

Looking out onto the fairway, I saw what looked like a pleasant fall afternoon. People were scattered everywhere. Some lay on their backs, soaking up the sun. A few jogged. A couple of elderly folks sat on benches, just staring into space. It could have passed for a typical day in a town park, except for the high chain-link fence topped off with a coil of razor wire that circled the perimeter.

This was the recreation yard of a prison.

Armed SYLO soldiers were stationed everywhere, silently watching the inmates.

"Follow me," my escort said.

He led me along the row of huts toward the north end of the fairway. As we walked I stared out at the people, wondering why they were there. Had they crossed Granger too? Did they know too much, just like me? I saw no obvious link between any of them. There were older folks, both men and women, and some as young as me. I recognized a few people who lived on the island, but most were strangers. That wasn't odd since so many off-islanders had stayed to enjoy the warmer-than-usual autumn and were trapped because of the quarantine. I guarantee they all wished they had cut their vacations shorter.

Everyone wore their own clothing. There was no "prison garb" that would have helped to complete the image of a prisoner-of-war camp. It was odd to see everyone dressed in casual vacation clothing like shorts and T-shirts and sandals. A few even wore tennis whites, as if they had been plucked off the courts. There was only one thing they all seemed to have in common: They were all alone. There were no couples talking or strolling. Nobody playing catch. No groups sharing conversation. From what I could tell, all of these people were on their own.

"Through here," the soldier commanded as he opened up a gate in the fence.

I was about to step through when my eye caught something that froze me.

Kent Berringer was standing on the far side of the compound, staring at me. He must have been watching me walk the whole length of the fairway. I should have felt it sooner because the heat of his gaze was that intense. The last time I'd seen him, he was pissed, thinking I'd turned him and his parents in to SYLO for using the Ruby. I hadn't, but that didn't matter to him. He'd wanted to take my head off and from the look he was giving me, he still did. At least he was alive and looking somewhat normal. The effects of the Ruby were gone.

I didn't wave to him or acknowledge his presence. Not because I wanted to continue our feud, but because Granger was so interested in our relationship. That couldn't have been a random question he asked. I figured I had to be careful around Kent Berringer for all sorts of reasons.

The soldier led me through a narrow walkway between two fences until we were let through a gate on the far side and into another section of the SYLO base. What was once a driving range was now occupied by large, temporary structures that gave the area the feel of an instant city. The place was teeming with soldiers and civilians alike. When did all these people arrive? They must have been transported to the island from the naval ships at night.

The civilians all seemed to have purpose, hurrying between buildings. They wore red jumpsuits with a four-inch SYLO logo over their hearts. Most carried papers, clipboards, and tablet computers that they read while walking. It was a wonder that there weren't any collisions. There were no smiles. No laughs. It was all tense and urgent. Everyone was busy; nobody seemed happy.

The soldiers weren't as busy. They were watchful . . . and armed.

A truck was being unloaded that was stacked with large crates, all with the SYLO logo stenciled on the outside. It seemed like there was a steady flow of deliveries coming in from the mainland. There had to be. How else would the people of Pemberwick be fed? I watched as one large wooden crate was cracked open and saw that it contained smaller boxes with markings that indicated what each held. I saw: Wheat Cereal, Light Bulbs, Hand Soap, and Marshmallows. Marshmallows? Like it was important to bring in marshmallows to a prison camp? Whatever. The variety of stuff made it seem as though SYLO had been doing some damage at Walmart.

I was led into the one and only building that had been there before the occupation—the clubhouse. It was a big old white structure that had probably been around since the turn of the last century. It was a place where the wealthier residents of Pemberwick Island socialized, along with the type of visitors who stayed at the Blackbird Inn. The kind of people Tori hated. The place was all polished wood and overstuffed leather furniture with oil paintings of whaling ships on the walls and beautiful scale-model ships inside glass cases.

Normally it was crowded with men wearing navy blazers or loud golf clothes and women in tennis outfits but those people were nowhere to be seen. Instead, the place was overrun by SYLO soldiers and civilians. The antique furniture in the large sitting room was gone, replaced by rows of steel desks. Each one was occupied by a soldier or civilian busily filling out paperwork or talking on a cell phone.

I was led past the front desk and down a flight of stairs. Our journey ended in the men's locker room, where a few temporary walls had been set up to create a makeshift doctor's examination room. There was a padded table with sanitary paper stretched along its length next to a counter with a sink. No sooner had I entered the room than three men wearing medical-looking white lab coats arrived.

"We need to do a thorough exam," the first guy announced. "Please try to relax. Your cooperation will make this a simple process."

I looked at the soldier, who gave me a blank stare that said, "Do exactly what he says or I'll hurt you."

"Whatever," I replied.

What followed was an experience that gave new meaning to the word "thorough." The three of these guys operated quickly and efficiently, as if they'd done this several times before—that same day. They didn't ask me a single question and barely spoke to each other. They weren't interested in my opinion, they were gathering data. While one entered the information into a laptop, the other two proceeded to take me apart. They began with the usual poking, prodding, deep breathing, eye-looking, tongue-depressing stuff that comes with a normal exam. It quickly evolved into something more annoying. Using long cotton swabs they took samples from every orifice I owned. The worst wasn't what you'd expect. One guy came at me with two swabs on the ends of long, wooden sticks. He grabbed my forehead then jammed them both up my nose, one in each nostril. He pushed them so high I thought they would hit the top of my skull. The only good thing I can say about it was that it was quick. Each sample was put into its own plastic bag, sealed, marked, and placed on a tray.

They also took blood samples. Lots of them. I don't know how many vials they filled, but it made me wonder how much blood they were leaving behind for me to use. I didn't say a word the whole time. I didn't want them to know how freaked out I was.

After the physical abuse in the exam room, I was taken down the corridor into a room with a huge device that looked like a human-size donut.

"MRI," the one examiner said. "It's a scan. There's no discomfort."

Fine. So long as they didn't go sticking swabs where they didn't belong, I didn't care what they scanned. I was strapped down onto a table so I couldn't move, then slid into the donut. The whole process took about twenty minutes and didn't hurt at all. When I was pulled out, the examiners were gone. The soldier wasn't.

"You're done," he said and led me out of the building.

I guess you could say that I felt violated. I wondered if the experience was anything like what those people said they went through after being abducted by aliens. There had been far too much probing going on. They gave me no clue as to what they were looking for or why they were being so thorough, but it made me wonder if we had been wrong about the Pemberwick virus. Granger knew that I knew it was bogus, so then why go through the motions of examining me like that? Was there really something scary that they were looking for? The whole process ended up leaving me more confused than I had been before.

While my anger grew.

The soldier led me out of the clubhouse, past the driving range, and back to the recreation fairway.

"You'll be called to dinner at seventeen hundred hours," he said perfunctorily. "After that you will be assigned a bunk."

"Any chance of you telling me why I'm here?" I asked.

The soldier ignored me, left through the gate, and locked it behind him.

"Guess not," I said to nobody.

I had no idea of what to do so I wandered around aimlessly, trying to think. I needed a plan. Finding Tori was key. I had to hope that she was being kept somewhere on the same compound. I had the horrible thought that something may have happened to her out on the water but I forced those ideas away. It wouldn't do any good to stress over something that might not be true. I also had to do all I could not to think about Quinn because as soon as my thoughts went to him, my heart started beating faster and my head started to spin. I couldn't let that happen. I had to think clearly, so I did my best to lock Quinn away in a remote part of my brain.

It was strange walking along the perfectly mowed and manicured fairway. This was a place for fun, not for holding criminals. I tried to make eye contact with the other prisoners, but everyone was making a distinct effort to avoid any interaction. My guess was that they were all just as angry and confused as I was and felt it was better to keep to themselves. Or maybe they were all plotting their own escape.

The sound of an incoming helicopter broke the silence. I looked up to see a chopper skim the treetops, headed toward the opposite end of the recreation compound. With nothing better to do, I picked up the pace and made it to the fence on the far side. Beyond was a landing pad with a windsock. I watched as the helicopter hovered and landed softly. A soldier ran up to slide open the door and the new arrivals began jumping out.

There were a few older soldiers who were probably officers, followed by two men wearing business suits. The suits were incongruous with anything I'd seen before. What were these guys dressed up for? A board meeting? I was about to turn and walk away when the last guy jumped out—and I did a double take. It didn't seem possible, but there was no mistake.

It was my father.

He carried a thick briefcase (like I'd never seen before) and was talking animatedly to the guys in suits. He wasn't wearing a suit himself—he had on his usual khakis and polo shirt. Between the whine of the rotors and the fact that he was a good fifty yards away, I couldn't hear what he was saying. It didn't matter. I was staring at proof positive that my father was working with SYLO. It took all I had not to scream. Or cry. Or puke.

"Just keeps on getting more interesting, doesn't it?" came a voice from behind me.

I turned quickly to come face to face with Kent. He, too, was staring at my father while casually tossing a white Wiffle ball into the air and catching it.

"Turn back around," he barked.

I did what I was told. I was too surprised to do anything else. I faced the fence and the helicopter beyond. Kent stood several feet behind me, facing the same way.

He said, "We don't want them to think we're talking . . . unless you're with them now."

"If I were with them, would I be on this side of the fence?" I asked.

I glanced around to see that several other people had gathered near the fence to watch the helicopter. It was the only game in town at the moment and better than staring at grass.

"So your father is with them," he said.

"I . . . I don't know," I said over my shoulder. "It looks like it."

"You didn't know?" Kent asked.

"Not at first, but I wondered. Now I know. I didn't turn you in, Kent."

"I know. I was out of my head."

"Why did your parents take the Ruby?" I asked.

"They were afraid. They thought there would be riots and the Blackbird would be looted. They were protecting their property."

"They got it from Feit?" I asked.

"Who else?"

"How are they?"

Kent didn't answer right away. I thought he might have walked away but a quick look back showed me that he was still there.

"My mother is fine, I think," he finally said. "I haven't seen her in a while. They keep us separate."

"What about your father?"

"Dead," was his simple, emotionless answer.

I turned quickly without thinking.

"Turn around," he demanded again, through clenched teeth.

I turned back to the helipad. Dad was still in an animated discussion with the suits.

"I'm sorry," I said.

"Why? It wasn't your fault."

"I tried to escape," I said. "To get off the island and tell people what's going on here."

If he was surprised, he didn't show it. "Yeah? And how did that work out for you?" he said, back to his usual sarcastic self.

I ignored the obnoxious comment and said, "There were three of us. I don't know what happened to Tori Sleeper. My guess is she's here somewhere. But Quinn is dead."

"Quinn who?"

I spun back to him. I didn't care what he or anybody else thought about it.

"Quinn Carr," I barked. "You know exactly who he is. Don't pretend you don't. He doesn't deserve that because he died trying to help the people on Pemberwick."

I expected some backpedaling from Kent. What I got instead was unexpected. He had tears in his eyes. I realized then that bold, arrogant Kent Berringer had also reached bottom and was barely holding it together. I turned back around to give him some space.

"They're watching us," he said, his voice cracking. "That's why we're all here. They want to see who's working against them. It's why nobody talks to each other. They don't want to be accused of conspiring against SYLO."

I glanced around at the SYLO guards. It suddenly seemed as though they were doing more observing than guarding. Was this why I was sent out to the recreation area? To see who I would talk to? To see if Kent and I were planning something?

"There was a battle," I said. "In the air. We saw it from out on the water. Something happened over the mainland. There were planes firing on one another. They had this weapon—it was like a laser or something. It's what killed Quinn."

"Who was fighting who?" he asked.

"No idea. SYLO was part of it but I don't know on which side. I don't even know what the sides were or what they were fighting over. The only thing I can say for sure is that the truth is being kept from us. There is no Pemberwick virus, Kent. It's all a lie. The world has to know."

"I want out," Kent said. "Out of this camp. Off this island. I want the world to know what Granger is doing . . . what *everybody* is doing that has anything to do with SYLO. I want to blow this place up."

As I let Kent's bold words sink in, I watched my father finish his conversation and get back onto the chopper. Oddly, it was a familiar scene. Not the chopper, but seeing my father in a discussion with guys in suits. It was the kind of thing I saw him do all the time when I was a kid and he worked for the town of Greenwich. He was always fighting for something he believed in. I wondered what he could possibly believe in that was happening on Pemberwick Island.

The rotors sped up and the craft lifted back into the air, headed for . . . who knew where? It was painful to realize I didn't know anything at all about who my father really was.

"Then we want the same thing," I said. "But it won't be easy. Like you said, we're being watched and we're stuck behind some very big fences."

"How badly do you want it, Rook?" Kent asked, suddenly sounding like his old, brash self. "What are you willing to risk to get out of here and get a little payback?"

"I think I already answered that," I said, trying to match his bravura. "I tried to escape, remember?"

"But how far are you willing to go?" he asked.

He was getting at something but I couldn't put my finger on it. "Why?"

"Because I can get us out of here," he said. "Out of this compound. I can even get us a shot at escaping from this island. But you have to want it, desperately, to take the risk."

I gave his ominous warning some thought then said, "I've already lost it all. What more is there to risk?"

"Just your life," he said.

"I already did that once," I shot back. "Maybe the second time will be easier."

There was a long silence. Kent was thinking it over.

"All right, Rook," he said. "We'll talk again. Until then . . . have a ball."

I stood there waiting for him to say something else.

"Kent?"

No reply.

I turned to see that he was halfway across the compound, strolling away casually. I didn't like that he was being so mysterious about what he knew, and what his plans were, but I guess when you're being watched, you can't be too careful.

I glanced back up to see the helicopter with my father onboard flying away. I was filled with both sadness and anger. I knew I would have to confront him at some point, but that wouldn't be soon. A reckoning would come, but not until I had taken back a little control.

I took a step to head back into the compound and accidentally kicked something on the ground.

Kent's white Wiffle ball went skittering across the grass. Had he dropped it without knowing? Or had he left it there?

Have a ball.

That's what he said. Was he being literal?

I picked up the ball and immediately realized that it felt off. The closed half, the half opposite the air holes, was heavier than normal. Something was inside. I casually lifted the ball, trying not to arouse suspicion from the ever-watchful guards as I peered through the air holes.

What I saw made my throat clutch. Kent's words suddenly made sense, as did his plan. He was right. Doing things his way was a risk. A huge risk. There was no guarantee that his plan would work and even if it did there was a good possibility that we wouldn't survive. The question was, was I willing to take the chance?

I needed to think. What was I willing to risk to expose SYLO, stop Granger, and get revenge for Quinn's death? What I held in my hand might give me that chance.

Nestled in the closed side of the seemingly innocent Wiffle Ball, glued firmly in place, was a thick layer of sparkling crystals.

Ruby red crystals.

NINETEEN

At five o'clock a horn sounded that was the call to dinner. I had no idea if it was actually five o'clock because I didn't have my cell phone, but that's what the soldier told me would happen. Everyone in the recreation yard stopped what they were doing and immediately started moving toward a gate that had swung open along the northernmost fence. Nobody said a word. They simply started walking as if it was a well-practiced routine. I didn't know what else to do so I followed. Besides, I was hungry.

"My name's Tucker," I said to the guy in line next to me.

He must not have been a local because he wasn't familiar. He gave me a quick glance then looked straight ahead without answering.

"Do you know why they're keeping us here?" I asked.

"Mind your own business, kid," the guy said, without looking at me.

"Why?" I asked, pressing. "Why won't anybody talk to each other?"

"Because we want to stay alive," was his sober response.

He pushed through the line to get further ahead—and away

from me. Just as well. His answer stunned me into silence anyway. I tried to make eye contact with a few other inmates but got the same response. They were scared. But why? They were prisoners. Why would talking to other prisoners get them into more trouble than they were already in? And why were they in trouble in the first place? It made me even more determined to escape, not just to save my skin, but to find out what was really going on.

We were funneled through open gates guarded by two SYLO sentries. I felt the weight of the Wiffle ball in my jacket pocket and hoped that the guards weren't doing body searches. I had a moment of panic when I feared that Kent had set me up.

To my relief I walked past the guards without a problem. We filed through a narrow walkway with high fencing on both sides leading to a large tent that had the distinct smell of cooking food. It actually made my mouth water. I couldn't remember when I had eaten last.

Once inside, the crowd split into two orderly lines that each led to a different serving station. I followed everyone's lead and picked up a sectioned tray and a flimsy plastic spoon. I suppose there were no knives or forks because they could be used as weapons, though I'm not exactly sure how much damage you could do with a plastic fork.

We had no choice with the food. Everyone got the same thing as they slid their trays past the steam tables manned by workers with white smocks that had SYLO logos on the arms. If you didn't like what they were serving, too bad. Kind of like the cafeteria at school. But the food was pretty good. There was sliced turkey with gravy, mashed potatoes, green beans, and a slice of pumpkin pie.

It was your basic Thanksgiving dinner, though at that moment I couldn't think of anything to be thankful for. There was only water to drink but that was okay. The portions were big and it all smelled delicious.

The whole setup was efficient and orderly. There was plenty of food and enough workers to keep it all running smoothly, which said to me that this operation hadn't been put together in a hurry. Food had to be ordered and delivered. Workers had to be brought in. Uniforms had to be made. You don't just slap something like this together overnight. It made me realize that whatever the truth was about SYLO being on the island, it had been planned and prepped for a good long time. When I left the line with my tray, I scanned the tent for a place to sit. There were long tables running the length of the space. Prisoners were filing in from different entrances so I got the chance to see some of my fellow inmates. I saw Kent but we didn't acknowledge each other. If we were being watched, it would be better not to be seen together too often. The person I really wanted to see was Tori, so I pretended to look for a place to sit while walking slowly along the rows of tables, checking faces.

SYLO guards stood silently along the walls, watching our every move. My guess is that there were a few hundred prisoners. Nobody spoke, which wasn't a surprise but it sure was eerie. The inmates all sat at their tables and ate without so much as looking up at anybody else or even asking for the salt.

I saw a few faces I recognized from around the island, but none that I had been friendly with. Most were strangers. I was about to give up on Tori when I spotted a USM cap. Yes!

I walked quickly to the end of the table and saw her there,

quietly eating. It was total relief. I didn't want to say anything to her because I would have been the only person in the whole room speaking, so I walked past her and cleared my throat to get her attention.

I thought I was being subtle, but when a room is mostly silent, any noise is jarring. At least ten people looked up. Thankfully, one of them was Tori. When she saw me, I could see the relief in her eyes. She was just as worried about me as I was about her. I gave her a wink and continued on.

Seeing her gave me the resolve to make a decision. I was going to trust Kent. I was going to escape with him . . . and Tori was coming with us.

I sat between a lady wearing a bright pink warm-up suit and a guy who looked like any of the hundreds of lobstermen who worked off Pemberwick. It was a bizarre assortment of people in that they were a cross-section you would see on any day on the island, not the types you would expect to find under military arrest.

The one person I didn't see was Tori's dad. If he had been arrested, why wasn't he there?

I followed everyone's lead and ate silently. It didn't take long. I suppose I should have taken my time and enjoyed it but I was starving. I was happy to see that people were going up for seconds and I wasn't shy about joining them. I marched right back up and doubled up on the meal. Not only was I hungry but there was no telling when I might get the chance to eat again.

The mealtime lasted twenty minutes, which was plenty. It wasn't like people were sitting around chatting afterward. When they were finished, they dropped their utensils and sat silently, staring at nothing.

A horn sounded. Everyone diligently stood up and filed out, depositing their trays in a bin by the door. I took a quick glance back to see Tori doing the same thing on the far side.

We marched out the same way we had come in and were herded toward the recreation yard. I wondered what the rest of the schedule for the day was. Were we just going to hang out on the fairway until somebody told us to go to bed? I hadn't even been shown where I was supposed to sleep. I entered the yard, prepared to do nothing, when I felt a hand on my shoulder. I spun quickly to see it was a SYLO soldier.

"Come with me," he ordered.

I figured I was about to see my prison cell and followed him without question. He led me back toward the row of huts and opened the door of one. I was about to step inside when I heard, "Hey! Tucker!"

It was strange to hear a friendly voice in the otherwise silent yard. I turned to see Kent jogging up. Oddly, he was all smiling and bright as if he were having a great time.

"My turn," he said. "Let's have the ball."

My brain locked. Why was he asking for the ball with the Ruby? The SYLO guard was standing right there. Was Kent throwing me under the bus?

"C'mon, man," he cajoled. "I'm bored out of my mind."

Not sure of what else to do, I reached into the pocket of my hoodie, took out the crystal-filled ball, and tossed it to him.

"Thanks!" he said. "We'll have a catch later."

He turned and jogged off, tossing the ball into the air and catching it like it was the most fun thing in the world. I didn't understand what had happened and wasn't going to get any answers standing there, so I continued into the hut. The soldier closed the door behind me and I was once again alone.

It wasn't my new home. At least I hoped it wasn't. It was empty except for a single chair in the middle of the room. There were three blank walls and one that was a floor-to-ceiling, wall-to-wall mirror. I stood there for a second, unsure of what to do, when the mirror turned to clear glass as a light came on behind it. It was a two-way mirror and standing on the other side was Captain Granger.

"Sit down, please," he ordered dryly.

I walked tentatively to the chair but didn't sit.

"Once again," he began. "Why were you out on the water last night?"

"What do you want to hear?" I said. "I told you. I was trying to escape."

"Why?"

"Are you serious? What don't you get? There's no virus. I know that. So that means we're prisoners. Not just in this camp, the whole island. We're cut off from the rest of the world and I want to know why."

"Who helped you escape?" he asked.

"Nobody. It was just the three of us."

"The boats you used belonged to Michael Sleeper. Did he plan the escape?"

"No! He was arrested before I even got to his house. You must know that."

"Was the escape planned before that?"

"No."

"Tell me who else was involved."

"Jeez, dude," I said, frustrated. "You can ask me the same questions over and over, but I'll keep giving you the same answers because it's the truth."

The door to the outside opened and two more medical guys in white jackets entered.

"Oh, man," I said. "Again? What else do you want to squeeze outta me?"

"Please remove your clothing," one of the guys said.

I looked at Granger, who had his eyes on his tablet. Glancing to the door, I saw the SYLO guard with his hand resting on his holstered pistol. I decided to cooperate.

"You're not gonna use Q-tips again, are you?"

"No," was the medical guy's simple answer.

I took off my jacket and handed it to the first guy. He immediately searched through it, turning out all of the pockets. They did the same with my pants and my shirt. Whatever it was they were looking for, it wasn't part of my physical body—which meant that Kent had just saved me by asking for the Wiffle ball. He must have known I would be searched.

I didn't have to drop my boxers, I'm happy to say. The two were satisfied that I wasn't carrying anything suspicious and handed my clothes back.

"Get dressed," the first guy said and the two left.

"What was that for?" I asked Granger.

"A random check."

"What did you expect to find?" I asked as I got dressed. "A weapon?"

"Information," was Granger's curt answer.

"How often are we going to be having these little chats?" I asked.

Granger's answer was to turn out the light. The clear glass turned back into a mirror.

"Okay! See you next time!" I called out cheerily. "I'll have the same answers for you!"

The SYLO guard opened the door and motioned for me to leave. I stepped out of the hut to see that it was getting dark. It may have been warm but it was autumn and the days were growing shorter. The guard led me back through the now-empty recreation area toward another gate in the fence. I followed silently until I caught sight of something beyond the fence near the food tent.

"Stop," I said to the guard.

He spun around as if surprised that I would challenge him. His gaze traveled to what I was looking at.

"Can I have a minute?" I asked.

The guard hesitated as if unsure of what to do. Finally, he relaxed and said, "Make it quick."

He stayed put while I walked to the fence. It was the longest walk I'd ever taken. Part of me wanted to get there faster, the other part wanted to turn and run in the other direction. My feet felt leaden, but I kept moving until I was standing right at the fence . . . directly across from my mother.

"Hi, sweetie," she said softly. "How are you doing?"

Her eyes were red and swollen from crying.

I didn't know what to say.

"I heard you would be by this way," she said, her voice cracking. "I wanted to see you."

"Quinn is dead," I said flatly.

Mom closed her eyes as if the words physically hurt her.

"I know," she said in a soft whisper.

It was all I could do to keep from crying myself. This was my mother. I loved her. She had taken care of me my entire life. She didn't even want me to play football for fear I might get hurt and here she was standing on the other side of a fence from me in every way possible.

"Why?" was all I managed to say.

She opened her mouth, but didn't answer.

"Did you know all along?" I asked. "Is that why we moved to Pemberwick? Was this all part of some plan?"

It seemed as though it was physically painful for her to keep the words in, but she did.

"Talk to me," I begged. "Why can't you tell me?"

I was starting to lose it. As much as I didn't want to cry, I couldn't help myself. Once I gave in to my emotions, I couldn't hold back and the waterworks began.

"You can tell me the truth," I said, pleading. "I mean, why not? It's over for me now, right? I'm in prison. What harm can I do here? I just want to know what's happening. You owe me that."

Her tears flowed too. I honestly believe that it pained her not to tell me what I wanted to know, but something was preventing her. She wasn't allowed to talk to a prisoner, even though he happened to be her son.

"Tell me!" I shouted.

The SYLO guard walked up behind me, took my arm, and said, "That's it. Let's go."

"No," I bawled and pulled away. My defenses were gone. I had become a desperate, lost little boy.

"Mom!" I screamed, my throat already sore from crying. "You're supposed to watch out for me! How could you let this happen?"

Mom put her hand up on the fence and said, "You're safe here. Tell them whatever it is they want to know."

"But I don't know anything! You never told me anything! Mom, what is happening?"

She pressed closer to the fence as if she wanted to get through to hold me. At least that's what I hoped she was doing. I couldn't be sure of anything. Not anymore.

"Tucker?" she said, crying. "Don't trust anyone."

Those words cut through to me. It wasn't what I wanted to hear. I wanted her to tell me that everything was going to be fine and that she and Dad would take care of things and explain it all. Instead, she issued a warning.

My tears stopped. My head cleared. That was the moment that I fully accepted the truth.

I was completely on my own.

"Really?" I asked. "Does that include you?"

Mom winced like I had punched her in the stomach. It felt good—and made my heart ache.

"C'mon," the guard said and pulled me away from the fence.

"I love you!" Mom called, sobbing.

I didn't turn back and it killed me not to. I loved her too. She was my mother, for God's sake. But she wasn't taking care of me. Not anymore.

"That was a mistake," the guard said. I sensed a touch of compassion.

He led me through the gate and along another corridor of fencing until we reached yet another fairway and a large, temporary wooden structure. He opened the door and gestured for me to go inside.

"What happens here?" I asked. "More questions? More searches? More tests?"

"It's your barracks," he said flatly.

Oh.

Inside were two rows of cots along the walls. It looked like a military barracks, with a small locker at the foot of each bed.

"Take number fifteen," he said. "Soap and towels are in the locker. There are clean socks and underwear too. Leave your clothes on top and they'll launder them overnight. There's a library in back next to the bathrooms. Take what you want. Three-minute showers. Lights out at twenty-one hundred hours. Breakfast call at oh seven hundred. Any questions?"

"Yeah. Why am I here?"

He left without answering—no big surprise.

I counted forty bunks in all, twenty on each side. I wondered if any of them belonged to Kent. A few guys read in bed while others showered. With nothing else to do, I wandered to the library. It wasn't much, maybe a hundred paperbacks tucked into a corner of the tent in a cheap bookcase, but it was more proof that this operation had been planned and prepared for. The books were brand new. Most of the bindings had never been cracked. They had been chosen, collected, and shipped to Pemberwick for the purpose of being used by prisoners in this camp.

I grabbed *The Catcher in the Rye*, one of my favorites. I sat on bunk fifteen and tried to focus on it, but it was a no-go. It felt too odd to be doing something as normal as reading. I was more interested in watching as the other men wandered in. I didn't recognize any of them. Like in the food tent, nobody spoke and I wasn't about to break the tradition. I decided to take a shower and grabbed a towel out of the footlocker, along with a new toothbrush and flip-flops. I put my clothes on top of the locker and went to the bathrooms.

It looked pretty much like the showers at school, with pump soap and shampoo dispensers on the wall. I took a quick shower in water that wasn't quite warm enough, brushed my teeth, and headed back to my bunk.

My clothes were gone. So were my cross-trainers. It struck me as a pretty effective security trick—taking the clothes from prisoners at night so they don't have anything to wear in case they decide to jump the wall at midnight. It made me wonder what Kent's escape plan was and if we were going to go at night. I couldn't imagine going anywhere wearing old-man white boxers and flip-flops.

I stretched out on the cot, let the squeaky springs settle, and stared up at the tent's ceiling. I was exhausted in every way imaginable. There was no telling what the next day would bring. I had to rest and be ready. I hoped for a long night of sleep with no nightmares because I sure couldn't stop them when I was awake. Sleep would be the only thing to stop me from seeing the image of my mother on the far side of that fence, not helping me. That would stay with me for a long time, maybe as long as the sight of Quinn about to jump from that boat . . . and disappearing in a lethal flash of light.

"No worries, my friend," I whispered aloud. "Somebody's gonna pay for that."

I didn't care who heard me.

By the time the lights went out, I was long gone.

The next time I opened my eyes, it was to the sound of another horn. It was the wake-up alarm. I opened one eye to see that all of my bunkmates were quietly rising and getting dressed.

True to the soldier's words, my jeans, shirt, sweatshirt, socks, and underwear were on the locker at the foot of my bed, freshly cleaned and folded. Even my cross-trainers were there and looked as though they had been buffed up a little. It creeped me out that little SYLO elves were scurrying around at night messing with my stuff. I dressed quickly and followed the others out, headed for the food tent. The breakfast experience was pretty much a duplicate of dinner, only with scrambled eggs, bacon, wheat toast with jelly, and juice.

Tori sat in the same spot. I tried to get a seat across from her but there were too many ladies crammed in. All I could do was walk by and give her a little smile. She winked. I took that to mean that she was doing okay.

I found a seat not far from Kent but we didn't speak. When breakfast ended, he made a motion with his head as if I should follow him. The whole group was let back out into the recreation yard, where everyone quickly went about their business of doing nothing. I walked to the far end of the fairway and up to the fence where I had confronted my mother. I'm not sure why. Maybe I was hoping that she had come back to see me.

She hadn't.

I scanned the compound to see that every so often a SYLO soldier would approach one of the inmates and lead them into a hut. I had to believe that everyone went through random interrogations the same as me, which was probably why nobody spoke to anybody else. If they had any secrets, Granger would do his best to get it out of them.

"It's why we're all here," Kent said. He had walked up behind me without my realizing it. "They're afraid of us."

"Of us?" I repeated, incredulous.

"They're afraid of what we know."

"I don't know anything," I argued.

"They don't know that," Kent said. "And who knows what anybody else knows?"

"That makes no sense," I said.

"C'mon," Kent said and took out the Wiffle ball. "Let's just have a catch."

"Is this allowed?" I asked. "I mean, nobody else is—"

"So let's give 'em something to think about," he said. Kent was back to being the cocky son of privileged parents. For once, I didn't mind.

He tossed me the loaded ball, and I tossed it back. It was about as innocent a scene as you could imagine. At least that's what I hoped. I also hoped that the guards didn't notice the odd wobble of the loaded ball.

"There's something about to happen," Kent said. "Something big and they're afraid somebody might scuttle it. That's why we're here. We're the suspects. They're looking for somebody to rat on somebody else and smoke the troublemakers out."

"I heard them call it an event," I said, showing Kent that I wasn't totally in the dark about what was happening. "Do you know what it is?"

Kent shook his head. "And I haven't met anybody else who does either, but that doesn't stop SYLO from asking."

"How did you get the, uh, the . . . ?" I held up the Wiffle ball. I didn't want to use the word Ruby in case we were being listened to.

Kent smiled. "Sorry, Rook. I've gotta watch my own ass. Until we get outta here, you're on a need-to-know basis."

I tossed the ball a few more times while letting his words sink in, then said, "Sounds to me like you might be one of those people who have information they'd like to know about."

Kent's answer was to smile. He tossed the ball back and said, "We go tonight."

He walked passed me but I grabbed his arm and said, "Tori's coming with us."

He pulled away quickly. "No chance."

"Then I'm out," I said and tossed the ball back to him.

Kent looked at the Wiffle ball, weighing his options.

"I can do this without you," he said.

"Then do it," I replied. "But I don't think you will or you wouldn't have asked me in the first place."

I'd seen Kent angry before. He wasn't good at hiding his emotions and just then he was clenching his jaw. It wouldn't have surprised me if he flipped me off, or took a swing at me. Instead, he lobbed the ball back.

"Okay, Rook," he said. "But she's your responsibility."

"So what's the plan?" I asked.

"The plan is for you to shut up and wait for me to get you," he said with a snarl.

He really was angry. I guess he didn't like it when "the help" bit back.

"What barracks are you in?" he asked.

"First one beyond the gate."

"Keep your clothes on," he said and walked off.

I watched him for a few seconds and was about to turn away when a SYLO soldier came up and grabbed him by the arm. Kent pulled away angrily, but then gave in and walked toward the row of huts. It was his turn to be interrogated. Was it because the two of us had been talking?

Before he went into the hut, Kent threw me a quick "See? I told you" look and stepped inside.

I was glad to be the one holding the loaded Wiffle ball.

The rest of the day was spent swinging between boredom and total stress. I wasn't pulled into a hut again, but I was nervous about what Granger might have gotten out of Kent. Was the plan still on? I had no way of knowing because I didn't see Kent for the rest of the day.

The Wiffle ball o' Ruby felt as though it weighed fifty pounds in my pocket. Whatever Kent's plan was, I felt certain that it involved us taking the stuff. With the Ruby doing its work, we would have an advantage over anybody who tried to stop us—so long as we didn't get shot. But the idea of putting myself under its influence again was terrifying, and not just because it was dangerous. I wasn't worried about overdosing. I knew how much I'd taken from Feit and would make sure I didn't take any more than that. I was more worried about losing control.

Though it had given me incredible strength and impossible speed, the experience was just that—incredible and impossible. There was nothing right about doing that to your body. It was frightening, yet strangely exciting. I didn't want to do it again, but to be honest, in some perverse way I was also looking forward to it. I wanted the feeling again and that scared me even more than the physical danger.

There was yet another wild card in the mix. Where did the Ruby come from? I was pretty sure that SYLO had brought it to Pemberwick based on the wreckage on the bluffs and the fact that they had total control of the island. But why? Were we all being used in some massive, sinister experiment by the government? Was that the deal? Were we just guinea pigs?

I wouldn't have considered taking it again if I hadn't been driven by a load of other factors. I was angry over so many things: Quinn's death and the betrayal by my parents, to name just two. The new reality of my life was that there was nothing for me on Pemberwick anymore.

Nighttime couldn't come fast enough.

At the end of the day, I lay on my cot, fully dressed, doing my best to pretend as though I was reading *The Catcher in the Rye*. I watched the various prisoners file in, take showers, or just hit their cots. I didn't know any of them from Pemberwick Island. They had to have been summer people who had been unlucky enough to be stuck on the island when it all hit the fan . . . or spies planted by SYLO. Was everyone there as innocent as I was? Or did some of them have a connection to the "event"? I had no hope of finding out because if all went according to plan, I'd be out of there that night and never have to see any of them again.

The lights went out at nine o'clock, and the barracks went dark. Soon the sounds of snoring filled the tent, but I was nowhere near sleep.

An hour went by. Two hours and then the door to the barracks slowly creaked open. I lifted one eyelid, hoping to see Kent but instead I saw a team of white-jacket-clad SYLO workers enter quickly and pick up the dirty laundry at the foot of the cots. One worker stopped by me and for a second and I feared he might wake me up and ask for my clothes. I hoped that pretending to be so deep in sleep that I couldn't be roused would work, but I didn't have to worry. The guy moved on and soon the team left with their bundles.

Another hour went by. And another. I was beginning to worry that maybe Kent's latest interrogation had broken him and the escape was off.

Finally, I felt a slight tapping on my shoulder. I was so surprised that I nearly screamed. I must have dozed off because I hadn't heard the door open. Kent put his hand over my mouth to stifle any sound, then left me and padded for the door. I slipped on my shoes and followed quickly.

The compound was lit by a series of lights on poles that reached up from outside the fences, but the place was not evenly bright like daytime. Only so much light could be thrown by temporary lamps and there were shadows everywhere. Kent was waiting for me in the shadow just beyond the door of our barracks.

"You got it?" he whispered.

I held up the Wiffle ball.

"The Porta-potty," he said. "Go inside and crush it with your foot. The seam is already scored. It should come apart easily. If anybody hears you, just tell them you had to take a leak."

"Why don't *you* do it?" I asked.

Kent frowned and shook his head. "I'm already on their radar. If they catch me in there, they'll know something is up."

I was too nervous to hang around and debate so I hurried to the portable bathroom and stepped inside. These toilets were all over the compound because it wasn't like they had time to bury sewer lines. Each had a white SYLO logo stenciled on the door, proving once again that the occupation had been thoroughly planned.

Once I went inside and closed the door, it was pitch black. And it smelled bad, no big surprise. I took the Wiffle ball out of my pocket, placed it on the floor, then lifted my right foot and brought it down hard in the general vicinity of where I thought the ball was.

I crushed it on the first shot, but the sound rang like a gunshot in that tiny plastic room. I debated about whether I should wait and see if somebody might come to investigate or to just take off. I took off. If somebody came looking, they'd find an empty potty.

I ran back to where Kent was waiting and handed him the two

halves of the plastic ball. He grabbed the half with the Ruby and dug at it with his fingers.

"It was glued in here," he whispered. "They dropped Elmer's down through the holes, then sprinkled in the goods."

"Who's 'they'?" I asked.

Kent smiled. "Let's hope you get the chance to find out."

He scratched out what amounted to a palm-full of the red crystals—about twice as much as I'd taken from Feit.

"Give me your hand," he instructed.

I held out my palm and he sprinkled half of the strange mineral into it.

This was it. The moment I never thought I would face again.

"You gotta tell me what the plan is," I whispered. "Or I'm not taking this."

"It's simple," Kent said. "They've got ambulances leaving from the clubhouse all the time. Day and night. I think that's how they bring in the prisoners. We'll make our way over there and—"

"How? The gates are all locked between here and there."

Kent held up his handful of crystals. "That's where this comes in. This isn't Alcatraz. They put this place up in, like, a minute. Those locks aren't any stronger than something you'd get at a hardware store. With this in our system, we can tear right through them. Or climb over. There's no razor wire on the interior fences, only around the perimeter. They don't have cameras here either. If we can avoid the guards, we can make it."

"And then what?"

"We stow away aboard one of the ambulances."

"What if there's somebody in back, like a soldier?" I asked.

"I hope there is," Kent replied. "I'd love to kick somebody's ass."

"Kent, that's, like, a really lame plan."

"It isn't," he argued. "Not with the power the Ruby gives us."

I was hoping for something a little more clever or ironclad than Kent's crude plan, but I wasn't about to back out.

"I've got to find Tori first," I said.

"That's a mistake," he said quickly. "The longer we're running around out here, the better chance we'll have of getting caught."

"Too bad," I said. "She's coming or I'm staying."

Kent clenched his jaw. "All right, but we'll go to the clubhouse first. I'll wait for you but if I get the chance to jump an ambulance, I'm going alone."

"Understood," I said.

The two of us looked to each other. There was no more putting it off.

"I'm trusting you, Kent," I said.

"And I'm trusting you."

With that, he lifted his hand and licked off the Ruby.

"Now you," he said.

I stared at the pretty red crystals. They looked so innocent. I thought of the rush of adrenalin I had gotten when I had taken it before. Adrenalin and power. I lifted my hand.

The last thought I had before licking it clean was the sight of two graves by the seaside that held the remains of two dead horses.

TWENTY

The effect from the Ruby was instant and dramatic.

As before, it felt like an electric charge had fired up every nerve in my body. Any trace of fatigue was wiped away. My head cleared. In a word, I felt powerful. There was a moment of fear as I remembered the dangers of what it was doing to my body, but it didn't last. I felt as though I could see better, hear better, and leap over any fence that stood in my way.

"I am so ready," I said to Kent.

"After you," he replied with a sly smile.

I scanned the area, looking for any SYLO guards. I was surprised to see that none were around. Did they really believe that once everybody went to sleep in their underwear, nobody would try to escape? That was fine by me. I took off sprinting for the gate that led to the seventh fairway and the women's section of the compound. The distance was maybe fifty yards but I was there in an instant. Anyone running that fast would have to appear as a streaking shadow to a guard who happened to be looking. My confidence soared.

The Ruby was doing its job.

The gate was locked, no big surprise, but Kent was right. It wasn't exactly a formidable device. It would have stood up to a normal person trying to break through, but at that moment I wasn't a normal person. I laced the fingers of my right hand through the lattice of the door and pressed my left hand against the frame. I knew I could break it open because I *had* to break it open. I gritted my teeth, gripped the fence, and pulled.

The lock snapped and the door opened as easily as if it were a flimsy latch on a dollhouse. The metal lattice of the door was bent and twisted by the sheer force of my grip. I had a feeling of complete dominance. I couldn't wait to use it again. I was ready to tear down an entire section of fence, if need be.

I turned back to see Kent running up behind me.

"Don't stop now," he whispered, breathless.

I ran through the gate, confident that Kent would close it to cover our tracks. I sprinted the distance of the corridor, sure that my fleeting shadow wouldn't be seen, until I reached a gate on the far side. Tearing this open was as easy as opening the first. We had arrived at the driving range, beyond which was the clubhouse where I had been repeatedly Q-tipped. An ambulance was parked in front.

Kent caught up and closed the gate behind us. Without a word we both sprinted for the safety of the shadows behind a row of Porta-potties. My confidence was high. I felt invincible. It took a load of willpower to stay calm, both physically and mentally. All it would take was being spotted by a SYLO guard and we'd be done. No amount of the Ruby would protect us from a bullet.

"You still want to go after Sleeper?" Kent whispered.

I nodded.

Kent frowned, then peered around the corner—and quickly pulled back. He held a single finger to his lips. There was no need to explain. Somebody was out there. He held his hand up as if to say, "Don't move."

I heard the door of the Porta-potty squeak open. Whoever was out there had come to take a leak. All we had to do was wait him out, but that was easier said than done. The Ruby was surging through my body, demanding that I move. It felt like a bomb had gone off inside of me and the only way I could release the pressure was to do something physical.

I heard the splash of the guy peeing and hoped that was all he had to do. If he had gone in there with a magazine, I'd have to scream. I looked at Kent to see how he was holding up. He was doing better than me. He held both hands out as if to say, "Stay calm." I clenched my fists, hoping that pumping them would help relieve the pent-up energy.

Mercifully, I heard the sound of the potty door slam. Kent got on his hands and knees to peer around the corner.

"C'mon," I urgently whispered.

Kent held up his hand to keep me back for a few more seconds, then motioned for me to come forward.

"He went inside the clubhouse," he whispered. "Let's make our way around the outside. I want to get close to the ambulance before you go after Sleeper."

He didn't have to tell me twice. I jumped up and ran for the fence, staying low, relieved to be moving. I ran parallel to the fence, jumping over obstacles, willing myself to appear as nothing more than a fleeting shadow. I wasn't frightened. The Ruby gave me a feeling of invincibility. This wasn't good because we were extremely "vincible." That much had been proven by Marty Wiggins. And Peter Nelson. And Kent's father. And, and, and.

I ran up to one of the large military trucks that were used as troop transports and hid there. From that vantage point I could see the ambulance parked in front of the clubhouse. A guy wearing a red EMT-like jumpsuit with a SYLO logo on the sleeve entered the driver's side. He wasn't armed, which gave me hope.

It didn't last. My stomach sank when I saw a SYLO soldier who *was* armed open the rear door of the ambulance and climb in back. He was riding shotgun. Literally. The ambulance rolled past the clubhouse and up to a small guard shack near the front gate of the country club. The driver spoke a few words to the guy in the shack, after which the iron gates swung open and the ambulance drove out. The gate remained open long enough for another ambulance to drive in and stop in front of the clubhouse. The back door opened and a SYLO soldier jumped out along with a lady who was the perfect image of somebody's grandma . . . except that her hands were cuffed behind her back. I didn't recognize the lady. She was yet another unfortunate victim of the quarantine—and now a prisoner of SYLO. The soldier roughly pulled her into the building and the ambulance drove off to get back in line.

"My God," I whispered. "This is just crazy!"

"They don't trust anybody," Kent replied. "Doesn't matter how old they are."

The ambulance did a U-turn and parked back in front of the

clubhouse. The EMT-looking driver got out and the ambulance was left unguarded.

Kent said. "I think they just wait there until they get called out to pick somebody up."

"So we could be waiting here all night," I said.

"Or it could take off a minute from now."

"I'm going for Tori," I said and started to move.

Kent grabbed my arm and said, "If that ambulance goes, I'm on it. With or without you."

"I'll be back," I said and took off.

The women's area was set up on the next fairway over from the medical area. I knew that from watching where the women went at the end of the day. It was easy to see pretty much everything through the fences. I made my way there quickly, always keeping an eye out for anybody in a uniform. I got as far as the gate that led through to the women's area when I saw my first patrolling guard. It was a woman who stood like a sentry near the closed and locked gate. She didn't look as though she was going anywhere soon, so I had to find another way through.

The answer was simple. I climbed the fence. None of the interior fences had razor wire. There was no way we could climb our way out of the compound to freedom without getting slashed, but moving between fairways was easy, especially when fueled by the Ruby. I was up and over the fence in seconds. Getting Tori back over wouldn't be as easy.

There were five barracks, all similar to mine, and I had no way of knowing which one Tori was in. My only option was to search. I had to hope that if any of the women prisoners were awake and saw me, they'd think I was one of the laundry elves coming to pick up the day's work. I sprinted to the first building, took a deep breath, and entered.

My only strategy was to get in and out fast. With luck I'd be moving so quickly that I would appear to be nothing more than a shadow, though I couldn't move too quickly or I might not spot Tori. I zipped in, sprinted between the two rows of cots, quickly checked out the sleeping women on one side then did an about-face and repeated the process while checking out the other side on the way back.

No Tori. At least I didn't think so. One sleeping lump didn't look much different from another. I was able to see most of the faces but some of the woman had their blankets up over their heads. I could have missed her but I had to play the odds and keep moving. I flashed into the next barracks and did the same thing. Still no luck. I was beginning to think I would have to come up with a different plan.

I went into the third barracks and sprinted along the row of cots. The last bed on the right held a woman with the blanket covering her face—and a USM cap resting on the footlocker. I moved quickly to the side of the cot, knelt down, and gently pulled back the blanket.

The sleeping woman wasn't sleeping. Touching her was like releasing the catch on a coiled spring. She lunged forward, hands first, and closed her fingers around my neck in a powerful grip that had to have come from hauling lobster traps her whole life. Her eyes were wild with fear and I have no doubt that she would have strangled me if I hadn't had ridiculous strength from the Ruby.

With one hand I grabbed her wrist; the other I clamped over her mouth.

Tori's mouth.

"We're getting out of here," I said with a strained whisper as her hand stayed clamped around my throat.

It took a second for her to register what was happening. I watched her eyes. They went from terrified to knowing. She released her grip. I let her go and without a second's hesitation she hopped off her cot fully dressed, slipped on her sneakers, grabbed her hat, and led the way out of the barracks. It was as if she had been waiting for me.

She didn't say a word until we left the building. I took her by the shoulders and guided her to the shadows on the side of the barracks and out of sight.

"What's the plan?" she asked in a whisper.

"Kent is at the clubhouse. We're going to hijack an ambulance."

Tori nodded in understanding. She didn't question. Just the fact that she was sleeping in her clothes meant that she was ready for anything. My coming to get her was far less of a surprise than I thought it would be. I suppose I would have felt the same way. It wouldn't have surprised me at all if she had come for me.

"I've got to find my father," she said.

"I don't think he's here," I replied. "I've been looking. He's nowhere in the men's area or the recreation fairway and I didn't see him at meals. Have you?"

Tori shook her head. "No, but I'm not leaving without him."

"I get it, but I wouldn't know where to begin looking. Not now. We've been lucky so far; nobody's seen us. That won't last."

Tori was staring right into my eyes.

"What's wrong with you?" she asked.

"What do you mean?" I replied, suddenly self-conscious.

She continued to stare at me as if searching for the answer to a question she couldn't quite grab hold of. Two seconds later, she had it.

"You're on the Ruby," she stated flatly.

"I am. Kent and I both are."

"Damn. Are you okay?"

"Sort of, though I feel like I swallowed jet fuel. I did it to get us out of here. If you want, I'll stick around to keep looking for your father, but whatever we do, we have to do it now."

Tori started to argue but then thought better of it.

"Thanks for that," she said. "And for coming to get me."

"I knew where to find you. I can't say the same about your father."

"Okay, I get it," she said. "Let's get out of here and hope the rest of the world will help us get him out."

I hate to admit it but I was relieved that we didn't have to find Mr. Sleeper. Not that I didn't want to rescue him, but looking for him would probably have sunk us all.

"One way or another, we'll get him out," I said. "I promise."

"You can't make a promise like that," she said sternly.

"I can promise to try."

Tori nodded. "I'll hold you to that. How do we get out of here?"

I grabbed her hand and ran for the fence that would lead us back to the medical fairway and the ambulances.

"Whoa, slow down," she whisper-yelled.

I had to consciously force myself to go slower because there was no way she could keep my Ruby-fueled pace. It didn't take long for us to get back to the area I had climbed over earlier.

"There's a guard outside the gate," I explained. "Can you climb up the—"

She finished my sentence by hopping up on the fence and scaling it with the confidence of a cat. I stayed below in case she slipped. When she reached the top, I hyper-climbed up and back down the other side to get under her again. A few seconds later, she joined me on the ground.

"That's just wrong," she said with dismay.

It was, but I wasn't about to stop and debate my decision to use the Ruby. We hurried back the way I had come, retracing my steps until we got back to the truck to find Kent still there, cautiously peering at the ambulance that hadn't moved.

"I was about to give up on you," he said without taking his eyes off the vehicles.

"Nice to see you, too, Kent," Tori said sarcastically.

"There's been some activity down there," Kent explained. "But no driver."

Tori looked around the enclosure, the wheels turning in her head.

"Why aren't there more guards?" she asked. "It's a prison. Shouldn't there be more security?"

"Who cares?" Kent said. "That's their problem."

"Maybe now's the time to get in the ambulance," I suggested.

"No," Kent shot back. "We could be sitting there for hours. We've got to—wait! Look."

A SYLO guard walked quickly to the ambulance, opened the rear door, and climbed in.

"They're getting ready to roll," Kent declared. "Get down there and take him out before the driver shows up."

"What do you mean, 'take him out'?" I said skeptically. "I'm not some ninja."

"You don't need to be. Not with the Ruby. Open the door fast and punch his lights out. He won't know what hit him."

"Why don't *you* do it?" Tori asked.

"Because I didn't take it."

At first I thought I hadn't heard right.

"Wait—what?" I asked.

"I didn't take the Ruby," Kent said.

I grabbed him and spun him around to face me.

"Are you serious?" I screeched in an intense whisper.

"Why should we risk both our necks? I took the chance of smuggling it in—the least you could do is use it. And one of us has to be thinking straight."

I wanted to punch the living crap out of him.

"That's why you needed me," I said, seething. "You didn't want to take it yourself."

"I nearly died on that stuff," Kent said through clenched teeth. "It killed my father. No way I'd take it again."

It suddenly made sense why he had been lagging so far behind ever since we had left the barracks. I was angry enough to hurt him, especially since I was fueled by the Ruby. He was lucky. Tori got to him first. She grabbed him by the throat and forced him to look at her.

Kent's eyes bulged under the pressure.

"If anything happens to Tucker because of this," Tori snarled. "I'm coming after you."

"Then let's make sure nothing happens and get the hell out of here," he said in a strained whisper.

Tori pushed him away and Kent fell back against the truck, hitting his head and letting out a pained whimper.

"We're on the same side here," he complained. "Try to remember that."

"I could say the same to you," Tori shot back.

I snuck a peek around the corner and saw a guy who had to be the driver walking down the clubhouse stairs, headed for the ambulance. There wasn't time to think or question.

"I'm going," I said.

"You sure?" Tori asked.

"No, but it's as good a plan as any. After I get inside, wait a second and then follow me."

"What are you going to do to him?" Tori asked, wide-eyed.

"I don't know. But whatever it is, it'll be fast. I've got that going for me."

I gave her a wink.

She gave me a nervous smile.

Before I could second-guess myself, I took off running. The more effort I put out, the more the Ruby produced. I covered the distance in what seemed like a second and yanked the rear door of the ambulance open. Kent was right about one thing—the guard didn't know what hit him. I jumped in and tackled him like I was headed downfield on kickoff coverage. That much I knew how to do. The guard let out a grunt because I probably knocked the air out of his lungs. He hit the deck so hard I wouldn't have been surprised if I'd broken some ribs.

Seconds later I was joined by Tori and Kent. They jumped inside and closed the door.

"What the hell are you doing back there?" the driver said.

There was a partition with a sliding glass window between the cab and the back of the ambulance . . . that the driver was sliding open. In seconds he would look back and see us all.

Kent reacted first. He grabbed the rifle from the dazed guard, jumped to the front of the cab, and leveled the weapon at the face of the startled driver.

"Drive," Kent said with a slight quiver in his voice that betrayed his nervousness. "Just like normal."

The driver's eyes went wide.

"No problem," he said quickly. "I ain't no hero."

The driver started the engine and a second later we were moving. I didn't believe for a second that Kent would actually shoot the guy. I doubt that he'd ever fired a rifle except maybe on a shooting range. But as long as the driver didn't know that, we'd be okay.

The stunned guard moaned. Tori stuck her knee on his neck and twisted his arm behind his back. Where did she learn to do that stuff?

"Easy," she said. "Your rifle is aimed at the driver's head. Don't do anything stupid."

The guard strained to look up and see who his tormentors were but Tori dug her knee in and he backed down. He wasn't going to be a problem.

I held my breath as the driver rolled up to the guard shack.

"I can hear everything you're saying," Kent warned him.

We came to a stop and the driver lowered his window.

"Evening," the guard in the shack said. "Got a lead on somebody?"

"Yup," the driver said casually. "They just keep turning up. It's gotta stop sometime."

"Let's hope so," the guard said. "Be careful. Good hunting."

Good hunting? These SYLO characters were cold.

I imagined the gate swinging open. We were seconds away from being outside. The driver had done exactly what we needed him to do. We could only hope that he hadn't given some secret signal that would have alerted the guard to the fact that there were a couple of escapees on board. I held my breath for what felt like an eternity, and then the ambulance rolled forward. A quick glance through the back window showed that we had left the compound.

"Now what?" the driver asked.

"The Blackbird Inn," Kent replied.

Tori and I exchanged glances.

Kent looked back at us and as if reading our minds said, "Relax. There's a reason."

I had put our lives into Kent's hands. He had already shown his true colors by lying about the Ruby and using me. It was difficult to know how far we could trust him. I had to hope that as long as we were together, we had the same goal. Staying alive.

It didn't take long to get to the Blackbird Inn. The driver pulled up to the front and stopped.

"Need some help with your bags?" he asked, sarcastically.

Kent jammed the barrel of the rifle through the window and clipped him on the side of the face.

"Ow," he screamed. "What was that for?"

"For being clever," Kent said coldly.

Kent scared me sometimes.

"You got the guard?" Kent asked.

"He's not going anywhere," Tori replied.

"C'mere, Rook," Kent ordered.

I moved to him and he handed me the rifle.

"If this clown so much as farts, shoot him."

I took the weapon and Kent moved to the back of the ambulance.

"Where are you going?" Tori asked.

"I'll be right back," he replied and jumped out of the van.

I turned my attention to the driver, who looked at me with wide, scared eyes. I had never held a gun on anybody before. It was a frightening feeling of power. I could pull the trigger and end somebody's life. Bang. Just like that. I could. But would I?

"You're not going to shoot me, are you, Chief?" he asked. "You look kind of squirrely."

With the Ruby surging through my body, I wasn't in my right mind and I think the driver sensed that. He looked at me like I was some deranged lunatic, and maybe at that moment I was. I had been sitting still for too long and it was driving me crazy. I kept fidgeting and shuffling, doing anything I could to keep from crawling out of my skin.

"Take it easy," the driver said. "We'll do whatever you want."

The guard that Tori was holding finally spoke. "Tell us what you want and we'll do what we can."

"I want you to shut up," I snapped at him.

It was like the words had come out of somebody else's mouth. Tori thought so too, based on the surprised look she gave me. The Ruby was doing a number on my body and on my head as I fought to stay in control.

Thankfully the rear door opened and Kent climbed in. He came right to me and took the rifle back.

"Drive out to Quahog Beach," Kent ordered. "Don't break any traffic laws."

"You got it," the driver said and got us back under way.

Nobody said a word on our way to the beach. I was dying to know what Kent had planned but didn't think he'd explain it to us in front of our captives.

Our captives. Up until that point, I felt as though we hadn't done anything wrong, but the fact that we had captured two people and were holding them prisoner changed that. We were kidnappers. I hoped the night would end before anything worse happened.

In my gut I knew that wasn't likely.

Kent glanced out of the window as we drew nearer to the beach.

"Drive us right out to the bluff," he commanded.

I could feel the ambulance bump as we drove off the road and started to travel over sand. We continued on for a minute or so, but then the driver pulled to a stop.

"That's as far as we go," the driver finally said. "Another few feet and we'll be wet."

"Get out," Kent said. "Everybody."

I took charge of the guard. Tori may have been more skilled at controlling people, but I had strength that came from the Ruby. As soon as I grabbed the guard's arm, he knew it. He was not about to try to fight me.

"Everybody move over there," Kent ordered once we were out.

The four of us stepped back from the ambulance and stood together facing him. I suddenly had a sick image: firing squad. What was Kent doing?

"C'mere," he said to me.

I was happy to see he was still aiming the rifle at the bad guys.

"What?"

"Put it in neutral, and push it over the edge."

Ordinarily I would have laughed at that, but not then. He was talking to the right guy. I opened the driver's door, put the gear shift into neutral, then ran to the rear.

"Yeah right," the driver said, scoffing.

I took that as a challenge. I leaned down, put my shoulder against the rear bumper, pumped my legs like I was hitting a blocking sled, and pushed the ambulance forward.

"Jeez!" I heard somebody exclaim in awe.

It only took five strides before I felt the ambulance begin to slide forward on its own. I stopped pushing and stood to watch as the white vehicle went over the edge and tumbled end over end down the steep bluff before crashing into the sea.

"That's, like, impossible," the driver exclaimed. "Can all you people do that?"

"You people?" Tori said quickly. "What's that supposed to mean?"

The driver didn't answer. He looked at the ground as if he had already said too much.

"Now what happens?" the guard asked.

"Drop your gear," Kent commanded. "Your walkie, cuffs, baton, everything."

The driver and the guard obeyed quickly.

"Now climb down the bluff," Kent ordered.

"What?" the driver exclaimed.

"Or I could shoot you," Kent said.

The driver and the guard exchanged nervous looks.

"You'll be fine," Kent said quickly. "All we want is a head start."

The two gave in and marched to the edge of the bluff. The driver went first, carefully climbing down the steep embankment. It was treacherous but not impossible. The guard was next, but before dropping over the edge, he looked up at Kent with hatred like I've never seen before.

"We'll never give up," he said defiantly.

Tori gave me a questioning look.

"Stop talking! Go!" Kent barked.

The guard began his descent.

"What did that mean?" Tori asked. "And what did he mean by 'you people'?"

"Who cares?" Kent replied. "By the time they make it back up, we'll be long gone."

Kent walked quickly to the edge and looked over to make sure that the two men continued to climb down.

I didn't know what to think about the guard's odd comment. I was too busy fighting to stay in control of my racing heart. I wondered how long the Ruby would be working on me. It seemed as though once it was in your system, so long as you called upon it, it gave you what you needed. It wasn't until you forced yourself to calm down that the effects would lessen.

But it wasn't time to calm down. Not yet.

"Oh my God," Tori exclaimed. "Listen."

At first all I heard was the sound of crashing surf. Before I could ask Tori what she meant, I heard it too.

"They're back," I said fearfully.

"Who's back?" Kent asked.

Once again the eerie music floated down from the sky. We all looked up to see another formation of dark shadows approaching from the east.

"What the hell is that?" Kent asked.

The shadows moved fast, headed west toward the mainland. There looked to be about a dozen of the stingray-shaped objects, each emitting the same incongruous musical sound. They were moving fast, far faster than what we'd seen two nights before. They flashed overhead and were gone in seconds. Moments later, the sky to the west lit up with the same kind of brilliant display we had witnessed before.

Kent took a few steps toward the light show, as if those few feet would give him a better view.

"What's going on?" he asked, numb.

"It's the same as the other night," I answered. "There's a battle going on but I have no idea who's fighting, or why."

Unlike the previous night, the light show didn't last long. Nor was there another dogfight. No fighter planes arrived to challenge the dark shadows. The light show soon ended and I expected to see the mysterious aircraft flying back our way, having completed whatever mission they were on. But they didn't.

The three of us stood there, staring west, trying to understand what it was that we had just seen. It was at that moment that a pair of headlights appeared on the sandy road in front of us, headed our way.

"Uh-oh," Tori uttered.

"It's okay," Kent assured us. "All part of the plan. Pick up their gear and toss it."

I snapped back into the moment, the disturbing light show momentarily forgotten. I didn't care about the handcuffs and the baton, but the walkie would cause us trouble if the guard got it back too quickly. I picked it up and heaved it into the sea. It was the longest throw I had ever made.

Kent did the same with the rifle. He wound up and tossed it away, spinning it into the sea. Part of me was relieved. I didn't like the way he was waving that thing around. I wouldn't have put it past him to use it on *us*. But we were on the run and could have used the protection, especially since somebody was driving toward us.

"C'mon," Kent said and ran toward the car.

"Do you trust him?" Tori asked.

"It's not like we have a choice," was my sober reply.

We followed Kent, who became a silhouette against the approaching headlights. He ran right up to the driver's side as the car came to a stop. The driver jumped out and threw her arms around him.

"It's about time," she cried.

It was Olivia. The stop at the Blackbird Inn now made sense.

"I've been so worried," she squealed while hugging Kent and giving him a big kiss. She was wearing her usual short-shorts with a halter top—not exactly a practical uniform for aiding a prison break.

"Are you okay?" she added when they came up for air.

"Fine," Kent said perfunctorily. "But we gotta keep moving."

Olivia looked at me and said, "I was afraid I'd never see you again, Tucker."

Maybe not as afraid as not seeing Kent again, but I appreciated her concern.

"Strange days," I said with a shrug.

"Who is *she*?" Tori asked me.

"Kent's girlfriend, Olivia," I answered. I guess that was official now.

"And who are *you*?" Olivia asked, giving Tori an appraising once-over.

"Kent's other girlfriend," Tori said without missing a beat as she walked past Olivia toward the car. "Didn't he tell you about me?"

Olivia stood stock-still with her mouth open, stunned. I would have laughed if my head weren't still exploding. Seemed as though Tori liked pushing buttons too. Quinn would have loved it.

Quinn.

Thinking of him snapped me back into the mission.

"Where are we going, Kent?" I asked.

"Someplace where all your questions will be answered," he said. He put his arm around Olivia's shoulders and said, "Tori's not my girlfriend."

Olivia smiled with relief. "I knew that."

We all got into the vehicle, which turned out to be a Jeep. Olivia sat behind the wheel while Tori and I climbed into the back seat. Olivia hit the accelerator and turned quickly, slinging up sand while the wheels spun. For a moment I thought she had no idea of how to drive and I feared we would follow the ambulance over the edge. But the tires bit, she spun the wheel back, straightened out, and we were on our way.

"Tell me everything," she said.

"Not until we get there. Turn out the lights."

"The lights?" she complained. "I won't be able to see."

"I'm more worried about somebody seeing *us*. Your eyes will adjust."

Olivia shrugged and killed the lights. It was disconcerting for a moment as everything went black. But our eyes adjusted quickly and Olivia kept us on the road to . . . somewhere.

Tori put her hand on my arm and said, "How do you feel?"

"Okay. I think I'm coming down."

"Perfect timing," Kent said.

"That was a rotten thing to do, Kent," Tori said to him. "You used him."

"And he used me. You both did. But we're out, right?"

"Yeah, we're out," I said. "So now tell us what's going on. How did you get the Ruby inside?"

"And where are we going?" Tori added.

Kent gave us a cat-that-ate-the-canary smile. "When you see where we're going, you'll know how I got the Ruby."

We had trusted Kent this far and it had worked out okay, mostly.

We had to let him play it his way. I took a deep breath and actually could feel the effects of the Ruby lessening. I had survived. At least that part of the nightmare was over.

Tori kept her hand on my arm and said softly, "Thank you."

I shrugged.

"You're welcome," Kent said.

Tori smiled. It didn't happen often, but when it did her face lit up. I was beginning to really like Tori Sleeper. She took my hand and gently rubbed my arm. I wasn't sure if it was an affectionate thing to do, or if she was trying to calm me down. Either way, I didn't hate it.

Olivia drove without saying another word. Thankfully. She must have been using all of her brain power to keep us on the road. I knew the island as well as anybody and saw that after moving along the Memagog Highway for several miles, we turned onto High Pine Road, the road that led due north and ended at Chinicook Island.

Chinicook was a desolate stretch of land that was technically part of Pemberwick but surrounded by water. The only access was by a long wooden one-lane bridge that had been built before the Second World War. Islanders never went out to Chinicook unless they were bird watchers. There wasn't much there except for miles of beach surrounding dense scrub. Tourists were the only ones who made the trip. It was supposedly romantic to pack a picnic and get away from the crowded island beaches. At least that's what it said in the guidebooks. But the drive took over an hour and then there was the half mile of narrow bridge. It was a trip that was daunting enough to turn back most casual explorers.

The longer we stayed on High Pine Road, the more certain I became that we were headed to Chinicook. The question was why?

Olivia drove fast, considering we were flying without lights and the road was covered with sand. I closed my eyes, suddenly feeling weary after losing my Ruby boost. Tori rubbing my arm helped with that. I think I might have fallen asleep because the next time I opened my eyes, we were approaching the Chinicook Bridge.

"Take it easy here," Kent warned. "We don't want to go over the side."

It was good advice. There was no rail to speak of, only a long wooden beam that ran the length of both sides a foot off the deck. One wrong move and—splash.

"You're awake, Olivia, right?" I asked.

"Wide awake," she replied quickly.

I sensed the tension in her voice. She was alert and locked in.

We had gotten maybe halfway across the bridge when she jammed on the brakes. Tori grabbed my arm as we skidded forward. I thought for sure that we were going over the side but Olivia managed to keep the Jeep going straight until we came to a stop.

"Why did you do that?" I demanded.

"What's that?" Olivia cried nervously, pointing forward.

Something was on the bridge ahead of us. In the dark it appeared to be a moving gray shape.

"Kent?" Olivia whined, her anxiety growing.

"It's okay," Kent said with confidence.

He got out of the Jeep, walked to the front, and stood directly between the two headlights.

"Flash the lights," Kent commanded. "Two short. Two long. Two short."

"What?" Olivia asked, totally confused.

"I'll do it," Tori said impatiently and reached forward.

She flashed the lights, just as Kent had instructed.

The gray shape offered a reply with its own flashing light. Two long. Two short. Two long.

"Very James Bond," I said.

Kent got back in the Jeep and said, "Drive. Slowly."

Olivia obeyed. She gently stepped on the gas and we rolled forward, staying a good thirty yards behind the gray shape that now looked to be moving back toward Chinicook.

"Friends of yours?" I asked Kent.

Kent didn't answer.

After a nerve-wracking few minutes, we reached the far end of the bridge and drove onto the sand of Chinicook Island. Now that we were closer, I saw that the gray shape was actually a group of four people.

Kent turned to us and said, "This is what SYLO wants to know about."

"What?" Tori asked. "A bunch of people hiding out in the dark?"

"Hiding out in the dark," Kent said. "And planning to take the island back."

Kent got out and went to the group. They all shook hands.

"This is just plain creepy," Olivia said.

I couldn't argue with her.

Tori and I got out of the Jeep and stood in front, not sure of what to say or do. If what Kent had said was true, we had found the people Granger referred to as "rogues." It sounded like some kind of revolutionary underground that wanted to fight back against SYLO. Knowing that, all of Kent's caution about saying anything about his plan made sense. It raised him up in my estimation. At least a little.

"Tori?" one of the gray shadows called. "Is that you, Tickle?"

Tori immediately tensed up. "Daddy?"

The man hurried toward us and I quickly recognized him as the guy who was sitting aboard the *Tori Tickle* working on his lobster traps when I first visited their house.

Tori ran into his arms and the two hugged.

"What are you doing here?" he cried, full of emotion.

"I gotta ask you the same thing," Tori said through her tears.

Another mystery was solved. We now knew why Michael Sleeper wasn't hanging around the SYLO compound.

"Young Tucker Pierce!" called another of the shadows. "Never thought I'd be seeing you out this way."

It was my turn to tense up, but not for the same reason as Tori. I knew that voice and as soon as I heard it, I realized that yet another mystery had been solved.

I knew where Kent had gotten the Ruby.

The man stepped forward and held out his hand to shake. "Welcome to the revolution," he said with a warm smile.

It was Mr. Feit.

TWENTY-ONE

I didn't shake his hand.

I punched the smile off his face.

"Whoa, dude!" Kent yelled with surprise the second my fist connected with Feit's chin.

I'll put the blame on the lingering effects of the Ruby. It's easier than saying I had lost control. Or maybe I wasn't the same guy I used to be, but in that moment, the smug smiling face of Feit represented all that had gone wrong on Pemberwick Island.

Hitting him felt pretty good.

Feit's head snapped to the side and he went down hard, landing on his butt. I hadn't knocked him out, but he wasn't in a hurry to get back up again.

At first nobody made a move. I think they were stunned and maybe afraid I might take a swing at them too. After a tense few seconds, Tori walked up to me and said softly, "Can I hit him next?"

Her words actually calmed me down, which I think she was trying to do.

Feit rubbed his aching jaw and when he looked up at me, the smile was gone. I had knocked it into next week.

"You can hit me again if it'll make you feel better," he said.

"I don't need your permission," I snarled.

Kent approached me and said, "I don't blame you, man, but you should listen to what he's got to say."

I looked around at the others. They were keeping their distance, staring at me with concern, wondering what I would do next. I liked the feeling. For a change, I was the one in control.

"Get up," I ordered.

Feit gingerly got to his feet, making sure that he was out of punching range. He looked the exact same as I'd remembered him, complete with baggy shorts, flip-flops, a hoodie, and a few days' growth of beard. He looked every bit the part of a surfer dude who was a little too old to be a surfer dude.

"I get it," he said, with no hint of his usual charm. He wasn't laughing either. "Some of the people who took the Ruby died. That's tragic and I have a lot to do with it. But it wasn't all my fault."

"*You* brought it here," I said.

"I did."

"And you were the one getting people to use it."

"Guilty," he admitted.

"And it was your company that made it."

Feit didn't reply to that right away.

"That's what you told me," I said.

"I know," he admitted. "I lied."

"So then where did it come from?" Tori asked.

Feit looked to Mr. Sleeper as if asking his permission to answer.

"Tell him," Mr. Sleeper said. "You owe him that much."

Feit let out a laugh, though it was more out of nervousness than anything else.

"I do work for a company that makes sports supplements," he said. "It's my own company. I'm the only employee. I'm a bio-chemist. MIT graduate."

"If you're trying to impress me, I might have to hit you again," I said.

"Okay, sorry," he said, laughing.

I almost clocked him again just for that annoying laugh, but I held back.

"About a year ago this guy came to me. Said he worked for a well-funded private think tank that was developing a revolutionary dietary supplement. He said it was light years ahead of anything else out there, but they were running into problems getting it tested and quickly approved by the government. He said if I helped them, I'd be a joint patent holder when it finally got approval. Do you know how much money something like that is worth?"

"No," I said flatly.

"A lot. Millions. Many millions. To a guy who is struggling just to get by, it's too tempting an offer to resist."

Tori asked, "What did he want you to do?"

"Run a test. A secret test. In a contained, controlled environ-ment . . . like an island community."

"Like Pemberwick Island," Kent added.

"Yeah. He wanted me to casually introduce it to the popula-tion, take notes, record all the results, and then get back to him.

He said with that data they could streamline their testing and cut years off the approval process. He promised me it was safe . . . and offered an incredible future. So I went for it."

"But the tests didn't go so well," Tori said.

"They went *too* well!" Feit said. "A lot of people took it. Most you don't even know about. The Ruby did everything it was supposed to do. The problem was dosage—and controlling it. It wasn't until Marty Wiggins that . . ."

"That people started to die," I said, finishing the thought.

"So the Ruby has nothing to do with SYLO?" Tori said. "Or the quarantine?"

"Oh, no," Feit said quickly. "SYLO has everything to do with the Ruby being here."

"How's that?" I asked.

"The guy who came to me with the offer was Captain Granger."

I thought my knees would buckle.

"No!" Tori said with a gasp.

"Yes," Feit said. "I had no idea he was actually working for the government. With the military. There wasn't anybody more surprised than me when he stepped onto this island with an invasion force. I've been hiding ever since."

"But . . . why?" was all I could say. "Why would our own government poison us with that stuff?"

"Or invade us," Kent said. "None of this adds up."

"Whatever the reason, you're still responsible," Tori said to Feit with disgust. "You're going to prison for this."

Feit shrugged. "I'm already in prison. We all are. Irony is, the Ruby might be our only hope of getting out."

"No," I declared. "No way."

"Easy there, Rook," Kent said. "It helped us break out of the SYLO camp, didn't it?"

"We smuggled the Ruby into the SYLO compound," Mr. Sleeper said. "We've got a lot of people on our side."

"Who is we?" Tori asked.

"People who are ready to fight back," Mr. Sleeper said. "Many of them were picked up by Granger and his thugs and stuck in that camp. He doesn't want anybody challenging his authority."

I thought back to how all the prisoners kept to themselves and wondered how many of them were part of this group . . . whatever this group was.

"Look," Kent said. "I hate this scum. The Ruby killed my father, remember? But if it gives us a way to fight back, I say we use it. Use *him*. Just like we did tonight."

"You mean just like *I* did tonight," I corrected.

"Whatever. After that he can hang, for all I care."

There was a long moment of silence, and then . . .

"I don't know about you people, but I would really like to get off this crappy island and go home," Olivia said softly.

Tori's father stepped between the two of us, but faced me.

"You should see what's going on here, son," he said. "This Feit character is only part of it."

"I thought they arrested you," I said.

"They took me out of the house, but we never quite made it to the golf course," he said, then smiled knowingly. "Somewhere along the route there's a wrecked Hummer and a couple of soldier boys with severe headaches."

"You don't mess with my dad," Tori said proudly.

Mr. Sleeper was a big guy with thick arms and huge hands that came from a lifetime of working on boats. There was nothing complicated about him. When he spoke, he looked you straight in the eye, and if he was anywhere near as good as his daughter at taking down people who crossed him, I had no doubt that the SYLO soldiers who had arrested him regretted it.

"C'mon," he said. "Let me show you."

I looked at Tori, who shrugged and nodded. She didn't like Feit any more than I did, but she wasn't about to argue with her father.

"Okay," I said and instantly felt the tension melt away from the group.

Mr. Sleeper looked to the other men and said, "Get that Jeep out of sight."

The guys got right on it and took charge of the Jeep while Mr. Sleeper led us along the sandy road, headed deeper onto the island. He had one arm around Tori, while I walked on his other side. Kent was next to me. The rest followed, including Feit.

"We started this group a couple of days after SYLO landed," Sleeper began. "It was casual at first. A bunch of us old-timers got together to try and sort it all out. Nobody bought the story they were feeding us about the quarantine. We tried contacting the state and even made some calls to Washington but kept hitting stone walls or getting doubletalk. We started holding meetings every couple of nights at a different location for fear of Granger catching on to us."

"How did I not know about this?" Tori asked.

"I didn't want you involved."

Tori snickered. "Great. I thought I was protecting you and the whole time you were in way deeper than any of us."

"My father was part of it," Kent added. "That's how I knew all about it."

"I kept thinking it would all just go away," Mr. Sleeper went on. "Of course, it didn't. More and more frustrated folks started showing up to vent. Not just locals either. Many of them were tourists who came here for vacation and got stuck. It got to be tricky keeping it all quiet. Those SYLO goons were always poking around, asking what we were up to. It came to a head when communications to the mainland got cut."

"The riot in town," I said.

"The anger just boiled over. We never bought the virus story. It wasn't until Feit here paid us a visit that we knew for sure."

"Knew what?" Tori asked.

"That there was no virus."

Feit came forward and said, "I told them why people were dying. I wanted to . . ."

His voice trailed off.

"Just say it," Mr. Sleeper demanded.

"I wanted to confess," Feit said, barely above a whisper. "I told them how everyone who died had taken the Ruby . . . and that Granger was behind it all."

I glanced at Kent. He kept his eyes on the ground but I could feel his anger bubbling.

"That's when we knew we had to do something," Mr. Sleeper said. "Sitting back and waiting for it all to blow over wasn't going to happen. So we mobilized and came out here. It took a while. We didn't want to raise any suspicion. We could only move at night and had to cover our tracks. But we made it. Been here a couple of days now."

"You're all just camping out here?" I asked.

"Not exactly out," Sleeper said. "More like camping under."

We were met in the road by a guy carrying a shotgun with the stock against his shoulder, up and aimed.

"It's okay," Mr. Sleeper said to him. "It's my daughter and her friends."

I knew the guy. He worked at the drugstore in town. He lowered the gun and said, "Welcome."

We walked past him and then by five other men and women who were stationed on the road to keep out unwanted visitors. I knew them all. One guy worked on my dad's car. I recognized a woman who taught algebra at the middle school. There was even a husband and wife who owned one of the ice-cream stores in Arbortown. Seeing them guarding the desolate island, with weapons, was like stepping into a surreal dream.

"Won't it be easy for SYLO to find us?" Tori asked. "I mean, they have helicopters."

"And we got camouflage," Sleeper replied proudly.

We arrived at the edge of what was normally a dense scrub forest. Even in the dark of night, I could see that camouflage netting had been erected in the trees.

"We only travel at night, and keep the lights out," Sleeper said. "During the day we're hidden beneath the canopy. Besides, we won't be here long."

We stepped into the forest to see an elaborate camp filled with small tents. There were no campfires to give them away. Instead there were multiple containers stacked everywhere for storing food. Dozens of camp chairs were scattered about. Most were empty because it was so late, but there were still plenty of people awake and talking in hushed tones.

Calling this a camp for guerilla fighters seemed silly, considering that the people didn't look anything like hardened revolutionaries. It seemed more like a campground for parents who wanted to get away for the weekend. All that was missing was the beer. The only sign it was something more ominous was that most of them carried guns.

"What's the point?" I asked. "I mean, you're not really planning some kind of revolution, are you?"

"Depends on your definition of revolution," Mr. Sleeper said and kept walking.

As we moved through the campground, we kept getting suspicious glares from the people we passed. There were no smiles or waves or words of welcome. These people were living on the edge—and they were scared. I recognized a few more faces, but there were just as many people I had never seen before.

Mr. Sleeper led us to the largest tent in the campground. Inside were several portable picnic tables. It could have been a food tent, or a meeting hall. The only light came from shielded camp lanterns that were hooded to keep the light contained.

"Take a load off," Mr. Sleeper said.

Tori and I sat at one table, Kent and Olivia at another. Feit sat by himself.

"We're not kidding ourselves here," Mr. Sleeper said. "We have no hope of bullying SYLO off the island. But we can make ourselves heard."

"How?" I asked. "They're an army. You guys . . . aren't."

"We're going to kidnap Granger," Mr. Sleeper said as nonchalantly as if he had said, "Pass the salt."

None of us reacted. I think we might have been in shock. I know I was.

"Why?" Tori finally asked.

"To force their hand. You know as well as I do that we're isolated here on Pemberwick. Nobody on the outside knows what's happening. They haven't since the day communications were cut. We figure that if we can pull in SYLO's most important player, somebody somewhere will finally listen to us."

"But there's no guarantee of that," I argued. "Even if you get Granger—and I'm not so sure you can—we'd still be cut off. Nobody outside of Pemberwick would even know."

"Exactly. That's why we wouldn't keep him here," Sleeper said with a satisfied smile. "The plan is to bring him to the mainland. We've got a half dozen speedboats ready to make the run. We'd send them all at once so they won't know which one's got Granger. Once we get to the mainland, we can parade him in front of every camera we can find and let the world know what he's been doing here."

"Awesome," Kent said. "I can't wait to see that guy squirm in front of TV lights."

I wanted to tell Mr. Sleeper what a crazy plan that was, but the more I thought about it, the more I realized it wasn't much different from what Quinn, Tori, and I tried to do. We wanted to get to a radio or TV station to blow the whistle on SYLO and that was exactly what Mr. Sleeper was planning. The only difference was that he wanted to do it armed with some serious evidence. Granger.

Tori must have been reading my mind because she looked at me and said, "It's not bad."

"Where are the boats?" I asked.

"Out here on Chinicook. Hidden in Crescent Bay. It was a hell of a risk getting them out here at night, but we pulled it off."

My mind raced—and it had nothing to do with the Ruby.

"Is there a plan to get him?" I asked. "I mean, sneaking a couple of people out of that compound is one thing. Breaking in and nabbing the boss is a whole 'nother ball game."

"We've got a lot of people on our side," Mr. Sleeper said. "Out here and on the inside."

"Prisoners?" Tori asked.

"That's how we smuggled in the Ruby. SYLO doesn't know who is innocent and who they have to be afraid of. People have sacrificed themselves just to get inside. We have total surprise on our side. And something else too."

Sleeper nodded to Feit. Feit walked to the side of the tent where a tarp was stretched over a bulky object. He grabbed one end of the tarp and yanked it off to reveal eight clear plastic containers, each the size of a cooler—and each packed solid with the Ruby.

"Oh, man," I exclaimed and jumped to my feet. I couldn't help myself. Seeing that much of the deadly substance was a shock.

"It's like making a deal with the devil," Mr. Sleeper said

ominously. "But if used properly, it'll give us the advantage we need to get Granger, bring him to the mainland, and end this nightmare."

"I like it," Kent said enthusiastically.

"Shut up, Kent," I snapped.

Kent was ready to jump at me but thought better of it and backed off.

"Let me make one thing clear," Mr. Sleeper said. "I'm only telling you this so you know what's been going on. You all are not going to be part of the operation. You've been through too much as it is."

"You get no arguments from me," Kent said.

I shot him a dirty look but he avoided eye contact.

"When?" I asked.

"Tomorrow night. There's no telling how long we can keep Chinicook a secret so we have to move fast. One last thing we need before we move is something from the three of you."

"Anything," Kent said quickly, but I didn't think that extended to him taking the Ruby.

"You've been inside the compound," he said. "We need maps and any other information you can give us about how it all works. Hopefully between the three of you, we can get a good idea of what we'll be faced with."

"What about me?" Olivia asked. "How can I help?"

Kent took her hand and kissed it. "You've already done your part by getting us out here."

Tori rolled her eyes and said, "I think I just threw up a little in my mouth."

Olivia ignored the cut.

There was so much to digest. What had started out as the search for answers about a mysterious virus had become something far bigger.

"There's something else," I said. "Have you seen those flying shadows?"

"We have," Mr. Sleeper said. "We think they have something to do with SYLO."

He looked at Feit, as if expecting him to add something.

"They do," Feit said. "I don't know what kind of aircraft they are, but they're SYLO all right."

"How do you know?" I asked.

"Two weeks ago I was supposed to get a shipment of the Ruby. I got a call to be out on the bluffs on the east side of the island at midnight. I drove out there and saw this shadow fly by—and it exploded. Scared the hell out of me so I just took off."

"And the next day a boatload of the stuff washed up on shore, along with the wreckage," Mr. Sleeper added.

"And killed my horses," Tori said.

"The pickup truck," I said. "The one we saw on the bluffs. That was you?"

Feit nodded. "I didn't think anybody saw me."

"But that doesn't explain what the shadows are, or what they're doing," Tori said. "There was a dogfight over the mainland. If those shadow planes were SYLO, who were they fighting? And why? Planes were blown out of the sky. People died."

"Quinn died," I said.

"What?" Olivia exclaimed. "Quinn is dead?"

Tori ignored her and said, "Even if you get Granger and make it to the mainland, what are you going to find there? Whatever SYLO is doing, it's not just about Pemberwick."

"We thought about that," Mr. Sleeper said. "All of it. I'm sorry to hear about your friend, Tucker. And your father, Kent."

"I can't believe that Quinn is gone," Olivia said, genuinely upset.

"And I'm sorry about my parents," I said. "They're working with SYLO."

That shut the conversation down. With each new revelation about SYLO, I kept thinking about my mom and dad and wondering what part they were playing in this nightmare. For me, that *was* the nightmare.

"We don't have a whole lot of answers," Mr. Sleeper said. "But we all feel certain that the only way to get the truth is to blast off of this rock and get back to civilization. Nobody knows what we're going to find there and who might be on our side, but what other choice do we have?"

"None," I said quickly. "I'll help. I'll draw you as many maps as you want and tell you every last thing I learned about the place, but I want something in return."

"What's that?" Mr. Sleeper asked.

"I want Tori and me to be on one of those boats going to the mainland."

"What about me?" Kent asked.

"And me?" Olivia chimed in petulantly.

"You do whatever you want, but Tori and I will be on one of those boats."

Mr. Sleeper frowned and shook his head. "No. Too dangerous."

I stalked toward him and said, "It's no more dangerous than

what we've been through already. We've been out there, Mr. Sleeper. In your boats, in the middle of a battle. One of them was vaporized with my best friend on board. *That's* how Quinn died."

Mr. Sleeper went white. "You made a run for the mainland? Tori?"

"We did," Tori said. "The *Patricia* was hit by a light that vaporized it, along with Quinn."

"Seriously?" Olivia said, stunned. She looked whiter than Mr. Sleeper. "Evaporate? Like . . . poof?"

"I don't know who is fighting who," I said. "Or why. But they're not taking prisoners. We saw it all, which means we have a hell of a lot more experience making a run for the mainland than any of your weekend warriors here. We will be on one of those boats, Mr. Sleeper. In fact, Tori will be the captain. I trust her more than anybody. It's not a request, it's a fact. Accept it or you won't be getting any map from me."

Tori stood up and said, "Or from me, Dad."

I looked toward Kent. He saw how serious I was. He gave a resigned shrug and said, "Or me. I don't want to be stuck here either."

Mr. Sleeper was speechless. Tori went to him, wrapped her arms around his waist, and pressed her cheek against his chest.

"Don't think that leaving us here is the same as protecting us," she said. "We stand just as good a chance of surviving by making a run as staying on the island."

Mr. Sleeper closed his eyes and hugged his daughter. She was all he had in the world. It must have pained him to think that he would lose her. But he wasn't the kind of guy who would step back, hope for the best, and let fate play out on its own.

"All right," he said softly, then looked at me and added, "You know how to pick 'em. If anybody's got a chance of piloting a boat through a crapstorm, it's my daughter."

"That's what I figured," I said. "Do I have your word?"

He nodded. "You do." He wiped his brow and added, "Let's get to work on those maps."

We spent the next hour drawing, talking about what we saw in the SYLO compound, and answering questions thrown at us by a group of people that Mr. Sleeper brought in. Most I knew from around town. They were Mr. Sleeper's buddies, and now they were his lieutenants. It was clear that Mr. Sleeper was the boss. He'd grown up on Pemberwick; he knew every inch of the island and most of the people. He also had a very strong personality. When he spoke, his buddies listened.

They didn't fill us in on the details of their plan to snatch Granger. I think they were still figuring it out, especially since we had dumped a boatload of new information on them. All we knew was that once the team left Chinicook, we would move down to the boats and wait.

Feit was not part of this discussion. When the lieutenants showed up, Feit was asked to step out. Obviously, nobody trusted him. He wasn't going to play a critical role in the kidnapping other than to provide a boost from the Ruby. I got the feeling that nobody liked him much. Made sense. As far as I was concerned, the guy was a murderer. I hated that the good guys had to rely on him and worried that they were going to take the Ruby, but it was a small risk compared to everything else that was going on.

It didn't help my opinion of him that he was such a good liar.

Everything he first had told me about the Ruby was bogus. It made me wonder where his lies stopped and the truth began. We accepted everything he told us about SYLO and Granger because it fit and helped to explain some things. Still, I couldn't help but wonder if everything he said was the absolute truth.

It was nearly four in the morning by the time we finished. I hadn't slept much earlier that night and I was definitely feeling low after coming down from my adventure with the Ruby. Olivia had already crashed somewhere because she didn't have anything to offer. Kent got bored quickly and was asleep on the floor of the tent.

"Get some rest," Mr. Sleeper said. "If you think of anything else, you can tell me later. And sleep in. We don't move around much during the day. We're like a camp of vampires."

The lady from the ice-cream shop came in with a couple of sleeping bags and pillows for us and started to lay them out near the crates of the Ruby.

"Thanks," I said. "But I'd rather not sleep near that stuff."

She glanced at the Ruby and nodded. "Right. Sorry."

She laid both of the bags down on the opposite side of the tent and I went right for one, ready to crash.

Tori gave her father a playful poke in the chest. It reminded me of when she pushed his hat over his eyes on their dock. "I'm proud of you, Dad," she said. "If anybody can pull this off, it's you."

"It's not like I have a choice," he said. "I've gotta take care of my little girl."

He kissed the top of her head and headed out of the tent.

Tori came over and lay down on the sleeping bag next to mine.

"Did you ever imagine that your father would be the leader of a revolution?" I asked.

"No, obviously," she said. "But if there's gotta be a revolution, there's nobody better to run it. People listen to my dad."

"Seriously. I can't imagine telling him what to do."

Tori leaned over, kissed me on the cheek, and whispered, "But you *did* tell him what to do. And he listened. Not bad."

She lay down on her sleeping bag and was asleep in seconds.

It wasn't fair. I was about as exhausted as I'd ever been in my life, but I had been jolted awake by a kiss that I never saw coming.

There was so much rattling around in my head, good and bad, that I feared I'd never get to sleep. I probably lay there thinking for, oh, a solid eight seconds before dropping off.

I didn't sleep for long though. Can't say why. I definitely needed more downtime but my brain needed my body to be awake so we could both get back to stressing over the situation.

It was still dark. I saw that Tori was fast asleep. Kent and Olivia were, too. I wanted to fall back to sleep but knew it would be impossible so I got up and left the tent.

The sky was slowly growing lighter. The sun would soon rise on what promised to be a dramatic day—maybe the most important day of our lives. Witnessing the dawn on that kind of day felt like the right thing to do, so I walked through the campground, snaking past tents, looking for a trail that would lead me out from under the protective canopy. The entire camp was surrounded by dense scrub trees. There was no way to bushwack out. I had to walk halfway around the perimeter until I found a trail.

I followed the narrow meandering path for at least thirty yards until I broke out into the open to find a wide expanse of sand and grass that stretched to the ocean. From the end of the scrub where I stood to what looked like the edge of a bluff was about fifty yards. Luckily I had come out on the east side of the island, the side where I would see the sunrise.

It was spectacular.

The sky was growing brighter by the second. I thought about walking out to the edge of the bluff but remembered Mr. Sleeper's warning. It wouldn't have been smart to be spotted by a passing Navy ship. So I stayed close to the edge of the scrub, where I had a perfect view of the sunrise.

Standing alone with only the sounds of the ocean and the occasional squawking seagull to keep me company, I felt oddly at peace. As uncertain as I was about how the day would unfold, it was good to know that there was a plan. I wasn't so naïve as to think that we would put a quick end to the nightmare, but at least we now had direction. And friends. We weren't alone anymore. I guess you have to appreciate the good stuff when it comes because there was more than enough bad stuff to go around.

If there was anything positive to take from recent events, it was that in some small way I had proven to myself that I was able to rise to a challenge. That's saying a lot. I guess you could say that I had been floating. I didn't like to fail—at anything—which meant I usually didn't try. Quinn loved to point that out about me. When I was faced with a challenge, I backed off, whether it was in school or with girls. It was always easier for me to pretend as though I didn't care than to put myself on the line and risk falling on my face. If I had known I was going to land in the spotlight on the football team, I never would have joined in the first place. Maybe it was because I didn't want to look bad. Or to be seen as somehow lacking. I think that's why I never allowed myself to have the kind of dreams that Quinn had: to leave Pemberwick and make a difference somewhere. That was the kind of stuff other people did. I didn't think I had it in me—whatever "it" is.

But that changed when life changed. I could no longer sit back and say, "Really? The island's been invaded? Oh well, pass the popcorn." Maybe you have to have things taken away before you can truly understand how valuable they are . . . or however that song lyric goes. I had been pushed. Hard. I'm proud to say that I finally pushed back. And I would continue to push back. It was a strangely exciting feeling. It made me wonder what I might be capable of once we got past all of this crap and life settled back to the new normal. Maybe I'd start thinking more like Quinn and start looking around to see what could be accomplished. I'm not sure if that kind of thinking frightened me before, or if I just couldn't see myself succeeding. But after what we had been through, I no longer had those doubts. I felt confident that I could rise to the challenge. Any challenge.

I wanted the chance to prove it . . . for myself, and for Quinn.

While I stood there contemplating the wonders of my new-found enlightenment, the sun began to peek up over the horizon. The strip of sky above the sea quickly turned orange, lifting the curtain on a new day. It was a day that would set the course for the next chapter in this strange adventure. I felt certain that the next time the sun came up it would be on a whole new reality—one that we all had a hand in shaping because we were about to make another Pemberwick Run.

Then I saw something on the horizon.

It started out as a black speck on the sun . . . that soon turned into two specks.

I stared at the aberrations, not sure of what I was seeing as the mysterious blots grew larger. It was the sound that brought it all into focus. It took a few seconds after I had registered the black specks for me to hear it because the speed of sound is painfully slow.

It was a steady, low thumping sound. It was incessant. It grew louder. Fast.

I don't know why it took so long for me to react. Maybe it was ignorance or disbelief or wishful thinking—or stubborn resistance to the fact that all of our carefully crafted plans were about to go into the toilet.

The black specks were flying out of the rising sun.

They were helicopters.

SYLO had found us.

TWENTY-TWO

"**W**ake up! Get up! We're under attack!"

I ran through the camp screaming like a lunatic, trying to roust the dozens of people who were sleeping peacefully, totally unaware that the game was about to change. People crawled out of their tents, wiping sleep from their eyes, looking more annoyed than worried.

"Get up! Helicopters are coming this way!"

Nobody reacted. Maybe they were still asleep and didn't trust the ravings of a guy they didn't know. They wandered about, grumbling, rubbing their eyes and generally looking dazed. I had the odd thought that this was what it must have been like on Pearl Harbor just before all hell broke loose.

"Tucker!" Mr. Sleeper called as he crawled out of his tent. "What's going on?"

I opened my mouth to tell him, but didn't get the chance.

His answer came from the sky as the first helicopter swooped in low and unleashed a torrent of machine gun fire on the camp.

They hadn't come to capture anybody. This was an all-out attack.

Nobody saw the flying beast. The camouflage cover worked both ways. What we saw instead was the sky falling and the ground torn up by two lines of bullets that raked the ground, splintering trees, tearing through tents, and sending small explosions of dirt into the air.

That woke everybody up.

Some people went for their shotguns. Others turned and fled into the scrub. Still others crawled out of their tents with looks of shock, as if the reality was too much to comprehend.

I hit the ground but didn't know why until I realized that Mr. Sleeper had grabbed me and thrown me down while shielding me with his body.

"Get Tori," he said. "Go for the boats."

I jumped up and started running for the big tent just as the next helicopter made its attack run. I hit the ground on my own this time, grabbing my head for protection—not that that would have helped against a white-hot bullet. The stream of bullets strafed the camp, pulverizing the plastic coolers, blowing them into the air with a shattering barrage. This time people were hit. I saw a guy running through the center of the camp, headed for his shotgun. He didn't make it. At least one and probably more bullets hit him, dropping him instantly. A red cloud that seemed strangely pretty erupted from his back. My mind wouldn't accept it for what it really was. The poor guy hit the ground and didn't move.

"Go!" Mr. Sleeper yelled to me.

I scrambled to my feet and sprinted for the big tent.

Inside, Kent was just starting to wake up. Fool.

"What's all the noise?" he asked, groggy.

"Get up!" I shouted. "We're under attack."

"Attack?" he repeated dumbly as if it didn't register. "By who?"

"Where's Tori?"

"Here!" she called.

Tori was huddled under one of the picnic tables with Olivia, who looked like a deer caught in the headlights with wide, frightened eyes.

"New plan," I said, breathless. "We're going for the boats now."

"I knew it," Tori said angrily. "That's why we escaped so easily. They let us go."

Kent crawled over and scrambled under the table.

"No way," he argued. "My plan worked perfectly."

"Because there weren't any guards around, you idiot!" Tori screamed. "They knew exactly what we were doing. We were set up. They followed us here."

Her words stunned me, but made total sense.

"Kent?" Olivia cried with confusion. "Are we going to be okay?"

Kent didn't get the chance to answer as another strafing run hit the camp. The pounding sound of the helicopter flying low over the trees was broken up by the nasty chatter of its guns. I jumped under the table just as the surface was hit, sending splinters of plastic all over the tent.

Olivia screamed. Kent did too.

I grabbed Tori and held my breath, bracing against the pain I expected to jolt me at any second. But the strafing run ended and I was still in one piece.

"Anybody hit?" I asked.

I was answered with wild, frightened gazes.

"We gotta go," I declared.

"No," Olivia cried, shaking her head like a petulant two-year-old. "I'm not moving."

I grabbed her and stuck my nose right in her face.

"That's your call," I said. "But if they keep pounding the camp, this might not be the safest place to be."

She was on the verge of hysteria but she had enough sense to understand that staying could mean death.

"Okay," she said, nodding quickly. "I'll go."

I pushed her toward Kent and said, "Watch out for her."

"Seriously?" Kent snarled. "Who's gonna watch out for me?"

I don't think I could have hated Kent any more than I did in that moment.

"I gotta find Dad," Tori said as she crawled out from under the table.

"No," I said, grabbing her arm. "He's okay. He told me to get you and head for the boats."

A helicopter roared over. Olivia grabbed her head and screamed again as Tori and I dove beneath what was left of the table. This time the helicopter didn't unload.

"They're just messing with us now," I said.

"They're doing a good job," Kent whined.

"I can't believe this is a mass execution," I said. "They're going to land and try to round us up. Our best bet is to get lost in the trees and bushwack out."

Nobody disagreed. They needed guidance and mine was as good as any.

"Then let's go," Tori shouted.

We headed out of the tent to witness total chaos. Many people had shotguns pointed to the sky at . . . what? Sunlight streamed through the bullet holes in the camouflage, making it look like a giant spaghetti colander. At that moment I was more worried about getting shot by a trigger-happy friend than by SYLO. There were a few people down and hurt, or worse. Others huddled together, staring up, waiting for the next attack.

"This way," I said and started for the trees on the north end of the camp.

Tori didn't follow. She stood still, staring at something.

"C'mon!" I yelled.

She took off in the other direction.

"Let her go," Kent demanded.

There was no chance of that.

"Tori? What are you—"

I saw where she was headed. Lying in the dirt on his back, unmoving, was her father. She ran to him and fell to her knees. I hurried up behind her to see that he was alive, but barely. His eyes were vacant and dreamy. His mouth hung open and, worst of all, a thick pool of blood was growing under his back. Tori lifted his head and put it on her knees.

"Dad?" she said, holding back tears. "How bad is it?"

Her father focused on her. Surprisingly, he smiled.

"Not bad," he said in a weak whisper. "But I won't be paying Granger a visit tonight."

"We'll get help," she said, her voice cracking. "I'll stay with you until the soldiers get here and—"

"No," he said and grabbed Tori's hand. "Go. Now. While there's still a chance."

"I won't leave you," Tori argued. She was losing the battle to keep from crying.

"You have to," Mr. Sleeper said and winced. The guy was in serious pain.

"Don't move," Tori pleaded.

"I lied, Tickle," he said. "I'm hurt. Bad. You staying here won't change that."

"I'm not leaving," Tori argued as she stroked his hair. "Not until we get help."

"If you wait for me to get help, then they've got you," her father said with as much urgency as he could offer. "We'd both be done and then this was all for nothing."

A voice came booming at us from a loudspeaker that was somewhere outside of the campground.

"Attention in the camp," the voice called. "Place your weapons together in plain sight. We will discontinue the attack so long as there is no resistance. At the first sign of aggression, we will resume the strafing. Do not make the mistake of underestimating our resolve."

The voice belonged to Granger. There was one thing I could say for that guy: He did his own dirty work.

"There you go," Mr. Sleeper said. "You've got a window. Please, please use it."

Tori tried to say something but it caught in her throat.

"I couldn't be any more proud of you, sweetheart," Mr. Sleeper said. "I know it's been rough for us but you've been strong and smart and I couldn't have made it through without you. You've always taken care of me but now it's time to take care of yourself."

"I can't," Tori sobbed.

"Yes, you can. I know you can. Go. Get to the mainland and put a stop to this nonsense. I'm counting on you."

Tori leaned over and hugged her father tight.

"I love you, Daddy," she said softly.

"I love you, Tickle," he said. "You've always made me proud. Don't stop now."

Tori nodded, gave him one last hug, then gently rested his head back down.

"Goodbye, Daddy," she said and backed away.

Her father didn't respond. I don't think he could bring himself to say those same words.

As Tori retreated, I knelt down next to Mr. Sleeper and said, "I'll watch out for her."

He smiled and gave a little chuckle. "I think she'll be the one looking out for *you*."

His chuckle turned into a cough. Pain creased his face. His eyes went wide and then blank. In that brief instant I saw the spark of life leave Michael Sleeper.

I steeled myself, stood up, and went right to Tori, blocking her view.

"I think he's going to be okay," I lied. "They'll take him to the hospital in the SYLO compound."

Tori nodded. I wasn't sure if she believed me or not.

Granger's voice returned, sounding closer this time. "We will allow two minutes for you to surrender your weapons. Our forces have gathered and will enter the camp after that. They are armed and have been ordered to shoot at the first sign of aggression."

Tori looked me right in the eye and declared, "We're getting out."

Glancing around the camp, I saw that most of the people were cooperating with Granger's demands. Men and women gathered toward the center of the camp and dropped their various rifles and pistols in a pile. Most of those who were cooperating I recognized as longtime islanders. It seemed to be the off-islanders who were the most reluctant to give up.

"If we're going, it better be now," Kent said.

I scanned the camp, looking for what I thought would be the best route out. I chose a spot where the scrub was dense and would provide us with some cover.

"C'mon," I said and ran for the trees.

Tori, Kent, and Olivia were right behind me. I dove into the thick brush, shoving aside the tangle of branches that blocked our way. Olivia was not dressed for this kind of adventure. The branches had to be tearing her legs up. But to her credit, she kept moving. Fear helps you do some crazy things.

"This is horrible," she complained. "We should take one of the trails."

"Sure," I said. "And meet a team of soldiers coming in from the other direction."

She stopped complaining.

We had only gotten a few yards into the brush when a gunshot sounded.

"Down!" I commanded.

Everyone dropped without question. I looked back to see that the two minutes were up. SYLO soldiers poured into the camp from three different trails. Unlike the guards back at the compound, these guys were dressed for battle, complete with deep red helmets and flak jackets. They also carried automatic rifles. This was a full-on combat unit. It struck me as overkill. The "rogues" were nothing more than a collection of pissed-off civilians. I'd bet most of them had never fired a gun at a target, let alone another human being.

The soldiers moved quickly and efficiently. They surrounded the people in the clearing, forming a circle around the perimeter of the camp. The frightened people huddled together, making sure to stay away from the pile of weapons so there would be no question that they had given up.

The last to arrive in the camp was Granger. He too was dressed for combat but didn't carry a weapon or wear a helmet. He strode around the frightened prisoners, making a full circle to inspect them all. He stopped over the body of Mr. Sleeper and nudged it with his foot.

Tori dropped her head.

If she hadn't known that her father was dead before, she knew it then.

"Is this Sleeper?" he asked anybody who would answer.

A few of the prisoners nodded or mumbled that it was indeed their leader. I thought back to when Granger interrogated me about our failed escape. He was asking questions about Mr. Sleeper and the boats and how it was planned. He knew Mr. Sleeper was involved with this group and wanted to know if I was too.

Granger put his hands on his hips and glared at the prisoners.

"Make no mistake," he announced coldly. "This is far from over. Do not underestimate our resolve. We will fight. There will be no surrender. No compromise. No negotiation. You have chosen the wrong road and you will pay for it."

Tori and I exchanged puzzled looks. Granger's speech wasn't making sense. It almost sounded as if *he* were the one on the defensive.

Granger continued, "I understand that not all of you are aggressors. Rest assured that we will separate the wheat from the chaff. Until then, you are all considered enemy combatants. You will be treated humanely, that I promise, though it is more than most of you deserve. Transport vehicles are waiting on the far end of the bridge that will take you to the SYLO compound. You will march in an orderly fashion, single file. Do not step out of line or you will be shot."

Not exactly my idea of humane treatment.

"And may the Almighty have mercy on your wretched souls," Granger added.

Granger waved his arm and the soldiers sprang into action, forcing the people to put their hands on their heads while funneling them into a line.

I wanted to keep going but I was afraid that any little movement might be spotted by a soldier. Precious time was ticking away. For all I knew there were SYLO soldiers swarming all over Chinicook and we had no chance of making it to the bay that held the speedboats. But until the camp was cleared, we had no choice but to wait it out.

The prisoners were marched out of the clearing and the dead were carried out.

Tori looked away when the soldiers lifted her father's lifeless body. I reached out and squeezed her arm. She closed her eyes and let the silent tears fall.

Soon the camp was empty except for Granger and two soldiers. Granger scanned the space, looking beyond the camp and into the woods. I held my breath, for whatever good that might do.

"Where are those children?" Granger asked one of the soldiers. "Sleeper's daughter and the Pierce kid?"

"We haven't seen them since they crossed the bridge early this morning," the soldier replied.

That confirmed it. We had been allowed to escape so they could follow us. We had led SYLO directly to the only people who had a chance of stopping them.

"They can't get off the island, sir," the soldier added. "The bridge is secure."

Granger nodded, thinking.

Hearing those words gave me hope. They didn't know about the speedboats that had been waiting to take Granger to the mainland. There was still a chance.

"Smoke 'em out," Granger said. "Burn it down. All of it."

No sooner did he give that command than he strode from the clearing and was passed by another soldier on his way in. This guy had a steel tank on his back and held a nozzle that was connected to the tank by a hose.

"Uh-oh," I whispered. "Is that—"

With a loud *woof*, a jet of flame shot from the nozzle.

"Yup," Kent answered.

The flamethrower sent out a monstrous line of fire that had to be at least ten feet long. The soldier strolled casually through the campground, sweeping the flame about, turning the place into an instant inferno.

"Move!" I commanded and jumped forward, hacking my way through the dense brush an instant before the soldier swept the flame in our direction and turned the dry scrub behind us into a wall of fire. There was no way to know how far we would have to fight through the tangle before breaking out into the open.

"Tucker?" Olivia called nervously. "It's getting hot."

I turned and was shocked to see the fire was spreading quickly.

"Keep moving," I said.

"Pick up the pace, Rook," Kent called. "Or we'll roast in here."

I tried to move faster but the tangle of growth was relentless. The very same thick foliage that was keeping us from being seen was also preventing a quick escape.

"How much further?" Tori asked.

"I don't know," was my honest answer. "But the longer it takes, the closer we'll get to the bay."

"Or burn trying," Kent added.

There was nothing we could do but keep moving and hope we were faster than the fire. I felt the heat at my back, which made me fear we were losing the race. I realized that we were no longer running from Granger—we were escaping from the fire.

"We've gotta get outta here," Tori warned.

I looked to either side but couldn't tell which way was the most direct route to safety. Going north would take us to the bay, so I kept leading us in that direction. My hands were crisscrossed with bloody slashes from pushing aside the branches, and I got whacked in the face more times that I could count. I didn't want to see how badly Olivia's legs had been cut. But she didn't complain. I guess having fire nipping at your heels makes a few cuts seem trivial.

Finally, with the flames growing so close that I feared my sweat-shirt would combust, we reached the edge of the scrub. I held up my hand to stop the others but with the fire so close it was a waste of energy. Nobody stopped and we all quickly leaped out of the thicket and onto a stretch of sea grass.

"Damn," was my first reaction.

There was still a stretch of at least a hundred yards between us and what looked to be the edge of a bluff that surrounded the bay.

"What do you think?" Kent asked.

"Don't think," Tori said. "Run."

She took off at a dead sprint. I was right after her and the others followed. There was nothing strategic about it. We needed to get to the bay before the SYLO soldiers thought to look for us this far north. A second one way or the other could mean the dif-ference between escape and death. I kept glancing back, fearing that I would see a helicopter headed our way or soldiers sprinting around the perimiter of what had become a monstrous fire. Chini-cook Island would soon be nothing but a charred ember.

Kent picked up the pace and ran up alongside me.

"You sure we're going the right way?" he asked, gulping air.

"We'll know soon enough," I replied.

We made it to the edge of the bluff, where we could look down on the crescent-shaped bay that was cut into the northernmost shore of Chinicook. It was a long way down to the water.

"Where are the boats?" Olivia asked frantically. "I don't see any boats."

"They wouldn't be out in the open," I said. "Or they would have been spotted."

"So then where are they?" Kent demanded to know. "This isn't the right spot."

"Yes, it is," Tori said. "Look."

She pointed down to the right, where we saw several people hurrying down a winding switchback trail, headed for the water.

"They have the same idea," she said.

"There's the trailhead," I exclaimed and ran twenty yards along the bluff's edge until we hit the narrow spit of sand that marked the beginning of the trail.

The path was steep and the footing was bad. One slip and it would be a very long drop to the rocky beach below.

"I'm wearing flip-flops!" Olivia complained.

"Take 'em off!" I yelled back.

I don't know if she did it or not, but she kept moving.

We had gotten about halfway down to the water when I heard someone yell, "Tucker!"

I stopped and looked back up to see Mr. Feit standing on the edge of the bluff. I had almost forgotten about the guy.

He started running for the trailhead and shouted, "I'm coming with you!"

"No, he's not," Kent growled. "Keep moving."

For once I agreed with Kent. I was about to continue moving when we heard a sharp *crack*. It was a rifle shot. SYLO had caught up.

I looked back up to see that Feit wasn't running anymore. He wasn't moving at all. He just stood on the edge of the bluff as if admiring the view.

"What is he doing?" Olivia asked.

The answer came quickly. Feit's knees buckled and he fell. Not to the ground—over the cliff. It was a grisly sight that I couldn't take my eyes off as he bounced from rock to rock, each impact changing his direction, spinning his body, until he landed with a huge splash in the bay.

Just like that, the pusher who had brought the Ruby into our lives was gone.

"I hope to God he was dead before that fall," Tori said.

"I hope he wasn't," Kent snarled. "He deserved to feel all of that."

The shock of witnessing Feit's gruesome death momentarily made me forget why it had happened. SYLO was closing in.

"Let's move," I ordered and continued the treacherous journey down the narrow path.

There was no way to know how close the shot came from. Was it long-range sniper fire? Or would SYLO soldiers be peering over the edge at any second and take aim at us? When we hit bottom, we found ourselves on a narrow, rocky beach with gentle waves lapping onto the shore. The curve of the bay knocked down the biggest waves, making it a cove that was just right for landing a small boat. Or hiding several.

"Where are they?" Kent asked anxiously.

We all looked up and down the coast, searching for the people who had gotten there before us.

"It's like they just disappeared," Olivia cried. "Did we really see them?"

I ignored her. But I didn't know where the boats were, either—

until the loud rumbling of an engine firing to life told us that we were in the right place.

"Where the hell is it?" Kent asked.

The sound intensified. The engine was throttling up.

"There!" Olivia shouted, pointing.

A sleek cigarette boat blasted out from behind a rock outcropping that had been shielding our view. The monster boat was at full throttle, headed out to sea. On board were four people I didn't recognize. The sight reminded me of the boat Tori and I had witnessed being blasted out of the water.

"You can't outrun the Navy like that," Tori said. "If we're going to make it, we have to be smart."

"Lead on, Captain," I said.

We took off running along the beach and quickly climbed up and over the rock outcropping. Beyond it, the bay curved back toward the bluff where a cave was cut into the steep rock wall that was large enough to accommodate several boats. All the craft were hidden in the shadows but I could see them lined up side by side, waiting. Without a word we scrambled over the rocks and splashed through the waist-deep water until we reached the mouth of the cave.

"That one," Kent said, pointing to the largest of the set. "That'll fly."

"No," Tori said with authority as she sized up the rest. "I told you, we can't outrun them. We have to be able to maneuver, and that thing looks like a pig."

"A fast pig," Kent argued.

"Sure, if we were taking a single heading," Tori shot back. "We're going to need more options."

"Listen to her, Kent," Olivia said. "She's, like . . . a boat person."

Tori made a quick appraisal of the small fleet and said, "That one."

Without waiting for anybody's approval, she hurried for the chosen boat. It was on the far right end, which made it easier to access. I have to admit that I wasn't so sure about her choice at first. It was a V-hull open-deck sport boat, about thirty-seven feet long with a center console and two padded pilot seats. There weren't any bells and whistles. All the boats were simple craft that were built for performance, not comfort. Mr. Sleeper and his rogues must have scoured the island until they found the five fastest boats on Pemberwick. Tori's choice looked like it could maneuver well enough, but at first glance it didn't look to have the same horsepower as the other, bigger craft.

That is, until we climbed on board.

"Wow," Kent said. "Never saw a rig like that."

The boat was powered by four identical 250-horsepower Mercury engines. Any one of them would have provided enough horsepower to make the boat fly. I couldn't imagine what they would do together.

"You say we can't outrun the Navy," I said. "But this gives us a shot."

Tori was focused on the console, familiarizing herself with the controls.

"That's not why I picked it," she said. "I want to maneuver."

"Can we go now?" Olivia asked.

"Cast off the line," Tori commanded.

I jumped to the stern to see that all the boats were anchored to a spot deep within the cave. I cast off the line and tossed it to shore.

"Clear," I announced. "It's deep enough to turn the props."

Tori fired up the first engine. Its low, throaty growl boomed through the cave and rattled my gut. She started each of the others in turn. The power these motors put out was almost scary.

"Kent, walk us out of here," Tori commanded.

Kent went to the starboard side, reached over the rail, and walked his hands along the rail of the next boat over to move us forward.

I sat down on the stern bench and looked forward as we slowly slipped from the protection of the cave. There was nothing for me to do but go for a ride. It was a sobering moment.

This was it. Our last shot. We were going to make a run for the mainland in broad daylight. There was no halfway. No moral victory to be had. No Plan B. We were either going to make it . . . or die.

I felt strangely at peace, much like I had felt that morning as I watched the sun rise. The plan may have changed but the feeling that I had that morning remained true. This was the end game. It was an oddly peaceful feeling, though I knew it was the calm before the storm. The final storm. One way or another, it would soon be over.

I thought of Quinn and said, "*This* is the Pemberwick Run."

"Buckle up," Tori barked.

The boat crept into the sun, slipping out from its hiding place, purring, ready to launch. I got up and sat next to Tori, who was buckling her seat belt. What kind of boat had seat belts? It was yet another clue that we were in for a wild ride. I sat to her right and did the same. Kent and Olivia sat directly behind us on the seat that ran the width of the stern. They too buckled in.

"You sure you know what you're doing?" Kent called.

"I don't see anybody else on board who knows more," was Tori's cocky reply.

I had total faith in her, and in her father's opinion. He said that if anybody could pilot a boat through a crapstorm, it was Tori. I also put faith in Quinn's opinion. Tori could sure as hell tie knots.

"Ready?" she asked me.

"Absolutely," I replied.

Tori turned her baseball cap backward and hit the throttles. The engines roared, the boat lurched forward—and the crack of a rifle cut through it all. I spun around to look back at the bluff to see a SYLO sharpshooter sitting on top, with his rifle trained on us.

"They're here!" I shouted over the roar of the engines. "That must have been the guy who got Feit."

I looked at Tori. She was slumped over the wheel.

"Tori?" I called.

She didn't answer.

A blossom of blood was growing on her back, soaking her shirt.

TWENTY-THREE

My brain locked.

I didn't know if I should shake her or scream for help or grab the wheel. I probably should have done all three, but I felt as though I'd been hit in the head with a baseball bat.

It was the second gunshot that pulled me back into the moment. I heard a *crack* and then the fiberglass console directly between the two of us was shattered by the impact of a bullet.

"Kent!" I shouted.

Turning around I saw that both Olivia and Kent were huddled down on the seat, beneath the stern rail and the engines.

"She's hit, help her!" I screamed.

He didn't move.

"Now!"

I tried to gently pull Tori back off the wheel but this was no time for being careful. We were flying over the water's surface under full power and nobody was steering. First priority was to take control.

Kent finally came forward and grabbed her by the shoulders.

Tori moaned in pain.

"What do I do?" he cried. He was near brain-lock as well.

"Get her back there and lay her on the deck," I screamed. "And stay low!"

He unbuckled her seat belt, then reached under her arms and dragged her off the seat. I didn't have time to worry about her. We were under attack. I undid my own seat belt and slid into the captain's chair.

"She's bleeding!" Olivia cried, as if she was more worried about getting blood on her clothes than about Tori's life.

"Get us outta here!" Kent yelled.

Thank you, stater-of-the-obvious. I hoped that with each passing second we were getting further out of range of the sharpshooter. Just to be sure, I made a short turn to keep from traveling in a perfectly straight line and making us a perfectly easy target. I barely touched the wheel and the boat responded instantly.

"Whoa, easy!" Kent hollered.

Tori had called it. This boat could maneuver. The slightest adjustment made a dramatic turn.

No more shots followed. We were definitely out of range. But now I was the captain of the boat so I set a course that would take us out of the mouth of the bay. Chinicook was north of Pemberwick Island and the bay was to the northernmost shore of Chinicook. All I could think to do was get out of the bay, round the top of the island, and then head west, staying as close to the island for protection for as long as possible before turning into the open sea and the five-mile crossing to the mainland. It was the best I could come up with.

"How is she?" I called back.

"I don't know," Kent replied. "She's bleeding bad. Front and back. The bullet must have traveled straight through her shoulder."

"It freakin' hurts," Tori moaned out.

She was conscious. At least that was something.

"Put pressure on it to stop the bleeding," I ordered. "Then find something to bandage it."

I didn't know anything about bullet wounds, but it seemed like Tori may have caught a break if the bullet went through her shoulder without hitting anything vital—like her heart or her lungs. If she could talk, I had to believe we had some time to get her help. But where? There were no hospitals in the ocean, and we definitely weren't going back to Arbortown. It made getting to Portland all the more critical.

"What do I use?" Kent cried. "There aren't any bandages back here!"

"Look under the seats," I ordered.

Olivia responded and started lifting up cushions. It wasn't an easy job because we were bouncing over the swells, but she stayed focused.

"Here!" she exclaimed and pulled out a first-aid kit.

"There's gotta be gauze or something," I said. "Pack the wound and then use a bandage to tie it up."

"Got it, got it," Kent said. "Jeez, there's blood everywhere."

"So shut up and stop it," Tori ordered.

It was good to hear her voice. She was with us and alert. But for how long?

We were nearing the mouth of the bay. It was time to turn but

I had no idea how shallow the bottom was. The last thing I wanted to do was run aground or hit a rock, like I did the last time I was in command of a boat. To be safe I steered a wide course that I hoped would get us out of the bay.

I kept glancing back to see how Tori was doing and was surprised to see Olivia really stepping up.

"I don't think it's so bad," she said to Tori, though it sounded like a lie to make her feel better. "It looks like the bullet went clean through. We'll stop the bleeding and you'll be okay."

She gingerly took off Tori's sweatshirt and then her flannel shirt to reveal the wound. Olivia used some alcohol on cotton pads to clean it up. It actually seemed as though she knew what she was doing. Once the blood was wiped away, the wound didn't look quite so bad.

"Jeez," Kent said. "It really did go clean through. It's just a hole on either side."

"Yeah, a hole that's bleeding," Tori pointed out.

Olivia made two thick pads out of gauze and placed one in front on the wound just below her collarbone and the other on her back, just inside of her bra strap.

"Get the bandage," she instructed Kent.

There was an Ace bandage for wrapping sprained ankles that Olivia used to hold the gauze pads in place. She wound it under Tori's armpit, covering both gauze pads.

"Sorry, I've got to make it tight," she said to Tori kindly. "It's the only thing that'll stop the bleeding."

Tori said, "It's like you've done this before."

"You learn all sorts of things in the Girl Scouts," Olivia answered casually.

"Really?" Tori said. "I don't remember going for the gunshot-wound merit badge."

Olivia wrapped the bandage several times around then secured it with adhesive tape.

"I think that's got it," Kent declared.

"I do too," Olivia said.

"Looks like you really dodged a bullet," Kent said. "So to speak."

"Shut up, Kent," Tori barked. Then looked to Olivia and softened. "Thank you."

"No problem," Olivia replied, then staggered to the side of the boat, leaned out, and puked.

Kent gave me a surprised look and a shrug.

Olivia could have puked on my shoes for all I cared. She had earned it. Fixing up Tori like that was probably the hardest thing she'd ever done in her life, but she didn't back down. It gave me new respect for her. She wasn't the liability I thought she would be.

With Tori stable I turned my attention to the hardest thing *I* was ever going to have to do—getting us somewhere safe. I hadn't seen any trace of the other boat that had blasted off before us. They must have taken another route. Or maybe it was already on the bottom of the sea.

I worried that the helicopters might come after us, but there was nothing in the air. As far as I could tell, we were alone on the ocean.

There was a moment . . . a perfect moment of peace in which I allowed myself to believe that we were only small fish in the general scheme of things. Granger had invaded the rebel camp and had either killed or captured most of the people he was after. The revolution had been squashed; his hold on the island was secured. Did that mean we didn't matter to him anymore? It was a nice thought that I tried to convince myself was true.

We were approaching the northernmost spot of Chinicook. Once we rounded the point and turned west, we'd be able to see the mainland five miles away and begin our run to freedom. I gripped the wheel and gently eased the hurtling boat into a turn. The craft responded instantly. Tori had chosen well. I looked ahead to see the rocky promontory that was the tip of Chinicook. I had to be careful not to cut it too close. I eased the wheel to port, made the gentle turn and . . .

. . . my moment of peace instantly vanished.

"Oh my God," Kent said with an incredulous gasp.

Though we were facing due west, we couldn't see the mainland because the view was blocked by a line of naval warships that stretched across the horizon for miles.

"Please tell me this is a bad dream," Olivia muttered.

There was every kind of ship imaginable: cruisers, destroyers, assault ships, frigates . . . it looked like the entire Atlantic fleet had arrived at the Maine coast. Pemberwick Island was blockaded. Access to the mainland was completely cut off.

"Turn back," Kent said.

I didn't react to his demand. I think I might have been in shock.

"Turn back!" Kent screamed into my ear.

"Why?" I yelled back at him. "To end up back in that prison?"

"Tori needs help," Olivia announced. "We can get her to a hospital on the island."

"We *all* need help," Kent argued. "They're gonna blow us out of the water!"

"Stop, all right," I shouted. "I gotta think."

"There's nothing to think about," Kent shouted. "This is suicide."

"No," Tori called in a weak voice. "Going back is suicide. Out here we've got a chance."

"Seriously?" Kent replied. "There's us—and the entire freakin' Navy. What kind of chance is that?"

As we argued, we continued to speed toward the fleet. It was hard to tell how far away the ships were. A mile? Two miles?

"My father died fighting back against SYLO," Tori said. "He didn't give up and neither will I."

"Hey, my father's gone too," Kent yelled back. "We've all lost family. Except Tucker. His parents are fine. They're working for the bad guys."

I let go of the wheel and nailed Kent with a punch that sent him to the deck.

"Stop it!" Olivia shouted in tears.

I grabbed the wheel again and kept us heading west—toward the blockade.

"That's just great," Kent said, rubbing his sore jaw. "Are you *trying* to get us killed?"

As I stood at the wheel, I honestly didn't know what I was trying to do. Going back meant prison, assuming we even made it to shore without getting shot or blown out of the water. Going forward meant sailing into the teeth of the Navy. There was no third option. I didn't think that the situation could get any worse until—

It got worse.

"Oh no . . . no," Olivia cried with despair.

I turned to see that she was looking back toward Pemberwick, where another boat had just rounded the tip of Chinicook and was headed our way.

"Please tell me that's one of the boats from the cave," she whined.

Kent stood up and took a hard look back.

"It isn't," he replied soberly. "That's a fast-attack military boat." He turned to me and said, "What do you want to bet that Granger's on board?"

"I hope he is," Olivia said hopefully. "We can surrender to him."

Any thought of surrender being a good idea was shattered when the pursuing gunboat opened fire on us. The clatter of a machine gun was unmistakable, even above our roaring engines.

"Jeez!" Kent yelled and fell to the deck along with Olivia.

I started to do short, quick course corrections to make us a difficult target. I had no idea of the range of that gun, or if we were fast enough to stay ahead of them, or if I even knew what I was doing. I was acting out of instinct rather than experience. I knew boats, not hurtling pieces of machinery. Or guns.

"Still want to go back?" I yelled.

I got no answers.

The hope of escape was fading rapidly. It was now about survival.

"I'm going for the fleet," I said. "Maybe there's somebody there with a cooler head who will capture us instead of—oh my God."

"What now?" Kent yelled.

I pointed west, to the sky over the mainland, where a long line of what looked like black dots had appeared. They were high enough that they could be seen above the warships—and they were growing larger.

"They're back," Tori said, aghast.

"I don't think the Navy's going to worry about dealing with us," I added soberly.

"Why?" Kent asked anxiously. "What are they?"

There was too much engine noise for us to hear the musical engines of the incoming aircraft, but there was no mistake: A formation of the mysterious fighter craft was headed our way. Behind us the gunboat was closing but had stopped firing. I didn't know if that was because they were waiting until they could get a better shot, or because they had seen the incoming aircraft and were just as stunned as we were.

"What do we do?" Olivia asked in a shaky voice.

I had no idea and didn't have time to wonder because the war was about to begin.

TWENTY-FOUR

The first shot was fired by the Navy.

A missile was launched from one of the ships. Followed by another and then another . . . all aimed at the incoming swarm of planes.

As the dark spots in the sky grew close enough for us to make out their stingray shape, they quickly scattered to evade the missiles. There were far more of them than we had seen in the earlier battle. It was an invasion-level force with multiple waves of planes. Several missiles found their mark, hitting the dark crafts and turning them into spectacular fireballs in the sky. The fiery wrecks plummeted to earth, splashing down in the ocean on the far side of the line of Navy vessels.

Kent joined me at the control console, his eyes fixed on the mayhem in the sky.

"What are they?" he asked numbly. "Stealth bombers?"

"I don't know. They're not like any planes I ever heard of. According to Feit, they belong to SYLO."

"So that would make the Navy the good guys," Kent said. "But

SYLO is part of the Navy, so why would they be shooting at their own planes?"

My mind raced, calculating the possibilities.

"It doesn't make sense. Unless . . ."

"Unless what?" he pressed.

"Unless Feit was lying."

We shared sober looks. That possibility turned everything on its ear, once again.

"So who do we root for?" Kent asked.

"I wish I knew."

The clatter of a machine gun added to the mayhem. I whipped around to see that the attack boat had drawn closer and had opened fire on us. I'd almost forgotten about it. Almost. I took another quick turn, nearly throwing Kent off of his feet.

"Stop that!" he complained.

"Do you want to get shot?" I yelled.

Kent started to argue, but held back and said, "Do what you gotta do."

The Navy kept launching an intense barrage of missiles, creating a daytime fireworks display in the sky. Some hit, most didn't. The black fighters were amazingly agile as they quickly veered to avoid being hit. I had the fleeting hope that the Navy's attention would be so focused on the aerial attack we would be able to slip past them unnoticed.

Behind us, the attack boat was still closing but had stopped firing again. All I could do was keep pushing ahead.

From the south, four new fighters entered the fight. They were traditional military jets that had probably come from an aircraft carrier. With their arrival the sea-to-air battle turned into a dog-fight. The streaking military jets broke formation and made runs at the black crafts, launching their missiles, then pulling out to set up for another pass. Several more shadow planes exploded and dropped from the sky.

"This is horrible," Olivia said with a gasp. "We're watching people die."

"Why aren't they fighting back?" Tori called.

Her answer came seconds later, when the black planes went on the attack. I expected them to unleash the laser-like weapons we had witnessed before. Instead, what we saw were explosions on the Navy ships without any sign of the missiles that caused them. There were no flashes of light, no smoke trails, no clatter of guns. But the black planes were definitely firing, for they would swoop down low for an attack run and then seconds later an explosion would erupt on one of the ships. The only thing I can say for sure was that they were not using the weapon that made the *Patricia* evaporate.

The four fighter planes were given the same treatment. A black plane would chase one down, and then seconds later it would be blown out of the sky without warning.

Tori struggled to join us at the console. She was in pain and needed to hold on to the control panel for support but she fought through it to be with us.

"I don't get it," she said. "Why aren't they using the weapons they used before?"

Nobody had the answer. Instead of the ships lighting up and dis-appearing, the results were much more conventional. Fires burned everywhere. The ships finally started to take evasive maneuvers as the long line that had blockaded Pemberwick Island went ragged. Within minutes most every ship had been hit and was damaged to one degree or another. Some fatally. A few listed and started to sink. Smoke billowed from the ships and settled over the ocean like a dense, dark fog. The smell of burning oil hit us quickly.

"This is our chance," I exclaimed. "We can try and make our way through."

"You want to drive us through that mess?" Kent said.

I glanced back at the attack boat that was still on our tail.

"It's either that," I said, "or face off with them. I'd rather take my chances picking our way through."

I had seen movies of battles at sea, but nothing compared to the reality of what we were barreling toward. The Navy was taking heavy losses. We were still maybe a half mile from the first ship but we could already see lifeboats in the water. The jet fighters weren't doing much better. Several more rocketed in and took down their share of the black planes, but every last one of them paid the price and was blown out of the sky. Still, there was no sign of the deadly laser weapons.

"It's daylight," Tori said.

"Yeah, so?" Kent said.

"Maybe that's why those laser-light weapons don't work. They might not function when it's light out."

"Doesn't matter," Kent said. "They don't need any laser guns. The Navy's getting their ass kicked. "

"Are they?" Tori argued. "They're knocking a lot of those planes out of the sky."

"But the planes keep coming," Kent shot back. "There could be thousands of 'em."

"And that's as far as they're getting," Tori said thoughtfully. "The Navy's targeting the lead planes like they're trying to prevent them from getting any further. None of them have made it past the ships."

"Why would the Navy care?" I asked. "If they're protecting the mainland, it's back the other way."

Tori looked me dead in the eye and said, "But Pemberwick Island is *this* way."

The idea rocked me.

Was it possible that the Navy was here not just to quarantine Pemberwick Island, but to protect it?

The sound of machine gun fire brought us back to our immediate trouble. The attack boat had closed considerably and was firing at us again.

"Doesn't that guy ever give up?" Kent asked angrily.

"We gotta go for it," I said. "I'm driving us through the battle. It's our only chance of losing him."

I changed direction slightly to take us on a more direct path to the turmoil on the sea. Thick smoke from the burning vessels was growing. It would make perfect cover.

"When we hit the smoke, I'll change direction," I said.

"You gotta be careful, Tucker," Tori cautioned. "There's a lot of debris in the water."

Debris was a nice word for the mess we were speeding toward. Huge chunks of steel that had been torn from the warships were floating everywhere . . . and then there were the warships themselves.

Most were still under power and taking evasive action but many were foundering. Several were dead in the water or sinking fast. We didn't want to collide with a ship fifty times our size or run down a life raft full of sailors. It was a dangerous, moving minefield but navigating through it was our best hope for escape—and survival.

"I don't like this one bit," Olivia said the instant before we hit the leading edge of the smoke.

It was like driving into a fog—a dense black fog that smelled of death.

"Slow down, Tucker," Tori wisely suggested.

I eased back on the throttles and it was a good thing I did because no sooner did we drop our speed than our bow was crossed by a frigate that had no idea we were there. We were buffeted by its wake and Tori was thrown to the deck. She hit hard and yelped with pain.

Olivia instantly ran to her and helped get her into the copilot's seat.

"I'm okay," Tori said through gritted teeth.

"You should buckle in," I said.

Before Tori could respond, Olivia snapped the belt around her waist.

"That feel okay?" she asked.

Tori nodded, though she wasn't feeling close to okay.

Olivia gave her a comforting rub on her good arm. I was beginning to like Olivia, and it had nothing to do with memories of her bikini. She may have been totally out of her comfort zone, as we all were, but she showed a caring side that made me realize she was more than just a pretty, spoiled rich girl. I guess conflict brings out the best in people. Or in some cases, the worst. I won't mention any names.

It was no longer about speed. We had entered into a game of cat and mouse with an attack boat on our tail that was hunting for us.

"Relax Tucker," Tori said. "If you grip the wheel any tighter, you'll snap it."

"I'm fine," I said, lying.

"I know you are," she replied. "You're doing great."

From her, that was a huge compliment. It helped my confidence. A little. My entire concentration was focused on the few feet ahead of our bow.

"I'm changing course," I announced. "Or it'll be too easy to track us."

Visibility was near zero but not being able to see the action didn't mean that it didn't exist. The steady *whoosh* sound of missiles being fired and tearing through the sky, exploding planes, and watery crashes meant that the fierce battle was still raging. Being in the center of the conflict, blind, was beyond nerve-wracking. There was no way to know if we were on a collision course with a ship, beneath a burning plane that was tumbling out of the sky, or about to be strafed by Granger.

"Keep headed west," Tori said, tapping the compass.

I listened for the engine of the gun boat, but there was too much else going on for me to pick it out. For all I knew it was only a few feet back, ready to blow us out of the water.

"Look out!" Kent called.

Too late. We smashed into a chunk of floating debris that looked to be a hull section the size of a VW. We hit it hard and our boat rocked so violently that I thought we would capsize. I spun the wheel to my left and managed to regain control—in time to run head on into a massive gray wall. The impact sent us all tumbling forward. Kent and Olivia fell to the deck. I was thrust onto the steering wheel so hard it knocked the wind out of me. The only one who didn't move was Tori because she was buckled in, but the sudden jolt was painful for her just the same.

The gray wall was the hull of a ship that was so monstrous I couldn't see up to the deck. Gasping to fill my lungs with air, I spun the wheel hard to the right and we quickly came around until we were traveling parallel to the ship. But we were still so close that we scraped against the steel hull, creating a shrieking sound that made it seem as if our boat was being ripped apart.

"Pull away, Tucker," Tori said coolly.

Her calm voice helped me get my head back together enough to steer away from the behemoth and end the torturous noise. It took another minute for my heart to stop thumping.

"Anybody hurt?" I called out.

Nobody answered, so I took that as a good sign. Tori gave me a smile. I looked at her bandage and was grateful to see that no blood was seeping through. Maybe Olivia had earned a gunshot-wound merit badge after all.

"I'm fine!" Tori yelled, as if annoyed by the fact that I had been looking at her for too long.

"Kent, go to the bow," I commanded. "Check for damage."

I expected him to complain and refuse but he immediately crawled forward, knelt on the seat, and leaned over to inspect the bow.

"The fiberglass buckled," he called back. "There are some cracks but I don't think it's fatal."

"Stay there," I called. "You gotta be my eyes."

Kent didn't question and stayed where he was, his attention focused ahead.

Olivia crawled back to us and stood behind Tori's chair, holding the back for support.

"Let's not do that again, okay?" she asked sweetly.

"We're headed north," Tori pointed out. "We want to go west."

"We're still on the outside of the blockade," I said. "The ship we just hit is between us and the mainland. We have to get around it. As soon as we clear it, I'll make the turn west."

The big ship seemed to be still in the water. As we moved alongside, I could hear the thrum of its engines and the occasional shudder as it launched another missile. This appeared to be one of the ships that had not yet been hit. Yet. I hoped its luck would hold out—at least until we got by.

The thick smoke was burning my eyes and making it hard to breathe. Both Olivia and I kept coughing. Tori did too and it was clear that the pain caused by each cough was excruciating. Olivia saw how much trouble she was having. "I'll see if I can find you some water," she said.

She never got the chance.

A shrill, screaming sound grew quickly.

"Hang on," I yelled. "Something's coming in."

A moment later one of the black planes fell out of the sky and crashed into the water not twenty yards from our starboard side.

The force from the crash created a wave that rushed at us and drove us into the big ship again. The violent impact threw Olivia onto the deck and nearly flipped us. I managed to hang on to the wheel since I already had a death grip on it.

Kent was sent sprawling to the deck and lay flat on his stomach.

"Are you hurt?" I asked.

He didn't answer.

"Kent?" I called, more insistent.

"I . . . I'm not moving," he replied.

Kent sounded shaky, as if the last near-miss had finally blown away whatever courage he had managed to find up to that point.

"You gotta get up, man," I said. "I can't see where we're going."

"I—I can't. I won't. We're going to die here."

"We're not going to die," I yelled angrily. "But if you don't get your act together, we might!"

It wasn't the most diplomatic way of handling somebody who had a legitimate excuse to panic, but I was tired of dealing with Kent. And I didn't want to die. But my tirade didn't get through to him. He lay on the deck, his face down, shivering.

It was Olivia who once again saved the situation. She crawled forward and sat on the deck next to him. She stroked his head gently and spoke in the sweet voice of a little girl. "I need you, Kent. Now more than ever. I'm so scared. Please don't let me down."

Kent slowly raised his head and looked up at her with frightened eyes.

"Please?" Olivia added sweetly.

Kent nodded. He wiped his eyes then managed to pull himself up and get back to his post in the bow.

Olivia came back to the console and gave me a smile and a knowing wink. She had totally played Kent.

"Now let's get the hell out of here," she commanded with confidence.

"I think I see the bow of the ship," Kent called back. "Maybe another twenty yards to go."

The smoke had momentarily thinned enough for us to see more than just a few feet ahead. Of course that meant we could be seen as well.

"Ten yards," Kent called out. "Get ready to turn."

I didn't want to cut it too tight in case the ship started moving.

Kent called, "And . . . we . . . are . . . clear!"

I continued on for another two seconds for safety and was about to turn to port when the gunboat came charging from the direction we were about to turn toward. It was under full power with its dark bow riding high, appearing out of the smoke like some vengeful demon.

"Turn hard!" Tori screamed.

I spun the wheel, missing the speeding boat by only a few feet as it flew by. We must have surprised them as much as they surprised us, for as they sped by I saw a guy on its deck spot us, start with surprise, and then scream at his men to change course.

It was Granger.

In that one fleeting moment, the hope that we no longer mattered to him was shattered. From the very start he had proved that he was ready and willing to do his own dirty work and this was no different.

He wanted to be there for the kill.

Granger stood behind the wheelhouse with the mounted machine gun and the soldier who manned it. The soldier looked just as surprised to see us as Granger did. He quickly swung the machine gun toward us and began firing, but there was little chance of them hitting us as we were flying in opposite directions. They were traveling at a dangerous rate of speed, considering the bad visibility. I hoped they'd hit some debris and bye-bye Granger.

"They're turning," Kent called out. "And coming after us."

They had been going so fast that making the one-eighty would take some time . . . time we desperately needed.

"Throttle up, Tucker," Tori said calmly.

I jammed the throttles forward and the four mighty engines roared. It was still too dangerous to be traveling so fast, but at least the smoke had cleared enough for me to see several feet ahead. It was a chance we had to take because once Granger made the turn, he wouldn't be moving cautiously.

Though the military ships were in disarray, they still made a formidable gauntlet that blocked us from an easy run to the mainland. We were trapped on the outside of a dozen foundering ships with Granger about to close in.

"Up there!" Kent screamed, pointing skyward.

I looked up to see a flaming black plane falling from the sky directly in our path. I turned the wheel to the right and banked the agile boat hard before the doomed shadow splashed down only a few yards to our left. This time we were gone before the surge of water could hit us.

"Where's Granger, Olivia?" I called.

Grasping the back of my chair, Olivia looked back for our pursuers.

"I can't see them. I think they had to make a really wide turn so that big ship is blocking them now and—no, oh no, here they come. They're moving past that ship now."

"We can't outrun them forever, Tucker," Tori said, still calm.

"I'm open to suggestions."

Tori scanned the watery battlefield and the endless line of ships while I did my best to dodge obstacles. We were traveling so fast that I nearly ran down a life raft carrying a dozen sailors. They screamed at me angrily as we flew by but I wasn't about to stop and apologize. Besides, they were the bad guys. I think. We kept getting bounced and thumped as we flew over pieces of junk. It would only be a matter of time before we ran into something more substantial, and at that speed it would mean catastrophe.

"Kent, come here," Tori called.

"No, I'm the lookout!"

"Come here," Tori said more insistently.

He reluctantly joined us.

Tori was oddly calm. I feared she may have been in shock from the injury, but her eyes were clear and she seemed focused.

"We could die out here," she said to all of us.

"Gee, you think?" Kent shot back sarcastically.

Tori gave him a withering glare and he shut up.

"Granger isn't going to give up. Even if we get past this line of ships, he could follow us all the way to the mainland and shoot us down on shore."

Nobody said a word because she was saying what we all had been thinking.

"If we don't do something drastic," Tori said. "We're dead."

"Drastic like what?" I asked. "It's not like we can turn and fight."

Tori looked forward. We were still traveling north along the line of foundering ships that stood between us and the mainland. Far ahead was a destroyer in flames. It was perpendicular to the mainland and listing to its side, away from us. Beyond it was a battleship that was dead in the water, parallel to the destroyer.

"Drastic like we could die," she said. "But we're going to die anyway."

I looked at Kent and Olivia. Both looked sick.

"Do you have an idea, Tori?" Olivia asked with surprising calm.

Tori said, "I do. But it has to be now—and you have to trust me."

Kent looked back and announced, "That damn black boat is right on our tail. They're going to start shooting any second."

"Do it," I said to Tori.

"Hurry," Olivia added.

Tori glared at Kent.

Kent said, "Go."

Tori instantly unbuckled her seat belt and said, "I'll take the wheel."

"You sure?" I asked.

Her answer was to push me out of the captain's chair and grab the wheel with her right hand. Her injury was to her left shoulder, making that arm useless, but I trusted Tori with one hand on the wheel more than any of us with both.

"Take the throttle," she commanded.

Tori gently nudged us to port, getting us closer to the line of ships. She had to make two quick course adjustments to dodge floating debris, and with each movement of the wheel, I saw her wince with pain. Yet even with the handicap, she could maneuver the speeding craft with an expertise that I couldn't match.

"Olivia! Tell me what's happening back there," she commanded.

"They're getting closer," Olivia cried.

"Maybe fifty yards back," Kent added. "And closing."

I looked ahead at the destroyer that was perpendicular to the mainland. Its entire superstructure was ablaze and it was listing hard to starboard, away from us. It would roll onto its side at any second—and probably hit the battleship that was lying next to it.

That's when I knew.

"You can't be serious," I said to Tori.

"Everybody hold on to something," was her response. She was locked in, calculating the physics of what she was about to attempt. I hoped she was working with something more solid than guesswork.

I buckled into the copilot's seat. Kent and Olivia each grabbed safety rails.

"What are you going to do?" Olivia asked nervously.

Tori ignored the question and called out, "How far back are they?"

"Forty yards," Kent replied. "The guy's standing at the machine gun. He's lining us up."

Tori said, "Tucker, when I tell you, power down by half but keep your hand on the throttles."

"Got it," I replied though my mouth had gone dry.

The doomed destroyer loomed over us as we came up quickly on its stern. I saw sailors jumping for their lives off the port side.

"Thirty yards!" Kent called out.

The machine gun behind us opened fire.

We were about to cross the stern of the flaming destroyer when—

"Now!" Tori called.

I pulled back on the throttles as Tori spun us into a sharp left turn. We had been traveling so fast that I feared we would flip, but with an expert touch she kept us righted as we side-slipped forward, passing the stern of the doomed ship . . .

. . . with our bow now pointed toward the mainland.

"Throttle up!" Tori yelled. "Go, go, go!"

I thrust the throttles forward and the monstrous engines roared back to full power. The jolt of acceleration was so sudden that Olivia and Kent were nearly thrown over.

"You're crazy!" Olivia shrieked in terror.

I couldn't argue with her. The listing, burning destroyer was now to our left. To our right was the battleship. Between them was a narrow corridor of water. The battleship was doomed. Even if it had power, it wouldn't be able to clear in time. The burning superstructure of the destroyer was seconds away from toppling onto the deck of its neighbor—with us sandwiched in between.

"My God," Kent screamed. "We're in hell."

The heat was quickly becoming unbearable as the listing ship tilted toward us. The flaming superstructure loomed directly over our heads, creating a ceiling of fire.

Tori didn't show a hint of fear or concern.

"Are they coming?" she asked.

I twisted to look back and was shocked to see Granger's gunship sliding into the same maneuver we had just made. It was about to follow us into the suicide corridor.

"Yeah, they're coming," I called out. "They fell back a little making the turn. I don't think they expected us to do that."

"Neither did I," Kent wailed. "We're gonna be incinerated."

Tori stayed focused. I kept my hands on the throttles, pressing down hard as if that might help us go faster, but the engines were already wide open.

We made it to the mid-ship point—and Olivia screamed.

A chunk of flaming metal fell off the superstructure and dropped toward us. It would have landed directly on the deck if Tori hadn't made a subtle but lifesaving shift toward the battleship. The flaming mass hit the water to our port side, the hot metal sizzling as it slammed into the water.

"The whole thing's coming down on our heads!" Kent screamed.

The destroyer had reached the tipping point and was on its way over. Our engines roared and dug into the water that was being churned up by the massive ships on either side of us. Bits of molten metal fell like sparkling rain all around, each drop as dangerous as acid. Some hit our front deck and quickly melted holes in the fiberglass. We huddled under the canopy to avoid the burning shower, but the thin top would do nothing to protect us from the tons of flaming metal that was seconds away from hitting us.

Above the pounding of our engines and the white noise of the inferno, I could hear the panicked shouts of sailors from both sides who were abandoning ship.

I reached out and held on to Tori's shoulder. I wanted her to know that in spite of what was about to happen, she had made the right move. The only move. Besides, I wanted the last moment of my life spent making human contact with someone.

She looked at me and I gave her a smile. "It's okay," I said with surprising calm.

"I know," she said with a cocky shrug. "We're gonna make it."

She gave me a wink . . .

. . . as the superstructure came down.

It hit the battleship and we were instantly enveloped in a cave of fire. The heat was so intense I feared it would melt the fiberglass boat. The screaming sound of a thousand tons of wrenching, burning metal cut through the roar of our engines. Above it all I could hear the panicked cries of sailors from both doomed ships who were desperate to escape the death trap.

I braced myself, ready to be crushed or burned alive . . . as we cleared the destroyer's bow and charged into open water.

Safe.

"Yahhh!" Kent screamed in triumph as we flew on, leaving the carnage behind.

Olivia screamed too, out of pure joy.

The superstructure erupted like an angry volcano, shooting massive spikes of flame high into the sky. A powerful wave of heat hit us in the back as the two ships collapsed into each other to create a single massive floating inferno.

"Granger?" Tori asked while keeping her eyes straight ahead.

I focused on the flames at sea level, expecting to see the attack boat come charging out of the fire.

A second passed. Then another. The destroyer was nearly on its side, its burning superstructure having hit the battleship and crumbled into the space between the ships. Kent had called it. It was hell.

Olivia said, "Do you think they—"

An explosion erupted in the space that had once been the corridor between the ships. A cloud of debris blew from the impact point, creating a fiery bloom of burning metal. For a fleeting instant I saw the dark silhouette of a machine gun spinning out of control. The one thing I *didn't* see bursting out of that explosion . . . was the attack boat.

Olivia, Kent, and I kept staring back, not daring to believe what we had seen. Seconds passed as the two massive ships burned as one.

"There's no way they turned around in time," I finally said.

"And they sure as hell didn't make it through," Kent added.

We all shared stunned looks.

"Is it possible?" Olivia asked.

"I think it is," I said, hardly believing it myself. "They're done. Granger's dead."

The four of us let out a spontaneous cry of triumph. Kent threw his arms around me and lifted me off my feet.

"We did it, Rook," he said with tears in his eyes. "We beat him. We won."

Olivia wrapped her arms around the both of us. She was sobbing. I think she said, "We're not going to die," but it was hard to tell because she was such an emotional mess.

Tori stayed focused ahead.

I leaned down to her and whispered, "You know something? You are crazy."

Tori gave me a quick look—and a smile.

"I told you we'd make it."

Olivia gently put a hand on each of her cheeks and kissed her on top of the head.

"Sister, you are my new hero," she said. "But I will not go on a boat with you ever again."

"Take a break, Sleeper," Kent said as he put one hand on the wheel. "You earned it."

That's as big a compliment as Kent was capable of giving.

Tori hesitated, as if not wanting to give up control. Or maybe her hand was frozen to the wheel after having gripped it tightly for so long. She leaned forward, winced with a twinge of pain in her shoulder, and eased back on the throttle.

"She's all yours," she said to Kent. "Get us the hell out of here."

We had done it. We'd escaped. And as a bonus, we had cut off the dragon's head. SYLO's leader was on his way to whatever level of hell he belonged in.

It was a moment filled with relief and joy. I walked to the stern of the boat, alone, to look back on the miles of floating devastation that had once been a fleet of ships spread across the horizon. Several were still intact and under power, though just as many were foundering. The sky had grown dark with the smoke of a hundred floating fires.

Pemberwick Island was completely blocked from view. I wondered if I would ever see it again.

"We did it, Quinn," I whispered. "We made the Pemberwick Run."

Against all odds we had survived. But the feeling of triumph was soon replaced by another nagging thought.

Was this the end of our journey, or just the beginning?

TWENTY-FIVE

I took control of the boat from Kent.

Driving actually helped calm me. The battle seemed to be over but I wouldn't be able to relax until we hit dry land. Tori lay across the stern seat with her head in Olivia's lap. Kent stood over them, staring back at the war zone.

Several of the black planes flew overhead, their incongruous music now clearly audible as they headed west, back toward the mainland and away from what was left of the naval blockade. They were no longer flying in perfect formation but instead were scattered across the sky like shell-shocked soldiers staggering back from the battlefield after having lost most of their comrades.

Casualties were heavy on both sides. Looking back at the line of damaged ships that grew steadily smaller the further we moved away made it clear that the Navy had taken just as bad a beating as the invaders from the sky.

"How many people died?" Olivia asked wistfully, to nobody in particular.

"I only care about one—Granger," Kent replied without a trace of sympathy.

"What was the point?" I said. "Who won? Those planes came from over land. Don't invasions usually come from the sea?"

"I guess that depends on what's being invaded," Tori pointed out.

That reminded me of something she had said earlier.

"Is that possible?" I asked. "Could those Navy ships have been trying to keep the black planes away from Pemberwick Island?"

Kent snickered and said, "Possible? Are you serious? Why use logic now? I'm thinking *anything* is possible."

"But then . . . why?" I asked. "More important, who? We just saw two huge military forces going at it. Who has the kind of technology we saw with those singing planes?"

"We know the United States is involved," Tori offered. "President Neff himself set up the quarantine."

"So then who was flying the black planes? Were they from SYLO, like Feit said? Why would they be attacking their own navy?"

"It could be the Chinese," Kent said. "Or the Russians."

"What about that laser weapon we saw the other night?" I asked. "Where on earth did that come from? And why didn't they use it today?"

"Maybe you hit it, Rook," Kent said soberly. "Who on earth has that kind of technology? Maybe nobody. What if that attack came from somewhere else?"

I didn't register what he meant at first but when it finally struck me, I had to laugh. "You can't be serious. You think this is, like, an alien invasion?"

"This is real life, Kent," Tori admonished.

Kent stiffened.

"No, it isn't," he said with absolute conviction. "This is fantasy. There's nothing that happened over the past few weeks that has anything to do with real life. At least not the life I know. When you cross that line, I don't think you can rule anything out."

I'd disagreed with pretty much everything Kent Berringer had said and done since I'd known him—until then. In the absence of any real explanations, how could we rule anything out, no matter how wild it seemed?

"So then, what do we do now?" Olivia finally asked.

Tori said, "All we can do is stick with our original plan. We go to Portland, find a TV station, and talk to the world. Let somebody else figure this out."

Now that her adrenaline spike had left her, Tori was left looking pale and fragile. She was right, we had to stick with the plan, but that plan had to include finding a hospital to get her help. For that we had to get to Portland, so we pressed ahead, drawing ever closer to the mainland and hopefully to answers.

It took us another hour to make land and find a dock to tie up to. Part of me wanted to continue up the coast until we reached Casco Bay and the city of Portland, but none of us wanted to be on the water, and vulnerable, anymore. Having dry land under our feet would be a good thing.

We motored a short way north until we came upon a rickety old private dock with a float. I brought the boat around and Kent jumped off to tie us up.

"How are you feeling?" I asked Tori.

"I'm good," she said.

She wasn't. She was white. I didn't think she had lost a dangerous amount of blood, but until she saw a doctor and got patched, we had to worry about her.

We had landed in a wooded section of the coast. It wasn't the middle of nowhere, but there weren't a whole lot of houses around either.

"We gotta find transportation into Portland," I said. "Olivia, wait here with Tori. Kent and I will go looking."

I figured that Kent wouldn't want to do anything but sit on the dock and vegetate, but I couldn't have been more wrong. He jumped from the boat, ran off the dock, fell to his knees, and leaned over until both his hands were on the ground. He then started to laugh. He couldn't control himself. He laughed until tears ran down his cheeks.

I exchanged nervous looks with Olivia and Tori.

Tori shrugged. She didn't know what his deal was any more than I did.

"Dude," I called out. "You all right?"

He turned to us and sat on the ground.

"I never thought I'd set foot on land again," he said through gasping breaths. "We could have died like a couple of dozen times back there but—here we are. How awesome is that?"

I couldn't help but smile. I looked at Olivia and Tori, who were suddenly beaming. I took a deliberate step off the dock onto the dirt and gravel to plant my foot firmly on the mainland. It felt good.

I laughed too. That's how relieved I was. It wasn't until I felt solid ground under my feet that I truly believed we had made it. We had escaped. It was a great moment. One I hadn't expected. There was no way to know what the future would bring, but it was good to be able to stop and take a few seconds to appreciate what we had done.

"All right," I finally said, trying to control the giddiness. "We're awesome. Yay us. Let's keep going and end this for good."

I walked to Kent and held out my hand. He took it and I helped him to his feet.

"Yeah," he said. "Let's end this for good."

Kent and I climbed up a steep hill from the dock to find that we were at the end of a desolate but paved road.

"We'll walk until we find a house," I said.

A few hundred yards in from the coast, we came upon a big old rambling white house that had probably stood there for a hundred years. It was the kind of place that usually belonged to wealthy boating people. They probably owned all the land right up to the shore and the dock where we were tied up.

I hurried up the driveway and rang the doorbell. Nobody answered so I knocked. Hard. If somebody was inside, they would have heard.

"They're probably at work," Kent said. "Or maybe they're weekend people."

"Or maybe they're hiding in the basement because, oh, I don't know, there was just a huge battle raging off shore."

"Or that," Kent said soberly.

I left the porch and rounded the house to the detached garage.

"We're trespassing," Kent said nervously.

"Do you really care?" I asked.

"I care about getting shot by somebody who doesn't appreciate people snooping around their house."

"I am way beyond worrying about that," I said and continued on to the garage. Looking in through the window, I saw two cars parked inside, an old Saab and a Subaru Outback.

"Maybe they really are hiding in the basement," Kent observed.

"Then they'll come out when they hear their car starting," I said and lifted the garage door.

"What are you thinking, Rook? You want to steal a car?"

I threw the garage door up the rest of the way then looked straight at Kent. "I'm thinking about borrowing one of these cars, and I hope there are people inside who are watching and that they call the police and the police will show up and arrest us so we'll get a ride into town and Tori to a hospital, which would save us the trouble of getting there on our own. And when they give us our one phone call from jail, I'll call the *New York Times* and tell them what's been happening on Pemberwick Island. What are *you* thinking?"

Kent rolled that over in his head, then said, "Yeah, that's pretty much where I was going."

I looked into the Outback and, sure enough, the keys were in the ignition. Gotta love the country. Nobody expects a car thief to mosey by.

"You've got a license," I said. "You're driving."

"Seriously?" Kent exclaimed. "After that big speech, you're worried about getting in trouble for driving without a license?"

"No," I replied patiently. "I'm worried about wrapping us around a tree because I have zero experience driving on the highway. But if you want to take that risk—"

"Enough, enough, I get it," he said, throwing his hands up.

Kent got behind the wheel and started up the car. As he backed out of the garage, I kept my eyes on the house to see if anybody was watching, but there was no sign of life. It was looking as though we would have to make our way into Portland on our own.

I hopped in and Kent drove us back to the shore. Olivia had already helped Tori up from the dock and they were sitting in the grass waiting for us. I guided Tori into the back seat and slipped in next to her. Olivia sat in the front with Kent.

"Whose car is this?" she asked.

"Friend of Tucker's," was Kent's curt reply.

Nobody questioned further. Kent hit the gas and we were on our way.

Portland, Maine, is more like a big town than a booming metropolis. It was built around fishing, turned to manufacturing, but then eventually became one of those cities that you don't really know why it exists other than to take care of itself. The population was only around sixty thousand, but that still made it the biggest city in Maine. Mom and Dad and I would take a trip there every once in a while so we could remind ourselves what it was like to be part of the outside world. Mom liked Portland because it was culturally diverse and had a great art scene. Dad liked the architecture of the Old Port and its cobblestone streets. He always pointed out that the streets, technically speaking, were made with paving stones, not cobblestones. Me? I liked the Italian sandwiches at Amado's. We always found something in Portland to keep us happy.

On this trip the only thing that would make me happy was a hospital for Tori and a reporter who would help us get our story out to the world.

Kent drove us along winding wooded roads following signs for I-95. There was probably a faster way into the city using local streets, but none of us had much driving experience or knowledge of the area so we figured the most obvious route was the best, even if it took a little longer.

Tori put her head down on my lap and closed her eyes. I didn't mind. I watched her, wondering which of us had it worse. Years before, her mother had abandoned their family and that morning her father had been killed by SYLO. Was that worse than finding out your parents were liars, playing a part in a conspiracy that was responsible for the deaths of dozens of people—including your best friend? In my mind it was a toss-up.

Though we did have one thing in common: neither of us had parents to take care of us anymore. We would have to look out for each other. I brushed Tori's hair back from her forehead. She didn't open her eyes, but she smiled. I wished we could get to the hospital faster.

"What day is it?" Kent asked.

Nobody answered because nobody could remember.

"Why?" I asked.

"Must be Sunday," he said. "There's no traffic."

I hadn't noticed because I had been lost in my own thoughts, but once he said that, I started looking around. We drove through a fairly rural area but every once in a while we'd pass a row of shops or a gas station. Not once did we see another car moving on the road.

Or another person.

When we turned onto the interstate, the lack of activity was even more obvious. There were no other moving cars. None. Several were pulled over to the side as if broken down, but nobody was with them. The stretch of I-95 outside of Portland wasn't a typically busy interstate, definitely not like the section that runs past my old home in Greenwich, Connecticut, outside of New York City. Still . . .

"I'm getting a creepy feeling," Kent said.

For the second time that day, I didn't disagree with him.

We switched from I-95 to I-295, which went past downtown Portland. Since we were getting closer to the city, I kept expecting the traffic to pick up. Or to see another person—or any sign of life, for that matter. I didn't. Portland may have been a sleepy city, but on that day it was downright comatose. The only increase in activity was the growing number of abandoned cars on the side of the road.

"My God, look," Olivia said.

Tori struggled to sit up. She needed to see what we were seeing.

Not all the cars were abandoned. Olivia pointed to one that had driven off the highway and slammed head-on into a tree.

"Pull over," I said.

Kent eased the car off the highway and came to a stop.

I got out to see if anybody needed help. It was a horrible wreck. The entire front end was caved in and wrapped around the tree. All the doors were still closed, which meant whoever was in the wreck was probably still in there. I slowed down and approached cautiously. I could only imagine how gruesome the scene would be. I got closer to the car, squinted, and looked inside to see . . . it was empty.

"Are they dead?" Kent called.

"They're not even here," I replied.

I felt the hood of the wreck. It was stone cold. There was nothing more to do so I hurried back to the car.

"How could they have gotten out?" Tori asked.

"I have no idea, and I'll tell you something else—the engine is cold."

"So what?" Olivia asked.

"So that means it didn't happen during the sea battle. That wreck's been there for a couple of days. Whatever happened here happened a while ago."

We all exchanged looks but nobody knew what to say to that.

"Can we please keep going?" Olivia asked nervously.

I got back in the car and Kent got us back on the highway. We passed several more wrecks like the one we first saw. It seemed like the people had driven off the highway, hit something that destroyed their vehicles, and somehow magically disappeared.

"Things are not right in Portland," Kent said ominously.

"You think?" Tori said. "Look at *that*."

She was pointing to the side of the highway, where a hole the size of a swimming pool was cut into the ground on the edge of the forest.

"Is it a construction site?" Kent asked.

"Doubt it," I said. "What would they build on the highway in the middle of nowhere? It looks more like a—*look out*!"

There was another crater in the center of the road.

Kent looked forward in time to yank the wheel and swerve around it. We missed falling in by inches.

"Hell of a pothole," Kent said nervously.

"Or a bomb crater," I said. "There were missiles flying everywhere. Some of them must have hit land."

Tori said, "So does that mean Portland was attacked too?"

Nobody had an answer to that, but we'd find out soon enough.

As we traveled closer to the city, we passed several more craters. Not all were harmless looking. Some still had smoke drifting up from within. Not all the stray missiles had hit empty stretches of land. We passed an industrial building that was on fire and another that had been reduced to rubble.

"This was recent," I said. "It must have happened during the battle."

Olivia said, "So where's the fire department?"

Good question.

Out of the corner of my eye, I caught movement and looked toward the far side of the highway. What I saw seemed impossible, yet it wasn't. It looked like a giant jellyfish moving across the barren landscape.

"What exactly is that?" I asked.

It moved slowly, its tentacles brushing against the ground.

"It's a parachute." Kent answered with dismay.

The large, white half dome of silk was full of air, which made it float gently on its own. The tentacles were the lines that hung down to the ground.

Kent stopped the car to let it cross in front of us. It seemed to be moving in slow motion as the soft breeze gently pushed it along, its silk skin rippling. It was a strange and haunting sight.

"So where's the pilot?" Tori asked.

"Keep driving," I said to Kent.

We were nearing downtown. I looked ahead to the skyline, fearing that I would see buildings going up in flames. Thankfully, nothing looked out of the ordinary.

"I don't think the city was attacked," I said. "Everything must have happened out over the ocean."

"Almost everything," Olivia said soberly and pointed ahead of us.

There was another wreck. This one was in the center median. It wasn't a car.

It was a gray jet fighter.

"I guess that tells us where the parachute came from," Kent said, numb.

The plane must have slammed into the ground going full blast because there was little left of it but wreckage. Flaming wreckage. This plane hadn't been down for long. There were a few recognizable parts, like the tail fin and . . .

"The cockpit," Kent said. "I gotta see."

Before anybody could protest, Kent turned onto the median and drove right up to the largest piece of the wreck.

"The canopy's gone," Kent said. "They must have ejected before they—oh, *man*."

Of course we all looked . . . and wished we hadn't. Kent was right. One of the pilots must have ejected because the front seat was empty. The rear seat wasn't. We could clearly see the outline of a charred body slumped forward, still strapped into the seat.

Tori turned away and buried her head in my shoulder. I looked forward, already regretting having seen it for only a brief second. Kent did the same.

"I . . . I'm sorry," he said as he jammed on the gas and peeled out.

The only one who didn't take her eyes off the grisly scene was Olivia. She kept staring back at the poor victim until we were far past it. I couldn't tell what was going through her mind. Was she in shock? Or fascinated by the horror?

"We are so stupid," Tori said, battling tears. "How could we have thought that everything would be normal here?"

"Because that's what we wanted to think," I said.

"This doesn't change anything," Kent said. "We've still got to get the word out."

"We'll go to Maine Medical Center first," I said. "Tori's got to—"

"No!" Tori shouted. "There's plenty of time for that," she said as she struggled to sit up. She may have been in pain, but she was still stubborn. "I'm okay. Go to the TV station on Congress Street. WCSH."

Olivia turned around and in her best mothering voice said, "We need to get you to a doctor."

"We need to do what we came here for," Tori said adamantly. "Until then I'll be fine."

End of discussion. We were going to WCSH.

"Do you know where Congress Street is?" I asked Kent.

"I'll find it," was his reply.

"Center of town," Tori offered.

The closer we got to the city, the more my stomach twisted.

I kept looking ahead, fearing that I would see damaged buildings or more bomb craters or fires or any other kind of destruction, but there was nothing. Though there were no obvious signs of an attack, things still weren't right.

Besides the distinct lack of activity, the first definite sign that something was truly off was that none of the street lights worked.

"The city looks wrong," Kent said.

"You think?" Tori said sarcastically.

"I don't mean because we're not seeing anybody. That's plenty weird, but I'm talking about the city itself. I've been here a hundred times and something about it doesn't look right."

I couldn't imagine what Kent was talking about, but then again I didn't know Portland as well as he did.

"It's, like . . . abandoned," Olivia said. "Maybe people are hiding in their basements. I know I would be."

That made sense. We were so focused on Pemberwick and escaping from Granger and the quarantine that we didn't give much thought to how the people on the mainland would be reacting to the naval blockade and the battle in the sky.

"Even if that's the case, the TV stations will still be operating," I said. "That's what they're there for. If there's a war, you don't shut down the TV stations unless . . ."

"Unless what?" Kent asked.

"Unless there was an evacuation," I replied.

With that sober thought left hanging, we drove into town.

There wasn't a single soul on any of the streets. There was no life behind the windows. Trash blew across the cobblestones . . . or the paving stones.

"Congress Street," Olivia said, pointing to a sign.

"Take this right," Tori directed. "The station's a few blocks down. It's the building with the big NBC peacock logo on it."

Kent made the turn, not bothering to stop at the dead light, and continued down Congress Street through a gauntlet of abandoned or wrecked cars.

"It's up there on the right," Tori said. "Just past the—oh my God."

"What?" Olivia asked nervously.

"The building. It's . . . it's not there."

The spot that Tori had directed us to was nothing more than a giant hole in the ground.

"You must be wrong," I said. "Maybe it's further down—"

"No," Tori said adamantly. "I came here with my father about a month ago when he did an interview. Look, there's the NBC logo."

There was a parking sign with a WCHS logo and the rainbow peacock, but there was no building. No WCHS.

"That's it," Kent declared. "That's what's wrong."

"What?" I asked with growing fear.

"It's the skyline," he said. "It isn't the same."

"How can that be?" I said. "A whole skyline can't change."

"It can," he said. "If buildings are missing. That's what I sensed. Some of the buildings aren't here anymore."

Without waiting for a response, Kent drove us back through the city, where we passed many similar holes in the ground, just like the site of the former WCHS. Each time it was the same thing. There was no rubble, no signs of destruction, no smoke from an exploded bomb, and no building—not even a foundation.

Nor was there any damage to the buildings on either side of the holes.

The grim reality was that several of the city's buildings had been cherry-picked out of existence.

"It's like they just . . . disappeared," Kent said, his voice shaking.

"The weapon," I said.

"What weapon?" Kent asked, his voice shaking.

"The one that vaporized the *Patricia* . . . and Quinn. That night we saw the lights flashing over Portland, those planes could have been attacking Portland. But not with bombs, with that laser weapon."

"This war started before the battle on the ocean," Kent said, numbly. "That's why the car wrecks were cold. This happened days ago."

"Go to the Old Port," Tori said. "If there are still people in town, they'll be there."

Kent jammed on the gas and with a squeal of tires we launched forward, headed for the easternmost end of town and the most popular and populated district in the city. Along the way I noticed many more empty lots. Had they always been empty? Or was it the work of the strange marauding planes that came at night and serenaded a sleeping city with their murderous song?

We drove down Pearl Street until we hit the intersection at Commercial Street, the street that ran parallel to the shore and the downtown piers. This was the quaint tourist center of Portland. People came from all over the world to sample lobster rolls and Moxie soda, to buy miniature lighthouses and bibs with smiling lobster designs. It was the heart of Portland.

It was deserted.

When we made the turn onto Commercial Street, Kent hit the brakes hard and screeched to a stop.

"Oh, this isn't good," Olivia said with dismay.

Lying in the dead center of the empty street was another wreck.

It was one of the black shadow planes.

The thing wasn't huge, maybe the size of a Hummer. It squatted like a giant roosting bird of prey that had decided to make its nest in the middle of the wide street.

"It's been here for a while," I observed. "There's no smoke or anything."

"It must have crashed when the city was attacked," Tori said, stunned. "Does that mean the city's been empty since then?"

"I gotta take a closer look," I said and started to get out of the car.

Tori grabbed my arm to stop me, which made her wince with pain.

"Don't," she said, gritting her teeth to fight the sting. "That thing could be ready to explode."

I looked ahead at the mystery wreck. It seemed dead.

"We want answers," I said. "That thing might give us a couple."

Kent added, "There's gotta be markings. At least we'll know what country we're at war with—or what universe."

I smiled at Tori and said, "I have to."

Tori nodded and reluctantly let go of my arm.

"Be careful," she warned.

"Seriously," Olivia added.

I got out of the car. Nobody followed. Tori had an excuse. The other two were just scared. Can't say I blame them. I was too. But that wasn't going to stop me. Not anymore.

I rounded the Subaru and walked slowly toward the dark wreck, ready to bail at the first sign of trouble. There was no smell and no sound. There didn't seem to be danger of an explosion, and if it was leaking invisible radioactivity, we were already doomed.

Its rounded lines reminded me of a B-2 bomber but with no obvious wings or engines. There didn't appear to be any hatches or windows either. It was like a giant clamshell with absolutely no aerodynamic qualities. Kent's crazy theory of these craft being from another world was beginning to seem *less* crazy. I walked with caution, hoping that there wasn't an injured alien trapped inside preparing to defend his craft.

As I drew closer, I actually thought of Marty Wiggins. This had all started with his final moment of glory. The crowd was going crazy. Marty was on top of the world—until he fell off. It didn't seem fair that somebody's life could end at a moment of such triumph.

Or maybe that was a good thing. What better last memory to have than the joy of hearing the cheers of adoring fans? In light of all that had happened since, he might have been the lucky one.

Marty's death was the beginning.

Or was it?

I had to accept that my parents had moved us to Pemberwick Island years before to prepare for SYLO's arrival and some big event that was planned long before Marty had taken a fatal dose of the Ruby.

The event.

What was the event? Was it the battle between the Navy and the dark aircraft? Was it the attack on Mr. Sleeper and his band of rebels? Or did the event have something to do with the lights in the sky and the fact that sixty thousand people from Portland seemed to have disappeared, along with some of their buildings?

Had the event already happened? Or was it still to come?

I stopped a few feet from the edge of the dead aircraft and scanned its surface, looking for any clues that might help me understand. It was coal-black, with seams and rivets that told me it had been manufactured. This was no organic, alien creature. Check that off the list. I took a chance and ran my hand across its surface. The cool skin looked and felt like the pieces of wreckage that had washed up on the beach, along with a ton of the Ruby. That made it more likely that the exploding shadow Quinn and I saw on our midnight ride was indeed one of these alien-looking planes. Had it actually been loaded up with the Ruby and on its way to make a delivery to Pemberwick, courtesy of SYLO?

That's what Feit said. But he was a liar.

I circled the wreck, looking for something. Anything. This was one of many lethal weapons that had attacked a fleet of warships from the United States Navy. Was it because the Navy, under the command of Granger and his SYLO goons, had blockaded Pemberwick Island? Were they trying to blast past the Navy to rescue us?

Or had they meant us harm and the Navy's mission was to protect us?

Either way, why would anyone care so much about Pemberwick Island? The reason for the battle may not have been obvious, but this much was clear: These aircraft had flown over Portland

and lit up the sky. Now a major city lay empty and several massive buildings had been vaporized.

Between the deaths on Pemberwick and those from the air and sea battles, there was no way to know exactly how many people had died. Wars are fought for many reasons: religion, power, land, riches, prejudice . . . Name a basic human conflict and you can bet that a war was fought over it. But what was the issue *here*? There had to be a good team and a bad team but it was impossible to know which was which without knowing who was fighting and what was at stake. I was hoping that I would find something about the aircraft that would at least tell me where it had come from and maybe open a few doors that would lead to understanding.

I walked further along and saw something on the skin of the craft that was totally out of place. It looked like somebody had crudely scrawled a line of graffiti using white paint. I didn't understand the words because it definitely wasn't English, but the letters were recognizable.

Sequentia Yconomus Libertate te ex inferis Obedianter!

Was it Latin? I had no idea. Who could have done it? Someone from Portland who was angry over the attack on their city? If it were me, I probably would have just thrown a rock at the downed plane or hit it with a baseball bat. I was looking for answers and found yet another maddening mystery.

"Anybody know what it says?" Kent asked.

I turned quickly to see that he had joined me, along with Tori, who leaned on Olivia for support. Tori looked pale and I didn't think it was from the blood loss.

She was staring at the graffiti.

"Do you know what it says?" I asked.

"No," she said, sounding numb. "But I can guess what it means."

She picked up a stone from the street, leaned down to the plane and underlined four letters, scraping a mark under each.

"Sequentia yconomus libertate te ex inferis obedienter," she said, sounding it out awkwardly.

"Oh my God," Olivia said, stunned.

The four letters Tori had underlined were S – Y – L – O.

"SYLO," Olivia gasped.

"So what the hell does that mean?" Kent demanded.

Since the moment of Marty's death, I had been grasping at pieces of a hundred maddening clues, desperately trying to understand what was happening to us. It took the revelation of those four letters for my brain to finally start putting the pieces together.

"It means Feit was lying," I said with confidence.

"How do you figure that?" Kent asked.

"Somebody scrawled this after the plane crashed, marking their kill. These planes aren't SYLO. That never made sense. SYLO is part of the Navy. They wouldn't battle themselves."

Tori said, "So Feit lied about Granger asking him to bring the Ruby to Pemberwick?"

"Absolutely," I said with total conviction. "I don't think SYLO has anything to do with the Ruby."

"How can you be sure of that?" Olivia asked.

"When Quinn and I were on our midnight ride, just before the black plane full of the stuff exploded, there was a steak of light that came from the ocean—"

"I saw that too," Tori said. "I have no idea what it was."

"I think I do," I declared. I'll bet it was a missile fired from a submarine. I think SYLO blew that plane out of the sky, just like all the others they've been shooting down since."

"Whoa," said Kent.

"That makes total sense!" Tori exclaimed as the realization hit her. "The battle began long before anybody was aware of it. Before Portland was attacked."

Kent asked, "So if these aren't SYLO planes, what are they? *Who* are they? And why were they bringing the Ruby to Pemberwick Island?"

"Whoever they are," I said, "Feit was one of them."

"But that doesn't matter anymore, right?" Olivia offered hopefully. "Feit's dead."

"Yeah, he is," I said. "But if he was waiting for a delivery of the Ruby, whatever he was up to, he wasn't doing it alone."

Pieces of the puzzle were falling together quickly and the implications were frightening.

"There were a lot of strangers on the island," Kent said thoughtfully. "Way more than normal. I thought it was because of the late summer and the quarantine but . . ."

He let the thought hang.

"Who *were* all those people?" Tori asked. "Strangers were being arrested all over the island, and being held prisoner in the SYLO camp, and rioting downtown, and plotting with my father on Chinicook Island and—"

"It's like there were two invasions of Pemberwick," I said soberly. "One obvious, one not. I don't think SYLO is the only enemy on Pemberwick Island."

Olivia was on the verge of tears. She leaned into Kent and said, "I don't want to be here anymore."

I took a long look around the Old Port and at the once lively city that was now very dead.

"So where do we go?" Kent asked.

"We have to find somebody who knows what's happening," I replied. "And somebody who can help us tell the world what we've been through. I say we go to Boston. That's the closest big city."

"And what if Boston was attacked too?" Tori asked.

"Don't even think that," I replied quickly. "But if it was, we'll keep going. To New York. Or Washington."

"Maybe my mother went back to New York," Olivia said hopefully.

I doubted that, but I didn't say so.

"Maybe," I said. "I don't know. But one thing's clear—there's nothing for us here."

"And we sure can't go home," Tori added.

That was the most sobering thought of all. I can't speak for the others, but as much as I wanted to escape from Pemberwick, my goal was to find the truth, blow the whistle on SYLO, and get them the hell off our island so we could get back to normal. Seeing what had happened to Portland made me doubt that would be possible. Ever.

Kent kicked the plane in anger. "Who the hell *are* you?"

"Let's get Tori to the hospital," I said. "Even if it's deserted, we'll get medical supplies."

We started back toward the car, finishing the full circle around the downed plane.

That's when I saw it.

I stopped short.

"What?" Kent asked.

It was a simple clue, but unmistakable. If the sun hadn't been hitting it at just the right angle, I probably wouldn't have noticed it because it was the same shade of black as the skin of the craft. It stood out only because it had a slick sheen that reflected the sunlight.

It was a logo, no more than ten inches wide. There was a star inside a circle with two flaps, like wings, to either side with three stripes on each. Normally it would be red, white, and blue but there was no mistaking the monochrome version.

"This is no alien spaceship," I declared, pointing to the logo.

Kent joined me, took a look, and gasped. "Oh, man."

It was the logo of the United States Air Force.

We had been in the middle of a monstrous battle between two different branches of the military from the same country. My country. It was no drill. It was no training exercise.

"So what does that mean?" Kent asked.

"It means that the United States of America is at war with itself."

Tori said, "It's the second Civil War."

It was almost too much to accept that such cataclysmic events, events that were sure to shake the world, had begun in my own backyard, at a high school football game, on a warm fall evening that turned out to be the perfect night for death.

The first death.

How many more were to come and how far would we have to go before it would end?

"Do you hear that?" Olivia asked.

We all held our breath and listened.

Portland was dead. Dead quiet. There were no normal sounds of life. No traffic. No voices. No screams or laughter. All we could hear was the forlorn cry of seagulls floating on the ocean breeze . . .

. . . and music coming from the sky.

TO BE CONTINUED . . .

Keep reading for a sneak
peek of the next book in
The SYLO Chronicles!

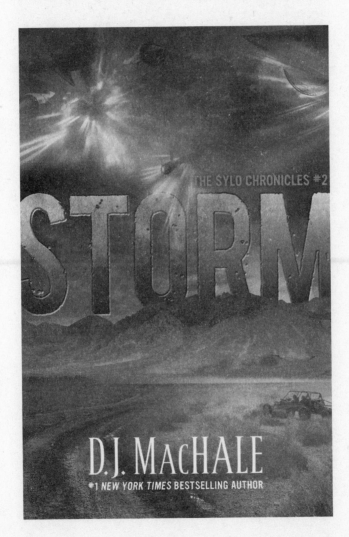

ONE

High noon.

    The sun floated directly above us on a warm, clear, mid-September day. The street was bathed in an intense white light that cast no shadows . . . until the world suddenly went dark. The warm, comforting rays of the sun had been blocked by what appeared to be an unscheduled lunar eclipse.

    The music that came from the looming shadow told me otherwise. The dark shape had appeared from over the tops of the brick buildings of the Old Port and hovered above us like a rogue storm cloud preparing to unleash its fury.

    "They found us," Kent said with a gasp.

    High noon.

    Showdown time.

    "Back in the car!" I commanded.

    The four of us scrambled to get to the Subaru we had "borrowed" after making our escape from Pemberwick Island.

    Tori Sleeper was hurt. She had been shot through the shoulder and needed to lean on Kent Berringer and me in order to keep moving.

Slowing down to help her saved our lives.

The black attack plane fired, sending an invisible pulse of energy at the car that rocked it onto its side and ignited the gas tank. The wave of heat from the violent explosion knocked us back, shaken but alive.

"This way!" Olivia Kinsey shouted while running toward a row of low brick buildings.

We had been standing in the center of Commercial Street, which ran past the busy piers of Portland, Maine. The *normally* busy piers.

We hadn't seen a single living soul from the moment we hit town. Stranger still, many of the buildings in Portland had vanished. They weren't destroyed or bombed, they were just . . . gone. We knew this was the result of the attack we had seen several nights before when an enormous fleet of these flying black predators put on a light show over the city. Tori and I had witnessed the attack from her father's fishing boat as we were making our first attempt to escape from Pemberwick Island. It wasn't the only horror we saw that night. We also got a close-up view of the lethal power of these planes when three of them fired a laser-like weapon at a fishing boat that was making the escape with us. The light enveloped the defenseless craft. Seconds later it was gone . . .

. . . along with Quinn Carr.

The black planes had killed my best friend.

They had devastated Portland.

Now one of them was coming for us.

The hovering plane fired another shot that tore up the ground behind us as we sprinted for the safety of a building. It was close.

I felt a sharp sting across my back as I was hit by a wave of pulverized street.

"The alley!" Kent shouted.

With one arm around Tori's waist, I changed direction and ran toward a narrow alleyway between the old buildings.

"You okay?" I asked her breathlessly.

She nodded, but I didn't believe her. Tori had lost a lot of blood. She needed to be lying down in a hospital, not running for her life.

As we ducked into the alley, I glanced up to see if the plane was following. I expected to see it loom into view above the buildings. Searching. Hunting. These beasts could fly with the speed of a jet fighter, hover like a helicopter, and cause unfathomable damage. What seemed impossible was all too real.

Several seconds passed. No plane appeared, nor did the signature musical sound of its engines. Had it given up that easily?

The streets of the Old Port were narrow and paved with rounded stones, giving the area the feel of an old-time fishing town, which is exactly what it used to be. Now it was a tourist destination where the vintage brick buildings held restaurants, bars, and souvenir stores.

Olivia ran for one of the shops. She yanked the door open and held it so I could get Tori inside. Kent followed quickly and slammed the door shut . . . as if a closed door would keep out the boogeyman.

We found ourselves in a store packed with Maine souvenirs. Every last inch of counter and wall space was taken up with displays of model lighthouses, saltwater taffy, kitchen-magnet lobsters, scrimshaw snow globes, and anything else that would remind visitors of their trip to the Pine Tree State.

Kent hurried to the large front window and peered out with caution.

"Why are they after us?" Olivia asked anxiously. "Because we escaped from Pemberwick Island?"

I helped Tori into a chair behind the sales counter. Though she appeared slight, she was a strong girl who had spent most of her life working lobster boats with her father. But at that moment she was as weak as an old lady.

She looked at me with glazed eyes and muttered, "I need some water."

I searched the shop, hoping they stocked bottled water as well as flip-flops.

"Tucker!" Olivia cried impatiently. "I asked you a question. Why are they after us?"

"How should I know?" I replied, annoyed.

"Because you have all the answers," Kent commented with his usual dose of sarcasm.

Everyone looked at me, hoping for words of wisdom. I hated being the one who was always expected to come up with solutions.

Moments before being attacked, we had learned a frightening truth while examining the wreck of one of the black planes. The craft looked like a giant stingray, with no aerodynamic capabilities whatsoever. I thought it might have come from an alien world . . . until I saw the logo on its skin.

It was the symbol of the United States Air Force.

That morning the four of us had escaped by speedboat from

our home on Pemberwick Island and found ourselves in the middle of a sea-air battle between killer planes from the U.S. Air Force . . . and warships of the United States Navy.

"What can I say?" I answered tentatively. "It looks like the Navy and the Air Force are at war with one another."

"We were running away from SYLO," Kent said. "And SYLO is part of the Navy, so that means the Air Force are the good guys."

"How can the Air Force be good guys?" I shot back. "They just wiped out Portland."

"Yeah, and SYLO turned Pemberwick into a prison," he countered. "Oh, and they also killed Tori's father. Did you forget that?"

I didn't. I couldn't bring myself to look at Tori for a reaction.

"Maybe there *are* no good guys," Olivia said gravely.

We let that sobering thought hang in the air for a few seconds.

Tori then added in a weak voice, "Or maybe we're in the middle of the second Civil War. One side's got the Air Force, the other has the Navy and SYLO."

None of us commented. The possibility was mind-numbing.

"What are we going to do?" Olivia whined.

"Stick to the plan," I replied. "First we get to a hospital and patch Tori up. Then we head to Boston and tell the world what's been happening on Pemberwick Island. After that I don't know what—"

"Git out!" came a threatening voice from deeper in the store.

We all spun to see an elderly man standing in the doorway leading to the back room. He was a typical Mainer with a plaid flannel shirt and jeans. There was nothing unusual about him . . . except for the shotgun he had leveled at us.

"Whoa, take it easy, gramps," Kent warned.

"Don't *gramps* me," the old guy snarled. "Git outta my store."

"We will," I said, trying to defuse the situation. "But one of those planes was shooting at us and—"

"That's why I want you out," he snapped. "I've been ducking them things for days. I don't need you kids bringing 'em down on me."

"Wait," I exclaimed. "You're alive."

"Keen observation, Rook," Kent said sarcastically.

"I mean, you survived the attack," I said to the man, ignoring Kent. "What happened that night?"

"You don't know?" he asked suspiciously. "Where you from?"

"Pemberwick Island," I replied. "We saw the—"

"Pemberwick!" the guy exclaimed as if I'd said we just dropped in from Alcatraz. He held the shotgun higher but took a frightened step back and added, "You got the disease!"

"There is no disease," Tori said weakly. "The quarantine was just an excuse they used to keep us there."

"Who?" the old guy asked.

"SYLO," I answered. "You must have seen it on the news. They're part of the Navy. They took over the island and were gunning down people who tried to escape so the truth wouldn't get out."

"Truth about what?" he demanded.

"There was no virus," Tori said weakly. "We were prisoners."

"We think they were experimenting on us with this stuff called the Ruby," Kent added. "It was killing people, so we left. That pretty much sums it up."

"What about your parents?" the guy said with suspicion.

The answer would only have confused him more. Tori's father and Kent's father were dead, and my parents were part of SYLO. How could I explain that to him? I couldn't even explain it to myself.

"Look," I said, ducking the question. "Tori's hurt. Can I give her some water?"

The man's gaze jumped between us as he debated what to do. He finally looked to Tori, who sat slumped in the chair behind the counter.

"Over there," he said, jabbing the shotgun toward another counter.

There was a case of bottled waters on the floor. I grabbed one, cracked it open, and brought it to Tori.

"Thank you," she said and took a few small sips.

"Now, on your way," the guy commanded, hardening once again.

"We have to get to Maine Medical," I said. "If her wound gets infected—"

"Then go!" he barked.

"We'll never make it on foot. We're going to need a car or—"

"Look!" Olivia screamed.

The black plane was outside the window, at ground level, moving slowly along the street like a giant black shark searching for its next victim.

Nobody moved.

The lethal shadow floated by, the sound of its musical engine growing louder as it moved closer, providing eerie accompaniment while searching the streets for us. Was there a pilot? Or was it an unmanned drone being controlled from a command room miles away?

Seconds passed. The music receded. The plane moved on.

"Now go," the old man said through clenched teeth. "I didn't live through an attack on my town just to be given away by a couple of fugitives from a leper colony."

"Put the gun down," I barked. "We're not going anywhere."

The old man wasn't sure of how to react to my bold order.

"You can't shoot, or that plane will come right back here," I said boldly. "And I doubt you're a killer anyway. What's your name?"

The man blinked a few times, as if he was having trouble processing what was happening.

"Whittle," he answered tentatively.

"All right, Mr. Whittle, we'll be on our way. I promise. But first we need a car." I looked to Kent and said, "Go get one."

Kent stiffened. "*You* go get one!"

"I'm not a good driver. You've got a better chance."

Kent looked around, as if searching for an argument. He was a few years older than me, and I didn't even have my driver's license. He knew I was right.

"I'll go with you," Olivia offered. "This guy makes me nervous."

Whittle slowly lowered the shotgun, as if embarrassed.

"I'm just trying to protect myself is all," he said apologetically.

Kent stuck a finger in my face. "You are not in charge."

I shrugged. "I don't care who's in charge as long as we're smart about what we do. Right now the smart move is for you to get a car."

Kent's eyes flared. For a second I thought he might take a swing at me, but Olivia put a hand on his arm and gently pulled him away.

"C'mon," she said softly. "The sooner we get a car, the sooner we'll be out of this horrible city."

Olivia kept surprising me. I don't think many people told her no . . . especially guys. She was a spoiled rich girl with cute short blond hair who was used to getting her way. It didn't hurt that she was gorgeous. She was no dummy either. She always seemed to know the exact right thing to say to calm people down, and she was quick to help when it was needed. I guess you'd call her an enigma. Maybe that was why I liked her. That and the gorgeous part.

"We'll be back as soon as we can," she said to me, then looked to Whittle and added sweetly, "Don't go shooting anybody while we're gone now, 'kay?"

"Sure enough," Whittle replied meekly.

Olivia had worked her magic on him too.

"Be careful," Tori called out.

"Gee, you think?" Kent shot back. He looked out of the window to scan the street, then cautiously opened the door and peered outside.

"It's clear," he announced and stepped out.

Olivia gave me a small smile and followed him.

There was an awkward moment when nobody knew what to say.

"We're sorry to give you grief," I said to Whittle, hoping to get him to lighten up.

"Grief?" he said with an ironic chuckle. "You kids can't bring on any more grief than we've already got."

"Tell us what happened that night," Tori said gently.

Whittle softened.

"They came out of nowhere," he began. "No warning. No explanation. No chance to run for cover."

"Three nights ago, right?" I asked.

Whittle nodded. He spoke as if in a daze, relating a story that must have been too stunning to believe.

"It was prime time in the Old Port. Early evening. Restaurants were full, saloons were buzzing, people were out strolling, enjoying the warm night. Then the sound came. Like music. Folks stopped and stared up at the sky, pointing. It looked like a wave of bats flying in from the west. They were all perfectly spaced up there, like a pattern. It seemed like a show in the sky. But it was no show. It was a . . . a storm."

Whittle's eyes started to water. It was a painful memory.

"We were out on the ocean," Tori offered. "We saw the sky light up over the city."

"It lit up all right," Whittle said, his voice cracking. "So many people. Families. Little ones. One minute they were out enjoying the evening, and then . . . they weren't."

He looked to the ground, suddenly seeming very tired. He lifted the shotgun and for a second I was afraid he was going to turn it on himself. Instead, he placed it down on a table, pushing aside a bunch of snow globes that fell to the floor and shattered. He didn't care.

"Did they use that laser weapon?" I asked tentatively.

"Is that what it's called?" Whittle snapped. "All I saw were streaks of light coming out of the sky. The beams would join up and grow stronger, like they were coming together to build up energy. It was almost pretty, like a holiday spectacle. But there was nothing pretty about what those lights did. Whatever they hit would light up and then . . . poof. Gone. Whole buildings were there one second and gone the next. It seemed impossible, especially since it was all so silent. There were no explosions or sounds of buildings crumbling. All you could hear was the music of their engines . . . and the screams."

I knew exactly what he was describing. It was how Quinn died.

"But the buildings meant nothing compared to what happened to the people. So many of 'em were just . . . what? Disintegrated? Vaporized? Whatever you want to call it, bottom line is they're gone. Killed. Thousands of 'em."

Whittle's throat clutched. It was a tough memory to relive.

Tori said, "So sometimes buildings disappeared, and other times it was just people?"

Whittle nodded. "Being inside didn't help. It was like those evil beams could penetrate walls to grab their victims. Whole apartment buildings were left untouched, but every last person inside was wiped out. At least it was quick. They didn't suffer. Can't say the same for those who watched it happen. They knew their time was coming. Panic took hold real quick. People ran every which way, but it made no difference for most of 'em."

"How did you make it through?" I asked.

"I ducked inside here and hid down in the basement. Seems like that was the only way to protect yourself. You had to be underground. Not that I knew that beforehand. It was the only place I could think of to hide. I was just lucky, I guess. Or maybe the lucky ones are those who got gone. They don't have to live with the nightmare."

"Are there other survivors?" I asked.

"Plenty. If they were underground during the attack, they're still around. But you won't see 'em 'cause they're hiding like scared cockroaches. Those planes came back a couple of nights later for a second go at it. They're rooting out the survivors is what they're doing. Lately they've been showing up during the day. You never know when a plane might pass by. They don't use that laser-light thing during the day, though. Seems as though it only works in the dark, but what do I know? Nothing makes sense anymore. There's no TV or radio. No power. There's running water, but who knows how long that'll last? You'd think the Army would have shown up by now. I mean, we were invaded, right? Shouldn't the cavalry be riding in?"

I didn't have the heart to tell him that the cavalry was part of the problem because our own military was at war with itself.

"It's like we've been abandoned," he cried, his nerves starting to fray. "It makes me wonder if . . ." His voice trailed off.

"If what?" I pressed.

"Maybe we weren't the only ones who got attacked. What if those things hit Washington? Or New York? Or London, for that matter? If that happened then nobody's gonna care about little old Portland, Maine, because it'll mean the whole world has gone crazy."

"I hate to believe that's true," Tori said softly.

Whittle looked to her with sadness, and I could see him for what he truly was: an old man who was as scared as he had ever been in his life.

"You okay, sweetheart?" he asked warmly. "You're looking kind of fragile."

Tori shrugged. "Better than most people who get shot, I guess."

"Drink more of that water," he said with genuine concern. "You remind me of my granddaughter. She's down in Boston. I wonder if . . ."

He didn't finish the thought, but I knew what he was thinking. He was wondering if she was still alive.

"Come with us," I said. "After we hit the hospital we're going to Boston. I gotta believe we'll find answers there and—"

"Look out!" Tori shouted.

I spun to look out of the front window in time to see that the black plane had returned. I had been so focused on Whittle that I hadn't heard the musical engine. It hovered outside of the window, filling the frame. Its nose was facing us.

It knew we were there.

I dove for Tori. The second I wrapped my arms around her, the shop exploded. We fell down behind the counter as the window blew in and the world turned inside out. I felt the force of the powerful blast as the counter was knocked over on top of us. It wasn't firing the laser weapon. If Whittle was right, that only worked in the dark. Instead, it was shooting the same kind of gun it had used in the battle with the Navy. It fired an invisible pulse of energy that didn't disintegrate its target—it blew it apart. The weapon itself was absolutely silent, which meant all we could hear was the sound of the shop being torn apart.

Tori and I rolled over in a jumble of arms and legs.

"You okay?" I asked.

She nodded. "The back door."

We crawled through the rubble of plastic beach toys, twisted picture frames, and smoldering T-shirts. There was so much dust and debris in the air that it was impossible to tell which way to go. I crawled on my hands and knees and pushed aside a metal shelving unit to discover . . . Mr. Whittle. He was on his back, staring up at the ceiling with lifeless eyes. I can't say what had killed him, but as with all the other victims, it had been fast.

By his standards, he was now one of the lucky ones.